1/4/1990

D1333074

NO SAD SONGS

NO SAD SONGS

Sarah Lyon

Barrie & Jenkins
London

First published in 1990 by Barrie & Jenkins Ltd,
Random Century House, 20 Vauxhall Bridge Road,
London SW1V 2SA

Copyright © Sarah Lyon 1990

All rights reserved.
This book is sold subject to the condition that it shall not, by way of trade or otherwise, be reproduced, stored in a retrieval system, transmitted in any form or by any means, electronic, mechanical, photocopying or otherwise, nor be lent, re-sold, hired out or otherwise circulated in any form of binding or cover other than that in which it is published, without the prior permission in writing of the publisher, and without a similar condition being imposed on the subsequent purchaser.

This book is a work of fiction. Any resemblance between the characters portrayed and real persons, living or dead, is purely coincidental.

Sarah Lyon has asserted her right to be identified as the author of this work.

British Library Cataloguing in Publication Data
Lyon, Sarah
No sad songs.
I. Title
823′.914 [F]
ISBN 0–7126–3478–9

Printed in Great Britain by Mackays of Chatham

For Julia

Acknowledgement

I owe a particular debt of thanks to Michael Lewer, QC, for his very generous and much-appreciated offer to look at the pages in this novel dealing with the murder trial, also to Isolde Victory, clerk in the House of Lords' Library, London, for answering my numerous questions about Trial by Peers.

Inevitably, exact parallels to the fictitious arraignment of Lady Frances Obsorne are not available; the only two this century have been the Earl Russell for bigamy in 1900 and Lord de Clifford for manslaughter in 1935 (when, ironically, Sir Henry Curtis-Bennett appeared for the Defence and Sir Thomas Inskip, as Attorney-General, appeared for the Crown, as they do in my imaginary reconstruction in this book), and earlier examples from previous centuries have been discarded as inappropriate. Trial by Peers in the House of Lords was abolished by the Criminal Justice Act, 1948.

Because of this, where I have been unsure of any particular detail I have simply improvised, and therefore all resultant errors and omissions are entirely mine. For this, and any other unintentional mistakes, I ask my readers' indulgence.

Sarah Lyon
May 1990

PART ONE

1

Everyone was calling it 'The Wedding of the Year'. For the past six months, ever since the engagement had been announced, every newspaper, every popular women's journal, every society magazine had carried regular, lavishly illustrated stories that many were saying eclipsed even the pre-nuptial press interest of the last Royal weddings in 1922 and 1923, when the Princess Royal had married Viscount Lascelles and then Albert, Duke of York, had married the Earl of Strathmore's youngest daughter, Lady Elizabeth Bowes-Lyon.

It was the proverbial fairy-tale marriage with all the glamorous ingredients that the public adored; the bride, Lady Elizabeth Osborne, eldest daughter of the Earl and Countess of Cultrane, was blonde, beautiful and daringly modern. Her father was a leading Tory politician, one of the most powerful men in Stanley Baldwin's Cabinet and a senior member of one of England's richest Catholic families; her mother had been a famous Edwardian beauty in her heyday and was now a leading social and political hostess whose invitations were more prized and sought after than those of Lady Colefax, Lady Cunard, or Lady Londonderry.

The bridegroom, William Vaux, Lord Banbury, was a senior political colleague who had held high office in India under Lord Curzon and was a fabulously wealthy widower with vast estates, tipped by people whose business it was to know such things, to rise high in the present government.

In every photograph, at every social function that the couple appeared together, it was clearly obvious to their delighted onlookers that they were very much in love.

As early as seven o'clock in the morning of the wedding the crowds had already begun to muster, lining the route from the Osborne mansion in Belgrave Square to Westminster Cathedral; because of the bride's religion the fashionable Anglican churches of St Margaret's, Westminster, and Holy Trinity, Brompton, were not used on this particular occasion. But none of the happy, avidly curious and rapidly swelling crowds who patiently waited for a fleeting glimpse of the much-talked about, much-photographed bride, could have cared less about that. All that mattered to them after the grim post-war years of depression, falling exports, mass unemployment and general pessimism, was that they were in for a visual treat likely to live in their memories for a long time to come.

Many of them had not only come to cheer the beautiful, aristocratic bride and her groom; for not only had the entire British Cabinet been included on the distinguished guest list but also the ever popular Edward, Prince of Wales and his younger brother Prince George headed the long list of glittering personalities.

After the service the reception was to be held at the Goldsmith's Hall; then, after spending the night at the Osborne mansion the couple would leave London next morning to catch the boat train to Paris, where they were to spend their honeymoon.

The wedding dress, the bridesmaids' gowns, the wedding ensemble of the bride's mother and her entire trousseau had been designed and made by the celebrated new Queen of English haute couture, Mrs Anne Turner, at her exclusive New Bond Street establishment which was patronized by the most fashionable and wealthy women in England.

On the morning of 13th April 1927, the most talked about subject was not only the wedding itself but the feverish speculation on that highly guarded professional secret, the bridal gown itself.

Laura Asmussen squeezed herself nearer to the car window and craned her neck to get a better view of the tall, elegant buildings as they flashed by. The excited chatter of the other girls Mrs Turner had chosen to come and assist with the packing of the trousseau and putting the last minute touches to the bridesmaids' gowns receded into the background as she went on staring from the window, entranced.

She had never seen this part of London before; the massive, imposing colonnaded fronts of three-storeyed mansions where the titled and the wealthy lived in cocooned luxury with their armies of servants, the famous landmarks that until now she'd known only by name: Downing Street, the Admiralty, Horseguards, Buckingham Palace, the Foreign Office and Westminster Abbey, all another world away from the dull, dreary little rows of terraced villas in suburban Kilburn where she lived with her parents and her brother Kit.

She thought of him now as she glanced down at the wristwatch he'd bought her for her last birthday, remembering how he'd said in that gay, teasing way he had that now she was one of Madam Turner's élite it would never do for her to be late. She wished he could see her now, being chauffeur-driven through the best part of London on her way to the mansion of a famous Cabinet minister, to help his daughters dress for the wedding of the year. She was so excited and bursting with pride that she could scarcely believe it herself. But knowing her brother as she did she knew that he'd just laugh and say that under all the grandeur and rich trappings the Osbornes were just flesh and blood like everyone else.

She knew how pleased and proud her parents were that, after only a single year, Mrs Turner thought so highly of her original ideas that she'd allowed her to design three of Lady Elizabeth's evening gowns – there were twenty-eight in all, one for every night of her honeymoon – although, of course, Mrs Turner herself had naturally taken the credit. But to Laura that didn't matter. It was an honour that she still hadn't really got over. And she'd been so nervous about being included in the party of girls for today that she'd scarcely slept for a week.

It was half-past eight now; any minute the car would arrive in the Square.

Half-past eight. Her mother would be thinking of her, she knew; talking animatedly about the imminent wedding with Mrs Grady, who came to 'do' for her daily, showing her the articles in *Good Housekeeping* and the *Women's Journal* that had been publishing a succession of photographs of the bride as a debutante, and eagerly speculating about the design of her dress . . . How could the new, daringly short hemline for women be reconciled with the traditional, decorous length required and expected for a bridal gown? Laura smiled; she was one of the few who knew the secret, and what a genius Mrs Anne Turner really was. When the designs for the Osborne wedding became public in a few hours, she guessed, rightly, that the name of Anne Turner would be on a par with all the top French fashion houses. To be part of that was one of the most thrilling things that had ever happened to her.

She looked again at her watch. Five minutes had passed, and she thought now of her father. He would have left the house thirty-five minutes ago. At every moment of the day she knew what he would be doing because he was obsessed with punctuality, and because her brother was not it was one of the things that made them constantly at odds with each other. Breakfast at seven forty-five; ten minutes to look at *The Daily Herald*, then he would go into the dismal, narrow little hall with its shiny linoleum floor covering and maroon, cream and brown paint, and wait for Mrs Grady to hand him his coat, briefcase, umbrella and hat. Then he would thank her and say good-bye, close the front door behind him and take the four steps it took to reach the front gate. It would take him thirty-five minutes at a brisk walk to reach Notting Hill Station where at eight forty-three he would board his train on the Hammersmith and City line to West Smithfield Street, and the offices of Lacy, Hartland and Company, one of the city banks.

And Kit? A broader, more lingering smile played on her lips now. The moment their father was out of the house Kit would be downstairs making his own breakfast, then off he'd go up West with his clarinet and a pile of sheet music under one arm to practise for his evening's performance in the orchestra in the basement of the Embassy Club.

Laura hugged her knees in mounting excitement and anticipation as the car began to slow down. Up ahead, she could see uniformed policemen, Mrs Turner's own car some way in front of theirs, turning into Belgrave Square. Then she had her first look at Osborne House, and her heart began to beat faster.

It was huge, double-fronted, magnificent. It seemed to tower upwards into the strong spring sunshine, dwarfing every other building in the square.

She knew nothing about architecture so she didn't know that the mansion had been built by the renowned William Kent in the mid-eighteenth century for Sir Edward Osborne, later first Earl of Cultrane, and that at the time it was hailed as the finest example of the Palladian style in existence anywhere in London. All she knew was that it was the grandest, the most breathtakingly beautiful house she had ever seen in her life, with its massive pillared portico in marble and stone, the great door with its gleaming brass knocker and letter-box, the rows of large, glittering windows. In her wildest thoughts she could never begin to imagine what it must be like to live here, surrounded by every possible luxury, an army of servants to gratify your every whim. She was so used to doing everything for herself that she found it difficult, almost impossible, to imagine the everyday life of women such as Lady Elizabeth Osborne and her mother Lady Cultrane, who had personal maids to help them dress, arrange their hair, fasten on their jewellery, to fetch, carry, and tidy up after them. She wondered what it felt like to eat breakfast, lunch and dinner while half a dozen footmen stood at attention along the wall, looking like statues but surely seeing and hearing everything that was done

14

and said. As much as she would love to be a lady like the Osborne women and their kind, she was certain she would hate that.

She looked ahead to where Mrs Turner's car had stopped. The uniformed chauffeur had got out now and was holding the car door open for her. As usual she looked magnificent; an elegant, understated version of the wealthy women she dressed, in a tailored costume with fur trimming and a velvet cloche hat pulled down over her bobbed fair hair. She swept up the flight of steps to the front door which opened as if by magic: Laura caught a tantalizing glance of rich interior, a footman in uniform with gleaming brass buttons, then Anne Turner disappeared inside and the door closed behind her. Following the car in front, they turned into the mews.

There were already several large cars parked there: clearly most of the bridesmaids had already arrived. Walking in sedate pairs the girls followed Mrs Turner's assistant to the side entrance where another, junior footman was already waiting for them. Then something up above, a sudden movement, a curtain being drawn aside, made Laura glance upwards to one of the big windows above. For a moment a young girl's face looked down at her; a brief, fleeting impression of blue eyes and fair hair. Then the curtain fell back into place and the face was gone.

A gramophone somewhere in the house was blaring out *Bugle Call Rag*; maids were rushing backwards and forwards, carrying armfuls of flowers. Enormous Chinese vases of blooms seemed to stand everywhere, and their exotic, heady fragrance filled the air. Laura gazed all around her in stunned silence, trying to take in everything she was seeing, while the older girls gasped and giggled in whispers.

They had been shown up to the second floor by the back staircase, but looking down from the landing she could see the state staircase at the front and the marble hall beyond it, a lake of rich, scarlet carpet and priceless antiques, oil paintings in heavy, ornate frames lining the walls. She thought inadvertently of the hall at home, too narrow even for a table, dingy behind its door panel of mass-produced stained glass, the single hatstand, the solitary picture of the King and Queen in its plain wooden frame. Though Laura had always loved her home and been happy with everything in it, she would have been less than human if she hadn't made comparisons between it and what she was seeing now. The rich were certainly different. She'd caught glimpses, of course, of women like Lady Elizabeth Osborne and Lady Cultrane at the New Bond Street showrooms just as she had other well-known society figures – Lady Diana Duff Cooper, Princess Helene von Sondeburg, musical theatre star Evelyn Laye – and she'd always taken for granted that they lived in beautiful houses surrounded by beautiful things; but coming face to face with reality was still a revelation.

The music was almost deafeningly loud now. The maid who had shown them upstairs paused in front of one of the doors and knocked – though nobody inside could have possibly heard her – then she opened it and stood back for them to file through. It was the most breathtakingly beautiful room Laura had ever seen, and the largest; one entire wall was mirrored from floor to ceiling, the big windows were festooned with elaborately swathed pelmets and matching curtains in sky-blue brocade. Every piece of furniture was upholstered in the same material and trimmed with gold bullion fringe. The room was filled with giggling, half-naked young women, being helped by their maids into their bridesmaid's gowns. In one corner Lady Elizabeth's maid was standing by the cabinet gramophone, ready to wind it up when it ran down. At the far end of the room a pair of double doors stood open on to the bedroom beyond, where Laura could see Lady Elizabeth Osborne herself sitting at her dressing table in nothing but a white silk slip and stockings, engrossed in painting her face with meticulous care. Beside her stood Anne Turner, smoking a Turkish cigarette in an elegant holder. Instructed in what she had to do the previous day, Laura left the other girls helping the bridesmaids and walked nervously towards them. She knocked, then hesitated uncertainly in the doorway.

Lady Elizabeth, brought up to regard servants as part of the furniture, simply went on with her conversation and painting her lips a vivid scarlet; Mrs Turner made a sign for her to wait.

'The trouble with William is that he's so old-fashioned . . . just like Daddy! He's been a widower for so long that the house is simply crying out for a woman's touch. Of course, his first wife didn't have an original idea about decoration in her head . . . but then wives just didn't in those days, did they?' She leaned back to survey her face in the mirror. 'I told him, the minute he took me to see the house – I want Syrie Maugham to redecorate everything while we're away in Paris.'

'The whole house in white, from top to bottom? Won't it get terribly grubby?'

'But Anne, darling, Syrie's all-white rooms are all the rage now! As soon as it starts to look a little tarnished we'll just have it done all over again.' She finished darkening her eyelids and then began to powder her face. Her skin was already so dazzlingly white that the powder, against the darkened eyelids and brilliant red lips, gave her almost a garish look which Laura thought detracted from her considerable natural beauty, the perfect bone structure, the pale blonde hair, the dazzlingly blue eyes; but all the most fashionable young women painted their faces shamelessly and Lady Elizabeth was one of the most up-to-the-minute and stylish of them all. She was so elegant, so chic, so sparkling. Laura gazed at her in silent admiration, amazed that, surrounded by this frenzied activity, with crowds and pressmen already gathering along the wedding route in the streets, she seemed no more nervous or excited than if she were dressing to go out for an evening at the theatre.

She stood up now and walked over to the full length cheval mirror. She regarded herself admiringly, turning this way and then that.

'I suppose it's all quite exciting, really, isn't it? Not so much for William, of course, because he's done it all before. At least he'll be getting his money's worth, this time.' A peal of laughter. 'The only thing I know I shall positively *hate* is having to entertain all his boring old political cronies ... Austen Chamberlain and Stanley Baldwin, I ask you! Daddy absolutely loathes Baldwin privately, but of course when he got in as PM instead of Curzon Daddy had to pretend he was pleased ... I mean, it would have been so undiplomatic not to. But it must be very galling for him ... he'd make such a marvellous Prime Minister himself. Well, he's bred to hold a position like that, isn't he? Baldwin really is a tatty little man in trade.'

Anne Turner, conscious of Laura's presence, discreetly made no answer. Instead, she beckoned her further into the room. 'I've sent Blanche to supervise the packing of Lady Elizabeth's trousseau ... run along and make sure that everything's running smoothly.' Through the half-open dressing room door, Laura could hear the suppressed sound of chatter and giggling.

'Yes, Mrs Turner.'

Elizabeth Osborne's voice followed her into the next room. 'You were *so* wonderfully clever with all the designs! Did I tell you I teased Mummy and Daddy and told them I was determined to have my wedding gown up to my knees? You should have *seen* Daddy's face ... ! Mummy, of course, realized I was just joking ...' 'I went to the Embassy last night. The Prince was there with Freda Dudley Ward. He asked me to dance with him, and of course I did ...' she giggled conspiratorially. 'And guess what he said? That it was such a pity I was a Catholic and that the Royal Marriage Act stopped him from ever marrying one! Just think. I might have been Princess of Wales. Oh well. Fate and all that. Just imagine . . . this time tomorrow we'll be in Paris.'

Katherine, Countess of Cultrane, had been born Katherine Ernestine Maria Josepha Tribe in 1882, the only daughter and heiress of a millionaire Catholic industrialist, who had been knighted by the Queen for his outstanding services to British trade and industry. He was a handsome man and his only daughter had inherited the family good looks, to such a striking degree that she had had more than fifteen proposals of marriage before she was twenty. She had been Débutante of the Year in 1900 and had not unexpectedly caught the Prince of Wales' eye, but she was far too astute to encourage the attentions of any already married man, even if he was the heir to the throne himself; young as she was, she understood the value of a woman's reputation. On her nineteenth birthday, her doting father had her full length portrait painted by the leading society portrait painter of the day, and it was unveiled at her coming-out ball – a year late because of her mother's death – the most lavish, glittering event of the Season. As the eager male admirers crowded round to admire the canvas and the golden-haired, blue-eyed original, the Honourable Katherine Tribe cast her haughty, self-possessed and calculating gaze over the plethora of assembled matrimonial possibilities and shrewdly assessed that Thomas, Viscount Osborne, heir to the politically powerful and enormously rich Earl of Cultrane, was most definitely the pick of the suitors. Not only was he good looking, cultivated and charming – and conveniently Catholic – he was well on his way to following in his father's footsteps at Westminster and politics to Katherine meant power. She also sensed in him a large degree of malleability, an overwhelming desire to please – for a girl who had been indulged and spoiled all her life and always had her own way in everything, that, maybe, was one of the most important assets in a husband of all.

She saw herself as the power behind her husband, holding sway at her own political and social soirées, dispensing or witholding favours at her whim, making or breaking other men's aspirations and careers with a single blow. A leader of fashion, more copied, envied and admired than any other woman of her day, her husband – and every other man – willing putty in her hands.

Thomas Obsorne never quite got over his wonder that someone as

18

beautiful and sought-after as she was chose him in preference to all the others who had clamoured to marry her. Her real motives stayed carefully hidden until it didn't matter to her anymore whether he knew or not. In the beginning he was as fooled by the angel's face and soft-spoken demeanour as everyone else; only the years after their marriage revealed the real Katherine Tribe in her true colours; a woman obsessed by herself, ambition, power and sex.

In the beginning she was far too clever to be indiscreet; she played the dual roles of political hostess and devoted wife with a consummate skill any professional actress would have admired; it was second nature to her. Even after the birth of their second son when the mask began to slip a little, Osborne was too engrossed in his own rise to power to notice the subtle change in her, or to suspect that her practice of encouraging and grooming promising young men for political careers had a less than innocent motive.

In bed he no longer satisfied her; though she still found him physically attractive, his lovemaking was tame and unadventurous compared to the varied skills of her wide range of lovers; he was spending more and more time at Westminster; her vanity demanded constant flattery and the need to be desired by other men. In those circumstances her infidelity was almost inevitable. She felt no sense of guilt. She'd been brought up to believe that whatever she wanted, she should have: a belief she held on to for the rest of her life.

She disliked children and loathed being pregnant: after each birth she'd hastily handed over each baby to the waiting arms of its nurse, and the very size of Osborne House in London and the Cultrane mansion in Essex meant that she only had to see them at rare intervals; even the girls, as soon as they were old enough, had been packed off to exclusive boarding schools in the country. Henry had died in 1909 and Margaret in 1915, but neither death had really affected her; she was one of those rare women almost devoid of any true maternal feelings. Freddie – her eldest son – was her favourite; he reminded her of her father and always agreed with everything she said. She'd derived enormous pleasure from arranging brilliant matches for him and for Elizabeth. Banbury was Baldwin's man and ever since Baldwin had been chosen as Prime Minister in preference to her husband's friend and erstwhile colleague, Lord Curzon, it had been imperative to find someone within the Party capable of smoothing his path into Baldwin's favour and trust . . . Banbury was the perfect choice. Elizabeth had balked at the idea at first; after all, Banbury was three years older than her own father; but her mother's will and duty to family had prevailed. True to character she'd sulked for a while and even threatened that she wouldn't go through with it; but when her mother applied pressure as only she knew how and Banbury started showering her with jewellery and other expensive gifts, she had a sudden change of mind; this was a man only a fool would let slip through her fingers.

When Anne Turner was shown into the luxurious room where Katherine Cultrane was dressing, her sharp eyes noticed the jewel case lying open on the satin ottoman by the door, revealing a diamond bracelet and a card bearing Banbury's name. Another of his grateful offerings to the mother of his bride.

A maid was holding out the box that contained the jewellery Lady Cultrane had chosen to wear for the wedding.

'All right, leave that. I can put these on myself.' The girl curtsied and backed away. 'Come back in half an hour.'

'Yes, my lady. Will there be anything else?'

'Mrs Turner and I don't want to be disturbed.'

The door clicked shut and they were alone.

Anne Turner smiled. 'I knew that shade of blue was exactly right for you. Lapis lazuli. Not even Elizabeth could carry it off.' She could tell by the expression on the Countess's face that what she said pleased her; saying exactly the right words at exactly the right moment was one of Anne Turner's many talents; that was why she had climbed so high so quickly.

'Sit down and have a cigarette; we've tons of time.'

They'd first met when Anne Turner was Anne Corder, and they were both eighteen; she'd been a seamstress in the Tribe household, but even she had her sharp blue eyes on higher things, and the beautiful daughter of the house had astutely assessed her as a kindred spirit. They were both ambitious, ruthless and irresistibly attractive to men. That Anne Corder had a remarkable talent for drawing, then making up ladies' gowns that were both striking and highly original soon elevated her from her position of modestly paid seamstress to highly paid personal dressmaker to the future Countess of Cultrane. Though most of Katherine's wardrobe came from Paris, she recognized something special when she saw it.

Dressmaking was by no means Anne's only talent; after her mistress's marriage – when she was bored and starting to take a succession of lovers – the ever obliging, ever discreet Miss Corder willingly took on the role of confidante, go-between and courier of

20

clandestine messages; her skill at telling lies was as adept as her skill with a needle. The bond between them was sealed. When Anne Corder became Anne Turner she was given five hundred guineas and a pearl necklace as a wedding present; after her husband's death her ever-grateful mistress introduced her to an equerry in the Royal household who not only set her up in business but, unknown to his wife and family, kept the attractive widow in expensive style with a generous allowance. Yes, Anne Turner had come a long way since she'd first gone into service as a thirteen-year-old girl without a penny to her name.

She caught sight of her reflection in the mirror and involuntarily stroked her sleek cap of golden hair; vanity was another thing the two women shared. The face that looked back at her pleased her . . . soft, smooth, the proverbial English rose, with only the faintest trace of lines; no, she didn't look a day over thirty-five . . .

She took the Turkish cigarette that was offered and searched in her handbag for her own ivory holder. 'Well, you can congratulate yourself . . . your eldest daughter off your hands, and a brilliant marriage to boot . . . even better than the Asquith girl you got for Freddie.' She leaned forward and let Katherine Cultrane light her cigarette. 'Elizabeth gets a titled millionaire and you get a short cut straight to Baldwin. Nice going.'

'I was always good at chess . . . if you remember.' They both smiled. 'But Tom isn't home and dry quite yet, more's the pity. Baldwin knows he voted for George Curzon as Party leader four years ago, and politicians have long memories.' She lit her own cigarette and leaned back in her chair. 'Tom said openly that Baldwin was a disaster for the Party, that he didn't have the experience, that he'd had serious misgivings about his competence right from the start; and that he just didn't have what it took to do the job. George Curzon did. Baldwin isn't likely to forget that or who said it.'

'But George Cuzon died two years ago.'

'That's not what I meant. If he'd been chosen as PM in '23 when Bonar Law had to stand down, he'd have made certain things weren't left to deteriorate the way they were left under Baldwin. George Curzon was always a man of action, the finest Foreign Secretary we ever had, a man with a lifetime's public service behind him . . . only the back-biting and petty jealousies in the Cabinet prevented him from having the job all those qualities made him fit for, the job he should have had by right. Because he was the kind of man he was he never spoke in public about his bitter disappointment at being passed over; the injustice of it must have been galling to his pride. What none of them could bear was the fact that he was ten times the statesman and ten times the man that any of them could ever be . . . and that rankled.' She stubbed out her cigarette forcefully and immediately lit herself another one. 'His death put Tom's political career back at least five years.'

Anne Turner was so practised in the art of saying soothing things hat it had become second nature to her. 'Oh, surely not . . . ? Tom has got where he's got entirely on his own merits. Lord Privy Seal. Senior member of the inner Cabinet. It wouldn't surprise me if at some time in the future when Baldwin goes out of office . . .'

'Tom, Prime Minister? A marvellous thought, yes; and I've thought about it so often . . . but I doubt it could ever happen . . . there's so much against it. It's Tom himself. It always has been. He has wonderful ability, acumen, even sometimes flashes of genius . . . but that isn't enough. A successful politician has to be capable of being ruthless, being able to discard his conscience when expediency dictates it, he has to have the killer instinct. And Tom hasn't.' She crossed her shapely, elegant legs and made a faint gesture of despair. 'It's something a man either has or he hasn't; it can't be learned, it can't be acquired. Tom's uncle has it. And so do I. Sometimes I wonder what would have happened if I'd been born a man. I've done everything in my power to try to influence him, to instill things in him that he wasn't born with . . . but it makes no difference still. He is what he is, a highly competent statesman and no more. He's so complacent sometimes that I want to scream . . . he's got the Privy Seal and he's content to rest on his laurels. But I want much more for him than that; much, much more.' A bitter note crept into her voice.

'When I look at a man like Baldwin, a man with no more qualifications or right to be head of the Government than the most insignificant back bench MP, it makes my blood boil. And there's Tom, with his background, with his experience, like George Curzon a man with all the proper advantages, but he's passed over because the Cabinet think a commoner can do the job best . . . and he won't fight. He just accepts it as inevitable. He says that if it's meant to be it'll happen, that there's nothing anyone, least of all himself, can do about it.'

'Isn't that just like a man? But now Banbury's a member of the family . . . in a manner of speaking . . . shouldn't that make it all easier?'

'It will if I have anything to do with it. If things had been left to Tom, Elizabeth would have been allowed to throw herself away on the first smooth-talking, good-looking young man she was infatuated with; someone with an empty title and empty prospects, without enough money even to keep her in shoes for a single season. With her looks, I was determined that that wouldn't be permitted to happen . . . Banbury was a fish that we just couldn't afford not to hook. He's the perfect husband for Elizabeth . . . old enough to be grateful that he's marrying such a young and beautiful girl who could have married anyone she chose to; rich enough to indulge her tastes and powerful enough to make Tom's passage into the higher corridors of Westminster a comfortable ride.'

Anne Turner stretched, lazily, sensuously, like a sleek, self-satisfied cat. 'I told her when she first came for her fittings at New Bond Street that she was the envy of every young woman in London.'

'Elizabeth was born stubborn; and she has no sense of responsibility. Spending every evening at Ciro's or the Embassy Club, dancing the night away and coming home in the early hours with a different escort every time . . . after Banbury came on the scene I told her that it had to stop . . . for a while. The occasional evening out, at the opera or the theatre with maybe supper at the Savoy afterwards with a group of friends; that was acceptable while she was engaged and even more in the public eye. But any hint of scandal . . . Banbury would be sure to hear it.' Anne Turner nodded in agreement. 'As you and I both know, it isn't what you do . . . it's the getting caught at doing it that counts. And Tom's made enough political enemies in his rise to the top who'd be only too delighted to drop a word in Banbury's ear. That must never be allowed to happen. Once the wedding ring's on her finger then she can do what she likes – as long as she's discreet. In the beginning, I've no doubts she will be . . . what worries me, knowing as I do . . . is her ability to keep it up.'

'Oh, but she's such a bright girl, and so clever . . . she knows what the rules are – and how far she can bend them. She's already got Banbury eating out of her hand. Anyone can see he's besotted with her. And you know the old saying: *There's none so blind as they who will not see.* Besides, when the House resits he'll be so absorbed with constituency business, he won't have the time or energy to keep track of what she's doing.'

'But people still talk.'

'Well, Elizabeth was Débutante of the Year and she's always been a leader of fashion . . . of course people talk about her. I've never opened a copy of *Vanity Fair* or *The Tatler* yet that didn't have some picture of her in it looking absolutely ravishing. She's the darling of the press and never more so than now. What she does, where she goes, is always news. She's in the Prince of Wales' smart set, on intimate terms with all the best young people . . . what she wore at Ciro's or the Savoy or the Embassy Club . . . well, people want to read about it.'

A wry smile. 'And you, of course, love the publicity about the clothes . . . your exclusive designs . . .'

'Well . . . it does help.' Anne Turner returned the smile, showing perfect white teeth. 'But that wasn't the point I meant to make. It's that Banbury is *used* to having her talked about. And I'm sure he adores it all almost as much as she does. After all, what other men of his age can boast a young, beautiful wife like Elizabeth? She's given him a new lease of life. Twenty-odd years a widower, piling up his money and not spending it, nothing to look forward to except old age and death. You'll see, he'll indulge her like a pampered child. And when she gives him what his first wife couldn't, a big strapping male heir, she'll be able to do anything she likes with him.'

'Your optimism is always like a breath of fresh air. But I still worry about Baldwin. Getting Banbury on our side through Elizabeth was one thing . . . but will Baldwin see through it? More to the point – in time – will Banbury?'

'Elizabeth will take care of Banbury and Banbury will take care of Baldwin. You'll see.'

Katherine Cultrane dotted the ash from her cigarette in a nearby marble ashtray. 'You can imagine how it stuck in my throat to have to invite Baldwin and his wife to the wedding . . . along with all the others who supported him against George four years ago . . . but there you are, that's politics. Eternally being forced to hold the candle to the devil, eternal compromise.' As she spoke one of the beautiful French clocks chimed the half hour and they both looked up. 'Goodness, is it as late as that already? Where's that stupid girl?' She stood up and rang the bell impatiently; Anne Turner stood up with her.

'I must go and supervise all the last-minute touches with the gowns . . . but let's meet as soon as Banbury and Elizabeth have gone on honeymoon.' A roguish smile. 'I'll need to arrange another fitting for these summer gowns . . . and I can't wait to hear what ghastly get-up Lucy Baldwin wore . . .'

The dressing room was already a hive of activity when Laura arrived; housemaids as well as Mrs Turner's girls were busy checking, folding and then carefully packing the exquisite clothes into Lady Elizabeth's monogrammed trunks, in between layers of tissue and scented sachets.

Blanche Stephens put Laura in charge of the evening gowns.

'Make sure you look every one of them over carefully, just in case there's a bead or a sequin missing; you know how easily that happens! Mrs Turner's orders.' She went back to her own job of looking over the other girls' shoulders.

'Watch the knitted dresses! No snagging them on the trunks! Yes, that's it . . . lay the sachets in the middle and then use plenty of tissue in between.'

'What about the accessories?'

'Leave those for the maids. They're not our job.'

'Some girls get all the luck!' someone was wailing on the other side of the room. 'Wouldn't I like to wear some of this lot!'

'You'd never squeeze into them; you're arse is too wide!'

'Come on, get on with it you lot! Mrs T says we've to be finished and out of here by half past four at the latest!'

'Put your horse whip away, Blanche!'

Laura smiled at the gossip and went on with what she was doing, loving as she always did the unique, exquisite pleasure of handling beautiful materials. The trousseau was certainly any young woman's dream. With pride, because she was responsible for a good part of it, she looked around the sumptuous room where every surface seemed to be covered with some garment or other, all waiting to be packed.

There were *haute couture* day dresses in a vast array of expensive materials and styles, every one with the unique Anne Turner touch: her distinctive, hand-sewn label with the large italic *T* and the single name, *Turner*, said all.

There were chic, minimal two-piece suits in gabardine, linen, cashmere and pure wool in Elizabeth Osborne's most favoured colours – burgundy, indigo, saxe blue, turquoise, *eau-de-nil* and aubergine; smart frocks in bugle-pleated chiffon and *moiré*, a selection of coats to take account of every possible change of weather: a tailored black moleskin with sable collar and cuffs with matching muff and hat; a merino coat with astrakhan trimming and matching epaulettes; a lighter coat in oyster velvet and a variety of evening coats and wraps in glossy fabrics, all with a wealth of specially designed accessories: shoes, handbags, gloves. Laura's favourites were the evening gowns she'd designed herself – but for which Anne Turner had taken the credit – and the exquisite lingerie all in pure gossamer silk and crêpe de Chine.

Most of the evening gowns were of silk, satin, voile, chiffon, georgette and organza, worked with sequins, *diamanté* or beads, every one of them striking in their design, beauty and originality.

There was an aubergine moracain silk shift with matching satin inserts, stunning in its stark simplicity except for a striking S-shaped spray of rainbow flowers which covered the gown from neck to hem and glittered like gemstones in the light as the wearer moved; an *eau-de-nil* shantung silk shift covered with tiny sprays of blue and green beaded shapes which changed colour as the wearer walked; a topaz princess line in shot silk with accordion pleated hemline, one complete half of the gown embroidered in gold and silver beads; and each creation had a matching evening cloche which could be worn or not according to the wearer's pleasure.

She was in the middle of laying the last one in its bed of pale pink tissue in one of the trunks when the adjoining door burst open and a young girl of about her own age burst into the room.

'Please, could somebody help me? I've caught my hem on this stupid heel and it's ripped it to blazes!' She turned to Laura and Laura recognized her at once; it was the face of the girl who'd been watching them from an upstairs window when they were coming into the house from the mews. She smiled, suddenly aware that all the girls behind her, including Blanche Stephens, had fallen silent; although the girl's hair was a darker gold than Lady Elizabeth's and her eyes a much deeper blue, the likeness was still striking. It had to be Lady Frances Osborne, the younger sister.

'Yes, of course; I'll be glad to help. I'll fetch my needlework case straight away.' She picked it up; every one of Mrs Turner's girls carried one, in the event that they might have to deal with some last-minute crisis just like this one.

'You'd better come back with me to my room,' Frances Osborne said. 'If my mother sees what I've done, she'll be furious.'

'It could have happened to anyone. I've done the same thing myself.'

'You don't know my mother. She can't abide clumsiness. She'll say that if I can't walk properly in a long dress than I shouldn't be a bridesmaid at all.' Laura followed her quickly through the outer room lined with mirrors, where the rest of the bridesmaids were chattering and giggling and busy getting dressed. Disjointed pieces of their conversation drifted towards her as she hurried by.

'. . . well, everyone *knows* she's only marrying him for the money . . . his family are frightfully rich . . . my dear, her father's a car salesman or some such ghastly thing . . . just imagine! All those dreadfully common relatives at the wedding . . .'

'. . . it's just like Mummy always says . . . put a beggar on horseback . . .'

'. . . surely he can't possibly go through with it..?'

'. . . and then when we arrived to play tennis it absolutely poured down cats and dogs and we were all marooned in the summer house . . .'

'It's this way,' Frances Osborne said, leading the way towards double doors at the end of the picture-lined corridor. She pushed them open and Laura found herself in an enormous bedroom decorated in pale lemon and green chintz that was at once less ostentatious than Lady Elizabeth's but far more welcoming.

The two oval tables on each side of the bed were covered with little silver and wooden framed photographs; groups of children, family gatherings; an assortment of cats and dogs. In between there were little hand-made knick-knacks: a velvet and satin pin-cushion, polished horse chestnuts, little coloured glass bottles and enamelled boxes. A battered old teddy bear and a faded china doll were propped up against the pile of embroidered pillows that decorated the head of the bed. Laura noticed a bookshelf with novels, books about gardening and history and, most intriguing of all, a pile of sheet music.

Frances Osborne's eyes followed hers, and she smiled.

'Did you see Evelyn Laye in *The Merry Widow* at Daly's theatre? My sister-in-law took me to the matinee and I loved it! Evelyn Laye's *so* beautiful, don't you think? I know she's one of Mrs Turner's clients because I saw her once at New Bond Street when I went there with Elizabeth . . . oh, drat! This tear is much worse than I thought it was!'

Laura knelt down and examined the ripped hem.

'Don't worry, Lady Frances; I'll restitch it so that nobody will ever guess it was torn in the first place.' She opened her needlework case and selected one of the smallest needles and silk thread to match the lace. 'Embroidered lace like this is much easier to repair when it's damaged than materials like silk or satin . . . the embroidery disguises the stitches.' She began rapidly pinning it together. Behind them, the doors opened again and Frances Osborne's maid came in with her bouquet.

'Grace, I don't think I'm ready for those yet. You'd better put them back in water with all the others . . . oh, goodness, if only I hadn't been so clumsy!'

'Lady Cultrane says you've to be ready to leave for the Cathedral in half an hour, my lady. Shall I fetch a vase and put them in water in here?'

'Yes please, Grace. Heavens, I wish I didn't feel so nervous. If I do anything wrong today my mother will never forgive me.'

Laura had taken an immediate liking to her and thrashed around in her mind for something comforting to say. She seemed almost afraid of her mother. 'Everyone suffers from nerves now and then. Even people like my brother who never ordinarily seems nervous about anything. And me. I was a bundle of nerves when I first went to work for Mrs Turner. That first morning at New Bond Street I remember my hands were shaking so much I could scarcely hold my pencil.'

'*Pencil?*'

'I was making up sketches for evening gowns for Mrs Turner's collection; I pressed too hard on it and I broke the lead three times.' She was intent on what she was doing and didn't see the expression of surprise on the other girl's face. 'Luckily Mrs Turner understood about beginner's nerves.'

'You mean . . . that *you* designed some of the pieces in the collection? By yourself?'

Briefly, Laura glanced up. 'Yes. As a matter of fact, Mrs Turner used three of my designs for your sis . . . for Lady Elizabeth's trousseau. Three of the evening gowns were my design.'

'I thought she designed everything herself?'

'Well she does . . . mostly. Until I went to New Bond Street.' Laura momentarily stopped what she was doing. 'It's odd how I even came to work there in the first place. Fate, my brother Kit would say! You see, I went into a florist shop near Marble Arch one day, wearing a suit I'd designed and made myself . . . and Mrs Turner just happened to be in there. I was buying daffodils for my Mother's birthday and she was buying gardenias. She struck up a conversation with me . . . she wanted to know where I'd bought my suit. She looked so astonished when I told her that it was just one of my own. Not so astonished as I must have looked, though, when she asked me if I'd like to go and work for her at New Bond Street.' She re-threaded her needle. 'My parents were very much against me working at all, to begin with; but they knew how much I enjoyed designing and making my own clothes . . . and, of course, it was such a great privilege even to be asked by somebody as well known as Anne Turner. That was how it all started.'

'But it isn't fair that you should design gowns that she takes all the credit for.'

'It isn't quite like that. She *is* my employer. She pays me to do a job. She has all the expense of buying the materials and paying the out-workers . . . I'm very lucky to be there at all.' She smiled. 'If it wasn't for Mrs Turner I'd never get to work on all those wonderful commissions. My clothes allowance from my father wouldn't run to satin and pure silk!'

'I still don't think it's fair. I'd hate to see someone else's name on the labels of clothes that I'd designed myself. Don't you mind?'

'I've never thought of it that way. I just feel terribly pleased and proud when I see one of Mrs Turner's famous clients wearing it. It's such a thrill!' Laura took her scissors and snipped off the end of the thread. She stood up. 'There . . . you see? I told you nobody would ever notice the hem had been torn in the first place.'

Frances Osborne bent down and examined it, almost incredulously.

'Gosh, you're so clever! Even my mother wouldn't be able to tell. Thanks so much, you've really saved my life.' The doors opened again and the maid appeared with a large vase full of water. Laura began putting away her needlework tools.

'I suppose I'd better go back and finish helping to pack the trousseau. Mrs Turner says we have to be finished by half-past-four.'

Frances Osborne sat down at her dressing table while her maid brushed her hair and pinned flowers into it.

'Oh, I wish you didn't have to go. But I don't want to get you into hot water with Mrs Turner. If I make you late and she notices, she'll tell my mother and then we'll both be in hot water.' She pulled a face in the mirror. 'You're *so* lucky to be terribly talented and have a fascinating job . . . none of my friends do! I wish I was good at something.'

'You play the piano and sing beautifully, my lady,' the maid Grace said, standing back to admire the effect of her handiwork. 'I've heard you.'

'My brother's a musician.'

There was a sudden silence. Frances Osborne and her maid both

29

turned and stared at Laura and she wondered what was so incredible about it that they should look so surprised.

'A musician? A *real* musician? I mean, a professional musician?' The blue eyes were round and wide. She got up from the stool. 'He plays in an orchestra?'

'He plays at the Embassy Club, actually.'

'*The Embassy?* Gosh, how thrilling! Elizabeth goes there all the time. I wish one of my brothers did something exciting like that.'

'It's hard work, really. And very late hours. I think it's only because Kit's so dedicated that he sticks it at all. My parents . . . my father, in particular . . . well, they were both very much against him working there. I'm afraid Daddy doesn't exactly approve of nightclubs.'

Frances Osborne was just about to say something else when the double doors unexpectedly opened and her mother, followed by Anne Turner, came into the room. Instantly Laura sensed tension. Without glancing in her direction she could feel Mrs Turner's eyes fixed on her, and the unspoken question . . . what was she doing here?

'Well, what's all this? Only ten minutes before you leave for the Cathedral and you're still not ready?' Laura had never seen Lady Cultrane so close before; only in newspaper photographs, or glimpses at the showrooms in New Bond Street; she was strikingly beautiful but she had the coldest, haughtiest face she'd ever seen; she could well understand why Frances Osborne seemed almost afraid of her.

'Oh, no, Mummy . . . I am ready . . . well, almost.'

'And what are you doing here, Laura?' asked Anne Turner in the voice that had been honed to an almost-perfect imitation of a born aristocrat's by the elocution lessons her late, elderly, besotted husband had paid for. 'I left you helping to pack the trousseau.'

'*I* asked her to . . .' Frances Osborne broke in before Laura could stutter an answer. She felt the colour rising in her cheeks, as if she was back at school and standing before the headmistress for some unknown transgression. 'I wanted someone to check that the underskirt was hanging right.' She realized how improbable that sounded and added, quickly, too quickly, 'It was all a false alarm, though . . . a bit of it had caught up on my petticoat . . .'

Katherine Cultrane nodded at her maid to fetch the corsage.

'Elizabeth's ready to go. You'd better come and wait with the others.'

'We're coming straight away.'

Someone had turned off the gramophone, but the noise of the women's shrill voices and laughter was almost as deafening. From downstairs, Laura could hear more chatter and laughing as the wedding guests who were going to the ceremony from the house all poured out from the morning room into the marble hall. Laura found herself caught up in the crowd of bridesmaids, all chattering like starlings. Standing there, listening to them, she realized how far apart she was from their own privileged, exclusive world.

She was suddenly startled by an unexpected touch on her arm; but it wasn't Anne Turner.

'Lady Frances!'

'Look . . . I'm sorry about just now . . . having to fib to my mother and Mrs Turner . . . I didn't mean to involve you.' They stepped back, away from the others. 'I just hope I haven't dropped you in it.'

'No, of course not. It's all right, really . . .'

'Thanks ever so. For mending my dress and everything. I'm terribly grateful.' She smiled, her eyes flitting nervously towards the open doors that led out onto the crowded landing. No sign of her mother. 'You really did get me out of a hole, and my mother would have been absolutely furious if she'd found out what I'd done.'

'You don't have to apologize, I do understand. I'd have done the same for anyone.'

'You're a real brick. Look, I'll try and fix it so that you can come back, without Mrs Turner, and measure me for some new gowns. My mother always orders me tons about this time of year . . . supposed to last me for the whole season. I'll wait till my sister's left on her honeymoon, and then I'll ask. I'd love to hear all about your brother . . . you're so lucky to have someone in the family who does something exciting! I get bored stiff hearing about politics all the time . . . oh, by the way, what's your name?'

'Laura Asmussen.'

'Asmussen? That isn't English, is it?'

'My grandfather was Danish; *his* father emigrated here for some obscure reason, and he was born here.' She smiled. 'That's about all I know.' They were suddenly separated by a group of taller, older bridesmaids making their way outside onto the landing, ready to go down to the waiting cars. Then a hush fell on everyone in the room and every pair of eyes turned avidly towards the open bedroom door: sweeping theatrically through, a heavy lace overskirt over a satin underdress that stopped at the knees, giving tantalizing glimpses of her legs, her twenty feet long embroidered Chantilly lace train billowing out behind her, came Lady Elizabeth Osborne. There were gasps of admiration, voices talking all at once. Mrs Turner's assistants rushed forward to adjust the hemline and the train; one of the bridesmaids straightened the veil, another handed Elizabeth her bouquet of hothouse flowers. The bride, fully aware that she was holding centre stage, cast a self-satisfied glance at her reflection in the wall of mirrors.

'Well, I suppose I'd better not keep William waiting,' she quipped, without a sign of pre-wedding nerves. Her composure was almost unnatural. 'If we're late getting to the Cathedral he might think I've changed my mind and jilted him.'

There was a general outburst of laughter. 'Anne, darling, you've absolutely surpassed yourself,' Elizabeth smiled.

Laura watched as she went out of the room and down the scarlet-carpeted stairs, followed by the bridesmaids, then the servants who had been given special permission to watch the wedding party leaving the house from the first floor landing that overlooked the marble hall.

There were more gasps of admiration and surprise from the rows of maids leaning over the banisters on the upper floors. As she reached the bottom of the magnificent staircase, Lady Elizabeth exchanged a single glance with her mother as the Countess left for the Cathedral. Her father was standing ready for her to take his arm. The wedding car rolled majestically up to the open door.

She swept out of the hall through the doors that two liveried footmen were holding open into the spring sunshine, to the waiting press photographers and the cheers of the crowds in the square outside.

2

The moment she found herself cut off from the other bridesmaids and surrounded by hordes of virtual strangers, talking politics and drinking champagne, the old nervousness hit her: the nervousness that made her gauche and tongue-tied on school speech days; the nervousness that made her blush violently and stammer in a room of important guests, that exasperated her father and made her mother rage. The harder she tried to conquer it, the worse it became. If she could have closed her eyes and had a single wish it would have been to be back in her bedroom at Belgrave Square, listening to Laura Asmussen telling her all about her musician brother. She wondered what Laura was doing now.

All her life Frances had envied other people and wished she could change places with them; the endless succession of nannies who seemed to come and go as they pleased; the governess who'd kept a secret scrapbook about sensational murder trials and been sacked by her furious mother; her godfather's daughters who had had so much more freedom than she would ever have; Laura Asmussen, with an exciting brother and almost as exciting a career. She watched her sister Elizabeth and her mother moving with effortless self-confidence and ease among the wedding guests, and she suddenly wanted to run away.

It would be even worse when the sixty or so special guests were invited back to Belgrave Square after the glittering reception; at home, imprisoned in the big drawing room, she would never be able to escape them. Among the hundred who were here now at least she could hide in anonymity.

But not for long. Suddenly, from nowhere, materializing from the gorgeously dressed crowds of chattering, laughing, noisy people, Frances saw her great uncle, Lord Henry Osborne, who regarded himself as the head of the family, come purposefully towards her, and her heart sank.

He was smiling at her, but there was no warmth in the smile; there was something unnerving about the cold, shrewd, calculating look she always saw in his eyes. Almost as if he had the power, like her mother, to look into her mind and know everything she was thinking . . .

His long, cool fingers gripped her wrist like a vice.

'Well now, what's all this? The prettiest bridesmaid hiding herself away like a schoolgirl at her first dance? Whatever will people think, my dear?' The note of censure was unmistakable. 'Come along now . . . you must mingle with the guests and talk to them . . . before anyone has occasion to think that you're neglecting an essential duty.' His voice was very soft, and deceptively pleasant; in all her life Frances had never heard him shout. But like her mother, he had no need to; a single look was enough to make her heart hammer faster and bring the blood rushing to her cheeks. She was fifteen, and he made her feel as if she was a five-year-old.

'I'm not very good at talking to people. I don't know about politics.'

33

'Nonsense. There are dozens of people here that you've met already.' He took her by the crook of her arm and propelled her towards the throng. He gave her a slight push that was more purposeful than gentle. 'Come along now, Frances. Mingle with the guests and show off that charm I know you have; you can't just reserve it for special people. Look at Elizabeth; and your mother.' Her sister was laughing at some remark one of their father's colleagues had made; even above the noise Frances could hear her light, familiar, tinkling laughter. Her mother was expertly moving from group to group of distinguished guests, entirely at ease. 'You see what I mean?'

'If you can point out anyone who'd rather talk about music than politics, I'll do my very best.' She could see by the look in his eyes that the note of defiance hadn't pleased him; she'd meant to sound obliging and compliant, but the words merely came out sounding surly. She could see him looking towards a particular group of guests that contained more than one eligible young man, and her heart sank. She wouldn't be sixteen until Christmas, and already it had started: the accepted, inevitable path that all young girls of her age and class were expected to follow . . . to marry as early as possible, and marry well. Like her mother. Like Elizabeth. It seemed ironic to her that such an indefatigable match-maker as her great uncle should never have married himself.

'Come along, my dear, let's circulate together.' Again, the cold, calculating smile. 'Remember. Next time, it'll be your turn.'

She bought copies of every evening paper and ran home all the way from the station, only stopping for a few minutes at the corner of Suffolk Street because she was out of breath and had a stitch. She pushed open the garden gate, fumbled in her handbag for her doorkey and was so excited that she had difficulty in getting it into the lock. Then she burst in, calling to her mother at the top of her voice, even forgetting to wipe her shoes on the doormat in the hall. She collided with Ethel, their live-in cook-general, on her way in to the lounge where she knew her mother would be.

'Glory be, Miss Laura! You gave me the fright of me life!'

Laura thrust one of the newspapers at her excitedly. 'Have a look at that, Ethel! Oh, she looked so *lovely*! But you can't see how beautiful the dress was from these pictures; talk about an eyeful! After this, Mrs Turner's bound to have every débutante in London clamouring for her to make their wedding gowns. Not to mention all the rest of the guests!'

34

Ethel held the paper in her chapped, work-roughened hands. 'Don't she look a picture, miss? Oh . . . bridesmaids look pretty, too. Wouldn't mind changin' places, I wouldn't!'

Laura found her mother reading. She bent down swiftly and kissed her on the cheek.

'What a day!' She flung down her handbag and flopped down on the couch beside her. 'Here, look at these . . . Mummy, she looked absolutely out of this world . . . I wish you could have been there to see her. I was just telling Ethel . . . you can't see how lovely the dress was by these. None of them do her justice.'

Violet Asmussen adjusted her reading glasses and picked up one of the newspapers.

'My word . . . and look at the crowds! More people turned out than when the Duke of York got married. Or the Princess Royal.' She read the picture caption, then glanced up. 'How did you get on?'

'It was so thrilling . . . going into their house. Golly, *what* a place! It was like a palace . . . the pictures and furniture and the carpets . . . huge vases of hothouse flowers everywhere; must have cost a small fortune. Still, I suppose to them it was nothing. Lady Frances Osborne tore the hem of her bridesmaid's dress and I had to repair it without Mrs Turner knowing. I can laugh about it now!'

'Why couldn't Mrs Turner know?'

'Because she'd tell Lady Cultrane and Lady Frances would get into hot water. So I promised not to let on. But Lady Cultrane . . . she came into the room after I'd finished . . . she looked a real dragon! Really beautiful, but very severe. I wouldn't like to get on the wrong side of her.'

'She was a well-known beauty as a young woman. I was always seeing pictures of her everywhere.'

'Yes, I know; you told me. Lady Elizabeth's gorgeous, too. When she walked down that huge staircase with her lace train behind her on the red carpet . . . what a picture!' She handed her mother the rest of the newspapers she'd bought. 'But do you know something . . . in spite of her being Débutante of the Year and all that . . . I thought her sister was much better looking. I liked her, too.'

'Goodness, this list of guests . . . foreign ambassadors, European royalty, most of the Cabinet . . . the Prime Minister and his wife . . . and the Prince of Wales and Prince George were there, too . . .'

'While I was helping to pack the trousseau I heard some of the maids talking. They were saying that if the Osbornes hadn't been

Catholics Lady Elizabeth could very well have ended up Princess of Wales.'

'I daresay . . . I daresay . . . oh, she's a lovely girl . . .'

A sudden noise overhead made Laura look up.

'Is Kit home?'

'Yes. But not for long. He has to go to rehearsal.'

'I'll go up and see him then.' She left her mother engrossed in the newspapers and ran up the stairs to her brother's room. She went in without knocking, and found him sitting cross-legged on his bed sifting through a pile of dog-eared music sheets. He glanced up and smiled.

'So, you're back from the event of the year. How did it all go, then?'

She took a playful swipe at him.

'Kit, why didn't you come down when I got in? You must have heard the front door. I bought every paper I could lay my hands on on the way home . . .'

'That's exactly why I didn't . . . catch me listening to you women gossiping about wedding dresses and bridal bouquets.'

'You should have seen their house! It's like nothing you'd ever imagine . . .'

'Course not. They're filthy rich, aren't they?' He said it without a trace of resentment.

'Lady Elizabeth looked absolutely ravishing . . . but what amazed everyone was that she didn't show a trace of nerves. She walked out to the car on her father's arm as calm as you please. I met her sister . . . she was one of the bridesmaids. She had an accident with her dress and I stitched it for her. She was really nice, not stuck up at all . . .'

'What's she got to be stuck up about? She's just flesh and blood, isn't she?'

'Kit . . . you know what I mean! The others were all very polite, but she was different. Really friendly. She was the one with the nerves! I don't think she was looking forward to the wedding at all . . .'

'Poor little rich girl!'

'*Kit..!*'

He got up and kissed her swiftly on the cheek.

'Got to run. Late already. New numbers to rehearse.' He picked up his music and started off down the stairs with Laura behind him. He called a cheery goodbye to his mother.

'Kit, it's cold out, take an overcoat!'

'Don't need it. I don't feel the cold!'

'So you're tough.'

'You said it.'

'I could walk part of the way with you, as far as the station, and we could talk some more . . . I haven't finished telling you everything . . .'

He smiled at her as they stood side by side in the hall, their profiles reflected in the mirror. They looked very much alike; the same dark, well-defined good looks, the same intelligent eyes. The only difference was in colour; she had inherited her mother's green ones; his, like their father's, were brown.

'You don't have to tell me anything else. I see them almost every night when they come dancing at the Embassy in your Mrs Turner's scandalously expensive gowns . . . with just about any man except their own husbands.' He winked at her.

'Kit, you're wicked!'

'Just truthful.' He gave her another peck on the cheek, picked up his clarinet case from where it was standing against the wall, and opened the door.

'Have you had anything to eat?'

'I always play better on a half-empty stomach.'

She looked at him, exasperated.

'You take care, do you hear?'

He turned round as he reached the garden gate and winked at her.

'I promise not to talk to any strange women. And I'll walk on tiptoe so I don't wake you up when I come in . . .'

Frances closed her eyes, bent her head forward, clasped her hands tightly together and repeated the Lords' Prayer in Latin, as she did every morning and night in the small private chapel that the family always used for Mass and private devotions when they were in residence at Osborne House. It was the only place in the whole house she felt she could come to escape the wedding revelries that were still going on upstairs.

She leaned forward on the pew in front of her and stared at the statue of the Virgin Mary, the rich altar-cloth in red and gold, the tall silver candlesticks at either end of the altar, then she closed her eyes once more.

She rose to her feet, made the sign of the Cross and genuflected in the aisleway. Time to go. As she turned to walk out of the chapel she caught sight of her sister's small hide-bound prayer book, left lying on one of the opposite seats; she'd come down to the chapel earlier, after changing out of her bride's gown. As Frances picked it up, it fell open to reveal a small folded square of paper, with some hastily scrawled lines in an unfamiliar, but unmistakably masculine, hand.

'*Make an excuse to slip away for a few minutes later. Meet me in the blue bedroom. Darling, I love you madly!*'

Elizabeth's laughter rang around the crowded room, rising above the background chatter of guests and the clink of champagne glasses. She clung flirtatiously to her new husband's arm, gazing up into his face with a rapturous expression; her blue eyes gleamed with pleasure and excitement at the diamond necklace Banbury had just a few moments ago fastened around her neck. As Frances slipped back unnoticed into the room, everyone crowded around her to admire it.

'Perfect.' His eyes never left her face. He touched her cheek with the tips of his fingers. 'I've never seen it in a more breathtaking setting.'

'Darling, you say the most divine things!' Elizabeth danced over to the huge gilt mirror to admire her reflection.

'You're an extremely lucky man, Banbury,' said the Prince of Wales, with a broad smile and a wink towards Elizabeth. 'I suppose you realize that if it wasn't for that confounded Royal Marriage Act of George III, I'd have been fighting a duel with you over this exquisitely beautiful and charming young lady!' There was more light-hearted laughter among the guests. 'As it is, I propose another toast. Long life and happiness to the bride and groom!'

'Hear, hear!'

'To William and Elizabeth!'

Elizabeth looked at her future King through eyelashes lowered with false modesty, as if the thought had never occurred to her.

'Oh, Sir! You really oughtn't to say such things!' There was more hearty, all-round laughter. But Frances was carefully watching her mother's face; how galling it must be for a woman of her ruthless ambition and family pride to have a daughter who, but for her religion, might well have been the future Queen of England.

Elizabeth went on accepting the endless congratulations and good wishes, displaying the considerable reserves of charm that always stood her in good stead; across the milling heads, Frances saw her exchange a brief, almost imperceptible glance with Edward Vaux, her husband's young nephew. He put down his half-empty glass of champagne and left the room.

'Of course, at this time of the year there are bound to be the odd showers . . . even in Paris. But Anne's been so *clever* with things for my outdoor wardrobe . . .'

'Darling, there's the most sweet little accessories shop on the rue de Bondy . . . the handbags are out of this world . . .'

'I must get William to take me there . . .'

'. . . I bought one in blue leather, with the most ingenious little touch . . . a diamond-studded watch set in the side; only the French, my dear, could have possibly designed such a novelty! *Everyone* asks me where I got it . . .'

'William, darling,' Elizabeth kissed him on the cheek. 'I simply *must* dash upstairs and powder my nose!' Pausing here and there to talk to one of the guests, she gradually made her way towards the door and out of the room.

Frances had half-moved towards her as she'd passed; the little leather-bound prayer book, with its curious little note tucked away inside, was in the beaded clutch bag she'd had with her when she'd gone into the chapel. But Elizabeth was clearly in a hurry; or was that just her imagination?

Thinking of the date, only one thing continued to puzzle her; strange nobody else seemed to have thought of it before. Today was April the thirteenth and thirteen was supposed to be unlucky . . . but then, how could it be unlucky for the golden couple who not only had everything but who were so much in love?

It was icy cold in the big unheated guest bedroom on the third floor; the blue bedroom, named for the sky-blue satin drapes and colour scheme that matched down to the tiniest detail, was one of fourteen on the same floor that were rarely used, even on an occasion like this one, for most of the Osborne family had their own houses in London; but neither of them felt the chill. The very remoteness of the room, the dust-sheet covered furniture, made them feel safe, secure, undiscoverable, like two wild animals in their lair.

Elizabeth lay against the door, quivering, eyes closed, panting with passion, holding on to his shoulders while he knelt at her feet and slowly removed her high-heeled shoes, then her silk stockings, rolling each one down her soft, silky smooth legs with tortuous slowness, kissing her flesh as his lips continued on their journey towards her thighs. Every now and then he paused, whispering her name against

39

her hot skin; then he drew off her silk camiknickers and began to draw her down towards him on the floor, moaning in ecstasy.

'Eddie . . . I must go . . . back downstairs . . . someone might come looking . . . if I'm gone too long . . . he mustn't ever suspect . . . or my parents . . . if they found out . . .'

'What the hell did they expect, marrying you to an old man . . ?'

'I can't bear to leave you! I don't want to go to Paris with him!'

'Four weeks won't last for ever.'

'Oh, God, I want you so . . .' As the pleasure of the nearness of him became unbearable she suddenly pushed him away almost violently, angry that there was no time to make love; all at once, her whole life had been taken over by time and her husband's obsession with the observance of it; another mark of the wide gulf between their generations. Time to say goodbye to her guests, time to leave her family, time to drive to the station to catch the boat train to France. Was it only now that she'd noticed Banbury's maddeningly irritating habit of looking at his gold fob watch every few minutes?

She thought of the sumptuous bridal suite in the luxury hotel in Paris that was already waiting for them, the rich décor, the big, satin-draped double bed she was condemned to share with an ageing man who revolted her, and she shuddered.

'Eddie, I can't bear it,' she gasped in a voice of strangled self-pity. 'I don't know if I'll be able to pretend . . .'

'You'll do it. I know you'll do it. Because you remember what I told you; ever since he had rheumatic fever ten years ago his heart hasn't been strong and he's been on those special pills.' Contempt came into his voice. 'An old man trying to claw back his lost youth by marrying a girl nearly thirty years younger than he is – it makes me sick! But it won't last forever; it can't, you know that. One day he'll be dead and you'll be alive . . . with me. Think of all the fun you'll have spending the old bastard's money!'

'Eddie, I must go now.' Her voice held panic, her skin felt like fire. The thin silk of the dress she'd changed into after the reception at the Goldsmith's Hall stuck to her body with perspiration. She wanted Edward Vaux more than she'd ever wanted anything: being a rich old man's darling, being Countess of Banbury, being covered with jewellery that he lavished on her day after day; suddenly material things didn't matter anymore. If only they could slip away – just the two of them – away from this house, the hated marriage her parents had coerced her into. But it was impossible. She dare not tell him that only a few weeks ago, racked with guilt, she'd made

40

up her mind to break off their affair before the wedding; but she'd found that when the moment came she didn't have the strength to go through with it. She needed him. How much easier it had all seemed on those countless, stolen afternoons and evenings when Anne Turner had let them use her house at Putney for their secret meetings, covering for her by pretending that she was at New Bond Street for after-hours fittings. How much she owed to Anne Turner already . . .

'I'll try and telephone you from the hotel.' She was getting to her feet, smoothing down her silk dress. 'I know he sleeps in the afternoons . . . but I can't promise. If I don't manage to get through to you you'll know why. I can't ring you from our suite because they'll put it on his bill and he'll ask questions.'

'I know all that.' He pulled her towards him and the diamond necklace Banbury had given her dug into his chest as he held her close. 'Elizabeth, I want you so much.'

'When we come back, you can always get a message to me through Anne Turner; she'll let you know when it's safe to meet. I see her all the time, and he's given me *carte blanche* to order anything I want from her . . . she's the perfect excuse . . .'

He was only half listening to her.

'Make me a promise?'

'Do I even need to?'

Mockingly, he touched the thick ropes of diamonds around her neck with the tips of his fingers.

'Promise me that when you've buried him you'll let me take you to the Embassy Club and use that thing to buy roulette chips.' A smile, his eager lips against her damp hair. 'You'll be the perfect widow . . . you'll look so beautiful in black.'

3

Someone had already turned off half the lights in the place, but except for the chandeliers in front of the orchestra box and the gold Art Deco lamps along one side of the club wall, the rest were still burning. Some of the staff were starting to stack away the chairs and pile them on top of the tables ready for the cleaners when they came in; one waiter was busy taking off the white tablecloths, another was sweeping up discarded cigarette butts, several more were collecting empty glasses and plates from the tables that lined the dance floor.

Kit Asmussen flopped onto the nearest seat, put his feet wearily on the table top and took out a packet of cigarettes; he'd been longing for one all evening, but nobody in the orchestra was allowed to smoke while the club was open; a bit ridiculous, he'd always thought, when ninety nine percent of their regular customers did. But then the orchestra weren't treated like the customers.

He broke open the wrapping and offered the packet to the two musicians with him before taking one for himself.

'Thanks, Kit.'

'Don't mind if I do.'

Kit drew out his monogrammed lighter and flicked the top.

'Nice. Present, was it?'

Kit shook his head.

'No. Bought it myself . . . some swanky jewellers in Albemarle Street; they engraved it for me as well, no extra cost.'

'All right for some. I can only afford matches,' the fair-haired trombone player teased.

'You haven't been playing here as long as we have.'

'OK, don't bite my head off. What's got in to you tonight, anyhow? You've hardly spoken all evening.' A knowing grin. 'Got some girl trouble?' He nudged his other companion in the ribs.

'I'm just tired, that's all. And I've got a stinking headache,' Kit said irritably, and drew deeply on his cigarette. He glanced at his wristwatch. 'Time for one drink, then I'd best make tracks.' He called to one of the waiters who was still clearing the debris from the tables. 'Fetch us some black coffee, will you?'

'Fetch us some scotch, too, will you?' one of the others shouted after him. He turned back to Kit.

'Hey, Kit . . . you still living at home? You must be out of your mind, travelling all that distance four times a day.' The dark-haired double bass player turned and got himself an ashtray from the table behind. 'This time of night it's still dark outside – no trains are running; you got to get a taxi. And that all mounts up. Besides which, you're always clock-watching.' He dotted his ash. 'All that hassle for nothing, when you could get a nice little place a few minutes walk away, easy.'

'A nice little place at West End prices!'

'Not *right* here, I didn't mean. Say twenty minutes, half an hour's walk away. Like me. I got these digs in Halkin Street, two big rooms, use of bathroom, landlady doesn't care what time I come in, and 'cos she's got mostly other musicians in the house, she never grumbles when I practise. She's a real brick. It's about thirty minutes walk if you don't hurry, half that time if you do. In a cab, two, three minutes at the most. And for eight bob a week, I don't reckon I'd find better.' He leaned forward and tapped Kit on the arm. 'Why don't I have a word with the old duck and ask her to give me the nod when a room comes free? I'll vouch for you. Blokes are coming and going all the time. Well, how about it?'

'I'll give it some thought,' Kit said. But that was only a half truth; in the last few months he'd thought about little else. While the other two chatted about the next evening's numbers and times for rehearsals, he leaned back in his seat and turned the idea over again in his mind, like a record going over the same well-worn grooves.

It wasn't that he was exactly unhappy at home, that he was dissatisfied with the way things were; except for his frequent falling-out with his father he was much luckier than most, everything was done for him. Meals, laundry, clean bed linen, things that if he lived on his own he'd somehow have to arrange to do himself. But he pushed mundane thoughts like that to the back of his mind; it was the freedom, the independence, that mattered. He loved his mother and his sister – and his father after a fashion – and he'd miss them, he'd be sorry to go. But all his life he'd had special instincts about things, and his instincts now were to break free.

There was so much he wanted to do, to learn, to perfect, to achieve; he couldn't do it unless he was allowed to strike out on his own. He knew it wouldn't be easy; but then anything worth having never was. Most of all, he was tired of having his father tell him to be satisfied with what he had instead of trying to understand what it was he wanted to do with his life. To write his own music instead of playing other peoples', to have his own band instead of being just a clarinet player in someone else's, to have his name as well known as all the other legendary musicians and composers he copied and admired. To his father all those things were simply daydreams; foolish things that only happened to other people. To him they were ambitions that he knew he was capable of attaining, and he was determined that one day he was going to. But first, he had to be free of all the old ties, however painful it was to break them.

The off-duty waiter coming back with their tray of drinks broke into his crowded thoughts.

'Penny for 'em,' he said, dumping the tray on the table and slurping the coffee into the saucer.

'Hey, watch it, Tony! You trying to scald us or something?'

'I'm not paid to wait on you lot, just the customers.'

'This coffee's got a film on it.'

'Don't worry. I won't charge you extra.'

Kit sipped the brew and pulled a face.

'It isn't even hot. If you served this up to the customers tonight no wonder the place was half-empty.'

Tony stopped what he was doing and leaned on his broom.

'The place was half-empty, genius, because all the top nobs was away at that wedding you said your kid sister helped make the dresses for. Forgotten?'

Kit took the jibe in good humour.

'So I did. The cigarette smoke from the other half of *Burke's Peerage* that didn't get invited must have addled my brain. Sorry.'

Tony gave him a thumbs' up sign and went on with the sweeping up.

'Hey, you two, take a look at this!' The fair haired trombone player had produced a dog-eared copy of *Melody Maker* from somewhere and was pointing at the small print in the advertisement columns at the back. They both crowded close to him to look. 'They want a second clarinet in the orchestra for that Jessie Matthews musical, *One Damn Thing After Another*!' He nudged Kit in the ribs. 'Matinées and evening performances, either or both! Why don't you get yourself over there first thing tomorrow? Hey, look at the rates of pay! Not bad, eh? You'd be a bloody fool not to.'

'*One Damn Thing After Another*; that's the new Charles Cochrane review, isn't it?'

'Yeah, that's right. Go on, Kit, give it a whirl! Just think. If you only did afternoons and here, you'd be doubling your pay. Find out what time the evening performances start and you could get a taxi straight here afterwards. Nothing easier.'

Kit went on staring at the two lines of print, making mental calculations in his head. So much he wanted to do, but without enough money saved behind him, he was trapped. If he auditioned and got the job he could triple his earnings at one stroke and everything that up until now had just been ideas in his head, could be made to happen. But he wasn't counting his chickens.

'Maybe I will get over there tomorrow,' he said with much more flippancy than he felt. Suddenly his headache didn't seem so bad, suddenly he didn't feel so tired. 'Can I cut that bit out, if you've finished with the paper?'

'Sure, Kit. It's only adverts. Nothing doing for trombones this week.' He downed the half measure of scotch. 'Well, I s'pose we'd best be making tracks.' He stood up and slapped Kit on the back. 'Glad I don't have the journey home that you do.'

Kit smiled a little wearily.

'If I get lucky tomorrow at the audition I just might take you up on that offer of a room.'

'Good luck, then!'

'Yeah, good luck, Kit!'

He called goodnight to the others, slung his overcoat over one shoulder and went out into the street to find a taxi.

'Surprise!' A little flushed, Elizabeth burst into the crowded drawing room and instantly claimed everyone's attention; deliberately, she avoided looking in her mother's direction. She and Eddie Vaux had taken such care, not to be seen talking together too often, to leave the room separately, several minutes apart . . . surely nobody could ever faintly suspect . . . ?

Behind her, two sturdy young footmen were carrying in the big, solid walnut cabinet gramophone that Banbury had bought her, just one among a torrent of engagement presents. She was holding some records in her arms.

'Daddy, you've got to give in today!' Gaily she positioned herself next to the Prince of Wales. 'He absolutely *loathes* jazz, Sir . . . but I know how much you love it . . . just like me! Do you know that ever since William bought me this, Daddy complains like anything every single time I play it . . . he says he can't concentrate on his state papers!' Laughter rang around the room. 'So tonight I'm shamelessly taking advantage of the fact that you're guest of honour and there's absolutely nothing he can do about it!'

'What's all this, Cultrane?' the Prince joked, waving his cigarette towards the gramophone. 'You don't like modern music?'

'Nothing but a raucous din, Sir! And I'm sure His Majesty would agree with me!'

'Don't be beastly, Daddy! His Royal Highness is on *my* side . . . and there's nothing you can jolly well do about it!'

'What about you, Banbury – do you share your wife's musical tastes? Well, it's too late now, even if you don't!'

'I'll suffer uncomplainingly, Sir.' Almost unnoticed, Eddie Vaux came back into the room; taking a glass of champagne from a footman, he went casually over to the records Elizabeth had put down, and pretended to look at their titles. He lit a cigarette.

'Frances, you're in charge of the music!' For the first time all day Elizabeth was taking some notice of her, now she could make herself useful. 'Be careful how you handle those top ones! William had them especially imported from America for me and they're simply like gold dust . . .'

Frances chose one of her own favourites and laid it reverently on the green baize turntable, then she wound the machine up and placed the arm, with its thick needle, on the edge of the spinning record. After a few seconds of loud crackling, the jaunty strains of the Savoy Orpheans' *Dinah* filled the room, mixing with the laughter and chatter from the guests. This was more like it. Feeling happier than she had all day, she began to swing her foot and tap her fingers on her knees in time to the beat of the music.

Elizabeth turned on all the lights in her room and went through the chest of drawers beside her bed for the second time, impatiently tossing out their contents on the floor. She slammed each one angrily. She went into her dressing room, where the dozens of trunks, already packed, were waiting to be carried downstairs in the morning ready for the boat train, and opened the two smallest of them where her maid had put away her more personal things. The silver-backed hairbrushes and combs, the stockings, garters, suspender-belts and brassières, more boxes of cosmetics and different jars of expensive face creams that she'd ever use; she rummaged among them and slammed down the lids when what she was seeking wasn't among them. Behind her, she'd hardly noticed that the door of her bedroom had opened. The sudden, totally unexpected sight of her mother standing there in the doorway made her jump. A gasp of surprise escaped from her lips.

'Is this what you're looking for?' Katherine Cultrane closed the door behind her and leaned against it. She was holding up a book.

'You've been going through my things! *You've no right . . !*'

'*Contraception: its Theory, History and Practice.*' Her voice was harsh with barely suppressed outrage. 'To think that a daughter of mine could lower herself to read this filth! Have you any idea what would happen if I showed this to your husband?'

'It isn't filth! You don't understand! For God's sake, mother . . .

46

this is 1927! Women are tired of being drudges, worn out by the time they're thirty-five or forty with having a child every year!'

'Do you really think I'd read a single page of this obscene trash?'

'It isn't what you think . . . she believes that women have a right to choose . . . choose when they want to have children, not just have it thrust on them by their husbands. And I happen to agree with her.' Elizabeth tossed her head in a gesture of defiance; for so long her mother had dictated how she had to behave, how she should live her life. She was twenty-one. She was a married woman. But the old nervousness in her mother's presence that went back to when she'd been a child hadn't quite vanished. There was sweat on the palms of her hands. 'Everything Marie Stopes writes makes perfect sense. Lots of eminent people happen to think so, too. Besides which, I don't intend to be a brood mare for Banbury!'

Her mother's eyes were as cold as ice. 'Have you actually been to this notorious clinic of hers?'

Elizabeth coloured violently. 'Of course not! Do you think I'd go there in person with all those working-class women? I'd be recognized in a minute. I'd never do anything publicly to jeopardize the name of the family, or Daddy's position . . . surely you know that? But my own private beliefs are my concern and nobody else's . . .'

'It seems that your "private beliefs" are completely different from everything you've been brought up to believe in!'

'Oh, come off it, Mummy! There were plenty of spaces between all our births, and you married Daddy when you were nineteen. Don't tell me you didn't cheat now and then!' Her last words were stifled by a stunning crack across her cheek. She cried out.

'How dare you speak to me like that. And don't lie to me, either. I know very well why you've suddenly taken to reading this disgusting trash; I can tell by the state of the cover and how well thumbed the pages are that you've had this book for some time. Ever since you started sleeping with Eddie Vaux, in fact.' Elizabeth's face turned white. 'You really thought I didn't know what was going on?'

'Mother, I swear . . .'

'You bloody little fool! Have you any idea what would happen if Banbury ever found out you were having an affair with his own nephew? See how besotted he'd be with you then!'

'All right! *All right* . . . it's true. But we've been discreet. We've never once dropped our guard and been careless. All this time and nobody's ever guessed except you.' She sank down on the side of the satin-covered bed and covered her face with her hands, trying to rally her failing courage. 'I promise, William will *never* find out!'

'You'd better be sure that he doesn't.' Her mother's voice held a note of threat. 'I've invested nearly a year and a half of my time in getting you where you are now . . . there were others Banbury could have married. Rich widows, still young enough to give him the heir he wants and attractive enough to manipulate him . . . all of them after the prestige of being the next Countess of Banbury. You don't realize your luck, do you? We get you one of the richest men in England and all you can do is complain about how hard done by you are!'

'You only wanted me to marry him because he'll help give Daddy another shunt up the political ladder, because he's hand in glove with Stanley Baldwin.'

'That isn't the only reason and you know it.'

'He's older than Daddy, for heaven's sake!'

'That didn't seem to bother you when he was falling over himself giving you expensive presents.'

'I wish I'd never let any of you talk me into it! I'd rather be shut up in a convent.' Slowly, sulkily, Elizabeth bent forward and retrieved the book from the floor; she sat there cradling it in her arms as if she was afraid her mother would snatch it away. The side of her face still smarted from her mother's slap.

'I can think of no one less suited to take the veil than you are.' A mocking tone. 'Not that any convent I know would even be willing to have you . . . if not the devil, you're far too fond of the world and the flesh. But let me warn you here and now, duty to your family comes first. Always first. You're an Osborne; don't ever forget it. Play around with Eddie Vaux if you have to, but don't ever let your husband find out. If he does, then remember exactly what any kind of scandal would mean not only for you – but for all of us.' Her slim, beautifully manicured hand rested lightly on the door knob. 'I haven't spent my entire married life trying to push your father to the top to have it all destroyed by someone as selfish and egotistical as you.' She let herself out.

4

The first thing he was aware of was the brilliant sunshine; through the chink in the curtains where they weren't drawn all the way across, it shone across his face in a single piercing line, making him squint and curse and turn over on his other side, one limp, still sleepy hand clamped across his forehead.

Downstairs he could hear the familiar sounds of pots and china and cutlery being washed up in the kitchen, the voices of Ethel the live-in maid and Mrs Grady as they chattered while they worked.

He opened one eye and focused it on the clock. Twenty to eight. His father would have already left for work but Laura would still be here, busy getting ready to walk to the station and catch her train. At the very same moment that he was thinking about her the bedroom door swung open and she put her head round it.

'Still in bed?'

He winced. 'I got in much later than usual.'

She came in and perched herself on the edge of his bed. 'Bear with a sore head. You look awful. Why were you so late last night? Or should I say "this morning?" '

'Oh, you know how it is . . . after the club closed I stayed behind for a quick drink with the other chaps and we got talking.'

'Anything interesting?' She smiled.

'Nothing for your innocent ears.' He gave her one of his half-wicked, half-enigmatic smiles that made her long to hug him. 'Tell you what, though; I'll meet you at New Bond Street at one o'clock and take you to lunch at the Holborn restaurant . . . my treat. Might let you into a secret if you're a good girl.'

Excitement leaped into her eyes. 'Tell me now! Go on, don't be such a spoil-sport!'

'Sorry, can't. Won't know what I want to know myself till then.' He blew her a kiss. 'Just have to be patient and wait and see, won't you?'

He started to climb out of bed.

'*Kit* . . ! You can't keep me in suspense for the next five hours, it isn't fair. Give me a clue.'

'Nope. Go on, shift. I've got to shave and get dressed and I'm late already. Got something special on at rehearsals this morning.'

'Rotter!' she called gaily as she went downstairs singing *My Heart Stood Still*, from the latest Charles Cochrane musical at the top of her voice. She checked her appearance in the hall mirror, went into the breakfast room where her mother was drinking tea and sat down to wait for Ethel to bring her another cup. As she'd expected she was plied with an endless stream of questions about the Osborne wedding.

'Ooh, she looked *lovely*, the Lady Elizabeth, didn't she, Miss Laura? Big picture of 'er right on the front o' the mornin' paper . . . they looked ever so 'appy . . .'

'Everything seems a terrible anti-climax today, after all the excitement yesterday . . . just about now they'll be leaving on the boat-train for Paris.'

'Paris! Wish I could 'ave 'id meself in the luggage!' She went off, carrying Richard Asmussen's egg-stained breakfast plate, nearly colliding with Kit at the door.

'Good morning, Mama dearest,' he said affectionately but in the tongue-in-cheek way that exasperated his mother and annoyed his father. 'Sorry I'm late.'

'Really, Kit. You could make more of an effort to be on time for meals. It isn't fair on Ethel.'

'I stand chastized.' He helped himself to toast. 'I might be late tonight, by the way. Later than usual.'

'Oh, Kit!' His mother lay down her knife and fork with irritation. 'The Murrays are coming for bridge tonight; we're having dinner half an hour earlier. If you're going to be late, you'll have to eat in the kitchen. I'm sorry, but your father arranged this weeks ago.'

'No problem, it doesn't much worry me where I eat. I might even have a meal somewhere before I come home with some of the boys from the club.'

Violet Asmussen's lips were pursed with disapproval. 'I really don't like the idea of you socializing with those fellows who play in the band, Kit. You know very well your father doesn't like it, either. It's one thing to work with them; but most of them aren't really the sort of young men that we think you ought to be mixing with.' Laura and Kit exchanged glances. 'Coming home all hours of the day and night doesn't give the neighbours a very good impression. That's the chief objection your father and I have to you working at that place.'

'It's good enough for the Prince of Wales.' A sly glance in his sister's direction while she pretended that she hadn't noticed; they both knew that people of their parents' class and generation had a proper respect for the royal family and the aristocracy.

'The Prince of Wales doesn't hang about with undesirable company.'

'That's a matter of opinion.' Kit sipped his tea.

'Kit, I'm not in the mood for your witticisms this morning; with this bridge party this evening I've far too much to do. You know exactly what I mean. With your ability you could get a good respectable place in the orchestra at somewhere like Covent Garden; you know that. But anything your father or I suggest is automatically not a matter for consideration.'

'Mummy, Kit doesn't want to play classical music . . .'

'You stay out of this discussion, Laura. It's high time you were leaving for work. If you miss your train you'll turn up late at New Bond Street, and that won't go down very well with Mrs Turner.'

Kit wiped his lips on his napkin and got to his feet.

'Ah, Mrs Anne Turner, purveyor of clothing apparel to the upper classes, *nouveaux riches* and anyone else who can pay her exorbitant prices! She must be feeling pleased with herself this morning.'

'Kit, do you always have to make disparaging remarks about other people? You seem to forget that Mrs Turner is Laura's employer.'

'I haven't forgotten the fuss Father made when Laura wanted to go and work for her. And you agreed with him. If she hadn't been making clothes for half the English nobility, you wouldn't have let Laura accept . . . it was the magic name "Turner" that changed your minds. Besides, employer or not – she's done very well out of Laura's talent, hasn't she? Everything she designs Mrs Turner passes off as originals designed by herself.'

Ten minutes later, walking beside him in the street on their way to the station, Laura caught him by the sleeve.

'Kit, I wish you wouldn't say things like that! She'll tell Father now and then there'll be an almighty row when you come in from work.'

Kit grinned.

'Not if the Murrays are here playing bridge, there won't. You don't really think our esteemed parents would actually behave naturally in front of guests, do you?'

'Kit, I think you say those things to Mummy on purpose!'

They walked on, side by side. Kit checked his wristwatch. 'I only tell her what she doesn't want to know.'

51

'I know she annoys you saying all the time that you ought to work in a classical orchestra . . .'

'It goes in one ear and out the other; don't worry.'

'. . . but you weren't very fair about Mrs Turner. I get really good wages, more than some men with families . . .'

'Oh, and doesn't she get her money's worth!'

'Look, it isn't like that. Other girls would give their right arm to work for Anne Turner.'

'Do you mean to tell me she'd employ workers with only one arm?'

'Kit, will you be serious?' He was walking too fast and she had to increase her pace to keep up with him. 'And slow down, please; I'm wearing heeled shoes. What I mean is, she did *me* a favour by offering me a job. Not only the prestige of working for someone with her reputation, but the rate of pay. I could never do better.'

'Well, it's your brain she's picking, not mine. I just don't happen to think it's very fair.'

'Funny you should say that; Lady Frances Osborne thinks that, too.'

'The poor little rich girl? Well, well. So she's got a brain in her aristocratic head!'

'I'm *lucky* to have the position at New Bond Street, Kit. Where else would I get the opportunity to design clothes in the kind of expensive fabrics I could never afford to buy? And see titled ladies and European royalty actually wearing them? Oh, you don't understand!'

He slowed down as the station came into sight.

'When I'm rich and famous I'll set you up in your own business and you can turn Mrs Turner on her head . . . how's that?'

She smiled as they walked towards the ticket office together.

'The day *anyone* takes business away from Anne Turner, I'll walk down the whole length of Oxford Street with a pineapple on my head!' They laughed together. 'She's in business to stay!' She hooked her arm through his. 'Anyhow, when you do come home tonight, for goodness sake don't rub Daddy up the wrong way with quips about the idle rich . . . you know he has no sense of humour. If the Murrays are still there everyone will be bound to be discussing the Osborne wedding; for the last few months nobody seems to have talked about anything else.'

'The Osbornes!'

'You forget that Lord Cultrane is in the *Cabinet*, Kit! He helps run this country . . .'

'Oh, is that what you call it?'

'I'm not going to get into an argument about politics because I don't understand anything about them – but if you despise the upper classes so much then why do you work at the Embassy Club entertaining them?'

'A little thing called necessity. Besides which, I don't play for *them* . . . I play for myself.'

'You could say that if they didn't patronize the nightclubs you wouldn't have a job at all.'

'Is that what you think? If they shut every single one tomorrow I'd just pack up my clarinet and my music and go somewhere else; there are plenty of places crying out for good musicians: theatres, music halls, hotels. And just because the Prince of Wales and his hangers-on patronize the Embassy, it doesn't mean it's the only nightclub in London. In any case, anybody can stay in one place too long.'

Something in his voice alarmed her.

'Kit? You wouldn't throw up a good job like that just because you didn't like the people who went there . . . would you?'

'I don't even notice the people that go there; they're just glitter and noise.' She moved closer to him as they were jostled by other commuters hurrying to catch the train. 'Oh, come on! Don't look at me like that; why do I always manage to say the wrong thing? Look. When I take you to the Holborn at lunch time I promise you can choose all the most expensive things on the menu. How's that?'

She had to smile at him.

'I'd be just as happy going to Lyon's Cornerhouse and being content with a mixed grill.'

'Wouldn't hear of it. Besides, think big! Look where it got Anne Turner!' Before she could say anything else her train came hurtling into the station and everyone rushed towards the doors. She didn't even have time to kiss him goodbye. She turned round in her seat as soon as she was inside, and waved; he waved back to her across the heads of the crowd.

Even Kit's father had heard of Charles B. Cochrane; there couldn't have been anyone in London who hadn't. His name was emblazoned, along with the title and the names of his leading lady in his latest big musical show, *One Damn Thing After Another*, in huge letters over the imposing entrance to one of his many theatres, the London Pavilion. It was only a short walk from Piccadilly Station to the theatre, on the corner of Coventry Street and Shaftesbury Avenue;

crossing the street, Kit looked around him at the familiar sights and places. Twenty minutes, half an hour's brisk walk in any direction and you were in the very heart of theatreland. But the London Pavilion was the biggest and his own personal favourite; most of the big Cochrane musicals had been staged there.

He remembered Noël Coward's *On With the Dance*, two years ago, and *Phi-Phi* and *Fun of the Fayre* three years before that; 1921, the year he'd got his first real engagement, playing in the orchestra at the Savoy where he'd stayed over a year before a better place had come up playing at the New Oxford. Then there'd been a spell at Chiswick Empire, the Comedy and the Lyceum, before working at the Holborn Restaurant, until his father insisted he leave after the sensational Thompson and Bywaters trial; the Holborn had been one of the ill-fated lovers' favourite meeting places and, he'd argued, as such no longer a suitable place for the son of a respectable bank clerk to work in; notoriety stuck to places like that and notoriety was what people remembered. When Kit had answered that if every place where illicit lovers met was to close down there wouldn't be a restaurant or a theatre left open in the whole of London, his father hadn't been able to think of a suitable reply; although Kit had bowed to his wishes and left – reluctantly – a gulf had opened up between them that had slowly but surely become more unbridgeable year by year.

Thinking about his differences with his father made him think again about what he'd decided to do, if the production manager at the London Pavilion took him on; and he was keeping his fingers crossed. With wages from the theatre and from the Embassy Club he'd have enough for his own lodgings in the West End and plenty to spare.

There was a broad smile on his face as he reached the theatre and told the doorman why he was there.

'Got an audition for the orchestra, 'ave yer? Just go through that door at the end an' follow the sound of the music.'

Most theatres backstage looked very much like any other: long, narrow little stone corridors and warrens of tiny dressing rooms; trunks, baskets, props, rows of costumes; men in their shirt sleeves rushing from one end to the other and groups of pretty, giggling, scantily-clad chorus girls going up and down backstage stairs. Behind him their raucous laughter faded as he walked into the aisle and along it towards the orchestra pit. He stopped halfway.

Three men were reclining in the front row of seats, a few musicians sat in their places in the orchestra pit and someone was already being auditioned on stage. He was playing a Cole Porter melody and Kit thought that he played very well, not a note out of place but the overall effect to his mind was mundane and unexciting. But then maybe that was what they wanted; for a brief moment he felt a flush of rare self-doubt. He waited until the other musician had finished before walking the rest of the way down the aisle to where the three men were sitting, then he put down his clarinet case and his music and held out his hand. One of the three men sitting in the front row of seats looked up disinterestedly.

'You come for the clarinet audition?'

'Yes, my name's Kit Asmussen.' Nobody offered him their hand so he let his own fall to his side again. 'I can play you something I wrote myself or else one of the numbers from the show.'

'We don't want a one-man band, sonny,' one of the other men said, dismissively. 'We just want someone who can play the clarinet and play it good.'

Kit shrugged. 'That's OK with me. Do you want me to go up next?' The other musician was coming offstage. He glanced at Kit, then at the men in the front row seats.

'All right, that was good. If you want to wait around for a while with the others, we'll let you know.' The first man turned his attention back to Kit. 'So you play clarinet? Are you out of work or are you playing somewhere now?'

'I'm playing at the Embassy Club, but I've worked at a few other places . . . before I went to the Embassy I was in the band at the Holborn, before that at the Comedy and the Lyceum. I've worked at the Chiswick Empire, the New Oxford and the Savoy.'

'You played with the Savoy Orpheans?'

'For a while, yes.'

'So why did you leave?'

'I just fancied a change; playing the same kind of music night in, night out isn't my idea of going in the right direction.'

The other man frowned.

'We advertised for a reed man and that's exactly what we want; no frills and fancies; if you get the job you play as part of the whole orchestra, not your own one-man-band. Understood?'

'Understood, sir.'

'I'll take a look at your music, then.'

Kit handed him the selection he'd brought along and he leafed through it, pausing to frown every now and then. He glanced at the others over his shoulder. 'This one's going to play *My Heart Stood Still*. All right, sonny. Let's see what you can do.'

They came from every corner of the theatre to listen; the box office and the men from the prop rooms; the technicians from backstage, the chorus girls from their dressing rooms; the theatre manager, the assistant manager, the dressers, the stagehands, even the cleaning women. When he'd finished playing he looked down into the front row and saw that even Charles B. Cochrane had come out of his office to hear him.

Everyone broke into thunderous applause.

As he came back down the stage steps with his clarinet in his hands, the impresario stood up and smiled.

'Nice playing, boy. Very nice playing. I reckon you've just got yourself a place in my orchestra.'

5

Frances stood at one of the windows that overlooked the square and watched as the Rolls Royce that had taken her parents to the station to see Elizabeth and William Banbury off on their honeymoon, drew up outside. Only her mother got out; her father would have been dropped off at his office in Westminster. Behind her, the three clocks in the room all chimed the half hour simultaneously, and she thought of what she'd been doing, thinking, feeling this time yesterday. Now everything had changed as if the wedding had never happened at all.

The whole house was so quiet; the only sounds she could hear were the ticking of the clocks, the faint noise of traffic from the street outside, distant sounds in the depths of the house of familiar, background things: servants going along the corridors, the house-maids cleaning rooms. She turned and walked out into her sister's suite of rooms and felt a lump rising in her throat as she went through them; in a family of prosaic, forward-thinking women she was the only one cursed with soft emotions and incurable sentimentality. She had already found out how painful both could be.

They had never been close. All her short life, always in the background, she'd looked up to and fervently admired Elizabeth, the elder sister who was so different from herself: quick, clever, witty, beautiful; she drew other people to her like a magnet, she was always perfectly at ease with everyone she met. Although Frances adored her, Elizabeth barely ever acknowledged her existence; like a housemaid or a footman, she was little more than part of the background, someone young and unimportant and therefore not worth bothering with; Elizabeth was only interested in people who could do things for her, people with influence and power.

But despite the offhandedness, Elizabeth was Frances's heroine; in her wildest imagination she could never even think of anything her sister might do that could ever change that. After all, as other people said, blood was thicker than water. Avidly reading about her, as if she was a stranger, in the gossip columns and the daily newspapers, Frances had secretly cut every photograph and every article about Elizabeth that had been printed since she was first presented at Court, and pasted them into an enormous album; nobody else knew of its existence. No doubt Elizabeth would have been as astonished as she might have been flattered if she'd ever seen it.

Frances looked around the empty dressing-room where this time yesterday the bridesmaids had been noisily and excitedly getting ready, at the wall-to-wall mirrors that now only reflected herself; she thought of Sabine winding up the gramophone, Anne Turner supervizing her seamstresses from New Bond Street; and Laura Asmussen. For several moments her thoughts dwelt on the girl she'd instantly liked and felt comfortable with. Curious, how well they'd got on when they were complete strangers who'd never met before and might not ever meet again. She found herself wondering what the other girl was doing now, right at this very moment; perhaps sewing beads and sequins on to some other client's exclusive evening gown, maybe cutting out some garment or other ready to be put together. Whatever it was it was undoubtedly something interesting, something useful, something that made her independent and fulfilled; just looking at the magnificent sight of the wedding gowns she'd helped to create yesterday, Frances thought, would be more than enough to make her feel proud of the work she'd done. *Not like me . . .*

Wistfully, wishing it was hers, she lay a hand reverently on the shiny polished top of the expensive cabinet gramophone Banbury had bought Elizabeth, and looked longingly at the pile of records stacked neatly beside it. She squatted down on the floor and began to look through them, handling each one as gently as if it was made of glass.

There were half-a-dozen Scott Joplin piano rags, jazz and blues songs recorded by all the most popular favourites: Paul Whiteman

57

and his orchestra, Bix Beiderbecke, King Oliver, Jelly Roll Morton and Louis Armstrong. There were two versions of the Charleston, one with vocal refrain and one without; Abe Lyman, Jean Goldkette, Ted Lewis and his band, a dozen or more orchestrated versions of popular tunes by Cole Porter and Irving Berlin. Frances went slowly and methodically through every one, pausing to read the names of all the musicians, even the minor players. Looking at the records reminded her of what Laura Asmussen had said about her brother, and she wondered how good a player he really was. She sighed. How she'd love to play these records that Elizabeth had so carelessly left behind; but she couldn't do that unless she first asked permission from her mother.

She bit her lip and went on staring down at them. At breakfast her mother had mentioned expecting a visitor from the Foreign Office at eleven; and it was almost eleven now. Then she was lunching out at the Savoy and going straight on afterwards to visit Lord Henry Osborne. Frances's French lessons weren't until two o'clock and her mother was unlikely to be back till past five. With the lesson lasting two hours, that gave her a whole hour to listen to her sister's records, provided her mother would agree.

She got up and smoothed down the creases in her dress. She went downstairs and knocked on the morning room door.

Katherine Cultrane was sitting in one of the big hide club chairs smoking a cigarette in a long jewelled holder when Frances came into the room. A copy of the *Tatler* was lying open on her lap, a tray of coffee and biscuits sat on a small table in front of her. She glanced up, then her eyes went back to the magazine and she spoke without looking away from the page she was reading.

'Shouldn't you be busy practising your French for this afternoon?'

'I've been practising. Besides, my tutor won't expect me to do much today . . . not the day after the wedding.'

Her mother shut the *Tatler* with a snap. 'Oh? And why not, may I ask? It was your sister's wedding, not yours.'

'Can't I have just a single day off?'

'You certainly *cannot*. By the time he was thirteen − two years younger than you − your brother was fluent in not only French and German, but Italian too. Even Elizabeth's French is much better than yours.'

'She's got a French maid . . .'

'Don't be insolent, young lady.' Katherine Cultrane got angrily to her feet and rang the bell. 'Or you'll find that you're not too old for a spanking. Go back upstairs and practise.'

'I came down to ask if I could play some records on Elizabeth's gramophone.'

'When you've finished the exercises you were set last week . . . and only then. I have to go out in a moment – but don't think I won't know if you've been slacking. I've asked your tutor to report directly to me.'

'It isn't fair!'

'I'll decide what is fair or what isn't in this house. I advise you not to forget that . . . or to whom you're speaking.'

Diplomatically, Frances bit back an angry retort.

'The French Ambassador and his wife – and son, I might add – are among the guests of honour at our party on Thursday night. I want you word perfect by then.'

'Oh, now I'm beginning to see . . .'

'It isn't your business to "see" anything. Just to do as you're told. Now. Your father expects you to converse with the Ambassador's son in his own language, for at least part of the evening . . . so go back upstairs and practise.'

'If I could play some of Elizabeth's records first, it . . .'

'I said *practise*, Frances. Your tutor leaves at half-past three. I've arranged for someone to come over from Mrs Turner's to see to the final fittings for your dress for our party at four o'clock. I shall be back at around seven.'

'Is Daddy sitting late tonight?'

'Yes, he is. But don't think that because neither of us will be here, you can idle your time away playing that execrable noise that passes for music! I shall want to look over your work for this afternoon when I get back.'

Frances smiled with false submission; as soon as her mother had left the house, she wound up the gramophone.

'You dark horse, Laura! Never told us you had a boyfriend!'

Laura smiled enigmatically, taking their teasing in good part. Then she tied the sash belt on her coat and carefully adjusted her cloche hat in one of the elaborate showroom mirrors.

'Sorry to disappoint you, girls. He isn't my boyfriend; he's my brother.' She laughed at the expressions of astonishment on their faces as she went down the stairs to meet him.

'*Brother?*'

'Getting hard of hearing in your old age, Blanche Sanger?' At the bottom of the stairs where Kit was waiting to collect her for lunch, she paused and looked back at them. 'Anyhow, don't tell me you can't see the family likeness!' She threaded her arm through his and they went out together into the crowded city street.

'What a morning! After all the publicity over the Osborne wedding, the telephone hasn't stopped ringing! Mrs Turner has fourteen new orders for wedding gowns and complete brides' trousseaux today alone.'

'Bully for Mrs Turner!'

'This afternoon the Duchess of Northumberland and Lady Westmorland are both coming for fittings for period costume gowns for Lady Londonderry's fancy dress ball.'

'That should be a sight worth seeing.'

She looked up into his face and saw that he was laughing.

'Kit, you're being sarcastic again!'

'Me? Never! It just amazes me that so many rich, overweight women enjoy dressing up like children going to a tea party . . . and all of them trying to outdress the other.'

'Fancy dress balls are all the rage with the aristocracy! Ivy Tree told us that when the Duchess of Sutherland gave a Baby party this new year, Lord Portarlington and his son turned up dressed as a Victorian dowager and her daughter, with no hideous detail omitted . . . can you just imagine it? She said the Prince of Wales and Prince George went as little boys, and Lord Ednam got himself up as a nanny and wheeled his wife about in a perambulator!'

'It just goes to show what I've always said about the royal family and most of the titled lot was right . . . they're all stage struck. But in this case although they've got the money to throw away on their fancy dress get-ups, none of them has got what it really takes to get up and go on a stage – talent.'

'I suppose you're right.' She squeezed his arm. 'Well, don't keep me in suspense for a minute longer . . . let's hear what this secret of yours is. I've been watching the clock all morning.' A sudden suspicion. 'You haven't just been pulling my leg, have you?'

He winked at her as they quickened their step and deftly wound their way through the busy lunch-time crowds. 'When you're sitting comfortably in the Holborn restaurant . . . then I'll begin. OK?'

Laura gazed down onto the ground floor below them, watching other people as they talked and ate, at the band on their raised platform at the far end of the restaurant, playing the latest Cole

Porter and Irving Berlin tunes. Waiters flitted back and forth across the floor with trays of food, and just watching them made her remember how very hungry she was.

Eagerly, she took up the menu. 'Hm ... grilled sole sounds delicious. Just what I fancy. Or the skate with butter and caper sauce.'

'Don't you want a starter? Or are you trying to spare my pocket?'

'Well ... the chilled melon isn't too terribly expensive ... but if I have a starter as well as cheese and biscuits and coffee afterwards, I'll feel guilty. And I don't want to put on any weight.'

'You women and your slimming diets!'

'If I don't want my figure nobody else will.'

'You don't need to watch it.'

'Flatterer.'

'Just being truthful.'

'Tell me this terrible dark secret then. What have you been up to?'

There was a pause. A waiter came up and took their order. She looked astonished when he asked for two glasses of champagne.

'What's all this in aid of?'

'Isn't champagne usually what people drink when they've got something to celebrate?'

'What is it? What's happened?'

He leaned back in his chair and gave her a beaming smile that had a touch of mock smugness in it. 'Guess who's just landed a prime job in the orchestra at the London Pavilion for the whole run of *One Damn Thing After Another?*'

'Kit, you haven't?'

'Had an audition at half past nine this morning. At nine-forty they gave me the job.'

Her eyes lit up with excitement and pleasure. 'Oh, Kit, I'm so proud of you! Were there a lot of other musicians auditioning for the place, too?'

'Dozens of them.' The smile on his face faded a little. 'Pity only one of us got picked. Still, there're other orchestras around.'

'When do you start? And what about your job at the Embassy Club? Won't the hours clash?'

'I start tomorrow ... it's a matinee and then the evening performance at the Pavilion, then I have to grab a taxi and go straight to the Embassy just in time for opening ... admittedly, it'll be a bit of a rush. But they both pay well and I do need the money.'

'But you'll be whacked out! And you've still got rehearsals for both

61

of them to cope with . . . will you get enough time to eat and sleep? Kit, you know I'm thrilled for you but are you sure two jobs at once won't be too much?'

'I'll manage.'

There was a pause while the waiter brought their champagne and took their order. Kit raised his glass in a toast. 'To us. Success, good health, fame, lots of money and not forgetting happiness as well!'

'Are you sure that's enough to wish for?' She was laughing now. 'Kit, seriously . . . I just don't see how you're going to manage with all the travelling, constantly rushing backwards and forwards without time to draw breath. I know you think you can cope with it now but when you actually have to do it every day, day in and evening out, I can't see you keeping it up without dropping from sheer exhaustion . . .'

His face was suddenly serious again. For a moment he didn't answer. But she could tell that by his expression and the way he was toying with his glass that he had something else to tell her, something that she wasn't going to like.

'Laura . . . about the travelling . . . I've given it a lot of thought . . . not just because I've managed to get the job at the Pavilion; it's been on my mind for weeks . . . I'm not going to be able to manage coming home every day . . . it wouldn't make sense.' He reached out a hand and lay it on top of hers. 'I've asked around and I've managed to find myself some really nice digs . . . not far away from the Pavilion, as a matter of fact. All the other blokes in the house are musicians or actors . . . so the landlady's used to eccentrics! And there's a piano that she says I can use if I like to pay to have it tuned myself. Isn't that just the ticket? I could hardly believe my luck!'

Laura was so stunned by his news that she couldn't trust herself to speak; a lump had risen in her throat. So he was going, he was leaving home, nothing would ever quite be the same again. All the small, mundane things they'd done together were about to become part of the past, and because they were, she was suddenly made aware of how much they had all meant to her.

'Laura . . . ?'

She waited until the waiter had gone away again before she looked up at him across the table; tears were stinging at the back of her eyes.

'What is it, what's wrong?'

'Do you . . . do you have to leave home? Do you really have to? Kit, we'll miss you so much . . .'

'Dad won't, that's for sure!'

'Is that the real reason you're leaving? Because of him?'

'No, of course not!' He reached across the table and took her hand in his. 'Don't be silly. Whatever he says to me is like water off a duck's back . . . if I took any notice of him I'd have given up what I'm doing years ago! Look. It doesn't change anything. It doesn't make either of us different. All it means is that you live at home and I live somewhere else. It isn't as if we're never going to see each other ever again.'

There was a long silence before she spoke. 'When are you leaving?'

He squeezed her hand more tightly. 'I thought I'd break the news to Mum and Dad this evening before I have to leave for the Embassy. That'll give me time to pack my things and sort out my music. I can take most of it with me and call back later for the rest.'

'So soon?' There was a break in her voice; she was almost grateful when the waiter came back with their food and gave her a few moments respite so that she could compose herself; if she embarrassed Kit by breaking down and crying in public, she knew that she'd never be able to forgive herself or come here ever again. Slowly, she picked up her knife and fork and tried to make her voice sound normal. 'I'll help you, if you like.' *You're selfish*, a little inner voice reproached her, *You only care about how you feel. This is his chance to better himself and all you can do is sit here feeling sorry for yourself and spoiling it all. You should be ashamed.* She swallowed, and tried to force herself to eat, but the food tasted like paper in her misery. And she'd been so happy all morning, she'd so looked forward to having lunch with him.

'It isn't the end of the world just because I'm leaving home,' Kit said with a smile. She looked up into his face and knew that without her saying anything, he understood; they'd always been like that, understanding what the other was thinking, feeling, going through, almost like a kind of telepathy. He laid his knife and fork down and folded his arms in front of him on the table. 'Laura, it doesn't change anything. You know it wouldn't, not even if I was on the other side of the world. We're too close for that.' He reached out and touched her chin so that she had to keep looking at him. 'I'd never let anything come between us. Trust me.'

She made herself smile. 'Yes, I know that. It'll just take a bit of getting used to, that's all.' She had to change the subject, she had to talk and think about something else. 'So tell me about theatre. They were rehearsing the new Revue. Did you see Charles B. Cochran himself?'

'He came out of his office to hear me play.' Kit sipped his champagne. 'You know, whatever people say about him, you can't help admiring a man like that; someone who started right at the bottom of the heap and worked his own way up. He never had a penny to his name when he started, he didn't have any rich or influential family or friends. Now he manages more than half the theatres in London and lays out thousands on each of his productions . . . amazing what you can do if you're determined to try, isn't it?'

The conversation seemed to have taken an even more ominous turn. Laura pushed her plate away, the food only half finished. 'But you wouldn't do anything like that? Go to America, I mean?'

'Not right now I'm not thinking of it, no.'

'But if Cochran took one of his shows to New York and you were expected to go, you would?'

'There wouldn't be any point . . . shows in London keep their own orchestras even if the principal stars go on Broadway. Very often they'll use different leading men and ladies in New York to the ones that have made the show here. I'm one of a team, not a solo act . . . why should Cochran want to go to the expense of sending musicians from London to America when they've got plenty of their own musicians there already?'

'But you always said that you wanted your own orchestra . . .'

'Band. My own band, playing my own music. That's what I've always wanted; at the moment all I'm doing is biding my time and waiting for the right opportunity to come along. The kind of music I write and play isn't what's happening now . . . but it will. The only place I'd be able to play and be listened to is somewhere like Chicago, or better still, New Orleans. That's where jazz musicians like Jelly Roll Morton and Sidney Bechet'll be. Louis Armstrong, Buddy Bolden. King Oliver and Red Allen. They're the ones who play my kind of music.'

The mention of Chicago and New Orleans in a single sentence electrified her. 'But you just said you weren't thinking of going to America!'

'Not *now*, no. But it doesn't mean that I won't sometime in the future.' Her face fell. 'Look at it this way; if Mrs Turner suddenly opened a big showroom in Paris and wanted you to manage it, wouldn't you jump at the chance? Course you would. Just because

64

you travel the world doesn't mean that you're never coming back again . . . does it?'

'I suppose not.'

'Well then, drink up your champagne and let's order dessert.' Kit caught the eye of a hovering waiter. 'Did you know they're famous for their chocolate mousse here?' He'd got her smiling again. 'Now, that's better!'

'Whether they're famous for it or not I can't have any. Got to watch my figure. I'll just have cheese and biscuits. And coffee. Any more champagne and it'll make my head swim. I'm not used to it.'

'You know what? I reckon if I took you back with me to the Pavilion old Cochran'd offer you a top place with his Young Ladies just like that! For looks alone you'd knock all the others into a cocked hat.'

'Flatterer.'

'Dad'd have a fit, of course; just the mention of the word "chorus girl" is enough to do that.' He smiled the smile she could never resist. 'But if you ever get fed up with sewing sequins on Mrs Turner's gowns for the spoiled aristocracy, you know where to come.'

She wasn't really sure whether he was teasing her or not.

6

Lord Henry Osborne settled back into his favourite hide chair, slowly and methodically began to fill his pipe with his favourite brand of tobacco, then listened to his nephew's wife with great attention, thinking as he always did whenever he saw her, what a beautiful woman she still was. Today, as always, she was dressed in the height of style and elegance, a combination that most women of her age aspired to but rarely achieved; either they dressed dowdily and out of fashion like pre-war matrons, or looked like mutton dressed as lamb. She was wearing a chartreuse cashmere suit with matching high-heeled shoes and silk scarf around her neck, fastened with a vibrantly multi-coloured brooch, the single splash of colour exaggerating the stylish plainness of her outfit. The tradition of family solidity and loyalty had always been strong in him; and he was fond of his nephew. But he'd always thought that Katherine Tribe with her striking looks, acidic wit and brilliant mind, was far too good for him. Naturally, he'd kept his opinion to himself; but if he had ever married – and he knew that at his age he never would – she was exactly the kind of woman he would have chosen.

As a younger son he hadn't succeeded to the enormous wealth and vast estates of his nephew's father; a pity, he'd always thought – without rancour – since he had an inborn talent for administration and a passion for detail that other men found boring; but after excelling at Eton and Oxford and embarking on a lucrative diplomatic career in India, he'd discovered that international intrigue was much more to his liking than the dull day to day running of a family estate.

With the family's Catholic background, he could easily have chosen a career within the church; indeed, with his inpenetrable veneer of piety and brilliant mind he could no doubt have risen high in the graded hierarchy of the church. But that, too, he decided to turn his back on. Though he acted the hypocrite frequently and publicly he knew that to devote a lifetime to pretending to be something he was not would be a sure recipe for disaster. He knew his limitations. Instead, his years of distinguished overseas service in foreign embassies and his flare for flattery and intrigue had brought him the position to which he was most perfectly suited. As Lord Chamberlain, he enjoyed access to all the privileges of power in high places, and the confidences of royalty; and he was in the unique position of hearing gossip that he never hesitated to turn to his own or to his family's advantage. It suited him well. There was nothing he loved more than knowing other people's secrets. And when the secrets involved the highest in the land the knowledge merely added to his pleasure.

His dark, intelligent eyes moved appreciatively over Katherine as she spoke, but there was no sexuality in the way he thought of her. Like his priceless paintings, his antique furniture, his rare china and his beautifully bound library of books, she was a thing of beauty to be admired. He looked at her as he might look at a sculpture or a work of art, and enjoyed her presence in the same way that he derived pleasure from his favourite brand of tobacco or a particularly fine wine. All his life, women had meant very little to him in the physical sense; power had always seemed so much more attractive than passion.

He knew, of course, how different other men were; and therein lay their weakness. Henry Osborne's head – like that of his nephew's beautiful wife – had always firmly ruled his heart. That she was consistently unfaithful to Thomas Cultrane bothered him not at all;

she had cuckolded Cultrane almost from the beginning of their marriage and never once had there been a breath of scandal, never once had she allowed her affairs to intrude upon her married life; Henry Osborne admired that. If his nephew had ever suspected anything, then he was far too well-bred ever to mention it. Certainly, he had never given any sign that he knew the truth.

She crossed one shapely ankle over the other and took out her ivory cigarette holder. Then she inserted a Turkish cigarette and let him lean forward to light it for her.

'I hear the King and Queen have been invited down to Chequers this weekend; didn't you and Tom receive an invitation too?'

'Yes, we did . . . but I left him to make our excuses.' She lay back her head and let a cloud of blue grey smoke spiral upwards from her nostrils. 'We gave Elizabeth and Banbury as our excuse.'

Henry Osborne laughed out loud.

'My dear, you have such a wonderfully succinct way of putting things.'

'God alone knows what Banbury will think of his house when he gets back . . . probably he'll take one look inside and think he's gone to the wrong address . . . everything, every room, stark white, from top to bottom. Elizabeth has asked Syrie Maugham to decorate it in her new style. Can you imagine anything more dreadful? If he wasn't so infatuated with Elizabeth I'd swear he'd never have agreed to let her go ahead with it.'

'The whole house, *all of it*, decorated in *white*?'

'Except the staff rooms and Banbury's study; they'll be left as they are.'

'A most impractical colour . . . and insipid. Whatever made Elizabeth think of such a thing?'

'Oh, you know the way she is . . . if something's in vogue then she simply has to have it. She has to be the first to do everything. Banbury's very tolerant, of course; he's besotted with her and he still can't get over his luck. When the Prince of Wales said, 'If it wasn't for that stupid Royal Marriage Act that old George III cooked up I'd marry you myself,' I saw the way Banbury looked at him. Nothing worries or pleases a man as much as when other men show a desire for their wives. On the one hand they take it as a compliment; on the other they're constantly afraid that the woman will fall in love with someone else. As long as Elizabeth doesn't do anything completely foolish, everything should be all right.'

His sharp ears sensed a note of tension in her voice. 'Is anything worrying you about her?'

There was a long pause. Katherine set down her half-finished cigarette and drew a deep breath. 'She's sleeping with his nephew. Edward Vaux.' Another pause. 'I've known for months that she's been flirting with him, that he's been acting as her escort. After all, with Banbury nearly always in the House or too tired to take her himself after sitting all day, he was the obvious choice. And can you see Banbury dancing the charleston at two o'clock in the morning?' She gave a short, dry laugh. 'Besides, his Father was Banbury's brother – who'd make a more fitting companion? In Banbury's eyes the whole thing's entirely innocent. What worries me is if other people start talking. Then he might very well look at the whole thing with very different eyes.'

'Not if Elizabeth's too clever for him.' Henry Osborne was not shocked by her revelation; nor had she expected him to be. His thin, cat-like face showed no surprise; nor had she expected that, either. Infidelity and adultery were simply the ways of the world.

'I wonder if she will be. When I was looking in her room on the night of the party I found a copy of that woman Marie Stopes' book on contraception.'

His smile faded just a little. He did not answer immediately. He got up from the comfort of his chair and went over to the window; sitting for a long period in the same position tended to give him cramp. In the street below people and vehicles trundled by.

'I shall speak with her . . . if you want me to, when she gets back from the honeymoon. I'm sure you can trust her discretion. She's a clever girl, Elizabeth. Not up to your standards, of course, my dear . . . but I doubt if she'll forget that she's an Osborne.'

'If Banbury ever found out anything . . . or Tom . . .'

'Yes, of course; anything that rocked the boat with Banbury would have a disastrous affect on his own career, especially since Baldwin's government can't in any way be guaranteed to win the next election. Ever since the General Strike the radicals have been gathering more popular support, highlighting social ills and all the other things that reformists love to bleat about. In the next two years anything could happen on the political scene . . . particularly since I can't remember anyone so inept as Baldwin being Prime Minister . . . maybe Asquith excepted. If Lloyd George hadn't taken over when he did – and I hold no brief for the Liberals – Asquith would have lost us the war.'

'That's exactly what Thomas Holland used to say.'

He smiled without answering. Holland was a name he rarely mentioned at length when he talked to Katherine; as a young girl of seventeen her father had taken her to India when Curzon was Viceroy and Holland his right-hand man, and Henry Osborne had his own opinion of their relationship then and since. Astutely, he changed the subject by offering her another glass of sherry.

'No, I won't. I should be going. But before I do there was something I particularly wanted to ask you. About Frances.'

'Such a pretty girl. A credit to you, my dear.'

'I'm not so sure. She's getting distinctly lackadaisical about her studies, and lately she's shown a habit of answering back which I don't like at all.'

'Some small measure of mild rebellion is quite usual in the young.'

'I have my doubts that when the time comes she'll prove as tractable as Elizabeth was over the marriage with Banbury. I told you on the telephone about the French Ambassador . . .'

Slowly, he poured sherry for himself.

'You have your eye on his son for Frances . . . at some future point in time? A very good match. His wife is a second cousin to the Montfort family, if my memory serves me correctly . . .'

'Yes, it does. And that's why I'm anxious that Frances makes the best possible impression. By the time she's ready to be presented at Court, the choice of a suitable Catholic husband might have become even more limited than it is at the moment . . . unless we're prepared to compromise on the subject of religion. 'And one needs to pick a match that will prove . . . advantageous.'

'That may be something we might have to consider. But let's think more seriously on the subject a little closer to the time.'

'I'd rather prepare the ground now . . . if they seem to get on together . . .'

'I shall be here myself, as you know . . . leave it to me to keep an eye on the Osborne interests.'

She smiled as she rose and he kissed her lightly on the cheek. He rang for his butler to show her out.

Katherine Cultrane lay back on the leather upholstered seats of her car a few moments later, reflecting on their meeting; she was too astute not to have noticed when he'd carefully turned the conversation from the subject of Thomas Holland. He'd always been so clever, so understanding; and he was very fond of her, she knew. But had he ever really guessed the truth?

Hyde Park Terrace was a smart, fashionable row of elegant Georgian town houses halfway between Marble Arch and Piccadilly, with Green Park on one side of it and Rotten Row on the other. On the journey from Henry Osborne's house they passed Carlton House Terrace and Katherine felt a stab of emotion and painful nostalgia as her eyes fastened unwillingly on one of the tall, elegant, white façades; even the sight of the house where he'd lived could still bring back that part of her past that she thought could be forgotten now he was dead. Defiantly, she turned her head away in the opposite direction; she had always despized sentimental women; women who cried in vain for lost loves, women who foolishly clung to the past. Thwarted only once in her life, the sudden sight of the house and the memories it evoked for a moment caught her off guard. As if to exorcise them, she rapped sharply on the glass panel that divided her and the chauffeur in front.

'It was Hyde Park Terrace, my lady?'

'Yes . . . number twenty.' After a few more seconds the house was behind her, and she lay back in her seat with a sense of relief. She could have asked the chauffeur to take another route; but that would have been a sign of weakness and weakness was something that she scorned in others; a failing she would never tolerate in herself. Driving past his house and forcing herself to remember was like wearing a hair shirt; an essential exercise in self-discipline, something that was painful to do but which must still be done.

'Number twenty, my lady,' said the chauffeur's voice, breaking into her thoughts. He stopped the car, opened her door and stood behind it while she got out. For a moment she stood there right on the pavement looking at it; then she went up the short flight of steps to the front door and rang the bell.

A manservant answered; of course Edward Vaux, on a bachelor's limited income, would not go to the unnecessary expense of engaging a butler. A waste of money. She guessed, shrewdly, that Vaux had no more than a handful of servants: the manservant who doubled as a valet, a cook, and a couple of maids. The manservant showed her into the drawing room and while she waited for Vaux to appear she looked around it with a calculating, practised eye.

Yes, he had taste; she had to give him that. There were sporting prints on the walls and the furniture was Chippendale; her eyes rested with interest on a particularly fine cabinet bookcase filled with hide-bound first editions that she guessed Henry Osborne would have appreciated. There was a late eighteenth-century longcase clock in unusually fine condition. The room was comfortable without being over-furnished; a piano in one corner, cabinet gramophone, a pile of records, photographs in silver frames on a round library table; several of them, her sharp eyes registered, were of Elizabeth.

When he came into the room she was holding one of them in her hand. The look of astonishment on his face was so great that she wanted to laugh out loud.

'Lady Cultrane, what an unexpected pleasure . . . can I offer you something to drink?' He was covering his surprise well.

'Thank you, no; I've just come from visiting someone else and I had tea with them. May I sit down?'

'Why, yes, of course . . .'

She took her time, enjoying his discomfiture. Slowly, she took off her gloves. She smoothed down her silk, fur-trimmed coat and crossed her ankles. Then she looked up into his face. With her uncanny intuition, she could almost read what he was thinking. How much did she know?

Stiffly, he sat down opposite her and clasped his hands on his knees.

She smiled. 'How long have you been having an affair with my daughter, Edward?'

With a kind of perverse satisfaction she saw the colour drain from his face. 'I don't know who told you such a thing but . . .'

She settled herself more comfortably in her chair.

'Please, don't insult my intelligence by trying to deny it; I saw the way you were looking at each at the wedding. And when we came back to the house after the Goldsmiths' Hall you both disappeared at the same time for more than half an hour; even the Prince of Wales asked where you were. You came back into the room within minutes of each other . . . something of an extraordinary coincidence, wouldn't you say?' She opened her kid handbag and took out her ivory cigarette holder, and then a cigarette. 'When I made a discreet check of the guest rooms upstairs – the blue bedroom to be precise – there was really no other reasonable conclusion I could have come to about what you were doing there . . . was there?'

He ran a hand through his dark, wavy hair. He got up and stood stiffly by the mantlepiece, staring into the empty grate.

'Are you going to tell my uncle?'

She laughed, softly and mockingly. 'Do you really think I would ever do anything as stupid as that?'

He spun round, astonished. 'But . . . isn't that why you've come? To tell me that if I don't give her up you'll tell him about us?'

Her smile disappeared sharply. 'I came here to tell you that if either of you ever do anything indiscreet, anything that in any way at all could jeopardize my husband's political career, I swear I'll ruin you both. I don't need to tell you how things stand; because of the marriage between Elizabeth and your uncle, he's giving her father all the support and influence in the party that he's got; all the political ground my husband lost when Baldwin was elected Prime Minister has been regained . . . because of Banbury's close friendship with him. If he thought for one moment that Elizabeth was sleeping with his own nephew, laughing at him behind his back . . . Have you any idea of what the consequences would be not only for you but for my husband's political future? The scandal that would break would not only force him to resign . . . it would destroy our entire family. And the last twenty-five years that I've spent pushing Tom further up the ladder towards the top will all be for nothing. If you think that I'd allow that to happen because you and my daughter can't control your lust, then you're both sadly mistaken.' He opened his mouth to speak, but she held up her hand. 'Don't misunderstand me; I couldn't care less what you do in bed, or who you do it with; as far as I'm concerned Elizabeth can sleep with every man in London; you're not her first lover and I doubt if you'll be the last. But you both know the rules. It isn't what you do . . . it's getting caught at it that matters. Do I make myself perfectly clear?'

She put the silver tip of the ivory cigarette holder between her lips, and he leaned forward, lighter in hand, and lit the cigarette for her.

'I swear . . . we have been discreet. Both of us. We couldn't have been more careful. Nobody would ever suspect . . . if anything, the fact that she's the wife of my uncle makes it all easier. He has late sittings in the House, Cabinet meetings at Downing Street . . . he'd never expect Elizabeth to sit waiting for him at home. He loves her to enjoy herself, to go to parties and nightclubs . . . it's all part of her charm to him, don't you see that? He's a different generation, he's flattered that someone as young and beautiful and daringly modern as Elizabeth is married to him . . . in a way I think it excites him . . . seeing her photograph in all the newspapers, reading about all the outrageous exploits of the "Bright Young Things", that she danced with the Prince of Wales at the Embassy . . . for a man of his age that's like an aphrodisiac. He doesn't mind not being able to be there himself; even if he could go, he hasn't got the stamina to keep up with her – and he knows it. He'd fall asleep halfway through the evening . . . and then what an old fool he'd look in front of all her racy friends. He'd never risk that. So he's well content to let her have a long rope . . . and while I'm there, a member of the family, the perfectly respectable and acceptable escort . . . what could be better? I'm the one man he'd never dream of suspecting.'

She dotted the ash from her Turkish cigarette. 'Yes, very true. Not many men would suspect their own nephew of fornicating with their wife.' She'd meant her words to sting him and they did.

'It can't be easy for a young woman like Elizabeth to be married off to a decrepit old man!'

Katherine couldn't resist smiling. 'Harsh words. Unfortunately, very few of us in our station of life are free to pick and choose. Including myself when I was her age.' Yes, that had surprised him. 'Be that as it may; even if duty and family obligation force us to marry in one direction, that doesn't mean that we can't – if we are discreet – follow our natural inclinations in another. You both have far more freedom than young people of my generation ever did; be sure that you appreciate it. And you're far luckier than most. Banbury is much older than she is and his heart is weak. Even if he manages to live for another ten years – which I doubt – Elizabeth will be a very rich widow, still young . . . and you'll be ready and waiting in the wings . . .' another smile. 'Unless, of course, you've tired of waiting for dead men's shoes.'

The barb went home. 'I love Elizabeth and she loves me!'

'Time will tell.' Katherine disposed of her cigarette in his ashtray and stood up, ready to leave. 'Well, I've taken up enough of your time. And I do have one final call to make before I go home.' She drew on her gloves. 'Before I go, just a last suggestion . . . when she comes back from Paris, you make no mention to Elizabeth of this conversation at all.'

He held the door open for her and she walked out into the hall without waiting for him to answer. As she went down the short flight of steps to the pavement outside, she turned and gave him a dazzling smile. The chauffeur opened the door for her, she got in and in a few moments the car had driven off in the direction of Regent Street and Cavendish Square.

The chauffeur dropped her outside Liberty's; she instructed him to come back and collect her when she'd finished shopping in two hours. From inside the store, she watched him as he climbed back inside the Rolls Royce and drove away. Then she came straight out again and hailed a taxi.

Five minutes later, it drew up outside a house in Manchester Square. She got out, paid the driver, then walked up to the gate and opened it. A moment later she was ringing the bell. While she was waiting for the door to be answered, she got out her powder compact and checked her appearance in its tiny mirror.

In front of her, the door opened, and the man's face in the doorway broke into an appreciative smile. 'Katherine, how lovely you look. As always.' He leaned down and kissed her lips. 'How long can you stay?'

7

In Anne Turner's richly furnished main fitting-room, Laura stood waiting while Mrs Turner carefully measured and re-measured one of her most important clients for a new evening dress; but for once her mind was a long way removed from her job. All she could think about was Kit.

'Waist . . . twenty-five inches. Hips . . . thirty-four inches . . . length, from shoulder to knee . . . thirty-seven.' Anne Turner nodded towards Laura and Laura wrote them down in her small, neat handwriting as she dictated. She wondered what Kit was doing now. She wondered what it would be like the day after tomorrow, when he'd left home for good.

'I suggest a straight box neckline, cut low; and the single strap decorated with the same black silk fringes that we have at the front of the gown . . . a very low back, with a specially designed ornament to make a striking statement whichever way the gown is viewed . . . from back or front.' Mrs Turner stood back, considering. 'As to colour and material . . . I know you favour pastel colours, my lady . . . but have you ever considered black? Stark black chiffon, with the addition of silk chiffon fringes and ornaments for decoration will make a stunning contrast to your natural fair colouring. The entire effect will be sensational.'

'Black?'

Anne Turner made a sign to Laura, who turned and picked up a roll of black silk chiffon, then spun it around in her hands several times until the material spilled out across the floor. Mrs Turner lifted one end of it and held it up against her client; they all studied the effect in one of the enormous gilt mirrors.

'Mrs Turner, you're a genius! Black chiffon will be absolutely perfect!'

'Laura, fetch me the sketches please.'

While the women chatted and studied the drawings for the gown, Laura stood back, studying the short, petite figure of Lady Irene Stanton, and wondered not for the first time why she was such a celebrity in society.

The youngest daughter of the Duke of Cheshire – and Laura had overheard backroom gossip that she was really the daughter of her mother's good-looking lover – she was the wife of a minor politician and one of the "Bright Young Things" who inhabited the orbit of the likes of Lady Elizabeth Osborne and her ilk. She was very pretty, certainly – the proverbial English rose type with fair hair, blue eyes, and delicate pink-and-white skin – but there were many other young women both in society and on the fringe of it whose looks far eclipsed her own. Lady Cunard, the well-known society hostess, might always introduce Irene Stanton as 'the most beautiful woman in the world', but Laura, studying her face and figure intently, thought that beside Elizabeth Osborne she looked insignificant and ordinary.

The real secret of her celebrity, she'd heard people whisper, was her talent for self-advertisement, catching the imagination of the newspaper-reading classes who adored tales of the artistocracy, and feeding gossip columnists with cleverly calculated snips of information about her own daring transgressions of 'polite behaviour' which everyone passed off as lovable, delightful eccentricities. But her obvious self-obsession and high, tinselly laugh irritated Laura; even more so her widely publicized boast that despite being terribly 'hard up' the Stantons wined and dined at all the best places and were never in debt. Easily done, Laura thought, when friends and relatives footed all the bills and fashionable dressmakers fell over themselves to keep her supplied with expensive and exclusive gowns. Lady Irene Stanton was no more or less than a society parasite.

Anne Turner handed the roll of black silk chiffon back to Laura and helped her client to get dressed.

'Shall we say a first fitting in ten days? Of course, if that isn't convenient . . .'

'Mrs Turner, if we were dining with the King I'd still be here. I can't *wait* to see it! Do you know, I'd never have thought of myself wearing black . . .'

Anne Turner smiled. 'In my experience the very ladies who most favour the colour are the ones least suited to wear it. You could carry off anything.'

Outside, well out of earshot, Laura looked back at the closed fitting room door with an expression of relief at her escape.

She went along to the sewing room. Thirty seamstresses were busily bent over their work. Machines were whirring in the background as Anne Turner came into the room a few moments later.

'Laura, let Blanche have Lady Irene's measurements and get the gown cut out today. I'll check the pieces over myself before we close.'

'Yes, Mrs Turner.'

'When you've done that I want to see you in my office.' The two girls exchanged glances. 'Blanche . . . give Dora the sketches for the Sondeburg costumes so that she can make a start on them before tomorrow. The Princess has an appointment at eleven to choose the materials and colours.' She glanced at the busy workforce with satisfaction, then turned and walked out of the room.

'I wonder what she wants me for?'

Anne Turner was sitting writing behind her desk when Laura knocked on her door and was told to come in, instantly aware as she closed it behind her of the distinctive, overpowering scent of her favourite perfume.

The room itself was a fitting testimonial to the woman's remarkable success in her chosen profession as designer and purveyor of beautiful clothes to the rich, the famous, and the aristocratic. Everything in it was exclusive and very expensive. It was a perfect blend of the best of the antique and the modern; Mrs Turner's desk could have come directly from one of the gilded rooms in the Palace of Versailles; every other piece of furniture was modern Art Deco. Silk lined the walls instead of paper; hanging alongside framed photographs of her impressive clientele wearing her creations were original paintings by a variety of French artists, and a madonna by Rubens. The last seemed particularly appropriate to Laura; the smooth white skin, golden tresses and blue eyes of the woman in the picture were strikingly similar to Anne Turner herself.

She stopped writing and looked up with a smile. 'Please, take a seat.'

Laura sat down and folded her hands on her lap.

'Well, over the last few months you've certainly come up with some very creative and innovative designs.' She closed the book she'd been writing in and lay down her platinum and gold pen. 'Your progress has been astonishing . . . as I always thought, you have real talent. Rare talent.' She gave Laura the dazzling smile that was normally only reserved for clients or men. 'You've more than borne out my initial faith. In view of that I think it's time to give you a little more responsibility.'

Laura flushed with pleasure. 'Thank you, Mrs Turner . . .'

'Lady Cultrane's youngest daughter . . . you'll perhaps remember her from the wedding . . . is due for an evening dress fitting this afternoon – at Belgrave Square. I want you to see to it personally. Take a taxi there and back – I'll give you the fare from petty cash. Lady Cultrane also wants a series of designs made for a range of outfits . . . for the coming season.'

'For Lady Frances?'

'Yes, for Lady Frances. While you're there today, you could take down a few details from her about colour preferences, and styles; go to work on them when you get back. Lady Cultrane would have to give them her final approval, of course.'

'Yes, I see.' She was thinking about the lunch date with her brother. 'Have I to be there by any particular time?'

'Oh, after lunch will do.' At that moment her telephone rang, and she nodded towards Laura as she picked it up, signifying that she could leave. 'Come and see me when you get back.'

As she closed the door behind her Laura heard Anne Turner's voice become even more aristrocratic, and she guessed that the client was an important one.

'Duchess! But how wonderful to hear from you . . .'

Nervously, she got out of the taxi and paid the driver, then stood there on the pavement looking up at the house for several minutes before she mustered sufficient courage to go up to the front door. From its background of glossy white paint, the gleaming brass letter-box and massive lion's head glittered in the afternoon light, and she went on looking at it uncertainly, wondering whether or not she should use the back entrance in the mews.

Behind her in the street she heard the sounds of the engine as the taxi drove out of the square, leaving her standing alone on the wide stone steps beneath the marble portico.

She'd meant to ask Mrs Turner which entrance she should use before she'd left, but she was still talking on the telephone and couldn't be disturbed. Taking a deep breath, Laura reached out a gloved hand and knocked on the door.

Almost instantly it was opened by the Cultranes' butler. 'May I help you?'

'Thank you.' She tried to move her lips in a smile but his stony expression forestalled her. 'Yes, please . . . Mrs Turner sent me to see Lady Frances Osborne . . . about some dress designs . . .

His face remained expressionless; except for his eyes. Laura shrewdly guessed that his demeanour would have altered considerably if she'd been somebody higher up the social scale. She felt as if she was back in school. 'Kindly use the mews entrance, Miss.' He pointed. 'Turn to your left and keep walking until you reach the gate at the back. One of the servants will show you where to go.'

'No,' said another voice from somewhere behind him in the hall. 'Miss Asmussen doesn't use the back entrance.' They both turned in the direction of voice; Frances Osborne was standing halfway down the grand staircase. 'She'll come up this way with me.'

The butler's manner changed immediately. 'Very good, my lady. Of course.' He stood back to let Laura walk in. 'Will there be anything else, my lady?'

'Will you please have a tray of tea sent up to the old nursery in half an hour?'

'Yes, my lady; I'll attend to it right away.' He took Laura's hat and coat and disappeared with them into the cloakroom on the other side of the hall. Frances' face broke into a smile.

'I'm sorry about that.' She beckoned Laura up the stairs. 'You might as well follow me.'

'It's all my fault . . . I should have gone round the back way like we did when we came with Mrs Turner. I wasn't really sure what to do . . .'

'Oh, don't take any notice of Saunders . . . he'll remember next time. I'm so glad you're here! I've been bored stiff all morning, writing exercises in German and French. My mother's orders. She's gone out but she'll check everything when I get back, and talk to the tutor who comes here if she thinks I'm slacking.' She pulled a face. 'She's threatened to send me to a language school in Kensington four times a week if my work doesn't improve.' She opened the door of her room and Laura followed her inside, gazing round at the exquisite furniture and paintings she remembered from the day of the wedding. 'When I told my mother that if any French or German people want to talk to me at one of her parties, then they'll just have to do it in

78

English, she went into one of her rages.' When she grimaced, Laura had a good idea just how intimidating those rages would be. 'I'd much rather play records on Elizabeth's gramophone!' They both laughed together.

'I can't believe Mrs Turner's given me this to do . . . me, designing clothes for the Earl of Cultrane's daughter! I never thought about being given anything so important . . .'

'Important? Me?' She started to laugh. 'Well, I suppose my mother and my sister are important to Mrs Turner. Or, rather, their custom is. Being able to say she dresses the Osborne women is quite a feather in her cap, isn't it? Did you know she used to work for my grandfather as a linen maid when she was young?'

'No! I never knew that . . .' Laura was genuinely startled; she'd heard different rumours, gossip from the other girls, but never anything like this.

'I didn't mean that to sound disparaging; after all, she's a very clever woman; not only at designing clothes every woman in London wants to wear . . . I admire people who fight their way to the top, and get there, from sheer talent and hard work. No, it's something else. Something else about her that I can't quite like.' Frances motioned her to sit down. 'Anyhow, let's talk about these dresses . . . and your brother; please, tell me all about your brother. I was dying to ask you so many questions at the wedding, by my mother and Mrs Turner came in and spoiled everything. How did he come to play at the Embassy Club?'

'He always loved music, he was always determined to be a musician . . . he could play the clarinet and the piano like a professional when he was thirteen or fourteen years old. Of course, our father never approved of it at all; he wanted him to go into an office. Kit in an office! There were some awful rows, I can tell you , but Kit got his way in the end. Mind you, Daddy was against me working too . . . it was only Mrs Turner's reputation and the names of some of her clients that won the day. Mummy and I somehow managed to persuade him that it was an enormous honour even being *asked*. Secretly, I think he's quite smug about it now. With all the publicity about the wedding, he was able to boast to his colleagues at the bank that I had a hand in it all.'

'You're so lucky to be independent.' There was real feeling in Frances's voice. 'If you wanted to leave home you could, couldn't you? You could pay your own way.'

79

'But I'd never leave home . . . I've never even thought about leaving . . .'

'If I had your talent, I jolly well would. Even though Mummy and Daddy would probably hang draw and quarter me; in our family you just don't *do* things like that! Unless you happen to be my brother Freddie, who gets away with just about everything because he's my mother's favourite.'

'Does he live here?'

'No, he got married last year and has his own house . . . and one in the country. It was a wedding present from his in-laws.'

She smiled, apologetically. 'I'm sorry. I don't want to bore you to death. Come on, let's go and talk about the dress designs in the old nursery . . . it's cosier in there. And it'll almost be time for Saunders to bring up the tea.' As they got up to go out, Laura noticed a photograph on the table beside the satin-draped bed in a particularly elaborate frame. Her curiosity got the better of her manners.

'Who's that?'

'It's Sir Thomas Holland, the War Secretary . . . Lord Curzon's deputy in India. He was my godfather." A tinge of sadness came into her voice. 'He died four years ago . . . curiously enough, in the same year as Lord Curzon did. When I was away at boarding school, he was the only one who used to come down to visit me. It was right in the middle of nowhere but my godfather always seemed to manage time off from whatever he was doing to drive down and take me out to tea. The night before, I'd be so excited that I couldn't sleep, and all the other girls would be green with envy!' She went to a drawer, rummaged in it, then took out a small, faded picture. 'He got someone in the village to take this of us together . . . it's my favourite, because he's smiling. In all the photos the newspapers published of him – the official photos, he was never smiling.' Laura looked down at it; Thomas Holland, one arm around a much younger Frances, sitting on a rustic village bench with a quaint little tea shop in the background. They were both smiling at the camera, and looked incredibly alike.

'He's awfully handsome; and he's got such a kind face.'

'Yes, he was kind,' She put away the photo and they went out. 'The old nursery's this way . . . next floor. There are so many stairs in this house.'

Different to all the other rooms in the house, the old nursery was clearly furnished for practicality and not decoration; everything was big, solid, serviceable. There was an enormous dolls' house, a tallboy, a chest of drawers; a table and stout chairs. A rocking-horse with faded paint, a clutch of old toys and books, an old Victorian horsehair sofa with loose covers, ranged around the faded walls.

'I've always loved this room. Sit down and make yourself comfortable. You can spread all your things out on there.' She indicated the table. 'I used to adore the nursery teas in here with my nanny, then my governess . . . she was *so* fascinating to talk to . . . just like you . . . from a different world to us. I used to be so jealous of her on her afternoons off, when she could simply put on her hat and coat and go out wherever she liked! I always wished I could go with her . . . but of course I wasn't allowed . . .' she was fishing through the deep drawers of the tallboy, looking for something. 'here it is! I wanted to show you this . . . it belonged to her.' Laura took the large, dogged-eared scrapbook and lay it on her lap. Slowly, she turned to the first page, where neatly cut out pieces of yellow newsprint had been pasted carefully in place.

'Goodness, it's from the *Daily Mail* . . . 1922 . . . the trial of Edith Thompson and Frederick Bywaters . . .'

'Yes . . . my Mother would go mad if she knew I had it . . . look . . . there are all sorts of famous murder cases here . . . my governess used to collect them . . . then one day my mother found it and there was a dreadful scene; she was absolutely furious. She gave her notice straight away, told her she wasn't fit to be in charge of children, and dismissed her even without a reference. I can remember her leaving by the back entrance with her suitcase, in floods of tears. My mother wouldn't even let us say goodbye.' Had it dated from then, the irrational unease of being in her mother's presence . . . or had she always been afraid of her? The far-off figure, like Elizabeth, a glamorous idol to be adored, admired and envied. The disgraced governess and Thomas Holland had been so much more real to her.

'Did you ever hear from her again?'

'No. I never knew what happened to her. But I always wondered. I thought how dreadful it must be to be dismissed without a reference . . . how would she be able to get another job? I wished that I could have helped her, but there was nothing I could do.' Laura looked at her appraisingly; she doubted that anyone else in the Osborne family had given that a second thought. Frances was different to them.

'My brother always says that everything happens for the best.'

'He sounds nice. Like you. You're lucky to have a brother like that. I have three and I don't get on with any of them. The two

81

youngest are away at school, so I don't see them very often; but when they do come home all we do is quarrel. They have a lot more freedom than me, and I always complain that it isn't fair. Not that anyone ever listens!'

At that moment, Saunders came in carrying a silver tea tray spread with a lace cloth which he set down in the middle of the table. Both girls looked at it at the same time: there was a silver hot water jug, a china teapot, milk jug and sugar basin toast and cakes; but only a single plate and cup. The deliberate omission was not lost on Laura.

'Saunders,' said Frances Osborne politely, only the two bright spots of colour on her cheeks giving away her anger at the slight, 'you seem to have forgotten to bring another cup.'

His face never moved a muscle; but Laura caught the expression of outrage in his eyes. 'Yes, my lady.'

When he had gone, Frances poured the milk and then the tea into the solitary cup, then handed it to Laura.

Anne Turner got out of the taxi at the entrance to the mews and handed the driver half a crown.

'That's all right. Keep the change.' She gave him one of her dazzling smiles, the smiles she reserved strictly for members of the male sex; even a humble taxi-driver. It had always amused her to see the way they reacted to her veiled sensuality, boosting her sense of personal power. Above all, there was that glorious sense of slumming . . . She'd never forgotten that tall, muscular, handsome young footman who'd been in service with the Tribes at the same time as she had . . .

As the taxi drove off in the direction of Maida Vale she closed her handbag and began to walk in the direction of the Mews. There was a distinct chill in the air now it was near dusk, and she pulled her silver fox fur closer around her shoulders. As always, she was dressed in the height of fashion but with an understated elegance that hall-marked an Anne Turner original at a glance; with a complacent smile, as she walked she remembered the famous names of the celebrated couturiers of her youth, and those of a few years ago who her own fame had now virtually eclipsed. There was Madame Hayward, whose New Bond Street premises she'd taken over in 1923; Reville and Rossiter in Hanover Square, who'd made the wedding gown for the Princess Royal; her nearest rival. But the fact that the Royal family chose to patronize the more traditional dressmaking establishments worried Anne Turner not at all; she could afford to do without

82

their custom. It was the 'Bright Young Things', the sophisticated theatrical and society beauties who got their names in the popular newspapers who were her most cherished clients; they were the ones who mattered. Dull, conventional women like the Queen and her daughter were scarcely leaders of fashion.

She paused when she reached the house she was seeking, and pressed the bell. After a few moments a housemaid opened it and smiled with immediate recognition. She stood aside to let her walk in.

'Oh, Mrs Turner. Good evening. Turned chilly now, hasn't it?' She closed the door behind her and led the way through the hall. 'Dr Forman's still in his consulting room, going over some notes. He's expecting you . . .'

The hall was large, white and clinical, its severity broken only by one large and very strikingly ornate inlaid table and a row of neat watercolours depicting botanical subjects. Their footsteps echoed on the polished parquet floor.

'Is Mrs Forman at home?'

'Oh, no, ma'am. It's Thursday; Mrs Forman always goes over to Lambeth to see her sister of a Thursday. Never gets back till late.' They reached the large white door at the end of the hall and the girl knocked and opened it.

'Mrs Turner's here, Dr Forman. Shall I make some tea?'

The man who rose from behind the desk to greet her was middle-aged, immaculately dressed and suavely good-looking; his hands were beautifully manicured and smooth; his dark hair attractively turning grey at the temples. He kissed her lightly on the cheek and helped her take off her coat and hat.

'Take these for Mrs Turner, Lily. And I think it's just a little late for tea. Bring me a whisky and soda and get Mrs Turner a pink gin, will you?'

'In here, Dr Forman?'

'Yes, in here. And when you've done that tell the other servants that Mrs Turner and I have some business to discuss and don't wish to be disturbed.'

'Yes, Dr Forman.' She went and closed the door softly behind her.

'My dear, do sit down and be comfortable.' He sat down again behind his desk. 'As always, you look absolutely ravishing. But then, you always do. For you, it's second nature.' He pushed a large silver cigarette box on his desk towards her and she opened it and took one.

'You're so good for my ego, Simon darling . . . that's what I've always loved about you.' She let him light her cigarette and then smiled at him, showing white, perfect teeth. 'You know, courtesy in men always had this extraordinary effect on me . . . it always makes me want to go to bed with them.'

He lay back in his chair and regarded her with pleasure; despite her humble origins, she'd always had style. Born into another class and she'd have been a society beauty, the mistress of some titled, wealthy aristocrat or politician, maybe even of a king; she had brains as well as looks. And he'd always admired intelligence and ambition in a woman.

'Well,' he said, tapping a newspaper lying on the desk in front of him,, 'I see you've really excelled yourself over the clothes for the Osborne wedding. According to this, Banbury took his young wife to the Paris opera and her evening gown created a major sensation.'

'Can I see that?' She took the paper and spent several minutes reading the article and studying the photograph of Elizabeth Osborne; while she was looking at it the maid came back with the tray of drinks.

Forman sipped his whisky and soda reflectively. 'How long do you give the marriage? Six months? A year? Two, if Banbury's lucky?'

Anne Turner put down the newspaper and took her glass of pink gin from the tray. She crossed her shapely ankles. 'You mean how long will it take Banbury to find out that she's sleeping with his nephew? He's so besotted with her, he wouldn't believe it even if someone told him to his face; there's no fool like an old fool, don't they say? In any case, she's too sly to be caught out . . . unless she loses her head and does something really stupid. Sometimes, the risks she takes, I wonder if she's perfectly sane . . .'

Forman got up from behind the desk and came over to where she was sitting. Gently, he took her by the arms and raised her up; their lips met and opened in a long, passionate kiss.

Slowly, without speaking, he suddenly released her and went to the door. Then he turned the key in the lock. His caution amused her.

'I thought you told me that no one would dare come in here while you're consulting with a client. Even that jealous, provincial, suspicious-minded little wife of yours . . . ?'

He came back to her and slowly began undressing her. 'My dear, of course they wouldn't dare . . . but then, as you always tell me, one can never be totally sure of anything . . .'

He raised her pale rose linen top over her head, then her silk slip. With practised skill, he deftly unhooked the matching rose silk brassière, revealing her full, pointed breasts. He bent his head and kissed them, then ran his tongue over her nipples.

'You could at least have let me finish my pink gin.'

Smiling, she put one long, shapely leg on the chair and began to unfasten her suspenders. With sensuous slowness, she rolled each silk stocking down towards her ankles, then flung it off, while he stood there watching her. Finally, she slid off her pink silk and lace cami-knickers and stood in front of him naked. Her body quivered with pleasure as she felt his cool, light touch on her hot skin.

His fingers lifted the exquisite sapphire necklace that she'd been wearing beneath her clothes. He raised his eyebrows questioningly. 'How lovely . . . and it matches the colour of your eyes. I've never seen it before . . . a gift from one of your admirers?'

She smiled as she reached out and began to unbutton his shirt. 'Just a little token of appreciation . . . from Elizabeth Osborne. Banbury gave it to her and she didn't care for it . . . so she gave it to me.' Another smile.

'With a little prompting, of course?'

'A little reward for certain services rendered . . .'

The moment she took her key out of the door and went into the hall, she knew that he'd got home before she had; his clarinet case was propped up against the wall underneath the stairs, beside it sat a battered carpet bag stuffed with sheet music. She could hear his voice, then her father's, coming from the dining room.

Taking off her hat and coat, with a quick glance in the mirror to check her hair was tidy, she went and found them.

'Laura, you're more than half-an-hour late! And you knew we were having dinner early because the Murrays are coming for bridge . . .'

'Yes, I'm sorry, Daddy; but Mrs Turner gave me a special assignment today and I didn't want to leave until I'd finished. I just missed by usual train.' She exchanged a glance with Kit; so he hadn't told them he was leaving home yet. Her mother looked fussed and her father was clearly in one of his bad moods. 'The Murrays aren't coming until half-past seven, are they?'

'That isn't the point, Laura. Punctuality is a most important thing. If we're late sitting down to dinner then Ethel will be rushed in the kitchen, and she'll barely have time to get everything ready for supper when we've finished our bridge.'

'I thought Mrs Grady was coming in for an extra few hours this evening.'

'Her daughter's ill. She had to go over to Streatham at short notice, and Ethel's going to have to manage on her own. Really, it's just too bad! And this evening of all times . . .'

Laura and Kit exchanged another glance; he pulled a face behind his father's back and Laura fought with herself not to giggle. She sat down and spread her napkin on her lap. Neither of her parents spoke; for several minutes, while Ethel brought in the soup, there was a painful silence, broken only by the noise of the spoons in the soup dishes.

'So . . . what's this special assignment the great Turner's lined up for you?'

She threw Kit a grateful glance, but her father scowled.

'Kit . . . if you can't speak about the lady in a civil manner, kindly refrain from speaking about her at all. I'm in no mood for your sarcastic comments this evening!'

'I stand chastised. I'll rephrase the question . . . that's what barristers say, isn't it? What's the special job Mrs Turner gave you to do today, Laura?'

She described her afternoon at Belgrave Square.

'Oh, the poor little rich girl again! You have to design evening dresses for her so that she can attend all those political parties her mother's so famous for! Cinderella *will* go to the ball!'

'Kit, please . . .'

'Sorry, Ma. No, I take it all back. She sounds un-Osborne like. Especially when she put the butler in his place. I'd love to have been a fly on the wall.'

'Kit, have you told Mummy and Daddy about your audition at the London Pavilion yet?'

There was a sudden silence around the table. Kit grinned.

'I was just going to, as a matter of fact.'

'Audition at the London Pavilion?'

'I went there this morning to audition for a place in the orchestra. I got it.'

'What about your job at the Embassy Club? Won't the hours of work clash?'

'I can do it.' There was another strained silence while Ethel came in to clear the dishes and serve the next course.

'We've got a really rushed day tomorrow,' Laura tried again to dispel the atmosphere her father's bad mood had cast over everyone.

'Lady Ednam's coming in for a fitting in the morning . . . Mrs Turner asked me to put down a few ideas for designs in styles she likes . . . so I'm keeping my fingers crossed. I do like Lady Ednam. She's not exactly one of the regular clients, but she's so pleasant and cheerful . . . and she has the most beautiful translucent complexion and lovely eyes . . .'

Her mother lay down her knife and fork. 'Wasn't she Lady Rosemary Leveson-Gower before she married? The Duke of Sutherland's daughter?'

'Yes, that's right. Blanche Stephens was saying that the Prince of Wales wanted to marry her just after the war . . . he met her when she was a Red Cross nurse in France. But the King was supposed to have vetoed the marriage because he didn't approve of her relations; her mother was divorced twice and her uncle gambled. And he was bankrupt three times over.'

'Goodness me!'

'What's that got to do with her marrying the Prince of Wales?' Kit spoke unexpectedly and their father frowned with disapproval. Divorces weren't spoken about at the dinner table. 'It wasn't her fault what her mother or uncle did. If I'd been HRH I'd have gone and married her anyway. If the King didn't like it, he could lump it.'

'You'll be good enough to speak of the King with respect, if you don't mind.'

'My apologies,' Kit answered drily, but Laura kicked him under the table in warning; to their father any criticism of the Royal Family was like waving a red flag at a bull.

'I'm sure the King was simply worried about the risk of a scandal,' Violet Asmussen said. 'After all, neither he nor Queen Mary could possibly receive a divorcée under any circumstances . . . it would be unthinkable!'

'Blanche said that the uncle's gambling was so notorious that they named that popular song after him, *The Man Who Broke the Bank of Monte Carlo*.'

Kit burst out laughing, but her father looked ferocious. 'Are all Mrs Turner's employees such inveterate lovers of idle gossip?' he said with heavy disapproval, giving Kit an old fashioned look. 'I'm sure she'd take a very poor view of her staff repeating such things about a client, whether they're true or not.'

'It was Mrs Turner who told Blanche in the first place, Daddy.' She lay back against her chair and dabbed her lips with her napkin.

'What a pity the Prince couldn't marry the girl he loved, though. Such a shame!'

'Pity he didn't. That's what he needs, a good wife, a family to think about. Give him some stability. All this galivanting about all over London, in and out of nightclubs till all hours . . . what kind of an example is he setting to the younger generation? I can sympathise with his parents all right – anyone less suitable to be heir to the throne I can't imagine!'

'If the King had minded his own business and left him to marry who he liked, he wouldn't be galivanting about all over London, would he?' Laura shot her brother a warning glance, but it was too late. 'He's only got himself to blame if the Prince hasn't turned out the way he expected; just because King George married for political reasons and not from personal choice doesn't mean to say that his son has to do the same. Good luck to him. That kind of thinking went out with the Victorians.'

'A little more of the good old fashioned Victorian virtues are something you *and* the Prince of Wales could do with cultivating! You think too much of your own pleasures and not nearly enough about your duties and responsibilities.'

It was clearly a challenge and Kit rose to it. 'Oh? Perhaps you'd care to tell me what you think they are?'

'Kit, please . . .'

'Consideration for other people, to begin with; when I came home this evening I noticed that you'd left your instrument case and music in the hall. It looked unsightly and slovenly. As I pointed out to you before dinner, I expect it to be taken immediately after we've eaten to where it belongs – upstairs in your room. If the Murrays saw it when they arrived goodness knows what impression it would make on them.'

'One clarinet case and a bag of music hardly constitutes a slovenly and unsightly mess. Besides, I left them there for a good reason. After dinner I'm going out.' He hesitated for a moment. 'I want to leave them in my new digs at Halkin Street before I go on to the Embassy.' His parents both stared at him, open-mouthed. 'I suppose I should have told you straight away, when I first came in. I'm sorry. But I had to make arrangements pretty quickly, if I wanted to hold onto both jobs. It's the travelling, more than anything. We're a bit out of the way here, and I really need to live somewhere close to both places. A pal at the club fixed me up.'

'Well, Christopher . . . I suppose we should congratulate you on

88

getting taken on at the London Pavilion . . . but you might have had the courtesy to give us more than a few hours notice that you intended to leave *today*.' He knew by his father's use of his full name how angry he was. 'But then, knowing you as I do that would have been too much to expect, wouldn't it?'

'Look, Dad, I said I was sorry! I didn't know for certain I was going to get that job today. How could I have given you more notice? They wanted me to start straight away. I can't afford to turn down a chance like this . . .'

'But, Kit, are you sure this . . . these digs in the Halkin Street are . . . well, respectable?'

'Mum, will you please stop fussing? Everything's fine. And I'm old enough to take care of myself now, OK?'

Richard Asmussen's face was purple with barely suppressed fury. 'Don't speak to your mother in that impatient tone of voice; and kindly refrain from using execrable American slang while you're in this house!'

For a moment Laura thought Kit was about to lose his temper, and she squeezed his arm under the table; but the moment passed and he got up, pushing back his chair.

'I don't want any more, thank you. If you'll excuse me I'll go upstairs and pack.'

'Sit down, Laura, and finish your food.' Slowly, reluctantly, she did as she was told. 'I think we've had more than enough interruptions for one evening.' He resumed eating angrily. 'Any more and the entire meal will be stone cold.'

'But I want to help Kit.'

He went on eating without looking up. 'As your brother has just pointed out to us he's old enough to take care of himself.'

'Kit, I'm sorry. I wanted to come up straight away and help you with things, but he wouldn't let me.' She leaned against the door frame, watching him.

He finished fastening his suitcase and smiled, a little grimly. 'I guessed he wouldn't. Well, I suppose I shouldn't have expected him to take it gracefully. He can't bear to think of me being independent of his charity!'

'He was angry because Mummy was upset about you going!'

Kit swung the suitcase from the bed to the floor, wincing at the unexpected weight of it. 'Oh, come on, Laura! You know it wasn't that. If I'd have given him a month's notice that I was leaving he'd still have made a fuss. That's just the way he is.'

'*Shh*, he'll hear you!' She came in and closed the bedroom door. She could feel the lump rising in her throat again. 'Kit . . . do you really have to go? I mean, right now? Couldn't you wait a bit, see how things work out? You might not like it, you might find it's too much rushing from one place to another and then back again. Your job at the Embassy . . .'

He stopped what he was doing. 'I might not be at the Embassy for much longer.'

'What do you mean?'

'I got talking to some of the other musicians while I was at the theatre today; they were saying that the 43 Club was looking for a solo clarinet . . . and they're offering half as much again as I get from the Embassy. Besides which, in all the time I've been there I've never once been offered a solo spot.'

She was shocked. 'Kit, you can't! Not the 43 Club in Gerrard Street! It's notorious. I've heard the girls at work talking about it . . . it's run by this awfully shady woman and it's even been raided by the police! If Daddy so much as heard you'd set foot in it he'd bar you from coming home for ever!'

Kit waved his hand in dismissal. 'That's a chance I'll have to take. Besides, what Dad doesn't know won't hurt him, will it? Most nightclubs have been raided by the police at one time or another.'

'How can you sound so casual about it?'

He shrugged his shoulders. 'Laura, live and let live, that's the way I look at things. I don't believe in going around the way Dad does, narrow-minded and blinkered, condemning everything that gives people pleasure and saying that anyone who goes to a place like the 43 Club is loose and damned. He's so dogmatic about everything, he never listens to anyone else's point of view . . . he's right and they're wrong. I can't live by his rules anymore, I just don't want a nice, boring, respectable job at the bank like his, or in some office in the city, sitting at the same desk day after day for the next forty years, getting a permanent stoop and bad eyesight. Doing everything by the clock, catching the same train to work every day and coming back at the same time every night; it'd drive me crazy.

'If I was a classical musician, It'd probably be different . . . sitting in an orchestra at Covent Garden playing Puccini . . . he'd approve of that. Respectable people go to the opera. But nightclubs are at the other end of the line; the wrong end, as far as he's concerned. It's only because the Prince of Wales and other well known people frequent the Embassy that he allowed me to work there at all.'

'But he can't help the way he is! Three quarters of fathers in this country would think in exactly the same way. He doesn't even really approve of women being independent and running their own businesses, like Mrs Turner. Remember the fuss he made when I wanted to work there? But if she'd been a man he wouldn't have batted an eyelid . . . people of Daddy's generation are so full of different prejudices; things have changed so much, so quickly since the war ended, they can't keep pace with them any more. But Kit, *please*, don't go and work at the 43 Club . . . I can't bear the thought of you working in a place like that . . .'

He laughed teasingly but for once she didn't respond.

'Oh, come on Laura! Get rid of that long face. The Crown Prince of Sweden's one of their most important patrons . . . Prince Nicholas of Rumania, Michael Arlen, they're all on the members' list . . . if it was some low dive do you think people like that would patronize it?'

'Now you're being sarcastic!'

'Just truthful, my beautiful little sister. Just truthful.' He kissed her lightly on the cheek. 'Get me a piece of paper and a pencil and I'll write my new address down for you. And the telephone number . . . as long as you promise not to give it to Dad.'

8

Rushing ahead into the house in front of her husband, leaving the footman to struggle in with the mounds of heavy trunks and suitcases of luggage, Elizabeth ignored her maid who was standing waiting to take her sable coat and hat from her in the hall and went straight into the drawing room. She stood there on the threshold, surveying the decorations Banbury had put in hand before the honeymoon, her blue eyes bright with sudden pleasure.

'William! Just come and take a look at this.' She walked around, turning this way and that, examining everything. 'You'd never believe this was the same old, fusty, antiquated drawing room that was here before we went to Paris!' She turned to him, waiting for his approval. 'It's absolutely the very latest look.' From the corner of her eye she saw the expression on his butler's face as he hovered in the open doorway, waiting to speak. 'William darling, you simply have to admit that I was right to have it all changed!'

Banbury, still weary from the journey, looked all around him, at all the white walls, white curtains and white covers on the furniture. 'It's certainly very different.'

'You don't like it!' Her face clouded into a frown, her voice had a sudden accusing edge to it. 'But I told you . . . it's all the rage now. *Everyone* wants Syrie's white interiors.'

Banbury went over to the fire and rubbed his cold hands together. The sun was brilliant outside the window, but the wind was unusually cold for the time of the year; surrounded by icy, pristine white in the once cosy, old fashioned room with its warm comforting mauves and plum-reds, he felt colder still. But all that mattered was that Elizabeth was happy. For most of the honeymoon, she'd seemed curiously subdued for a reason he couldn't understand and hadn't liked to ask.

'It's very attractive, my dear. Stunning, in fact. But after living with the room the way it was for so many years you'll have to allow me time to adapt to the change.' He went over to her and kissed her, but she didn't respond. 'I shall be afraid to sit down in case I make it dirty.'

She went back into the hall and let Sabine take her coat and hat. 'Oh, what nonsense! We can always have it cleaned.' She flopped into an armchair. 'Did they remember to collect my gramophone from Belgrave Square while we were away, Seddon?'

'Yes, my lady. His lordship left no specific instructions, so I had it placed in the music room.'

'Oh, good; at least they remembered to do something right. Could you please have a tray of tea sent in? I haven't had a decent cup of tea since we left England . . .'

'Now, you're exaggerating, my dear.' Banbury turned to his butler with a smile. 'Everything running shipshape while we were away, Seddon?'

'Yes, my lord. I've had this morning's post laid on the desk in your study – your secretary came in every day to deal with all the most pressing matters, but there was a message from Downing Street this morning.' He handed a folded piece of paper to Banbury who opened it, read it, and sighed.

'Back to the grindstone. Never let a chap rest, not even on the day he gets back from his honeymoon. I'm sorry, darling, but I shan't be able to join you for tea. Baldwin wants to see me as soon as possible. Damn infernal nuisance!'

'What is it? What's wrong? A major revolt by all the backbenchers?'

'God knows. But it sounds urgent so I'd better leave straight away. I've been out of the country for a month, and a month is a long time in politics. I'm afraid it's something you'll have to get used to, being married to a politician.'

He kissed her long and lingeringly on the lips before he went out.

The moment she was alone she pulled out a handkerchief and wiped her lips with an expression of disgust, then stood behind one of the curtains watching until his car had drawn away from the pavement. She rushed across to the telephone and dialled the exchange. But before she could speak, Seddon had come unexpectedly back into the room. She put down the receiver quickly and went over to the fire.

'Do you wish me to pour, my lady?'

'Where on earth did you dig out that hideous china from?' Her parents had always instilled into her from childhood that one was always courteous to servants, but for the past few weeks her nerves had been frayed and raw; the strain of hiding her real feelings over the honeymoon made her want to lash out at someone she knew dare not answer her back.

'This is the best Crown Derby china, my lady.'

'It looks as if it's come out of the Ark – or the British Museum! Where's the Limoges service my uncle gave us?'

'Lady Banbury always used the Crown Derby, and it is his lord-ship's favourite china . . .'

'Well, it certainly isn't mine. And *I* am Lady Banbury now. Kindly take it away and get rid of it, then bring me a fresh tray with the Limoges.' Stiffly, she sat down in the chair; she'd disliked Seddon on sight and every time she saw him her dislike intensified; he'd been in service with the family ever since Banbury had brought her prede-cessor here as a bride and she knew instinctively that Seddon was comparing them to each other.

He lowered his eyes so that she couldn't see his expression. 'Of course, my lady. I'll attend to it immediately.'

The moment she was alone again, Elizabeth rushed across the room to the telephone. The exchange seemed to take ages to put through her call to New Bond Street. After what seemed an eternity, the line clicked and she heard Anne Turner's voice.

'Anne, it's me. We just got back. I have to see you right away. Yes, today. It's urgent. Where is it safe to meet?' The voice at the other end of the line was surprised. 'No, he isn't here. There was a message from the PM waiting and he had to leave, thank god! With any luck Baldwin will keep him at Downing Street all night.' Still looking furtively towards the door, she lowered her voice. 'No, I can't talk now. Someone might hear. At the showrooms then, in half an hour. Yes, I'll get a taxi.' There was a pause while Anne Turner spoke at the other end of the telephone. 'I'll call Eddie from your office; it's too risky to do it from here. There's an extension in his study and in the butler's pantry. Yes, yes, all right. Goodbye.'

The moment she put down the receiver, there was a knock at the door and Seddon came in carrying the tea. With maddening slowness, he set it down and then stood up. His face was impassive, expressionless, but she could read the dislike and disapproval in his eyes. He thin scarlet lips turned up slightly at the corners; Seddon's days in the house were certainly numbered; she made a mental note to speak to William tonight when she got back.

'Leave that, Seddon; I'll pour for myself. Is there any mail for me?'

'Yes, my lady. Shall I fetch it from his lordship's study?'

'If you will. Oh, and Seddon . . .' Her voice halted him at the door. 'Please tell Sabine to bring down my outdoor things in fifteen minutes, I'm going out.'

'Do you wish me to instruct the second chauffeur to bring round one of the other cars, my lady?'

'No, I'm going by taxi.'

After he'd brought her the mail she fumbled in her crocodile handbag for her ivory cigarette holder and cigarettes. She sat down and lit one, then paced up and down the floor. She stubbed it out, poured herself tea and sat sipping it nervously, while she flicked through a pile of letters in her lap.

There were belated letters congratulating her on her marriage; she threw them into the fire. Invitations to lunches and dinner parties, half-a-dozen forthcoming events at the start of the Season and four country house weekends; several invitations to house parties for Ascot. Nothing of interest. She flung them down on the chair and got to her feet again, leaving her tea half finished. Sabine came in with her hat, coat and gloves.

'Close the door.'

'My lady?'

Elizabeth beckoned Sabine further into the room. 'Get one of the footmen to call me a taxi. If my husband telephones or comes back early and wants to know where I am, say I've gone out shopping, and that I'll be calling in to see my mother at Belgrave Square. And be careful of that old fool Seddon. He doesn't like me and I don't trust him an inch.' The girl's large, sleepy brown eyes flickered; she understood. 'And make sure that you never tell anyone here – including my husband – any of my business.' She checked the time by the platinum and diamond wristwatch Banbury had bought her in Paris, then let Sabine help her on with her coat. A footman called a taxi and held the door open for her as she climbed inside. In less than fifteen minutes she was in New Bond Street.

The porter took her up in the private lift to Anne Turner's spacious office on the second floor. Pulling off her gloves, barely listening to Anne Turner's fulsome greetings and enquiries about her honeymoon and the Paris shops, she sat down abruptly on one of the beautiful brocade-upholstered chairs.

'Elizabeth, you look blooming! Paris clearly agrees with you. But I didn't expect to hear from you so soon after you got back . . . you sounded so strange on the telephone.'

Elizabeth opened her handbag and took out her cigarette and ivory holder. Her hands were shaking. '*I can't stand him . . .* '

'Whatever's happened? Whatever's the matter?'

'He's disgusting, revolting. The things he does in bed . . . if only I'd known what he was really like I'd never have let my parents persuade me to go through with it.'

Anne Turner was immediately intrigued; anything to do with sex – particularly other people's – held a lurid fascination for her. Her imagination was already working overtime. 'Elizabeth, darling . . . whatever do you mean?' She reached for her own ornate cigarette box and took out a Turkish cigarette. 'Look, let me pour you a drink.'

'Not champagne. I need something much stronger. Whisky, if you've got any. Without water or soda.'

'Tell me about it.'

'I couldn't. Not the details. Not even you.' She took the double whisky and drank half of it down with a gulp. 'The disgusting things he wanted me to do . . .'

'I don't know what to say!'

'It was all huge fun at first, when we got engaged. He kept buying me presents, jewellery, sending bouquets of flowers . . . anything I even hinted that I wanted, the next day it was there. It was easy while all that was happening to think that the age difference didn't matter . . . that my parents were right when they told me how lucky I was, that he'd be dead years before me and then I'd have all his money, be free to marry anyone I liked . . . It was only when I saw him undressed for the first time that I realized what a terrible mistake I'd made . . .' She gulped down the rest of the whisky and started to cry. 'Anne, you don't know what it was like! I nearly panicked. I wanted to be physically sick! I just wanted to run away! Only the thought of what would happen if I did stopped me . . . you know why they wanted me to marry him, that if I messed things up they'd never forgive me . . .'

Anne Turner came out from behind her desk and put an arm around Elizabeth's shaking shoulders. 'I do know, I do understand; believe me, I understand. My husband was old enough to be my father.' Elizabeth looked up at her through her tears. 'I married him because he was financially secure and I wanted to better myself. What I had to submit to in the bedroom was just part of the price I paid for both those things. But I comforted myself with the thought that one day he'd be dead and I'd be very much alive – and that much richer. And – very discreetly, of course – I took lovers. Men my own age, men who I found attractive. However miserable you are now, my dear, don't forget that nothing lasts forever; Banbury isn't immortal.'

'But I loathe it when he touches me!'

'Think of something else. Pretend he's somebody else. Eddie Vaux, for instance.'

A hard look came into Elizabeth's face. 'That would be beyond anyone's ability! My God, when I think of having to share the same bed with that disgusting old man every night of my life . . .'

Anne Turner had moved away so that Elizabeth couldn't see her face.

'Well, as I see it, there are two things you can do . . .' Immediately, Elizabeth stopped crying. 'The first . . . have a child as soon as possible. The moment you announce that you're expecting one, he'll have to leave you alone; and you can always invent and embellish to make him believe that you feel so ill with the pregnancy, you want to sleep alone.' Her face was composed now; she turned around and they looked at each other. 'Of course, there's nothing to stop you pretending that you're pregnant before you actually are . . .'

'But he'd rush me straight round to Theodore Mayerne at Harley Street!'

'You could tell him you prefer your own family doctor.'

'Paul Lobell? Well, yes . . . but as soon as he examined me, he'd know I wasn't really pregnant.' Anne Turner restrained a sigh of impatience. How slow witted she was! And she'd always thought Elizabeth was so clever.

'You don't actually have to go and see him; just tell Banbury that you did.'

'But wouldn't he check?'

'Why should he? Why should he disbelieve anything you tell him when he's madly in love with you?' It was beginning to irk her to continually state the obvious. 'He'll be so overjoyed that you're giving him the heir he's wanted at last, that he won't even think of doubting you. You'll be rid of him for nine months at least . . . and for several months after the birth you can make up all sorts of reasons why you're not ready to go back and sleep with him.' A sly note crept into her voice, tinged with amusement. 'With any luck, he might have a heart attack at the happy news.'

'If only wishing it could make it happen . . . But you said there were two things I could do. What else?'

'Try numbing reality a little. Lots of young women I come into contact with do it, now and again. Or regularly, if they want to. Besides,' coolly, she poured out more drinks, 'it's really getting quite smart, in certain sophisticated circles . . .' Their eyes met in understanding. 'If you like, I can introduce you to a very good friend of mine . . . a doctor . . . he's the most discreet man, and he can supply you with anything you might care to try . . .' She gave Elizabeth one of her sickly-sweet smiles. 'He used to have a private practice in Paris . . .'

9

Stanley Baldwin got up and opened the doors of the small cupboard behind his desk, then brought out a bottle of vintage sherry and two glasses. He was smiling as he poured.

'You look so well, William; better than I've seen you looking for years. The Parisian air obviously agrees with you.' He handed a glass of sherry to Banbury who was sitting on the opposite side of his desk. 'But most of all, I'd say it was all down to your charming young wife. Here, a toast for the future. May you enjoy many happy, healthy years together.' They touched glasses and Banbury chuckled.

'Elizabeth is absolutely marvellous! Never a dull moment with her.

Of course, like most women, she *is* a little over-fond of shopping.' He went on to relate his experiences in the couture centres of Paris. 'But I went with her uncomplainingly. After all, a woman only has a honeymoon once.' He sipped his sherry appreciatively. 'Sometimes, just sometimes, the big gap in our ages worries me; I know I can admit that to you . . . after all, how long have we been friends? Realistically, I know she's a young woman and she needs to live a young woman's life . . . shopping, dancing, all that sort of thing; of course she'll settle down when we have a family. But just because I get tired easily and can't always keep up with her, I don't want to spoil her pleasure. She's such a wonderful, lively girl. Incidentally, as soon as we finish with these blasted decorators in the house, you and Lucy must come and dine with us. I know Elizabeth would love that.'

Baldwin laughed, softly. 'And how was the Syrie Maugham drawing room?'

'Just between you and me, bloody awful! I almost had a fit when I first laid eyes on it. But how could I say that to Elizabeth? She was so enchanted with it that I simply didn't have the heart to tell her I didn't like it. Wait until you and Lucy see it . . . my dear chap, it's the most ghastly thing you ever saw!'

Baldwin roared with laughter. 'Don't worry, I'll keep the secret! These fads and fashionable fancies . . . white rooms, indeed! I think I should be afraid to sit down in case I marked the furniture. But when the craze passes, Elizabeth will no doubt have it all redone just the way it was before . . . you'll see.'

'I sincerely hope you're right. Now, enough of my newly-found marital bliss. What's all this I hear about you being laid up in bed while we were away? I ran into Trenchard at the War Office before I came over here, and he told me you were taken ill at the Royal College of Surgeons dinner just after we left for Paris . . . you really should have cabled me . . .'

'Oh, nonsense! It was nothing; nothing at all. The doctor said it was just a case of a tired man going on strike. Nothing a good rest in bed wouldn't cure. Now, I'd like you to read that report on the Rhodesian copper deposits that Lord Sydenham's new secretary prepared.' He opened a drawer in his desk and shuffled some papers. 'Carr. Robert Carr. Now there's a young man who shows immense promise. No wonder Sydenham thinks so highly of him. His grasp of the situation there is astonishing, considering that he made a single visit in January and was only promoted from the Scottish Office three months before that. Sydenham tells me that he has the most incredible capacity for work in a young man that he's seen for a very long time.'

'Robert Carr. No, I haven't come across him. But I'll ask Cultrane to keep an eye open for him; he sounds the very type of young man who deserves every encouragement.' Baldwin slid the report across his desk and Banbury took it. 'I'll take it home with me, if I may. After I've sorted through all the work that's built up over the last four weeks with my secretary at Westminster, it'll be one o'clock in the morning before I can get back to Elizabeth. I don't want to leave her by herself on our first day back.'

'Of course.' Baldwin smiled and stood up. 'I understand perfectly; give her my warmest regards.' A moment's hesitation. 'Incidentally, the Cultranes have invited Lucy and me to dinner on Thursday evening; I gather you'll be there too. I must admit that in spite of everything that's happened in the past, I quite like Cultrane. He has a great sense of duty; while you were in Paris he dealt with all the most pressing papers that arrived in your office, as well as his own work.'

Banbury was opening his attaché case and putting in the report prepared by Robert Carr. He snapped down the locks. 'I know you're not a man to bear grudges; a man after my own heart. And I know you realize that when Cultrane supported George Curzon against you for the premiership, it was nothing personal. In his heart I'm sure he knew that you were the best man for the job, but in public he could hardly admit it . . . after all, he and Curzon had been close friends for years. It would have been unthinkably disloyal for him to vote against Curzon and support you.'

Baldwin nodded, and they shook hands. 'I understand perfectly, William; as I said . . . and I mean it sincerely . . . it's all water under the bridge. I look forward to seeing you and Elizabeth at Belgrave Square on Thursday evening.' Side by side, they walked together to the door. 'Don't go working too late tonight, will you?' He clapped a hand on his friend's shoulder. 'One thing I can tell you women never forgive is if you neglect them.'

Banbury smiled broadly. 'Thanks for the advice, Stanley; but I don't intend to. I can't wait to hurry back to her.'

She lay against him with her eyes closed, her damp, silver blonde hair a white halo against his dark head, their hands entwined. They'd made love so passionately and wildly that it was several more moments before either of them got back their breath. The loud ticking of the bedside clock and its hateful reminder that time was slipping away and she soon had to leave, brought Elizabeth back sharply to reality.

Pressing her lips against his cheek, she rolled over, sat up and fished in the semi-darkness for her lighter and cigarette. 'Dear god, I can't bear the thought of going back to that bloody house!' Suddenly tense and irritable, she lay back against Anne Turner's sumptuous padded satin headboard. 'Play-acting the devoted wife to that disgusting old fool, pretending I'm in raptures with his company . . . if only he'd stay at Westminster with bloody Baldwin and work all night. Maybe with any luck a bit of overwork might kill him!' She ran a beautifully manicured hand through her tousled fair hair. 'I called on my mother on the way back from Anne and she mentioned that she'd invited us – and the Baldwins – to one of her dinner parties on Saturday evening; if only I could get out of it and meet you here instead!'

Eddie Vaux reached up and gently traced the outline of her face with his finger. 'Darling, you know you can't. It would look too obvious.' Uncomfortably, he recalled his confrontation with Katherine Cultrane, the confrontation he was going to keep to himself. 'We simply can't risk it.'

She turned to him passionately. 'If only he'd go with Baldwin on this Canadian trip with Prince George and the Prince of Wales. If he could get posted to one of the foreign embassies . . .'

'If he ever did then you'd be expected to go with him.'

Elizabeth fell silent, toying with the ivory and platinum cigarette holder in her fingers; they'd been married for barely five weeks and already she felt trapped, a prisoner with invisible chains. After the first misgivings about marrying Banbury, she'd started to enjoy the game that she thought she'd be able to play, and play well – his slavish devotion, the endless round of flowers and expensive gifts, then the excitement of the wedding, the frenzied interest of public and press that had all been fuel to the fire of her vanity and self-importance; making love with his good-looking nephew behind his back; but now it was all over and the fleeting glamour had palled; she was really his wife and the pretence had become reality. The panting, sweating elderly man who had shocked her in the hotel bedroom in Paris had shown her that. She shivered in disgust at the hateful memory. For how long could she possibly bear it?

'Come on.' He was reaching out for her, drawing her back into his arms. She raised her hand and deposited her cigarette and its holder in the ashtry at the side of the bed. 'Forget about him. He's nothing. One day he'll be dead and we'll still be alive . . . how many times have I told you to keep remembering that?'

How could he understand? How could she make even Eddie understand what Banbury had put her through, the revolting things that he'd wanted to do that she couldn't even begin to describe to Anne Turner, or even her mother. At the brief visit to Belgrave Square to see her parents, she'd got no sympathy there. Nor had she expected any. They were only concerned with their own selfish ambitions. She only wanted to be happy.

'I was thinking, on the way over here in the taxi . . . the estate in Kent . . .'

'Greyfriars?'

'. . . I've only visited it twice, when we were engaged; I made him promise to let me have the entire place redecorated, in any way I want, ready for entertaining during the Season. . . . He can't get away while Parliament's sitting, but I can. I could use it as an excuse to keep the distance between us. You could motor down and we could meet somewhere . . .'

He kissed the tip of her nose. 'Darling, you're a devious vixen and I adore you. What a capital idea. And he'd never guess, either. Of course, we couldn't take the chance of meeting at the house just in case any of the servants start talking . . .'

'I don't trust that supercilious old fool he's got as a butler, either; Seddon. I could tell straight away that he didn't like me.' She related the incident of the tea service. 'He said *Lady Banbury* as if he was talking about someone else. And I saw the way he was looking at the redecorations in the drawing room . . . he didn't approve of my taste at all!'

'It's none of Seddon's damned business how you choose to have the drawing room redecorated. He should know how to keep his place. God knows, he's been in service with the family for long enough! Uncle William always did let him take liberties.'

'To him, I'm an outsider. Not to be compared to the first Lady Banbury.'

'Do you really care what a servant thinks?'

She was already thinking of something else and the coming evening, then the night that she'd be forced to spend with Banbury in the big double bed. She shivered, even though the room was warm from the electric fire. 'I'd better get dressed . . . I daren't be out when he gets back . . .' She contemplated her clothes, draped over one of the boudoir chairs, her silver high-heeled shoes lying side by side on the floor where she'd kicked them off. 'I'll try and ring you tomorrow, from New Bond Street. It's too risky to call from the house.'

'I know.' He swung his legs over the edge of the bed and reached for his trousers and shirt. 'If I want to reach you quickly, I'll contact Anne Turner.' He got up and went over to her, then he took her gently into his arms and kissed her lips; so softly this time that it was like the touch of a feather.

'Eddie,' she ran her hands over his naked shoulders hungrily. 'If only I could have married you instead . . .'

Kit sat cross-legged in the middle of the narrow bed, flicking through the pile of music sheets in front of him. Every now and again he paused, took one out of the pile and put it to one side. When he'd finished he picked up the sheets that he wanted and went over to the upright piano that stood against the wall on the opposite side of the room. Halfway through playing one of his own compositions, the door opened and a young man with straight, fair hair stuck his head around it.

'Hi! Can I come in or do you want to be by yourself while you're playing?'

'Please yourself,' Kit said, without taking his eyes from the keyboard. 'Damn. That bar's not right.' He reached for a pencil from the top of the piano and scribbled, then replayed the same piece again. 'You want some thing or are you just at a loose end?'

The young American sat down on the nearest chair. 'Don't mind me. I just heard you playing and I liked the sound. Thought you was a reed man?'

'I play piano too. Sometimes it's more soothing.'

'Yeah, I guess it is. You play that thing better than the guy Kate Meyrick pays to play piano all the time at the 43.'

Kit stopped, and turned to him with a knowing smile. 'So that's what's brought you back in here? Trying to twist my arm to go for an audition at your place again. I told you; I've already got two jobs; holding both down at the same time stretches me enough. There isn't enough of me to go around for three. But thanks anyhow.'

'Look, man. I told you. You got something special. You're different. You're a cut above all the other guys and it shows. The other cats in those bands – they're good, sure; but they're the run of the mill. Now, if you wanted to play your own stuff at the Pavilion or the

Embassy, they'd tell you to go take a runnin' jump, right? But you take it to Mrs Meyrick and she's a lady that'll pay big bucks for something out of the ordinary . . . her customers'll go wild for your kind of music; they'll never get to hear anythin' like it this side of America. I'm tellin' you, you don't think big, you never going to get where you ought to be. I know. Just come with me one afternoon when you're free and let her hear you play some of your own stuff . . .'

'That's just the point, Rudy . . . I'm never free. I've got rehearsals at the Pavilion, rehearsals at the Embassy; I just get time to eat and sleep. There's only twenty-four hours in a day, for christ's sake!'

'You can make the goddamn time! Look. You said it. Being one of the crowd in the band isn't your style . . . you want your own band and you don't want to take your whole life trying to get it. I know the short cuts. You got to go out and grab what you want in this world, Kit. You said that yourself. So why not give my idea a whirl first?'

'Rudy, I know what I said . . .'

'So what's stopping you?'

'So what are you saying? That if I take all this stuff to Kate Meyrick at the 43 Club she'll make me the toast of London?'

'I'm sayin' . . . let her hear you. She's got connections. If she likes you she'll pull strings. Do you know some of the big shot names she's got on her members' list?'

'Yeah, like "Brilliant" Chang the dope-dealer, for starters; she did six months in Holloway three years ago for letting him run his operations from the club.'

'Kit . . .'

'. . . and don't tell me again for the fiftieth time that her three daughters all married into the aristocracy. I've heard it all before.'

'Look, let me get a word in edgeways, will you? OK. So she's done time. But she's still a lady. She's got guts. She clawed her way to the top and she's still right up there with the best of 'em. People admire that; if they didn't she'd have closed down years ago. She tried to put the brakes on Chang but he kept dealin' behind her back. So she owns the club, so the law comes down on her like a ton of bricks and Chang slips away free as air. It happens. Don't tell me the Embassy was never raided by the cops because I know different.'

'Yes, it's been raided; what nightclub hasn't? The difference is they don't peddle dope to their customers.'

'So who says? What do you know what goes on all the time? You can't know everything, Kit. The nobs like a snort of cocaine and where there's a market there's dealers. Not every guy dressed in a Savile Row suit is squeaky clean . . . come on, don't play dumb with me!'

Kit sat staring at the sheet of music in front of him without really seeing it. 'All right. You win. I'll give it a try. Maybe then there'll be some peace around here. I'll do it just to shut you up – OK? Fix something up with Kate Meyrick but do it so it fits in with rehearsals . . . otherwise it's off.'

Rudy Loew's face crumped in a smile. He slapped Kit on the back. 'Now you're talking, boy! And I promise you won't be sorry. Hey, what about a bet that she offers you a job?'

Kit ran a hand through his thick, dark hair and gave Rudy an exasperated look. 'Rudy . . . thanks for the enthusiasm . . . but let me finish this, will you? If I don't get it right I won't be going to any audition at the 43 at all.'

The American was already at the door.

'OK. OK. I hear you. But promise you won't welsh on this? If I fix it up for Mrs Meyrick to hear you, you won't get cold feet and back off?'

Kit smiled and rested one arm on the piano keys. 'Promise. Now will you cut along and give me half an hour's peace?'

He turned back to his music. Behind him the door closed.

10

Frances moved unobtrusively among her parents' guests, a glass of champagne in one hand, smiling and nodding as she weaved in and out; pausing now and then, as her mother had told her to, to exchange brief conversations with the most important of them. Her father had given her stern instructions, half an hour before anyone had arrived, to be particularly charming to the Baldwins.

Ever since she'd been thirteen she'd been allowed to attend all her mother's political dinners and cocktail parties; but she never enjoyed herself. Most of the guests were people she'd overheard her parents talking about in a disparaging manner – she was perfectly aware that the only reason they'd been invited was because they were important to her father's career; she loathed the play-acting and the practised hypocrisy. True, there were always plenty of good-looking young men

– her mother's special 'protégés' who would ask her to dance or follow her with their eyes; but she was never certain about their sincerity. Were they being nice to her because they liked her for herself or because she was the Earl of Cultrane's daughter?

She spotted the daughters of two of her father's colleagues across the room, whom she'd first met at boarding school, and made her way through the throng towards them.

'Frances, I absolutely adore your dress! Is it one of Anne Turner's?'

'Yes, that's right.'

'I simply love it when Mummy and Daddy come to one of your mother's parties and I get invited, too . . . She's a positive genius at parties! Do you think your sister will start having them, now that she's back from her honeymoon? I mean, Lord Banbury's in the Cabinet so she's bound to, isn't she?'

'Elizabeth doesn't need that as an excuse to have a party. Besides, nobody will be able to talk about politics . . . the music will be so loud nobody will even hear themselves speak.' The other two girls let out shrieks of high-pitched laughter and several heads turned their way.

'Shut up, Winnie, you silly ass!'

'I think that champagne's gone straight to my head.'

'Not so much I can't see that good-looking threesome over there, talking to old Joynson-Hicks! Who on earth are they, Frances?'

'Some of my mother's protégés, I expect. She did introduce them to me when they first arrived but I can't remember their names.'

'The one in the middle's rather super, don't you think? Quickly, don't stare, he's looking this way.' They retreated into a corner giggling together. 'Listen, I've been waiting to ask you . . . Frances . . . you know your parents are going to that boring weekend in two weeks time to Chequers? Ours are, too. So we thought of an absolutely marvellous idea that we could get up to while they're all out of town!'

'Louise, what are you up to?'

'My cousin Archie is a member of the 43 Club . . . and we thought that if he invited a couple of chaps along, we could all go . . .'

'It'd be an absolute hoot!'

'The 43 Club? But it's *terribly* fast . . .'

'Oh, fiddlesticks! It'll be huge fun. We can paint our faces and wear high heeled shoes and lots of pearls, and have an absolute whale of a time. Well, are you game?'

Frances lowered her voice to a whisper and glanced towards where her mother was standing deep in conversation with the Home Secretary. 'My parents would *kill* me if they ever found out.'

'But that's the whole point, you goose. Nobody will!'

'But we're not old enough. They won't let us in.'

'Of course they will, silly! With clothes and make-up we'll look positively years older than any of us really are. Besides, we'll be with Archie and nobody will even bother to ask. Oh, come on. Don't be such a wet blanket. Archie says the lights are awfully dim inside the club anyway . . .'

'Supposing there's someone there who recognizes us? They'd tell our parents.'

'Who do you know who belongs to the 43 Club? In any case, if we see anybody we know we can always slip out!'

Frances smiled. 'All right, I'm coming.' She gave another glance over her shoulder and saw that her mother was looking at her. 'Telephone me as soon as your parents have left, and we can arrange what time you're picking me up. Gosh, Mummy's giving me daggers – I'd better go and talk to the guests.'

She put down her half-full glass and began to mingle with the groups of people, stopping to have short, polite conversations with those who her parents had told her were the most important. She took a smoked salmon canapé from a maid and stood nibbling it a few feet from where her brother Freddie was talking to one of the lesser-known guests. She was more intent on thinking how handsome and debonair he looked than on what the elderly member of Parliament was speaking to him about. She'd already noticed how many of the women in the room kept glancing his way. In the background, diamonds flashing on her earlobes and around her wrist and neck, she caught sight of Elizabeth.

'Trouble is, none of those damn country bumpkins have the slightest idea what goes on in town, let alone the Commons,' the unknown member of Parliament was complaining to Freddie Osborne who, with his head on one side had assumed an expression that made his listener believe he was riveted by his boring conversation. 'Damn agents can't even keep my constituency books in order!'

'Jolly bad show, old chap! Wouldn't have your job for the world.'

'Never hear anything except damn complaints. Damn working classes are never satisfied. Try and bring 'em into line and the damn fellows go out on strike. Always having to listen to their complaints. Damn bad show all round.'

Freddie had caught sight of Frances and had turned to include her in the conversation. She spoke without really thinking of the consequences.

'But surely, that's the whole idea of them having a Member of Parliament? So that they have somebody to represent their views in the House of Commons.'

There was a sudden embarrassed silence all round; everyone in earshot had stopped talking and was staring at her. Her great-uncle materialized from nowhere, smiling the smile that never reached his eyes. Instinctively, Frances stepped away from him.

'You can see why we can't risk giving the vote to females under thirty!' he joked, patting the other man genially on the back. He fixed her with an icy stare; she knew what would happen after all the guests had gone home. 'No more champagne for this young lady, Katherine.' Her mother appeared beside him but she dare not look at her. 'It's clearly gone straight to her head.'

'You little fool! Have you any idea who that was. Sir John Zouche. A leading and very important backbencher whose support I heavily rely on in the Commons!'

'Daddy, I'm sorry; I didn't mean to be rude. I was talking to Freddie, not him . . .'

'Don't back answer me. What you said was tantamount to an insult to the man – and half the guests in the room overheard.'

'That's not fair!' She looked wildly round at all of them as they stood there glowering at her. 'What I said was true. That's why we've got a Parliament, isn't it? So that all the people in the country can have someone of their choice sitting in it to give them a voice. Isn't that why we had a civil war in the 17th century because the King wouldn't let the ordinary people have a voice in Parliament?' She was suddenly very angry. 'That man was grumbling about having to go down and listen to his constituents at election time, as if they didn't matter; as if they were just a nuisance that had to be humoured just so he could go on getting their votes – that's why I said what I did. If he doesn't like representing the people who vote for him then he shouldn't have put himself up for election in the first place. He should resign and let someone else do it. Someone who really cares!'

For a moment nobody spoke. Only her brother had a trace of a smile on his face. But he took care that only she saw it. Her father's face was completely white, which showed her how angry he really was. 'Go up to your room immediately and go to bed.' She went to the door without speaking, where her mother's cold voice halted her.

'I've told Grace to make sure you're up and ready to leave the house at nine o'clock tomorrow morning; you're going to the language school in Kensington to meet the Principal. I've already instructed her about the clothes you'll wear. Don't be even one minute late.'

'But . . . what about my tutor?'

'Your progress in French and German isn't nearly good enough. I've arranged for you to attend the school four days a week, until you come out. Now do as your father says and go upstairs.'

'I'd better be off myself, now,' Freddie Osborne said when Frances had gone. 'Lottie's back from Great Marlow in the morning and I promised to meet the train, then take her to the Savoy for lunch. We'll see you for dinner when you get back from the country.'

Katherine Cultrane kissed him on the cheek. 'Goodnight, darling.'

'Goodnight Mother. Father, Uncle Harry.'

'Don't drive too fast in that infernal motor of yours.'

As the door closed behind him, Thomas Cultrane sighed and leaned against the mantlepiece; Katherine lit a cigarette. Henry Osborne had sat down and crossed one long thin leg over the other.

'You must remember that Frances is at the "difficult" age . . . I've no doubt that next time she'll be careful to think before she speaks.'

'She's old enough to know better.'

'I know Zouche well, and he isn't the kind of man to bear a grudge; and is there a parent in England who can say that his children never embarrass him? Look at King George and the Prince of Wales.'

'Freddie never caused us a moment's worry!'

Henry Osborne smiled. 'Ah . . . we all know that Freddie's perfect, my dear. But Frances is a very intelligent girl and she'll learn by her mistakes. I've been watching her very carefully for the past year; and she's not in the least like Elizabeth . . .'

'A damned good hiding to knock some sense into her wouldn't come a miss by a long chalk.' Thomas Cultrane's face had become very red. 'Half the people in the room overheard. It's not her stupid blunder that worries me . . . it's the possibility that anyone who heard what she said might think she's merely repeating what she's heard from me. You know how easily rumours start and facts get garbled at Westminster; supposing it got put about that Thomas Cultrane thinks the majority of backbenchers in the Commons are only paying lip service to their constituency duties? What the hell would that little snippet do for my popularity? God knows, I've made enough enemies already . . .'

His uncle raised a hand in a conciliatory gesture. 'All men who rise to the top make enemies, Tom; you know that as well as I do. But you're taking this too much to heart. Leave it to me to smooth things over in the right quarters . . . to begin with, I've invited Zouche to lunch tomorrow at my Club.'

Thomas Cultrane ran a hand through his thick dark hair. 'Yes, I suppose you're right. I'm sorry . . . it hasn't been a good day. There was that damned disagreement at the Foreign Office . . .'

'A week down at Audley will do you both good.' He stood up. 'Are you taking Frances with you?'

'Goodness, no, she'd just be in the way. Besides, her French and German are abysmal. If you ask me, that confounded tutor she's had for the last eight months has taught her nothing at all. She needs the daily discipline of being in a class with other students and being given specific exercises which have to be finished in a given time. By the time she's ready to be presented at Court I want her fluent in both languages. Elizabeth could speak French like a native when she was far younger than Frances.'

'But Frances is far more accomplished in music. I've heard her play.'

'That's the trouble . . . she spends too much time at it. When she ought to be practising the lessons the tutor sets, she's sitting in front of the piano. Well, she won't this time. While we're away I'm leaving instructions to the servants to keep the music room locked.'

'As you think best, Katherine my dear.' He kissed her on the cheek as he made his way to the door. 'Well, I shan't see you again until you get back . . . have a good journey.'

Frances stared dismally at her reflection in the dressing table mirror while Grace, her maid, went on brushing her hair; ever since she'd come upstairs after the guests had left, she'd seemed unusually quiet; not like herself at all. Taking advantage of her year and a half's service with the family, Grace paused, cleared her throat, then asked, lightly, 'Nice party was it, my lady?'

'It was until I put my foot in it. My parents are absolutely furious with me now.' She gave her a condensed version of the evening's happenings. 'I didn't do it on purpose. Offend that man that Daddy says is so important, I mean. In any case, I *was* right! If someone doesn't want to be bothered with listening to people who voted them into Parliament, then they shouldn't be allowed to be an MP.'

'That's just what I think too, my lady.'

'Mummy says I'm terribly behind with my French and German

and the tutor hasn't got me to make any progress, so now I've got to go to this horrid boring language school in Kensington, whether I like it or not . . . four days a week.'

'Never mind, my lady. Just think how it'll be when you can talk fluent French and German.' Grace lay down the silver-backed hair-brush and stood back to survey the results. 'That'll do. I've laid out your fresh nightdress, my lady; the silk one. It's a bit warmer tonight.'

'Thank you, Grace.' Frances unclipped the bracelet around her wrist and handed it to her maid to put away. 'I've got something else to tell you . . . but you must promise . . . you must *swear* not to repeat a single word . . .'

'My lady! Whatever is it..?' Before Frances could tell her about the secret evening she and her friends had planned when her parents were away, the bedroom door opened and her mother came in without knocking. They both fell silent.

'You may go, Grace,' Katherine Cultrane said.

Slowly, Frances got to her feet and faced her mother across the floor. Grace went out so quietly that neither of them heard her leave.

'I've come to tell you the arrangements I've made while your father and I are away.'

'The language school?'

'Benson will take you to Kensington every morning in the car, and bring you back again in the afternoons. After lunch I shall expect you to study.'

'But I . . .'

'To ensure that you don't idle your time away tinkering with the piano instead of attending to your lessons, I've instructed that the door of the music room is to remain locked while your father and I are out of town. Is that understood?'

Frances was overwhelmed by the injustice of it all. 'But if I'm at the school all morning why can't I play the piano in the afternoons?'

'I didn't come here to argue with you. Just to tell you what I want you to do while we're away. Frances, I'll brook no disobedience. And don't think you can get round the staff the moment we're gone. I've made it perfectly clear to them that you're not to be given the key of the music room under any circumstances.'

'It's not fair!'

'When you learn to apply yourself to the subjects that matter, then you can expect concessions. Until then you'll concentrate solely on perfecting your German and French. When we come back I shall expect to see a marked improvement.' She went out without kissing her or saying goodnight. Grace had been hovering behind the dressing room door. She came back in again as soon as the Countess had gone, speaking in whispers in case she was still outside the bedroom door.

'Never mind, my lady; you could get Benson to take you over to see Lady Elizabeth; Lord Banbury's got a grand piano over there.'

'Yes, I suppose I could.' Frances kicked off her shoes and sat down on the edge of the bed. 'Except that now they're back from their honeymoon they'll be going out a lot, if I know Elizabeth, or else have dinner parties every night.' A sudden thought struck her. 'Do you think you could find out where my mother's put the music room key? It'll either be hanging up in the butler's pantry or in Daddy's study in the top drawer of his desk; he keeps all his spare keys in there. Grace, please, say you will . . .'

'My lady, I daren't . . . I'd lose my place if her ladyship found out, you know that . . .'

'No, you don't understand. If I know where it's kept I can take it and unlock the room myself; I'm not going to involve anyone else. Don't you see? I'll hang it back where I found it and nobody will know I've been in there. Please, Grace. I can't go a whole week without playing the piano.'

'I wouldn't say nothing about it, nor would anyone else downstairs. But you know Madders. He'd be telling his lordship you'd been playing that piano against his orders the minute they got back.'

'Yes, I suppose you're right . . .' She thought suddenly of the secret outing that was planned to the 43 Club and she smiled. 'Never mind, Grace . . . I'm going to do something else while my parents are away, something much more exciting than playing the piano . . .'

'My lady? What are you hatching up now?'

'Help me off with this dress and I'll tell you . . .'

11

Coming in from the sunny street outside, the sudden dimness inside the club made Kit squint. He waved to Rudy Loew who was already there, sitting in front of the piano where the band played, talking to the other musicians. Lounging around on chairs were some of Mrs Kate Meyrick's girls, hostesses, Rudy had told him with a wink and a nudge, which Kit interpreted on his own without any further elaboration of the services they provided for Mrs Meyrick's exclusive list of guests. When they caught sight of Kit, he saw them whispering and grinning among themselves.

'Hi,' Rudy said, getting up. He turned to the rest of the band. 'This is Kit Asmussen, boys. And ladies. Kit, this is the 43 band and these are the club's lovely ladies.' Kit put down his clarinet case and his music. 'Pete Mercer, drums. Jack Bailey, trombone. Tommy Hyde, piano. Harry Stern, double base. Me, of course, the one and only on trumpet.' There was another round of laughter from everyone.

'What about introducing us?' said one of the girls, without taking her heavily made up eyes off Kit's face. She got up from her chair and came towards him, smiling. She put a hand on his arm and squeezed it. 'My name's Amy.'

'The lovely Amy,' said Rudy Loew, winking at Kit. 'Violet, Ruby, Estella. And last but never by any means least, Irene. I already told you, Mrs Meyrick only picks the best looking girls.' Kit glanced down at the hand still on his arm and noticed the fingernails, varnished deep red, were at least three-quarters of an inch long. She tightened her grip on him.

'What are you doing after the audition, Kit?' He glanced down at her. She wore thick black mascara on her short, spiky lashes, and pancake make up; her vivid scarlet lipstick was put on carefully, in a fashionable cupid's bow. There was a pencilled beauty-spot on her left-hand cheek and she was wearing too much of a perfume that he couldn't identify but didn't like.

'I have to leave straight after for the London Pavilion.'

'And what do you do after that?'

'I play at the Embassy Club.'

She moved closer to him until she was pressing against his side. 'My flat's only a fifteen-minute taxi ride from there. Why don't you drop in for a drink after you've finished?'

He smiled, thinking how shocked his parents would be if they could see him now. 'Sorry. I don't finish at the Embassy until three-thirty or four. All I want then is to go home and go to sleep.'

A hand crept up his back and rested on his shoulder blade. 'My place is nearer than yours. Rudy told me.'

He moved forward so that her arm dropped away suddenly. 'Why don't you ask Rudy back for a drink instead? He needs less sleep than I do.'

112

'Hey, Kit!' shouted Rudy from across the room, saving him. 'Come here. There's a very important lady I'd like you to meet.' Kit glanced at the woman standing at Rudy's side, and smiled; even without being told guessing who she was; he'd already seen her photograph in the newspapers.

'Mrs Meyrick, this is Kit Asmussen, who I told you about. Kit, this is Mrs Kate Meyrick.'

She shook his hand and smiled. 'That's not strictly true, Kit . . . Rudy didn't just tell me about you once; he never stops talking about you.'

'I hope he hasn't been exaggerating.' They exchanged glances over Kate Meyrick's shoulder. 'It's an annoying habit of his.'

'Oh, I never take too much notice of what other people tell me. I always prefer to judge things for myself.'

'Well, you're very kind to spare me some of your valuable time. I hope I won't disappoint you.'

She looked up into his face and he could feel the shrewd, humorous grey eyes assessing him. He'd already decided that despite everything he'd read and heard about her, he liked her. 'I'm sure you won't.'

She was much smaller than he'd imagined; tiny, almost birdlike, with a little heart-shaped face and beautifully-kept hands. If he hadn't known who she was he would have made the vast mistake of grossly underestimating her; she looked so fragile and vulnerable. But he knew that she was one of the most astute and tough businesswomen he was every likely to come across. He gestured to his clarinet case.

'I brought some of my own music as well as one or two other pieces.' He glanced at Rudy. 'There's a rag and a blues that Sidney Bechet's already recorded in America; both my favourites. I thought I'd start off with one of those and then play a couple of my own pieces in between.'

'It sounds fine to me. Rudy? Give the boys the music and let them take a look at it.' She smiled at Kit. 'They're pretty good . . . even if they don't know a number it doesn't take them long to follow it.' She sat down on the chair someone had brought her and her girls came and stood around her, like maids in waiting at Court. 'So you write your own music? How long have you been doing that?'

'For as long as I can remember. A lot of things I've thought over twice and thrown away. There's a limit to how much you can store in one room. When I was living at home my father wouldn't let me keep too much music around; he said piles of paper cause dust and dust breeds germs.'

She laughed, softly. 'Now I *can* sympathize . . . my father was exactly the same. From what I hear from Rudy, you don't live at home anymore?'

'I moved out just a little while ago. Rudy put in a good word for me with his landlady.' He could feel the girls' eyes watching him and he deliberately kept his fixed on Kate Meyrick's face. 'He's been twisting my arm to come and meet you ever since I got settled in.'

'Well, I'm glad he did. Even if I don't like your music I certainly like you.'

From behind them somewhere he heard Rudy's voice calling him. 'Excuse me. When you're ready then?'

'I'm ready.'

He went across and took his clarinet out of its case, then spent a few moments chatting to the band about the music. 'We'll start with *Shake It and Break It;* then one of yours . . . isn't that what you said?'

'If it's OK by you, boys?' A murmur of general assent went round. 'All right. Let's take it from the top. A-major key.'

Kit took his position at the front of the band. He could see Kate Meyrick still sitting there, chin in hand, watching him intently. The girls were talking behind their hands and whispering. Amy's eyes were fixed unwaveringly on his face. Like he always did when he was playing, he looked past them all, the first notes of the music making him totally immune to all the sights and sounds around him. Halfway through the first loud, hypnotic bar, he might as well have been there alone. He didn't notice the beads of sweat that broke out across his forehand and soaked his dark, wavy hair; he forgot the time, that he was due at the London Pavilion in less than three-quarters of an hour; Kate Meyrick, the girls, the other staff and waiters, even the band behind him spun to insignificance as he played every note as if he was possessed, going through every bar and every cadence like a man in a trance. At the end, when the sights and sounds of his surroundings gradually began to come back to him, he was only aware of the sudden, deafening outburst of applause. Rudy was slapping him on the back, Kate Meyrick was getting up from her chair and walking towards him. Slowly, he lowered the instrument in his hands.

From all the other voices clamouring around him, Kit heard hers alone. She had to look up to him, because she was so short and he was tall. 'I've heard plenty of musicians in my time, young man; but never anyone like you.' She smiled. 'You must be a reincarnation of the pied piper.' Around them, everyone laughed.

'Thank you, Mrs Meyrick.' Before she asked him he knew by the expression on her face that she was going to offer him a job. And he already knew what his answer was going to be.

'Only a fool would let you walk out of that door. How much do they pay you at the Embassy?' He told her. 'I'll pay you double . . . to begin with.' The shrewd grey eyes twinkled. 'When can you start?'

'As soon as I've worked out my notice at the Embassy.' He was already telling himself that this was something that his father must never be allowed to find out. And nor, for a long time in the future, must his sister Laura.

Elizabeth climbed out of the taxi and left Anne Turner to pay off the driver. Looking around her, she pulled her cream mohair cloche hat down further over her eyes, the huge sable collar of her fashionable coat close up around her face; though the street was virtually deserted, she was taking no chances. It was still only early evening and hers was a face that had been a long time in the public eye. Thankfully within a few minutes they were inside the house.

From her small lizardskin clutch-bag Anne Turner took out a key and unlocked the front door. Elizabeth stood staring round the big, clinically white hall, acutely aware of the almost sinister silence. A clock was ticking somewhere but she couldn't see it. Their high-heeled shoes echoed on the polished parquet floor.

'This way.' Anne Turner smiled and took her arm; but before they reached the end of the hall the large door at the bottom opened and a man stood there. For a moment Elizabeth hesitated; then she felt the small, almost imperceptible push of Anne Turner's hand. She felt curiously stripped of all her natural superiority: at New Bond Street, at Belgrave Square, she was the Countess of Banbury, who was treated and spoken to with deference and exaggerated respect. The moment she'd stepped out of the taxi and through the front door, she felt that her position had been completely reversed; here, she was on Simon Forman's ground and she felt nervous and unsure.

'Elizabeth,' Anne Turner's soft, cooing voice spoke from somewhere behind her, 'this is Dr Forman.'

'My dear Lady Elizabeth – or should I call you Lady Banbury? What a pleasure this is. What a striking resemblance you have to your mother. The newspaper photographs of your wedding really don't do you justice . . .'

Anne Turner had never mentioned that Simon Forman had ever met her mother. She turned to her questioningly.

'Do go in, Elizabeth, and sit down.'

She went on staring into his face, at the heavy-lidded, hypnotic eyes, eyes that refused to let her own go. Behind him, she was dimly aware of the room itself. The rosewood partners' desk, the leather upholstered chairs, the gilt statue of the nude goddess Aphrodite in the centre of the mantlepiece. Slowly, she dragged her eyes away from him and looked around her. There were other statues; statues in gilt, in bronze, in stone; on his desk a naked man and woman entwined together in an intimate and explicit embrace; she was shocked and fascinated at the same time. With difficulty, she dragged her eyes away from it.

He smiled at her from his chair. 'Anne, pour Elizabeth a glass of sherry.' Already she was merely 'Elizabeth'. He had relegated her in the social scale to his own middle-class level. 'Anne tells me that you'd like my professional help with a little private matter . . . and that there might be other services I can offer you?'

All the way here in the taxi, she'd thought of this moment and what she would say. 'Yes. The trouble is . . . as you may already know . . . my family and my husband are Catholic . . .'

'Of course. Not disciples of Dr Marie Stopes.' He drew his chair closer to her and reached out unexpectedly to take her hands in his. 'Relax, Elizabeth. Let yourself go . . . you're among friends. Anne and I both completely understand . . .' She felt herself responding to him. Somehow, the way he'd taken her hands in his didn't seem impertinent, or an imposition; after all, he was a doctor. 'You're young. You're a leader of society. You want to enjoy life for a while . . . before the inevitable restrictions of starting a family . . . you'd be surprised at the number – and the rank – of the women among my patients who are in exactly the same position.'

'Anne said you'd understand! That I could tell you anything, and it would be all right . . .'

'My dear, this consulting room is like the confessional; whatever is said within these four walls remains strictly between us three; I gather from Anne that you want me to give you an examination this evening . . . so that we can make sure the device is exactly the right size for you. I can't stress the importance of that. If it doesn't fit exactly there's an ever-present risk of the pregnancy occurring that you're so anxious to avoid.'

'I'll leave it all to you.' She drank the sherry that Anne Turner handed her with a gulp. She'd missed lunch because she was nervous

116

about meeting Simon Forman, and it went straight to her head. She saw him through a slightly fuzzy haze.

'Now, Elizabeth . . . if you'll just go behind this screen and take off your clothes . . . the couch is over here . . .'

His hands were cold and dry; she flinched when she first felt him touch her skin. He kept up a constant flow of conversation in his low-pitched, soothing voice; despite the initial discomfort and embarrassment, she was beginning to feel relaxed. On the other side of the screen, she could hear Anne Turner moving about the room.

'Of course,' he was saying, as he moved away and washed his hands in the gleaming white sink behind her. 'Fitting devices for my lady patients is merely one of my services . . . as I believe Anne's told you . . .' She still felt faintly giddy from the sherry; she heard herself respond. Surely he'd finished now? When would he tell her that she could get up? Somewhere beyond the screen a door closed and everywhere seemed unnaturally silent; Anne Turner had left the room. 'Some years ago, I had the privilege of advising your mother . . . Anne introduced her to me, of course . . .'

She raised herself up on her elbows. 'My mother? You've met my mother? But she would never . . .'

He went on as if she hadn't spoken. 'All my consultations – and the identity of my patients, needless to say – has to remain totally confidential . . . I know you'll understand that. But I can tell you . . . the last time I saw her was in 1911 . . . when she consulted me about a possible termination.' Elizabeth stared at him, suddenly realizing the implication of what he was saying. 'All the arrangements were made. Everything was ready. And then, for some reason which she never told me, she suddenly changed her mind.'

12

Laura sat curled up in one of the armchairs in the little back parlour, a magazine open on her lap, vaguely aware of her parents' conversation from across the room. It was so dull without Kit around in the early evening, the whole house seemed so quiet and lifeless without the familiar sounds of him whistling in his room as he got ready for his nightly appearance at the Embassy. Now that he'd gone for good, she suddenly realized just how much having him here had meant to her.

Unenthusiastically, she turned over another page of her mother's *Good Housekeeping* magazine. She'd just half-heartedly finished reading an article about women's clubs, and two-and-a-quarter pages by Arnold Bennett on editing a woman's paper. She'd hesitated, her interest momentarily caught, by the cookery editor's comments on a suitable menu for anyone catering for a dance. A more promising article entitled *To Marry or not to Marry*, caused her to pause, and begin reading again. At the top of the page was a black-and-white line drawing of a large, sumptuously dressed dowager getting out of a chauffeur driven Rolls Royce, advancing towards a shabbily-dressed navvy in the process of sweeping up leaves, and the caption: '*If you are a Duchess and your mate is a dustman, track him down and marry him . . .*'

'You haven't heard anything from Kit, I suppose?' her father was asking from the other side of the room; momentarily she glanced up, only to realize that the question hadn't been directed at her. She looked back at the article.

'No, not since he left. He did say he was probably going to call in and see us later this week . . .'

Laura focused her eyes on the page, wondering why she felt so depressed and tired this evening; thinking about it, she'd been feeling depressed all day. When Kit was here, she'd always looked forward to coming home again. . . . *There are only two occasions on which a woman is unhappy in this life . . . when she is married, and when she isn't . . .*'

'Typical of him. Completely thoughtless. I suppose the young puppy thinks he can breeze in and out of here just as it suits him. Well, he can't.'

'I'm sure he doesn't think that, Richard.'

At the mention of her brother, Laura set down the magazine. 'Oh, Daddy, I don't think you're being very fair about Kit . . . I mean, he must be terribly busy, what with moving all his things and rehearsals on top of that . . . it isn't as if he can telephone us to let us know when he's coming, because we don't have a telephone.'

'No, we most certainly do not have a telephone, and I have no intention of acquiring one. Such luxuries don't come within my budget for this house, young lady, nor are they ever likely to. There is such a thing as the post, in case you've forgotten. Don't waste your breath defending your brother because his conduct is quite indefensible. If he chooses not to have the courtesy of keeping in proper touch with your mother and me after being looked after, clothed and fed ever since he was born, there seems little I can do about it; he's over twenty-one. And, last but not least, my remarks weren't addressed to you. I was speaking to your mother.'

Laura felt her face flush, but she stood her ground. 'Kit isn't thoughtless, he's busy, that's all. You just have no idea how busy a musician's life is . . .'

'Oh, I see! So he's completely different to the rest of us who go out to work to earn a living? I leave this house at eight-thirty every morning and I don't return to it until forty-five minutes past six; with the sole exception of one hour for lunch I work every single minute of the day . . .'

'I didn't mean that kind of work, Daddy . . . I know you work very hard . . . but Kit's kind of work is different . . . it takes so much more physically . . . and he works much harder than most other musicians because he works at two different jobs . . . two sets of rehearsals, two different places to travel back and forwards from every day, and working all night until two or three or maybe even four o'clock in the morning. When he has a moment he'll get in touch with us, I know he will. He didn't just walk out of here and forget all about us. He wouldn't do that. But you have to try and understand . . . he must get very tired doing everything he has to do. I don't know how he does it; I couldn't. The travelling alone would knock me for six.'

She'd been so intent on her passionate defence that she'd barely noticed the rising colour on her father's face. Before she could say anything else he was on his feet. 'That won't be the only thing that'll knock you for six, my girl, if you don't remember to whom you're speaking! As old as you are I'm in two minds to give you a damned good spanking for your cheek. How dare you presume to lecture me. I can see that that brother of yours has been nothing but a bad influence on you all along; his leaving is clearly a blessing in disguise.'

'I'm sure Laura didn't mean to argue with you, Richard . . .'

'This is entirely my own fault, I can see that now; I should never have allowed him to take up music. Not that I ever would have permitted it if I'd known that he was going to turn out like this, completely undisciplined and absolutely thoughtless in every way. But it can hardly be wondered at, the company he must have been keeping . . . I should have put my foot down and forbidden him to work in that damned nightclub in the first place. Mixing with heaven alone knows who, working at a time when decent, respectable people are asleep in their beds, playing that awful ear-splitting noise he calls music . . .'

119

'Kit's a first-class musician. When he auditioned at the London Pavilion Charles B. Cochran himself came out to listen to him. I've heard him, I know. You ought to be proud of him, Daddy. And as for working at the Embassy Club, all the very best people in society patronize it, from the Prince of Wales down: and you can scarcely say he isn't respectable.'

'Laura, please! You really mustn't answer your father back like this . . .'

'It isn't my place to make comments on my betters, young lady, least of all on a member of the Royal Family. Be that as it may, His Royal Highness's behaviour in general does leave much to be desired. For one thing, it gives a very bad impression and an even worse example to the young people of this country on standards of accept-able behaviour. But simply because the Prince of Wales does some-thing that is questionably reprehensible, that does not follow that others have to copy him. I never approved of Kit working at the Embassy Club, no matter who it's members are, and I don't approve now.'

'But, Daddy!'

'Not so long ago I was reading in the newspapers about the number of police raids on certain nightclubs in the Mayfair area . . . not the Embassy, granted; but simply because the raids were carried out on far less morally reputable places and not at the club where your brother works is neither here nor there; in the public mind these places are all tainted with the same brush. My goodness! Illegal gambling, drinking spirits and allegations of *drugs* . . . it scarcely bears thinking about.'

'But Kit isn't involved with anything like that.'

'Guilt by association, Laura. People naturally think that if such dreadful things go on at such and such a place, anyone who has anything to do with them must be involved too.'

She could barely contain her anger. 'Well, they'd be wrong, wouldn't they?'

'Laura, you'll oblige me by going straight to your room. I hope,' he took his place in one of the vacant fireside chairs and opened his evening paper. 'When you're there you'll reflect on your behaviour and take care that it's never repeated.'

Wearily she went up the little narrow staircase and hesitated at the top. Away to the right was Kit's bedroom door. Unable to stop herself, she took hold of the door handle and opened it.

A thin ray of moonlight fell across the floor and the bed through the undrawn curtains. Everywhere seemed so neat and tidy, all his possessions, all the little things that had made the room his, were gone; the room might have belonged to anyone. There was a lump in her throat as she closed the door and went on to her own room.

13

'Is this it?'

'Yes, isn't it absolutely top hole? Gerald Hunter said their musicians are out of this world.'

'Go on, it's your turn to tip the driver!'

'What if someone's in there we all know?' giggled Diana Gunnis, and the other girls collapsed into fits of nervous laughter. 'Mummy and Daddy will positively skin me alive if they found out!'

'It was all your idea in the first place, Diana.'

'Oh come on, everyone, we're all in this together. Frances hasn't got cold feet!' She looked at Frances defiantly. 'Have you?'

'If my sister's in there I'm coming straight out again.'

'You said she was going to a dinner party at the Moseleys.'

They piled out of the taxi and filed into the foyer of the 43 Club. The dim lighting was the first thing that struck Frances; it made her feel safe, cocooned from the danger of discovery. She felt slightly sick with excitement, there were butterflies in the pit of her stomach and she wished she'd eaten something before they'd left. The unfamiliar cocktail Bertie Gunnis ordered for all of them went straight to her head and made her feel dizzy.

'Bertie, whatever *is* this concoction made of? It tastes absolutely excruciating.'

'That, my dear, is what is known in nightclub circles as a screw-driver.'

'Well, I'd much rather have champagne.'

Cigarettes were being offered around, but Frances shook her head. The smoke threatened to make her cough and her eyes began to water. The club was beginning to become more crowded now; loud laughter, the chink of glasses and the noise of peoples' voices vied with the music from the band. Curiously fascinated, Frances began to gaze around her, suddenly shocked by what she saw.

Women were dancing with their partners in poses verging on the indecent; some were openly kissing, or smoking as they danced, holding their long, elegant cigarette holders over their partners' shoulders. In a far corner, one of the women was sitting on a man's lap, her evening gown pushed up so high that Frances could see the tops of her suspenders. Blushing violently, she dragged her eyes away. Suddenly, she wished they hadn't come; but she was the only one in the party who wasn't enjoying themselves.

Diana Gunnis was on her second cocktail and had helped herself to one of her brother's cigarettes. 'Oh, do have one, Frances, it's terribly chic. Bertie, give Frances one of your Turkish cigarettes.'

'No, really, I'd rather not.'

'Enjoy yourself, silly. Vivien, you haven't finished telling us about Dorothy Saint-Albans. Didn't you say she'd been on one of those super new cruise liners and come back brown as a nut? She says it's going to be all the rage this summer . . .'

'What? Being brown?'

'Oh, shut up, Bertie!'

Suddenly, into the noise and clamour the sound of a lone clarinet cut across the mayhem and voices. People began to talk in whispers; everyone turned, like Francis, in the direction of the lowered stage where the club band sat. A young man in an evening suit with thick dark hair and brown eyes stood up in the centre of the other musicians and played a wild, thrilling piece of New Orleans jazz that made her heart beat faster and sent tingles up and down her spine, then went straight into a novel interpretation of the very latest Cole Porter song, then another and another, barely pausing to draw breath in between each one; when he'd finished, there was a deafening burst of applause to which he almost imperceptibly responded, before sitting down with the rest of the band to play a slower, softer melody for the dancers. For Frances, the whole evening had changed; she had never enjoyed herself so much in all her life. She couldn't take her eyes off of him.

'Frances, what about a dance?'

'No, really . . .'

'Oh, come on! Don't be such a dashed wet blanket!'

'In a minute, then . . .'

'I'm going to powder my nose. Frances, are you coming?' Diana Gunnis grasped her by the wrist. 'Then you've simply got to give Alistair a dance.'

Frances looked over her shoulder as they went towards the powder room, at the lowered stage where the club band sat. The dancing couples, gyrating constantly to and fro to the rhythm of the music, partly obscured her view so that she couldn't see him clearly, but she knew he was still there. She longed to hear him again; the tunes he'd played on the clarinet were going round and round loudly inside her head. Suddenly, the evening seemed to take on a new meaning.

It was only when she came out of the powder room again just before three o'clock that she realized something was wrong; the table where everybody had been sitting moments before was deserted; only her pale blue silk wrap was draped across the chair where she'd left it; all her friends' evening wraps had gone. Barely a dozen or so couples were left on the dance floor; her eyes sought a familiar face frantically, but they were all total strangers. Fighting down the feeling of rising panic, she ran out into the foyer and found the cloakroom attendant.

'Excuse me . . . please . . . the party I came in with . . . do you know where they are? Is there another room in the club?'

'Mr Gunnis's party left a few moments ago, miss; if I might say so, in something of a rush. They all got into a taxi while Mr Gunnis was paying the bill.' He looked at her intently, as if suspecting her real age beneath the carefully applied make up that Diana had assured her aged her by at least two years; she suddenly felt very frightened and very alone.

'Could you . . . ?' she began to say, then abruptly stopped; she had no money for a taxi to take her home; Diana's brother had paid for everything and Diana had told her that she didn't need to bring any. She fought down the urge to cry. She felt incredibly stupid and ridiculously young, foolish and naive.

'Did you require a taxi, miss?'

'No, thank you.' She clutched at her evening bag to keep her hands steady. 'No, it's perfectly all right. My friends will be coming back for me.' She went out into the chilly street, drawing the flimsy wrap around her shoulders, frantically looking this way and that. Surely they wouldn't just have left her like this, surely they'd come back? Was it a joke of Diana's to have rushed off and left her here, knowing she had brought no money and had no idea which way to go home? And even if she had, she could never walk back to Belgrave Square on the other side of London in high-heeled shoes. Behind her, people were beginning to come out of the club, jostling her as they went by, the sound of their laughter only emphasizing how much she was alone. It must be near closing time; the hands of her wristwatch were pointing to three o'clock. Her feet ached unbearably, the garters holding up her silk stockings were cutting unmercifully into her thighs. She had no money and she had no idea how she was ever going to get home again. She should never have let Diana Gunnis talk her into coming.

Covering her face with her hands she burst into tears.

'Well, what's all this?' said a voice from somewhere behind her. She turned round and found herself face to face with the dark-haired young musician who'd so enthralled her in the club. 'Here,' he took a handkerchief from the pocket of his evening suit and handed it to her. 'Now, supposing you tell me what's wrong. Then maybe I can help you.'

She stared at him, torn between relief and astonishment. 'I . . . I was with some friends. We all came here together. Then a little while ago I went into the powder room, but when I came out again, they'd disappeared.' She wiped her eyes, blotting the borrowed handkerchief with mascara smudges and the blue and gold cosmetic paste Diana Gunnis had painted her eyelids with to make her look older. 'I don't know what happened to them, why they went. But I can't get a taxi home, you see, because I haven't got any money. They told me I didn't need to bring any.'

He smiled at her, and in spite of her distress she felt colour coming into her face; he was very good-looking, even more attractive than he'd seemed in the band box. 'OK, don't panic. I live just a few minutes walk from here; you can clean up your face in my bathroom and then I'll call you a cab.'

She turned to him eagerly in the dim light. 'You're so kind! I don't know how to thank you!'

'I don't think the price of a taxi ride home is going to make too big a hole in my pocket.' She glanced at him sideways as they walked and he was grinning. 'So your chums went off and left you high and dry . . . if I was you, they'd be ex-chums from now on.'

'I'm sure they must have had a really good reason . . . except that I can't think what it could be. I suppose it might have been their idea of a joke, except that they knew I didn't bring any money . . .'

'They've got some sense of humour.' He stopped walking as he noticed she was shivering and put the overcoat he'd been carrying around her shoulders; it was absurdly too big for her. 'Here, take this before you freeze to death in that flimsy thing.' She gave him a grateful glance. 'Another couple of minutes and we'll be there.' It never occurred to her for a single moment to think that here she was, unchaperoned for the first time in her entire life, in a part of London completely unfamiliar to her at twenty-past-three in the morning, with a perfect stranger.

She read the street sign as they turned down another corner and stopped outside a large house with a stained-glass fanlight over the top of the door: *Halkin Street*. The young man had produced his door key and the large front door creaked open to reveal a wide, black-and-white tiled hall furnished with a hatstand and a hall table that had a vase of flowers and a telephone on it, and smelled faintly of polish. A narrow carpet runner in red, dark green and blue made a pathway to the staircase ahead of them.

'Try and walk on tiptoe, if you can in those shoes. We don't want to wake everyone else in the house if we can avoid it.' Two floors up, he took out another key and let her into a large room. He switched on the electric light and the single bar fire.

'Make yourself at home.' She looked around her, still nervous but curious now, at the single iron bedstead, the piles of sheet music on the table and on the upright piano that stood in the opposite corner of the room. It was a typical man's room, like her brothers' when they lived at home, without any unnecessary adornments; no photo-graphs, no sentimental knick-knacks. It was simply serviceable and practical. He was rubbing his hands together and holding them over the fire.

'Well, I suppose we ought to introduce ourselves. My name's Kit Asmussen.'

She stared at him in disbelief. 'Asmussen?'

'It's Danish. My father was born in Copenhagen, but he was brought up here. My mother's as English as cricket and cream teas. So, who are you, then?'

She'd been rescued by Laura's brother. 'Frances . . .'

'Ah. Frances. A mystery girl with no second name.' He smiled and sat down beside her. 'OK. So you'd rather not tell me; I understand. Tell you what. I'll call you Frankie.' She was clearly a girl from some upper class family, judging by the way she talked and the quality of her clothes, but it didn't bother him; if she wanted to be anonymous he couldn't really care less. He shrugged his shoulders. 'I'll make us some cocoa while you wash your face, then I'll get you a taxi to take you home. Let me show you where the bathroom is.'

'I'll try not to make a noise.' She wondered if his landlady would mind him inviting a strange girl to his room at this time in the morning; some would have given him notice, she'd no doubt. But he didn't seem worried. 'All right, Frankie?'

'Nobody's ever called me that before.'

'You never met me before.'

She blushed. 'Thank you for being so kind.'

'You didn't expect me to leave you there on the pavement crying your eyes out, did you? I'd have done the same for anyone.'

'I don't know what I'd have done if you hadn't been there.'

In the bathroom, she took off her shoes so that she made no noise, then she splashed cold water on her swollen eyes. She looked at her reflection in the mirror above the hand basin, and although it was long past her normal bedtime her eyes were sparkling and bright. There were still traces of mascara on her eyelids and the cosmetic paste on the lids of her eyes; did she really look eighteen or nineteen, as Diana Gunnis had assured her she did? He first reaction when she'd found out that Diana and the others had gone off and left her stranded had been panic and fury, but now she was almost pleased; how else would she have found herself here, with Laura's brother, who also happened to be the most handsome young man she'd ever seen? She desperately wanted to know what he really thought of her. When she'd tiptoed quietly back to his room, she cradled the enormous mug of hot cocoa in both hands and knelt down beside the single bar of the electric fire. She was wondering why Kit Asmussen was playing at the 43 Club when Laura had told her that he played at the Embassy.

'Have you been in the club band for very long?' she asked shyly, watching him over the rim of the mug. He stretched. Unlike her, he seemed completely at ease in a stranger's company.

'No, not long; I used to play at the Embassy but they never gave me the chance to play solos. Kate Meyrick also pays me more; not that I came to her club just because of that. After I'd auditioned for her she said I could play my own stuff straight away. That decided me.'

Frances felt sure that Laura didn't know. 'Do you like it better?'

'The clientele are different.' He grinned. 'So is the atmosphere. So far we haven't been honoured by a visit from the Prince of Wales'

She caught the disapproval in his voice. 'Don't you like the Royal Family?'

'How can I not like people I don't even know? That'd be prejudice. Let's just say I don't approve of what they represent; unjustified privileges . . . privileges should be earned, not inherited.' He gave her a broad smile. 'Mind you, if I said that at home and my father heard me, it'd be high treason.' Those three sentences told her a lot about him. 'When I played at the Embassy the Prince was always there, and from a distance – the band are high up – anyone could see that whatever else he might be, he's no stuffed shirt. The King probably disapproves of his lifestyle as much as my father disapproves of mine.'

She recalled the unpleasant scene with her parents after her mother's dinner party, and felt an instant affinity with him. 'Don't you get on with your father? Is that why you live here?'

'He was partly the reason I left home, yes. But there were other reasons . . . getting in at all hours wasn't really fair on my parents or my sister. Often as not, however quiet I tried to be, I'd wake somebody up. And there were always arguments if I left sheet music around the house or practised in my room . . . definitely didn't go down well with my Mother's bridge parties. We live in Kilburn, and that's a long way to travel backwards and forward when you work in the city; and have two jobs like me. I'm also first clarinet at the London Pavilion.'

She forced out the words she'd wanted to say ever since she'd met him. 'I think you're the most wonderful musician I've ever heard!'

He laughed out loud, forgetting that everyone else in the house was asleep. 'You can't have heard many.'

'My sister has dozens of jazz records, a lot specially imported from America, and none of them played like you did!'

'Well, thank you, Frankie.' He put down his empty cocoa mug and got to his feet. 'I hate to have to say this, but I think it's high time I was getting you home . . . what the hell are your parents going to say when you turn up at this hour and tell them your chums ditched you? I'd better come with you and explain, hadn't I?' He saw the horrified expression on her face and used his imagination. 'Don't tell me . . . they don't know about tonight. If they found out you'd been within five miles of a nightclub they'd skin you alive.'

She looked down shamefacedly. 'Something like that . . . but I thought . . . well, if I could use the telephone in the hall – very quietly, I promise! – I could ring my sister, and she'd take me back. I know she won't have gone to bed yet, because she was going to the theatre tonight and then on somewhere for supper . . . the thing is, my parents are away, but there are people in the house . . . if I came back on my own so late, I know they'd tell them when they came home and then I'd be in awful trouble . . .'

'Yes, I expect they would; my mother's got a maid called Ethel and she couldn't keep a secret if her life depended on it.' He picked up her flimsy evening wrap and draped it around her shoulders. He couldn't help thinking what beautiful skin she had, and he'd have sworn her hair was naturally blonde; Kate Meyrick's girls at the club would have killed for it. 'Of course you can use the telephone. While you're getting through to your sister, I'll go outside and find you a taxi.'

Alone, she picked up the receiver nervously and dialled; when she was put through to the Portland Place number, the bell at the other end was ringing for a long time. When she was about to give up and put it down it suddenly clicked, and a very sleepy, slightly querulous voice answered.

Frances swallowed; she realized how late it was and that she'd obviously got Seddon, William Banbury's butler, out of bed. 'I'm very sorry to disturb you; but could you please tell me if Lady Banbury is at home? It's rather urgent.'

There was a slight pause at the other end of the line as if Seddon was trying to work out what that was. He cleared his throat. 'Lady Banbury went out for the evening and hasn't returned yet.' Was that a hint of disapproval in his voice? 'His Lordship has an all-night sitting in the house and isn't expected back until tomorrow. May I enquire who is speaking?'

'Thank you,' Frances said quickly, and replaced the receiver guiltily. At the same moment Kit emerged from the street.

'Taxi's waiting outside when you're ready. Isn't your sister there?'

'It doesn't matter . . . I'll just have to face the music on my own; I could say the car broke down and the others put me in a taxi . . . there's no need for you to come, really.' Whatever happened, he mustn't find out who she was or where she lived, or how young she really was. She wanted desperately to see him again 'I must pay you back; for the 'phone call and the taxi fare . . .'

'One cab ride and a two-minute telephone call are hardly going to make a hole in my pocket.'

'Please, I want to. If you're here tomorrow could I come back and return the money then? I don't want to get in your way . . .'

He was laughing softly now, his dark eyes full of amusement; her obvious *naïveté* and her fresh, unspoiled looks both appealed to him; she was certainly very different to the girls he usually came into contact with.

'Come if you insist.' He opened the front door a little wider so that she could walk through. 'I come back from rehearsals about half-past eleven. Make it any time after then . . . up till about one-thirty.'

128

They walked out onto the pavement where the taxi was waiting and he opened the door for her. She watched him lean forward to speak to the driver and pass him a handful of coins. 'Take the young lady where she wants to go.'

'Righto, gov'nor!'

He stood back away from the kerb as the engine came to life and the vehicle started off, raising a hand to wave to her as she turned and gazed back through the rear window. In front of her, the glass panel separating her from the driver slid open with a bang.

'Where to, miss?'

On the pavement behind her Kit had gone back into the house.

'Fifteen Belgrave Square, please.'

She went on gazing from the back window at the spot where he had been.

Eddie Vaux parked his two-seater MG sports car in the most shadowed part of the street, then turned off the engine and took Elizabeth into his arms. Though they'd spent most of the evening in bed making love, they kissed passionately for several more minutes before finally, breathlessly, drawing apart. Immediately Elizabeth began rummaging in her lizardskin clutch-bag for her lipstick and powder compact.

'Eddie, darling, you've kissed off all my lipstick! I can't possibly go in like this . . .'

'You look beautiful just the way you are.' He stroked the back of her neck with the tips of his fingers. 'Besides, they'll all be in bed now. He's away at the House.' He sat watching her while she repaired her make-up and combed her hair. 'When am I going to see you again?'

She put away the lipstick and compact and snapped the bag shut. 'Darling, we've got to go on being careful. I told you about Seddon . . . I just don't trust him. God, if there was some way I could get rid of him.'

'Don't bother trying. He's been in the family for God knows how many years . . . my uncle's devoted to him. As he is to anything that's antique – it makes him feel young by comparison.' There was bitterness as well as contempt in his voice. 'I always did hate the old bastard. Most of all when I found out that he was marrying you.' He could see her looking at her diamond and platinum wristwatch; every time they met, every stolen moment, evening, afternoon, was governed by time, and he hated it. He was the one who had a moral right to her. If she hadn't been an Osborne, if her family hadn't been ruthless and ambitious enough to sacrifice her to the arms of an old man older even than her own father, they could have been together, they could have been happy. He took an almost vicious pleasure in deceiving his uncle every time he went to bed with her.

'Darling, I'd better go . . . I'll ring you. Or get Anne to send a message. If anything urgent comes up you know you can always reach me through her first.'

He smiled and they kissed again. 'I love you,' he whispered to her as she climbed out of the car.

'Don't get out. Someone might see you.' She blew him a kiss with her fingertips and then began to walk in the direction of Banbury House. Behind her in the deserted street she heard the car driving away.

Silently, being careful to walk on tip-toe, Elizabeth let herself into the house and closed the front door. Just as carefully and quietly, she drew the bolts across, then for a moment she leaned against it and looked around her. Everywhere was in darkness, the only sound the ticking of half-a-dozen clocks. She paused, took off her high-heeled shoes and began to walk stealthily towards the staircase. She was glad she'd told Sabine not to wait up; another moment and she could throw off her clothes and go to bed.

It was then that a sudden, unexpected movement at the other end of the darkened hall made her jump, and she almost cursed aloud. Seddon, a lamp in one hand, came slowly towards her.

'*Seddon?*'

'Good evening, my lady.' Was it her imagination or was there a slight, sarcastic inflection of that second word? 'I took the liberty of waiting up for you . . .'

She fought down her fury at being caught out, tiptoeing up the stairs with her shoes like a guilty maidservant, late back from her evening out. She was so angry she could have struck him. 'Really, Seddon, you shouldn't have bothered.' How dare he try and make her feel guilty. 'I rarely come in until this time when I have an evening out . . . I just slipped off my shoes to avoid disturbing anybody . . .' She knew by the expression in his eyes that he didn't believe her.

'Very good, my lady. Is there anything you require?'

'No, I don't think so. Only a good night's sleep.' She was fighting a

130

losing battle to contain her sense of outrage. But Seddon's deceptively bland expression never changed.

'Before you retire, my lady, I should perhaps mention that there was a telephone call this evening, while you were out. For you.'

Alarm shot through her. 'My husband?'

'No, my lady. It was a lady caller. Unfortunately she rang off before I was able to ascertain her name, and if she wished to leave a message. She wanted to know if you were at home.'

'What time was this?'

'About an hour ago, my lady.'

It could only have been Anne Turner; who else would telephone her at half past three in the morning? But whatever could her reason have been for ringing at such an hour? Her fertile imagination instantly began to work overtime. Perhaps it had been someone else?

'All right; thank you, Seddon. You can go back to bed now.'

'Thank you, my lady. I trust you had a pleasant evening.' She looked at him sharply. 'Goodnight, my lady.'

She ran up the enormous staircase without answering him. When she reached her room she collapsed on the bed without getting undressed and closed her eyes, after hurling her shoes across the floor in a fit of temper. Waiting for her, spying on her, trying to catch her out; she'd taken an instant dislike to Seddon on the first day they'd come back from their honeymoon and now she hated him implacably, never mind that hate was a mortal sin. He deserved it. Whatever it took, she was determined to get him out.

A wave of nausea came over her, and she sat bolt upright, cursing the fact that before she could sleep she had to face the bathroom ritual of washing and cleaning her teeth. Perhaps she should have told Sabine to wait up for her after all.

The unknown telephone caller was still worrying her. First thing tomorrow morning she must ring Anne Turner.

Sliding down beneath the satin sheets, she closed her eyes and wished that Eddie Vaux was still in bed beside her. In a few minutes, she fell into an exhausted sleep.

14

Kit yawned as he walked through the warren of passages and dressing rooms backstage, half-heartedly raising a hand in acknowledgement or a tired smile as people along the way recognized him.

'Late night, Kit?' One of the stage-hands stopped shifting a pile of props and lit a woodbine.

'You could say that.' He walked on towards the auditorium, clarinet case under one arm, glancing to one side as one of the dressing room doors opened and a chorus girl leaned against the side of it, watching him.

'You're five minutes early today!'

'That's better than being five minutes late.' He suddenly realized that she was following him.

'Fasten me up, will you? I can't reach the top.'

'What's the matter . . . your dresser gone on strike?'

'She's having a tea break.' She tossed back her thick red hair and looked boldly up into his face. 'Besides, I want you to do it.'

Kit put down his clarinet case with a sigh of impatience. 'OK. Stand still. Lift your hair up off your neck or it'll catch in the clip.'

'Ouch! Your hands are cold!'

'Teach you to wait next time for your dresser.'

'Kit Asmussen, you bastard!'

He laughed as he walked away towards the auditorium. 'Tut, tut . . . uncensored words from the lips of one of Mr Cochran's Young Ladies!'

The double-doors to the auditorium banged shut so he didn't hear what she yelled after him.

'Morning, Kit! You been upsetting the girls again?'

'Nothing they can't handle.' He smiled, taking a seat halfway down the aisle with a group of the other musicians while they watched Charles Cochran directing a line of dancers on stage.

'You're a fool, you know that? You could take your pick from the chorus if you wanted to . . . ever since you started here, they've been falling over themselves to get near you. Give me the chance!'

Kit couldn't resist a wicked smile. 'I don't think the Boss would like it.'

'What the eye doesn't see the heart doesn't grieve over. Think of all that beautiful, warm, willing flesh. You want your bloody brains tested!'

'There isn't much CBC's eye doesn't see, you can bet on that!'

'He can't sleep with all of them!'

'Want to bet?'

'Every time Iris looks at you, you can see her temperature go up.'

Kit turned to his companion, unable to resist teasing him. 'So why don't you make sure you're near at hand, holding a thermometer? She isn't my type.'

'Are you kidding?'

'No. Are you?'

'You mean you wouldn't go to bed with her?'

'Maybe if she was the last female on earth I might reconsider it.'

'You don't go for redheads?'

'It's got nothing to do with the colour of her hair . . . which might or might not come out of a bottle. She just doesn't do anything to me . . . satisfied?'

'Don't tell her that.' They all rose as the bandmaster beckoned them over to the orchestra pit.

'Asmussen, I want you to play piano to start off with; Hutch is off sick today. Rest of you take up your places, please!' The choreographer suddenly smiled, and turned towards the petite, dark-haired girl with enormous brown eyes who'd that moment come from the wings onto the centre of the stage. 'Ready when you are, Jessie.'

Frances had been awake since before dawn, long before Grace brought in her morning tea and drew back the curtains. She was astonished to find her sitting up in bed and unbelievably bright-eyed.

'And after that late night, too, my lady! What a shame, Mr Gunnis's car getting a flat tyre. Goodness knows what time he and Miss Diana managed to get home, then.' She opened the wardrobe and began getting our Frances's clothes for the day. 'That's the trouble with motor cars, isn't it? With a horse and carriage you know where you are!'

Frances was eyeing the outfit Grace had laid out on the satin counterpane of the bed. 'I don't think I'll be wearing that today, Grace.'

'Oh, but my lady . . . Lady Cultrane was most positive about what you were to wear to the language school . . . she brought me up here and pointed it out special.'

Frances gave her a conspiratorial smile. 'Well, she isn't here, is she? And I promise I'll wear what she wanted me to, tomorrow. But not today.' She flung back the bedclothes and stretched. Sunlight beamed into the room from the windows, outside in the long garden that stretched away into the distance for as far as you could see, blossom was waving on the tree branches in heavy, abundant clusters. 'You see, I'm not going to the language school straight away. I want to go over to Portland Place and see my sister.'

Anything that wavered from routine, especially anything against Lady Cultrane's orders, always worried Grace. She looked unhappy. 'But her ladyship said you was to go straight to the language school in Kensington. The chauffeur's got his orders, my lady.'

'He can have the morning off instead. I think it would be much better if I took a taxi. In any case, it'll be boring for him to sit in the car and wait for me while I'm with my sister. I don't want any breakfast, just more tea, please. Will you ask Madders to make sure I have a taxi for eleven o'clock?'

'Her ladyship left the chauffeur his orders, my lady . . .'

'Oh, balls of fire, Grace! Will you please ask him or shall I?'

'If her ladyship comes back and finds out everything's been done different to what she said it was to be done, she'll have our guts for garters!'

Frances forgot that up until last night she'd always been as afraid of her mother as the servants were. All she could think of was seeing Kit Asmussen again. 'If nobody tells her then she'll never find out, will she?'

The sound of someone playing *Maple Leaf Rag* on a piano drifted loudly down the stairs towards her as his landlady showed her into the hall.

'Yes, he's back, dear; got back about ten minutes ago.' She smiled and pointed towards the stairs. 'Know which room it is, do you? Would you like a cup of tea?' Her total lack of formality took Frances slightly aback; at Belgrave Square, after morning tea and tea at breakfast, no tea was served again until four o'clock.

'Yes, please. If you're sure it's no trouble.'

'Trouble? No trouble, duck. I was just goin' to put the kettle on for meself.' She went off in the direction of the kitchen steps singing in a flat, tuneless voice.

Left alone, Frances looked around frantically for the mirror. Yes, the broad-brimmed fawn moiré picture-hat she'd chosen because it made her look older, suited her; but would she still look too suspiciously young without Diana Gunnis's lipstick and eye-paint? She had none of her own and Elizabeth had taken all her cosmetics with her when she'd left the house more than a month ago; she dared not touch anything of her mother's. Well, there was nothing for it; she'd have to do as she was. She pinched her cheeks to make the colour come into them and with a deep breath mounted the stairs. She hesitated outside his room.

The music came from inside, and for a little while she stopped where she was, thrilled by the sound and the way he played. When he'd finished the final bar she managed to summon up enough courage to tap gently on the door; instead of calling to her to come in, he got up from the piano stool and opened it himself.

'Hello, Frankie.' He smiled and she felt her face begin to burn like fire. 'So you got home all right. Did those so-called chums of yours phone up and apologize for leaving you in the lurch?'

She hadn't even thought about them again. 'No, not yet; but I expect they will later.'

'They're all probably too ashamed to make the first move and call you.' He motioned her to a chair and perched himself on the edge of the piano stool. She noticed the half-smoked cigarette in the ashtray on top of the piano, the stack of music laid out on the bed. His thick dark hair was slightly dishevelled, he was wearing a tie but it had come loose at the neck, and his shirt sleeves were rolled up; she gazed at his bare forearms and the place below his neck where she could see his chest, and she suddenly wanted to touch him. She fumbled in her handbag for her purse.

'Here . . . please take it . . . is it enough? And thanks so much again for helping me . . .'

He laughed. 'Don't be silly. You keep it.'

'You must take it, really . . .'

He reached out and enclosed her hand over the coins, and the sensation of his touch sent all her pulses leaping.

'My pleasure. Now let's forget about it.' He stood up, releasing her hand. 'You know, I wasn't sure whether you'd really come back or not.'

She looked at him aghast. 'But I said I would! I asked you and you said it would be all right!'

He laughed again, softly. 'In my experience young women often say one thing and do quite another.' She felt a stab of jealousy; so he'd known lots of young women. But then, of course, he would, with

135

his good looks, charm, and bohemian way of life. This was only the second time they'd met so why did the thought of that hurt her so much?

'Are you sure . . . I mean . . . you didn't mind me coming back? I'm not interrupting you, or stopping you from doing something else..?'

'If I hadn't wanted you to come back I wouldn't have invited you, would I?' He was having difficulty in suppressing a broad smile; she was so sweet, shy, so endearingly unsophisticated; so utterly different from all the girls he knew. He thought of Kate Meyrick's 'girls' at the 43 Club, the dancers at the London Pavilion with their scanty clothes, vivid scarlet mouths and wordly, heavily kohled and mascara'd eyes, and thought that in comparison she was like a breath of fresh air. She intrigued him, and had done ever since last night when he'd come out of the club and found her crying on the pavement.

The way she spoke, her manners, her clothes; in fact virtually everything about her, proclaimed she came from an upper-class home, and most of the young women he'd seen at the clubs where he'd played were ones he'd usually steer clear of; but she was different. There were a lot of questions he'd have liked to have asked her from mere curiosity, but not now. As he looked at her in the clear light of day he realized that she was much more striking than he'd thought her last night when she'd been dishevelled, frightened and tired. She was beautiful. As he looked at her he realized, with not a small amount of amusement, that she was very much in awe of him. For Kit that was an entirely new experience where women were concerned.

'OK Frankie, he took her hand and led her towards the piano. 'What do you want me to play for you?'

She gazed up into his face, her blue eyes sparkling. 'I thought you played wonderfully last night, at the club. But I didn't know you played the piano too. I think you're very clever.'

'All this flattery is going to go straight to my head.'

There was a pause while his landlady came in with the tray of tea. She smiled as she looked across at Frances. 'What a lovely 'at you've got on, dear; I thought that the minute I saw it downstairs, when I let you in. And a very smart outfit. Very stylish indeed. Don't you think so, Kit?'

'Yes, she looks beautiful.'

'Drink this while it's nice an' hot. I've put a plate o' biscuits on, too. Plenty more in the pot if you want it.'

'Thanks, Mrs B.'

Frances was still blushing at the unexpected compliment when the landlady had gone. 'Did you really mean that?' All her life she'd lived in the shadow of her mother and Elizabeth.

'When you know me better you'll know that I don't make a habit of saying things I don't mean.' He got up and came over to her, then gently, carefully, he lifted off the broad-brimmed hat; for a moment she felt almost naked. 'There, that's better. It's a beautiful hat and it suits you – like Mrs. B said – but I like the face underneath much better.'

Involuntarily, Frances put a hand up to touch her hair. 'My sister's the best-looking one in our family . . . everyone says so. When I'm old enough my mother says I can have my hair shingled, just like hers . . .'

'I don't like shingled hair; I like it the way you've got it now. Besides, with any luck, maybe it'll have gone out of fashion by then.'

For a moment she was tongue-tied; all her life, she'd yearned to look like her mother, or Elizabeth; to her they were the epitome of beauty, sophistication, and style; two unattainable, almost impossible ideals to look up to, both something that she never thought she could ever be herself. Now here was someone telling her that he liked her just the way she was. To cover her confusion she blurted out the first thing she could think of, but it wasn't what she wanted to say at all. 'Fashions do change so quickly, don't they? My sister's dressmaker says that hemlines are going to go down to mid-calf length by this time next year.'

He laughed, and the awkward moment was passed. 'So long as the Tories and Stanley Baldwin go out of fashion by the next election, that'll suit me.'

'Do you think the Labour party might win the next election?' A heretic thought for a Tory Cabinet Minister's daughter.

'As long as Baldwin doesn't get re-elected, I don't care who wins it. Baldwin's another "Wait and see" man. When he got sent to Washington to negotiate terms for repaying our war debt, he came back with a mess of pottage; a better politician would have got us a better deal.'

'Is that the only reason you wouldn't vote for them?'

'No.' He paused for a moment. 'A long time ago when I was just a boy at school, someone in our class lost his mother in childbirth; she needed a caesarian operation but she couldn't afford the doctor's fee for performing it . . . so she died. I swore then that when I grew up I'd never vote for a government that let something like that happen. She was too poor to pay and it cost her her life. Public schools, expensive medical treatment, all perogatives of the upper classes because they're the only ones who can afford them; it shouldn't be that way. That's what I thought then and that's what I thought now. I haven't changed my mind.'

'It's terrible!'

'It's a cruel world.' He put down his teacup and turned back to the piano. Strange that she was the first person he talked to about something that had happened so many years ago and yet he'd never forgotten it. 'I always knew what I wanted. To be a musician. Not just someone who played a certain instrument in a band. I wanted to rise above that. Every day I realize more how far I've got to go; sometimes I feel like Jack and the Beanstalk, climbing something that reaches into the sky and I can't see the end of . . . but if I didn't believe I could do it, I'd have given up long ago. Of course, my father doesn't approve; in his vocabulary, jazz is synonymous with sin. Which is why I left home not long ago. I can't stand atmospheres. Now, if I was in the orchestra at Covent Garden, he'd think that was a real achievement, never mind that I'd stay in exactly the same position with the same status till I was sixty.' He laughed, unexpectedly. 'If he ever found out that I worked at the 43 Club, he'd most likely never allow me over the doorstep again.'

'He doesn't approve of nightclubs?'

'There isn't much that's modern that he does approve of. But that's the way he is . . . mostly like all his generation. He only approved of me working at the Embassy because it's patronized by the Prince of Wales; I suppose he thought that gave it respectability.'

He was sitting down at the piano now, and the morning sunlight was playing on his hair and face. She wanted to go and sit down beside him, but somehow she didn't quite have the courage. Nice girls were never 'forward.' His fingers moved over the keys expertly. 'I only heard this one today . . . catchy, isn't it? Noel Coward's working on another revue, but it probably won't see the light of day till next year. It hasn't even got a title.'

'Don't you ever get tired playing all night?'

'Frequently. The secret is you mustn't give in to it. Can you imagine what the customers would say if the band kept falling asleep?' They laughed together. 'Do you play or do you sing, Frankie?'

'I play a little, not anywhere as good as you. I'd practice all day if I could; but when my father's at home he grumbles because of the noise.'

'I take it he isn't musical? You must take after someone else.'

'It depends what mood he's in when he comes home.'

'Now who does that remind me of?' He stopped playing, and smiled at her. He tapped the piano stool beside him. 'Do you sing?'

'Not in front of other people.'

'But I'm not "other people". Come here.'

'No, really, I couldn't . . .'

'I won't bite your ear off if you sing the wrong note. Sing something for me, Frankie.'

She came across to him shyly; their arms touched, an exquisite sensation. She'd forgotten everything else that she was supposed to do today, where she was supposed to be. Nothing mattered except here and now.

'Do you know this one from Jessie Matthews's latest musical, *My Heart Stood Still?*'

'Yes, I know it.' Her voice was a whisper. Unexpectedly, he stopped playing and they looked at each other. Then he took her face in his hands and leaned forward and kissed her. In her surprise her mouth opened under his and her arms slid around his neck. She reached out instinctively as she'd long to do, and touched his hair. His skin through his shirt was warm and firm against her chest. She could feel his heart beating. Suddenly, he stopped kissing her; their lips drew apart. She looked up into his face. She wanted to read what he was thinking.

'All this and heaven too.'

'Kit. Please, don't joke about it.'

'I'm not joking, Frankie.'

His face moved downwards towards hers; she closed her eyes and clung to him.

Before the taxicab reached the entrance to Belgrave Square, Frances got out and pad the driver; for a moment she stood there after he'd driven away, savouring the sudden, blissful moment of freedom and space, the sound of birds singing in the trees and shrubbery of the park nearby.

As she walked along the pavement towards Osborne House, she felt as if she was walking on air.

The telephone had begun to ring just as one of the footmen had let her into the hall; it was Madders' afternoon off, she remembered.

139

Was it her mother telephoning to check up on her, to ask her about her progress with the French and German lessons at the language school that morning, the lessons she hadn't gone to? For a moment a brief tremour of fear spoiled her elation. But the caller wasn't Katherine Cultrane.

'For you, my lady. The Honourable Diana Gunnis.'

All the anger Frances had first felt when Diana and the rest of her friends had abandoned her at the 43 Club had long since spent itself; if Diana hadn't persuaded her to go she would never have met Kit Asmussen. She took the receiver coolly. 'Diana?' There was a gush of embarrassed apologies at the other end of the line.

'Frances! I tried to ring earlier, but you were at that language school in Kensington so I said I'd call back. Look, I'm *terribly* sorry about last night . . . I wanted to telephone and explain everything first thing, but Mummy was hovering about and I simply couldn't risk it . . . the thing is . . . while you were in the powder room this chap Daddy knows came in with a lady friend and some other people and we were absolutely *terrified* he might recognize us. He's only met me once at one of Mummy's cocktail parties but you never know . . . well, if Mummy or Daddy found out we'd been in the 43 there'd be absolute hell to pay. The only thing we could do was make a bolt for it . . . of course, when we got back, I remembered you didn't have any money and I felt positively *beastly* about leaving you . . .'

'It doesn't matter, really. It was a bit of a shock but I managed OK.'

'It's awfully good of you to take it like that . . . look, why don't we plan something else? Your parents aren't due back for another week.'

'I'm sorry, Diana, I just can't; I have to improve my French and German while they're away or I'll be for the high jump. I'll telephone you later and let you know.'

'Oh . . . well, all right.'

Frances ran up the staircase in twos and threes and dived full length onto her bed when she reached her room. She tossed off her hat, kicked off her shoes and grasped one of the satin pillows tightly to her while she lay back against the padded headboard and smiled to herself. Grace appeared in the doorway from the little dressing room next to her, with a stunned look on her face. She was holding some towels in her arms. 'Goodness, my lady! Did you enjoy the lessons as much as that?'

15

Laura was engrossed in watching Blanche Stephens demonstrating how to adapt a paper pattern to a different dress length when Anne Turner sent down for her.

'A call from Belgrave Square,' the girl said, who brought the message. 'Lady Frances Osborne. Mrs Turner says you're to collect the taxi fare from petty cash and go over there right away.'

'Well, who's the blue-eyed girl of the upper classes, then?' Blanche teased, but good-naturedly. 'You want to make sure you play your cards right; I would! Keeping pally with an Osborne's bound to come in handy.' She started refolding the paper pattern. 'In a couple of years when she's presented at Court, she might even ask you to design her clothes instead of Madam Turner – you'll be in clover. A few private commissions under the carpet . . . give me the chance!'

'I don't like her because of anything she might do for me in two years time; I like her for herself. Besides, I couldn't do anything underhanded like taking one of Mrs Turner's clients . . . what would people think of me?'

Blanche laughed. 'You're green, you are! Do you think her upstairs'd be so fussy if the boot was on the other foot? Besides, what's to stop you settin' up on your own account? You don't owe her anything. All right, so she gave you the job – but that was for her own benefit, not yours. Those designs of yours that Lady Cultrane fell in love with made her a nice little packet, I can tell you!'

'Setting up on your own takes money . . . which I haven't got. Anyhow, who'd buy clothes from me when they can go to someone as famous as Anne Turner?'

Blanche gave her an exasperated, parting look. 'Ten years ago nobody had ever heard of her, either.'

'I'm so glad she let you come! I made up a story about a damaged beaded dress . . . gosh, I've never told so many white lies in all my life.'

Laura was still mystified. 'What is it? Is something wrong?'

'Laura, I have to tell you this.' They sat down opposite each other, almost simultaneously. 'The other night I met your brother, Kit . . .'

'The 43 Club! But he said he wouldn't play there!'

'Honestly, it isn't anything like as racy as people make out; if it was Bertie Gunnis wouldn't be a member. There was some scandal a while ago when some Chinese man got the owner into trouble because there were rumours drugs were sold there . . . but I'm sure none of it was true. Anyway, my sister Elizabeth's been there lots of times . . .'

'. . . he never said a word to me about leaving the Embassy Club. Not a single word.' She felt Kit had deliberately deceived her and she was devastated by it. 'Did he say why? Was it because they offered him more money?'

Frances found herself rising to Kit's defence. 'I'm sure that wasn't why he left. No, he said the chief reason was because at the 43 he was allowed to play solos, his own compositions; that was what was important to him. Laura, I know you said he was clever . . . but he's so brilliantly talented! I never heard anyone play that way before . . .'

'If my parents found out . . . Daddy would be so angry he'd bar him from coming home!'

'But *why?*'

'They were never happy about him playing in any nightclub . . . Daddy only agreed about the Embassy – Kit wasn't twenty-one then – because of its high reputation, people like the Prince of Wales being members and all that . . . if he had any inkling that he'd left to go to the 43 Club . . . my parents have very definite views on what's acceptable behaviour and what isn't.' She looked thoroughly miserable; he hadn't told her first and that was what hurt most of all. 'Didn't you tell him your chums took you there for a lark?'

Frances flushed. 'I couldn't.' She found herself trying to explain her feelings with difficulty, even to a friend. The truth was that she'd developed an enormous crush on Kit Asmussen. 'I was going to, I suppose. But somehow what I'd meant to say in the beginning never got said. I didn't want him to know how old I really was, because I thought if I told him, he wouldn't want to see me again; and he certainly wouldn't if he knew my father was Thomas Osborne – he's such a radical! He despises the Tories and Daddy's a leading member of the reigning Tory cabinet – I couldn't bear him to find out the truth! Laura, you won't tell him anything, will you? Please promise me that you won't tell him?' For the first time, she'd put her feelings into words.

'Did he ask you to go and see him again?'

'I went today . . . although I have to admit, I sort of invited myself.

142

I just hope he didn't think I was terribly forward. Laura, I simply had to see him again!'

'But didn't you say that you were starting classes at that language school in Kensington?'

Frances sighed. 'I was meant to start today. This morning, but I bunked off. I rang the Principal from the telephone at Kit's place to pretend I had a migraine headache – just in case someone rang the house to enquire why I hadn't turned up. If they'd done that, Madders would have given the message to my mother. Then I'd be in hot water!'

'But what about the lessons? You're bound to get terribly behind.'

'I don't care about that. I had to see him, to pay back the money. In any case, if the ambassadors and foreign diplomats who come to Mummy's dinner parties can't speak to me in English, then they'll just have to lump it.'

Laura hesitated before she spoke. 'Are you bunking off from the language school because you hate French and German or because of my brother?'

For an answer, Frances sat down beside her and seized her hand. 'Please, Laura, don't tell him the truth about me. For goodness' sake don't tell him who I really am.' She paused for a moment, struck by the enormity of her own words; and she'd only met him last night. 'If I couldn't see him again, I think I'd go mad.' A sudden thought. 'You don't mind me seeing him, do you?'

Laura made herself smile, but she was fraught with misgivings. And why was it that she felt as if something was going to go horribly wrong? But she couldn't say anything that would wipe the happy smile from Frances' face. 'Of course not. Besides, it's up to Kit who he sees.'

'And you won't say anything? You promise not to tell?'

'I don't think you really need to ask me that, do you?'

Elizabeth found herself shaking as Anne Turner helped her out of the taxi in the twilight, and took her arm. She took a deep breath, pulling the high collar of her coat closer around herself; even though the day had been warm and pleasant, she was shivering.

Behind her she heard the driver's voice as he thanked Anne Turner for the fare and tip, then the sound of the vehicle driving away. There were few people about in the quiet street: she caught sight of a bowler-hatted man in the distance, a young woman putting a letter into a post box. Then Anne Turner's hand guided her forward.

'There's no need to be nervous. It's really a very simple procedure. Simon does dozens. It'll be over before you even know it.'

'Will it hurt?' She didn't see the other woman's blue eyes light up with contempt. What did a pampered socialite like Elizabeth Osborne know about pain? She had to look away so that she couldn't see her face.

'You'll hardly feel a thing. I didn't.' She smiled, enjoying her own vivid, erotic thoughts; after he'd fitted the contraceptive device inside her, Simon Forman had made love to her on the operating couch. 'All you'll feel, if you feel anything at all, is a light twinge; Simon's so gentle.' She was exciting herself by remembering the touch of his cool, strong, surgeon's hands. 'Just think of all the benefits. No children until you choose the time.'

'I can hardly believe I'm doing this. My God, if my mother only knew . . . William . . .' She felt no guilt at all; only incredulity. And she would never reveal what she had had done to anyone, even at confession.

'It's your body, not theirs. With Simon's help, you have total control of your own fertility. Think of how women have suffered for hundreds of years, being forced to bear a child every year. Old and worn out before they were forty.' They were at the front door now. 'We've come a long way from then, haven't we?'

The white-painted door with its gleaming brass lion's-head knocker and letter box shone in the early evening light. She thought of that clinical white, almost spartan hallway on the other side, the stark lines of the table and the prints that lined the wall; she had only been here once before and yet already she hated it. Then, suddenly, Simon Forman himself opened the door.

The suave, charming manner she guessed came of deep and long experience with the opposite sex; every gesture, every movement proclaimed a man who was totally sure of himself with women. And he knew exactly how to put nervous female patients at their ease. He took her coat himself and handed it to Anne Turner.

'Anne darling, do fetch Elizabeth a glass of brandy.' A meaningful smile. 'It's the perfect antidote for a lady's nerves.'

Inside the spotless surgery, she allowed him to gently push her into a chair.

'What is that, in the syringe?'

The alarm in her voice amused him, but he took care that she didn't see the expression on his face. He was holding it up to the

144

light, staring with satisfaction at the pale amber colour liquid. 'Just a little something to help you to relax.'

'But you said the brandy would do that.' Anne Turner was beside her now, she could feel the silk sleeve of her dress being pulled up to reveal her slim white arm. The sudden pain as the needle penetrated her skin made her cry out; all her life she had been terrified of physical pain; an aching tooth, a bruised knee, had sent her into a swoon. Her nanny had always told her that she had to be a brave girl and not cry. But she always had. She closed her eyes tightly and gripped the sides of the chair.

'There . . .' The room was fading now, slipping away before her eyes; their voices were strange and hollow, like echoes in a dream. Her body no longer seemed to belong to her; it floated, somewhere beyond her reach. Only a while later, when she was slowly come out of the mist-filled daze, could she make out their shadowy outlines, one on each side of the couch. Simon Forman was holding a little glass phial, half filled with white powder, in the palm of one hand. His voice was saying, very gently, coaxingly, 'Do try some of this, Elizabeth . . . here, I'll show you how to use it . . . I'm really quite addicted to it myself . . .'

16

She caught sight of him suddenly, through the trees, waiting by an empty seat. Excitedly she called his name and waved, then broke into a run. When he saw her his face broke into a smile.

She reached him, laughing and trying to catch her breath. 'I never thought I'd get here. A greengrocer's cart broke a wheel and shed its load all over the road in Grosvenor Place . . . all the traffic was held up while they tried to clear it away. I got out of the taxi and ran all the way here. I'm sorry if I'm late.'

'I forgive you.' He took hold of her hand and the touch of his skin on hers sent all her pulses leaping. 'Let's walk for a while. Then I'll take you to one of my very favourite places for lunch.'

She laughed and gazed up into his face, adoration shining from her eyes. 'Kit, I'm so happy I could jump over the park railings.'

He winked at her, then squeezed her hand more tightly and kissed her cheek. 'I wouldn't try it if I was you.'

'All right. I won't. Not unless you promise to help me down if I get stuck.'

'It's a dangerous game making promises to women.' He put his arm around her waist and they walked on, every tree, bush, flower in the park seemed to Frances, that afternoon, more beautiful, fragrant, special, than any she'd seen in her entire life. How was it that she'd been here so many times before and never noticed all the things she was noticing now?

She never wanted anything to change; only her youth and naïvete stopped her from realizing that nothing, especially people's lives, can ever stay the same at all. But now she was happy; even tomorrow seemed far away. When they reached the gates of the park he stopped to buy her a bunch of violets from a flower-seller.

'You still haven't told me where you're taking me.'

'Ah. You'll just have to be patient, won't you?'

Suddenly everything was threatened by a cloud of apprehension. Supposing they went into a restaurant where there was someone she knew? 'Please tell me.'

'I'll give you a clue.' He raised his hand and hailed a taxi. 'It's got three floors, you can have a table for two on the balcony and its own resident band.' He grinned as he helped her into the back of the taxi and gave the driver the destination. He took her hand in his and held it, and a thrill of excitement went through her. Outside trees, people, other traffic flashed past, but she was living in another, a different world. She felt the same delicious sense of unreality as, holding his arm, they walked into the Holborn Restaurant together. She'd already noticed the way women looked at him.

'You'll have to meet my sister sometime,' he said, suddenly and unexpectedly as they were being shown to their table, one floor up. 'She's younger than you, but I know you'd like each other.' He didn't notice the way her face turned pale.

As Madders opened the front door and Frances stepped into the hall, the signs of her parents' imminent departure were everywhere; trunks, hat boxes each with a different hat for every day of Royal Ascot, suitcases littered the polished floor. Three footmen were in the process of carrying them out to one of the cars in the mews. She had almost forgotten that they were leaving.

She was only a few steps up the staircase when she was halted by her mother's voice. 'Come into the drawing room.'

146

The first thing she realized was that they were alone; her father was still at Downing Street.

'I hope the weather stays fine for the racing . . .'

'Where have you been?' Each word fell like a stone into the sudden yawning silence.

'To the language school, of course.' She tried to make her voice sound normal; she thought she'd been so careful, so clever; nobody could possibly have found out . . . 'Moore just brought me back in the car . . .'

'Don't lie to me! I had a telephone call from the Principal this morning, asking when you'd be well enough to resume your daily lessons.'

Frances felt all the colour drain from her face. After her parents had come back from Essex, she'd let Moore drive her to Kensington in the car, then hidden in the school entrance until he'd gone. Making sure nobody saw her, she'd gone off to meet Kit. When Moore had come back to collect her she'd been waiting, demurely, at the gates of the school.

'I'm waiting for an answer.'

'I didn't feel like going this morning, that's all. Is that such a crime? I'm fed up with German and French. Who cares about stupid boring foreign languages? English is more important, anyhow; why can't everyone learn to speak in English? I don't want to go back there!'

For a moment her mother was taken aback at her unexpected, uncharacteristic defiance. Even Elizabeth had never spoken to her like that.

'How dare you speak to me in that manner. How dare you argue. Do you have any idea what embarrassment you've caused me? I was forced to lie to the Principal to save your face.' She took a step towards her but Frances stood her ground. 'I can see how devious you've been, hoodwinking everyone into thinking that you'd been attending the school when you were gadding about by yourself, unchaperoned, over half of London, no doubt. I suppose you think this makes you grown up? On the contrary: truancy is the clearest indication of an infantile mind.'

'Stop treating me like a child!' The slap across the face she received shocked her into silence.

'While you continue to behave like a child you'll be treated like one. One, moreover, who clearly can't be trusted. Goodness knows what you'd get up to while we were away for Ascot if there was no responsible person to keep an eye on you.' Abruptly, she turned away. 'I've arranged for you to stay with Elizabeth at Portland Place during Ascot week. I telephoned her after I spoke with the Principal at the school . . . she'll take you to the classes herself to make sure you go there . . . and also collect you. I expect to see dramatic progress in your work when I get back.'

Frances stood there, holding a hand to her stinging cheek. 'I'll never be good at languages because I hate them. I'd rather do other things.' All she could think about was getting away to see Kit; how was she to manage it now? And wouldn't Elizabeth resent having her foisted on her at a moment's notice? 'I thought Elizabeth and William would be going to Ascot . . .'

Her mother ignored her last remark. She had already gone to the door. 'You were born to a certain position in life; never forget that. And only doing the things you want to do is a luxury rarely accorded to any of us.

<h1 style="text-align:center">17</h1>

Violet Asmussen had laid Sunday afternoon tea in the 'best' room, the front room, that through the lace net curtains looked out onto the small beat garden at the front of the house. Laura noticed that one of the special tablecloths had been used, the starched, snow-white Irish linen with the exquisitely hand-embroidered scalloped edges, which only came out, usually, at Christmas, birthdays, or for very special guests.

When Kit eventually arrived, he stood almost awkwardly, staring at the impressive spread of home-made cakes and sandwiches: cucumber, anchovy paste, sardine, tomato and cheese; madeira, lemon sponge, layered angel cakes and macaroons. Laura noticed that the best tea service – used so infrequently that she'd even forgotten what it had looked like – had carefully been taken out of her mother's china cabinet and given pride of place on the table with the three-tiered cake stand; a wedding present from a long-dead aunt.

Kit kissed Laura and then his mother.

'Really, you shouldn't have gone to all this trouble . . . you've put on enough food to feed the whole orchestra and chorus at the London Pavilion.'

'But it's so long since we've see you, Kit! Here, sit down and let me pour the tea. Laura, be a dear and go and find your father . . . we were going to lay tea in the garden but I felt a few drops of rain. The weather seems very unsettled.' She smiled, almost nervously, as if he was an unexpected and not very frequent guest, not her only son. 'Kit . . . I know you've been busy, but couldn't you have managed to come home and see us before this? It's been weeks and your father takes a dim view of it . . .'

'Where I'm concerned when does he ever do anything else?'

'Kit, that's not true and you know it. Your father has very strong views on how things should be done. And how you should behave. He was very angry when you simply upped and left, without giving us proper notice . . .'

'I explained all that.'

Laura had come back into the room.

'Daddy's coming in a minute, he said; when he's washed his hands.'

'Your father and that garden! Anyone would think he was going to exhibit at the Chelsea Flower Show! of course, the Edgeworths along the road think their chrysanthemums are the last word . . . ever since he won first prize at the church fete last year . . . nasty, vulgar little man.' she poured more hot water into the tea pot. 'Mrs Lafone at the Finches told me that their daughter was engaged to some fellow who worked in Hackney at a printer's shop . . . not a very good catch, one might be tempted to say. Goodness knows how they come to live in a district like this.' Across her bent head, Laura and Kit exchanged glances. 'Now, dear, help yourself to cake. What's left over I shall take to Kilburn Ladies' Guild with me on Tuesday.'

Kit sipped the scalding hot tea and watched his sister over the brim of his cup; was it just his imagination or did she seem uncharacteristically quiet today, as if something was on her mind? It had been so many weeks since they'd talked that he began to feel faintly guilty that all the free time he'd had had been spent with Frances and not his family.

'How are things at New Bond Street?'

'More or less the same.'

'You're still happy there?'

'Why shouldn't I be?' There was an edge to her voice he hadn't heard before; and she still hadn't smiled.

'Aren't you going to have any of this cake or are you on one of those ridiculous diets that most women seem to be on nowadays?'

He was trying to make her laugh but for once it wasn't working. At that point, their father came in.

Immediately, Kit sensed an atmosphere in the room.

'Hello, Dad. Been working hard in the garden?'

'Making hay while the sun shines.' Richard Asmussen sat down at the tea table and morosely accepted a cup of tea. 'Nice and strong, just the way I like it. So. What's it like living away from home? Got used to looking after yourself for a change?'

'Just about.' He was determined not to quarrel, even though he sensed his father's barely-disguised antagonism. 'I manage. Not that I'm there all that often. As soon as I finish at the Pavilion it's home for a quick change act and off to more work.' Laura noticed at once that he called his lodgings 'home' and that he didn't say 'the Embassy'.

'I wish you'd managed to get home before,' their mother said, as she cut a slice of lemon sponge and placed it on her husband's plate. 'We were worried about you; no, don't laugh, Kit. I'm serious. I didn't know if you were all right, if you were ill, or getting enough to eat, even . . .' However had he lived here so long and endured her eternal fussing? It was a question he'd never be able to answer.

'There are such things as restaurants; and although my landlady's cooking isn't a patch on Ethel's or Mrs Grady's, it'll do.'

'Well, he looks healthy enough,' Richard Asmussen said. There was a long, uncomfortable silence, broken only by the chinking of the plates and cups. Kit glanced at the mantlepiece clock; had he really only been here for just half an hour? It seemed so much longer. Nobody spoke, Laura still refused to come to his rescue. He could have cut the atmosphere with a cake knife.

'Are you working on any more society wedding dresses or just the usual Turner *haute couture*?'

'I didn't know you'd developed such a sudden interest in women's clothes,' Laura answered with the same cutting edge to her voice. 'But maybe you've been noticing the evening gowns some of you aristocratic patrons have been wearing at the Embassy Club; most of them are Mrs. Turner's clients.'

He looked at her sharply; there was clearly a double meaning to her words but only he and she were aware of it. He had to speak to her alone.

He turned to his mother. 'Look, I'm sorry I haven't been over before. It's just that with engagements and then rehearsals, endless

150

rehearsals . . . well, you know how it is. It's not as if I could telephone . . .'

'Oh, nonsense! We're delighted to see you, dear. You're welcome at any time, you know that; well, after all's said and done this is your home. Now, this show that's on at the Pavilion with Jessie Matthews? I was saying to your father a few days ago, why don't we see it? Mrs. Edgeworth's niece and her husband at The Gables have seen it three times, they can't stop talking about it. My son's in the orchestra, I said. Playing the clarinet. You must be very pleased about that, very proud of him, she said; Oh, I am, I told her. Think of all the musicians there are that are out of work.'

'I hope I never am.'

'You do still enjoy it all, Kit? I mean, having two jobs at once can't be easy, as I said to your father. And it's so late at night that you have to work to . . . cats woke me up fighting in next door's garden at half past two this morning, and when I saw what time it was I couldn't help thinking of you. Kit's still working, I thought to myself. At this time in the morning. All those people that go to these smart nightclubs . . . they must sleep all day!'

Kit smiled. 'I don't get paid to worry about what the customers do in the daytime. Just to keep them entertained at night.'

'Damn nightclubs! Never heard of such places in my day.' His father put down his tea cup a little too heavily. 'Like all those modern, new-fangled things. I blame the war . . . women's hemlines up to their knees! My father would have turned in his grave to see some of the things that are going on now.'

Laura stood up and excused herself with a headache. 'It's been so oppressive today, like a storm's coming on and it can't quite break. I'll take a couple of aspirin and lie down for a minute.'

'Oh, what a shame, dear! And just on the day Kit's here, too.'

Kit guessed there was another reason. He, too, stood up. 'That reminds me. I think I left a pair of cufflinks in my room. When I unpacked, I couldn't find them anywhere.'

'Mrs Grady gave the whole room a thorough spring clean after you'd gone . . . she never said she'd found anything.'

'Maybe Laura found them first?'

'But what about your tea?'

'Pour me another one; I'll be down again in a minute.' He was out of the room and up the stairs in a trice.

She was standing at the window, staring out onto the long, neat

151

lawn, the packed flower beds on each side of the winding stone path; he could see a pigeon perched on the roof of the summer house, his father's wheelbarrow and tools where he'd left them to come in for tea. A woman in one of the neighbouring gardens was playing with her children on a home made swing. Somewhere in the distance a dog barked.

'You haven't really got a headache at all, have you?'

She spun round to face him, her green eyes alight with rage. 'You lied to me, Kit!' Her voice shook. There were tears in her eyes. 'You broke your promise! How could you?'

'What's all this about, for christ's sake?'

'You've left the Embassy, haven't you? You left it to work in that den of iniquity! *That awful place*.' She forgot that Frances had been there, that she'd told her it wasn't anything like rumour said. 'The woman who owns it has even been in jail . . . how could you lower yourself to go and work for somebody like that? Don't you have any pride?'

'Who told you?'

It was time to lie. It was the first time in her life she'd told him less than the truth and it hurt her. But she didn't have any choice. Besides, he'd been less than honest with her. 'I wanted to see if we could meet for lunch and I tried to ring you at the Embassy. They told me you didn't work there anymore.'

He sighed deeply and sat down on the bed. 'Laura, you don't understand . . .'

'You said you wouldn't go there. You promised.'

'I said I'd think about it, and I did. Kate Meyrick liked my music, she let me have a solo spot and she offered me twice what the Embassy were paying. But it wasn't the money. It was the chance to play my own songs . . . if I'd stayed where I was all I'd have ever been was just another musician in the band. I want more than that; I don't want to stay at the bottom of the heap with everyone else all my life; and if they wouldn't give me that chance to better myself, I reckoned the most logical thing to do was to go to someone who would. All right, Kate Meyrick spent a few days in Holloway a long time ago . . . but that doesn't make her one of the most wicked women in the world; there are plenty, I can tell you, who deserve a stint behind bars far more than she ever did. She had to do time because one of the members in the club was peddling dope there; she tried to put a stop to it but he just kept doing it; the police raided the club one night and the stuff was found. She was held responsible. Anyhow,

I thought I'd explained all that before. What she does – or what anyone else does there for that matter – is nothing to do with me, Laura. I'm paid to play the clarinet and that's what I do.'

'But how can you work in that place knowing what sort of things go on there? I can't bear to think about it. However much she's paying you, do you really think it's worth giving up your self-respect?'

'Well, you've certainly turned into a little moralist, haven't you? You must have been brainwashed by dad.'

'Don't you dare make fun of me!' Despite her anger, she began to cry. Once she started, she couldn't stop.

'Laura, please . . .'

'What hurts, Kit . . . what hurts more than what you've done, is that you lied to me . . . you went and you never even told me. We were always so close, before you left home. It's barely two months, and now I feel as if I don't know you any more . . .'

He came across to her and put his hands on her shoulders. 'I didn't tell you because I haven't seen you to tell you anything, have I?'

A tear ran down her cheek and into her mouth. 'But would you have told me? Or would you have kept it from me and just hoped that I'd never find out?'

'You haven't told Mum and Dad, I know.' He nodded downwards towards the room below. 'Otherwise they would never have let me in the house.'

'Kit, if Daddy ever finds out . . .'

'He won't if you don't tell him. Listen to me . . . you know how much I love you, how I'd rather do anything than hurt you or make you think I didn't care? That's still true. But I have to stick it out; for a while, just a while. And believe me, if there's anything going on in that club that shouldn't be, I haven't seen it. I'm not saying everyone who goes there is lily-white . . . but I'm just speaking as I find. Like I said downstairs, I'm just one of the musicians.'

Slowly, she wiped her eyes on the back of her hand. He reached out and stroked her hair. 'OK. No more crying. What do you think they'll think when we go back downstairs? Just remember. Because some shady Chinese in an evening suit sold dope to some of the members at the club a long time ago, it doesn't mean that everyone wanted to buy. I wouldn't, for one. So if that's what's worrying you, put it out of your mind.

'You asked me if I had any self-respect just now – the answer is, yes,

I have. Too much to even think about getting involved in anything as stupid as that. Dope destroys and it kills.'

She lay her head against his chest; for a moment she came close to speaking about Frances. But she'd given her friend her word and even for Kit she could never break it. She looked up into his face. 'Kit, I'm sorry. Please forgive me for the things I said.'

'Nothing to forgive. Just a misunderstanding. You might not believe me, but after we'd had tea I was going to find a way to get you on your own, and tell you I'd left the Embassy Club. I didn't know that you'd already found out.'

'We'd better go back downstairs. Mummy will be devastated if you don't let her stuff you with sandwiches and cake!'

'That's a thought.' He glanced out of the window. 'It seems different here, somehow. Maybe because in spite of what Mum said, it isn't really my home any more. It's funny, when you go away and come back to a place it seems smaller than you remembered it. I suppose it looks different because of the flowers that have come out since I've been gone.'

'Are you happy where you are? Tell me the truth, Kit. If you could choose would you rather be here, or where you are?'

'It's different.'

'That's not a proper answer and you know it.'

'It's the only one I can give you.' He looked at her a little sadly now. 'That's the trouble with life, Laura. Nothing ever stands still. It has to change, it has to move on. Even if we don't want it to.'

18

Katherine Cultrane sat at her small French escritoire in the morning room, carefully reading through the pile of invitations that had come while they'd been away; Thomas Cultrane's private secretary had sent all his correspondence down to the country.

Most of them were the seasonal invitations that she was well used to: Cowes, débutante dances, charity functions. Deftly, she made two separate piles; the first for invitations that she intended to accept, the second for those she would turn down. From one of the pigeonholes in her desk she took out her engagement diary and began to note down the dates of the invitations in the first pile. It was all routine to her, the habit of most of her lifetime.

A maid had brought her a tray of coffee and set it down on the table; while she waited for it to cool, she methodically opened and went through the drawers of her excritoire where old letters, photographs and obsolete diaries were kept; strange, that a woman as unemotional and practical as she would keep them at all; they had no further use, except to revive old memories, times and places and people in her life that were long forgotten, or dead. Her hand hovered for a few minutes over a small, leather box with faded gold tooling; then she took a key from one of the pigeonholes and turned it in the tiny lock.

The paper of the letters was yellow with age now; the ink, once black, had turned to a faded, uneven brown; gently she picked them up and looked through them, at the tall, proud, sloping and painfully familiar hand, then to the photographs beneath. She sat staring down at the first one, her tray of coffee, the pile of invitations waiting to be answered forgotten; had that fair-haired, laughing face, the beautiful girl in the cream silk dress, once been her?'

She gazed at the smiling face of the man beside her, his arm around her miniscule waist, and felt the faint tingling of tears behind her eyes. He was the one she'd loved, the man she'd wanted; Katherine Tribe, the spoiled rich man's daughter who had had everything in her life that she'd ever asked for, except the one thing she'd wanted most of all . . . the only thing her father hadn't been able to give her.

Angrily, she dashed a hand across her eyes and put the letters back in the box on top of her photographs; then she quickly locked it and pushed it back in its obscure place at the back of the drawer.

Why did it still hurt, why did she still feel angry and bitter, after so many years? It was the tantalizing thought of what might have been, the certainty that if she'd married him and not Thomas Cultrane he would have made her happy; because she was not happy now.

She got up and went back to her tray of coffee, but it was half cold. She was about to ring the bell for the maid to take it away and bring her more when the door opened and her husband came into the room.

She did not want to see him. She desperately longed to be alone and wallow in the rare luxury of nostalgia in the same way that a drug addict or a drunkard craves loneliness so that they can indulge in their secret vice. She looked at him, unable to resist comparing him to the other Thomas, the Thomas she had seen first but who had already been married. How passionately she'd been jealous of and hated his American wife.

'I must dash over to the Foreign Office now, darling; some problem or other. In case I bump into Boyd-Carpenter, are we accepting their dinner invitation for next Sunday night?'

'I suppose so. I have it here somewhere.'

He was hovering in the doorway and the gesture irritated her unbearably.

'And the weekend party at Iden Lodge? I know Baldwin gave us a tentative invitation down to Chequers for the same date, but Iden's heir is a bright young spark on the up and up and, well, he's only four years older than Frances. A little discussion with Iden on that score wouldn't come amiss . . . what do you think? She could hardly do better than end up as the next Countess of Iden. And he's the only son.'

'He was certainly taken with her at my last garden party . . . it's high time I arranged another one. But I don't know what's got into her lately . . . she walks around in a dream. And her results from the language school are appalling.'

'Katherine, there's plenty of time.'

It was second nature to them, plotting and planning other people's destinies as if they were no more then pieces on a chess board. Less than two years now before Frances was presented at Court; with her looks and the Osborne name she'd be one débutante who'd have no trouble at all finding a rich, titled husband who, ideally, would be catholic and have significant political power. If only she was eighteen now! Sometimes Katherine almost hated her because she reminded her of something that had happened in her life she would much rather forget, or pretend had never been. Married, out of the way, perhaps the pain would be more bearable then.

If only he'd go away, if only he'd leave her alone. 'You'll be late for the Foreign Office if you don't leave now.' She turned back to the waiting pile of invitations and pretended to look at them.

'Yes, of course.' He checked his watch. 'When you see her, give my love to Elizabeth.' She didn't answer and he closed the door behind him.

She spent the next three-quarters of an hour answering the invitations, then she rang the bell.

'Make sure these are taken to the post, will you? Take this tray away and then tell Moore to bring the car round to the front.'

'Yes, my lady.'

It only took her twenty minutes to dress; then she went down to the street where the gleaming Bentley stood waiting at the kerb outside the house, the chauffeur standing stiffly to attention.

'William said you hadn't been feeling well, and you didn't return my three calls. Seddon told me you were "not at home" when I rang yesterday.' Katherine sat down uninvited and opened her handbag where she kept her holder and cigarettes. 'Is there something you're not telling me that I should know?'

Elizabeth's cool blue eyes showed only surprise. But then Elizabeth always had been sly, even as a child. Katherine could remember her looking straight into your face and swearing something wasn't true when it was. She remembered a broken Meissen cherub which Freddie had sworn Elizabeth had knocked over, but Elizabeth had maintained that her brother was to blame. Of course, Katherine had believed her son.

Elizabeth sat down in one of the huge all-white armchairs and crossed her slender legs. She reached for the silver cigarette box beside her. 'I really don't know what you're getting at, Mother.'

'Are you pregnant?'

A hoot of derisive laughter. 'Good God, no! whatever gave you that idea?'

'You've been married for more than three months. It's perfectly possible.' They were watching each other carefully, like two cats sitting on either end of the same wall.

'Do we have to talk about this? I find the whole subject distinctly unsavoury.'

'One of the reasons Banbury wanted a much younger wife was so that she'd provide him with an heir. If you're putting into practice any of that immoral tosh you learned from Marie Stopes' scandalous book, I'd advise you to think twice about continuing it. Banbury isn't a fool.'

'You don't have to tell me what he is; I'm married to him, remember?'

Slowly, without taking her eyes from her daughter's face, Katherine placed her Turkish cigarette in its holder and flicked her lighter. The flame wavered. 'You think you're very clever, don't you?'

'I'm cleverer than he is.' With provocative smugness, Elizabeth lit her own cigarette. 'That's what you always taught me, mother; where men are concerned you always have to stay one step ahead. I'm simply putting your words into practice. Do you really think I'd be stupid enough to spoil my entire first year being hostess in my own right by becoming bloated with that disgusting old man's child? Not jolly well likely! He can wait for his precious heir. Hasn't he waited nearly thirty years already?'

'That isn't the point.'

Elizabeth blew smoke rings into the air. 'You can't manipulate me into doing what you want me to do any longer. You and Daddy – and dear Uncle Henry – virtually coerced me into marrying someone I detest and despise – all to further Daddy's political career, of course; haven't I done enough in the name of family duty? I suppose you'll try and do the same thing with Frances, if she lets you. Did I or did I not overhear Uncle Henry saying the other evening something about a possible match with the Earl of Iden's son?'

'Frances will do her duty to her family when the time comes.'

'Oh? I wouldn't be to sure of that. She's already dug in her heels over the language school thing. Oh yes, you can make her go there, but do you realize she's deliberately not concentrating on what they're trying to teach her? You know the old saying, Mummy . . . you can lead a horse to water but you can't make it drink.'

'I want you to look after her while your father and I are away.'

'Again?'

'I've already telephoned William at Westminster and confirmed that it's convenient.'

'I see. Well, I suppose I don't really have any choice, do I?'

'She is your sister.'

'Well, I'll give the staff the necessary orders, but I can't act as chaperone every minute of the day. Sabine will have to go with her to the school in Kensington. I've a thousand things to do before we go down the Ormsby-Gores next weekend.'

Katherine got up and began drawing on her white kid gloves. She looked around her. 'God, this room is a mess!'

'Syrie Maugham's white drawing rooms are the last word in good taste! Everyone's having theirs redone . . .'

'The last word in tastelessness. How does William live with it?'

'He isn't here most of the time. Besides, he told me I could have *carte blanche* with all the interior decorations. I intend to transform the house in Kent.'

Her mother went towards the door, then stopped. 'Does doing what you like still include sleeping with his nephew?'

Elizabeth flushed. 'I really don't think that's any of your business.'

'You may not think so at the moment. But take care I don't have to make it my business.'

As soon as her mother had left, Elizabeth stubbed out her cigarette and went to the door. Nobody in sight; one never knew when and where Seddon might be hovering, hoping to overhear something that she didn't want him to. She'd suggested, tactfully, that he was getting on and might be better managing the household at the estate in Kent, but to her fury and irritation Banbury had said he preferred Seddon to remain butler in London. Elizabeth would have to think of something else.

She picked up the telephone receiver and asked the exchange to connect her with Anne Turner's number. It was engaged and she had to wait five minutes before calling again. This time she was luckier.

'Anne, darling! It's me, yes. I had to call . . .' A few effusive sentences on the other end of the line. 'He's dragging me away next weekend to some boring houseparty . . . one of his colleagues and all that. No, of course I don't want to go. When I'm away from London how can I see Eddie? But that isn't the reason I rang.' She hesitated for a moment, then lowered her voice. 'It's the . . . supply from Simon; I'm running out. I must have just a little to take with me to buck me up. Otherwise I simply couldn't face it . . .'

In her New Bond Street office, Anne Turner smiled. 'Yes, of course I'll ask Simon. It may be a little more expensive this time; it's in such great demand and there never seems to be enough to go round. But for you, I know he'll do anything. Don't worry if you can't get your hands on the money immediately . . . you could always . . . well, find a small piece of jewellery . . . something you're not really keen on. Banbury won't notice, will he?'

Elizabeth put down the receiver and went upstairs. She invented an errand for Sabine and then locked the bedroom door. There was only a tiny amount of the white powder Simon Forman had given her left in the small enamelled pill box that she kept at the bottom of the locked drawer, and she sprinkled a few of the precious grains onto the back of her hand; then she lay back against the pillow and sniffed it in deeply.

In a few moments she was drifting, floating, suffused with a feeling of peace and happiness that was comparable only to the times when she was making love with Eddie. Simon Forman had to get her more. She didn't care how much it cost. It blotted out that part of her life that depressed and revolted her, the nightmare attentions of the sweating, panting old man whose demands in bed sickened and disgusted her. If only she didn't feel so miserable and drained when the effect wore off . . .

19

'My parents have gone away again, so I'm staying at my sister's house . . . it's much easier for me to do what I like when I'm there. She hasn't been feeling very well lately . . . in fact she's spent of of the last week in bed.'

Kit ran his hands over the keys of the piano and smiled. 'Why do your parents go away so much? Is it business?'

She'd become adapt to prevarication. 'Yes,. it's all to do with Daddy's business. I don't really understand it, it's all a terrific bore.'

'Why don't they ever take you with them?'

'Oh, I'd just get in the way. Besides, I have to go to that awful school in Kensington.'

'But don't you go away on holiday together?' He thought of the annual family holidays with Laura and his parents on the Isle of White or in Torquay, staying at the Laburnum Guest House near the Esplanade, outings to the pier, playing with buckets and spades on the sand; the Punch and Judy shows, the donkey rides, the theatre and cockles and whelks with brown bread and butter for supper in the evenings, walking along the shore when the tide was out. He reached out and caught hold of her hand. The upper classes treated their children so differently: hadn't she ever had any of those things?

'Kit, that's lovely! Is it a new song?'

'I invented it just for you. Do you like it really?'

'Oh, yes.' She was almost childish in her delight and artless enthusiasm. 'I wish I could write songs, compose tunes. It's so easy for you.' She came and rested her hand on his shoulder; she was rapidly losing her shyness when they were together. 'I think you're an absolute genius, so there!'

He laughed as he went on playing. 'I wouldn't go as far as that.'

She went on listening until he came to the end of the tune. 'Kit . . . do you ever . . . well, regret leaving the Embassy Club to work at the 43? I mean, if they'd let you play solos while you were there and

paid you exactly the same money as you get now . . . which place
would you rather be?'

'That's a question only a girl could ever ask.'

'Does that mean you can't give me an answer?'

'They're both different; owned and run by different people, patronized by different sets. The Embassy is bright, bigger, it attracts the
rich, royal and famous, but then you know that. The 43 has foreign
princes and self-made millionaires on its members' list but the atmosphere isn't the same. It's more . . . how can I put it? Daring, less
Establishment, *avant-garde*. The music is more unconventional, experi-
mental; pure New Orleans jazz doesn't get on the musical agenda at
the Embassy; the management are too conservative to try it. Me? I
don't really care where I play as long as I'm happy with the music.'

'Do your family know you changed jobs?'

'My sister does; she rang the Embassy to see if I could meet her
for lunch one day and they told her I'd moved on. Last Sunday I
went home for tea and she read me the riot act for not telling her
first. But she'd never tell either of our parents, I know that. Not
unless I wanted her to.'

'Would they really be that much against it, if you explained that
you had to move on because someone else had offered you the chance
to play your own music?'

He smiled. 'If you knew my parents – especially my father – you
wouldn't have asked that. To them things are either good or bad and
the 43 Club is bad. Middle-class prejudice, intolerance, call it what
you like. That's them. They can't help the way they are, I suppose;
their generation was different. Anyway, maybe they won't need to
know.' He folded up the music sheet and lay it on top of the piano.
'As grateful as I am to Kate Meyrick, I won't stay at the 43 Club
forever.'

'What do you mean?' Her voice had gone very quiet.

'I want my own band; sooner rather than later. I don't care how
hard I have to work for it or where I have to go to. But I mean to
get it.' Her face had turned pale. 'If that means leaving London,
even leaving England, so be it. New sounds have to happen in the
States, first.'

'America? But you wouldn't drop everything and go there, would
you?'

'I wouldn't be dropping everything, Frankie; I'd be picking up
something new. You can't open another door without shutting the
one behind you.'

161

'But what about your family?'

'They'd still be here.'

'But . . .'

'It isn't a matter of what I want . . . it's simply a means towards an end. If the opportunity came then I couldn't very well turn it down. That would be stupid.'

She felt the absurd, childish need to cry, as if something that she prized and cherished more than anything else was about to be snatched away from her. Since she'd met him she'd never thought beyond tomorrow; now he was talking calmly about going to the other side of the world. But what about her? 'I couldn't bear it if you went away.'

He turned and stroked her face gently. 'Hey, steady on . . . I'm not flying to the moon. I said might, that's all. And if I ever had to go away that doesn't mean I'm never coming back again. You have to trust me, Frankie. I'd never go away without telling you first.'

'Please, don't go . . .'

He put his finger over her lips. 'Let's not talk about what might never happen. OK?' He turned back to the piano and played the first tune that came into his head. It was beginning to happen, the thing he'd dreaded, the thing Rudy Loew had already warned him about; he'd allowed himself to get involved with her almost without thinking, virtually without realizing what might happen, and she'd become emotionally involved. He'd been a fool not to see it coming, to put a stop to it before it was too late. But if he was brutally honest with himself he'd have to admit that he probably wouldn't have done anything other than what he'd done, because already she meant more to him than he cared to admit. Only the violent way she'd reacted when he'd mentioned going to America – in exactly the same way that his mother and Laura were bound to react – sounded a warning bell inside his head.

He was already beginning to feel guilty; if she'd been one of Kate Meyrick's girls or just another pretty face in the chorus, he wouldn't have been concerned; women were always running after him and there'd never been anyone, until he met her, who'd taken up more than a passing thought; but she was different. From the first time he'd seen her she'd completely intrigued him with her peculiar *naïveté*, the way she acted and spoke, and he strongly suspected that her strange reluctance to talk about her family merely confirmed the obvious fact that they were upper class – everything about her, her clothes, her speech, her presence at the 43 Club at all, made that a foregone conclusion; only the upper classes patronized nightclubs. Not that any of that particularly worried him, except that where could such a relationship as theirs go? Would her strict, conservative parents approve of her walking out with a nightclub musician? He already guessed the answer.

It wasn't that he felt inferior; they came from totally different worlds, that was all. And for the first times since they'd met Kit realized that he was rapidly becoming very much aware of it.

When she gazed up at him with her wide blue eyes he suddenly had the uncontrollable urge to kiss her. When he did, she slid her arms around his neck and he instinctively knew that he'd stepped over a precipice from which he ought to have backed away.

Her honey-gold hair smelt clean and fragrant against his face; the adoration in her eyes as she looked at him both moved and terrified him. But it was too late.

'Kit, I love you. I do love you.' She blinked, then swallowed, as if she couldn't quite believe herself the enormity of what she was saying. 'I shall love you until I die.'

20

Richard Asmussen sat down and spread out his evening paper on his lap while Laura and her mother sat opposite, chatting. Violet Asmussen lay down the tray cloth she'd been embroidering and looked at the clock.

'Come upstairs with me, dear, just to have a look at that dark green taffeta . . . you know, the one I'm thinking of wearing to the Flavels on Friday night. The last time I wore it was for your Aunt Edna's anniversary, and I've put on a little bit of weight. It might want letting out, just a trifle . . .'

Laura followed her mother to the big double front bedroom. The windows were open and the net curtains fluttered gently in the soft evening breeze. She helped her into her gown.

'It's a bit tight just *there* . . . I'll do it for you as soon as I get home tomorrow. But what about your navy blue satin? I thought that was the one you used for best?'

'It's a bit fancy, really, for just dinner. Don't you think? With the

163

frilled cuffs and panels in lace . . . well, I'd hate Mrs Flavel to think I was overdressed.'

Laura sat down on her parents' bed. 'Why should she? Who are these Flavels, anyway? He's only someone Daddy works with, isn't he?'

Her mother gave a sharp look of admonishment. 'He's only Chief Clerk, that's all! And Mrs Flavel's uncle was a rural dean! Your father works under him at the bank so it's very important that we make a good impression. There's a vacancy one grade up that your father's hoping to be promoted to . . . and apparently, according to him, whether he gets it or not depends on Gerald Flavel.'

Laura smiled, thinking how amused Kit would be if he was here. 'Looks like you'll have to watch your P's and Q's, then. No using the wrong knife and fork when you go there. Where do they live, then?'

'One of those lovely new houses over at Cricklewood. Semi-detached, too. Your father says they have a son about Kit's age – he's already got a very good position in a firm of solicitors in Holborn; then there are two daughters, both married. The elder one's husband is quite well off, by all accounts. Works in his father's business and they've just bought one of those brand new houses on a private estate at Twickenham. Detached, I believe. Now, you can't get a place like that for less than £750 or £1,000, I can tell you. Mr Flavel was telling your father how modern it is inside . . . the builders have thought of every convenience: sliding doors connecting all the downstairs rooms, lots of built-in cupboard space, and lovely big windows to let in more light. Mr Flavel's son-in-law must be earning good money to afford that kind of luxury, mustn't he?' How important appearances were to her mother.

'They're probably buying it on a mortgage; how many people can afford to pay £700 odd or £1,000 outright? Blanche Stephens says her sister and brother-in-law are buying a detached £1,000 house near Richmond, and the repayments are 5/11d without the rates.'

'Good gracious! However can they afford that much? It's a small fortune?'

'I think they're both working; he's a clerk in an accountant's office and she works at the London Telephone Exchange, full time.'

'And what happens when she has to give up her job to start a family? I never did agree with married women working and I never will; their place is in the home.'

'Things are changing, Mummy . . .'

164

'Well, not for the better in my opinion. I'd say that young couple have definitely bitten off more than they can chew. Now, Mr Flavel's daughters don't have to go to work; their husbands are in good enough positions to be able to support them at that standard of living. If Blanche Stephens' brother-in-law needs his wife to go out to work to be able to afford the repayments on a house that seems to me quite out of their league, then he's completely irresponsible.' Laura decided it would be more diplomatic to remain silent. She helped her mother out of the green taffeta dress. 'Of course, Mr Flavel was very impressed when your father told him that you worked for Mrs Turner at New Bond Street . . . he's very proud of you, you know. Naturally, they'd read all about the big Osborne wedding . . .'

'Don't forget it was Daddy who was against me working in the first place. Anyway, if you run out of conversation you'll have plenty to talk about on the subject, won't you?'

'Naturally, we'll invite them back for dinner here. It'll mean a fair amount to do . . .'

'Why don't you have a garden party – the weather's glorious. The Osbornes are having one at Belgrave Square on Saturday.'

'Such a pretty girl, that Lady Frances. She went with her parents to open a new wing at the Charing Cross Hospital yesterday, and there was a picture of them all together in your father's newspaper. I cut it out especially to show you.'

'And the Flavels, of course?'

'Well, you're quite friendly with her, aren't you? Mrs Flavel's bound to be terribly impressed. I was only saying to Mrs Connaughton last week at the Ladies' Guild . . .' Downstairs, Violet Asmussen found the cutting. Slightly apart from her parents, Frances stood behind them, half facing the camera, dressed in a tailored coat and neat, simple cloche hat.

'She seems rather a self-effacing girl, not like her mother and sister at all..almost as if she didn't want to be photographed.'

Laura looked down at the cutting from her father's newspaper, praying that Kit would never see it.

Sitting with his feet resting on one of the tables, Kit played a few bars of an aimless, unfinished tune on his clarinet that had been going around in his head all afternoon. Someone was practising that evening's numbers on the club piano; two more were having a game of cards. In one of the corners, a group of Kate Meyrick's girls were gossiping and busy painting their nails.

'You thought about what I told you yet, Kit . . . I mean *seriously?*'
Rudy Loew sat down in the chair opposite him, cradling a glass of
beer. 'Look . . . we'd both be goddam fools not to, you know? Listen.
When a chance like this comes up, you just grab it with both hands.'

'Are you on about that yank who was signing on talent at the
Trocadero?' Kit laid his clarinet down on the table. 'If you are, then
what I told you when you first asked me the other night still goes . . .
the answer's no.'

'But why, for christ's sake? I mean, isn't this the kind of chance
we've both been waiting for? You, especially. I know I could leave
today and get work just like that,' he snapped his fingers, 'in some
band in New York or in New Orleans. But if you come with me we
can do better than that; we can form our own. With you writing the
melody and me the lyrics, we'll take 'em all by storm. Kit, you're
never going to get any place sticking around in the mud in London,
don't you realize that?'

'The time isn't right, that's all. Not for me. But if you want to go
and you think you can make it with the competition, why not go
ahead on your own? I'm not stopping you.'

'Say, what's wrong with you anyhow? What's with you all of a
sudden? You were the one who said that what you wanted most was
your own band, not playing in some other guy's . . . so what's
changed? I told you Mrs Meyrick'd love your music – and she did.
I told you she'd give you your own spot just like that – and wasn't
I right? And I said she'd pay, and pay well, for something that was
really different; and special . . . so when have I ever been wrong?'

Kit only looked irritated. 'Rudy, will you give it a rest? You know
why. I'm not ready to leave London yet. I've got commitments.'

'Guys who want to get on can't afford commitments. So you got
cold feet all of a sudden? One minute you say you want more than
anything to get to the top; the next breath you're telling me you can't
even be bothered putting your feet on the next rung of the ladder.
Commitments, my ass! So your mother'll miss you and your kid
sister'll cry her heart out if you go, and your old man won't even
think about you a couple of days after you've gone; they'll get over
it. You've got a name to make and places to go. They'll still be
here when you've done it all and come back.' He was watching the
expression on Kit's face. 'Oh, I get it now! Commitments, huh?
Wouldn't have anythin' to do with that cute blonde with the blue
eyes and the cut glass accent, would it? Yeah! I thought so!'

'Rudy, you don't understand . . .'

166

'She's really got you, hasn't she?'

Kit spread his hands on the table and nodded, slowly. 'I care about her, let's put it that way.'

'OK. OK, so you care. But stop looking at it through rose-tinted glasses, huh? You think you're goin' places with some girl hanging onto your coat tails for the ride? No way. Sure, she's pretty, she's cute, she's fun, she's got a brain in that beautiful head . . . but when you got your way to make, Kit, you've got to travel light. No excess baggage . . . you know what I mean? No one loves dames more than I do; but they just get in the way. And this one'll bring you nothing but big trouble; I can tell. She isn't like any of the others. She comes from nob stock who'd throw a fit if they ever found out that she spends time with you. Face it, Kit. It's no good. It was fun while it lasted but you come from two different worlds.'

Kit was silent for a long while; he knew all that; Rudy hadn't said anything different to what he'd already said to himself. All he knew was that whatever he did he couldn't bring himself to hurt Frances.

Finally he spoke. 'I thought it was you who said there's always something you can do about everything. Any more advice on the subject?'

'Come on, Kit; you know I mean it for the best. Look. You and me, we're a great team. The guy who's been listening in at the Troc is coming here tomorrow night, to listen to Guess Who? Why not talk to him about what he could do for us? It only makes sense.'

'No harm in talking. But I meant it, Rudy; don't try and rush me into anything I'm not ready for . . . understand? Otherwise you and I are going to be two halves of what used to be a beautiful friendship.'

Rudy drank down a long draught of his beer. 'You know, that's the trouble with you English guys. You need to think about something for five years before you even do it.'

'Half English.' Kit picked up his clarinet and started to play a tune; when Rudy started talking again Kit increased the volume so that all he could see were his lips moving, without hearing a single word. He went on playing for several more minutes, fighting down the laughter that was bubbling in his throat, then he put the instrument down.

'You know the trouble with you Americans? You always want to do something five years before you've even thought about it.'

'Kit, be serious! When you get a chance to break away from the rest of the ordinary fishes in the pond, you don't pass it up. If you do, I promise you . . . you're going to spent the rest of your life regretting it.'

'Rudy, please. You've made your point and I hear what you're saying. But this is something I need to be alone to think about, something I need to work out for myself. Maybe I'm a bit of a fatalist; I've always believed that if something's meant to happen it'll happen no matter what. I know what I want. I know exactly what I want to do. We've talked it over so often that I don't need to go over it. But one thing I *am* sure about: to get what I want I don't intend riding rough-shod over the feelings of people I care about, people who are important in my life.'

'Your family'll still be here when you get back.'

'I was thinking about Frankie.' He sighed. 'There she was, standing alone crying on the pavement that night; and I had to be the Good Samaritan who gave her a shoulder to cry on. If only I'd put her straight in a taxi and sent her home. I suppose if I was honest I didn't do that because I just didn't want to, and when she asked to come back the next day I said yes for exactly the same reason. And that was it.'

'That's all it takes; I know. But remember what I told you, Kit. There's no future for it, is there? If you want to get to the top of the tree you have to travel light, not let yourself get distracted by every pretty face that comes along.' He wasn't smiling now, nor was Kit. 'Don't forget what I said just now, about those two different worlds. Fire and water, Kit . . . they don't ever mix.'

21

The sun had been shining all morning, with no hint of cloud. A gentle breeze was blowing as Frances made her way downstairs and out into the garden to stand with her parents as they greeted the endless line of guests. In a pale lavender silk afternoon dress with a matching voile picture-hat and lace gloves, she felt as near as she had ever felt to being a young woman and not a little girl.

Many of the guests she recognized from her mother's political soirées and dinner parties, some faces were new. The Prime Minister and his wife, both looking as they always did, as if their maid and valet had forgotten to press their clothes, were chatting to a group of backbenchers and their wives; there was the Home Secretary and his wife and two daughters, both older than Frances by a year or two.

Her mother's young political protégés were everywhere; she looked across the lawn to where Katherine Cultrane was talking to half a dozen of them, and Frances couldn't help noticing that she gave most of her attention to the best looking ones. As she'd been told to do she began to mingle among the crowd, laughter and disjointed sentences came across the warm, still air.

'He's an absolute genius with figures, so he's been promoted from the Foreign Office to Junior Minister at the Treasury . . .'

'. . . she went with her sister on one of these new luxury liner cruises, and they both met millionaires . . .'

'. . . my dear, she's got herself elected to so many Committees, I doubt if she can remember which ones they are . . .'

'. . . all my gloves come directly from Fauriez in Paris, on the rue de l'Echiquier . . . I'd never buy them anywhere else . . .'

'. . . we loved Gertrude Lawrence in the new musical at the Alhambra . . . are you going up to Inveraray this autumn for the shooting?'

The voices and clinking glasses went on around her, while she walked and nodded and smiled, and thought of Kit. She wondered if he was thinking about her now. Only when a tall, lean shadow fell across her path did she stop day dreaming and look up.

'Frances, my dear, how enchanting you look in that wonderful floating dress,' said Lord Henry Osborne. She looked from his thin, catlike face to the two young men standing beside him. 'May I introduce Mr Robert Carr, who's just been promoted to junior minister at the Treasury, and Mr Thomas Dreikhorn, his private secretary. Mr Dreikhorn has already distinguished himself at the Scottish Office on his own account.'

They shook hands with her politely. Frances had heard their names mentioned before at one of her mother's dinner parties as rising young men; but then there were so many. Robert Carr was very fair, pale-skinned, with light blue eyes and the very slightest of Scottish accents; Thomas Dreikhorn was dark-haired and dark-eyed. A few words were exchanged and then she moved on, her great-uncle still beside her. Ahead of them on the lawn she caught sight of her mother going back into the house.

'You've conducted yourself admirably this afternoon, my dear.' He smiled the smile that never quite reached to his eyes. 'A little more attention to your studies while you have the opportunity, wouldn't come amiss. Of course, one realizes that one can't be good at every subject; but I'm sure you can use the time you have left before being presented, to better effect.' His cold, dry hand was on her wrist. 'Ah, the very young man I wanted you to see.' He gently propelled her forward. In an undertone and without hardly moving his lips he whispered, 'You already know him: Viscount Staughton, the Earl of Iden's heir. Your father's very keen on the possibility of that match.' The pressure on her wrist grew heavier until it hurt. 'Be especially charming to him, my dear . . . like Elizabeth with Banbury, you'll soon have him twisted right around your little finger . . .'

In the morning room Katherine Cultrane closed the door behind her and leaned against it. Henry Osborne took out his monogrammed gold lighter and lit her cigarette.

'I left her with him, chatting on the lawn. I could see he was more than taken with her.'

Katherine sat down and crossed her slim ankles. The pearl and garnet brooch on the shoulder of her dress glittered as it caught the afternoon light. 'I don't think we need to worry about them over-much, do you? I'd be willing to bet Iden's heir would be happy to wait for Frances. Tom should be sounding out the ground with Iden about now.'

'I left Frances with the young man on the lawn . . . he's not much of a conversationalist, true, but he has great ability, according to all the enquiries I've made. He should reach the Cabinet one day, at least.' He sat down opposite her. 'There remains only one question . . . Frances herself. Will she be as biddable as Elizabeth or will she take it into her head to want a say in matters herself?'

'She'll do her duty to her family just as Elizabeth and Freddie have done.'

He smiled at her; she was looking particularly striking today, in a parti-coloured dress of green and blue georgette, a long rope of pearls and a peacock-blue organza picture-hat with an enormous brim and lawn veil. He had no doubts at all that his great-niece would do exactly what her mother decreed when the time for decisions about her future came. No doubts at all.

'My dear, you've managed everything so brilliantly; shall we return to your guests and toast the Iden match with champagne?'

She got up, ground out her cigarette in an onyx ashtray and pecked him lightly on the cheek. 'It's such a pity you never married; I always thought so. You understand women so very well.'

He laughed, softly. 'Which is precisely why I've never wished to marry any of them, my dear. Wives are like other people's dogs and children . . . far more enjoyable when they belong to someone else.'

22

'Kit, it's so long since I've seen you! Longer since you came home to see Mummy and Daddy. Is it really because you've been too busy or because of what happened last time you came?'

'You mean when all the best china came out and I was treated like a distant visiting cousin that nobody wanted to invite but had to put a good show on for nonetheless?'

'You know that's not true! They were so happy to see you.'

Kit kicked at a stone and sent it spinning. All the things Rudy had said had been preying on his mind and he was in a bad mood. He felt guilty at once for taking it out on Laura. 'Look, forget I said that. But coming back only showed me one thing. How far apart we are now. When I lived at home I didn't notice it so much, but I can't face another of those Sunday afternoon teas, not yet.' They walked on in silence, side by side. In the distance Laura could see a boy walking an Aberdeen terrier, a uniformed nanny wheeling a perambulator. On one of the wooden park seats two young women, heads bent, were deep in animated conversation.

She told him all about the Flavels. 'Mummy's getting herself into such a tizzy about this dinner party; and Mrs Flavel only plays whist, not bridge. Isn't it silly?'

'It'll be another feather in dad's cap if he manages to impress the boss.'

'You look tired, Kit. And you don't seem yourself at all. You're not working too hard, are you?'

'Do you know how many musicians there are who're out of work?'

'It's not worth killing yourself for, is it?'

He didn't answer. When they reached the park gates he kissed her on the cheek and they said goodbye, then she watched him walk off in the opposite direction, head down, his hands in his pockets, and she fought down the urge to run after him and ask him what was wrong.

All the way back to New Bond Street she wondered what it could be.

Dinner was almost over; on the whole, the evening had been a great success. Mrs Grady had come in to help Ethel the day before and had stayed behind tonight to finish the mountain of extra washing-up, and unexpectedly Laura had enjoyed herself. Not that Mr and Mrs Flavel were particularly scintillating company; but their son Maurice, who they had brought with them and was the same age as Kit, had turned out to be a more than pleasant surprise.

'Perhaps I could take you to lunch one day,' he said, smiling at her from across the table. 'If Mr Asmussen approves, of course.' Laura had glanced momentarily at her father and saw that he did. 'Holborn isn't that far from New Bond Street. And if you like the cinema, there's going to be something very special showing in a week or two . . . the first talking picture!' There were exclamations of surprise from around the table. 'Yes, it's true; since you like music it'll be right up your street . . . Al Jolson. All the chaps in the office are talking about it.'

'I'd love to! That'll be all right, won't it, Daddy?' She could tell that her father liked young Maurice Flavel.

'It most certainly would. I might even take your mother!' They all laughed. 'Isn't it incredible, these new inventions? Of course, this Jolson fellow is never going to oust the likes of Mabel Normand or Mary Pickford; they're far too popular.'

'There's no reason why Mary Pickford can't make talking pictures, too, is there?'

'I suppose not; after all, can't stand in the way of progress. Mind you, it's quite scandalous what some of these Hollywood actresses earn. I was reading an article the other day in the *Herald*; I thought it was a misprint . . . then I read virtually the same thing in the *Daily Express*. Do you know that the joint income of Mary Pickford and her husband Douglas Fairbanks comes to almost £50,000 a year? A chorus of disbelief rang around the table.

'Oh, Richard, surely not!'

'As true as I'm sitting here. They'd hardly publish it if it was wrong, would they?'

'I think Daddy's right,' Laura said. 'I can remember Kit telling me that the American actress Gloria Swanson earns £500 a day . . .

172

that's £4 for every second's work . . . more than the President of the United States!'

'Oh, it's perfectly scandalous, isn't it? It's totally out of all proportion. Nobody's worth an amount of money like that, I don't care who they are.'

Gerald Flavel nodded in agreement. 'That's these Americans for you . . . everything done to excess. The trouble is they just have absolutely no sense of moderation. It would serve them right if these ridiculously extravagant film studios all went bankrupt. And it wouldn't surprise me in the least.'

'I really prefer the musical theatre to the cinema, don't you? So much more tasteful. I think I mentioned that our son is in the orchestra at the London Pavilion. He's doing very well.'

'What a pity he was working this evening; we would have so enjoyed meeting him . . . we've never met a musician before. You must be very proud of both your children, Mrs Asmussen . . . my daughters were fascinated when I told them that Laura worked for Mrs Anne Turner in New Bond Street . . .' she turned towards Laura. 'Do any of the ladies in the royal family patronize Mrs Turner's establishment?'

Laura smiled. 'I'm afraid the sort of high-fashion clothes that Mrs Turner designs are not the kind of thing Queen Mary would wear; or the Princess Royal and the Duchess of York, for that matter. Their tastes are much more conservative and conventional. But we do have a lot of foreign royalty as clients, yes.'

Maurice Flavel leaned towards her across the table. 'I doubt if Queen Mary could manage to squeeze into one of those *haute couture* gowns even if she wanted to; she is a rather large lady. And neither the Princess Royal or the Duchess of York exactly have suitable figures.'

'Maurice!'

'No disrespect intended to the royal ladies, mother. No slight intended at all. On the contrary, I think the Queen and the Duchess – and the Princess Royal, for that matter – all dress in the styles that suit them best. Not all ladies are so sensible, are they?'

'Maurice, you really mustn't criticize other people like that!'

'Oh, I think Maurice is right,' Laura said, pouring oil on troubled waters. What a prig Mrs Flavel was! 'One of our best customers – I suppose I shouldn't give her name – is really far too short for the gowns she commissions. But of course Mrs Turner can hardly tell her so.'

173

The Flavels were hanging on her every word, but her mother looked distinctly uncomfortable. 'Laura, dear, you really oughtn't to repeat gossip. I'm sure it's meant to be confidential.'

The good-looking Maurice came to her rescue. 'I should like to meet your brother, he sounds jolly interesting.' She gave him a grateful glance. 'Not that I can play a note of anything myself. But I admire people who can.'

'And what about your job? Do you have to write out briefs for robbers and murderers?'

Her parents were aghast. 'Laura! Really!'

'But Maurice Flavel only smiled. 'It's all right, Mrs Asmussen. You'd be surprised how many times I get asked that question. In fact, most of our work is just routine and boring; litigation, conveyancing, and the odd affidavit to be sworn. Not very exciting at all.'

At the end of the evening when the Flavels had left, for the first time in months Laura found herself thinking of somebody other than Frances or Kit.

'What a nice young man Mr Flavel's son is,' she overheard her mother saying and couldn't resist pausing to eavesdrop. 'Now, he's the kind of steady, responsible type that I thoroughly approve of. Oh yes, he's completely reliable.' A sigh. 'If only Kit could be a little more like that . . .'

Richard Asmussen was smoking his pipe. 'Very nice people. Very nice indeed.'

In the hall on her way to bed Laura passed Ethel, taking down the last of the dishes to the kitchen. 'Good lookin' young gentleman, that Mr Flavel's son,' she said, cheekily.

'Ethel, stop match-making!' She went to kiss her parents goodnight.

'I was very proud of you this evening, Laura . . . the Flavels were extremely impressed . . .'

She pecked him on the cheek. 'Was that because I work for Mrs Anne Turner Court Dressmaker of New Bond Street, or was it just because they liked the sunshine of my smile?'

'Both, I'm sure. But then I think you know that already. Of course it impresses people that you have such a good position.' He looked at her under his eyebrows in a meaningful way that she understood. 'Young Maurice seemed very taken with you . . .'

'Daddy . . . he only invited me to the cinema.'

He reached out and stroked her hair. 'That was the first place I invited your mother too . . .'

Kit gathered up his sheet music and placed it on the table beside his clarinet. He glanced at his wristwatch; still plenty of time to get to rehearsals. Before he forgot again, he'd best go downstairs and find his landlady to give her the rent.

She was dusting in her sitting room when he put his head around the door and tapped on the doorframe so that he didn't make her jump. He waved a ten-shilling note at her. 'Thought I might as well pay up to the end of the month. Sorry I haven't got any change.'

'Oh, it's you, dear!' She put down her house cleaning tools and wiped her hands on her pinafore. 'Just off to the Pavilion, are you?'

'In a while, yes. I thought if I got there half-an-hour early today they might let me leave before eleven o'clock. I have to pick up a new evening suit in Oxford Street.'

'Oh, I'm sure they will . . .' She took the ten shilling note and stuffed it in her pocket. 'I've got some loose change in my jar in the kitchen . . . why don't you come down and have a cup of tea before you go? I was just going to put the kettle on anyway . . .'

Kit smiled. 'If it's no bother . . .'

She chuckled as she led the way down the kitchen steps. From the half-open door Kit could smell a stew cooking. 'Always got time for a nice cup o'tea.'

Kit sat down on the bench while she filled the big kettle and lit the gas. 'That American friend of yours was off early today . . . I never even heard him go out; nice young bloke, he is. Said something about meeting a chap from . . . ooh, now, I've forgotten the name. Somewhere back home . . . wherever that is.'

'He's thinking of joining another band that specializes in jazz back in America . . . Chicago, New Orleans, I don't remember exactly where. He was going to meet up with someone at the Trocadero.'

'Well, he was certainly up and about early . . . and after coming in so late at night.' She took a jug of milk out of the fridge safe. 'Really, I don't know how you young chaps do it . . . still, that's being young, isn't it?' While she waited for the kettle to boil, she fished through a pile of old newspapers. 'Here . . . I knew it was about somewhere . . .' she was holding one out to him. 'I wanted to show you this, duck. Didn't you tell me your sister worked at that posh dressmakers in New Bond Street . . . the one what made all the gowns for that Cabinet Minister's daughter when she married some lord a few months ago? Can't remember the name now. But it was in all the papers . . .'

'My sister, Laura. Yes, she works for Anne Turner.'

'Laura! That's right. Pretty name. Well, when I saw this picture in the paper, it made me think of her. It's Lady Whatsername's parents and sister . . . ooh, I can't see this print proper without my glasses . . . opening a new wing at the Charing Cross Hospital . . .' Kit took it from her. 'It says there, the caption, that the outfit Lady Cultrane's wearing was designed by Mrs Anne Turner . . . I thought that name rang a bell.' She turned back to the kettle; steam was pouring from the spout and misting up all the kitchen windows. 'The father, you know . . . he's a bigwig in the government . . . and her, well, I can remember reading about her when she was young; her father was a millionaire. Stinking rich. Beautiful woman, though. Now, my husband, he always voted Liberal . . . thought a lot of old Lloyd George, my Bert did . . .'

Kit had suddenly gone very quiet. 'Here you are, dear. Tea up.'

'Would you mind if I kept this?'

'Oh no! You have it! Only goes out for the salvage man . . . your sister'll like to see that. That's why I saved it for you, you see . . .'

So that she wouldn't notice anything was wrong, he made his lips smile. 'Yes, it was very kind of you to do that. I'm glad you did.'

She left the taxi at the opposite end of the road and ran all the way to Kit's front door. It was already half open, a galvanized steel bucket three-quarters full of hot, soapy water, standing against it as a doorstop. There was a bar of household soap and a scrubbing brush beside it on the step. Frances stepped over them, peering around the hall for a sign of Kit's landlady; from the bottom of the kitchen stairs she could hear women's voices. Praying that he hadn't left for rehearsals at the theatre, she ran up the two flights of steps to his room and knocked on the door.

There was no answer, even though she could hear someone moving about inside. She tapped again, and waited; then opened it and went inside.

He was standing in the middle of the room, clearly ready to go out. He wore a jacket over his shirt and Fairisle pullover, his music and clarinet case stood beside him on the floor. But there was something different about him, something in his face that stopped her in her tracks. Her heart sank. Although he was always delighted to see her, she'd burst in on him at the wrong time. Clearly he was late.

'Kit, I'm sorry to turn up like this . . . but it was the only way!' She was still out of breath after running up the two flights of stairs. 'I'm supposed to be somewhere else, so I can't stop long; but I missed

176

you so much that I simply had to see you . . .' He went on staring at her; no greeting, no smile. 'Kit, what is it? What's wrong?'

There was a newspaper lying on top of the piano. He picked it up and thrust it into her hands. 'You tell me what's wrong, Lady Frances Osborne.'

All the colour drained from her face. 'Kit, please . . . listen to me. You don't understand . . .'

'Understand? I understand you lied to me! Right from the very beginning. Your real name, your family, your age; who you were, *what* you were!' His voice was husky with rage. 'For Christ's sake, Frankie! Do you realize what you've done? You're sixteen, virtually the same age as my sister! Have you got any idea what your parents would do if they found out you'd been seeing me?'

'They won't find out. They can't.' She struggled against her tears, the lump in her throat. She couldn't bear him to look at her like that, as if he hated her. 'They don't know anything. Not even where I am now.'

'And where the hell are you supposed to be?'

'In Kensington. At the foreign languages school. But I gave the maid my mother always sends with me the slip . . . when the chauffeur took the car around the back to park it, I ducked out without anybody seeing me . . .'

'You're going straight back there. Now.' He took hold of her arm. 'And you're not coming back here, Frankie. Not ever.'

'*No!*' The tears coursed down her cheeks. She didn't care if his landlady overheard. He couldn't send her away like this. 'I have to see you again, don't you understand? Kit, please. I love you.' The enormity of the sudden revelation momentarily silenced him. 'I meant what I said before. I mean it now. I didn't want to lie to you but I knew if I told you the truth you wouldn't let me come back.'

'You're damn right I wouldn't!'

'I begged Laura not to tell you, and she swore she never would . . .'

He swung round. 'You know my sister?' Sudden revelation. 'Of course. The Osborne wedding. And she knew all the time!'

The newspaper lay open at Frances's feet; she bent down and picked it up.

'My landlady thought I might like to see the picture because the Countess of Cultrane was wearing an Anne Turner outfit, and my sister works for Mrs Turner. Truth will out, huh?'

There was a long silence between them. He came over and lay his hands on her shoulders. 'Frankie, you know that I'd rather do any-

thing than hurt you; but you must realize we have to say goodbye.
No, please don't try and argue, don't try and make me change my
mind . . . because I won't. I'm going downstairs to get you a taxi
and you must go back to where you came from. For both our sakes.'

'You couldn't send me away if you loved me; you wouldn't. Not
after all the things we've shared between us.' She looked up at him,
blinking through the haze of tears. 'Say it, Kit. Say that you don't
love me. Tell me that you never did . . . that you only felt sorry for
me because you found me crying on the pavement that night. If you
can say that then I'll turn round and leave without another word.'

He heaved a deep sigh; what a fool he'd been! Giving way to his
emotions, letting her fall in love with him; blinkered, thoughtless,
never seeing where it would end. Rudy had warned him often enough,
and he'd been right.

He wished there was some other way he could cut himself out of
her life gently, without hurting her anymore than he'd hurt her
already, but there wasn't. Whatever he said or did now, he was going
to leave her with a scar.

'Frankie, I never meant to hurt you; or for us to get involved like
this. I take all the blame. But it's no use, don't you see? We belong
in different worlds, you and I . . . I don't belong in yours; you don't
belong in mine.'

When Anne Turner's secretary came to tell Laura that there was a
young man on the telephone asking to speak to her, her heart sank;
it was Maurice Flavel, she thought disconsolately, on her way to take
the call, ringing to cancel their evening at the cinema. Obviously he
hadn't been as taken with her as she'd thought. The depth of her
disappointment forced her to admit to herself how much she'd been
looking forward to it. With a resigned sigh, she picked up the receiver.

But it wasn't Maurice Flavel's voice on the other end of the line;
it was her brother's. Even as it buzzed and crackled so that she had
to strain her ear to hear what he was saying, she could tell that
something was wrong. He'd never telephoned her at work before.

'I want you to come here, today, as soon as you finish work. You've
got the address.'

'But, Kit . . . can't you tell me what it's about now?'

'I'll tell you later.' He rang off, abruptly, without saying goodbye.

Laura got off at the wrong bus stop and had to walk half a mile out
of her way to find the right road; three times she stopped people in

the street to ask the way. After the long day at work, her head was beginning to ache with tension, her feet were sore where her high-heeled shoes had rubbed. As she turned into Halkin Street, she opened her handbag to check on the piece of paper Kit had given her that she'd come to the right address.

Two young men carrying instrument cases were coming out of number five; they held the front door open for her and glanced back over their shoulders as they walked away with appreciative smiles. But she was too worried about her brother's strange telephone call to notice. In her preoccupation she almost collided with one of the other tenants coming down the stairs.

'I'm so sorry, it was all my fault. Could you please tell me which room Kit Asmussen has? Is it this floor?'

The young man tipped his hat. 'No, next floor up. Second door on the right.'

'Thank you.'

It was open a few inches and Laura pushed it and walked in, but there was no sign of Kit. The room was large, light, very neat and tidy; not like him at all. The bed was made; there were two suitcases and a carpet-bag, the same things he'd taken with him when he'd left home, standing side by side on the floor. On the piano was a single sheet of music, a packet of cigarettes and a newspaper, folded so that the front page lay topside up. When she went over and looked at it her heart sank.

'So, you managed to get here all right?' She spun round as the familiar voice made her jump; Kit was standing in the open doorway.

'Kit . . .'

He nodded coldly towards the newspaper. 'How could you, Laura? All the time you knew who she was and you never told me! Don't you have any idea what might have happened if I hadn't found out? The under-age daughter of a titled Tory Cabinet Minister, here, in my room! God,' he slammed the door behind him so hard that it made her flinch, 'the high and mighty bloody Osbornes would have loved that, don't you think? My career as a musician in London would have been well and truly finished. You knew all that, everything . . . but you still said nothing. And I still went on believing that she was someone else, two years older than she really was . . .'

'Frances told me what happened that night, how you helped her. She begged me not to say anything because she wanted to see you again, and she knew you'd never agree to it if you found out the truth.'

'Lucky my landlady gave me that newspaper, isn't it? She'll never know what a big favour she's done me!'

'Look, will you listen to me for just a moment? Please? I know you have a right to be angry, but neither of us wanted to lie to you. When Frances first told me she'd met you she pleaded with me never to say anything to you, and I agreed because I understood why and because she's my friend.'

'You could have made her understand the risks she was taking – not just for herself but for me, too. If her precious family had found out, who do you think they would have blamed? Yes, that's right, Laura! Me. Didn't it ever occur to you that you owed me just a little loyalty as my sister, enough to warn me about what I was getting myself into?'

'That's not fair!'

'Whether it is or not it doesn't matter anymore. Because just after I saw that picture, she came here herself and I confronted her with it.'

Laura turned pale. 'Frances knows you've seen this?'

'I told her what I thought of her for lying to me . . . and what her family would do if they found she'd been here. Then I told her that I didn't want her to come here ever again, and I meant what I said. You can tell her that when you see her, if she still has any doubts.' He snatched the packet of cigarettes from the top of the piano and lit himself one. 'I'm leaving here tomorrow. And no telling her where I've gone. In fact, it might be better if I didn't tell you anything at all. That way you won't be tempted to betray my trust again.'

'Oh, I see . . . everything's my fault now, is it? You've conveniently forgotten it was you who brought her back here in the first place . . . why didn't you just call her a taxi and send her straight home? You didn't have to let her come back, but you did. Because you liked her, because you wanted to see her again. She's a person, Kit, whoever her parents are, whatever her father does, regardless of whether her family are entered in *Burke's Peerage* and *Debrett*. You're the one who's putting up fences and blowing down bridges, not her!'

'She's out-of-bounds, for christ's sake! I don't need to have to keep telling you that! She doesn't belong here. And she doesn't belong with me.'

'Is that what you told her?'

'Yes . . . what else did you expect me to say?'

She gave him a long, withering look before she spoke again. 'I don't know you anymore, Kit. You changed much more than your

180

address when you left home. You're another person.' She glanced down at her wristwatch. She suddenly felt very tired and drained. 'I'm sorry, I have to go home. I'm late already and they'll start worrying if I'm not in by seven.'

His voice stopped her at the door. 'Laura ... I'm leaving for Chicago on Thursday week. That was the other thing I wanted to tell you.'

She was stunned, unable to believe her own ears. '*Chicago?*'

'I won't go into details ... but a friend of mine got talking to someone who was over here, in London, looking for musicians for his new band. I met him at the Troc a few days ago and everything's all fixed. I was going to come over on Sunday and break the news to Mum and Dad.'

The sudden threat of him going out of her life for good momentarily quelled all her anger. 'Kit, you can't! Mummy will be heartbroken ... and why, when you're doing so well here, in London? It doesn't make sense.' Sudden realization. 'Are you doing this because of Frances?'

'Laura, my mind's made up. And I don't want to argue about it.'

She nodded, slowly. 'You're quite callous, aren't you? I never saw it till now. You can coolly cut someone who cares about you out of your life and turn your back on your family, all your friends. Well, *bon voyage*, Kit. I hope you think it's worth it.'

She'd hurt him and she knew how much by the flash of pain that came into his eyes, but she was still too angry with him and too shaken by his news to care.

'Well, there's nothing left for us to say to each other, is there?' As she reached for the door handle the door itself opened and a young American with a thatch of straight, straw-coloured hair put his head around it.

'I did knock first, you didn't hear me.'

He grinned at her. 'Sorry.' A glance at Kit. 'Say, am I interrupting anything?'

'I was just leaving.'

'Blonde last time, brunette today! Hey, anyone ever tell you you're the dead spit of Louise Brooks? You can sure pick 'em, Kit!'

'Rudy, this is my sister.'

'My mistake.'

He followed her out onto the landing and halfway down the stairs. She turned and gave him her coldest look. 'You know where we live if you want to see us, but don't telephone me at work again, will

181

you? Mrs Turner doesn't like us having personal calls during working hours.' She walked down into the hall and out of the house without looking back.

Her father rarely ever sent for her unless there was something wrong, so she knew when Grace brought her the summons to his study that she was in trouble. No doubt the Principal at the language school in Kensington had been on the telephone to her mother, wanting to know the reason for her bad attendance; but she was far too miserable to care. Kit never wanted to see her again and Laura had told her he was leaving, for good, for Chicago. This time tomorrow morning he'd be gone.

She knocked on the door and heard her father's voice ordering her to come inside. Her mother was sitting at the side of him, fixing Frances with a cold, stony stare. 'Close the door and come here.' She did as she was told, too unhappy to feel afraid at the way they were looking at her. Thomas Cultrane was toying with a silver paper-knife in his hands.

'Grace said that you wanted to see me.'

'I understand that you refused breakfast, lunch, tea, and now say you don't want dinner. Are you prepared to give me an explanation?'

'I wasn't hungry.'

He stood up suddenly, so unexpectedly that a pile of papers toppled from his desk. 'Confound your damned insolence!'

'I'm not being insolent, Daddy. You asked me a question and I answered it.'

He slapped her face.

'Then perhaps you'll kindly answer another question for me? Why your mother received a telephone call from the Principal of the language school enquiring why you haven't been turning up for your lessons? This isn't the first time you've played truant, is it?'

'No.'

Behind him, Katherine Cultrane got to her feet. 'Frances. Because of what happened before I instructed Mary Peters to accompany you in the car to the school . . . but you've obviously been too clever for her.' There was a cruel smile playing about her lips. 'If you refuse to explain where you were when you should have been in school, I shall dismiss her, without references, for dereliction of duty.'

'*No!*'

'That's better . . .'

'You can't sack Mary, it wasn't her fault! How could you even think of doing anything so petty?'

'How dare you speak to your mother like that!'

'I suppose you'd think nothing of turning her out without a character and then going to the chapel for evening Mass?'

She received a second slap across the face.

'Be quiet at once. And kindly answer my original question before I lose my temper.'

'All right. I walked around London, I don't remember where. Well, I could hardly come back to the house, could I? Why did I do it? Because I hate that school. I hate French and I hate German and hate the Principal.' They were both staring at her. 'I never want to go back. If you make me go I shall sit there and I won't do anything. They can't make me learn something I hate, can they? And neither can you. I don't want to go back there!'

There was a long yawning silence before her mother spoke.

'We were planning to take you with us for Cowes week . . . but after your disgraceful behaviour, that is out of the question.' She glanced at her husband. 'Instead, you're being sent down to the country, alone, for as long as it takes you to achieve a complete reformation of your character. Father Hennessy will be coming every day to tutor you in the subjects you refuse to learn here.' A look of triumph; how could Frances play up a priest? 'He'll also instruct you in the necessary spiritual guidance.' She turned away. 'I think that's all for the moment.

'When are you sending me?'

'Tomorrow morning. Grace has her orders about the packing.'

In the first-class reserved compartment, Frances lay back against the seat, a magazine open on her lap, gazing woodenly from the train window as the landscape flashed by; every field, every village, every stretch of woods, swiftly taking her away from where she wanted to be. But did it really matter where she was when she could never see him again? In a few hours they would be in Saffron Walden.

She looked down at the magazine without reading it, imagining the huge, rambling, empty house when they eventually reached it, with a skeleton staff and the big echoing rooms like rooms in a museum, the endless miles of countryside only emphasising her isolation and loneliness. Not that any of it really mattered, not now.

The jolting of the train was making her feel tired and she lay back and closed her eyes. Every now and then, she could sense Grace looking at her anxiously, wondering what was wrong. But no one except Laura would ever know that, either.

Lulled by the chugging sound of the engine she could almost let herself slip away, back to the room in Halkin Street, and see him sitting there, smiling at her, his hands moving across the keys of the piano. She remembered the way the light from the window would steal across the floor, the way a strand of his hair fell across his forehead on the left-hand side, the movement of his hand as he constantly brushed it away. The texture of his Fair Isle pullover, his eyelashes, the cadences of his voice. Strange that those memories of him hurt more than the memory of that last, angry scene.

Laura, embarrassed and almost shamefaced, had told her that when he'd settled in Chicago, when he'd had time to get over his anger at what had happened, he might write to her; but even though she longed to believe that, to clutch at straws, in her heart she knew he never would.

Every day, starting from the big leaded windows up the drive of the house, eyes straining for the postman on his bicycle, she waited for a letter from him. But none ever came.

PART TWO

23

As he stepped out of the car and onto the pavement, William Banbury was suddenly aware that most of the downstairs rooms were ablaze with lights. The raucous din of laughter and loud jazz blared from the direction of the drawing room, and through the curtains he could see that some kind of party appeared to be in full swing. For a moment he stood there clutching his briefcase with shock and astonishment; the headache that had been growing steadily worse all afternoon beat mercilessly against his temples. As his chauffeur drove the car away into the mews, he went up the steps to the front door and knocked loudly. He had to stand for several minutes after knocking and ringing the bell again before Seddon answered it.

'For God's sake, Seddon! What on earth's going on in here?' The drawing room doors were wide open; the room was crowded with young people drinking, smoking and dancing. One young woman in a backless beaded dress was sitting on someone's lap with her bare arm draped suggestively around his shoulders; several other couples were kissing openly; a girl with short black shingled hair was lying full length on the sofa, blowing rings of smoke from her Turkish cigarette into the air and shrieking with laughter. He could clearly see the tops of her silk stockings.

'I'm sorry, my lord, but Lady Banbury is having a party.'

At the very same moment Elizabeth, with his nephew Edward Vaux behind her, came out together into the hall. 'Darling! Come in and join the fun! Eddie will mix you one of his wicked cocktails, won't you Eddie?' She ignored the amazement on his face and hooked her arm through his. 'You told me you'd be late back tonight, so I invited a few friends in for music and drinks . . . you don't mind, do you?'

He had never lost his temper with her but he came very close to losing it now. 'Elizabeth, I really do wish you hadn't done this! I have a splitting headache, a briefcase full of important papers to go through, and I can't so much as hear myself think! Do you realize that damn music can be heard halfway down the street?'

'Oh, darling, don't you like it? It's the very latest band from New

Orleans . . . Eddie got it for me. Now, stop looking so cross and come and meet everyone.'

'I'm sorry, I've far too much to do.' He handed his hat and coat to Seddon irritably. 'Please be good enough to turn down that infernal racket and get rid of all these people as soon as possible.'

'What's the matter, Uncle? Things not going too well for His Majesty's Opposition?'

'My dear boy, being a member of the Opposition can often be far more trying than anything we have to go through when we're actually in office. Now, if you'll excuse me . . .' He stalked off towards his study, but they went after him, exchanging a look between them that he didn't see.

He shut the door against the din from outside. 'I suppose there's no point complaining; we lost the last General Election so there's nothing any of us can do but grin and bear it. It won't be the first time.'

Elizabeth perched herself on the edge of his desk. 'Beastly voters, letting Labour back in after all your hard work! Darling, they simply don't deserve you or Daddy!'

He sat down heavily. The slight, nagging pain in his chest that had started on the journey home from Westminster, was making him short of breath now, and he could feel the beads of perspiration starting to form across his forehead. He poured himself a glass of water from the jug on the desk and took out his heart pills.

'I say, Uncle . . . are you feeling quite A–1?'

'It's nothing, Edward. Nothing at all . . . just a bit of tension after a long day.' He managed a brief smile. He'd always been fond of his dead brother's son. 'Listening to Churchill going on for the last two and a half hours about why he thinks the Liberal vote is sure to decline over the next two years is enough to make anyone feel ill. From pure boredom.'

'If you ask me, I think Winston just loves the sound of his own voice.'

'That's the most sensible remark I've heard all day!' He put one of the pills on the tip of his tongue and took a swig of water. 'Darling, I do have an awful lot of work to go through . . . and I brought it home because I imagined I was going to have peace and quiet.' He was already sorry that he'd been angry with her; he reached out and patted her hand. She was looking exceptionally beautiful tonight, with her shining, silver gilt hair in the new, short and curly style and wearing a mid-calf ice blue sequinned cocktail dress. 'Why don't you go back to your guests?'

She dropped a kiss on the top of his head. Was it just her imagination but was his hair thinner on top than it had seemed a week or two ago?

'I only followed you in here to remind you about Tuesday night, that's all.' He looked blank. 'Oh, William, really! Don't tell me that you've forgotten!'

'Forgotten? We have nothing planned for Tuesday night . . .'

'I knew you had! You promised to take me to see *Bitter Sweet* at Her Majesty's, with supper afterwards at the Savoy Grill. I was so looking forward to it, and I wanted to wear my new pink beaded dress! You know how I adore Noël Coward!'

'Elizabeth, if I'd promised to take you to the theatre, I would have written it down in my diary. Here.' He opened the thick, leather bound book and flicked over the pages. 'You see? There's no entry for Tuesday evening at all.'

'You forgot, didn't you? Monday we're dining with my parents at Belgrave Square; Tuesday you were taking me to Her Majesty's; Wednesday, I have an appointment with my hairdresser and lunch with Dora Sutherland at the Grosvenor Hotel. You've been so engrossed with your horrid papers at Westminster you completely forgot. Don't argue with me, William . . . I know you forgot because I've already booked the tickets.'

He sighed heavily. 'I'm so sorry, my dear . . . it must have slipped my mind somehow.' He glanced up at his nephew. 'The trouble is. I've arranged to dine at my club on Tuesday evening. Eddie, I don't suppose I could possibly ask you to stand in for me, if you've nothing else on?'

'Well, of course . . . I'd be delighted . . . if Elizabeth doesn't mind making do with me . . .' They were careful not to look at each other. 'I was going to make a fourth at bridge with Eva Scott-Montagu at the Winchelsea's but I think I can probably make an excuse and get out of it . . .'

'I'd be terribly grateful if it doesn't put you out . . .'

Vaux smiled, but he noticed a change in Elizabeth's face. She was glaring at him.

'I'll give her a ring when I get home this evening; I'm sure she'll be able to find another partner for next week. Half the chaps in London would probably jump at the chance to step in.' He followed Elizabeth out into the hall.

'In here!' She grasped him by the sleeve and opened the morning room door. When he was inside she slammed it after him ferociously. 'You bastard! You never told me you were taking Eva Scott-Montagu to the Winchelsea's for dinner!'

'Elizabeth, for Christ's sake what's the matter with you?'

'Are you sleeping with her?'

'Of course not.'

'Then why are you taking her out behind my back?'

'I'm not taking her out behind your back. Now, for heaven's sake, calm down before he hears you.'

'You never told me you were taking her out. Why not? Because you obviously didn't want me to know! *Half the chaps in London would jump at the chance to step in,*' she mimicked, 'What's so extra special about her, pug-nosed little bitch? No man in his right mind would bother to notice her if she stood naked in a nine-acre field.'

Vaux came to her and took her in his arms. 'Liz, will you calm down?' He kissed her. 'Listen to me. Don't you know by now that the only one I want is you? But I can't have you, not openly, not yet. Use your head. If we're seen together, in a group or not, he might think twice and start getting suspicious. And neither of us wants that.'

She laid her head against his evening jacket. 'I know, Eddie, I know that . . . I'm sorry . . . it's just that I can't bear the thought of you and her . . .'

'There's no "me and her" . . . there never was. It's just to throw him . . . or anyone else we know . . . completely off the scent.'

'I'd better go back and tell everyone the party's over . . .'

He caught her by the wrist as she walked away towards the door. 'Liz, it's not forever, you know that. I'd swear his heart condition's getting worse . . . did you see the sweat on his face before he took that pill?'

She paused in the doorway while she glanced out to see if any of the servants were watching. 'If he dropped dead tomorrow it wouldn't be soon enough for me.' He went after her into the crowded drawing room.

'Elizabeth! Eddie! Where have you two been? You haven't drunk your cocktails!'

'I've been trying to pacify my very irritable and impossibly bad tempered lord and master. And failed. Sorry, darlings, I'm afraid you'll have to drink up and go.'

190

She stood at the door, kissing her women friends on the cheek and waving goodnight to the men. Soon only she and Vaux were left.

'Come and have another drink before you go, Eddie. What about a scotch and soda?'

'Sounds capital. Yes, I will. Always was very partial to Uncle William's best malt.'

They both sat down. Elizabeth let him pour his own drink and mix her another cocktail. She opened the cigarette box, but it was empty.

'Oh, what a bore! They've had the lot, the vultures! Eddie, give me one of yours, will you? I don't want to have to ring for Seddon.' He left what he was doing immediately and handed her his silver cigarette case. 'Thanks, darling.'

'I'd better not stay too long now the others have left . . . with him in the house it might look suspicious.'

'Rubbish . . . he's stuck in his study with those boring beastly papers. I'd swear he thinks more of his damn constituents than he does of me.'

Vaux came over to where she was sitting, carrying their drinks in each hand. 'That isn't true and you know it; if he had the faintest idea about us . . .'

'Hopefully the shock would give him a heart attack!'

'Liz, you don't really mean that.'

'Oh yes I do! You've no idea what it's like, being married to a disgusting old man for nearly two and a half years . . . no, two years and seven months. Don't imagine I haven't counted every one. Like a prisoner, striking off each day to the moment when they open the gates and he's free. Yes, Eddie; that's exactly what it's like.'

'Shh . . . keep your voice down . . .'

'And that's another thing . . . I've begged him time and time again to get rid of Seddon. He's been in service too long. Always creeping about the place, suddenly appearing like the genie from the lamp when you least expect him to; I'm sure he's spying on me . . .'

'Liz, it's all in your imagination . . .'

'I even suggested that if William thinks so much of him, he send him down to the house in Kent, while I get a younger butler here . . . but he won't hear of it!'

'Seddon's worked for the family for ages . . . he's part of the furniture . . . and he isn't exactly a geriatric.'

'I don't care!' She inhaled the smoke from her cigarette furiously and blew it defiantly out of her nose. 'I want to get rid of him.'

191

Vaux sipped his drink. 'Look. Forget about Seddon. He isn't important. I want to know when I can see you again. When we can be alone.'

'William has a meeting at his club the day after tomorrow with my father and some other members of the Shadow Cabinet . . . I'll meet you at Anne's house then. Seven o'clock. Be on time. I don't think we'll be able to have more than a couple of hours . . .' she reached out her hand and touched his. The diamond bracelet Banbury had given her as a gift the day before glinted and glittered in the light.

'I've got something else to tell you before you go.' He smiled at her, waiting. 'I'm going to have a baby.'

'*Elizabeth!*'

'I thought that would surprise you.' She twirled her cocktail glass enigmatically.

'Does my uncle know? He'll be thrilled.'

'He wouldn't be if he knew that it isn't really his.'

Vaux stared at her. 'You mean . . . ?'

'Do you really think I'd go through with it if it wasn't yours? All that ghastly morning sickness, and having to wear horrid dresses like tents all through the best part of the Season? I'll miss Royal Ascot again next year, and I do so hate missing Ascot. When it starts to show I'll have to run away and hide myself at Greyfriars in Kent . . . I shall be bored to tears!'

'Darling,' he grasped her hand and in his. 'Are you sure, absolutely one hundred per cent sure about this?'

'Paul Lobell confirmed it this morning!'

'I mean, are you certain it's mine?'

'Do you really suppose I don't know the father of my own child?' She grinned, wickedly. 'Just think. Your son will be Earl of Banbury one day . . . and nobody will ever know!' She collapsed into bright, tinkling laughter.

'It might be a girl.'

'I'm sure it won't. And so is Anne. I had a dress fitting with her just after I left Harley Street . . . she said that she's going to leave out a bottle of champagne for us tomorrow night so that we can celebrate. Now, what do you think of that?'

William Banbury sat very still at his desk, sweat pouring from his face. The pain was gripping at his chest now like hot, burning fingers, and he fumbled clumsily to unfasten his collar and tie. It was agony when he drew the slightest breath, and the pill he'd taken ten minutes before had brought him no relief from the attack this time. Slowly, with shaking fingers, he unscrewed the top of the little bottle and tipped out another pill. He swallowed it and drained the glass of water in a single gulp. When Seddon came in to ask him about dinner, he felt fractionally better. Gradually, the hot, searing pain was receding. He heaved a deep sigh.

'Is everything all right, my lord?'

'Yes. Yes, thank you, Seddon. Is there something you wanted?'

'It's about dinner, my lord. Her ladyship said that she wouldn't be requiring any, and we hadn't expected you back until later this evening. Shall I instruct Cook?'

'Just something very simple for me, Seddon. Something light.' He took out his handkerchief and mopped the sweat from his brow. 'Has my nephew left yet?'

'A few minutes ago, my lord.'

A little unsteadily, he got up. The papers could wait until later. His headache was making it impossible for him to concentrate.

'That will be all, Seddon.'

She was sitting by the fire reading a copy of the *Tatler* when he went into the drawing-room; she didn't look up. For a moment Banbury stood there in the doorway, looking around him; the all-white Syrie Maugham drawing room, he thought gratefully, had long gone, discarded by Elizabeth for the latest Colefax and Fowler fashion and by the impracticality of its colour. He was glad. It was much more warm and welcoming now.

'It's very chilly tonight,' he said, going to stand in front of the roaring fire, holding his hands out towards the flames. 'I wouldn't be surprised if we had a fall of snow.'

At last she looked up. 'I hope not! It's all very well on picture postcards and greetings cards for Christmas, but in real life it's a bore. It'll all turn mushy and ruin my new white kid shoes.'

He bent down and kissed her. 'I may be rather late back tomorrow night. I'm sorry, darling, but it can't be avoided. We have quite a lot of subjects to discuss before we leave for the country for Christmas. I just hope the roads stay clear.'

'Oh, don't worry about me. Be as late as you like. I have a thousand things to do . . . I'm going over to see Mummy to discuss all the details for Frances' coming-out. Oh, it makes me think of when I was her age . . . all those parties, dances, ardent young men . . .' She suddenly realized that she'd been caught off guard and had made a definite verbal mistake. William hated anyone drawing attention to the differences in their ages. 'How boring they all were!' That was better, he was smiling now. 'Of course,' she reached up and stroked his face with the tip of her finger. 'I've always preferred mature men . . .'

'I'm very glad to hear it. Now . . . what's all this Seddon tells me about you not wanting dinner? You mustn't miss meals, Elizabeth. In fact, I wasn't going to mention this, but you look rather pale.'

'Too many late nights, darling . . . sitting up waiting for you to come back from your beastly political meetings. You're away more now than when the party was in office.' Let him think she cared, the old fool. 'I miss you so much.'

'I'm sorry, but when duty calls . . .'

'It'll be far worse next year, won't it, because you'll be gearing up for the next election? And I know how time consuming all that will be from Daddy!' She stifled a yawn. 'He hardly seemed to be home at all.'

He sat down beside her and took her into his arms, not noticing how she suddenly stiffened at his touch. 'I'll make it up to you, I promise. Don't I always? You remember that ruby and opal necklace in Asprey's that you liked so much?'

The maid left the tray of coffee on the low table by the couch, and went almost noiselessly out of the room. Katherine Cultrane lay aside the list that she'd been compiling and reached for the coffee pot.

'How did William seem to you today? I thought he was looking rather grey-faced . . . is he working too hard, do you think?'

Thomas Cultrane came over to her and sat down. 'Hard to say, really; he isn't the man to mumble on incessantly about every ache and pain. But I do know that he's been to see Theodore Mayerne a few times. He left the meeting half an hour early to go to Harley Street.'

'Elizabeth hasn't mentioned anything to me . . . but then she never would. Since that last mild heart attack two years ago, he's seemed to slow down. They don't go out and about nearly as much as they used to.'

'You mean *he* doesn't. I hadn't noticed Elizabeth curtailing any of her usual pleasures.'

She handed him his coffee. 'She is more than twenty-five years younger than Banbury. There was an edge to her voice that he recognized. 'All in all, I think she's handled things quite well.'

'William adores her. He'd never stop her going to nightclubs or the theatre with friends. You know that.'

'It would look better for appearances sake if he could tear himself away from Westminster to accompany her now and then.'

'My dear, it isn't really necessary, is it? Look at how many young, married women the Prince of Wales wines and dines.'

'I suppose you have a point. Elizabeth says he's hardly ever seen about these days without Thelma Furness. Did I mention that he invited Elizabeth and William down to Fort Belvedere for the weekend?'

'No, I don't think you did.'

'Elizabeth has accepted, of course . . . but whether William can tear himself away is another matter.' There was a silence while she sipped her coffee and glanced down at the list in her lap. At that moment the drawing room doors opened and Frances came in.

Her mother glanced up. 'You'd better look at this list of guests for your birthday dance at Claridges and see if there's anyone you think we need add.'

Frances came over and took the list from her. She was taller, more slender, much more self-contained and self-assured than she'd been at fifteen; the shy adolescent was now a sophisticated young woman. She wore her dark honey-coloured hair in a fashionable chignon, her face scarcely bore a trace of make-up, except lipstick; but she was striking. The only thing that puzzled and irritated her parents was her complete lack of interest in her fast approaching launch into Society; Elizabeth had been entirely different.

Her blue eyes with their dark brown lashes looked at the names on the list with hardly any interest at all. Then she turned the page and hesitated.

'Robert Carr? Who's that?'

Katherine Cultrane made a gesture of impatience. 'Surely you remember him? He was given a Junior Ministry in the last government, and he's been to several of my parties. If it hadn't been for Labour winning the last election he would have been promoted to a major post by now.'

'Marvellous talent for finance,' her father said from across the room.

'Well, it doesn't really matter, does it? You and Daddy have asked so many people I shan't have time to speak to half of them at all.'

'You'll make time to speak to Robert Carr; he's a distant cousin of the Earl of Rosslare.'

'Is that supposed to mean something?'

'Rosslare is one of the biggest and most important landowners in Scotland . . . and a widower with no sons. He isn't in good health. When he dies, Robert Carr inherits the title.'

Frances understood the implication only too well; looking down the alphabetical list she saw the name of Viscount Staughton, the Earl of Iden's son and heir. She glanced up with a sudden frown. 'I can't see Susan Hope-Sinclair's name down here, Mummy. We were at Croftly Hall together and she invited me to all her dances.'

'You can't see her name, Frances, because it isn't there; and the last dance her parents gave was nearly eighteen months ago. Since then her sister has become involved in a most unpleasant divorce case. Surely you see we can't possibly invite her?'

'But why not? Whatever her sister's done or not done isn't her fault.'

Her father lay down the papers he'd been reading. 'Your mother has explained *why* she hasn't been invited; kindly let us drop the matter. Whatever you think about the rights and wrongs of it all the fact remains that in this country people who go through the divorce courts are *not* received in polite society.'

Frances handed the guest list back to her mother with a tight smile. 'So. Let the sins of the sister be visited on one and all. Not a particularly Christian attitude, is it? Besides, I can't see what all the fuss is about; people make mistakes in everything else they do, why not in their choice of marital partner? Is everyone expected to get it right first time?'

'Frances, the subject is no longer open for discussion. And since you have to be at New Bond Street early tomorrow morning, I should have thought it was high time you went to bed.'

'Yes, perhaps it is.' She kissed both of them lightly on the cheek and went out.

'I'm afraid she's showing distinct signs of being distressingly wilful when the mood takes her,' Katherine Cultrane said, taking out her platinum lighter and reaching for a cigarette. She lay back in one of the deep winged-armchairs and crossed her shapely legs. 'I hope when the time comes we won't have the same trouble with her doing as she's told as we had with persuading Elizabeth to marry Banbury.'

'Oh, she'll come round when she gets into the swing of things. Girls are inclined to be moody at her age. She knows where her duty lies, in any case. And it has to be said that she has a better choice

196

than Elizabeth did; Iden's heir and Robert Carr are much nearer her own age.'

'You're really serious about Carr, aren't you?'

'My dear, you've met the young man often enough; Baldwin likes him, he hasn't offended anyone, he's modest, hard-working, very willing to be guided in the right direction. And he's almost certain to be the next Earl of Rosslare.'

'You prefer him to the Iden boy?'

'His prospects are distinctly brighter. He has admirers in high places. And as soon as we get back into office, I've been told in Cabinet – in confidence of course – that he's destined to rise straight to the top.'

Katherine dotted the ash from her Turkish cigarette in the crystal ashtray in front of her. 'What a pity he's so staunchly solid Scottish Presbyterian.'

'Oh, I think we can overlook his religion . . . after all, he'd be too big a catch to pass up.' Cultrane stroked his chin, thoughtfully. 'Can't say I'm too keen on that friend of his . . . his private secretary, Dreikhorn. There's an underlying touch of insolence in the fellow that I can't abide. Several chaps at the club have mentioned it . . . when you speak to him he looks at you as if he knows something you don't.'

'He has got under your skin, Tom. I thought he was quite deferential, when I spoke to him at my last garden party. They were together at the Scottish Office, weren't they, him and Carr?'

'Dreikhorn's uncle had quite an influential position there . . . of course, he's retired now. It was Dreikhorn I'm told, who got Carr a post there in the first place. Well, he's certainly come a long way since then.'

'Cynthia Moseley tells me that he's quite a ladies' man . . . every time he's seen out on the town, he has a different one on his arm.'

'Dreikhorn? Well, he's a dashed good-looking young chap, one has to admit. Comes from a good family . . . father was a circuit judge, Banbury was telling me. But as I say, a bit of a know-it-all . . . fellow's not half respectful enough for my liking.' He went back to his papers and Katherine picked up a copy of the *Tatler*.

'I thought of having a dinner party on Saturday night . . . just Freddie and his wife, Elizabeth and Banbury. He hasn't been looking terribly well lately . . . and there are several things I've been wanting to discuss with Elizabeth.'

197

Frances stood in the middle of the dressing-room lined with mirrors, while Laura and Anne Turner knelt on the carpet and made adjustments to the gown. Almost as if she was looking at someone else and not herself, she gazed dispassionately at her reflection, while the silver thread embroidery and sequins sewn skilfully across the ivory georgette overskirt winked and glittered in the light.

'It's perfect,' Anne Turner said, with a final, complacent smile. 'Just these final alterations to the hemline, and it'll be ready . . . shall we say in two days' time?'

'Thank you. It's lovely.'

Anne Turner stood back to study the effect; it had surprised her that shy, retiring little Frances had grown as tall as her sister and was so much more beautiful. But she bit back the fulsome remark that out of sheer habit, sprang to her lips; unlike her other clients, Frances Osborne seemed strangely impervious to flattery. She merely smiled and went out.

Laura stood up. 'You really do look stunning. I think this gown is even more striking than the one we made for your sister. Mrs Turner's definitely surpassed herself this time.'

'You mean *you* have. You designed most of it yourself.' Frances slid the lace-and-satin shoulder straps down to her shoulders and began to step out of it carefully. 'It may be her name on the label, but it's mostly your work, isn't it? It was your idea to have beaded and *diamanté* cobwebs on the overskirt and bodice. All she did was supervise the cutting.'

'Well . . . she does have a lot to do . . . and she did make several suggestions that I integrated into the basic pattern. It's a joint effort, really.' She smiled as she helped Frances to dress. 'She's the captain and I'm just one of the faithful crew.'

'You're good enough to open your own business! Haven't I said that dozens of times before?'

'Yes, and I've said where would I ever manage to get the capital from, besides all the other thousand and one problems I'd come up against. Anyway, Maurice expects me to give up work altogether when we get married.' Her smile faded significantly. 'In fact, we almost had words over it last night.'

'Oh?'

'Yes . . . but I was rather afraid he'd object; he can be surprisingly old-fashioned about that kind of thing. He has two sisters, both married now, and neither one of them has ever worked at all.'

'Why don't you just say you're going to? You enjoy what you do here so much.'

'Unfortunately, nobody else quite sees it that way. I was hoping Mummy and Daddy would back me up, but they're equally adamant that I should give Mrs Turner notice about two months before the wedding, so that we can get everything arranged.' She looked miserable. 'The way I look at it is that it'd be stupid for me to give up . . . at least, until we have a family. With both our wage-packets we could afford the deposit on one of those lovely terraced houses over at Holland Park; I'd quite set my heart on one. Maurice says we can manage perfectly well without my working and he refuses to hear anymore on the subject. It's a bit of stalemate at the moment.'

Frances lowered her silk chemise over her head. 'Have you set a date yet?'

Laura looked down wistfully at the small, simple diamond engagement ring on her finger. 'Well, no . . . Maurice wants to wait until next year when he gets the promotion he's expecting.'

'You know . . . you're so lucky to be engaged to someone who loves you so much. Much luckier than I am. For the last year my parents have been dropping hints as big as quarry stones about the various virtues of Jeremy Staughton, the Earl of Iden's heir . . . as if I couldn't guess why. Every dance I've been invited to and every party we've had at home, I turn round and there he is, almost treading on my feet.'

'You make it sound so funny.'

'It would be, if it wasn't so exasperating. And he's not the only one they've been pushing on me, by any means. That's why I envy you, Laura. Yes, I really do. I can't expect to be allowed to please myself . . . like Elizabeth and the boys, I have to make a 'good marriage' for my family's sake. It isn't fair, is it? Not that anyone I've met so far has given me any reason to want to spend the rest of my life with them. Far from it.'

Laura fell silent.

'You know, you could have invited Maurice to join us for lunch at the Savoy, if you'd wanted to.'

'Oh, I'd much rather we were on our own to chat. Fiancés tend to get in the way . . . and you have to be so careful what you say in front of them! Still, you could have backed me up about me wanting to go on working after we're married.' She laughed. 'He can't get over the fact that you asked me to lunch at the Savoy today. Nor can his mother. Every time I go to tea with them she plies me with

199

not very subtle questions about Mrs Turner's distinguished and aristocratic clients . . . not that I ever tell her anything I shouldn't.' She took the long, elegant, glittering evening gown carefully from the chair, and hung it up. 'I think she'll be quite starved for conversation when I have to give it all up . . .'

The Savoy Restaurant was crowded. As they walked in, following the head waiter to their table, Laura noticed the eyes looking their way, at the heads that turned. She was wearing a chic olive-green two-piece underneath her best coat, the new mid-calf length in black velour with white ermine cuffs and collar; it had taken her three months to save up for. Frances always dressed with a strikingly stark simplicity that was almost an affectation, shunning all frills and bows. She wore a chartreuse velvet cloche hat with feathers on one side, and underneath her full length sable coat a plain suit in crêpe chenille of the same colour. She wore very little jewellery. A wristwatch, a plain gold necklace with a single topaz stone, and matching earrings.

She smiled as the waiter handed them their menus. 'An aperitif, madam?'

Frances glanced at Laura; they knew each other's tastes by now. 'Two glasses of white wine, please. We're not quite ready to order.' The waiter departed. 'Will you live at home, when you first get married?'

'It *would* give us the opportunity of saving up, but I really can't bear the thought of living with his parents or mine, for that matter. I know most young couples do, to begin with. But I'd so set my heart on one of those houses at Holland Park . . . it's not the lack of privacy, really, that I'd mind so much if we had to share. My parents think the world of Maurice and I get on very well with his. But I'm afraid his mother is someone you can only bear in very small doses.'

Frances laughed. 'She sounds familiar.'

'Mrs Turner said I can design my own wedding dress, and the bridesmaids too, and she'll have them made up in house as a wedding present; when I wrote and told Kit about it he wrote back months later and said she wasn't the avaricious, money-making type he'd always thought she was . . . and I must say I thought it was very generous of her.' His name dropped between them like a stone; in her excitement and enthusiasm Laura had forgotten. Neither of them, almost by a sixth sense, ever talked about him, never mentioned his name. It had been an unthinking slip of the tongue, but the waiter came back to take their order and rescued her.

'I think the chilled melon and sole *meunière*. Thank you.' She smiled at Laura over the rim of her glass, as if the forbidden name had never been spoken. Her next words astonished her.

'Will he come back for your wedding?'

'I . . . I really don't know . . . he . . . in his last letter, he asked me if I'd go over to Chicago to see him. He said he'd wire the money for my fare.'

Frances was holding the stem of her glass a little too tightly. 'And what have you decided to do?'

'I wrote back and said I'd have to think about it. There's my job, for one thing . . .'

'Why not go there with Maurice for part of your honeymoon?'

'Gracious! Maurice would have a fit if I asked him to take me there! So would Mummy and Daddy . . . I didn't tell them about the letter. When you say *Chicago*, all they can think of is illegal drinking and gangsters.'

'Can't you pretend you're going somewhere else?'

'I couldn't lie to them. Besides, Maurice and Daddy would insist on knowing the name of the boat and the address of the hotel. They'd soon find out; then there'd be hell to pay when I got back.' She paused while their food was brought. 'By the way, are you staying in London for Christmas?'

'We're leaving for Essex on Christmas Eve. We usually spend Christmas and the New Year in the country. But what with the arrangements for my dance and all the new clothes to be fitted, everything's running a bit late this year . . . where will you go for your honeymoon, do you think?'

'Maurice has an aunt living in Torquay who's tentatively invited us to stay. She has a large house on the Esplanade. Actually, I'm not very keen. But Maurice says we'll offend her if we go somewhere else.'

'That's blackmail. And it's *your* honeymoon.'

Unnoticed by either of them on the other side of the restaurant, the two young men watched as Frances and Laura laughed and chatted over their meal. His dark eyes still on Frances, one of them took out his cigarettes and lighter.

'If you admire her so much, Robbie, why don't you go over and introduce yourself?' There was an underlying but distinct hint of sarcasm in his voice.

Robert Carr's fair skin flushed. 'I can't do that; we've spoken more

201

than half a dozen words. Besides, she might not remember me at all.'

'Who's the dark-haired girl with her? I don't recall her face from any of the Cultranes' parties?'

Carr's pale blue-grey eyes were still fixed unwaveringly on Frances' face. 'I've no idea; I've never seen her before. Some debutante, I expect.'

'Well, are you going to whack up the ginger to go and talk to her or not? Faint heart never won fair lady, and all that rot.' Thomas Dreikhorn flicked his lighter and held it to the end of his cigarette. He tipped back his head. 'Do you want me to do it for you?'

Carr looked annoyed. 'Don't be stupid, Tom. You know it's not on. She's Cultrane's daughter, for christ's sake!'

'I know who's daughter she is, Robbie . . . but don't they say a cat can look at a king? What's in a title but words, anyhow? Cultrane never had to work for what he's got; it was all handed down to him. And one thing I'm not – which you well know because it was me who got you promoted from the Scottish Office – is stupid.'

Carr sighed and drank down his brandy. 'I'm sorry, I didn't mean it like that.' He took a cigarette from his cigarette case and let Dreikhorn light it for him. 'Things were going so well, until we lost the last election and Ramsay MacDonald got back into power, just when Baldwin had given me that Junior Ministry. Bloody rotten bad luck. If we'd stayed in office I'd have been in a senior place at the Treasury by now.'

'Labour won't stay in power for ever . . . things are already beginning to look bleak. Like the American Stock Exchange two months ago, it's inevitable that MacDonald is going to crash.'

Carr's eyes were still on the two young women. 'I just hope you're right, Tom. I want that ministry back and I want it as soon as Baldwin gets into power again and can give it to me. A year-and-a-half is a bloody long time to wait, just kicking your heels.'

'If you're wise you can use that time well.'

'What do you mean?'

Dreikhorn nodded towards the table across the restaurant. 'You could do a lot worse than ally yourself to the Cultranes; they're the ones who have real power. With her Father's backing you could end up in the Cabinet . . . eventually.' He smiled. 'And where you go, I follow. I helped you at the Scottish Office, now it's your turn to help me. Agreed?' He flicked the ash from his cigarette. 'These things take

202

time . . . unfortunately; the qualifications for Cabinet Minister are a little more than youth and good looks.'

'More's the pity!'

'A pity your present lord and master isn't of the same persuasion as Lord Leith at the Scottish Office.'

Carr remained silent.

'Well, I can see it's going to be left to me, as usual, to direct operations here.' He caught the waiter's attention and asked for their bill. 'Pay this and then we can both be pleasantly surprised on our way out when we quite by chance catch sight of Lady Frances Osborne and Friend . . . and pause to renew the aquaintance. He took a ten shilling note from his wallet and they both got up. 'Don't look too eager . . . she might get suspicious. Women are like that.'

'But I thought the Cultranes had their eye on Lord Iden's heir for her?'

Dreikhorn tut-tutted without moving his lips. 'All the more reason for us to make sure that *she* has her eye on you.'

Frances caught sight of them as they came in the direction of her table on their way towards the exit. Robert Carr spoke first. 'What an unexpected pleasure . . . Lady Frances, isn't it? Lady Cultrane very graciously invited me and Thomas Dreikhorn here to several of her parties . . . and I have seen you – at a distance unfortunately – since. Please give her and Lord Cultrane my very best regards.'

Frances smiled; yes, she did remember him. Her eyes moved beyond him to where Thomas Dreikhorn was standing. Why was it that whenever she saw him, even at a distance, he had the knack of making her feel distinctly uncomfortable? Was it the dark hair and brown eyes because they reminded her of Kit or was it something else?

'I'm pleased to see you again, Mr Carr, Mr Dreikhorn.' She turned to Laura. 'Mr Carr was a Junior Minister at the Treasury before we lost the last election; Mr Dreikhorn is a colleague. Gentlemen, may I introduce my friend, Miss Laura Asmussen?'

They both smiled in her direction.

'Is your father in politics, Miss Asmussen?'

'No, in banking.'

'Ah, the banks,' Thomas Dreikhorn said, with a look of amusement in his eyes that left Laura wondering if he was mocking them or not. 'The mainstay of society. What would we do without them?' He looked directly at Laura. 'And what does your father think of the Wall Street Crash, Miss Asmussen?'

'He thinks it's most unfortunate for the Americans.'

Dreikhorn laughed, showing white, even teeth. 'It's been a pleasure meeting you, Miss Asmussen. Lady Frances.' They went on their way while the two girls stared after them.

'Well, I'll bet that one's a ladies' man,' Laura burst out as soon as they were out of earshot. 'And doesn't he know it, too!'

'What did you think of Robert Carr?'

'Handsome. Maybe . . . a little unsure of himself with women . . . but he looked far too young to be in such a high office.'

'Daddy says he proved such a wizard at the Scottish Office that if he'd stopped there he would have taken over Lord Leith's job.'

'And where does the other one come in?'

'Thomas Dreikhorn? Well, he worked there first – in fact it was through his influence because they'd been at Oxford together – that Robert Carr got there at all. Apparently he proved such a financial genius that he ended up overtaking everyone else . . . Lord Leith thought very highly of his ability. But he doesn't seem to me to be the usual egotistic, pushing type that most young politicians are . . . and I find that rather endearing. Anyone can see at a glance that Thomas Dreikhorn is a conceited know-all.'

'Like the two ladies who couldn't take their eyes off him as he walked past their table?' They both erupted into giggles and lowered their voice. 'Heavens! Wait until I tell Maurice's parents tonight! When they hear that I met a Junior Minister – well, an ex-Junior Minister, today – my future mother-in-law will make certain the entire road knows by this time tomorrow!'

'She sounds perfectly frightful!'

'She's very sweet, really, but I don't think she's ever had a mind of her own. Everything Maurice's Father says, she inevitably agrees with, like an echo. Unfortunately, I strongly suspect that they'll expect me to be like that, too. And I won't.'

'I'm sure Maurice would much prefer a wife with a bit of spirit.'

'Yes, up to a point. As long as it never clashed with his.'

Elizabeth was startled, unpleasantly, when she heard her husband's, then Seddon's voices down below in the hall. He should have been at a party meeting all afternoon and well into the evening. That was what he had told her this morning at breakfast. A swift stab of fear . . . did he suspect something? Had he come back, suddenly, unannounced, so that he could check up on her?

It was essential to keep calm, to behave as normally as possible.

But she was already late for her rendezvous with Eddie Vaux at Anne Turner's house in Putney, and she could hear Banbury's slow, laboured, heavy footsteps coming up the stairs. Somehow she kept the hand that was putting on her scarlet lipstick steady. She pretended complete astonishment when he appeared in the open doorway of her room.

'Darling! What a surprise. I was just off to Marshal and Snelgrove to pick up a few odds and ends . . . Cynthia Moseley said she *might* run into me at Brown's Hotel for afternoon tea.' She knew immediately that he suspected nothing by the way he kissed her. Inwardly, she shuddered at the touch of those flaccid, grey-tinged lips. 'I thought you were meant to be at some boring meeting?'

'It finished early, with not a little acrimony. Quite a few of the younger chaps simply don't see eye to eye with Baldwin. He isn't sufficiently right-wing for their liking.' She went on carefully applying her make-up in the mirror while he stood watching her. 'You know, Elizabeth . . . do you really think Cynthia is quite the sort of person you ought to be associating with? She's gone quite potty over the Socialists . . .'

'Oh, nonsense! I'm sure it's just one of her passing phases. I simply can't shun her altogether!' Elizabeth had caught sight of her wristwatch. She should have been in Putney fifteen minutes ago, and he was showing no signs of leaving.

'Did you come back here for something special, darling?'

'Only to see if some constituency papers I've been expecting arrived by the lunchtime post. But Seddon says not.' From the dressing-room, Sabine came in carrying her white fox fur coat, matching hat and white kid gauntlet gloves. 'You look especially glamorous for an afternoon's shopping at Marshal and Snelgrove.'

She laughed a little nervously. 'Got to keep up my image, darling. . . . Débutante of the Year and all that . . . What are you going to do? Back to another boring old meeting?'

'I've some constituency matters to sort out at my office, but I shall be home early this evening.' She tried to keep a straight face; this was nothing short of a disaster. After what he'd said at breakfast this morning, she'd arranged to spend the entire evening in bed with Eddie Vaux. Masterfully, she concealed her bitter disappointment. 'Well . . . that's wonderful! It's so long since they let you come home at a decent hour. The only trouble is . . . when you told me you were working late tonight I rather thought I'd go to Ciro's with the Bradley-Martins . . .'

He bent down and kissed the top of her head. 'I'd really much rather spend a quiet evening at home with you, darling . . . perhaps you'd ring her up and cancel it?'

'Of course.' She stood up, and Sabine helped her into her coat. She adjusted her hat in the mirror, biting back her furious anger, 'Well, I'd better be off, then.'

'I've got the car outside; I can get Philipps to drop you off right outside the store.'

She turned and faced him with a fixed smile. 'But it's in the opposite direction to where you're going . . .'

'That doesn't matter a jot. Philipps can come back when he's taken me to Westminster, and wait for you. If I can manage to get through those bally papers in an hour or two I might even join you and Cynthia at Brown's for tea.'

'Well, I might not meet up with her. It was just a tentative arrangement, really . . .' She was careful to keep her face straight and her false smile bright. 'You know what I'm like when I'm shopping.'

'I do indeed, my darling. I do indeed.'

'Elizabeth, calm down!'

'Calm down? He's ruined my entire evening, that's what he's done! God, how I detest him!' Angrily, she peeled off her gloves and flung them onto a chair. 'I had to endure the entire ride to Regent Street in the thick of the lunchtime traffic, and pretend to go into Marshal and Snelgrove until I saw them drive away. I had the most *awful* trouble getting a taxi!'

'It doesn't matter. You're here now. And Eddie's late.'

'Why is he late? Hasn't he telephoned? Suppose something's gone wrong?'

'Sit down and have a drink.'

'You'd better make it a stiff double brandy.'

'Why, are you celebrating something?'

'You could say that.' A pause while they looked at each other. 'I'm pregnant.'

'*Elizabeth* . . . !'

'Don't worry. It isn't his . . . it's Eddie's.' A brief smile of satisfaction. 'If it was his I think I'd have been sorely tempted to beg Simon to get rid of it for me.'

'How can you be so sure when you've been sleeping with both of them?' A mild look of amusement.

'Because I am. Ever since I got married, I've kept a diary . . . well, not a diary exactly. A sort of record book . . . the dates when I've slept with Eddie, the dates when I've had to endure *him*. Simon told me how to calculate the times when I'm most likely to conceive . . . certain days in the month, about four altogether, when it's most likely to happen. Banbury was away in Kent for two weeks and I slept with Eddie several times . . . so it has to be his.'

Anne Turner went and poured out two large glasses of brandy. 'Are you going to tell him?'

'Eddie? Well, of course! It's his, isn't it? If he thought there was any possibility of it being William's, he'd be frightfully jealous.'

'Well . . . congratulations.' They touched glasses. Anne Turner lit a cigarette. 'Now you've got two reasons to celebrate, haven't you?'

'Two?'

'I told you that when you gave him the son and heir he's always longed for – the son and heir his first wife couldn't give him – you'd be able to twist him around your little finger. And the second. That's really best of all.' She smiled her sickly-sweet smile, as if she was flattering a New Bond Street client. 'Now that you're having a baby, he'll have to leave you alone, won't he? No more of those ghastly nocturnal slobberings and other disgusting things he tries to do to prolong his pleasure.' Casually, she sipped the brandy. 'You'll point that out to him, won't you?'

24

'You went to lunch again, at the Savoy Restaurant, with Lady Frances Osborne?' Ida Flavel looked across the dinner table at Laura with rounded eyes, then she smiled; she adored the Royal Family and the aristocracy, every little snippet of information, wherever it came from, was like grist to her mill. Already, all the neighbours along the street knew that her son's fiancée worked for the famous couturier and Court Dressmaker, Mrs Anne Turner, and counted the Earl of Cultrane's youngest daughter, whose bridesmaid's gown for her sister's wedding she'd helped to make, among her closest friends. To be on terms of anything approaching intimacy with a peer of the realm's daughter, to come in daily contact with titled ladies who were household names and had actually dined with the Prince of

Wales, seemed absolutely incredible. And this was the girl who was engaged to be married to her Maurice.

'I expect the food's *wonderful* in there . . . the Savoy, I mean. Well, it would be, wouldn't it?'

Somehow Laura managed to repress a smile. They were all watching her. 'I daresay you could teach their French chef a thing or two!'

'Oh, go on!' Mrs Flavel almost blushed. 'I wouldn't know what to do with myself in a place like that. It must have been lovely for you, being asked out to lunch with Lady Frances . . .'

'She often invites me. She's one of the most generous and nicest people I've ever met. I liked her from the first moment I met her.'

'Her photograph's always in all the papers and magazines . . . I've saved them all to show you . . . she's certainly a lovely-looking young woman. I expect she'll marry someone high up, like her sister did. You know, somebody with a title.'

Laura lay down her knife and fork. 'I really couldn't say.'

'After she's . . . how do they call it? Presented, that's the word . . . you know, when all the cars line up along the Mall and all the débutantes have to go to Buckingham Palace in long white dresses and curtsey to the King and Queen . . . then they go to all those posh dances . . . I expect her family'll find a nice husband for her, then. I mean to say, with her being who she is, they'd want her to marry well. Not anyone ordinary, if you take my meaning.'

Laura was beginning to find the conversation a little tiresome. 'I can't imagine anybody making Frances marry someone she didn't want to, titled, ordinary, or not.'

Maurice distracted his mother's attention and rescued her. 'Well, now we're all here I might as well tell you my news.' He was beaming, looking particularly pleased with himself. He looked at Laura and winked. 'I've been bursting to tell you ever since you arrived, but I wanted to find the right moment . . .'

'Maurice, what have you been up to?'

'Got into Mr Keither's good books, that's what. From the first Monday of next month, I've been promoted in status with a salary rise accordingly. What a start to the new year!' He took Laura's hand and squeezed it. 'Now we can set a definite date for the wedding!'

'Oh, Maurice!' She was delighted more for him than for herself. 'I'm so pleased for you.'

'You've certainly worked hard for it, my boy,' Gerald Flavel said.

'You'll have a June wedding, won't you? June's a wonderful month for a wedding, and it's lucky too . . .'

'Mother, you and your silly superstitions!'

His sister joined in, everyone making suggestions at the same time, so that in the end Laura wanted to scream.

'I'd love June, yes,' Maurice said as soon as they'd all quietened down. 'But I think September would probably be better all round . . . from Laura's point of view.' They exchanged affectionate glances. 'I know how conscientious she is about her job; and I'm sure that the summer is Mrs Turner's busiest period . . . if Laura can give her as much notice as possible, I'm certain she'll appreciate it. Besides which, she's very generously offered to produce the wedding gown and the gowns for the bridesmaids as a gift.'

Laura had gone very quiet.

'Maurice, I thought we'd already talked about this. It would be madness for me to give up a marvellously well paid job before we're ready to start a family. With us both working, we could pay off a mortgage on one of those terraced houses in Holland Park in no time!' An uncomfortable silence had fallen around the table. 'I thought you'd agreed . . .'

'I'm sorry, Laura, but I'm totally against it. I've already made my views about working wives perfectly clear. It isn't as if you *have* to work after we're married. We'd be jolly comfortable *without* my promotion.'

'Oh yes, dear,' Ida Flavel said, and her husband nodded in agreement. 'Maurice is right. You surely couldn't think of going out to work after you're married, not when he's in the position he's in. You'll need all your time, I can tell you, to see to the running of the home.'

Laura took a deep breath. 'Maurice,' her voice was very soft but he heard the note of determination in it. 'I think we ought to talk very seriously about this.'

'What is there to talk about? I assumed you took it for granted that once we were married, you'd stop working for Mrs Turner. In fact, two or even three months before would be better still, to give you time to prepare for the wedding. Are you suggesting that without your income we won't be able to manage?'

'I didn't mean that at all . . . it isn't any reflection on your ability to support a wife. Maurice, please don't be silly. It's simply that I enjoy working there so much, and I do earn a very good salary.' She

209

could feel their disapproval crowding in on her. 'Do we have to continue this discussion now?'

'It appears to me that you've forgotten one extremely important thing in all this . . . who, pray tell me, will be running the home while both of us are out at work all day?'

'Well, we'd employ a cook-general, of course, what else? With us both working we could afford it.' His mother and sisters looked appalled.

'I see. So when I arrive home from the office I shan't find my wife waiting to greet me . . . just a cook-general?'

'Maurice, I think you're being completely unreasonable . . .'

'I'm sorry, but it's out of the question; as soon as we've fixed a firm date for the wedding, I shall expect you to tender your resignation to Mrs Turner.'

For a long moment she made no answer. They were all watching her, waiting for her to react. 'That was a delicious meal, Mrs Flavel.' Calmly, she put her napkin on the table. She took a deep breath. 'I feel like going for a walk, Maurice. Will you come with me?'

'A walk? But it's dark. And it's just started snowing again.'

'I always find going for a walk in cold weather helps me to clear my head.'

She was unfamiliar with the district, but she kept on walking; briskly, hands inside the deep pockets of her coat, her large fur collar drawn up around her face and chin. For several minutes neither of them spoke. She was only aware of the sharp tapping of her heels on the pavement and the whirling flakes of snow. She could have gone on walking for miles.

'Maurice, I'm sorry. I didn't want to start an argument, especially not in front of your family. But I meant what I said. I don't want to leave New Bond Street when we get married; I don't want to leave until we start a family. For me to stay at home all day doing nothing but being bored out of my mind would be completely pointless for both of us.' She didn't look at him. She was too busy concentrating on not slipping on the icy ground. 'I wish I could make you understand how I feel.'

'Being my wife and running my home won't be enough for you?' His voice was as cold and cutting as the chilly night air. 'I really do wish that you'd told me all this before.'

She stopped walking. 'I did. I tried to. But you seemed to assume that I'd just give in and do exactly what you wanted in the end.

Don't make me sound like some Suffragette, Maurice . . . of course I want to run your home, *our* home. Of course I want to set a date for the wedding as soon as possible. But my job is important to me . . .'

'More important than me?' His tone was petulant.

'No, of course not. But why are you so adamant that I give up working now? Why can't we wait?' His stubborn refusal to see her point of view was beginning to irk her. He'd always seemed so tolerant, reasonable. 'Maurice, *please?*'

'People will think I can't support my own wife.'

'Oh, is that what this is all about?' She was angry now. 'What *other people* think.' She looked up through the falling snow, catching sight of the lights from the Flavel's sitting-room through the curtains up ahead. Someone was standing at the window, watching for them to come back. She could imagine only too well what they'd all been saying, and none of it complimentary. 'Let's not talk about it any more this evening; not in front of your family. I think we should both go away and think it all through . . .'

'If that's what you want.'

He helped her off with her coat in the hall and his parents and sisters looked up anxiously as they came back into the sitting room. They were on his side, of course; but she didn't intend to give in. She was remembering what Frances had said to her earlier, about women hanging on to their independence.

And, in any case, her mother and father, when she told them, would be bound to agree.

She was wrong. When Maurice had taken her home and she was sitting drinking hot cocoa by what was left of the fire, she was astonished at their reaction when she told them about their quarrel. She could scarcely believe her own ears.

'But of course you'll stop working, Laura! All girls stop working when they get married. My goodness, no wonder poor Maurice was so cross. Whatever would people think?'

'Mummy, it isn't anyone else's business, so I really don't see that it matters what "people" think. And are you on his side or mine?'

'Laura, kindly do *not* speak to your mother in that tone of voice.'

'I'm sorry, Daddy . . .'

'I'm not taking sides. I never do, you should know that. But I do happen to think Maurice is right and you're wrong. Young women who go out to work after marriage. Well . . . it isn't the done thing. In fact it's considered rather fast. A woman's place is in the home after she marries, supervising the household, taking on the responsibilities of managing a home. It isn't something that can be done in half an hour: of course, you have no idea of the amount of work running a home of your own is going to entail.'

'You're jolly lucky to be marrying a fine young chap like Maurice Flavel, my girl. Thank your lucky stars. He comes from a very good family, he has an excellent position with very bright prospects . . .'

'Mr and Mrs Wintringham at The Oaks, in Fairlawn Avenue . . . you know that she's Chairwoman of the Kilburn Ladies' Guild? Well, her daughter Louisa is engaged to a young man in an accountant's office in the City . . . she happened to let slip to me at our coffee morning in the church hall last week that even after passing a special examination, his salary is only two thirds of Maurice's. You simply don't realize how lucky you are, Laura.'

'If Kit was here, he'd agree with me.'

'Kit is completely irresponsible and what he thinks or does not think on this subject is entirely irrelevant. I can't even remember the last time he bothered to write to us.'

'Daddy, he writes to *me*, and I show you the letters.'

'He should write regularly to *us*. But of course that would be too much to expect!'

Laura sighed; she was tired, she was worn out with arguing with Maurice and now her parents. All she wanted to do was to go to bed. But in her mind she'd already made at least one decision.

'Daddy, I've meaning to talk to you about this, I suppose now isn't the ideal time because it's nearly ten o'clock and we both have to be up for work in the morning. But this argument with Maurice about whether or not I should leave Mrs Turner's when we get married . . . well, it's made me think hard about something else.' They were both looking at her with puzzled expressions on their faces; was she about to do the entirely unthinkable and break off her engagement? 'I did have a letter from Kit a few weeks ago . . . the first in a long while. And it did make me realize how much I miss him; after all, it's been more than two years now. Because he has his own band and lots of commitments, it wouldn't be possible for him to come home to see us. At least not for a long while. Perhaps for the wedding.' Relief on both their faces. 'He said that if I wanted to go and see him, he'd wire the fare for my ticket.' She paused, knowing that both of them would immediately oppose the whole idea. 'I'd like to go. If Mrs Turner could give me a few weeks off in the New

212

Year . . . not just to see Kit again, but to sort out how I feel about giving up my job for good.'

They both spoke at once. 'You can't possibly go to a place like Chicago, Laura! All those gangsters. . . .'

'Mummy, I'm sure it's all exaggerated.'

'It's completely out of the question. A young woman travelling alone on a liner, halfway across the world? Anything might happen.'

'But lots of people do it! Lots of Frances Osborne's friends . . . she's told me. In fact it's quite the rage among the young Mayfair set.'

'You are *not* a member of the "young Mayfair set", they're quite different. They have maids, chaperones.'

'But Kit would be there to meet me when the ship docked.'

'Laura, I simply can't allow it. Think of your reputation, for goodness sake. What would people think? What would the Flavels think? We have a certain position in the district, after all . . .'

'I'm sure Jessie would agree to accompany her,' Violet Asmussen said suddenly. 'Richard? If a few weeks away would help her to see how ridiculous this idea of working after the wedding is . . . I'm sure she'd be happy to act as chaperone. And it would be comforting to have first-hand news of how Kit is . . . he never was a great letter-writer.'

'Aunt Jessie?'

'She lost your uncle last year, so she doesn't have any ties. I could write to her tomorrow.' She was waiting for her husband to show his approval, but he was still thinking out the implications in his mind.

'Daddy?'

'I'd go myself, Richard, but . . .'

'You most certainly will *not* go yourself. If your sister agrees to chaperone Laura and she's still of the same mind when the time comes to go swanning off to see Kit, that is one thing; for us to be forced to cancel all our social and domestic arrangements on a whim is quite out of the question.'

'Then I can go, Daddy?' She was having difficulty in holding back the excitement in her voice. 'I can write to Kit and tell him I'm coming?'

'If you're certain that's what you want to do . . . and if your aunt Jessie agrees to come with you. *Only* if she agrees, mind you.'

Laura flung her arms around his neck and kissed him. 'Daddy, how can I ever thank you?'

'By telling Maurice that you intend to do as he wishes. Remember

213

the words in the marriage service, Laura. A wife promises her husband to love, honour, and obey.'

Upstairs, alone in her room, she took out the pile of letters from her brother and re-read them all. A tear welled up in the corner of one eye; it was all there, from the very first day he'd arrived with Rudy in Chicago; all the disappointments, the trials and tribulations. Now and then, he'd mentioned a girl's name and Laura had read between the lines. Had he changed very much, she often wondered, from the Kit she'd known? People did, even the ones you'd loved and been close to. Was he still carefree, teasing, wonderfully easy to be with? Did he think of her a lot? By a conscious effort, she deliberately never mentioned Frances in any of her letters, and neither did he; she wondered if, after two years, he still felt guilty.

Carefully, she put the letters back into their envelopes and into the drawer where they were kept, then set her alarm clock twenty minutes earlier than the usual time.

She'd write to him before breakfast and post the letter on her way to work . . . how long would it take to reach him?

She got into bed and sat up against the pillows for a while, watching the snow falling steadily outside her window. Then she wondered how she was going to break the news about going to Chicago to Maurice.

Thomas Dreikhorn lay full-length on the leather couch, a cigarette half-smoked in one hand, a double brandy in the other. He was dictating a letter. Robert Carr sat at the writing table across the room, blank sheet of paper in front of him on the blotter, pen in hand. He was watching his friend's face earnestly.

'All right. That's the dutiful epistle to my unlamented distant cousin out of the way. Now, before we both fall asleep, what about the one you promised to help me with to her?'

Dreikhorn hooted with laughter; he was enjoying himself. 'No letter, Robbie. I've given it a lot of thought. A letter's too . . . dramatic, at this stage. You mustn't show her you're too interested. You mustn't let her know how eager to further the aquaintance you really are. After all, three-quarters of the bachelors in London are going to be hot on her heels after she's been presented at Court. If you play the game with subtlety, you'll leave them all standing. With me at hand to steer you in the right direction, of course.'

'All right, what are you suggesting I do, then?'

214

'You've got to impress her, but do it in a way that she'll remember when she's forgotten all the others. Remember . . . flattery will get you everywhere with women – they're so vain they believe every single word you say – provided it's never overdone. Be restrained. Low key. No purple passages. Flowers, as I suggested, and just the very briefest of notes . . . or a small verse. Something different . . . that's what she'll appreciate most.'

'What kind of flowers should I send her?'

Dreikhorn raised his eyebrows; sometimes Robbie could be very dim. 'Roses, of course. White, not red. And in a basket not a bouquet.'

'I'll do it first thing in the morning.'

'Write the card yourself. Put something like . . .' he thought for a few moments, even when he was tired after a long day behind a treasury desk, the quick, clever brain that never deserted him continued to work on. It was only the merest quirk of fate that Robbie had done much better than he had; but then his own dark good looks hadn't been as appealing as his friend's blue-eyed fair ones to the chief font of power at the Scottish Office in Edinburgh. A pity. More often than not, Robbie could be remarkably slow on the uptake. Like now. One didn't need to like women to be able to understand them. 'Shakespeare . . . who better to path the way for you to the lady's good graces?' Robbie looked at his friend gratefully; of course, one never knew when Tom was being sarcastic. 'Let's see. Ah, I know the very thing. *Let none say more than this rich praise; that you alone are you.* And your signature.' He smiled complacently. 'Then let fate take it's course. You'll see.'

Carr began to write, laboriously. 'Sorry, Tom . . . can you repeat the first line? I didn't quite get it all.'

Dreikhorn repeated the phrase slowly, clearly, without a hint of the impatience he was feeling. At last Carr glanced up, obviously pleased with his efforts.

'You don't suppose her father might object, do you? After all, even though we've been invited to her mother's political evening parties several times, she hasn't been officially brought out.'

'All to the better. That gives you four and a half months to get ahead of the Opposition'

'Maybe they've already got a husband picked out for her.'

Dreikhorn ground his cigarette into the ashtray on the floor. 'Don't be so bloody pessimistic! She liked you, I could tell. Nothing new in that; most women do, and don't say you haven't noticed.'

'I was still only Junior Minister in the last government.'

'But rising. And you've got an extra arrow in your quiver that counts for a very great deal with the Osbornes . . . your cousin's title. When the cancer that's been crippling him for more than a year finally kills him – and you know what his doctor told you himself – you'll be the next Earl of Rosslare.'

'Yes . . .'

'Come on, Robbie; he never meant anything to you. How many times in your life have you even been under the same roof? It isn't like you to be morbid. In any case, it'll be a happy release – think of it this way. He's spent the last eight months of his life as an invalid under morphine. And we all have to die sometime . . . even you. So enjoy all nature's bounties while you can get your hands on them.'

'You're right – as always.' Carr smiled, a little wearily. Four late nights in a row didn't agree with him. 'Let's have another glass of brandy before you go . . . or don't go, if you don't want to. You can always sleep on the sofa.'

Dreikhorn came to stand behind him, looking down over his shoulder at what he had written. He put a hand on his arm and held it there, just a fraction too long.

'Can't do that . . . what would the other tenants think? And Stanley Baldwin only lives a few doors away.' He laughed, softly. 'We have to think of your reputation.'

25

The basket of white roses arrived at the same time as Elizabeth.

'My goodness, I only left William half an hour ago and he had an appointment at Harley Street on the way back to Westminster. Talk about being a fast worker.' Madders tried to speak but she forestalled him. 'Oh, they're simply lovely. He knew I was on my way here to see you . . . that's why he sent them.'

Madders coughed and cleared his throat. 'The flowers are for Lady Frances, my lady.'

'What?'

'The basket of flowers has been sent to Lady Frances.' Frances had come out into the hall behind her mother and he held an envelope out to her. 'May I take your coat, my lady?'

Elizabeth pouted. 'Well, so they're not from William after all! My mistake.' She looked frostily at her younger sister. 'Aren't you going to tell us who sent them?'

Slowly, Frances broke open the envelope and read the neat, rounded handwriting on the card inside. She looked up, smiling. 'They're from Robert Carr.' Her mother and sister exchanged glances.

'Robert Carr? Isn't he one of your protégés, Mummy?'

'Not exactly . . . he had a Junior Ministry in Baldwin's last government; before that he was one of Leith's bright young men at the Scottish Office in Edinburgh, then he was promoted and came south. He's been rising fast ever since.'

'Isn't he related to the Rosslares?'

'A cousin. But next in line for the title. Rosslare's been in bad health for the last few years. From all accounts he's practically a recluse.'

'So young Carr's quite a catch, then?' Elizabeth was impressed. 'Is he good looking?'

'Most of the young women in London seem to think so.'

'Well, aren't you going to satisfy our curiosity and show us the card?'

'It *was* addressed to me.' Frances spoke quietly and politely, but her sister recognized the steel at the back of her voice. She shrugged. 'Sorry for asking.'

Katherine Cultrane turned to Madders. 'Get someone to put them in water, will you? And please bring in the tea.'

'Yes, my lady.'

Frances smiled at him and cradled the basket in her arms. 'It's all right, Madders. I'll see to them myself.'

She walked through the hall towards the garden room, wanting to be alone. Closing the door behind her, she set down the basket of roses on the tressle table and stood looking at them for a moment, then down at the card in her hand. It was the first time, since Kit had impulsively bought her a bunch of out-of-season violets from a street vendor in Green Park, that a man had given her flowers; the memory of the violets, like Kit, still hurt; she remembered hiding them inside her coat when she'd come home, keeping them beside her bed until they'd withered and died, then pressing them, lovingly, in the pages of a book of Christina Rossetti poems that her godfather Thomas Holland had given her. She could even remember the page, and the lines. *No sad songs* . . . the violets were still there, in the book. But she never looked at them.

She willed the image of his face away and replaced it in her mind with Robert Carr's. There was something solid and dependable about him, something she liked, something she felt she could trust. She must write a note to him and thank him . . .

The tea tray had arrived when she went back downstairs to see her sister.

'Well, there you are at long last! Come in and sit down so that I can tell you as well as mother my marvellous news.' Her long, slim legs were crossed elegantly; a Turkish cigarette was burning in her ivory and platinum holder.

'I'm sorry if I was a long time. I wanted to write a note to Robert Carr.'

'I'm afraid my first piece of news won't be much to your liking, but it really can't be helped. I shan't be able to stand in for Mummy when she can't chaperone you for the Season . . .' she smiled, clearly vastly pleased with herself. 'I won't be able to because Paul Lobell's just confirmed that William and I are definitely expecting the Banbury heir!' The expression on her mother's face never altered. Frances looked momentarily stunned, then congratulated her.

'That's why you thought my roses were for you, wasn't it? You thought William had sent them.'

'I must confess to being a trifle disappointed. Still, I expect the idea will come to him when he's knee deep in boring constituency papers in his office.' She dotted ash from her cigarette. 'I think he was so completely taken aback with the news that every other thought was erased from his head.'

Katherine Cultrane picked up her tea cup very slowly. 'Wonderful news, of course. I must telephone your father. An heir for the Banbury estate at last. Congratulations, darling.'

'Aren't I clever? Just think how long poor William was married to his first wife with nothing at all to show for it. I daresay the whole of Whitehall knows the news by now.'

'When did Paul Lobell say it's due?'

'July, of all months. Beastly bad luck, isn't it? I'd much rather have a winter baby and enjoy at least *some* of the Season. No Ascot next year. And I was so looking forward to it.'

Only Elizabeth saw her mother's expression. 'What a pity you and William didn't manage the timing a little better, then. Still, better luck next time round.'

Elizabeth deftly changed the subject. 'You must *all* come to my last dinner party in town before we leave for the Hall. Goodness, I hope those horrid little country roads won't be completely covered in snow. Frances, you're not absolutely desolate that I can't step in for Mummy over the chaperone thing, are you? I'm sure Cynthia Moseley would be delighted to oblige if Mummy telephones and explains what's happened . . . anyhow, I've asked her and David to my dinner party, so you could sort it all out then.'

'No, of course I don't mind.'

Katherine Cultrane had got purposefully to her feet. 'Why don't we telephone her now?'

'So, it's due in July?' Katherine closed the study door and leaned against it; Elizabeth felt trapped. 'It's Eddie Vaux's isn't it? Not Banbury's at all.'

Elizabeth perched herself on the edge of her father's desk. 'Not William's? I'm sure I don't know what you mean by that, Mummy.'

'Don't get clever with me. I know you too well. If you'd conceived a child on your honeymoon it would have been his, because Eddie Vaux was in England. But this one isn't.'

'Your proof?' She was infuriatingly cool and collected.

'The proof will be when it's born and shows a distinct dissimilarity to its putative father.'

'You're determined to spoil this for me, aren't you? You seem to conveniently forget that Eddie happens to be a Vaux too; his grand-father was William's father. There's almost bound to be a family likeness . . . unless it turns out to be blond and blue-eyed like me.'

'You're very smug, aren't you? And very sure of yourself. Be warned. If Banbury ever finds out about the double game you're playing not only is your marriage over but your father's political relationship with him would be damaged beyond repair. And I don't need to remind you what that means. The family name, our reputation . . .'

'Mummy, spare me the lecture!'

'. . . at the moment Labour are in power, but the situation is changing drastically . . . the next government could be either Conservative or even a national Coalition – that can't be ruled out. Whatever happens, I mean to see your father back in high office. Put that in jeopardy by cuckolding Banbury and I promise you, you'll bitterly regret it.'

'Do you really care if I'm happy or not, except for the benefits my marrying Banbury brought you and Daddy?'

'Not particularly. But that isn't the point, is it?'

'Is there anything that you really care about?'

'My generation, unlike yours, my dear, was brought up to put duty to the family above any other consideration. Even at the expense of personal happiness.' Unwillingly, she thought of her hopeless girlish passion for Thomas Holland. 'You really don't know the meaning of making personal sacrifices at all . . .'

He arrived a few minutes before seven o'clock and was astonished to find the drawing room empty. She stepped back from her bedroom window, hiding herself behind the velvet drapes where she'd been keeping watch in the street outside for his car.

She heard his voice calling to Seddon, then the sound of him coming slowly and heavily up the stairs. Jumping back into bed and pulling the covers up to her chin, she made a quick knowing sign to Sabine.

He almost burst into the room, his face beaming; then he frowned when he saw Sabine holding a cloth soaked in eau de cologne to her head.

'Darling, Seddon told me that you'd gone to bed! Whatever is it?'

'Just a headache, darling . . . and I've been feeling a little queasy. Paul Lobell said that I have to take care of myself.'

'Of course, of course . . .' he came and sat down on the chair beside the bed. The very nearness of him, the smell of pipe tobacco that hung about his clothes and clung to his hair made her feel sick. Sabine moved away noiselessly; she began folding up Elizabeth's silk underclothes on the other side of the room. 'Let Sir Theodore Mayerne come and have a look at you . . .'

'William, he's your doctor; I've always told you that I prefer my own. Paul Lobell's looked after me since I was a child.'

'It never hurts to have a second opinion.'

'I don't want a second opinion and I don't need one. I'm perfectly satisfied with the one I have.' She was watching his face carefully now. 'I might as well tell you that he advised that we sleep separately for the time being . . .'

Banbury's face turned blood red. 'Whatever for?'

'Sabine, you can leave that.' She waited for a moment, knowing that Sabine would be behind the dressing room door listening to every word, ready to come back at exactly the right moment as she'd been told to. 'William, it isn't simply what Lobell advised, it's how I feel. Besides which, we can't possibly risk anything happening to the baby after you've waited so long for an heir, can we?'

220

Banbury stood up, trying to contain his anger at what she was suggesting. 'Am I to understand that you're refusing yourself to me? I particularly asked Mayerne about the subject and he said there was no reason at all . . .'

'Well, he would, wouldn't he? He's your man. Paul Lobell is mine. And I'm sure you wouldn't like me to have to ask him if some of your personal practices are safe for the child or not?' She suppressed a smile. 'I see we understand each other.' As if on cue, Sabine appeared in the doorway holding a tall crystal carafe of water. 'I'm sorry, darling . . . for the time being I'm afraid you'll have to sleep in your dressing-room. I've already told Smithers to move all your things.'

'As you think best.' He moved towards the door. 'I'm sorry you're not feeling well, my dear . . . so I'll leave you to rest. And I'll be having dinner at my club.'

26

The room was stiflingly hot and airless, everywhere except the stage shadowy and dimly-lit. The black barmen sat around in groups, a few stragglers who knew the musicians in the band had stayed behind, as late as it was now, to listen.

'OK, you guys. We'll go through the numbers one more time.' Perspiration soaked Kit's hair and stood out in beads along his forehead. 'We don't quit tonight until every bit's note-perfect. You got it?'

Ben De Haan slumped over the keys of his piano, nodding wearily. 'Kit, we've been over every goddam piece for the last six hours, for Christ's sake; what d'you want . . . blood?'

Tension, exhaustion, something deep inside himself that drove him relentlessly on and on, made Kit snap back, brusquely. 'We'll stop when I say we stop and not one bloody minute before – OK? You guys fuck this recording session up tomorrow and I'll wrap your instruments around your heads!'

'OK, OK, so we'll do it all again . . .' De Haan picked up his music. 'Who cares if I drop down dead?'

'You don't need the music . . . you should know it all off by heart.'

Rudy Loew walked back towards the stage from the bar. 'Ready when you are, Kit. Are we recording tomorrow in the same order that we've been rehearsing tonight?'

'We start off with my re-write of *Maple Leaf Rag*; then *Shada, Sweetie Dear, Hurricane Blues, Dark-Town Strutters Ball*. The special piece. *Indian Summer*, then *One O'Clock Jump*. Think you can remember that?' His voice was deeply sarcastic but Rudy took no notice; they were all tired and irritable, Kit more than most; in between music sessions, playing all evening in the nightclubs in New Orleans, the endless succession of women and drinking more than Rudy thought was good for him, there wasn't much time left for sleep. He shrugged his shoulders and picked up his trombone; what Kit did was Kit's affair. It never affected his music or his almost fanatical perfectionism, and that was what counted. Kit was a real professional.

'OK. We'll take it from the top. *Shada* then *Maple Leaf Rag* one more time. We weren't all together on that on the last run through.' He glanced at his saxophone player, Johnny Pellini. 'Think you can remember to start off on A-major instead of D?'

'One more session like this one and I'll forget my own goddam name!'

'OK. Let's do it.'

All around them, the people who were left in the club had fallen silent. There were no clinking glasses, no scraping chairs. Kit picked up his clarinet from the top of the piano and took his place in the centre of the band.

'Ready when you are, Kit.'

His headache had got worse throughout the evening; now it was a tight, merciless collar of red-hot steel, cutting into his temples, clouding his eyes; he felt sick with exhaustion, thirst, lack of sleep. He couldn't remember the last time he'd eaten. He put the mouthpiece to his lips and closed his eyes, blotting out the dim lights, the moving sea of faces, the brash glitter of the instruments all around him, and felt his lungs fill with air, ready to play.

The music hypnotized him, pushed him on; like being in a state of trance, every loud, blaring note that came from the clarinet seemed to anaesthetize his pain. Why did he still think about her, why couldn't he drown the picture of her face in his mind that no amount of sex and whisky could erase? She was in the past, and the past was over, and he didn't believe in ghosts. So why, why, why, couldn't he forget?

It was almost, but not quite, dawn when they were finished; he watched them slowly file out of the half deserted clubroom with their instruments, Rudy the last to go.

'You coming, Kit? We all need some sleep before the recording session tomorrow . . . don't forget they want us there by eight.'

'I haven't forgotten. I'll be there.' He lay against the side of the bar while one of the barmen poured him a double whisky. From the shadows, the pretty girl in the white beaded dress came up to him and slipped her hand through his arm.

'See you tomorrow at eight, then.' Rudy gave him a weary smile and went out. In Montpellier Row he stopped and lit himself a cigarette, leaning against the wall while he smoked it. If Kit didn't lay off the whisky and the women he was going to go down for a fall.

The band was the biggest in New Orleans now, when the recordings were in the bag and the country-wide circulation began, things were bound to get even bigger; if Kit could hold himself together for long enough to make them happen. First class as all the musicians in the band were, Kit was the one that was special; without him, everything else fell apart.

Tomorrow he'd try and have a talk with him. Yes, tomorrow. It wasn't easy talking to Kit about personal things these days; he always took it the wrong way. But that's what friends were for, weren't they? And they'd been together, and been through a lot together, for a long, long time.

Rudy threw his half-smoked cigarette down in the gutter and walked on, in the direction of the hotel.

Kit lay back in the middle of the bed, a half full tumbler of whisky in his hand; he put it down on the table at his elbow and reached for his cigarettes.

'Kit, don't you think you've had enough of that stuff for one night? You said you had a headache back at the club. If you keep drinking straight sourmash one glass after another, you'll never wake up tomorrow.'

'Haven't you gone home, yet?' His lighter clicked in the darkness and she saw his strained, tired features illuminated by the single flame. 'The only thing that gives me a headache is your voice.' He was being cruel, callous, unreasonable, and he knew by the expression on her face that he'd hurt her; but he was past caring. She came towards him with the beads of her evening gown glittering in the weak light, sat down beside him on the bed and ran her hand soothingly, coaxingly, up and down his bare arm.

'I care about you, Kit.'

Through the haze of cigarette smoke he saw her face, framed by the cloud of soft, *clair brune* hair; her eyes were a very pale, luminous grey, like rabbit's fur, her lashes long and dark with mascara. A pretty face, a face you'd turn and look twice at. But the wrong face.

'If you came back with me because you thought I'd make love to you, forget it, Marcella. When I've finished this drink and this cigarette, it's lights out.'

'I thought you might need me, that's all. I thought you might want me to stay.' She slid her arms around his neck and kissed his cold, unresponsive lips. Her breath came in short, uneven little gasps. 'Kit, I want you so much . . . please let me stay with you . . . please let me . . .'

He pushed her away, swung his legs onto the floor and fished in the pocket of his evening jacket that was draped across a chair. 'Here!' He took out a bunch of keys and tossed them at her. 'Why don't you take my car and drive yourself home?'

'So how will you get to the session in the morning? Walk there?'

'I can ring Rudy and get him to pick me up.'

'I can't drive in these shoes.'

Kit shrugged. 'So drive in bare feet. There's no law against that, is there?'

Slowly, her face set with disappointment, Marcella put the keys on the table. She came back and stood close to him, so close that he could feel the warmth of her breath on his face. 'Let me stay, Kit. I'll make sure you get up on time in the morning; I always wake up early, remember? Even without an alarm.' She smiled at him and stroked his hair, but he brushed past her and walked away, back to the half drunk glass of sourmash whiskey. He took a long swig.

'If you don't want to take my car, take a cab instead.' He took out some cents from his pocket and flung them down. 'Just go, OK? I need to sleep.'

'Kit . . .'

He put the empty glass on the bedside table with a bang. 'See you around, baby.'

'I want to come back to Chicago with you when you go.'

He wasn't looking at her. 'We've talked about it before, and the answer's still the same. No way.' He sensed her lingering for a moment or two; then she picked up her fur wrap and the money on the table, and went out. Her shoes made a loud tapping sound on the stairs. Kit flung himself down, still fully dressed, and closed his eyes. In a minute, when he felt better, he'd get up and go to the bathroom and wash; in a minute he'd take off his clothes and go to bed. In a minute, when his head didn't ache so much, he'd get out the last letter Laura had written to him, and re-read it.

She never mentioned her name in any of the letters; never a single word. But, somehow, a sixth sense told him that they were still close friends. As he fell into a whiskey-sodden, restless sleep, her face with the halo of dark gold hair whirled around in his memory, the clear blue eyes swam out of the limbo of exhaustion and pain.

The special piece he'd written, the piece of music he'd so carefully composed that still had no name, that was hers. Frankie. Frances. Francesca. Latinized, nobody would ever guess. Except maybe Laura.

27

'Laura, you shouldn't have! But it's lovely.' Frances smiled and took the small, delicate pearl brooch fashioned into the letter 'F' from its case and pinned it to her dress. 'I'm going to wear it now – if you don't mind – even though I shouldn't have opened it for another ten days.'

'I didn't know what to get you. Then I just happened to stop and look in Jarrold's window in Charing Cross Road, and there it was. I'm glad you like it.'

Frances opened her handbag and took out a small, gift-wrapped box. 'An early Christmas present. I hope you like it as much as I like mine.'

'You shouldn't have!'

'Why not?'

Laura took it, a little hesitantly. 'I do hope you haven't spend an awful lot of money . . .'

'How does that prayer go that we used to have to recite at school assembly? Oh, yes; I remember. To give, and not to count the cost! Or something like that. I just spotted it when I was shopping and I thought it was just the thing for you. Green seems to suit you so well.'

Laura had opened the wrapping paper and was staring at the emerald earrings inside the box. 'Frances, you really oughtn't to have done this . . . they're absolutely beautiful!' She took one out and held it up and it glowed in the light. 'Goodness, they must have cost a fortune. Maurice will probably think I have a secret admirer!'

Frances sipped her tea. 'And has he come round to seeing things your way about staying on at work?'

'Not exactly. And what's more, Mummy and Daddy are on his side.'

'Surely they can see your point of view?'

'I think you're the only one who does. And my brother will.' All around them the sound of chatter and the clinking of cups and plates emphasized the sudden silence that had fallen between them as soon as Laura mentioned his name. 'I know Kit would understand. After all, he went to America because of his music. But then it's always easier for men to go off and do whatever they want to do, isn't it? We're the ones who are expected to give up things and conform.'

'Have you decided what you're going to do?'

'I suppose it would be fairer to both of us if we could agree on some sort of compromise. Maurice is adamant that I should give up working altogether at least a month or even two before the wedding. I really only want to give it up when I have to. I was thinking of asking Mrs Turner if I could design at home and take my work in to her once a week, but I haven't plucked up enough courage to ask her yet. Or tell Maurice.'

'It sounds perfectly fair to me . . . why should either of them object?'

'I'm beginning to find out, the longer I know him, that Maurice always expects to get his own way.'

'Then you'll just have to dig in your heels.'

Laura hesitated; the next thing was going to be difficult to tell her; she always fell silent at the mention of Kit's name. 'I thought I should mention that I'm going away for a few weeks in the new year. I'm going to see Kit in Chicago.' Frances looked startled for a moment. 'He wrote and asked me if I'd like to go a long while back, and I said I'd think about it. Mummy and Daddy made a dreadful fuss at first and gave all sorts of reasons why I couldn't even consider it; then Mummy saw how much it meant to me, and she suggested that if her sister could chaperone me, it would be all right.'

'I see.'

'My Aunt Jessie lives in Torquay. She's a widow; my cousins are all grown up so she doesn't have any ties. Mummy wrote to her last week and this morning she had an answer. She's agreed. So I've sent a cable to Kit.'

Frances looked down into the dregs of her tea cup to hide her expression.

'That's marvellous . . . I'm sure you'll have a wonderful time. As long as your Aunt Jessie isn't hopelessly stuffy.' She was trying to make her voice sound light, casual, as if the mention of Kit's name after all this time didn't still hurt her. 'I expect you'll find Chicago very different to London, though. But I'm sure all the things you read about it in the newspapers are dreadfully exaggerated.'

'Yes, that's what I tried to tell Mummy and Daddy.' Laura pulled a face as a sudden thought came to her. 'I'm really not looking forward to breaking the news to Maurice.'

'If he objects to you going so much, why doesn't he go with you?'

'Oh, he'd never leave that office of his. Work always comes first. Besides, with this early promotion he's just been given, it simply wouldn't do for him to be taking weeks off just to accompany me on what his boss would no doubt call a "frivolous, non-essential holiday".'

Frances laughed, and the slight tension since Kit's name had been spoken disappeared. 'That reminds me. Guess who sent me a basket of white roses recently?'

'The Earl of Iden's son? I can never remember his name.'

'Robert Carr.'

'The fair young man who spoke to you in the Savoy?'

'The very same.'

'Gracious!' A teasing smile. 'You're really quite taken with him, aren't you?'

'I have to admit I think he's rather interesting. Of course, Mummy and Daddy are all for encouraging him because he's the cousin of Lord Rosslare . . . who happens to be terminally ill and has no son to succeed to the title. When he dies, Robert will be the next Earl.'

Laura was immediately intrigued. 'Did he send a letter with the roses?'

'A card. It was quite funny, really. The roses arrived at the same time as my sister. Elizabeth thought her husband had sent them to her because she'd just told him she's going to have a baby, and he knew she'd be at Belgrave Square breaking the news to Mummy. She was quite picqued when Madders informed her that they were for me.'

'Your sister's having a baby? When?'

'Oh, she's only just found out. July, I think. She was terribly put out about it because it means she'll have to miss Ascot. But I'm sure my brother-in-law will be delighted; he was married to his first wife for years and she only had stillbirths and miscarriages, poor woman. Elizabeth won't be able to stand in as chaperone for my Season now; she was going to help out when Mummy couldn't do it. But Cynthia Moseley's offered, and I think she's sweet.' Her smiled momentarily faded a little. 'Actually, I'm not looking forward to any of it. All those debutantes dances, parties and formal balls, with eagle-eyed mothers on the look-out for the most eligible young men . . . it sounds fun, but it's really a bit of a glorified cattle-market.'

'You make it sound all very false and cynical.'

'Well it is, isn't it? Every girl has to make sure she ends up with the highest bidder. It's the ultimate disgrace, not to marry well . . . except for causing a scandal or committing murder.'

Laura smiled. 'I can't imagine anyone less likely to do either than you.'

'*Paris*? Marguerite Holland wants me to go with her to Paris?' Frances's blue eyes widened with surprise. 'Mummy, I'd love to! Did you tell her that I could?'

'I thought it would be a . . . useful experience for you, just before the start of your Season. Jack has business there and Marguerite always invariably goes with him . . . she's such a devoted Francophile. She invited Elizabeth to Monaco and Rome just before she had her Season, if you remember.'

'Yes; I remember how envious I was.'

They were interrupted by Madders calling her to the telephone. 'It's the Earl of Banbury, my lady, enquiring as to whether Lady Banbury is here this afternoon.' Katherine got up, warning bells sounding in her head.

'Thank you, Madders. I'll speak to him from the telephone in the study.' She went out, leaving Frances gazing dreamily into the fire. The unexpected sting of speaking about Kit again to Laura was beginning to recede now. It was merely foolish of her to still mind so much.

She began to look forward to her long-awaited birthday dance at the Savoy, the family Christmas in Essex, Boxing Day at Greyfriars, the Banbury country seat; New Year, a new decade, Paris, presentation at Court, then her coming out ball. And Robert Carr?

William Banbury drummed his fingers impatiently on the desk as he waited for his mother-in-law's voice on the other end of the line. He was being foolish, fussing unnecessarily, he knew that, and he was still suffering from pique after their near-argument last night when she'd insisted that she wanted to sleep alone. But she'd promised that she was spending the entire afternoon at home with her feet up and, because he was working late this evening, would be going to bed early with the latest romantic novel of Ruby M. Ayres. Each time he'd telephoned Portland Place the servants had told him that she was still out.

He'd already telephoned several places where he thought she might be; each time he'd drawn a blank. He was beginning to get seriously worried.

The line crackled a little, then clicked, and at last he heard Katherine Cultrane's voice. 'William?'

His fingers gripping the receiver had started to sweat. 'She isn't there? But I felt sure she would be . . . no, no; she hasn't been to New Bond Street. That was the first place I tried. I simply don't understand it. She said she was feeling very tired and intended to stay at home today . . . she was in bed before half past-seven last night! Yes, I appreciate she could be anywhere . . . I know how much she loves shopping . . . but I did tell her that she really must start taking things a little easier, after all . . . yes; yes, if she does call, will you ask her to telephone me here? Thank you, Katherine. Goodbye.'

He replaced the receiver with a bang and sat with his elbows on the desk. The pile of papers was still in front of him, routine constituency matters that he'd wanted to deal with before the Christmas holiday; he'd been so distracted by not being able to locate Elizabeth that half of them had not even been read through. With difficulty, he turned his attention back to the one that lay in front of him and tried to concentrate.

But all he could do was to wonder where Elizabeth might be.

The footman who was standing in for Seddon answered the door. Beyond him the vast hall, the whole house seemed almost deathly quiet. Unusually he was half deafened by the blaring of her gramophone. Banbury wiped his snow-covered shoes on the mat and let the young footman take his hat and coat.

'A bitter evening, my lord. And more snow on the way, or so I hear. It was coming down heavy this afternoon.'

'Yes, Harry, it's pretty general, I'm afraid. Quite beastly, and a damn nuisance for driving, too. I hope the roads are fairly clear for the journey down to Greyfriars next week.' He was having difficulty in hiding his agitation. 'Has her ladyship gone to bed yet?'

'No, my lord.' He took Banbury's coat and lay it carefully over one arm. 'Her ladyship's been out all day; she hasn't come back yet.'

'Not come back? But it's almost a quarter past eleven! Has she not telephoned?'

'Not to my knowledge, my lord.'

'Is her maid Sabine upstairs?'

'I believe Lady Banbury gave her the evening off, my lord.' He took Banbury's hat and cane. 'Will there be anything further, my lord?'

'No, Harry; I had a late lunch at my club. Just a large brandy in the drawing room.'

'Yes, my lord.'

The room was warm and comforting when he went in; the fire had been made up and the flames leapt and darted, casting long, flickering shadows around the walls. He sat for a long time in his favourite chair with the glass of brandy cradled in his hands but without drinking it. At twelve o'clock, when there was still no sign of her, he left the glass on the tray and went upstairs.

He stood on the threshold of her room, slowly looking around it. Sabine had turned on the bedside lamp; Elizabeth's silk nightdress and satin dressing gown trimmed with swansdown were laid out carefully on the satin cover of the bed, her satin slippers below them on the thickly carpeted floor. The curtains had been drawn and the fire made up for the night. On the Italian marble mantlepiece, the French *boulle* clock he had given her as a wedding present ticked away softly, then chimed midnight. He thought, irrelevantly, that the clock downstairs in the drawing room must be several minutes fast; or else this one was slow. It was then that he heard the sound of a car.

Quickly, breathing hard, he went over to the window and parted the heavy fringed curtains; a taxi had parked several yards away, its still-running engine muffled by the distance from the house and the thickness of the snow. His heart beating very fast, his breath coming in short painful bursts now, he watched unseen through the lace curtains as the driver opened the door and Elizabeth, muffled in furs, got out. For a brief moment he felt a marvellous sense of relief that she was safe; none of the dreadful accidents that his over-active imagination had conjured up during the day had happened. Then, just as he was about to come away from the window to go downstairs and greet her he hesitated, stunned, unable to believe his own eyes. She leaned forward towards a shadowy male figure still in the back of the car, and they kissed, passionately, on the lips.

For a moment he was too shocked to move. He stood there, staring down woodenly into the snow-swept street, as Elizabeth waved, then blew a kiss from her fingertips to the figure in the taxi as it drew away and drove off towards the Mall. When it had gone out of sight she turned and carefully picked her way over the slippery, snow-covered pavement to the front of the house.

He let the curtain fall back into place, then hurried as quickly as he could from her bedroom to his own. He lay back against the door, breathing hard, perspiration beginning to form across his forehead and down his back. The tight, sharp pain in his chest made him gasp for breath and stagger over to the drawer where he kept his pills. His hands were shaking as he poured himself a glass of water, put two of them on the tip of his tongue and washed them down in a single gulp. Then he sank onto the bed, panting, dizzy, sick, pulling feverishly at his collar and tie.

She would be coming up the staircase now; he reached out and turned off his bedside lamp. If she looked, there would be no light showing beneath his bedroom door.

He heard her soft footsteps; then the quiet opening and closing of a door. For a long time he lay there in the darkness, still fully dressed, grateful that he'd told his valet not to wait up. That anyone else besides himself should have known about tonight would have been unbearable to his pride.

He wanted, needed, to be alone to compose himself, to think. When he was certain that she would be in bed he turned the light back on; as he leaned forward to press the switch he caught sight of his reflection in the small swivel mirror. His face was grey, the lines deeply etched; there were thick, fleshy pouches beneath his eyes. His once dark hair was heavy streaked with grey and thinning.

He glanced down at the silver-framed photograph of Elizabeth on his bedside table, the photograph taken especially for their engagement; at the larger elaborately framed picture of their wedding day, on the steps of Westminster Cathedral. How young and beautiful she looked; he picked it up and stared at it, then at himself. Had he really looked so much older than she was, even then?

Slowly, he put it back in its place and put out the light. He lay down, only removing his shoes and the jacket of his suit. Old, blind,

231

egotistical fool. He should have remembered what Shakespeare once wrote about age and youth; they never mixed.

For the first time since his mother had died when he was fourteen, he felt tears of impotence and misery sting at the backs of his eyes. But there was no one to comfort him.

She was opening her mail at the breakfast table when he finally steeled himself to go in and join her. A footman was serving her with eggs and bacon, a maid was pouring her tea. She looked up brightly, her blue eyes sparkling and her soft, pale complexion translucently clear; why did he somehow expect it to bear the marks of her late night the evening before? He couldn't look at her.

'Darling, there you are! Not like you to be so late coming down in the morning. Did you manage to get all those fearfully boring papers finished off before you came home?'

He sat down heavily in his usual place at the top of the table. For a moment he didn't answer her. He let the footman and the maid serve him with toast and tea, but waved the tureen of bacon and eggs away. Then he dismissed them.

That was when Elizabeth realized something was wrong. 'Darling . . . whatever did you do that for?'

'Did you enjoy your early night yesterday?' His voice was strained, harsh. 'Tell me. How far did you get into Ruby M. Ayres' new book? Is it as well written as her last novel?'

'What?'

'You told me you intended to stay at home yesterday afternoon; have an early night and read a good book.'

'Oh, that!' She sipped her tea. 'Well, I *had* meant to, darling, but I got so dreadfully bored, I decided to go out visiting instead. After I'd called into New Bond Street I dropped by to have a chat with Cynthia, and then I was at a bit of a loose end, so I called in on mother.'

He sat watching her for several moments while she went on eating her breakfast, blithely unaware of the expression on his face. He could barely swallow. 'Don't lie to me, Elizabeth.' Her head jerked up. She stared at him with her mouth open. 'I tried to call you on numerous occasions yesterday afternoon . . . because I was concerned about you overtaxing yourself in your condition . . . every time I telephoned the house the servants told me that you weren't here.'

'I've just told you where I was.'

'I called New Bond Street first; Anne Turner's secretary informed me that you hadn't been there at any time this week; you weren't at Cynthia's either. And finally, when I telephoned your mother, she told me that you hadn't been to Belgrave Square since you called to tell her the news about the baby.'

Colour flooded into her cheeks. 'How dare you check up on me!'

'I'm waiting for an explanation, Elizabeth.' She'd never seen him like this before. His eyes were hard, glassy, like pebbles on a beach. 'I want to know where you were. And I want to know who you were with.'

She decided the only way was to bluff it out. 'All right, I was bored. I spent the whole afternoon in Oxford and Regent Street wandering through the big stores. I knew you'd make a fuss if you found out I was on my feet for so long, so I told a few little white lies.'

'Who is he, Elizabeth?' He saw her whole body stiffen with shock. 'Who was the man who brought you home last night?'

'I don't know what you're talking about . . .'

'When I came back from Whitehall at twenty-eight minutes past eleven last night, you were still not back. I waited downstairs for you for more than half-an-hour, then I reluctantly came upstairs to bed. But I heard a car draw up outside; a taxi. When I looked out of your bedroom window I saw you.'

She suddenly felt sick with fright, panic, rage. Please god, he hadn't seen Eddie! 'I told you I was frightfully bored; so I decided to go to the Silver Slipper. After all, while I'm still thin enough to be seen in public I might as well enjoy myself.'

He had never shouted at her before. He took her so completely by surprise that his voice made her jump. 'Answer me when I ask you a question, damn it! Who was the man you kissed in the taxi last night?'

'Someone who joined our party at the Silver Slipper. A diplomat from one of the embassies or something, I can't remember. He was very amusing and such fun and he offered to bring me home. We shared the same taxi, that's all.'

'Do you usually kiss complete strangers in the street?'

'It didn't mean anything. I'd had too much champagne and it went to my head.'

He stared at her down the length of the table, willing himself to believe her. She looked back unflinchingly into his eyes. But still at the very back of his mind doubt lingered. 'I see. Then why didn't you tell me the truth when I first asked you instead of a pack of lies?'

'Because I knew you'd make an awful fuss about me going out and stopping out late, that's why. And I was right. Treating me as if I was some kind of invalid, just because I'm going to have a baby.' Terrible suspicions, dark and horrible, were already beginning to form in the back of his mind, suspicions that a week ago, a day even, he would never have thought it possible to think. But they wouldn't go away.

'Elizabeth, have you ever been unfaithful to me?' He hated himself for asking it but the words came out almost before he realized he'd said them.

'No! Never!' She half-stood up. 'William, I swear it.'

He glanced down woodenly at the cold toast on the plate in front of him, the cold tea left untouched. He couldn't eat or drink anything now. He put his napkin on the table and stood up, then walked towards the door. As he reached her place at the opposite end of the table he hesitated.

'No doubt it's amused you, my dear, to laugh at me behind my back with your smart friends; running up enormous expense accounts all over London, dancing with the fast set into the small hours at your fashionable nightclubs, behaving as if you were a single woman with no domestic responsibilities or ties. But I'm afraid those days are over now. You are my wife, about to become the mother of my child, and I insist that you behave with the customary dignity and decorum one would expect from a married woman.' She stared at him. 'Your sister's dance at the Savoy will be the last time you go out socially in London; when I take you to Greyfriars for Christmas, I shall expect you to stay there until the child is born, and for a considerable length of time afterwards. I trust I make myself clear.'

She was outraged. 'You can't force me to stay in the country for more than a year. I won't do it. God, that house, stuck in the back-of-beyond! I'll go mad with boredom.' He didn't mean it. He couldn't. Somehow, she'd coax and wheedle and talk him round.

She clenched her fists until the nails cut into the flesh of her palms. If only the old bastard hadn't seen her from the window. How could she have dropped her guard and been so careless on the one night when he'd got home before she had?

'On the contrary, you'll have a great deal to keep you occupied. You've often complained to me how much you hate the old-fashioned interior at Greyfriars: I give you a free hand to make any decorative changes you wish. After that, your child should keep you busy.'

Like a cornered rat, she stood up and faced him. 'You're enjoying

234

this, aren't you? Playing the lord and master! Do you think I'm like your first wife, the dutiful, dull little woman contented to sit at home, obedient to your every word? If you think for one moment that I'm staying in that mausoleum for a day longer than I have to, then you're very much mistaken. I shall tell my father the way you're treating me and see what he has to say about it.'

He looked at her, thinking how hard and cold her face was, stripped of the aura of gaiety and charm. But which Elizabeth was the real one?

'Out of the respect I have for your family – and for your father in particular – I trust that this conversation will go no further than this room. Whether it does or not is up to you entirely. But if I were to tell your parents the true reason for leaving you down at Greyfriars – and the fact that you've insisted on my sleeping in my dressing-room – I have no doubt that both of them would be completely on my side.'

'You smug . . . !'

'Think yourself fortunate, Elizabeth, that I choose to believe you; many other husbands might not. In fact, your careless and irresponsible behaviour might not only have provoked a scandal . . . to a less understanding man it might well provide adequate grounds for divorce.'

'Surely you're not serious? Simply because I come home late from a night club with a foreign diplomat . . . who would have been grossly offended if I'd refused his kind offer to escort me to my door . . .'

'I shall be home at eight o'clock this evening.' He opened the dining-room door. 'And I shall expect you to be here.'

When she knew he'd left the house for good she went and poured herself a stiff drink to stop her hands from shaking. She felt sick. Her head swam. If he had any doubts and checked up on her story he would soon find out that the evening at the Silver Slipper was a complete fabrication. She sat for a few minutes trying to compose herself, then she went into his study and picked up the telephone.

She telephoned Eddie Vaux first. She's never risked ringing him directly before; it was too dangerous. But there wasn't much time. Whatever happened, however big the risk that someone downstairs might listen in on the call and overhear them, it was a chance she had to take. She glanced at the clock; if she was lucky she might catch him before he left the house. At long last he answered.

Her words came out in a torrent, falling out one over the other. 'Eddie, darling! Thank goodness I got hold of you.' She gave him a condensed account of what had happened with Banbury. 'No, of course he doesn't suspect you. The thought's never entered his head. Luckily he seemed to swallow my story about the foreign diplomat, but if he should take it into his head to check up . . . what I thought was, if you happened to bump into him and say *you* were at the Silver Slipper with some girl, and you saw me there . . . oh, darling, if you could! But for heavens sake don't make it look obvious . . . as if you're trying to get me off the hook . . . all right. I'll get a message to you somehow through Anne Turner before we leave for the country next week.'

She rang Anne Turner next. 'It was just pure bad luck, I could have spat. If only I'd had any idea that he'd be home before I was! He told me he'd be stuck at Westminster till the early hours . . .' A pause while Anne Turner spoke at the other end of the line. 'I must have some more stuff from Simon, before we go down to Greyfriars . . . yes, I need it this week. Just get it for me and then send one of your girls over here with a dress or suit or something . . . hide it in the parcel. Yes, I'll have the money ready.'

She put down the receiver and went back into the dining room. The teapot had been left on the hotplate to keep it warm, and she poured herself another cup, then lit a cigarette and bit hard upon her thumb.

She had a lot of thinking to do.

28

She moved through the laughing, chattering groups of guests, stopping now and then to talk to someone, pausing here and there for a few words or a smile. She knew it was important to circulate; she could feel her mother's critical eyes watching her and, every now and then, her sister Elizabeth's. Unlike her usual gay, flamboyant self, her sister seemed almost unnaturally quiet; keeping herself in the background, talking hardly at all, sitting out almost every dance. Obviously, she was feeling queasy. The quiet of the Kent countryside over Christmas and the New Year would do her good.

Somebody was standing in her path. 'I say, Frances. You haven't forgotten I've bagged the next dance, have you?' She suddenly found herself surrounded by a crowd of eager, admiring young men; and it wasn't by any means an unpleasant experience to be the centre of attention.

She held up her hand with a tolerant smile. 'I promise I won't forget which dance I promised to *anyone*.' Politely, she pushed her way gently through the crowd. 'Now, if you'll excuse me, gentlemen . . .'

Her ivory silk and *diamanté* evening gown winked and glittered under the lights of the chandeliers as she made her way to the ladies' powder room; like the gown being specially made for her presentation at Court, Anne Turner's contribution had been strictly minimal; it was mostly Laura's work. Frances thought of her now, no doubt busy packing for her two month trip to America; her ship sailed three days after Christmas.

It was then that Frances realized she was being watched from the other side of the enormous ballroom. As the groups of guests and dancing couples moved away and thinned out, she recognized Robert Carr. He got up from his seat and came towards her. They smiled at each other.

'Hello, Mr Carr. I hope you're enjoying yourself. I'm so glad that you could come.'

'Whatever other engagements I might have had tonight, I would have cancelled them all for the pleasure of seeing you.' They were Tom Dreikhorn's words, not his. He felt rather pleased with himself for remembering them. 'I suppose I ought to wish you many happy returns of the day?'

'Thank you! And your flowers were simply beautiful.' She noticed how other girls were looking at him. 'I've been so lucky. My room is full of them.'

'Then I envy the flowers.' Another of Tom's suggestions. He was desperately trying to remember what Tom had told him to say next, but he couldn't. 'Could I fetch you a glass of champagne, or something from the buffet?' Those were his own words, the first thing that had come into his head; he wondered if she'd think it was unromantic to talk about bouquets of flowers and then food and drink in the same sentence.

'No, thank you. If I have any more champagne my head will start spinning. And in any case I was on my way to the powder-room.' She looked around her, as if she'd just realized something familiar was missing. 'I don't see your friend Mr Dreikhorn. I know my mother invited him because I remember his name on the guest list.'

Carr smiled boyishly. 'I'm sorry to say Tom had a previous engagement – of long-standing. And as it was with a young lady he said he would feel very guilty if he had to disappoint her.'

So, Laura had been right; Dreikhorn was a ladies' man.

'Do I know her? I've noticed him about town with quite a few young ladies.'

'Oh, I doubt it; she's the daughter of a dean Tom met while we were in Edinburgh.' He tried to make his expression and tone of voice sound light-heartedly conspiratorial. 'Between you and me I think he's intending to marry her . . . but not quite yet. Tom's very much a believer in a chap enjoying his so-called days of freedom first.'

The attachment to the girl from Scotland softened Dreikhorn's image a little in Frances' eyes; but she still had a distinct feeling that Dreikhorn was after a more aristocratic bride; her brother Freddie had spotted him dining with Lady Dora Paget.

'Are you spending Christmas in London?'

'I'm leaving by train tomorrow morning for Ferniehurst . . . my cousin's Scottish estate. I suppose like everyone else you've heard he's very ill indeed? Christmas or not, I really feel that I should make the effort to see him again, despite the length of the journey.'

'Yes, I had heard about Lord Rosslare. I'm so sorry.' She could picture him waiting on the cold, snowy platform for the train north, resigned to spending a bleak, joyless holiday with only a dying man for company. 'Isn't there anything the doctors can do?'

'I'm afraid not, the cancer is deep-rooted; Ian's known that he's been dying for some time now. The trouble is, I'd have to be blind and deaf not to be aware of what everybody's saying.' Tom had stressed how important it was to get her sympathy. 'That I'm only making the journey out of a sense of duty, that I don't care how ill he is at all . . . because when he's dead I'll be the next Earl of Rosslare. But it means very little to me at all. My Father always did say that what you never have you never miss; I wish there was someone else in the family before me who could inherit it. Unfortunately, few people believe that.'

She admired his blunt honesty. 'Then they know very little about you.'

A flush of pleasure suffused his fair skin. 'It's most generous of you to say so.' A pause. Tom had told him that at all costs he mustn't seem to push himself on her. The roses and the card with the quotation from Shakespeare had caught her interest; now he had to tread carefully, very carefully, over the next step, obstacles and all. He'd been aware for several minutes that Viscount Staughton's heir was watching them. So had several other people. No doubt the polished toffs of London resented the raw Scottish boy for monopolizing her company. But the advantage was with him now. 'I suppose your next dance is taken, and probably the next half a dozen after that?'

She smiled. 'Yes, I'm afraid so . . . but I promise to save the last one especially for you.'

Casually, Eddie Vaux walked up to where Elizabeth sat, and handed her a glass of champagne. He remained standing, sipping his own and pretending to exchange polite smalltalk, while from the corner of his eye he kept a sharp watch on the stocky, greying figure of his uncle. He was well out of the way for the moment; Winston Churchill had cornered him near the buffet table and, from what Eddie Vaux knew of Winston, Banbury would be there for the next hour.

He glanced around them to make certain there was nobody likely to overhear them, then moved closer but spoke to her without looking down.

'The old man hasn't changed his mind, then? You're still going to be confined to Greyfriars until after the baby?'

Elizabeth didn't bother to hide the bitterness in her voice. 'Vindictive old bastard. If it hadn't been for Frances' party here we would already have left London. No doubt darling William would have loved to have packed me off to that bloody house in the middle of nowhere so that I missed even that.' She turned her head towards him. 'Eddie, I'll go absolutely crazy down there. I just can't bear to think of being away from you . . .'

'Look, don't worry. I've got a couple of old Oxford chums at Tunbridge Wells . . . they'll put me up. When he has to come back to town in the new year we can meet. Darling, I promise I'll manage it somehow . . .'

'But if you're in the country too he might start to suspect.'

'I'll hop back every now and then . . . Elizabeth stop worrying. Do you really think he could do anything to keep me away from you?'

The words of comfort pleased her and she smiled. 'If only Frances realized how luckily she is . . .'

She was watching her younger sister now, dancing with the Earl of Iden's heir, laughing as she danced at some amusing remark he'd made, the long, elegant evening gown with the exquisite silver embroidery on the overskirt of the white georgette winking as it caught the light. She looked so lovely, happy, carefree, it was almost impossible not to envy her. True, she'd have to fall into line over marrying one of the suitable candidates her parents had shortlisted, but at least they were all young men. The unfairness of it all brought a frown back to Elizabeth's face. How different her life would have been if only she could have married Eddie Vaux!

All around the edge of the ballroom, groups of young men stood watching her sister; once only she had been the centre of attention, and for a moment it hurt.

'I'd better circulate,' Vaux said, moving away from her chair. 'He'll bring Winston over here in a minute to congratulate you about the baby and it'll look better if I'm elsewhere.'

The faint, nagging sickness that she'd started to suffer from not only in the morning but at other, unexpected times of the day began fluttering ominously in her stomach now. She was tired and irritable and she wanted to go home to bed. Unreasonably, she wanted to hurt him without really understanding why. He could come and go as he pleased and it wasn't fair.

'All right, if you must. But if you dance with my sister or that bitch Eva Scott-Montagu, I'll never speak to you again.'

Marguerite Holland was already in the ladies' powder-room when Frances entered, busy titivating her make-up and hair.

'Frances, darling! It's an absolutely marvellous party and you look perfectly stunning. You just make certain you pack that gown when we got to Paris, won't you? It's bound to cause a sensation.'

Frances sat down beside her. 'It is rather super, isn't it?'

'Heavenly . . . an Anne Turner, of course?'

'Actually, a friend of mine designed it.' She told her about Laura. 'She has enormous talent and she designs and makes all her own clothes. She's done most of the work on my Court dress and coming out wardrobe. I don't know what I'll do when she leaves New Bond Street to get married. Unfortunately her fiancé doesn't approve of wives working after marriage.'

'Oh, these men! They can be so tiresomely unreasonable.'

'Marguerite . . . I've been meaning to chat to you all evening actually . . . there doesn't seem to have been time to draw breath since the party started. But I wanted to say how excited I am about Paris. It was awfully generous of you to invite me.'

'Nonsense! Jack insisted and I agreed. We'll have tremendous fun while he's taken up with his boring business. And it'll be first class experience for you just before you start your Season. We know most

240

of the hostesses, of course . . .' She took a comb from her beaded evening bag and began to rearrange her fair hair. For a moment their two reflections, side by side, looked startling alike in the mirror; Frances had always felt close to Marguerite because she reminded her so much of her godfather, Thomas Holland. Uncanny, almost, that they were both think of him now.

'You know; I do wish Daddy had been alive to see you tonight. He would have been so proud of you.' She smiled. 'You always were his favourite godchild, you know.'

The air was stuffy and overpoweringly smoke-filled in the crowded, dimly-lit basement club. All the tables were full, there was hardly a space to be had at the small, semi-circular bar. Waiters busily pushed their way through the packed bodies backwards and forwards, expertly balancing drinks on little trays. From a wind-up gramophone a saxophone wailed.

'Your eyes are watering,' Thomas Dreikhorn teased the slight, fair-haired boy who was standing at the bar beside him. He looked so uncomfortable, ill-at-ease and out of place that Dreikhorn wanted to laugh. 'Don't tell me smoke gets in your eyes?' He was holding a cigarette close to the boy's face and he started to cough.

'I'm just not used to it, that's all. My Father won't allow smoking at home.'

'Why don't you leave home?'

'I couldn't run to my own apartment; not yet, anyway. I suppose I could always share. With chums, I mean.' He glanced at Dreikhorn sideways from beneath long, silky white lashes. How much the boy reminded him of Robbie, when they'd first met; shy, gauche, eager to please. A pity a few seasons in London among the Mayfair set and the hope of money and a title had spoiled him, changed him. The raw Scottish lad had disappeared beneath the well-dressed, sought-after young man who graced ambitious mothers' drawing-rooms and was fast rising in politics through Dreikhorn's expert tutelege. Sometimes Robbie needed to be reminded of what he'd once been.

'Are you ready to leave now?' He was watching the boy with open amusement, deriving pleasure from his obvious embarrassment and self-doubt. 'Why not have one for the road?'

'No more, thank you. It makes me feel a bit . . . well, dizzy. Father doesn't approve of drinking spirits, you see.' He couldn't quite meet Dreikhorn's eyes. 'Look, I . . . I don't want to seem ungrateful; I

241

mean, it was awfully kind of you to invite me here for a drink. But it's getting on the late side and I'm . . . not really sure about this at all . . .'

'Your father naturally wouldn't approve of you doing something that you want to do?'

'It's not just that.' He was struggling with himself, with the weakness that he always tried to fight but somehow never could. The tall, dark fifth-former that he'd loved so much at Oxford . . . he thanked god that his strait-laced family had never found out. 'I go to church, you see. I know it sounds terribly old-fashioned; silly, really, to someone as sophisticated as you. I wasn't going to come tonight.'

Dreikhorn threw his head back and laughed out loud. 'You don't really believe in all that heaven and hell stuff, do you?'

'Please, don't joke.' He felt Dreikhorn reach out and touch his arm. He shivered.

'I told you . . . it's very discreet here. Look around you. Like I said, I'll bring you to a place where you'll feel perfectly at ease. They have rooms at the back, through that door. Yes, that's right.' The boy turned and looked. His face was very white.

'Isn't there any danger the club might be raided?'

'I told you, it's all perfectly discreet.'

The boy went on looking around him, nervously, as if he was having great difficulty in making up his mind. Propped up against the bar, cigarette burning in one hand, Dreikhorn watched him with a grin. Robbie wouldn't like it if he knew about this evening, but the feeling of revenge was sweet; serve him right for wasting his time away sucking up to the Cultranes at the Savoy.

'Well?'

'I've just noticed something. Over there, at the corner table. Two women. I thought you said women never came here?'

Dreikhorn smiled as he drew on his cigarette.

'You really are green, aren't you?'

Robert Carr went up the staircase that led to the door of his flat, and took out his key. But the front door opened before he could fit it in the lock. It swung back, revealing Thomas Dreikhorn's dark, laughing face.

'I saw you get out of the taxi from the window; you're much later than I expected.' He smiled, and Carr noticed the full glass of whisky in his hand. 'So. How did it all go? Did you beat off the opposition and sweep the fair Lady Frances off her white-slippered feet?'

242

Carr smiled wearily, tugging at his bow tie and throwing himself down on the leather couch; he was used to Tom's sarcasm.

'Opposition there certainly was; mainly bloody Iden's heir. I should think the Cultranes invited every eligible titled bachelor in *Debrett*. But I'm pretty sure that she prefers me.'

Dreikhorn sat down beside him, put down his whisky and began, slowly and gently, to massage the back of his neck. 'You do look all in. Still, a good night's rest should work it's usual wonders. Then, first thing in the morning you must put pen to paper and write her a love letter.'

'Tom, for god's sake . . . !'

'. . . not just any love letter; certainly not flowery and overdone like the sort of thing she'll get from the rest of the mundane opposition. No. This has got to be something very special.'

'Look, you know I'm a complete duffer at that kind of thing.'

'Have no fear! I shall write it for you. Or, rather, I should say, I'll compose it and you can copy it out. In your best handwriting, mind. Together with some suitable token of your undying esteem and admiration . . . again, it mustn't be overdone. Remember. Understate *always*. In letters. Gifts. Words. Otherwise it simply looks gross.'

'Why is it that you know exactly what women love and yet you hold them all in so little regard?'

'Because I'm a genius, Robbie; a true-born natural genius. And because women are so vain and stupid.' He reached for his whisky. 'If only Baldwin understood them as well as I do! Giving them all the vote at twenty-one instead of thirty has got him hoist with his own petard.' He laughed, loudly. 'He gives them the vote and then they all, the ungrateful bitches, cast it for the other side!'

'Frances?' She was surprised that her great uncle had come back with them after the dance at the Savoy; more surprised that he'd asked to speak to her alone. It was almost four o'clock in the morning and she was longing to go to bed. 'Could I just have a brief word with you, before you go upstairs. I'm sure you're quite worn out after this evening.'

She smiled a little wearily. 'Yes, I am.' A sudden thought. 'There's nothing wrong, is there?'

'No, my dear. Nothing wrong at all. I would say, wouldn't you, that your dance was an overwhelming success? You looked very beautiful.'

She had never quite lost that early feeling of not being at ease with him, the feeling that had been with her since she was a child.

'I was going to ask you what your feelings are about two certain young gentlemen . . . perhaps you might think that I've not chosen my time very well; after all, it's very late, and both of us are tired. But you'll be off to Paris after Christmas with Marguerite and I have my duties at Court . . . there may not be another opportune time.'

'I see.' She had an idea of what he was going to say, and she was ready. Had Elizabeth gone through this, too?

'Clearly I don't have to remind you of your duty to your family . . . as every young woman in your position knows, one is expected to marry well. You're more fortunate than most because you have a wider choice than most; including your sister.' Had it all been a sham, then, the publicity-emblazoned romance between Banbury and Elizabeth? How childishly naïve she'd been to believe, as she had three years ago, that they were marrying because they were so much in love. Banbury was so rich, so powerful within the Tory party . . . were those the only reasons why there'd been the fairy-tale wedding? It all seemed so orchestrated and cynical now, she almost shuddered with distaste. She was determined that it wasn't going to happen to her.

'Is this conversation anything to do with the Earl of Iden's son?'

'One would have to be of severely limited intellect not to have noticed that you reserved three dances for him this evening. More than you saved for anyone else.'

Frances shrugged. 'Mummy and Daddy told me to be nice to him. Besides, a few dances are one thing; spending the rest of your life with somebody is something else altogether.'

'There isn't a debutante's mother in London who wouldn't snap up the chance of Iden's boy as a son-in-law . . .' he smiled his ingratiating courtier's smile. 'Or for young Robert Carr.' He was watching her face carefully for a reaction. 'Both of whom, I believe, are more than interested in you. I know about these things. Do you have any preference in the matter?'

It suddenly occurred to her how tasteless and cynical this whole business was; he was trying to convince her that she had a choice, when it reality she knew that if Robert Carr hadn't been the heir to an earldom and a fortune, whatever his political successes were he would never have even been considered in their eyes. That, almost as much as the fact that she liked him, was drawn to him and felt nothing for Iden's son at all, made up her mind.

'If you really want to know, Uncle Henry, I'd much rather be the next Countess of Rosslare.'

Years later, she remembered her own words that night, and could have wept.

29

Frances stood at the window of their hotel overlooking the busy, bustling Champs-Elysées, watching the endless stream of traffic and people go by far below. There was so much restless energy about Paris it was impossible to spend even a few days in the city without being affected by it; it was so magical, so glamorous, so full of vitality, with none of the social partitions and prejudices of London. Poor artists and wealthy socialites co-existed, side by side; coloured entertainers, like the lovely, charismatic chanteuse Josephine Baker, were accepted everywhere. The shops in the rue de la Paix, the heart of the French fashion district, were a thrill and a delight to visit; already, the anteroom in their hotel suite was half-filled with ribboned hat boxes and packages.

Marguerite and Frances had fallen in love with the latest feminine spring styles that filled the windows of the rue de la Paix: Premet, Boulanger, Worth, Chanel; waists had definitely made a dramatic come-back, bustlines were more natural; dress lengths longer, evening gowns more elaborate and elegant; and so were the latest styles for women's hair. Gone was the severe, ear-length bob, the shingle and the Eton crop; the wire-curler, devised in a myriad of varieties, stamped the new decade with a message all of its own. Accessories were just as important as the elegant outfits they complemented; gloves from Alexandrine, Eisner and Fauriez were a must; silk shawls, scarves and stockings from André Gillier in the rue du Pont-Neuf. Maubossin jewellery, made from semi-precious stones and very much influenced by the oriental tradition, was very much *à la mode*. Marguerite had bought her, as a special present, a set of earrings, bracelet, necklace and hair fillet in cabochon rubies, sapphires and emeralds set in platinum, their brilliance enhanced by the clever addition of small diamonds and black enamel. From the generous present her great uncle had given her before they left London, Frances had not only purchased irresistible additions to her own wardrobe, but had spent nearly half of it in presents for her family and friends.

There was a black ostrich feather evening fan for Elizabeth, a diamond and opal bracelet for her mother; for Laura, a green silk evening wrap from André Gillier, with a matching bracelet and necklace to go with the earrings she'd given her for her birthday. A platinum pen for her father and Lord Henry Osborne; for Robert Carr, a platinum cigarette case with his initials.

'So,' Marguerite had said, teasing her a little, 'your mother was right. The good-looking Mr Carr has rather taken your fancy. I must admit I think he's so much more presentable than Lord Iden's son . . . I rather thought they were keen on you having him at one time.' She took out her powder compact and opened the lid. 'Mind you, in my opinion you've had a lucky escape there – have you ever met his mother?' They both laughed. 'Jack tells me Robert Carr's parents are both dead.'

'Yes, I believe they are. But he never told me himself. Daddy knew already.'

'It's always such a fearful ordeal, this coming out business . . . I was scared when I was presented at Court. But I had no idea then that that was the easy part; it was afterwards at all those endless dances that I found out you needed the constitution of an ox . . . and a hide like a rhino's.'

Frances came away from the window; it was almost time to dress. Marguerite's maid came in.

'Eunice, I still haven't decided which dress I'll wear tonight. Aren't I a ditherer?' She stood up. 'Frances, I need your advice. Shall I choose the coral or the magenta silk for this evening? Luckily, this jewellery goes with both. What do you think?'

'The coral's very delicate and pretty . . . I do like that. But I'd say the magenta . . . it's more definite and bold somehow. And with your colouring you can easily get away with it; so few women can really wear such a strong colour.'

'Right. The magenta it is . . . Eunice, do be a love and go and press it . . . I can see a few minute creases near the hem. Then fetch my silk high-heels; the ones I bought yesterday on the rue Charles.' She patted her waved hair with one hand. 'And what, may I ask, have you chosen for your last night in gay Paris?'

'The aquamarine organza . . . I've been saving it especially for this evening.'

'The Anne Turner?'

'Well, it has her label but it was designed, cut out and made up by my friend Laura Asmussen . . . she's worked for Mrs Turner for more than three years.'

'Good gracious, what talent! Why doesn't she start up on her own or something? So many enterprising young women are crossing the barriers and doing all kinds of things now.'

'Laura doesn't have that kind of capital. Besides which, her family and her fiancé would probably violently disapprove. She's already quarrelled with him because she'd prefer to stay at work after they're married.'

'What a tyrant he sounds! I'd ditch him in five minutes flat if he tried to dictate like that to me. Jack's such a darling, I suppose I'm terribly lucky to have him. He lets me do whatever I want to.' She pursed her lips in the mirror as she carefully began to apply her lipstick. 'That's the trouble with the middle classes . . . they have no imagination.' She suddenly stopped what she was doing. 'Why doesn't she simply just design for you, after she leaves Anne Turner's? It's worth thinking about. You get much more for your money – an original Turner is out of this world but then so is the price – and your friend gets the profit instead of Anne Turner. Besides which she won't be bored out of her mind all day because her husband wants to keep her chained to the happy home . . . what do you think? Jack will say it's definitely one of my brilliant ideas.'

'You could have something there.' Frances suddenly wished Laura was here so that she could talk to her about it. 'The only thing is . . . if she doesn't want to do it, I should hate her to feel I was trying to do her a favour just because we happen to be friends . . .'

'Rubbish! She'll love the idea. She loves designing, doesn't she? Ring her up when we get back.'

It was time for Frances to get dressed now.

'I can't. For the next two months she'll be in Chicago.'

An hour before they left, she started to get nervous.

'Silly girl! You look an absolute dream. Here. Walk up and down and let me see that divine dress! Golly, if that friend of yours could make me something like that, she'd certainly have another delighted customer.'

'It's so simple in style; but the way it's been cut makes it sort of fan out beautifully from the hipline when you walk. And I love the narrow, shoestring straps; it was so clever of Laura to embroider them with *diamanté*.'

247

Grace came in with her evening wrap and shoes.

'Now, this is our last night in Paris, so we've got to be absolutely determined to enjoy it. Jack will be joining us later. The Selkirks have the most ravishing apartment on the rue de Burgogne . . . the views over the Seine are quite breathtaking, especially at night. And they also have the most delightful villa in the south of France.' She picked up her Lalique perfume bottle of blue frosted glass and dabbed some of her favourite *Shalimar* on her wrists and behind her ears. 'They always have such utterly fascinating people to their parties . . . really, I know you'll adore them.'

She recognized the music instantly, loud and strong, as it pulsated towards them before they entered the apartment. As a black servant in livery opened the double doors, she saw the huge room crowded with laughing, chattering, dancing people; then she caught sight of the wind-up gramophone standing on an ultra-modern steel and sycamore low Le Corbusier table. Everything in the apartment was ultra-modern, including the very latest imported records of American jazz; the record on the green baize turntable could have been any band's; but instinctively she knew that it was his. That biting clarinet could only have belonged to him.

Her hands shook when she accepted a glass of champagne from one of the waiters; Marguerite was busy making introductions, but Frances responded mechanically and scarcely caught the names. Butterflies were turning over in her stomach; she was being childish, foolish, she reprimanded herself. Kit hadn't been any part of her life for almost three years.

Taking herself in hand she began to mingle with the other guests. From all directions of the vast room odd, disjointed pieces of other people's conversations drifted towards her.

'We saw the most sweet little cabinet in the Place Vendôme, all veneered in black macassar ebony and mother-of-pearl, and it was only a hundred francs . . .'

'. . . she was wearing the most awful shapeless Premet costume, darling . . . a positively ghastly shade of blue! Hasn't anyone *told* her that waists are going to be in again?'

Marguerite's voice now, bringing back a semblance of normality. Frances wanted to turn and run away, out of the apartment, away from the noise and voices, back to the quiet and sanity of their hotel.

'I adore your music, Louisa. Whatever is it?'

'Oh, it's the latest American jazz import . . . you know how mad

248

about jazz Norman is. Darling, do put on the other side, it's absolutely hypnotic. Do you know, they call the band leader the Pied Piper!' All the women in the room joined in as she hooted with tinkling laughter. 'Sylvia actually saw them play when Claude took her to New Orleans, and she said he was almost criminally gorgeous! Of course, all the women simply throw themselves at his feet . . .'

Why was this hurting so much, why should she care? It didn't matter what they said, did it? All he was to her now was simply a name on a record label.

'Norman, do hurry up; and don't forget to change that needle. If you make one single scratch on my favourite record I'll pour an entire bottle of champers down your trousers! That record is a positively sacred thing!'

Frances excused herself and asked the way to the ladies' cloakroom. There was nobody else inside and she sat down on one of the satin chairs.

'So, that's Tom and Katherine's youngest daughter . . . what a lovely girl! Very like Katherine . . . not a bit like Tom at all . . .'

Slowly, she eased off her satin high-heeled shoes and rubbed her feet. The hotel bedroom was in darkness; she'd told Grace not to wait up for them and Marguerite and Jack Holland had gone straight to bed when they'd come back from the Selkirks' party at one A.M. Frances eased off her evening dress and put on her crêpe de Chine dressing gown, then she went over to the window and parted the curtains with her hand.

Far below she could see the lights all over the city; the Champs-Elysées, Notre Dame, the Arc de Triomphe; parts of Paris that never slept. There was still the occasional, faint sound of passing traffic, but the sounds seemed a long way away, like distant noises during the dream.

Everything had been all right until she'd walked, all unwitting, into the Selkirks' apartment and heard him playing. It had stunned her to realize that even the sound of his music could still hurt.

It had only been a record. But to her it had seemed as real as if he'd been there with her in the room. It had hurt to hear other people talking about him; someone she'd loved, someone she'd never forgotten; it had hurt to hear other women speaking his name.

But she had to get over it, didn't she? She was being foolish, over-sensitive, silly. Kit Asmussen was part of the past and she had to think of the future. The future with Robert Carr.

30

Aunt Jessie Tremayne was confined to their cabin for the first four days of the Atlantic crossing with that bane of travellers, sea-sickness; but Laura, wandering the decks and sumptuous public rooms of the liner, was astonished at their sheer size, the number of passengers each could hold, and the striking likeness to the interior of a smart London hotel. She immediately thought of Brown's in Dover Street where she and Frances had met for tea.

She was nervous and excited at the thought of seeing Kit again; would he look the same as she remembered him, had he changed in any way? Three years in a foreign country were enough to leave their mark on anyone, even if they didn't notice it themselves. Three years this summer, and his letters had been so few and far between. Sometimes a few scrawled lines, the endings barely legible; occasionally a dozen pages that she'd scanned meticulously, hoping to find some indication that he was tired of America and planned to come home. But there never was.

When the liner docked and she caught sight of him standing near the end of the gang-plank, unable to help herself or contain her feelings any longer, she'd burst into tears, and so had Aunt Jessie; Kit had always been her favourite nephew and she'd always known he'd make good. While people milled all around them and the funnels from the Cunard liner belched clouds of steam, their voices were all but drowned by the deafening noise.

Slowly, he and Laura drew apart, and he hugged Aunt Jessie. Laura pulled out her handkerchief and dabbed at her eyes.

'Hey, none of that,' he said in his old, familiar, teasing way. 'You'll blotch your mascara.' He picked up their cases and made a sign to a waiting porter to carry the rest. 'Let's get out of this crush, shall we? The car's over here.'

'Are we spending just the one night here in New York like you said in your letter? Is Chicago a long way away?'

He grinned as he helped her into the back of the waiting taxi. 'A few times the whole length of England, that's all.'

The vast gilded foyer of the Waldorf-Astoria on Fifth Avenue was as busy and crowded as Oxford Street in the rush hour; all around her strange accents speaking in English made her head spin. She was continually exchanging surprised glances with Aunt Jessie; everything was so different to their own vague, preconceived notions of what America and Americans would be like. The pronounciation of familiar words were only one of the peculiar things they had to get used to.

Kit had burst out laughing on the journey to the hotel when Aunt Jessie had asked him why the traffic was driving on the wrong side of the street.

'They do things a little differently out here, Aunt Jess.'

Long after Aunt Jessie had gone to bed, they'd sat up talking until the early hours. She was worn out by the interminable trip. In London it would already be early morning. But there were so many things she still hadn't asked him that she had to know. So far all they seemed to talk about was her and Maurice.

'I met him at that dinner party Mummy gave for Daddy's boss and wife . . . and they brought Maurice along. Well, you were still at home, then, so you'll remember. He'd asked me to go to the cinema with him . . . Al Jolson's first talking picture. Funny, now, whenever I hear the name "Al Jolson" it reminds me of then. He was terribly sweet and interesting, determined to get on in the world; that part of him reminded me so much of you. I suppose after you left England and I saw more and more of him, he became a kind of substitute for your empty place.' She smiled, a little sadly. 'Not that anyone ever could, not really.' She reached out and touched his hand. 'I miss you, you know.'

'I've missed you, too. In fact I can scarcely believe that you're here.' He lit his umpteenth cigarette. 'I had a feeling Mum and Dad would put the brakes on as soon as I wrote suggesting you come out. I guess they came up with a hundred different reasons why you shouldn't?'

Laura nodded. How well he still understood them!

'Daddy immediately said that he wouldn't allow it under any circumstances, and Mummy went on and on about gangsters. Between you and me I think they were just as worried about what people would think of an unmarried girl sailing halfway across the world. And I knew Maurice wouldn't be at all keen! But then Mummy remembered Aunt Jessie and we all went down to see her in Torquay just before Christmas to talk it over. She jumped at the idea.'

Kit sighed. 'I always did get on much better with Aunt Jessie and Uncle George than I ever did with Mum and Dad. She always understood. The last time I went to see her before I left home, do you know what she said? That she wished me all the luck I deserved and she was certain I'd make good. If only Mum and Dad could have said something like that.'

'Kit, they do love you. And they do care. I know at times you might not think it; but they both find it terribly difficult putting into words what they feel, what they know they ought to say. And they can't help what they are, the way they think. They're different to you and I, that's all. And I could see by the expression on Mummy's face when I first told her I wanted to come out here and see you, that she wished she could come, too. When Daddy was being difficult, it was Mummy who brought up the idea of asking Aunt Jessie to chaperone me.'

He got up and poured himself a drink. It was a kind of American-style whisky, she could see that by the label on the bottle, and both the glass and the amount he poured into it was large. Since they'd arrived Laura had noticed how much Kit seemed to be drinking, and it worried her.

'Don't you think a mug of hot cocoa would be better for you as a night-cap than that?'

He threw his head back and laughed. '*Cocoa?* I've almost forgotten what it tastes like! If you rang room-service and asked them to bring some up they'd think you'd got bats in the belfry.' It was an old English expression that he'd often used at home, and she smiled; so much of his conversation, she'd noticed, was littered with strange expressions and Americanisms. She was desperate to convince herself that under the new, brash, inevitably changed Kit, the brother she'd always known and loved was still there, not altered at all.

He came back and sat beside her. 'So, what do you and Aunt Jessie think of New York? From the little you've so far seen of it? Chicago's very different, you'll find.'

'Kit, I don't want to talk about New York, or Chicago. I didn't come a few thousand miles just to do that. I'm not here for the sightseeing. I came because I couldn't bear any longer not to see you.'

'You're not going to go all sentimental on me, are you?'

For once, she wanted him to be serious. 'Kit, I want you to come home for my wedding. Please . . . for me. It simply wouldn't be the same without you.'

He was silent for a long while, staring into the pale brown liquid in his glass.

'I don't think I can do that, Laura. Not even for your sake. You see, the band have got commitments lined up for the entire spring and summer, and most of the autumn, too. Then come the winter RCA want us to do a couple of months more recordings. Got to make the brass while we can.' He was making excuses and they both knew it.

'Is it because of Frances?'

He got up and went over to the window and moved the curtain aside so that he could look out. Far below their fifteenth floor lights, people and traffic still moved; sometimes he wondered if American cities ever slept. Where were they all going to, where had they all come from? And why did just the mention of her name still hurt him after so long?

'Of course not. Why should it be? It was a long time ago. Besides, nothing could ever have come of it; we both know that. The musician and the cabinet minister's daughter . . . and never the twain shall meet.' Deliberately and too quickly he changed the subject.

'Aunt Jessie's looking well. It must be all that bracing seaside air. Did you say something earlier about you and Maurice spending your honeymoon down there?'

'Yes, I did. Torquay's always so much more peaceful in the autumn. When all the noisy holidaymakers have gone home.'

A look on his face in the dim light that seemed to her a little like nostalgia, flickered and then was gone. Was he remembering all the happy summers they'd spent on the beach there as children? Another life, another world away. He didn't move away from the window.

'I can still see the tide coming in across the beach, and the way it foamed and bubbled in the rock pools . . . do you remember how scared you were of jellyfish and crabs? And how you cried your eyes out when the sea swallowed up that great sandcastle we'd built? It took us the whole afternoon.'

'I remember that I built another one the next day and you trod on it.'

He was smiling again now. He let the curtain fall back into place, blotting out the skyline and Fifth Avenue. Then he came across to where she was sitting and kissed her gently on the cheek. 'Only a woman would remember something like that.'

253

The red-haired girl who was in Kit's tenth-floor apartment when they finally arrived in Chicago was a shock.

'Hi, I'm Anita Bronowski!' She'd opened the door as if she owned it, revealing a large, spacious room filled with sleek, modern furniture. Somehow Laura had been expecting something entirely different; something warm, homely, a poignant reminder of transplanted England instead of streamlined, ultra-modern American. She exchanged glances with her aunt. 'Say, you must be Kit's kid sister Laura, and this must be Aunt Jessie.'

Laura tried to recover from her surprise. 'Er, yes. We are.' Politely, she held out her hand. 'How do you do.'

'Say, you sure do talk funny. Must be that weird English accent.'

But Kit was scowling. 'What are you doing here, Anita?'

'Rudy let me in. I told him I wanted to be here to welcome y'all when you got in from New York.' She lit a cigarette without asking anyone if they minded.

But Kit was holding the door of the apartment wide. 'Maybe we'll run into you later. When we play down town at the club.'

She looked sulky but she left.

'I've never seen hair that colour before in all my life,' whispered Aunt Jessie under her breath.

The club where Kit played was another shock. When her eyes had got used to the darkness in the part where the public sat and dined, they were dazzled next by the lights that illuminated the circular stage. She remembered Rudy Loew from Kit's digs in Halkin Street, but all the rest of the musicians in his band were complete strangers. Aunt Jessie was wide-eyed at virtually everything she saw.

'My dear, will you look over there? They're *black* men!'

Kit grinned as he overheard her. 'Quite a few in this neck of the woods, Aunt Jessie. The further south you go, the more there are.'

'Well, I never! It would never happen in London. Did you know that famous Negro singer, Paul Robeson, was turned out of the dining room at the Savoy in the middle of having supper with his wife? They don't allow coloured people in there at all!'

'Hey, white boy,' called one of the black barmen as Kit walked by. 'Who are the two broads?'

'My Aunt Jessie and my sister Laura; over here to see me on a trip from England.' He drank down the double sourmash whisky in one draught. 'Get me another one of these, Koko.'

'Sister sure is pretty.'

'And spoken for. She's engaged to a solicitor from Cricklewood.' He laughed at the blank expression. 'In England we call laywers solicitors, thick head. And Cricklewood's a place.'

'Your sister's goin' to get hitched up wi' a *lawyer*?' He shook his head as he mixed cocktails and polished glasses. 'Man, that sure is cool!'

'See you after the show.'

'Hey, Kit! Dinah's bin askin' after you . . .' Kit was already walking away towards the band, but Laura had overheard. In between the thrill of listening to her brother play and her pride when he received thundering ovations after every song he performed, there was a growing disquiet; he was clearly drinking too much; there was more than one woman in his life. It was all too clear to her what was going on when she saw how the women crowded around him.

She had nothing against any of them personally; what Kit did and who he saw in his private life was his own business, not hers; but seeing him with them still hurt. They all seemed so wrong for him, somehow; shrill-voiced, brash, bold, almost aggressive in the way they pushed themselves forward. They drank, smoked and swore in a way that would have shocked and appalled Laura if they had been men. Because he always played into the early hours, Kit had arranged for a taxi to take her and Auntie Jessie back to his apartment; going into the ladies room at the club to fetch her coat Laura found herself unexpectedly face to face with Anita Bronowski.

'Well, hi again! I just got here. Came in to do a little re-touching job.' She pursed her lips in the mirror and liberally applied flame-coloured lipstick. 'Kit plays just great, doesn't he? Did he tell you RCA want to do another half-dozen records this fall? Wow, he sure is some guy!'

Laura stiffened. 'No, he hasn't told me yet. We haven't had much time to talk at all.' She forced herself to be polite; it was prejudiced and unreasonable to dislike somebody merely because of their appearance and the way they spoke. The girl couldn't very well help it; she was no different from most of the other American women Laura had noticed that night. And she was far from unattractive; quite the opposite. Willowy, smart, brash, pretty in a cheap sort of way with her flame-red bob and a mass of gold bangles and long beads that jingled like a harness when she walked. The sound irritated Laura unbearably.

'Have you known my brother long?'

'Six months, I guess. But the moment I laid eyes on him I knew he was the guy for me . . . I had to fight all the others off. I keep askin' him when he's gonna take me to England to meet his folks. All I ever get is stone-walled.' She lit a cigarette. 'Still, it's bin great meetin' with you. Kit says you're gettin' married come September time . . . maybe we'll make it a double event.'

A nerve had begun to beat furiously in Laura's temple. 'Really? You mean that you and Kit might get married?' The sudden thought of what their parents would think didn't bear dwelling on. And Maurice . . .

'Sure, why not? I'm just surprised a guy like Kit's been around so long on his own. Sure beats me.'

'I'd better go. Kit has a taxi waiting and Aunt Jessie isn't used to all these late nights.' She grabbed her coat and rushed out without saying goodbye.

Laura made herself a pot of strong coffee to keep herself awake until he came in. Aunt Jessie was snoring gently as she passed her door on the way back to the living-room from the kitchen. She'd drunk half the coffee and almost fallen asleep twice before she heard the sound of his key in the lock and he came in.

'Laura!' There were dark rings beneath his eyes; a single lock of hair fell across the left-hand side of his forehead, something that their father had always grumbled about when he lived at home, telling him either to have it cut off or brush it back. It made him seem oddly vulnerable, as if part of him hadn't changed at all. 'What are you doing still up? I thought you and Aunt Jess left the Club early because you wanted to get to bed?'

'I didn't realize you'd be back so late, that's all. I wanted to wait up for you.'

He put down his clarinet case and sank down on the sofa. He rested his feet on the arm. 'We never wind things up till around three. Later, sometimes.' He helped himself to the coffee and lit a cigarette. 'You don't mind, do you? I did warn you that I still had to work. Out here, you can't afford to let up. But I'll wangle some free time while you're here, I promise.'

'That's not why I want to talk to you.'

'Sounds serious. OK. Let's hear it.'

'Why didn't you tell me the real reason for not coming to my wedding?'

He sat up. 'Laura, what are you on about? I told you the reason. The band's got commitments that we can't break, engagements we can't slide out of. Not even for you. I'd be there if I could, you know that. Just to make sure this Maurice Flavel's good enough for my little sister.' He smiled wearily. 'Does that answer your question?'

'You don't want to come because you know what Mummy and Daddy would say about that girl?'

He stubbed out the half-smoked cigarette. 'I'm sorry. You've lost me somewhere.'

'That girl who was waiting here when we arrived from New York. Anita Bronowski. She was in the ladies' room at the club tonight. Among other things she told me that you were going to get married.'

Kit laughed. 'Who the hell gave her that idea? It's news to me.'

'She did. She seemed to be under the impression that it was all a foregone conclusion.'

'I'd better put her right then, hadn't I?' His flippancy suddenly made her angry. 'I made a mistake getting tied up with her.'

'You were the one who did the tying.'

He was suddenly as angry as she was. 'For Christ's sake, Laura. Do you expect me to live like a monk? I'm just flesh and blood, no different to anyone else. Would you rather I put on a show while you're here, and pretend that there're no women in my life . . . is that what you want?'

'No, it isn't what I want. But it hurts me to see you with someone like that, someone who isn't nearly good enough for you!'

'You don't like her, do you?'

'No, I don't. She's brash, she's loud, she doesn't know how to dress or how to conduct herself in front of other people. And I don't like the way she hangs on your arm as if she owned you. Is that enough to be going on with?'

'Quite a speech. But you're not in London now, Laura. Things are different out here.'

'I'm beginning to realize how much.'

It was their first quarrel and they were both upset by it. This wasn't how it was meant to be. On the boat coming over she'd had rose-tinted ideas of what it would be like; how they'd go sight-seeing, out to lunch, how she and Aunt Jessie would listen to him play, then go on to supper and a show. Nothing had turned out as she'd imagined it; other people, strangers she'd never expected to meet had intruded into the fairy-tale reunion she'd imagined and spoiled everything. She felt a sudden, unexpected stab of longing for home, and Maurice. She was so lucky that he loved her; all she wanted was for Kit to have that kind of love, too. But not with someone like Anita Bronowski.

'I'm sorry. I had no right to interfere. Can we forget what I said?' There were tears in her eyes. 'Kit, please forgive me. I really didn't come all this way to quarrel with you.'

He took her into his arms and held her and they squeezed each other tightly; she felt the touch of his lips against her hair. 'Nothing to forgive, little sister. And she means nothing to me. None of them ever do . . . I swear it. The only thing that matters to me anymore – besides you – is my music.'

She went to bed almost happy. Only long afterwards, when she was back in England, did she remember what he'd said and realize how desperately lonely he must have been to have said it.

They'd travelled back to New York three days before the Cunard liner sailed for Southampton. Kit had booked them a suite at the Waldorf-Astoria.

'It's gone so quickly, hasn't it? The two months I've been here. Gosh . . . it seems like two weeks, now.'

'I'm glad you came.'

All their luggage was ready packed and waiting for the bellboy to take it down in the hotel lift. Aunt Jessie was going through the drawers and cupboards in the bedrooms to make sure nothing had been left behind.

'She's been through them all three times already!' They both laughed, but Kit's face was quickly serious again.

'You and Maurice . . . you're sure?'

'Kit, if only you'd met him you'd never ask a thing like that.'

'So he's the first perfect man in the world. But you said you'd like to keep working for Anne Turner and he wouldn't let you.'

'He's no different to any other man on that subject. There's a . . . well, a certain stigma about working wives; you should know that. Only women whose husbands can't afford to support them have to go out to work . . . not wives of the solid, respectable suburban middle class. You remember what a dreadful fuss Daddy made when I first told him about the offer from Mrs Turner! It was only the fact that she dresses most of the aristocracy in London that made him change his mind at all.'

'And what does Mrs Turner think about you leaving her?'

'She understands, of course; although she doesn't want me to go. But she did suggest that I might persuade Maurice to let me work from home. I'd love to. I could design, prepare all the sketches, and then take them into New Bond Street once a week. But we haven't really discussed that seriously yet.'

'But why cut in Mrs Turner? She's made a tidy profit by exploiting your talent. Why don't you work for yourself?'

'But how could I? I'm completely unknown. Where would I get clients? Besides which, I don't have enough money to get started in any sizeable way . . .'

'Ah . . . but I have.' For a moment she just looked at him blankly while she absorbed what he was suggesting.

'Kit, I couldn't possibly take any money from you!'

'Why not? You're my sister. Who else should I help if not you? When you get back home you can go and see an estate agent to find you a shop; get all the details sorted out, then wire me and I'll arrange for you to be sent the money. Big oaks from acorns grow, don't they? Anne Turner wasn't born famous. With your talent you'll have her customers lining up in droves; and they won't have to pay through the nose for their dresses.'

He could see how excited she was. 'I'd have to talk about it to Maurice, to see if he minded. But I'm sure he won't!' A sudden frown. 'Mrs Turner wouldn't like it, Kit.'

'What the hell as it got to do with her?'

'Well, It seems so ungrateful, doesn't it? If I set up on my own. After all, she gave me the job at New Bond Street in the first place; I've learned so much there. I'd feel guilty about it; like biting the hand that feeds you.'

'All right, so she gave you a job. Why? For her own ends entirely, because she saw you had talent and she wanted to use it to her own advantage . . . how many of those famous gowns half of London Society are walking around in are your designs and how many are hers? Yes, I thought so. And how much profit has she made on each one? No, Laura. You don't owe her anything. It's Anne Turner who owes you.'

'It sounds different when you put it like that.'

'On the way home, you think about it. The money's here whenever you need it.'

31

For more than three hours, the endless procession of traffic virtually blocked the Mall. Nervous débutantes in their presentation gowns peered anxiously from the windows of their father's chauffeur-driven cars, trying to pass the spine-tingling waiting by chatting with their sponsors and looking out at the curious groups of bystanders who had gathered to watch the annual ritual all along the route to Buckingham Palace. One girl, *The Times* was later to note severely, was even smoking a cigarette.

No such trials and tribulations had been imposed on Frances; granted the special privilege of the Entrée, she was permitted to enter the Palace with her mother by a side door.

In the Throne Room, a page helped Frances to straighten and arrange her train. Laura's flair and skill in putting the finishing touches to her beautiful presentation gown, drew scores of openly admiring glances.

It fell gracefully from her shoulders in a slim, flowing line of snow-white silk and tulle, the overskirt meticulously hand-embroidered with pale gold and silver thread in a pattern of flowers and leaves; her train of white satin edged with velvet, three yards long, had also been hand-embroidered in the same painstaking, matching style. Her fair hair, drawn back from her face beneath her headress and the three compulsory white ostrich feathers, had been beautifully styled by Grace in a chignon of softly waved curls which rested at the nape of her neck; around her throat sparkled the white gold and diamond necklace from the Osborne family vault.

'You look absolutely ravishing, darling.' Her mother adjusted her *de rigueur* corsage of flowers and flicked imaginary specks of dust from her long, white silk gloves. 'Whatever you do, don't be nervous; there's positively no need at all. I've been through it, and I know. Like Elizabeth said, it's all over in a flash. When you reach the head of the queue, you simply hand your invitation to an official, then he shouts your name aloud and tosses your card into a rather common-looking wastepaper basket.' She laughed, and Frances felt a slight ebbing of the tension. 'After that, you just advance along the red carpet, stop and make two curtsies to the King and Queen – they'll be sitting on a low dais surrounded by a numerous assortment of relatives – and then walk on. Afterwards, you'll wonder why on earth you felt so nervous!'

'I know it won't take long. Diana Gunnis told me. Her sister Leonora did it last year, and she told us all about it. Poor Diana. She's probably stuck somewhere in the Mall in all that ghastly traffic.'

'Stand up straight, chin up, stomach in. And for goodness sake, remember the way you were taught to curtsy at deportment classes. You're an Osborne and you must never forget it.'

She saw him almost at once, standing in a group with her great uncle and Thomas Dreikhorn. Their eyes met and held for a moment; then he excused himself and she watched him make his way through the crowded room towards her. As if somebody had waved a wand, her mother had vanished. He reached her side and, taking her arm, brought her to a corner of the room where they were half-hidden behind a pillar.

She looked into his pale blue-grey eyes and for a moment neither of them spoke.

'You look breathtaking,' he said simply.

'Thank you.' She smiled, and felt her face grow hot. 'I have my friend to thank for that; she designed and finished off my entire outfit single-handed.'

'If you were wearing a sheet draped around you, you'd look more beautiful than anyone else. You don't need any embellishment.' It was the kind of thing girls dreamed of having said to them and for a moment everything seemed totally unreal. But Robert Carr was no ghost.

'Mr Carr . . . I mean, Lord Rosslare . . .'

'Robin, that's what my friends call me.'

'Robin.' Another barrier had been crossed. 'I . . . I was sorry to hear about your cousin's death; I know everyone was expecting it; but it was still sad and it was still a shock. I hope he didn't suffer too much pain before he died.'

'Nobody, even his own doctor, will ever know that. He never complained. He never once felt sorry for himself. It's only by a quirk of fate that I find myself with what was his. I've done nothing to deserve it at all.'

'I'm sure you'll be a very worthy successor.' She wished they were alone. She wanted everyone all around them to disappear. But why

261

was Robert Carr here today at all? He saw her look past his shoulder to where her great uncle and Dreikhorn stood.

'I wanted to see you. Officially, I'm still supposed to be in mourning; but my cousin would have understood. Frances . . . may I call you Frances?' He smiled when she nodded. 'I know the whole dashed Season's ahead of you, but I must say what I want to say now. I've been in love with you since I first saw you . . . I held back because I had no way of knowing if your family would object to you being courted by a Scottish Presbyterian.' A pause, while they took stock of each other. 'Your Great Uncle seems to think not.'

He was holding something out in both hands, a tiny, blue velvet box. She hadn't noticed him holding it; he'd simply produced it from nowhere like a magician.

'I'm not very good at flowery speeches; I'm a plain down-to-earth sort of chap. I have great nerve, I know that, saying this to you in such a public place, and on a day like this – right under the nose of the King and Queen, too. But when I saw you coming out of the Throne Room with all the lights shining on your hair . . . I simply couldn't hold myself back any longer.'

Slowly, hesitantly, almost afraid of what she was going to find inside, Frances opened the box. There, gleaming and winking against its velvet bed as it caught the light, lay a diamond engagement ring. She couldn't speak. 'If you would do me the honour of accepting this . . . I should like to speak to your Father . . .'

'Robin . . .' She was cut off in mid-sentence by the sudden appearance of her Great Uncle and Dreikhorn. The old man looked at her with his cunning, catlike grey eyes and she knew that he'd known Robert Carr was going to ask if he could marry her.

'My dear, I think you look even more beautiful than your mother did. And that, I assure you, is something than I never thought I would hear myself say to anyone.'

'Indeed not.' Was that a hint of mockery in Dreikhorn's eyes or was it only her imagination? He smiled, and gave her a slight, almost imperceptible bow. 'Lady Frances, you leave me hopelessly bereft of words.'

In that instant she knew that she didn't like him; anyone within earshot would have thought the words were merely a compliment but there was something in his voice and in his expression as he said them that told her they were completely insincere. Though he had the reputation of being a ladies' man, she strongly suspected that while he might admire a woman's beauty he had very little regard

262

for her intellect. Perhaps, like most politicians, he was so accustomed to saying one thing when he meant another that the habit of a lifetime was now impossible to break. But Dreikhorn didn't matter because Robert Carr loved her. And she was in love with Robert Carr.

32

Gunters was crowded when she met Laura there for tea. They found a secluded table tucked away in a corner, and Frances showed off her engagement ring.

'I've been dying to see you. It's seemed so long. There's so much to do with it being right in the middle of the Season and the wedding in September.'

Laura smiled to see her so happy. 'Where will you go for the honeymoon? Will you have to go and live in Scotland where his estates are? If you do I'll miss you so much.'

'Gracious, no! We'll live in London . . . where else? Robin's a politican and London is right at the very centre of things. If the Tories don't get a majority at the next election, he says there could be a National Coalition; and that means that, with his record, whoever is chosen to lead as Prime Minister is certain to offer him a key post. It's just the opportunity he's been waiting for.'

'With half the Season left to do, whenever will you find time to go house-hunting?'

'Somehow.' Frances sipped her tea. 'At first, we might have to simply rent somewhere furnished. Robin has a flat in Upper Brook Street, but of course that wouldn't be nearly big enough. There's only one bedroom. Quite a rabbit hutch, in fact. Of course, Robin should really have waited until the end of the Season before he asked me to marry him, but he confessed that he was afraid to wait in case I accepted someone else.' They smiled together. 'He was mostly worried that I really might prefer the Earl of Iden.'

'I remember you telling me about him.'

'His father died in March and he succeeded to the title; he and Robin glared at each other at my coming out dance. But I'd already decided in my own mind which one I preferred . . . still, all's well that ends well. He's going to marry Leonora Gunnis. My friend Diana's sister.'

'And what about your sister? Is she still down at Greyfriars in Kent? It sounds an absolutely heavenly place. I've always loved the country.'

'Well, Elizabeth detests it. In fact her letters are becoming more and more frenzied. She says that if she has to stay down there for another month, she'll go mad with boredom.'

'Couldn't she just as easily have the baby in London?'

'Staying on at Greyfriars was William's idea. He says that if he lets her come back to town she'll be too tempted by the bright lights. He doesn't want her to wear herself out.' She replenished Laura's empty cup. 'Anyhow, enough about my tribe. Tell me all *your* news. Have you and Maurice put a deposit on that house?'

'That was the easy part. I've been trying to continue my campaign to persuade him to let me go on with my work.'

'Laura . . . I've been thinking about that . . . I mean, if he's so dead-set against you carrying on at Mrs Turner's . . . well, what would you say to becoming my exclusive dressmaker? I'd pay for all the material, trimmings, your time, everything, before you made the clothes; that would only be fair. But you're so brilliant it would be absolutely criminal just to wilt all day at home . . . what do you say?'

She was about to tell her what Kit had said but stopped herself. 'Frances, do you mean it?'

'Of course. Will Maurice mind, do you think?'

'He jolly well better not!'

'Men can be very funny about some things . . . they feel threatened, somehow, by outgoing, independent women. Goodness knows why. Robin's friend Tom Dreikhorn is just like that. In his view we're simply put on this earth for pure decoration with no other use at all. Underneath I suspect he's just worried that we can do anything he can do, and better.'

'That sounds familiar.' Laura glanced momentarily from the window at the crowds of shoppers milling by. 'It reminds me of Daddy. And Maurice.'

She let herself into Robin's flat in Upper Brook Street with the key he'd given her, laying the flowers she had brought as a surprise for him on the hall table while she closed the door. It was then that she heard voices coming from the sitting-room. The first voice she instantly recognized as Thomas Dreikhorn's; the second belonged to a complete stranger. A friend, a colleague that Robin knew? It was young, high-pitched, hoarse with protest and emotion.

'But you said you'd speak to him, that it would be all right. You promised. That night I went with you to the club, you said the post was mine . . .'

Frances hesitated, listening, in the hallway, the flowers in her arms.

'You don't understand. We have to wait until things are more clearly defined after the next election. I'm doing all I can.' Dreikhorn's voice was a little louder now; he'd moved away from the window and further into the centre of the room. 'Remember; you were little more than a glorified messenger boy when Cultrane was at the Treasury. If Lord Rosslare acted on my recommendation and suddenly promoted you, people would be bound to ask why.'

'But I have two years' experience. You said you'd speak to Lord Rosslare, that everything would be all right . . .' The young, high-pitched voice had turned sulky. 'I know Lord Cultrane would have promoted me if he was still in office.'

'But he isn't in office.'

Taking a deep breath, Frances pushed open the sitting-room door and stood there; they both saw her at the same time and they were both equally surprised. As she might have expected Dreikhorn recovered from his surprise first.

'Why, Lady Frances, what an unexpected pleasure. I didn't expect to see you here.'

She met his mocking eyes squarely. 'I could say the same about you. For a moment I thought I'd come into someone else's flat by mistake.'

Dreikhorn turned towards the other man and Frances looked at him too. He was young, slight, fair; his grey suit looked a little too big for him around the shoulders. He flushed and smiled nervously.

'May I introduce Mr Lawrence Rankin, clerk at the office of the present Attorney-General. Mr Rankin, this is Lady Frances Osborne, Lord Rosslare's fiancée.'

'How do you do, Mr Rankin?'

'I'm honoured to make your acquaintance, my lady.' His handshake was weak, his hand sweaty and limp, like a week-old lettuce. 'But I really think I ought to be going . . .' He was clearly embarrassed and was making a very bad job of trying to hide it. Frances wondered why a mere junior clerk had been invited by Dreikhorn into Robin's private flat when Robin himself wasn't at home, and she could see by the expression on Dreikhorn's face that he had guessed what she was thinking.

'Time's getting on; yes.' He turned towards Frances. 'I just came by to collect some papers that Robbie wanted, and Mr Rankin spotted me going into the building.'

'Really? You're quite out of your way, aren't you, Mr Rankin? The Attorney-General's office is in the opposite direction.'

The young man flushed uncomfortably. 'I was actually on an errand somewhere else . . .'

'Oh, I see. Then I won't detain you.' When he'd gone Frances set down the flowers on the table and went to fill an empty vase with water. Dreikhorn was still in the sitting-room when she came back.

'Do you usually conduct interviews in Robin's flat, Mr Dreikhorn? Or did I misunderstand the end of your conversation?'

He gave her that slow, maddening smile. 'How much did you overhear?'

'I heard you mention my father's name.'

'Ah. Well, have no fear; I wasn't saying anything derogatory about his administration of the Treasury. I'm afraid I've found myself the meat in the sandwich with young Mr Rankin . . . His father cornered me at my club a few months ago and tried to make himself agreeable . . . I could see his real motive a mile off. Hinting how brilliant and hard-working his son was, when he knew I was in a position to recommend him for a certain vacancy to Robbie . . . but as I object to being press-ganged by ambitious fathers I was polite, but noncommittal. Now the young man's beginning to make quite a nuisance of himself. Damn cheek, following me in here.'

It all sounded perfectly logical, there was no reason at all for her to disbelieve him; yet at the back of her mind a single, inexplicable doubt lingered; yet why should he lie to her? She went on placing the flowers in water without looking at him.

'Wouldn't it have been better to have sent him packing? You could have made an appointment for him to see Robin at Westminster and he could have turned him down for the post – if he wasn't suitable – himself.'

'Robbie's very busy. With his own career. And with the plans for your wedding.'

'It was kind of you to think of that.' Why couldn't she bring herself to like him? After all, he was Robin's boyhood friend and he'd been instrumental in helping him in the first stages of his political career. Yet when she was with him she never felt entirely at ease. And why was he still standing there, watching her arranging the vase of flowers? Why didn't he take his papers and go?

'If there's any message you'd like me to take back to Robbie, I'd be glad to.'

'No, thank you. He's coming to dinner this evening at Belgrave Square. I'll see him then.' She glanced up briefly. 'Have you got the papers you came for?'

'Yes.' He came closer to her and she instinctively moved away. 'By the way ... Robbie did happen to show me something yesterday ... the guest list for your wedding. All the people I'd expect to have been invited, of course ... but I couldn't help noticed that you'd invited your dressmaker's assistant. Very commendable. Isn't she getting married in September, too?' She could hear the barely-veiled contempt in his voice and she wanted to hit him.

'How dare you speak to me like that! If Robbie was here he'd throw you out.'

'I wouldn't be so certain of that if I was you. Robbie and I have been friends for a very long while.'

'Too long, perhaps.' She meant to sting him by the remark and she did. Anger, then open hostility, flashed into his eyes. It was a declaration of mutual dislike.

'Dear me. I do hope Robbie isn't making an irredeemable mistake by marrying the wrong woman. That really would be most unfortunate for everyone involved.'

She put the last flower into the vase and picked up the paper she had brought with her containing discarded leaves and stems. Coldly, she walked past him to the door.

'I should like to say that it's been a pleasure seeing you, Mr Dreikhorn. But I prefer not to be hypocritical.'

Simon Forman handed her the glass of pink gin and sat down as she opened her small, snakeskin handbag. When he saw the money he smiled.

'And when does the unhappy young lady require the operation to be performed?'

'She isn't all that far gone ... she thinks about six weeks, eight weeks, something like that. I explained to her that you'd want to give her an examination first, and also that you'd have to charge her an additional fee.' She slipped the pink gin slowly. 'She's absolutely terrified that her family might find out; she's already started suffering from morning sickness.'

Forman smiled smugly as he took the money and placed it in the locked box that he kept in a drawer of his desk. 'The sooner the better, then. One evening next week would suit me best . . . when my wife visits her sister. Get back to the girl and make the necessary arrangements, then telephone me here.'

Anne Turner put down her glass. 'Simon, I have several clients needing more supplies of the powder . . . can I take some with me tonight?'

'Of course, my dear.' He went to his medical cabinet and unlocked it. 'You'll let them know, naturally, that prices – unfortunately – have gone up. Quite steeply, I regret to say.' They both smiled. 'Which reminds me. How is the unfaithful Lady Elizabeth?'

'Still sulking down at Greyfriars . . . awaiting the birth of her little bastard. She's on the telephone to me twice a day, snivelling about how hard done by she is.' She crossed her shapely ankles. 'I had thought of going down there to pay her a visit . . .' she nodded towards the phials of white powder in Forman's hands. 'You really have got her well and truly hooked on that stuff, haven't you?' Her voice suddenly became husky. He knew that sign so well . . . 'Your wife is away tonight, then. . . ?' She got up and walked towards him. 'You know, Simon . . . she really isn't good enough for you . . .' She reached out and stroked his cheek. 'What's she like in bed?'

'Regrettably inferior to you, my dear.'

Keeping her eyes on his face, she slowly began to unbutton the thin silk of her dress. When she was completely naked except for her stockings and suspender belt, she walked arrogantly across the room and stood on a chair. 'Well, what do you think? Do you think I'm still beautiful? More beautiful than your rich, aristocratic patients? I know you sleep with them, Simon. It must be so amusing to watch . . . you must let me, some time. Do they always believe everything you say?' He came over to her and touched her thighs. He ran his hands up and down each one, lingeringly; then he unfastened each suspender and rolled the silk stockings down. He pressed his lips to her skin and she closed her eyes in ecstasy.

'You're irresistible. So wickedly irresistible.'

She cradled his head in her beautifully manicured hands. 'I think . . . when I see Elizabeth . . . I shall make her believe that Eddie Vaux is being unfaithful to her . . . I'll tell her that I've seen him with another woman . . . how frightfully amusing! I can't wait to see her face . . .'

'That would be very naughty of you; and very cruel. And it isn't true, is it?'

She threw back her head and laughed. 'But such a wheeze . . . I couldn't resist it. She won't sleep, worrying that he doesn't love her any more, that she's lost her hold . . . there's no greater torture than that, for a woman who's in love.'

He took her into his arms and drew her down on to the couch. The leather was cold and hard, but she loved it. If he wanted to he could take her on the table, or on the floor. She enjoyed it more that way.

His lips were taunting, torturing, hot against her ear. 'My bad, beautiful Anne . . . come and be punished . . .'

Jane Forman held her breath, pressing her ear harder against his consulting-room door. The noises coming from the other side only confirmed to her what she had long suspected. Curious, that Mrs Turner and the other stream of wealthy, smart women who patronized his practice only seemed to have appointments when she was going out. She'd been on her way to the station to visit her sister when Anne Turner's taxi had drawn up at the entrance to the mews. That was when she'd decided to double back and find out if her long-harboured suspicions had been right.

Moving silently away from the door, she backed away, her shoes in her hand. She made no noise at all as she crept back the way she'd come, a faint smile on her lips. He didn't know it, of course; his vanity alone would never allow such a suspicion to enter his head; but for the past three months she herself had had a lover.

So he had a very profitable, illegal sideline, a sideline that he thought she knew nothing about. When the time was right, she knew exactly where his money was kept and what she intended to do. And he was no part of her future plans.

She made her way back to the street through the long, narrow garden, and out of the side gate. She'd missed the train she'd intended to catch; a taxi would do. Her sister would be waiting with supper, and she didn't want to be late.

The revenge she was planning in her mind would be all the sweeter for waiting for.

33

'It's very nice, isn't it, Richard? Very nice indeed. But I really did prefer the detached house in Richmond that you'd decided on first . . . so much more space, a bigger garden . . . and so close to Maurice's sister.'

Laura politely ignored her mother and followed the estate agent and Maurice inside. She was determined not to be balked. The villa here in Lansdowne Crescent was perfect; not too large to be unmanageable, close enough to local shops and public gardens but not too far from the underground if she wanted to go into town. It was more convenient for Maurice, too.

'I know that, dear . . . but with Maurice being promoted again so quickly, you'll be wanting to entertain . . . the house at Richmond *was* more impressive.'

The estate agent coughed. 'These villas are extremely charming, as you can see yourselves . . . in London, yet not in London, if you know what I mean! Holland Park is fast becoming, as I'm certain you already know, an extremely popular suburb with the business class . . .' they followed him into the front room. 'As you see, a charming room, plenty of cupboard space, and all newly decorated, sash-cord windows, tiled fireplace. Should you wish to convert to perhaps one of the modern electric fires, the tiling could easily be removed and boarded in with the minimum inconvenience, for a modest cost.' Their footsteps echoed on the bare boards as they followed him to the back of the house. 'A lovely, sunny room, this . . . for use as a parlour, perhaps, or a dining room . . . the choice is yours. And it looks out onto the garden . . .'

She and Maurice exchanged glances.

'A good-sized kitchen and scullery, with walk-in pantry as you see . . .' He rustled his notes efficiently. 'And, of course, three bedrooms on the first floor, and a most useful attic room on the second.'

'Could we see the garden, please?'

'Most certainly, madam.' Laura heard the jingling of keys. It was long and narrow, with lovely, neglected rose arches and an old dilapidated garden seat. 'There is a fish pond, right at the very bottom . . . and beyond that a vegetable patch. Compact, but very charming. Very charming.'

Laura clasped Maurice's arm. 'Maurice, do let's take it. Please. Then we have nearly six weeks to furnish and decorate before we move in.'

He smiled and squeezed her arm. 'I must admit I was rather tempted to plump for Richmond; but then, it was just a little more than we could afford.'

'Even if it wasn't it didn't have the right "feel". It wasn't homely. Besides . . . even if we could have bought it outright I still like this one best.'

They followed the estate agent back into the house and up the stairs to the floors above. While her parents were going from room to room opening and closing cupboards, and Maurice was deep in conversation with the agent, she stood at the window looking down.

It was a pretty, quiet spot; the crescent was lined with laburnum trees and there was a park; if she stood on tip-toe she could glimpse it through the foliage of the trees. She wanted to live here. She wanted a home that would be hers and Maurice's, alone. No trace of the previous occupants remained. The rooms were stark and bare, newly whitewashed and smelling faintly of paint. She and Maurice would make it their own.

She was already picturing the wallpaper that she'd choose for this room; in her mind she could see the different pieces of furniture, furniture that they would choose together. She would have chintz curtains at the windows, pictures on the sitting-room walls. Suddenly, she felt unbearably excited. If only Frances could be here to share it with her, too.

She glanced round and found Maurice beside her.

'Well, are you sure this is the one you want? Once I've signed the papers we won't be able to change our minds.'

'I love it! And this is going to be our room!' She kissed him impulsively on the cheek and he looked faintly embarrassed.

'Laura, for goodness sake . . . the estate agent . . .'

'Oh, fiddlesticks! I'm much to happy to care.'

'Really, do try to be more circumspect. Now come along and look at the other rooms again. I don't want you to say yes now and then tomorrow, when you've had time to think about it, tell me you've changed your mind.'

'As if I would.'

'Your parents preferred the one in Richmond.' She glanced over his shoulder and caught sight of her parents, gazing from the second bedroom window into the garden, the agent at their side. He was busily answering questions.

'Well, they would. They think a detached house is absolutely the last word. Anyway, it was much too expensive and I didn't like it. Besides which, it was too far away.'

'It had a lot more cupboard space.'

'Well, it would, wouldn't it? It's only just been built. This is fifteen years old.'

'You're sure now?'

'Absolutely. One hundred and fifty percent. And I'll be two hundred percent sure by tomorrow.'

He smiled.

'Anything to make you happy. And, I must admit, it does have possibilities. Besides which it's convenient for my office.'

'So it's settled then?' She hooked her arm through his and they walked back through the empty rooms. She restrained the temptation to shout 'hooray'.

Back in Kilburn, she curled up in an armchair and cradled the cup of tea her mother had made in her hands. 'I just can't believe it. Maurice and I have put the deposit on our first house!'

'It'll seem so strange not having you here. Two spare bedrooms, now. Your's and Kit's. Your aunt Jessie will be wanting to come and stay.'

'You and Daddy can come and stay with us . . . you will, won't you? When we come back from our honeymoon, you can come shopping with me, help me choose furnishing and things . . . oh, Mummy, I'm so excited! And so happy.' Her mother kissed her on the forehead. She was smiling.

'Maurice is such a wonderful young man. I have to confess I liked him from the very first. Of course, when I mentioned you were engaged, when it first happened, at the Ladies' Guild coffee morning, Mrs Prewitt was quite green with envy . . . she tried to hide it, of course; but I could tell. That daughter of hers, with all her airs and graces, is engaged to a most unsuitable young man – in the ticket office at Kilburn Station, if you please! All her boasting about how well her daughter was bound to do for herself . . . If you want my opinion, there's something not quite right about that girl . . . no better than she ought to be, I'll be bound!'

'Mummy!'

'Well, dear, Mrs. Fortescue, the vice-chairwoman did hint that

272

they were seriously considering asking Mrs Prewitt to step down from the local fund-raising committee . . . now you can't tell me that doesn't mean something.'

'Mummy, it's none of our business. Perhaps she fell in love with the young man in the ticket office. It's really nobody else's affair . . .'

'John Prewitt recently resigned from the tennis club . . . your father told me. Quite abruptly, by all accounts.'

'Maybe he doesn't want to play tennis anymore.'

'Or he's heard what people are saying about his daughter's obvious misalliance. I mean to say, letting her become entangled with a ticket office boy, when they have a semi-detached in Cedar Avenue . . .'

'Your Ladies' Guild sounds more like a hotbed of gossip than a fund-raising committee for local charities . . .'

'Laura, you've just reminded me . . . this . . . well, this difference of opinion you and Maurice have had about you continuing working after the wedding . . . you really must consider what people will say . . . it really wouldn't be right . . .'

'Well, whether it would be or not, I've already spoken to Mrs Turner. She was very sorry, of course . . . I told you before that she offered me the chance to design for her from home . . . but I turned it down.'

'Laura, I'm so glad.'

'. . . Because I recently – a few weeks ago, in fact, – had a much better offer.' For a moment her mother looked aghast, wondering what she was going to say, but when she told her what Frances had suggested instead, her face changed.

'But that's wonderful! Gracious . . . personal dressmaker to a member of the nobility! Have you told Maurice?'

'Yes, of course . . . when I'd worked out all the details in my mind . . . and after we'd settled on the house. I shall need a room to work in and the small box-room will be perfect. And it has such a lovely view over the garden. Maurice told his parents last night . . . no doubt the news will be over the entire length and breadth of Cricklewood by now.'

'I can't wait until Mrs Prewitt and Mrs Soames hear about this! There's a committee meeting on Thursday.'

'Mummy, I know it's an honour, but Frances *is* my friend. I didn't agree to do it just because she happens to be the daughter of one Earl and engaged to another.'

'Of course not! But all the same, there *is* a significant difference between your position now . . . I mean, there will be, when you give

273

up at New Bond Street. Being employed by Mrs Turner isn't at all on the same par as being personal dressmaker to someone like Lady Frances, after all . . .'

'No, Mummy. Do you know, I can't wait to tell her all about the house. There's a regular bus route; and the estate agent told us that they have a brass band in the park at three o'clock, weekdays and twice on Sundays.'

'Now that I would like to listen to. I do so love a brass band! So invigorating! And all those lovely old traditional tunes. Speaking of music, your father mentioned this morning that you'd had a letter from Kit.'

'It's so long since I heard from him.' Laura sighed. 'I know he isn't always the best letter writer in the world . . . but it seems ages this time. Daddy said it came after I'd left for work. I'd better go and read it, hadn't I? I suppose it's a good sign, really, that Kit doesn't have the time to write? His last letter was jammed full of all the news of the band's engagements and recording contracts. RCA . . . apparently they're the biggest musical recording company in America.'

'Fancy!'

'Kit wrote about engagements all over the place. California, Boston, New Orleans, New York. He was there the last time I heard from him.' She got up, eager to go and read his latest letter. 'By the way, how did Daddy get on at the caterer's? It's a real boon having Daddy *and* Mr Flavel working in the same place. Mr Flavel didn't mind him taking the day off from work.'

'There's still so much to do. We've booked the reception, of course . . . and your father gave the instructions about the wedding cake to the baker today. But don't you worry about a thing . . . you or Maurice. It's all very nicely under control.' She suddenly looked pensive. 'Such a pity that Kit can't get away for the wedding. I know how much having him here would have meant to you.'

'Yes, I know. But it couldn't be helped.' It had been one of the biggest disappointments of her life when his letter had come, postmarked Boston, saying that because of unavoidable commitments, he couldn't come. But then she had half-expected that.

Her mother had gone to fetch the letter. 'It feels much thicker than usual. The postmark's Chicago. But he must have written the envelope in a hurry . . . it doesn't look much like Kit's handwriting at all.'

Laura took it from her. 'It isn't.'

'What?'

'It isn't Kit's handwriting.' Slowly, while her mother watched her, she broke open the envelope and drew out the two handwritten pages inside. Folded between them were several newspaper cuttings. When she caught a glimpse of one of them on the top of the pile, her heart lurched.

'Well? Is it from Kit or not?'

'Er . . . no, from a friend of his.' So that her mother wouldn't see, she twisted the sheets of notepaper around the wrong way. 'Something here about Kit bruising his hand . . .'

'Oh, isn't that just like him? And he won't rest it, either . . . is there anything else? Is he coming home for the wedding or not?'

Thankfully, mercifully, Laura heard her father coming in from the hall. She got up, quickly.

'Daddy, you're just in time for tea.' She slipped the letter and its contents into her pocket. 'I'll be back in a jiffy. I've just remembered something I had to do upstairs.'

She rushed out, up the staircase to her bedroom. Then she sank down on her bed and spread out the clippings that were enclosed with the letter. She turned it over in her hands and read the signature: tall, scrawled, very artistic. *Rudy Loew.*

'. . . *I know that maybe I shouldn't have done this, but he talks about you a lot and I thought if I wrote and sent you these, you might be able to do something . . . I'm not sure what, but you're his sister and maybe he'll stop and listen to you . . .*' Her hands shook as she clutched the paper. '*It's the drink more than the women . . . they don't mean anything to him, but it's the hard stuff he lives on that really worries me . . . he can't go on like this; he doesn't eat, he doesn't sleep; he's a clarinet-playing machine and that's all that seems to drive him on.*

'*We've been friends for a hell of a long time, ever since London and Halkin Street and the 43 Club, and I hate seeing a guy like Kit just wasting everything away . . . there's a lot of anger inside him but I don't know what at . . .*' She lay down the letter, unable for a moment to read any more. Distractedly, she ran a hand through her hair. Then, slowly, she picked up the newspaper clippings one by one and spread them out side by side on the bed.

She could hardly bear to look at them, let alone read the details. It was like reading about someone else, a stranger, a Jekyll and Hyde, not the brother she knew and loved. A womanizer, a man who'd had affair after affair with singers, starlets, who drank to excess. Only his music hadn't suffered. Every piece that she looked at praised his genius, his talent, compared him to names she'd once heard him talk about with bated breath. The Pied Piper, Sidney Bechet had called him; and the name had stuck. Women threw themselves at him, everywhere he played was packed to the doors. She felt pride, love, pleasure, anger, despair, helplessness, all at once. He was so far away, so beyond her not only in distance but in what each of them had become, that she felt impotent to help him. What could she do? How could she make him change? Kit never did anything that he didn't want to; even if she did what Rudy Loew begged her to do would it make any difference? Was it already too late?

A tear had welled up in the corner of her eye and she dashed it away angrily with her hand. She caught sight of the particulars that the estate agent had given them on the little table beside the bed; they no longer seemed important. All the excitement, all the pleasure she'd felt earlier when they'd gone to look over the villa in Holland Park had dissolved away.

She picked up the clippings and put them back in the envelope with the letter. Then she went to find her writing paper and a pen.

She sat there, in the growing dusk, staring at the blank sheet of paper in front of her for a long while. Words eluded her, her mind refused to function. She knew what she was feeling inside, but how could she write down the words that she really wanted to say? One thing she knew for certain; her parents must never read Rudy Loew's letter, or see the clippings he'd sent her from the American press. She dipped her pen into the ink at last and bit her lip, hard.

'*Dear Kit . . .*'

34

Elizabeth had been walking in the gardens and on her way back to the house when she'd first heard the faint sound of the engine, the tyres crunching on the gravel as the car came slowly along the drive. Her first thought was that it was Eddie Vaux and she began to run towards it, considerably hampered by her bulk; but as it drew to a halt in the courtyard and the driver got out to open the door for his solitary passenger, her face fell. Elegant and stylish in a light, stone-coloured marocain silk costume and a large-brimmed hat, was Anne Turner. Elizabeth's face turned hard in disappointment.

She was wearing a simple, flower-printed summer dress, two sizes too big, and flat shoes; it was difficult, with the baby due imminently, to find anything suitable to fit her that she felt comfortable in. Confronted by a slim, elegant Anne Turner in the height of fashion only increased her irritability. Whenever she telephoned Eddie Vaux in London he was hardly ever there.

'Anne! What a surprise.' Anne Turner smiled. She could see by the expression on Elizabeth's face that she'd clearly hoped her visitor was someone else. 'You're the last person I expected to see down here.'

'I was dying to see you and have a chat,' she kissed the air beside Elizabeth's cheek and they walked together into the cool of the large hall, side by side. 'So I thought . . . be daring and take the day off. Of course, I really shouldn't have.'

'Aren't you terribly busy this time of year?'

The smile on Anne Turner's scarlet lips withered a little.

'I would have been more busy if I'd received the order I'd expected to from your sister.'

Elizabeth stared at her as they sat down. 'Whatever do you mean? You're making the wedding gown and all the trousseau . . .'

'I meant what I was expecting after that. She opened her clutch bag and extracted her ivory cigarette holder and the gold case containing her cigarettes. She lit one without offering them to Elizabeth. 'When I telephoned her the other day, she coolly informed me that the trousseau would be her last order with me. Without a word to me, she's asked my assistant Laura Asmussen – who's leaving me next month when she gets married – to design and make all her clothes.'

'But nobody could be a patch on you, Anne darling! Does it really matter?'

'This wedding to Rosslare is going to be the wedding of the year, make no mistake about it. Whatever Frances does, wherever she goes, she's written about, watched, photographed. How will it look when it gets out that she no longer patronizes Turner of New Bond Street? And that my ex-assistant from Kilburn is getting all my commissions instead?'

'But you've nothing at all to worry about. You have oodles of other important clients . . .'

'Who have been buying more from Paris couturiers this Season than ever. Don't think I haven't noticed. Ever since that sister of yours came swanning back from her little pre-Season jaunt in Paris with Marguerite Holland, both wearing French clothes, others have been only too quick to follow suit. Now it's considered the height of chic to go to the likes of Boulanger, Worth, and Chanel, and the up-and-coming French couturiers like Dupouy-Martin and Lucile Paray . . . instead of Turner of London. Who would have thought it? Shy, naïve little Frances blossoming into the chief exponent of the *dernier cri?*' Her beautiful face was sour. 'Fame is fickle . . . like men. My total orders are down on what they were this time last year. Thanks to your sister. And that doesn't please me at all.'

The baby was kicking hard; the headache Elizabeth had aggravated by walking in the sun was steadily becoming worse. She was having considerable difficulty in harnessing her temper. 'What exactly do you expect me to do about it? I can hardly tell her who to order her clothes from . . . you know as well as I do that Frances can be determinedly wilful at times . . . besides, I can't do anything stuck down here.'

Anne Turner lay back on the huge, comfortable couch and crossed her ankles. She'd already noticed that Elizabeth's were swollen.

'Actually, that wasn't the main reason I came down here . . . certainly not to bore you with my little troubles . . . when you rang me up earlier this week you said you were running a little short of certain supplies . . .'

Elizabeth's eyes brightened. 'You've brought some . . . ?'

'. . . unfortunately, no. You see . . . again unfortunately . . . the price has gone up considerably since last time . . . Simon wanted to know if you might have changed your mind . . .'

'No . . . no! Tell him to get me some. As soon as he can . . . it's the only thing that makes life bearable down here. God, I'm bored out of my mind! I don't care how much it costs . . . just tell him to get it.'

'He can't do that until you've given him the money.' Her sharp eyes were on the diamond and ruby brooch fastened to Elizabeth's dress. 'If you can't give me the cash, any little piece of jewellery will do.' She smiled, and reached out to touch it lightly with her fingers. 'Such a pretty piece . . . exquisite. I've always adored rubies.'

'No. Not that. Eddie gave it to me. I'll go upstairs and find you something else . . .'

Anne Turner smiled in an unpleasant way. 'Eddie . . . yes. I believe I saw him . . . well, I'm almost certain it was him . . . when I was passing Ciro's the other night in a taxi with a friend. He was with . . . now, what *is* her name? Eva Scott-Montagu. Dark, slender, very

278

attractive girl . . . wearing . . . I can't quite remember what she was wearing now . . .'

Beside her, Elizabeth had gone rigid and she pretended not to notice. 'You saw Eddie? At Ciro's? With her?'

'Oh, I didn't mean anything by it, darling . . . I expect he has to be seen out and about with other women, doesn't he? Otherwise William might start to suspect . . . Well, look at it from his point of view . . .'

'What time was it? Very late? Have you seen him with her before?'

'Only a few times . . . but then, he has to be circumspect, just in case that husband of yours started to put two and two together. If he did that, he might start wondering whose child you were carrying and that would lead to all sorts of unwanted complications . . .'

Elizabeth's face had gone very white. Her fists were clenched. She was so stunned and so angry that she felt sick. 'Do you want me to ring for tea?'

'Oh, heavens no, darling! I really ought to be getting back . . . duty calls, and all that. But I will take that piece of jewellery if you can go and get it . . .'

Ten minutes later, when Anne Turner's car had disappeared along the drive, Elizabeth hurried back into the house and picked up the telephone. Vaux's number was engaged. Who else would be ringing him at home at this hour in the afternoon? Immediately, she was suspicious. She replaced the receiver with a curse and waited a few minutes before trying again. This time his valet answered and told her that he was out. She banged it down and both telephone and table shook.

Angrily, she flopped into the nearest chair. Idly, resentfully, she wondered what Frances was doing now. On impulse she picked up the telephone again and dialled for the operator. Surprisingly, her sister was at home.

'So . . . you're not out and about with the handsome Lord Rosslare? Oh, yes, I know it's the middle of the afternoon and he's at Westminster . . . but I thought for you, his life and love, he'd cancel everything and carry you off somewhere. Too conscientious? Well, naturally! But couldn't he leave his workload in the no doubt wonderfully capable hands of that assistant of his who's perfectly brilliant, I hear? Yes, of course, I'm only joking, darling . . . what else?

'Why am I ringing? Well, to begin with I'm bored out of my mind, I'm sick and tired of looking out of every window in the house and seeing nothing but grass, trees, sky and cows. In fact I'm beginning to wish I'd gone to Marie Stopes' clinic and got one of those new-fangled Dutch caps or whatever they're called, that stop you getting pregnant in the first place; no, that isn't a joke . . . I'm deadly serious. Wait till you try it! How do I feel? Well, if you don't count feeling sick in the mornings, sick in the middle of the day and sick every night when I go to bed, you could say I feel wonderful!

'Why I'm ringing in the second place is that if I don't have some kind of intelligent conversation in the next twenty-four hours I think I'll be in grave danger of going completely out of my mind.' She paused, while Frances spoke on the other end of the line. 'Oh, that would be marvellous! You and Robin and Freddie might drive down next weekend . . . if you *could* drag yourselves away from all the hurly-burly in town it would just about save my sanity.' A pause. 'Speaking of visitors, by the way, you'll simply never *guess* who drove down here all the way from New Bond Street to see me this afternoon? Anne Turner. She isn't terribly pleased with you, darling . . . coming back from gay Paris with all those French gowns, and then getting her assistant to agree to design for you privately after she leaves . . . it's quite put her nose out of joint. Yes, she was definitely more than a trifle peevish. Anyhow, I told her, what did she expect me to do about it? I don't sound quite myself? Well, if you take into account the fact that I look like a balloon, none of my clothes fit me and I have goodness knows how many more weeks to go before I die of boredom, agony and torture before it's all over, you might begin to understand. No, I don't want to talk to mother!' She shifted position in the chair. 'Before I go, by the way, there was something I particularly wanted to ask you; just something Anne mentioned. I'm not sure if it was just idle gossip, but I did find it terribly amusing . . . she said that William's nephew Eddie Vaux had taken up with Eva Scott-Montagu . . . I suppose you don't know if there's any truth in it or not? I'm so dreadfully out of touch with all the latest gossip down here . . . of course, I don't know him *that* well, but I wouldn't have thought that she was his type at all . . . you haven't heard anything? Well, do let me know if you hear anything . . . I know William will be frightfully amused.' She asked a few more questions about the wedding out of politeness, and then rang off.

'Who was that?' Katherine Cultrane had just come into the room. 'You seemed to be talking for a long time.'

'Oh, just Elizabeth.' Frances put the receiver down gently. 'She's bored out of her mind, according to her. The waiting is driving her mad.'

'She never did have any patience; and if she takes much longer to have this baby she won't be able to come to your wedding.'

'It isn't until the end of September.'

'Babies don't arrive exactly to order.'

'She said Anne Turner was there today. She drove down especially to see her.'

'Oh?'

'It seems she was a little more than put out by the fact that I've asked Laura Asmussen to design my clothes after she leaves New Bond Street . . . I told you she was getting married at nearly the same time as me; four weeks after Robin and I, actually. Elizabeth says Mrs Turner isn't pleased at all.'

'Really? I wouldn't have thought it would have made much difference to someone as well-known and established as she is. She dresses everyone who *is* anyone in London.'

'Perhaps. But did you know that a great many of the designs that come out of New Bond Street to such acclaim are Laura's and not hers?'

Katherine Cultrane's curved eyebrows rose in uncharacteristic surprise. 'Really? She never told me.'

'Laura told me in confidence, of course, but I don't suppose it matters now that she's leaving. In fact the outfit you wore for Elizabeth's wedding was designed exclusively by Laura.' Her mother was looking thoughtful. 'That's the real reason she doesn't want Laura to leave . . . and why she's so piqued about her designing for me.'

'You don't like Anne, do you?'

'Is it that obvious?'

'Might one enquire why not?'

'I always thought there was something insincere about her; something not quite right. She's clever, of course; she would never have got where she is now by patronage alone. I have to admire that. The self-made business woman who's brought toadyism to a fine art. Oh, I know how charming she can be to her important clients . . . but that's just a façade. Secretly, I think she despises them.'

Her mother smiled. 'How very perceptive of you, Frances.'

'I'm sorry; I suppose I shouldn't have said that, should I? After all, she's very friendly with you and Elizabeth.'

'She's had her uses in the past.' She reached for the cigarette box. 'Did Elizabeth have anything else to say except for the usual string of complaints?'

'She did, as a matter of fact. Some piece of gossip that Anne Turner had heard. About Eddie Vaux.'

'Indeed?' Katherine had hesitated, about to light her cigarette. 'What kind of gossip?'

'Something about him having taken up with Eva Scott-Montagu. She'd seen them going into Ciro's together.'

'I hadn't heard anything. In any case it wouldn't interest Elizabeth . . . William and Eddie Vaux don't really mix all that often, socially.'

'She said she's starved of gossip stuck down there in the sticks. I felt rather sorry for her. When I see Robin this evening, I'm going to ask him if he'd mind driving down there next weekend to see her . . . I thought Freddie might like to come.'

Katherine smiled; she was already thinking of something else entirely. So Anne's creative ideas weren't entirely hers at all . . .

'Of course, darling, I'm sure Robin will agree. And Freddie. It's a splendid idea.'

35

A hush fell over the packed interior of Brompton Oratory as the first notes of music from the organ rose, then swelled, rising to the ornate, painted roof. Everyone moved and shifted a little in their seats, looking back over their shoulders to get a first glimpse of the bride.

Laura, with Maurice Flavel, moved in her pew halfway down the aisle and looked in the same direction, her eyes fastened expectantly on the arched double doors and the darkness beyond to the stone porch.

Maurice was looking discreetly around him at the glittering, the titled, the famous, with a stunned kind of awe; there were Cabinet Ministers, ambassadors, diplomats, every leading figure he'd ever read about in politics and high society; sitting beside the bride's mother, the Countess of Cultrane in the front left-hand pew, he could see the Prince of Wales and his younger brother Prince George; the bride's elder sister and brother-in-law, the Earl and Countess of Banbury; her great uncle, Lord Henry Osborne, then her brothers: Viscount Osborne and his wife, the Hon. Venetia Portland; The Hon. Harry and the Hon. Thomas, both down from Oxford for the wedding; the three pews behind were lined with lesser members of the Osborne family, and then all the leading peers. Maurice recognized, from seeing their pictures in the newspapers, Lady Cynthia and Sir David Moseley, close friends of the bride's family; Edward Vaux, nephew of Lord Banbury, who was married to the bride's elder sister Elizabeth; there was the Duke and Duchess of Sutherland, Stanley and Lucy Baldwin; the Duke and Duchess of Westminster, Lady Diana Cooper and her diplomat husband, several more whose faces were vaguely familiar to him from his perusal of the daily press.

In the front pew Elizabeth, resplendent in brilliant peacock-blue silk and matching pillbox hat, let her eyes wander to the front right-hand pew and rest morosely on the tall, fair, handsome figure of Robert Carr and his best man. Thomas Dreikhorn was leaning close to him and they were talking in low, rapid whispers, and smiling. Anger, resentment, stirred in her; it was all very well for Frances: Carr was young, personable, good-looking, set to rise high. William Banbury, his unhealthy pallor sharply accented by his grey morning suit, looked old and ill; distastefully, she inched away from him. He had suffered a mild heart attack shortly after the birth of her son; while he'd lain recovering at Greyfriars, everything had hung in the balance; every night she'd gone down on her knees and prayed for him to have another one; better still, to die. But he hadn't. He'd clung to life as stubbornly as she'd clung to her right to stay in London, visiting him only at weekends. She'd thoroughly enjoyed her protracted revenge; as soon as Banbury was out of the way and she'd recovered from the birth, she'd resumed her affair with Eddie Vaux with more gusto and passion than before; and it was clear that Anne Turner had only been malicious in telling her he'd been seen about town with Eva Scott-Montagu. A certain coolness had sprung up between the two women.

She would have loved to have turned in her seat and smiled at Vaux, two rows down; but she daren't. She looked away from the immaculately dressed figures of Carr and Dreikhorn and caught her mother's eye.

Katherine Cultrane was wearing the very latest Anne Turner suit in pale jonguil shantung silk; her shining, pale gold hair sleek against the chic, feathered hat and veil. She smiled slightly, as she glanced towards Robert Carr; the marriage was exactly what she'd hoped for her youngest daughter and, unlike Elizabeth, she hadn't needed to apply pressure to persuade her to agree to it. She had only two faint misgivings; Carr wasn't a Roman Catholic, and he would need to be

283

discreet about certain aspects of his private life, about which Frances knew nothing. But she was certain that he was intelligent enough to have already realized that. Satisfied, she looked away and at the same moment the music coming from the organ changed abruptly, then loudened, and everyone began turning in their seats to see the entrance of the bride on her father's arm.

The sunshine streaming from the tall windows and the wall sconces had turned Laura's painstaking months of delicate hand-embroidery on the wedding gown and its immense train into a dazzling myriad of silver-gilt light. Under her long veil of Honiton lace, Frances's dark honey-gold hair shone against the whiteness of her gown; a tiny blue silk bow that her godfather Thomas Holland had once given her as a child had been pinned to her white orchid corsage. Marguerite and Jack Holland were here to see her now.

Laura, swallowing down the lump in her throat, gripped Maurice's hand; Frances had never looked more beautiful.

As she drew level with the end of the pew where Laura sat, her eyes moved sideways in her direction beneath the veil, and she smiled.

Laura blinked back the tears that filled her eyes.

Frances lay back against the satin pillows and smoothed down the silk and lace front of her nightdress . . . a gift from Elizabeth. She was a little nervous, a little apprehensive; and Robin was taking such a long time. She looked across the semi-darkness of the hotel bedroom towards the half-open adjoining bathroom door, which spilled out a pool of light across the carpet. She could hear him humming, brushing his teeth, then the water coming from the tap. A long silence followed.

Anxiously, she glanced down at the clock ticking beside the bed; eleven o'clock. Robin had been fidgeting about in the bathroom for more than half-an-hour. Impulsively, she called out to him, 'Robin? Whatever are you doing in there?'

It was several minutes before he came to stand in the frame of the open doorway.

'Sorry, darling. Just getting myself spick and span.' He smiled boyishly. 'It isn't really all that late, is it? I thought I might take a chance and ring Tom.'

She immediately bridled with resentment. 'Ring Tom? In London? Now?'

'Well, there were those election papers that arrived on my desk the morning before the wedding . . .'

'Can't they wait until we get back? Surely he can deal with them. And, in any case, it's gone eleven now; won't he be asleep?'

'Tom doesn't go to bed terribly early; rarely before midnight. I'm sure he won't mind.'

'Robin, we're on our honeymoon!'

He came over and sat down beside her on the bed and took her face in between his hands. 'Don't tell me I've got myself a nagging wife?'

'Robin, be serious. Why do you have to worry about what's happening in London right at this minute? I've been sitting here for more than thirty-five minutes waiting for you to come to bed.'

'And ravishingly beautiful you look, too.' Gently, he kissed her. 'But with the election getting nearer and nearer I simply can't help having those papers on my mind . . . I'd feel much better if I just gave Tom a quick ring. Let me telephone down to the desk and see if they can get the operator to put me through.'

She sat back stiffly against the pillows again while he padded through to the sitting room that adjoined their bedroom. She heard him switch on the light, then the faint tinkle of a bell as he picked up the receiver.

His voice was firm and authoritative as he spoke to the desk clerk, then the hotel operator; then she heard it change as she pictured Dreikhorn coming onto the line at last.

She was angry, resentful; they had come away to be alone together and all he thought about was the work waiting for him in London, having conversations with his friend. She could hear him asking about the papers, then his voice became softer and less distinct, until finally she couldn't hear what he was saying at all.

On the other end of the line Thomas Dreikhorn lay full-length on the sofa in his Henrietta Street apartment, a drink on the floor beside him, an apple in one hand. He was smiling, picturing Robbie at the other end, and Frances, chafing with annoyance and impatience while they talked.

'So . . . how is the beautiful Osborne bride . . . or should I call her a Carr now?' He took a bite of the apple. 'Perhaps not; leopards never change their spots.'

'She's fine. Very well.' His sharp ears easily detected the note of strain in Robbie's voice. 'We were just about to go to bed.' Dreikhorn laughed, softly.

'When you come back, you must tell me what it was like. We'll have lunch together at the Ritz.'

285

'Tom? Are you alone?'

'What's the matter, Robbie? You're not jealous, are you?'

'Is someone there?'

'You could say . . . that I'm conducting a little late-night business.'

'Who is it, Tom?'

There was a lengthy pause, then the line crackled and hissed.

'No one you need bother about.' Dreikhorn was enjoying himself; it was such fun to tease Robbie. 'But I'm glad you telephoned. I was beginning to think that you'd forgotten about me.'

'You know I would never do that.'

Another pause, another smile. It was getting better and better. Foolish for him to even think of Frances Osborne as a rival now.

'Hadn't you better be getting back to your waiting bride; you really don't want to upset her on her honeymoon; she'll never forgive you.' He smiled at the slight, fair-haired young man sitting nervously beside him in a leather chair, cradling a barely-touched drink. 'Women are like that, I told you. They never forgive a slight.'

He replaced the receiver and picked up his whisky. Lawrence Rankin was watching him expectantly, uncomfortably, on the edge of his seat. How different the stupid little bastard was in bed. But he had an entirely different motive in inviting him here now.

'It was a good move, getting you into the Labour Party's offices . . . do you remember which parts of their next manifesto I want you to find and then copy?'

'Yes, I've learned them all by heart.'

'See that you don't forget.' He came and sat closer to him, and the boy flushed. He was getting a little too infatuated for comfort; continually ringing him at work, showing sulky jealousy if he mentioned someone else. But he hadn't finished with him yet. He was far too useful to be dispensed with.

'Drink up . . . and then we'll go down the East End . . . Limehouse again? Better if you're not seen too often coming in and out of here . . . you do understand that, don't you?'

'I saw you today. Going into the Grosvenor Hotel restaurant . . . with a woman. You didn't see me.'

Dreikhorn disguised the slight feeling of annoyance. He lit a cigarette.

'Lady Moira Avory; we had lunch.'

'You couldn't see me last week because you were taking her to the Criterion. It was someone else for the opera and supper the week before that.'

'I told you; it has to be this way. Do you really imagine that I enjoy it? Paying them empty compliments I don't mean, telling them how beautiful they are, how riveting I find their company.' He was sneering now. 'They bore me off my arse! But I have to do it, for the look of the thing. If I made the fatal mistake of remaining a bachelor and never being seen with a single woman, what conclusion do you think would be drawn? You do realise we could both go to prison if the truth was known?'

Rankin hung his head. 'I'm sorry . . .' He was staring miserably into his glass. 'I just can't bear it when I see you with someone else.'

'*You* can't bear it.'

'You don't . . . I mean . . . you don't do anything with them, do you?'

Dreikhorn hooted with laughter. 'They'd have to get me drunk first. And even then I don't think I could stomach it. But, like the perfect escort and the perfect gentleman I am, I never lay a finger on any of them.'

'You never kiss them?'

'Only very respectfully . . . on the cheek or the hand.'

'What about Lord Rosslare?'

'Ah . . . we've been friends for a very long time. Since the early days in Scotland. He'd never have got where he is now, you know, except for me. I got him appointed as private secretary to Lord Leith.' He grinned. 'If I'd been born with Robbie's fair hair and blue eyes, he would have given it to me.'

'You mean he didn't get it on his own merits?'

'I'll leave that to your imagination.'

The boy looked momentarily astonished; surely he wasn't that naïve?

'But I thought . . . I thought Lord Leith was married with a grown-up family?'

'So are a lot of men who prefer boys.'

'Does he know about . . . me?'

'Robbie? Of course not. And you won't tell him.' A warning note came into Dreikhorn's voice. 'Otherwise, as much as I'd like to keep seeing you . . .'

'I'd never say anything to him. Not to anyone. You know that. Just as long as I can keep seeing you. But I don't want to share you with someone else.'

Dreikhorn had gone to fetch their coats from the adjacent hallway. As he helped Rankin on with his, he paused and stroked the side of his face. 'I'm glad we understand each other . . .' It amused him to toy with the boy right under Robbie's nose. 'You know . . . you're very sweet, really . . .'

She saw the light in the adjoining room turn into sudden darkness as he turned off the lamp, then his silhouette as he came quietly into the bedroom and closed the door. It was a warm, tranquil night; the window was slightly open and a gentle breeze every now and then moved the curtains; the moonlight stole across the satin cover of the draped bed, casting shadows from the canopy above.

He stood over her for a moment without speaking; expectantly, wonderingly, she gazed back into his eyes. When he slipped off his dressing gown and lifted the covers, she instinctively slid down and lay there, waiting, in the middle of the bed.

His breath was cool, smelling faintly of the toothpaste he had been using twenty minutes before; his fair hair was clean and sleek, with the subtle tang of brilliantine. Hesitantly, still without speaking, she reached up and touched it.

In the semi-darkness she saw him smile at her, almost apologetically, before he took her in his arms and slowly drew her body towards his. She closed her eyes as he kissed her, waiting for the sudden wave of passion, longing, burning, the feeling she'd felt with Kit so long ago as if her entire being would burst, like an explosion, from inside her skin . . . but she felt nothing.

Slowly, the sun outside was setting, and the room was dark. Kit had closed the curtains. As she sat there, on the piano stool, watching him, he suddenly turned and came towards her, then took her hand and led her without speaking towards the bed. There were no noises outside the room; no voices, no music, no footsteps on the stairs. He smiled, then reached out his hands towards her, and slowly, very slowly, slipped the thin straps of her silk dress down from her shoulders so that they rested against her bare arms.

He whispered her name, he stroked her hair; his lips, his skin felt like fire against her flesh. His dark hair was damp as she caressed it with her fingertips, her whole body ached and burned and shuddered against his with a terrible, passionate yearning that she only half-understood; his body, hard and lean and strong, shivered with desire. She felt his mouth and tongue move across the hot skin of her cheeks, her throat, her earlobes, her breasts, her thighs, and she heard his voice in breathless, rapid whispers repeat her name, over and over again, before she woke, sweating, shaking, crying in the big canopied bed, trembling and sobbing out his name.

There was no one beside her in the bed.

36

She stared hard at her face in the dressing table mirror; then she turned, very slowly, and looked around the room. She had been a little girl here, then a woman; it was so tiny a space with so few things, but the memories it held for her would always be carried in her heart. Tonight would be the last night that she ever slept in here; tomorrow when she left with her father for the church, it would be the last time she left as Laura Asmussen; this time tomorrow she would already be Mrs Maurice Flavel.

With a smile playing at the corners of her lips she picked up her bridal headdress and laid it carefully away in its ribboned box; Maurice was downstairs with her parents and her uncle and aunt and everyone said it was unlucky to see anything before the wedding that would be worn by the bride. Kit would have laughed and teased her and told her not to be superstitious.

His last letter was still lying on the dressing table, read and re-read over and over again. If only he could have been here for her big day tomorrow, her happiness would have been complete.

She picked up the letter and stared down at the familiar writing; inside he spoke of new contracts, new venues, bigger crowds; but nothing of himself. There was no mention of any other person in his life except occasional, oblique references to Rudy Loew and other musicians in his band. There were no clues about his feelings for anything, other than his music; no mention of love, happiness or unhappiness; pleasure, hope. It was signed as he always signed, *Love, Kit.*

Her mother's voice, then Maurice's, called her name from the bottom of the stairs and made her jump.

'Laura! Hurry up! The car's just drawn up outside.'

She straightened her hair and dress and ran to the front bedroom window; a long, gleaming black Daimler had drawn up on the pavement outside; craning her neck she could see the uniformed chauffeur, the curtains of all the neighbours' windows along the street being pulled aside. People walking past the house stopped and stared, as the chauffeur got out, opened the back door of the Daimler and out stepped Frances, immaculate in a stone-coloured marocain silk suit and matching picture hat that fluttered slightly in the autumn breeze. On the opposite side of the street, everyone had come out of their houses to stand and look. Violet Asmussen had made certain that everyone within a five-mile radius of central Kilburn – particularly the ladies on the committee of the Kilburn Ladies' Guild – knew that her daughter's friend and patron, the Countess of Rosslare, was calling in to take afternoon tea when she arrived back from her honeymoon in the South of France. The Kilburn Ladies' Whist and Bridge Club, and the wives of the standing committee of the Kilburn Tennis and Golf Clubs were still talking about the discreetly passed news that Lady Rosslare had asked Miss Asmussen to design clothes exclusively for her.

In the post the following morning, there were more than twenty-two invitations addressed to the Asmussens to dinner parties, important local social events, and the vicar's house for tea.

How Kit would have laughed.

There was still no sign of them.

Her eyes searched the pews on either side as she walked along the little aisle on her father's arm; kneeling side by side with Maurice in front of the altar, only half listening to the vicar, the hymns and prayers. Where could they be? A sudden awful thought: even Bentleys and Rolls Royces occasionally broke down. But, please, God, not now on her special day. She so much wanted Frances to be here.

She listened intently to every little movement behind her, each separate noise. Here and there a whisper. An isolated and quickly muffled cough. At the back of the church one of the guests dropped their hymn book on the stone floor.

The vicar was looking at them benignly as he made the signal for them to stand up, and pronounced the blessing. Maurice's best man, a friend from the office, was standing ready to hand over the ring. Maurice, seeing her expression and thinking it was nervousness, looked down at her and smiled.

She forced herself not to turn round; the little church was packed to capacity, and they were all watching her. But was that because so many curious people she hardly knew simply loved a wedding, or because the news had leaked out that the chief guests were to be the Earl and Countess of Rosslare?

The vicar was joining their hands together when suddenly she heard noises of a late arrival at the back of the church. Unable to stop herself, she turned her head with almost all of the congregation, just in time to see Frances and Robert Carr slip inside the double-doors and sit down in their places on the bride's side of the church. For a moment their glances met and they both smiled before Laura turned back again.

Then at last the vicar pronounced the words that made her Maurice's wife.

PART THREE

37

'I'm not saying that Ramsay MacDonald didn't do a few useful things when he was in office with a Labour majority; even the worst Prime Ministers can manage that; he got through the Housing Act two years ago, and speeded up council house building subsidies and slum clearance; and his trip to the USA in '29 admittedly helped to heal the rift between us over our war debts – but that isn't exactly an arm's-length list. Good god, unemployment alone has shot up to over two point five million!'

Thomas Dreikhorn smiled and sipped his wine.

'Gentlemen, ladies . . . respect for the puppet Prime Minister, please! Let me compose a suitable epitaph . . . Few will regret him . . . Defiant at first, he soon took to grandeur and the high-life and wallowed in it like a man who has been starving all his life . . .'

Dreikhorn raised his glass and everyone around the table guffawed and giggled. 'At least he didn't make the same mistake as Baldwin . . . giving women the vote and then losing the election when they all voted for the other side!'

When the laughter her died down, Frances looked at him coolly from her place at the opposite end of the table. 'You seem to hold a low opinion of us ladies, Thomas.' Robin looked at her sharply. 'Is there something that makes women less intelligent than men when it comes to casting a vote?'

'Perhaps I can best answer that by saying that of the entire House of Commons, there is only a single woman Member of Parliament!'

Frances ignored the ensuing laughter.

'In ten or twenty years the situation may have drastically changed; so that in the entire House of Commons every member will be a woman with perhaps a solitary man.' Laughter from all the ladies around the table. 'What's the matter, Thomas? Surely you men aren't afraid to let us in? Or is it that you're worried we might be better than you are?'

There was a sudden silence.

'To quote someone whose name has momentarily escaped me . . . "It is contrary to Nature that the hen should crow before the cock," Dreikhorn riposted.

'Henry, Lord Darnley, second husband of Mary, Queen of Scots.'
Frances's reply was swift.

'How excellent your history is.'

For a long, painful moment nobody spoke; then Lord Bodley broke the silence by changing the subject to something else.

'My dear, I was so sorry to hear that your great uncle was in hospital with his old lung trouble . . . nothing too serious, I hope?'

Frances smiled, grateful to look away from the angry faces of Dreikhorn and her husband at the other end of the dining table.

'I visited him in his private room at Charing Cross. He seemed very cheerful. But my father says there's no possible hope of him coming home until well after Easter.'

'Just as well. Being where he is he'll get first-class care. And, of course, doctors on hand day and night. I must try and call in on him myself . . . he's permitted visitors?'

'I'm sure he'd be delighted to see you.' She chatted with Bodley, on her left, avoiding Robin's eyes. He was always annoyed with her when she tried to score points off Tom in public, but she hadn't been able to resist it. Later, when all their guests had gone except Dreikhorn, he rounded on her.

'Really, Frances. Why do you always have to have the last word? I must say I think it's in execrably bad taste.' He was pouring himself a drink. 'You sound like a damn suffragette.'

'I was merely standing up for my sex,' she answered him evenly.

'I know Tom's something of an acquired taste; not everyone appreciates his particular brand of humour. But I owe him a lot; much more than you can ever understand. And I'd be grateful if you remembered that he's a friend of many year's standing.'

Dreikhorn chose that moment to re-enter the room. Frances saw him first. As their eyes met and held behind Robin's back she knew he'd been listening at the door.

Carr turned and smiled. 'A brandy before you go home, Tom? It'll keep out the cold.'

'Perhaps just a small one.' He walked towards the trolley where the decanters and glasses were kept. 'Stay where you are; I'll help myself.'

'I'll go down and tell Lane to call you a taxi.'

'Don't bother, Robbie; it's a fine, dry night. I can walk back from here.'

'Nonsense . . . it's far too cold.' He went out, leaving them facing each other.

For a moment neither spoke; then Dreikhorn gulped back the brandy and lit a cigarette. He glanced towards the group of silver-framed photographs on the top of the grand piano, then he went over and picked one up. It was of her godfather, Thomas Holland, and she had to restrain herself from telling him not to touch it. He smiled, almost as if he could read her thoughts.

'You know . . . I never really noticed before. Foolish, when it's so obvious . . . but there's an incredibly striking likeness between you . . .' He held out, glancing at Holland and then Frances and back again. 'Really, the most incredible likeness . . .'

At the same moment Robin came back into the room.

'Your taxi, Tom! Right outside the door.'

'Really, old man, you shouldn't have bothered. The exercise would do me good.' Slowly, he put down his glass and stubbed out his cigarette. He gave a small, mocking bow towards Frances. 'The dinner was excellent and the company even more so. Robbie, was it your idea to invite the charming Margaret Grosmont or Frances'? I'm beginning to think the pair of you are determined to marry me off.' He winked at Frances. 'But I do wish you hadn't invited her sister-in-law and brother; if she'd come entirely by herself I would have had the perfect excuse to see her home.'

'I'll remember that for my next dinner party.' She forced herself to smile at him. Pity the poor girl he eventually married. She'd already told Robin that she was convinced he was waiting for the richest young woman he could find.

'You can scarcely blame him for that; don't tell me many of your illustrious family, my dear, married for love alone? Your mother was an heiress; and Elizabeth and Banbury's marriage wasn't made in heaven. They argue like cat and dog. As for your brother Freddie . . . everyone knows why he married Portland's daughter . . . well, it's true, isn't it? And your great Uncle Henry never bothered to marry at all. That's no doubt why he's lived so long.' He hadn't meant it to sound funny but it did and she burst out laughing.

'Robin, you say the most outrageous things, but I love you!' She kissed him and he held her and their earlier argument was forgotten. 'But you didn't marry me because I was an Osborne, did you?'

'You're the exception to the rule. But that scheming family of yours would never have let me get within miles of you if I hadn't been my cousin's heir. Now, admit it. A Junior Minister's salary would hardly keep an Osborne in the style to which she's been accustomed.'

'If they'd tried to make me marry someone else I wouldn't have listened to them.'

He kissed her hair. 'As I recall it, my darling, your mother was determined that you were going to be the next Countess of Iden before I came on the scene. Just think what I rescued you from! And you've only got Tom to thank for that, you know. If he hadn't introduced me to Leith at the Scottish Office in the first place, I wouldn't have been promoted and come south at all. And then I'd never have set eyes on you.' They walked towards the door together. He put his arm around her. 'Can you meet me for lunch tomorrow or are you busy with one of your interminable charity committees?'

'There *is* a fund-raising meeting at Queen Charlotte's in the morning, darling . . . I really have to be there. Arthur Watts, the hospital secretary, asked me to be there by ten. Then I'm meeting Laura for lunch and she's coming back here with me in the afternoon to fit me for those new gowns.' They both said goodnight to Lane on their way upstairs. He disappeared into the drawing room to clear away the glasses and turn out the lights. 'Then at four o'clock I'm meeting William Elliott . . . he's the director of the NSPCC. I'm one of their patrons and he wants to go over the Society accounts at Leicester Square.'

'A very worthy cause. But now I'm stuck with having lunch at the Traveller's Club with Winston Churchill.'

'I'm sorry, darling; you won't be able to use me as an excuse. Can't you get out of it somehow?'

'Well, I might as well suffer in silence. Besides, the food's good there and I won't have to say very much . . . Winston will talk enough for both of us!'

Grace was waiting to help her undress; Robin went to his valet in his dressing-room. She sat up in bed, a novel open on her lap, glancing at the light beneath the connecting door, waiting for him to come. It was nearly three-quarters of an hour and she was already half-asleep when he appeared.

'Oh . . . I thought you might have gone to sleep already. I didn't want to make a noise.'

She smiled at him, and closed the book she'd been reading, then put it on the table beside their bed. He climbed in beside her and turned out the light.

In the darkness he leaned over and brushed his lips on her cheek. But he made no attempt to make love to her.

'Goodnight, darling. Sleep well.' He turned his back towards her and within a few minutes she could tell by his deep, regular breathing that he was already asleep.

She lay staring up at the ornamental ceiling for a long while, wondering how long it would be until the next time.

38

She met Laura for shopping and they had lunch together at the Ritz. The cloakroom attendant took care of Frances' mountain of hatboxes and parcels.

'I shouldn't be so extravagant, I suppose; when I sit on the committees of the local hospitals and the NSPCC it makes me realize how terribly badly off so many other people are; and through no fault of their own. But this month and next there are so many birthdays and anniversaries in the family . . . only one of the hats is for me.'

'You're patron of so many charities, Frances. And the last person who should feel guilty.'

'Perhaps.' She sipped her glass of white wine. 'But there's so much poverty and misery in the world. I can't help dwelling on it somehow. Some of the conditions people are forced to live in, particularly in the East End . . . I saw some pictures . . . they look like something from the last century. I showed them to Robin and said that something really ought to be done about it. And what are the Government doing? He said with the National Coalition social reform has to take a back seat because there are more important issues. What could be more important than taking care of people who need help?'

'If he could do something I'm sure he would. Maybe the next election when the Tories get a majority and more power . . .'

'It's always "the next election", never now. Every Minister either says it's someone else's department, not his, or tries to shift the responsibility onto somebody else.'

Laura couldn't resist smiling. 'That sounds a bit like men all over.'

They both laughed.

'I'm so glad you were free to meet today. I was afraid you wouldn't be able to so often, not with Desmond teething again. How is he?'

'When I left this morning, still sleeping peacefully; no doubt he's woken up by now and driving Lily mad! But she's so good with him, and he does like her a lot. Of course we both tend to spoil him and

Maurice grumbles terribly, but he's such a darling. And it was a godsend finding someone as reliable as Lily. I never realized what hard work children can be – well, Mummy did warn me! Not that I'd ever be without him, even when he's kept me up half the night and I have circles under my eyes the next day.'

'He's adorable. I've put the photo of you holding him in a place of honour on my dressing table.'

They were interrupted by the sudden arrival of the Gunnis sisters; now both married – Diana to a wealthy industrialist and Leonora to the Earl of Iden. She could never look at Diana without being reminded of that evening at the 43 Club so long ago, nor Leonora without thinking that, had she never met Robin, she would almost certainly have married Iden instead. Diana had twin daughters and the Idens already had a son; how much longer would she continue to be the odd one out among all her married friends?

Diana was delighted to see her with Laura. 'Frances, darling, it's ages since we've all got together . . . let's arrange something. Now, I know this is that absolutely brilliant friend of yours who designs all your clothes . . . everyone's quite green with envy.' She turned to Laura after they'd all been properly introduced. 'You wouldn't consider designing for me, too, would you?'

'Don't leave me out, for goodness sake.' Leonora was fishing for her cigarettes. 'You don't mind if I smoke, do you? I know you don't . . . but Jeremy's so stuffy since Harry was born . . . he says the smoke is bad for children's lungs. So I have to do it secretly.' They all laughed. Frances glanced at Leonora; was she happy with Iden?

'It's very kind of you to ask me,' Laura said, feeling a little awkward that she'd have to refuse. 'But I don't really design and make clothes professionally . . . well, not anymore.'

'Laura has a young son, and her husband wasn't terribly keen on her doing any work at all after they got married,' Frances explained. 'You know how sticky husbands can be about wives being a bit too independent . . .'

'All too well, darling.'

'So she really only designs and makes my clothes as a sort of favour . . . because we've been friends for so long.'

'Lucky old you!'

'What a shame!' Diana was eyeing the midnight blue dress that Laura had designed and made for Frances. 'But I mean . . . if things changed . . . if you did have the time . . . it seems quite criminal to waste all that talent. Why don't you simply start up in business for yourself? Oodles of young enterprising women are doing it . . .'

'Yes, why don't you? We'd be customers for a start. And the word soon gets round, I can promise you. Well, that's how Anne Turner started. Word of mouth recommendation. And of course she had the patronage of Lady Cultrane. You have Frances's. I really would think about it, if I were you . . . you'll simply have to talk that hubby of yours round . . . besides, *everyone's* asking who your dressmaker is, Frances – surely you knew? Your clothes are streets ahead of Mrs Turner's, honestly; and the prices she's charging now for even simple gowns. Twenty-one guineas for an afternoon frock . . . it *is* a bit steep . . .'

'As much as that?'

When the Gunnis girls had gone to their table on the other side of the restaurant, Laura was pensive for a moment.

'They did have a point, you know,' Frances said, encouragingly. 'And people are starting to ask who makes my clothes. Didn't you tell me a long time ago that . . . that Kit said he'd put up the capital if you ever decide to work on your own? Really, you ought to think about it.'

'Yes. Yes, he did. It's just that I know Maurice wouldn't like it.'

'Maybe you should speak to him again. Things are different now. You have help at home, and you've got proof that people are more than just vaguely interested. And it could well be that Mrs Turner's fame has run its course . . . you heard what they said.'

'I'd still feel awful about undercutting her.' That, more than even Maurice's objections was still holding her back; it seemed so ungrateful to go into competition with the woman who'd first taken her on at New Bond Street.

'But that's what it's all about . . . competition. Otherwise there'd only be one dressmaker in all London. And what about all her rivals, ten years ago, when she burst onto the *haute couture* scene? Do you think she thought twice about taking away half their customers?'

'When you put it like that . . .'

'Why don't you sleep on the whole idea, and then discuss it with Maurice? I'm sure he'll want you to do something that you get so much pleasure from, and satisfaction. You could work out all the details first and then show them to him . . . ask his advice and so forth. It'll make him feel absolutely indespensible!' She smiled. 'Men like that.'

'All right, I will!'

'Good!' Frances caught sight of the approaching waiter with their order. 'Robin and I are having dinner with Mummy and Daddy tomorrow night. Telephone me the next morning and let me know what Maurice says.'

Maurice put forward all his usual objections, but she was ready with her answers.

'Darling, I really don't see why you should mind so much . . . it wouldn't interfere with home at all because I simply wouldn't let it. I could take Desmond with me to the shop, with Lily . . . and I'd only be there to meet clients in any case, just one or two a week . . .'

'Laura, I don't think you've begun to consider what an enormous undertaking it's all going to be. Admittedly, the way you put it makes it sound completely feasible. But the cost of it all, when you add it up . . .'

'Kit said that if I ever decided to work for myself, he'd put up whatever capital was necessary.'

'It's extremely generous of him, of course . . . but what if things go wrong? You'd be competing with the likes of Mrs Turner to start with . . . supposing these friends of Frances don't come to you, as they say they will? You have no firm orders at all, except hers.'

'I told you about what happened today when we had lunch at the Ritz . . .'

'Yes, that's all very well, darling. But did they mean it? That's what you have to consider before you take such an enormous step. Besides which, you know my feelings about working wives.'

'But it wouldn't *be* like that, Maurice! I wouldn't be somebody else's employee like I was with Mrs Turner; it would be my own business.' She sounded hurt. 'I thought you'd be proud of me, with the likes of Lady Iden and her sister asking me point blank if I'd design and make them gowns. And Frances says that all her friends keep asking her where she's getting her clothes.'

He came over to her and put his arms around her. 'Darling, I'm sorry to seem such a wet blanket. And I suppose I can't take wholeheartedly to the idea in the same way that you have . . . it's just that I don't want anything to change, to disrupt our life . . . and you do have Desmond to consider.'

'Do you really think I'd put the business before him? Or you, for that matter? Oh, Maurice . . . I wish you had more faith in me!'

'I have.' He drew her towards him and kissed her. 'All right. If you're determined and you want to go ahead, you have my blessing.

302

So long as you don't get too ambitious with this grand scheme of yours, and neglect us all. I don't want you changing into another Anne Turner . . . business first and last.'

'Darling, you're wonderful! I knew you'd see my point of view in the end.'

He stroked her hair and she kissed him.

'I'll write to Kit first thing in the morning.'

Later, upstairs, she went into the nursery and leaned over the cot, gazing down with a smile at the dark-haired, sleeping figure of her son. He looked so peaceful and vulnerable lying there, thumb in his mouth and a teddy-bear tucked beneath his blanket, and he reminded her poignantly of Kit. She bent down over the side of the cot and kissed him before quietly tiptoeing out.

Lying awake long after Maurice had gone to sleep beside her, she reflected how lucky she was to have a husband who loved her, a beautiful son, a lovely home; and Frances Osborne as a friend.

If only her brother could have had half as much . . .

It was unusual for her parents to invite only herself and Robin for dinner, and it was only afterwards, when the two men had left them to play billiards that Frances realized the real reason behind the invitation.

'So you're going down to Greyfriars this weekend to visit Elizabeth and the boys?'

'It would be lovely to have a quiet weekend in the country; and she wanted us to see the progress on the decorations. She was telling me on the telephone yesterday that the workmen have just finished re-painting the nursery.'

'Ah, the nursery.' Her mother sat down and lit a Turkish cigarette. She was looking pointedly at Frances. 'You and Robin also have a nursery at North Audley Street . . . but it's empty.' Wearily, Frances heard the veiled censure in her voice. 'That friend of yours who you met for lunch today, the girl who used to work for Anne Turner? Didn't you say that she had a young son about the same age as Elizabeth's?'

'Mummy . . .'

'. . . and she was married a month after you and Robin.' A pause. 'No children after nearly two years, Frances; it just surprises me, that's all.' She gave her a hard, penetrating look. 'You're not doing anything to prevent it, I hope?'

'As if I would!'

303

'Just before Elizabeth went on her honeymoon with Banbury, I caught her reading some atrocious book on contraception by that so-called doctor, Marie Stopes – the one who runs that infamous clinic in Holloway – the thought just crossed my mind that you might be doing the same.'

'Of course not!' Agitatedly, Frances went to the window and pretended to look out into the square outside, though it was too dark to see much at all. 'How could you even think I'd do something like that?'

'My dear, all your friends have children . . . some of them married quite a while after you . . . and Elizabeth now has two fine boys. Do you want Robin's title and estates to go to some distant relation?'

'That's not fair!' She was angry now. 'We haven't been married five minutes . . .'

'Two years is hardly five minutes.'

'I wish you'd stop saying that! We've been married for exactly one year and seven months; as for Elizabeth's two boys, she and William have been married for more than five years.' She turned away from the window at last. 'Is that the only reason why you asked Robin and I here to dinner tonight? I should have guessed you had an ulterior motive.'

Katherine Cultrane flicked the ash from her cigarette. 'There's really no need for you to be so touchy about the subject. I was simply going to suggest that you go along and see Paul Lobell.'

Suddenly Frances was very angry. 'Mummy, I'm not ill. I don't need to see a doctor. And there's nothing wrong with me; there's nothing wrong with Robin. You make it all seem as if we were in some kind of contest. Who can produce a child first! Who can produce the most in the least number of years!' Her voice was deep with sarcasm. 'I'm not a machine, for heaven's sake. And I do, believe it or not, have other things to think about.' At that moment her father and Robin came back and saved her.

'Robin definitely wasn't on form this evening,' Thomas Cultrane said, laughing. 'I beat him ten frames to seven.'

'I'll get even next time,' Robin said, lightly. 'I'm afraid I'm terribly out of practice. As a matter of fact, I've been thinking of turning one of the top rooms into a billiard room. I was going to ask your advice . . .'

The next morning, when Frances was supervising the packing for the weekend, Laura telephoned with her good news; Maurice had agreed to her going ahead with the idea of the shop. She'd already seen a smallish but likely place in Cavendish Street with a long lease. Someone in Maurice's firm who specialized in conveyancing had agreed to do the legal work and was already in touch with the estate agents.

'Well, congratulations! You're certainly a fast mover. Maurice has capitulated and you've got half the task completed already. I can't wait to see it.' She could sense Laura's barely-suppressed excitement over the telephone.

'I'm longing to show you. Why don't we meet early next week when you've come back from your sister's?'

'Bring Desmond along so that I can see him.'

'He'll be delighted to see his favourite godmother! We can stroll in the park and he can feed the ducks.' They both laughed. 'It looks like a fine weekend again. Have a wonderful time, won't you?'

It was warm enough on the first afternoon for the four of them to walk in the grounds. Banbury and Robin went ahead, chatting interminably about politics; Frances and Elizabeth strolled behind.

'Daddy was absolutely furious when Baldwin changed his mind after nearly resigning last year,' Elizabeth said, squinting at the strong sunshine in her eyes. She adjusted her hat so that she could see her sister's face more clearly. 'William said that the party would almost certainly have asked Daddy to take over in his place. It was just the opportunity that he's been waiting for.'

'What made him change his mind?'

'Goodness knows! Who knows why any politician does anything? Probably when it came down to it he simply couldn't let go. That kind of power must be terribly difficult to relinquish.'

'I'd heard that his health wasn't too good. Is that true?'

'Oh, he spent a few days in bed because of stress and strain; I'm sure he's really as strong as an ox.' They walked on, Frances admiring the flowers and the newly planted rose garden.

'It all looks so beautiful; I'd never have recognized this part. It was such a wilderness three years ago . . .'

'The whole damn place had been left to go to rack and ruin before I took a hand in it. William left all that sort of thing to his first wife . . . and whatever else she was, she was no gardener. Of course, that dreadful summer I had to spend down here when I was expecting Edward, bored out of my mind and without a thing to do, was when I first took an interest in it. I didn't have much else to occupy my mind. I ordered dozens of gardening catalogues, toured the grounds

305

and thought up a few ideas . . . then I called the chief gardener in and told him to get on with it. I'm rather proud of it now!' She had a pleased look about her lips. 'Besides, it's far nicer now when nanny takes the boys out . . .' Beside her, Frances had suddenly fallen silent.

'I think it's getting a little cold out here, Elizabeth . . . can we go indoors now?'

They went up to the nursery and played with the children before tea. Two-year-old Edward was already sturdy and handsome, with a mind of his own. Frances painstakingly helped him to build a castle with his coloured bricks. Thomas, just a year old, had recently learned to walk by himself and sent his mother into gales of laughter as he toddled lopsidedly across the floor like a drunken man.

'You're very lucky,' Frances said wistfully, helping her nephew up on his feet after he'd lost his footing and crumpled into an undignified heap. 'They're both beautiful children.'

'They're both little devils! You should hear them scream when it's time to clear away their toys and go to bed! I hide behind the door and leave it all to nanny.'

'My friend Laura has a little boy . . . Desmond . . . he's near their age . . .' she hesitated, finding it difficult to broach the subject, even to Elizabeth. 'When we had dinner with Mummy and Daddy the other night, she pointed out that Laura was married more than a month later than me . . . but she already has a child and I don't. Not to mention all my friends have children and you have two.'

'Trust Mummy to put her foot in it!'

'The point is, she's right. The deliberate way she asked just Robin and me to dinner, then got me alone when Daddy suggested a game of billiards . . . I know she invited us there just so that she could quiz me. She asked me if I was doing anything to . . . well, prevent it.'

The big, high-ceilinged room echoed with Elizabeth's laughter.

'She really is the end, isn't she? Did she tell you that she caught me with a copy of Marie Stopes' forbidden book? It was on the evening of the wedding, when I'd slipped upstairs just before we went away. She said she'd found it by accident but I know she'd been rummaging through my things. I was furious and so was she.'

'But . . . how could you do it?'

'Goodness, don't go all puritanical on me, please.'

'But *why* did you do it, Elizabeth? Why did you *want* to?'

'I would have thought that was obvious. God knows, if I hadn't put theory into practice I would have been pregnant on my honeymoon! That was the last thing I wanted. Just think . . . it would have absolutely ruined my Season! I'd have had to cancel Ascot, Cowes week, all those marvellous parties. Not to mention late night shows and then supper and dancing at the Embassy. You know how William hates all those kind of things. It was my first Season as a hostess in my own right and I was determined to enjoy it. Mummy's held sway over society for far too long. So I went to this marvellously discreet doctor that Anne knows and got myself fixed up.'

Frances was stunned. 'You mean . . . you actually used something artificial? But didn't William find out?'

'Gracious, no! Once it's in place a man hasn't the faintest idea whether anything's there or not.'

Frances was torn between disbelief and a morbid fascination; she'd been brought up strictly to believe that any form of contraception other than the rhythm method or outright abstention altogether was completely unacceptable. But here was her sister gaily giving her a detailed revelation of the process, and she didn't even feel guilty about it.

'Honestly, there's no need to look at me like that. Thousands of women do it all the time; half of them Catholics too, I shouldn't wonder. Surely you don't believe that a woman ought to be dragged down by being forced to have a child a year? Look at the high mortality rate among the working classes. That's the reason Marie Stopes started that clinic of hers in the first place.'

'When you put it like that it sounds different . . .'

'Of course it does, silly! Why shouldn't a woman be able to choose? You ought to have teased Mummy and said I'd taken you to have something fitted . . . I'd love to have seen the expression on her face.'

'Elizabeth, you're absolutely wicked.' But she was smiling. 'Do you mean to say that William's never found out?'

'That's the stumbling block – the husband – by law a wife has to get his permission before she can have any device fitted that prevents her having children; so can you imagine what would have happened if I'd trotted along to Paul Lobell in Harley Street before I got married and asked him to fix me up. He'd have had a fit!'

'This is all a game to you, isn't it? It isn't even serious . . .'

'Darling, surely you don't imagine I'm one of those maternal women whose only ambition in life is to fill a nursery full of shrieking children? Oh, I adore Edward and Thomas, of course. And now William can stop complaining because I've given him his son and heir – together with a spare; but I really don't want to have any more. Believe me, two is quite enough.'

'But what will William say if you don't have any more? Surely he'll want you to?'

'Who cares what he wants? Doesn't what I want matter at least as much? Fair's fair. I've done my duty and all that, so he certainly can't complain!' She walked over to the window and looked down into the gardens; William and Robin were coming back along the drive. 'You know how I always loathed being in the country? Now I look on being down here as a sort of retreat . . . at least when I'm not in Town I don't have to sleep with him.'

'You don't mean that.' The naïve, fifteen-year-old bridesmaid at the fairy-tale wedding who'd believed it was all a love match knew better now, but she was still shocked. 'Don't you care for him any more?'

'What makes you think I ever did?' They were interrupted by the boys' nanny, coming in to wash them for their tea.

'My saviour!' Elizabeth said brightly. She kissed each of her sons on the head and then signalled to Frances. 'I saw William and Robin coming back into the house. Let's go down to the drawing room and join them for tea.' A chorus of excited barking sounded from below in the great hall. 'Oh, heavens, who's let those dogs in again? And they'll be covered in mud, too!'

'Lord Banbury, my lady,' said the nurse, with a curtsey. 'He said it would be all right.'

'Oh he did, did he?' The two sisters made towards the head of the stairs. 'He's only let them in so that he can feed them with cake and he isn't tempted with it. Theodore Mayerne says too much extra weight's bad for his heart.'

Halfway down the massive, carved Elizabethan staircase, Frances could hear Robin's voice, and Banbury's coming from the hall.

'I thought he looked quite well; but paler than when we last saw him. He is all right, isn't he?'

'He is at the moment.' Frances glanced at her sister, anxiously. But Elizabeth didn't seem to be worried at all.

He had started to make love to her and she'd begun eagerly to respond, when all at once he suddenly stopped, ran his hands through his hair, and sat up. His fair, stony profile looked grim in the darkness. The huge, heavily curtained four-poster bed suddenly seemed unbearably confined, claustrophobic.

308

'Robin, darling . . . what is it?'

He'd covered his face with his hands.

'Are you ill?'

'I've felt better, admittedly . . . but it isn't that.' He flung back the scarlet brocade covers and got out. 'It's this damn bed. I wish they'd put us somewhere else. God knows this place has got enough bedrooms!' He was sitting on a chair somewhere near the middle of the room. 'Someone might have died in it.'

'Oh, Robin . . . don't be so silly.'

'People do die in bed, don't they? Especially old beds. My cousin had a bed like that at Ferniehurst . . . made by a master carpenter in the reign of James I . . . or was it Mary, Queen of Scots? I never could remember.' He was pouring himself a glass of water now. 'Whenever I stayed in that damn house as a child, I was always petrified . . . it was supposed to be haunted and I always expected the bed hangings to part in the middle of the night and some hideous ghost to appear, some ghoul waiting to get me. As often as not I'd wake up screaming, and bathed in sweat.' Her eyes were beginning to get used to the dark now.

'Robin, it's so late . . . please come back to bed. There's nothing we can do now, is there? I'll ask Elizabeth to put us in another room tomorrow night.'

'Don't do that. It isn't worth it, anyhow. We go back to London on Sunday afternoon. God, I hope Tom's sorted out all those appointments I had on Monday. So many people from the ministry to see . . .'

She lay back among the pillows. 'If that's all you're worrying about, you're worrying for nothing. You know how capable Tom is. You said so yourself. The perfect private secretary.'

'He'd laugh, if he was here. About me hating this damn bed. It's just that it reminds me so much of that great four-poster that belonged to my cousin Ian . . .' He'd put down the glass of water and come over to her. He leaned down and kissed her on the cheek. 'I'm sorry, darling. I was totally selfish, anyhow . . . it's been a long ride down and I really ought to have left you alone to sleep.'

'Robin . . .'

'. . . you turn over and drop off now. I'll just go through to the bathroom.'

Frances lay there in the darkness for a long time, waiting for him to come back. But when she finally fell asleep he still wasn't there.

39

They stood side by side with the estate agent, looking at the front of the bow-windowed shop from the opposite side of the street. The estate agent was visibly impressed by his client's companion, the Countess of Rosslare. Every time Frances spoke to him and he answered, he gave a funny little bow towards her which had the two young women exchanging glances.

'Shall we go inside again now, ladies?'

Already, Laura's imagination had filled the display with gowns and the interior of the shop and the workshop behind it was furnished, staffed, and in full production order.

'I knew this was the place the moment I set eyes on it.' She was as thrilled as a child. 'Frances, I'm so glad I let you talk me into doing this.'

'But I didn't. It was only a suggestion. Admit it . . . you've wanted to do this for a long time, ever since you left Mrs Turner's and got married. Only Maurice humming and ha-ing held you back. But I knew you'd persuade him in the end.'

'Well, yes I did manage to talk him round to the idea . . . but it was really his mother and sisters who clinched it.' She smiled. 'They simply mentioned the possibility of a procession of titled ladies of fashion being photographed in my creations, and how *terribly* impressed everyone at Maurice's office would be . . . including, of course, the head of the firm. That was enough to convince even Maurice that it was all a perfectly splendid idea! I'm afraid, as endearing as she can sometimes be, Maurice's mother is such a snob. Not to mention his eldest sister. I think their lives would become a social desert if they failed to receive their annual invitation to the vicar's garden party in aid of church funds.'

Frances felt as much pleasure as if the shop and the entire enterprise was her own; Laura so much deserved everything to be a success.

'I know it's all going to go splendidly, you'll see. Now, when we've finished here I'm dragging you off for lunch at Claridges, and then we can go back to North Audley Street for those fittings. I can't wait to see that divine oyster satin you measured me for last time . . .

goodness, after all those cream teas down at Greyfriars I hope I'll still be able to get into it.'

'Of course you will. Your measurements are exactly the same as they were when Mrs Turner took them for your wedding.'

'I suppose you know you're a genius?'

'Nobody's told me lately, no!' They both laughed, at the same time looking simultaneously into the mirror while Laura pinned the hem of the Nile-blue voile dress. Knowing Frances's acute dislike of over-embellishment of frills, fussy details and bows, she'd designed an evening gown that was at the same time striking but distinctly under-stated; cobweb-light bodice and transparent sleeves ended sleekly to the wrist, but from the elbow to the wrist gathered scallops of Nile-blue beaded chiffon flowed elegantly as the wearer moved, and yet at the same time were designed in such a way as to be completely unobtrusive; emphasizing the new elegant, flowing look, the gown fell starkly to the mid-calf mark, where the material subtly but distinctly evolved into a three-tiered effect that fluttered as the wearer walked. Frances was enchanted.

'Elizabeth would adore this! Blue was always one of her favourite colours. Mummy, too. I always did think that they both looked far better in it than I did.'

'You could really wear any colour. Even starkest, unadorned black. And you'd still look striking.'

'Flatterer! Goodness, is that Robin's car that's just drawn up outside? At this hour of the afternoon.' They both moved over to the window and looked down into the street. Rosslare and Thomas Dreikhorn were getting out.

'Perhaps the entire government's come to a complete standstill for the day, and Ramsay MacDonald has sent everyone home. Oh, let's leave them to it, whatever it is. We'll finish off here and then we'll go down and I'll ring for tea.'

Laura carefully helped her off with the half-finished gown, and then took the next one out of its tissue-lined box.

'Now . . . if you can just step into this one, there are a few adjust-ments to the darts I think I'll need to make.'

Frances reached out and touched the delicate fronds of material with her hand.

'Doesn't it look so much more stunning made up than when I saw the sketch? And you've almost finished it! Laura, you're marvellous.

311

Help me on with it and do the adjustments, and then I simply must go down and show Robin!'

'Tom, for Christ's sake, what the hell were you thinking of?' Robin had thrown his leather attaché case on to the couch and had begun to pace the room, agitatedly. 'You know how important Sewell-Barnet is . . . the PM never draws breath without consulting him first; they've worked together for years. And you have to go and offend him!'

Dreikhorn looked completely unruffled and simply lit himself a cigarette. 'He's a puffed up, pathetic little nincompoop, with a totally inflated view of his own non-importance. That Ramsey MacDonald thinks he's so indispensible is the most damning indictment of his own bloody incompetence and unfitness to be in office, let alone the leader of the Coalition. Robbie, he isn't worth worrying about; I told you. At the next election they'll both be out on their arses so what does it matter if I put him in his place? Concerning yourself with other men's underlings isn't really a very good way of passing the time.'

They had rarely quarrelled in all the time they'd known each other, but Rosslare was furious with Dreikhorn now.

'You just don't realize what you've done, do you? The position you've placed me in. When you told MacDonald's lackey that I was too busy to see him, he no doubt went straight back to Downing Street and told the PM that I wasn't willing to be co-operative over the new ideas for social reform. Don't you understand I'm trying to keep on the right side of him? You may dismiss him as Baldwin's puppet, but he's the one in the seat of power.'

'This really has got under your skin, hasn't it?'

His calmness only infuriated Rosslare more. 'For god's sake, Tom . . . just what are you trying to do? You were the one who was always telling me that I had to ingratiate myself with everybody.'

Dreikhorn had sat down and crossed his legs with a nonchalant air. Clouds of blue smoke from his cigarette slowly rose from where he was sitting, to the ceiling above.

'Let Cultrane and the rest of the almighty clan suck up to the Socialists if they want to; you're in a position now not to have to do that. No one got anywhere by grovelling to the wrong people.'

'Tom, you were bloody insulting to the man!'

'So, if it bothers you that much, why don't you go rushing round to Downing Street, cap in hand, and get down on one knee?' His voice was heavy with sarcasm now. 'You know, I hope I wasn't wrong about you, Robbie . . . I thought you had what it took for high office. But you're beginning to disappoint me.' He reached out and stubbed his cigarette in the chrome stand ashtray. 'Maybe you really only still have the errand-boy mentality after all.'

Before Rosslare could answer, the door opened and Frances, wearing the new evening gown, Laura behind her, stood there.

'Darling! I thought I heard voices from in here.' She glanced from him to Dreikhorn. 'What are you two doing back from Westminster at this time of day?'

Dreikhorn got to his feet but too slowly and reluctantly for good manners. Frances frowned.

'Well, ladies . . . this a very pleasant surprise!'

'It's all right, darling.' Robin came across and kissed her cheek, then smiled at Laura. 'Tom, I believe you already know Laura Flavel?'

'Of course! how could I ever forget it?'

'Laura's here for some fittings.' She'd wanted to come into the room and twirl around it to show off her new dress, but she felt awkward and embarrassed under Dreikhorn's eyes. 'This is one of her very latest designs . . . isn't it lovely?'

'Ravishing.' Dreikhorn was looking at Laura now. 'I understand that you're going into the *haute couture* business on your own account, Mrs Flavel? I wish you all the good luck that you're obviously going to need.'

Frances could have hit him. And what had he and Robin been quarrelling about?

'With Laura's talent and everyone I know asking me for the name of my dressmaker, I doubt if luck will play much of a part in it. Robin, can you ring for some tea please, while I go and change out of this?'

'Tom and I aren't stopping.'

'Oh, I see. Then just tea for us.' She hesitated in the doorway. 'By the way . . . you haven't forgotten that we're going to the Delavals' for dinner tonight?'

'No, of course not. But I may have to work on a little so it's going to be a bit of a rush.'

'Robin! Can't Tom finish off whatever it is that you have to do?'

Dreikhorn glanced at her and smiled; why did he always have that ever-present mocking look in his eyes?

'Certainly I can. I've been doing it for so long, haven't I, Robbie?'

313

'I can see why you don't like him. God, I think he's insufferable. And a typical male know-all. Maurice has one just like him at the office!'

'Could there be two Thomas Dreikhorns in the world?'

'Well, you know the type I mean. Whatever you do, they broadly hint that you'll never manage it. I didn't miss his little snipe about me.'

Frances poured them both more tea.

'Oh, don't take any notice; you're going to be a wild success. I know it already. In any case, Tom Dreikhorn is simply one of those men who absolutely hate to see a woman standing on her own two feet; and yet if they're weak and helpless they still despise them.'

'There's a word for that, isn't there? Mysogynist, or something like it.'

'Oh, he's certainly not that; he's escorted more women round London than the Prince of Wales. In fact he's managed to get himself quite a reputation. Typical ladies' man. Between the two of us I think he's a bit of a fortune hunter. I suggested it once, to Robin, as a joke; and of course he said it wasn't true. But friendship blinds people, doesn't it?'

'I hope it doesn't blind you about the success you keep predicting for my shop.'

'If you keep designing wonderful gowns like the ones upstairs . . . well, you simply can't go wrong.'

The workmen and fitters had finished their tasks by the end of May, and the first gowns appeared on models in the bow-fronted window two weeks after that. There was a rush of orders, and for a moment Laura almost panicked; the two experienced seamstresses and out-workers she'd managed to engage could barely cope with the sudden influx of work. Kit had sent her twice the amount of money she'd asked for, so she was able to take on more help to ensure that all her orders were completed on time.

One afternoon, just as she was getting ready to leave, a taxi drew up in the street outside, and out stepped a familiar figure.

'Blanche!'

'Well, well.' Blanche Stephens stood smiling in the small but beautifully furnished foyer, looking admiringly around her. 'You're a dark horse, Laura Asmussen – or should I call you Mrs Flavel now?' she sat down on a velvet upholstered chaise longue and peeled off her lace gloves. 'I always did tell you that you had a lot of talent, didn't I?'

'It's wonderful to see you. Why didn't you come sooner? You know I always meant to keep in touch . . .'

Blanche opened her handbag and took out a magazine, folded to show a large picture on the first page. Frances, Leonora Iden and the Countess of Airlie were standing in a group together in the Royal Enclosure at Ascot, all wearing Laura's unique gowns. She hadn't seen it and she gasped.

'Gosh . . . this will certainly please Mummy! Not to mention Maurice's mother . . .'

'But I know a certain someone who it won't please, I can tell you.' Laura glanced up from reading the caption beneath the picture. 'Madam Anne Turner, that's who . . . as if you couldn't guess. Well and truly put her nose right out of joint, this has.'

'But why? Her summer designs were absolutely brilliant . . . and I'll never have anything on the enormous scale that she has . . .'

'Don't kid yourself; what do you think she started as? Besides which, between you and me, I suspect she's beginning to run out of ideas. Talk was at New Bond Street that all her designs this year were just barely-disguised parodies of what's in vogue in Paris. And her prices have been going up and up . . . while our orders haven't. Yes, that's right. Between us, I wouldn't mind betting evens that Mrs Turner's had her day. Well, nothing lasts forever, does it?'

'I can't believe that, Blanche.'

'Neither could she when Lady Iden and half-a-dozen others in the same bracket didn't order from her this Season.' She lowered her voice. 'And you know who she blames for it all, don't you? That chum of yours, the Cultranes' youngest daughter, the one that's married to Lord Rosslare. Some of the things she's called her I wouldn't be caught repeating. She reckons things would have gone on the same for her business if you hadn't started as the Osborne girl's private designer . . . of course, nobody cared to remind her that while you were working at New Bond Street she was sewing her labels on your designs.'

Laura was outraged at the injustice of it all. 'But surely she can't blame Frances. It was nothing to do with her. Without my brother agreeing to put up the money I could never have got started in the first place. And even then the entire idea would never have got off the ground if I hadn't been able to persuade Maurice.'

315

'Oh, so you got round him in the end? Amazing what love can do!'

Laura managed to smile. 'Blanche, we must meet properly . . . look, I'll telephone. Not when you're at work, of course . . . but we'll have lunch or tea or something. I'm just so rushed off my feet . . . I never imagined it would turn out like this!'

'You're off somewhere now?'

'Tea at Cricklewood on the lawn. In-laws. Maurice's mother is a dear though . . . she's looking after Desmond.'

Blanche stood up, put her gloves back on and kissed Laura fondly on the cheek. 'Well, I'll wait to hear from you. I just had to come and wish you good luck – not that you seem to need it!' She pushed the magazine with the Royal Ascot picture back into Laura's hands. 'No, you keep it. I've got another copy. And you ought to frame it and keep it as a souvenir.'

40

Sabine had opened the bedroom windows, but the room was still hot and airless. Elizabeth poured herself a glass of water from the carafe, and closed the Ethel M. Dell romance that she'd been reading. She put it on the bedside table and kicked back the covers. At that moment the adjoining door opened and Banbury came into the room.

She glanced up in irritation; she was tired and in a bad mood after their dinner party this evening, and because of the humid, sultry weather, the boys had been fretful and difficult for nanny to get off to sleep. They'd both refused to lie down until she'd come up and read them a bedtime story. William had started to complain that she was spoiling them.

'I thought you were asleep,' she said testily. 'I was just about to turn off my light.'

He was naked beneath his dressing-gown.

'I've been longing for you all evening . . .' Reluctantly, she looked up into his heavily-lined face, and saw that he was sweating profusely; that, together with the thin, greying, brilliantined hair, and the way that his mouth was hanging slightly open, revolted her. A kind of disgust momentarily held her speechless.

'Elizabeth . . .' He reached out a thick, stubby, hairy hand and instinctively she shrank back in the bed.

'I'm tired, William. It's been a ghastly long day and an even ghastlier and longer evening. I said that I was about to go to sleep . . .'

The expression on his face immediately changed.

'How dare you pull away from me!'

'You've been drinking! I can smell it from here!'

'So what?' His speech was thick and slightly slurred. 'Isn't a man entitled to a few nightcaps? So you're too tired to make love? But not too damn tired to sit reading fairy stories to the boys, or to spend most of the evening flirting with all the men. Don't think I didn't see what you were up to, showing them all you've got in that low-cut gown? Don't think I'm some bloody old fool who's past it, who doesn't know what's going on . . . !'

Her anger matched his. 'Shut up, for God's sake! Don't you come into my bedroom at this time of night, shouting at me because you're jealous! Do you want to wake all the servants?'

'Bugger the bloody servants!' He made a wild lunge for her but she was too quick for him; in a trice she'd moved out of his reach and leaped up from the bed. 'Come here, you bitch!'

Furiously, she turned on all the lights in the room. For a moment they stunned him and he stood blinking. She forced herself not to look at the front of his gaping dressing-gown.

'You disgust me, do you know that? And you always have.' He stared at her. 'That's right, William. And don't look so surprised. Why don't you take a good look at yourself in the mirror?'

Anger, revulsion, five years of pretending had made Elizabeth reckless; her nerves were frayed and raw. The only thing he must never know about was her affair with Eddie Vaux, and that he wasn't the real father of either of her boys. 'You're an old man. You were old when I married you, and you're even older now. And you disgust me just as much now as you did then.' All the revolting things he'd done in bed, the things she'd had to pretend excited her, made her want to be vicious and cruel.

He began stumbling towards her with his hands outstretched, as if he was pleading with her to stop. But she couldn't now. 'You must have realized that I never loved you, that I just forced myself to go through with it because I had to make a good marriage and you were the best husband available . . . in a purely material sense, of course. Every other girl has to marry well, and so did I. What was it Mummy

317

said when I tried to argue? Marrying for anything as ridiculous as love is only for the working classes.' Suddenly she wanted to laugh. 'Surely you never imagined that I could ever have been in love with anyone as old and repulsive as you?'

'Bitch!' He staggered over to where she was standing and slapped her face. 'You damn bitch! My God, Margaret was worth twenty of you!'

'What? That barren old hag you were tied to for eighteen years? She couldn't give you the son you wanted, could she? I suppose she was pathetically grateful every time you wanted to sleep with her – after all, judging by her photographs I shouldn't think any other man would have wanted to! Tell me, William darling, did you ever try performing any of those disgusting bedroom habits of yours when you were married to her? Or did you need different things to make you excited then?'

'Shut up! *Shut up!*' He came forward to slap her again when he suddenly stopped, turned blue in the face, and bent double. With difficulty, he staggered backwards and flopped down heavily on the edge of her bed. 'My pills . . .'

She looked at him coldly, without a trace of pity. Her parents, the entire family, would be furious with her; but she couldn't pretend any more. Nobody would ever know that she'd been unfaithful, that the boys were Eddie Vaux's sons, not his; and, of course, there could never be any question of divorce . . . she was tied to him until he died. But she was determined that never again would she share a bed with him, that for as much time as possible they would live apart. Lord Henry Osborne, the head of the family, had once told her that a young woman could do more or less what she liked as long as it never became public; it was a motto that Elizabeth intended to live by. First thing in the morning, she'd pack her things and take the boys down to Greyfriars Hall.

'My pills, for God's sake! The brown pills Mayerne prescribed for me . . .'

She went over to the bell and rang it. Then she picked up her satin dressing-gown from the chair and put it on.

'Seddon can bring them. Not that they'll do you very much good. Theodore Mayerne may be a brilliant Harley Street doctor, but even he can't give you pills to prevent the effects of getting old. I'm going to spend the rest of the night in the children's room.'

She went out and left him there, struggling for breath. For the first time since she'd put on his engagement ring more than five years before, she felt free.

Surprisingly, Maurice hadn't reacted in the way she'd expected to the picture of Frances in the society magazine. On the contrary, the bad mood he'd come home from the office in grew more morose as the evening passed. He was clearly annoyed when she told him that she'd have to stay up to finish one of her evening-gown sketches, and picked an argument with her the moment she came to bed.

'I'm not surprised Mrs Turner's put out with all this business, Laura; I think I would be, in her place. After all, she gave you the opportunity to enter the high-fashion dressmaking business, and you must have learned a great deal while you were working for her. I expect she feels that in return you're simply stabbing her in the back. If what this Blanche Stephens says is true, you've taken away a fair number of her established clients.'

'Maurice, that isn't fair! Before Anne Turner came on to the scene ten years ago, Madame Handley-Seymour was the top ladies' dressmaker; do you seriously believe that Mrs Turner gave a hoot whether she took away her customers or not? Besides, she can hardly expect to be the only supplier of *haute couture* in the whole of London! That would be as unreasonable as expecting there to be only one bank, or only one firm of solicitors!'

He knew she was right and that only made him angrier and more unreasonable than ever. 'Well, if that's your attitude, Laura, then don't be surprised if you simply engender more ill-feeling. And all this high-society publicity is one thing, but have you thought of what might happen when these fickle ladies change their allegiance yet again to the next new dressmaker? If they deserted Mrs Turner so quickly, then don't suppose that they won't do exactly the same to you.' He sounded almost as if he hoped they would. 'Everything else aside, I'll jolly well tell you what I object to most of all. And that is you coming to bed at this unacceptably late hour because you've sat up drawing patterns! After a chap's been at the office all day, the very least he can expect is to enjoy his wife's company when he comes home. But no! You rushed through dinner and then rushed upstairs again to finish that confounded drawing!'

It was so unlike Maurice to be bad-tempered and carping that Laura harnessed her anger instead of giving rein to it. 'Darling, I'm so sorry you're cross. Did you have a bad day at the office?' She got into bed and lay back against the pillows. 'I didn't mean to neglect

319

you. It's just that I promised Frances this particular gown for the beginning of next month and I did so want to finish the sketch tonight.' She leaned forward to kiss him but he refused to be appeased.

'Frances! I might have known. And what, may I ask, is so terribly important about *this* gown that you have to sit up half the night designing it? I'm sure she won't be left without anything to wear!'

'Maurice, I'm too tired to argue with you. Certainly there's no point in my trying to explain while you're in this mood! But now that I'm running my own business, I do have certain commitments and obligations to my clients. When I promise a gown by a certain date, that promise has to be kept.'

He turned to her in the semi-darkness, his face taut with barely suppressed fury. 'Oh, I see! And what about your obligations and commitments to me? Of course I realize I'm only our husband, that I come a very poor second to all these grandiose schemes of yours! And what about Desmond? My mother spends more time with him than you do ever since you opened this confounded shop in Cavendish Street! You are the child's mother, damn it!'

Laura sat up in bed. 'Are you insinuating that I've neglected him?'

'I'm merely pointing out that the boy spends more time in the company of Lily and his other female relatives than he does with you. When is the last time you spent a whole day with him? A *whole* day, mind you!'

'I take him to Cavendish Street with me four times a week!'

'And leave Lily to play with him while you spend your valuable time flattering your rich, aristocratic customers!'

She stared at him through the patchy darkness, trying to understand why he was suddenly so against everything she'd worked for; in the beginning he'd seemed almost as happy and enthusiastic as she was. Yet now her name was beginning to become widely known and the orders were pouring in, he seemed to have mysteriously and abruptly withdrawn his support. Surely it wasn't anything as basic as jealousy?

'You mustn't let Maurice feel that he's being neglected,' her mother had said when she'd first told her about the idea. 'Men are strange creatures, darling. Just like spoiled, petulant little boys. They always want to come first, and sulk dreadfully if you don't let them.'

'Maurice isn't like that,' she'd answered, confidently. Surely what her mother had warned her about couldn't possibly be true? He'd seemed so pleased and so proud of her.

'Do you expect me to give it all up?' she demanded suddenly. 'Tell everyone that I'm very sorry but they can't have the gowns I promised them after all because my husband doesn't want me to finish them?'

'Don't be so damn childish!'

At that moment a loud wail rang out from Desmond's room across the landing. Instantly, Laura threw back the bed covers and pulled on her dressing gown. She tied the sash with a gesture of defiance. 'Thank you, Maurice. Thank you very much. Now you've woken Desmond. Lily said he's been fretful all day, what with this heat and his new tooth. If you'd kept your voice down he'd still be asleep.' She went out before he could answer her and sent Lily, who'd gone in to him, back to bed.

She cuddled him and stroked his hair and sat with him cradled in her arms until he fell back into an exhausted sleep. She was so tired that she fell asleep beside him on the little night bed.

She took a taxi to North Audley Street as soon as Maurice had left for the office next morning after breakfast. They'd eaten mostly in silence and what she had said to him had been answered in grudging, staccato monosyllables. Maurice was sulking. But what he'd said last night about Desmond had stung and hurt her. Leaving Lily to help Mrs Wilkinson, their cook-general, she'd dressed Desmond herself and taken him with her.

When they'd had coffee and Laura had got her to try on the gown and approve the new sketch, they took Desmond for a walk in the nearby park.

'I'm sure Maurice didn't mean to upset you. But I know how hateful it is when you have a row. Robin and I had a frightful argument after our last dinner party, and he made me so angry I could have hit him.'

'Did he say he was sorry?'

'I can't remember who said sorry first. But we did kiss and make up.'

'I tried to, but Maurice was still as bad-tempered this morning as he was last night. And I was furious when he woke Desmond!' They both watched the little boy as he toddled, uncertainly, a few steps in front of them.

'He's adorable! I do envy you.' She sighed and stared at the ground. 'All my friends seem to have children except me. As Mummy is forever reminding me.'

321

'You've only been married to Robin for two years . . . well, not even two years, not yet. Not until the end of September.'

'You and Maurice didn't get married until after we did.'

'Well, yes . . . but things don't always turn out the way you think they will. I could just have easily been childless, too. I mean, everyone's different, aren't they? We all take different amounts of time. Look at your sister Elizabeth.'

'Yes, I suppose you're right.' Not even to Laura could she say that Robin hardly ever made love to her. 'Maybe I'll never have any. Maybe I'm barren.'

'Oh, don't say that!'

'Well, why not? It might be true. At least Robin doesn't nag me about giving him a son and heir!'

'There you are, then.'

They sat down side by side on a seat, and Frances bent down and picked up Desmond in her arms. He gurgled happily and grasped hold of her pearl necklace. She studied his round, unformed childish face while they chatted. There was so much of Laura in him, but also she could see his father; and Kit. She wondered if Kit had looked like him as a little boy. She kissed him, and he laughed.

'Frances, tell me the truth. Do you think I made a mistake by opening the business in Cavendish Street? Am I trying to prove something to myself, am I taking on too much? Did I want to become a designer in my own right because I enjoy creating beautiful clothes for other people, or just to show Anne Turner that she isn't the only woman in London with a designer's brain? Was it all just an exercise in vanity? The way Maurice went on at me last night, I'm no longer sure. I thought he was so proud of me to begin with . . . but the more successful I become, the more he seems to object.' She gripped the edge of the seat with both hands. 'Surely he can't resent me for that?'

'Your mother was right. Men can be strange. Most of them simply don't like it when we go one better. There's still so much prejudice against independent, successful women. Anne Turner is a case in point. Not that I could ever imagine her being bothered by what other people think; she has too much self-confidence. I can remember a silly little thing that happened years ago when my brothers were home from school for the summer holidays and Elizabeth beat Freddie at tennis. He never forgave her! He sulked for ages and pretended it was something else, but we all knew why! Perhaps Maurice is afraid that you'll grow so successful that you won't need his approval.'

'But that's absurd! He's my husband! And he was so keen when I started . . .'

'Probably because he thought he was just indulging a whim, that you'd either give up half-way or that none of it would turn out as you expected. I'm sure he's as astonished by the way clients are flocking to you, as Mrs Turner is.'

Laura was silent for a moment. 'I was so happy about it all. I was so certain I was doing the right thing.'

'He'll come round, in the end. I'm sure of that. It's probably very difficult for him to think of you in terms of an independent, successful woman. Remember how he opposed you when you wanted to stay at New Bond Street? Perhaps he doesn't like the thought that one day you might be earning more than he does. In most men's eyes, that simply wouldn't be right.'

'But that's ridiculous. And even if it ever happened, would it matter?'

'He's just reacting against your sudden and totally unexpected success.' Frances smiled. 'The male ego is a very fragile thing – one of Elizabeth's sayings. And it's true. Oh, you'll simply have to get round him! But maybe you won't even have to. When he comes in from the office tonight he'll have probably forgotten all about your quarrel.'

'I wish I could believe that.'

Laura took Desmond's hand and the three of them walked back towards the gates of the park, stopping there while the little boy admired a passing dog.

'Do stay for lunch. I'll ask cook to make something special.' She laughed, suddenly. 'Do you know, I have absolutely no idea what year-old boys like to eat!'

'Anything sweet and sticky that he can get his hands on!'

When Laura and Desmond had left in the taxi she'd ordered to take them back to Holland Park, Frances went back into the empty drawing-room. It seemed so oddly quiet now that the little boy had gone, devoid of his restless energy. She felt suddenly lonely and depressed; unreasonable, perhaps. Then she was called to the telephone.

'Oh, good, you're in,' said Elizabeth's voice from the other end of the line. 'I was going to ring Mummy but on second thoughts, I'd rather you give her a message.'

'Is something wrong?'

'I've had a bust-up with William,' Elizabeth went on airily, with as much detachment as if she was discussing tomorrow's weather. 'I can't remember how it started, exactly, but the upshot of it all is that I told him I was taking nanny and the boys and going down to the country to sort myself out . . .'

'In the middle of the Season?' That didn't sound like Elizabeth.

'Oh, bosh to the Season! I just want a few weeks on my own, that's all, without him breathing down my neck. If you want me for anything, you know where I am.' A pause. 'He has his precious Seddon to look after him, and Theodore Mayerne to supply him with pills, so he can take his ill-temper out on them. Look, I must go, I have to tell Sabine what to pack. But be a dear and call Mummy later to tell her I've left town. I'd do it myself but all I'd get is total non-sympathy, and a lecture in wifely duty.'

'Yes, of course I'll give her your message.' Frances hesitated. 'Is there anything I can do?'

'No, thanks; I don't think so.' Her sister hung up abruptly without saying goodbye.

Frances wandered back into the drawing-room and sat down at the piano. She lifted the cover and let her hands move abstractedly across the keys; it was one of Noel Coward's compositions and the melody somehow soothed her; she wished Laura was still here, that Elizabeth hadn't chosen this exact moment to go away; her mother would be furious that she'd quarrelled with Banbury, and Frances was in no mood for family arguments. She wondered what their quarrel had been about.

It was then that she glanced up and saw the photograph of her godfather Thomas Holland. For some reason it reminded her of what Dreikhorn had said that evening after dinner, when they'd been alone. She'd refused to acknowledge that he was right about the striking likeness, because it was clear that he'd said it to insinuate something that was not only absurd, but a studied insult to her mother. Why did he always manage so successfully to get under her skin?

She forced herself to forget about him. Robin was coming back from Westminster early tonight and they were having dinner out, then an evening at the theatre.

It was almost time to think about getting ready.

Elizabeth lit a cigarette and took a final lengthy glance at her reflection in the mirror. Nanny had just gone downstairs to supervise the luggage they were taking in the car; Sabine was packing her clothes. She looked at her gold and diamond wristwatch; another half-an-hour and they'd be well on their way, long before Banbury was due home.

Seddon had given her a reproachful look when she'd informed him at breakfast that she'd decided, unexpectedly, to leave for the country that afternoon. 'His lordship made no mention of the arrangements, my lady.'

'His lordship didn't make the arrangements; I did.' She'd gone on sipping her morning tea without looking at him. 'Kindly make sure that the car is brought round at four o'clock.'

By the time Frances had told her mother, she'd be well on her way out of town. As soon as they reached Greyfriars she'd try to reach Eddie Vaux in Le Touquet; why had he chosen that particular week to go over and fly his plane?

Elizabeth hesitated by the telephone, tempted to ring Anne Turner. It was nearly ten days ago when she'd given her the jewellery for Simon Forman; but there was still no sign of the fresh 'supply' he'd promised her. While Eddie Vaux was away, a little occasional 'snifter' of cocaine was the only thing that made life bearable. But someone might overhear if she telephoned Anne now; better to wait until they got to the other end.

She looked all around the vast hall as she drew on her white lace gloves. The whole house and everything in it suddenly oppressed her, and she longed to be gone.

The footman held the front door open for her, and she turned and ran down the steps to the waiting car outside.

41

It was another warm, still evening, with barely a hint of a breeze; after dinner Richard Asmussen walked with Maurice in the garden, while Laura and her mother sat on the canopied swingseat outside, watching them and chatting.

Violet Asmussen poured them both homemade lemonade into tall glasses half-filled with ice. 'Maurice seemed unusually quiet this evening. There's nothing wrong at the office, is there? He's done so well since that first promotion . . .'

Laura lay back against the cushions cradling her lemonade, and sighed. 'He rarely talks about work anymore; unless it's to grumble about one of the other chaps he shares an office with. Lately everything seems to be getting on his nerves. Desmond's cutting another tooth and even Lily can't settle him; our sleep's been somewhat disturbed for the last few months. But I wish that was all.' She saw her mother's head turn sharply. 'I think he's sorry that he agreed to let me go ahead with the shop in Cavendish Street.'

'Oh, surely not, darling? It's such a success. Far more than you ever thought it would be. I'll admit, I was sceptical at first when you told us that Frances Rosslare's friends had promised to patronize you when you started. I thought it might have all been pie in the sky. But I'm sure you're wrong about Maurice being against it. He did agree, after all. And his mother was so impressed! When she saw the cutting from Vanity Fair that was taken in the Royal Enclosure at Ascot, she telephoned me especially! You're quite a celebrity in Cricklewood by now, you know!'

'Mummy, Ida Flavel is such a snob! If the whole venture had failed she'd probably have been one of the first to have said, "I told you so!" or "You should have listened to Maurice!" ' Laura kept her eyes on the figures of her husband and her father in the distance; Maurice was admiring the new rose arbour.

'You're not having regrets, are you?'

'No, of course not. Although sometimes I think Maurice would have preferred things as they were, with me just designing for Frances. But so many people kept telling me that I could be successful if I started up a business of my own . . . even Kit, all that time ago. Maybe if he'd never have suggested it I would never have taken the plunge.'

'I do see Maurice's point of view, of course; after all, taking work home with you isn't quite the done thing, Laura. I really wouldn't if I were you. You should keep your designing and your home-life completely separate.'

'It isn't always that easy. Maurice only wants me to spend a certain amount of hours at Cavendish Street each day; there are some things that simply can't be left to anyone else.'

They sat in silence for a few minutes.

'Did I mention that the Paulets have moved away? No? Well, it was quite extraordinary, really. But I must say I'm not in the least surprised. The daughter, you know, when all's said and done, married quite beneath her; it does make one wonder if she had to get married at all, if you take my meaning; the vicar's wife is quite convinced of it. Mrs Paulet always changed the subject at committee meetings if anyone asked her about her son-in-law. My dear! That such people could afford to live in Acacia Avenue at all is quite beyond belief! Your father was told that they were only renting, but Mr Paulet always put it about that the house was theirs. I never believed it, of course . . .'

It was half-past-ten when they got back to Landsdowne Crescent, and Laura went into the spare room where her sketches were kept to put them into her case for tomorrow. Downstairs, Lily was busy making cocoa.

'Do you have to do that now?' asked Maurice's voice from the open doorway behind her. She turned round.

'No, darling; but it'll certainly save some time in the morning if I do. I'll be down in a minute.' She closed the top drawer of the desk. 'It's just that Lady Airlie said she'd call by around ten o'clock tomorrow and I want to have these ready to show her.'

'You haven't forgotten about Friday night?'

She frowned. 'This Friday night?'

'I told you a week ago. We're dining with the Forsters over at Hendon.' The note of impatience in his voice that she seemed to be hearing more and more often these days was tinged with anger. 'Surely you've remembered?'

'Oh! George Forster from the office, you mean?'

'There's only Forster at the office, Laura. Only one of the senior partners, that's all!'

She smiled, a little wearily. 'Sorry, darling. Yes, I have it written down somewhere. I was going to have my hair done on Friday morning.'

'Well, for goodness sake don't choose a dress covered in beads or sequins. Mrs Forster is extremely conservative. And do try not to talk about women's clothes for the entire evening!'

'If Mrs Forster brings up the subject I can hardly be rude to her by ignoring it.'

'You know exactly what I mean.' He turned and went towards the stair head. 'Shall we have our nightcap and go straight to bed? I feel all in.'

'I'll be down in a minute. I'll just pop in and take a peek at Desmond.'

She closed the door of her son's room and leaned against it, watching his peaceful, sleeping form for several minutes before she went over to him and kissed his cheek, gently, so that she wouldn't wake him. For a moment he looked incredibly like Maurice lying there and she felt a sudden stab of nostalgia for the past, for the time when they'd first met; was it really only five years ago? Maurice had seemed so different to her then. Had it been when she'd first started designing clothes for Frances Osborne, when she'd come back from Chicago, that he'd gradually begun to change? It had happened so imperceptibly that she couldn't pinpoint the exact time, only that something intangible seemed to have come between them. Maybe it was merely her imagination; but over the past few months they'd quarrelled more over silly, inconsequential things; he seemed almost eager to find fault with the smallest of her shortcomings that previously he would have laughed at or ignored.

She sighed as she made her way back downstairs. Between the lighthearted, charming, laughing young Maurice who'd held her hand in the cinema and impulsively bought her flowers, and the stolid, dour Maurice who seemed to care about little else but impressing the senior partners in the firm, there was a wide, unbridgeable gap. Had any of it been of her making? All men, her mother had told her almost smugly, changed after marriage; had she been naïve to believe that her marriage would be different?

He was reading the evening newspaper when she got down. They drank their hot nightcap in silence. Impulsively, telling herself that his moodiness was all in her imagination, she got up and rested her hands on his shoulders.

'Why don't you go along to bed?' he said, without looking up from his paper. 'I have those notes from Forster to glance through. No sense in us both staying up.'

'Do you have to look at them now?' Her voice was soft, gentle. He still stayed where he was.

'Yes, I do, Laura.' He went on glaring at his newspaper without wishing her goodnight.

They'd stood for several minutes on the steps of the theatre after the show, chatting to the others in their party; then they'd all said goodnight and gone their separate ways. She'd thoroughly enjoyed the evening and clung affectionately to Robin's arm as he helped her into the waiting car.

It was only when they'd turned down a dimly lit side road to take a short cut to North Audley Street that they both caught sight of him, coming up the basement steps of a nearby house. They had a fleeting glimpse of him and his companion as their car drove by.

'Wasn't that Tom Dreikhorn?'

Robin was frowning slightly. 'Yes, so it was. He's out of his usual stamping-ground. Probably on his way to have late supper at the club.'

Pulling her sable evening-wrap closer around her shoulders, Frances sank back against the leather seats. There'd been something vaguely familiar about Dreikhorn's companion as he'd passed briefly under the light of a nearby street lamp. She'd seen him somewhere before; but for the moment she was too tired to think where or when.

'It was a wonderful show, darling; I'm so glad we went!' She turned to him and lay her hand on his arm. 'Marguerite said it was Noel Coward's best yet, and she was certainly right!'

Robin smiled vaguely, watching the buildings and late-night theatre-goers as they went by. He seemed to have gone very quiet. 'Yes. Yes, it was very enjoyable.'

Frances lay her head on his shoulder. She stifled a yawn. 'Goodness! I completely forgot to telephone Mummy and give her Elizabeth's message! It's too late now. I'll have to do it first thing in the morning.'

'Yes, you will.' Robin was staring out of the car window, unusually silent. He never spoke another word all the way home.

42

'Who is he, Tom?'

Dreikhorn lay back on the couch and crossed his legs while he casually smoked a cigarette.

'Who's who?' He held the burning cigarette in mid-air, smiling one of his maddening, teasing smiles. How amusing Robbie was when he thought he had a rival!

'Don't come that with me! I know you too well, remember? That young chap you were with last night. We both saw you, after we left the theatre in Piccadilly.'

'You and the fair Frances, I presume? Did you enjoy the show?'

'Tom, I want to know who he is.'

Dreikhorn smiled. How flushed Robbie's skin turned when he

was angry. That had enchanted Leith at the Scottish office too. He remembered the first time he'd brought them face to face, and the way the older man had stared and stared at him; lust at first sight. He'd laughed with Robbie, later, about that.

'Look, he isn't important. Just a boy I know. Satisfied? Actually, he was quite a find. When I first met him he was trying to twist my arm for a Ministry job, and I strung him along for a while. He's got brains, but he's not outstanding. It might have looked suspicious if I'd pushed him in by myself, but I found him something else instead. Now he's a junior clerk in Ramsay MacDonald's part of the Coalition. Perfect, isn't it? Who'd ever suspect some little clerk of copying certain private memos when he goes poking around in Labour Ministry files marked "private and confidential"? Isn't it a wheeze?'

One thing Dreikhorn had learned in his career, and by the unexpected fall of the Tory Party in the last election, was that as you rose you inevitably made enemies; and it was essential to know who they were. It was truly amazing what someone might say in an unguarded moment at the head of a staircase in Westminster, what another might write in a memo. Much of what Rankin brought him was rubbish; other things surprisingly useful. But Rosslare was unappeased.

'You're sleeping with him?'

'Is that a question or a statement of fact?'

'Well, are you?'

Dreikhorn grinned. 'Surely you're not jealous, Robbie?' He dotted the ash from his cigarette. 'Do I ever complain about having to share your body with that Osborne bitch?'

'Don't speak about Frances that way! She's my wife.'

Dreikhorn hooted with laughter. 'Well, well. That bloody high-and-mighty family of hers has certainly got you licking their boots!'

'She isn't like them.'

'Only time will tell, won't it? Her sister's a spoiled, selfish bitch; her mother's one of the biggest whores in London.' The grin had disappeared. 'Leopards don't change their spots!'

'Look, I know you don't like them. But don't forget it was your idea in the beginning for me to marry into the family. Your idea, Tom.' The crimson flush had spread from Robin's face to his neck. 'And you still haven't answered my question. I asked who the boy is I saw you with last night. Are you going to tell me or not?'

Dreikhorn uncrossed his legs. He shrugged. 'He doesn't mean

anything to me. It's just a little dalliance, something to pass the time.'

'Are you sure you can trust him?'

'You're worrying unnecessarily, I told you. All right. His name's Lawrence Rankin and I've known him for a while. I can't remember how long. I told you he's useful. He is. If I ask him to do something for me, he does it. He's so eager to please, it's really quite pathetic. You don't begrudge me a little fun, do you?'

'I don't think it's very clever of you to bring him back here.'

'I didn't. Do you think I'm stupid? There's a private club I know . . . very discreet . . . in Limehouse. Quite an amusing place, actually. Maybe you ought to come with me, sometime, and see for yourself.'

'*Limehouse?* The East End?'

Dreikhorn stretched. 'You're not shocked Robbie, surely?' Another slow, teasing smile. 'We all fancy a little slumming once in a while. You should try it.'

'For Christ's sake, what's the matter with you? Do you realize the risks? What if this place got known to the police? What if it was raided?'

'You're beginning to bore me, Robbie.'

'What would you do? How would you explain what you were doing there? You couldn't. Have you ever stopped to think of what kind of bloody scandal you'd let loose – and a trail leading straight back to me!'

Veins were standing out in Robin's neck; for a moment he looked singularly unattractive. How much better Dreikhorn had liked the young, naïve, uncritical Robbie Carr. Curious how suddenly coming up in the world, marrying into a rich, powerful family and acquiring a title you never expected to have, could so much change a man. The old Robbie would never have questioned anything he did or said.

'Bloody hell, Tom! Have you got a death-wish or something?'

Dreikhorn harnessed his anger; politics at least taught you how to dissemble. After all, he'd climbed this high by using Robbie and he intended to climb higher still before he'd done. All the same, he didn't like the way things were going. Was it that Osborne bitch who was changing him, or had the power simply gone to his head?

He got up and poured them both a drink.

'It's too early in the day for me,' Carr said, almost pettishly. 'I can't go in to Whitehall with the smell of whisky on my breath.'

'What would Lord Cultrane think?' Dreikhorn's voice was mocking. 'You're no fun any more, Robbie; you're getting too much like the bloody Osbornes!'

'Look. I didn't come here to quarrel with you.' His voice was softer, more conciliatory now. And he'd been upset seeing Tom with the boy. 'I'll come here this evening before I go home, and we'll have a drink together then. And maybe dinner later in the week. At the usual place.'

Dreikhorn smiled. Robbie still needed him. And in more ways than one. But he wasn't going to give up seeing young Rankin.

'Yes, why don't we do that?' He came over and stood close to him. They looked into each other's eyes. 'As long as you don't bring your wife.'

He didn't come home until gone midnight and she'd fallen asleep while she waited for him. She lay on one side of the bed watching for the light to disappear beneath his dressing-room door, but even when it had it was a long time before he crept silently into the room and slipped into bed beside her.

He'd thought she was asleep. When she whispered his name softly in the darkness and stretched out her hand, he jumped.

'Frances! You startled me.' Did he sound angry or was that just her imagination? 'I thought you'd have been asleep hours ago.'

'I was waiting for you.' She wanted him and she rolled over to his side of the bed and put her arms around him. 'Robbie, why are you so late again? You're working much too hard.' She kissed the back of his neck but he didn't turn over and face her.

'You'd better let me get some sleep, then.'

Slowly, she let her arms drop and moved away from him to her own side of the bed. Long after he'd fallen asleep she lay there, staring up at the ceiling, asking herself why he didn't seem to want her any more.

43

She had always loved Marguerite's lavish dinner parties and gay musical evenings, and, ever since she'd first been inside it, she loved this house. Her godfather's restrained good taste was stamped on almost every room: the elegant Georgian and Regency furniture had all been his; the sporting prints, the landscapes, the huge Canaletto that he'd been so proud of still hung in the room that had once been his study. Frances remembered being ten years old again, when her grandfather had died, and he'd left an important debate in the Lords to drive all the way down to her boarding school in Surrey because her parents were too busy, to collect her for the funeral. At the service she'd broken down and cried and he had been the one who had comforted her.

'Marguerite, you've got a new piano!'

'Isn't it heavenly? It's a Kaim boudoir grand, and the moment I saw it I simply couldn't resist it! It's a work of art.' Everyone gathered round it. 'Of course, Jack never let slip a single grumble, even though I play unimaginably badly!' Everybody laughed. The men had gone off into the smoking-room for their cigars and port and Marguerite begged Frances to play for them.

'She's always been far too modest! Have you ever heard her sing? She had the most divine voice, even as a child. But the only person she could ever be persuaded to sing in front of was Daddy. Come on, Frances, what about something from *Bitter Sweet*?'

'You're twisting my arm, Marguerite!'

'What about *I'll See You Again*? We heard Evelyn Laye sing it when we were in New York, and then we came back here and heard Gertie Lawrence sing it at the Criterion. It's quite Noël Coward's best.'

'Did you meet him at Connie's house party, darling? He has the most wicked sense of humour! He called HRH's little retreat in Windsor Park the Prince's Toy Fort! Everyone was in *stitches*!'

'Are you and Rodney going down to Somers Court this weekend?'

'No, we can't, the workmen are still there refurbishing the entire first floor . . . the time they're taking we'll be lucky if it's ready for habitation by the beginning of the Season!'

Marguerite sat down beside Frances on the long piano stool, and they played and sang a duet.

'Frances, you've been holding out on us! You're *far* better than Jessie Matthews!'

'Flatterer.'

'Mind Charles B. Cochran doesn't hear you; he'll grab you for one of his new shows!'

'From all *I* hear, darling, that isn't all he grabs talented young women for!'

At that point the drawing-room doors re-opened and the men came back in. Frances looked up into Thomas Dreikhorn's eyes.

'What the dickens are you girls up to now?' said Jack Holland, laughing. 'Are we back in time to join you for *God Save the King*?'

'Robin, I don't think you realize how talented your wife is,' Marguerite smiled. 'She can sail past top "C" easier than I can play the scales!'

Dreikorn leaned forward on the top of the piano. He glanced at Marguerite Holland, then back to Frances. 'You look like sisters, sitting there together.'

Nobody except Frances understood the veiled implication. She looked back at the piano keys without answering him. Everyone was shouting at the same time, requesting a different tune, and she played them all. When Jack Holland finally took over, she picked up her evening bag and went out into the cool of the hall and in the direction of the cloakroom.

She sat in front of the mirror, staring at her reflection for a long while. Of course Dreikhorn was only trying to hurt her, she knew that; the insinuations he'd made about the photograph of Holland, the remark he'd made just now about her and Marguerite. It amused him to hurt other people's feelings. He'd never liked her and she'd only forced herself to be civil to him because he was Robin's colleague and friend. She wasn't alone in her dislike; she'd overheard her brother Freddie saying that Thomas Dreikhorn enjoyed making sarcastic quips that got under other people's skin; he was trying to get under hers and she wasn't going to let him. Robin's patronage was beginning to make him arrogant.

Frances powdered her face, renewed her lipstick, then got up to go. Tom Dreikhorn was coming out of the drawing-room just as she was going into it, and they came face to face.

'Ah, you've renewed the war paint,' he smiled his slow, maddening smile, the smile that made her want to hit him. 'When Frances walks the fair spring flowers hide their faces from the sun.'

It was word for word from one of the letters Robin had written to her, before they'd become engaged, and she stared at him uncomprehendingly. Surely Robin had never allowed him to read something so intimate, something written privately and especially for her?

'Excuse me.'

'What's the matter? Didn't you like it?'

She let her hand fall away from the door. 'I don't like the insinuating remarks you've made twice now. You know exactly what I'm

334

talking about so I won't repeat them. And you might as well know that I don't like you.' She pushed past him and went back into the crowded room. When he eventually came back she avoided looking his way. Until she was forced to.

'I've always adored Noël Coward's lyrics. They're so much more genteel than Cole Porter's. Of course, so few of you chaps have any idea of how to write about love at all!'

'I say, that's a bit thick, Rosemary!'

'Darling, don't argue with me! You know it's perfectly true. Isn't it girls?' There was a loud chorus of laughing agreement. 'You know you're all absolute duffers when it comes to putting pen to paper and writing about love! Unless you happen to be George Byron, for instance! Or Noël Coward! Frances, you traitor! Why are you shaking your head?'

'Robin has quite a turn of phrase, although I say it myself. It must be all that Robbie Burns culture he came down from Scotland with!' Everyone laughed, and Rosslare coloured a little.

'Come on, Robbie, give us a sonnet!'

Suddenly Dreikhorn was standing beside her, smiling as if he knew something that she didn't. 'Robbie's more at home with state papers than love letters, Rosemary.' He glanced briefly at Frances. 'In the other department, he does need a little help . . .'

Her eyes looked straight at Robin's face, uncomprehendingly. But he'd already turned away.

As soon as they got back from Carlton House Terrace he went straight into the drawing-room to pour himself a drink. She went in after him and slammed the doors.

'What did he mean, Robin? You heard what he said in front of everyone tonight. What was he talking about?'

He waved an irritable hand at her. 'How should I know, for heaven's sake? You know what Tom's like. Always clowning around . . .'

'I wasn't laughing.'

'For God's sake, Frances! I don't want an argument. Why don't you go up to bed?'

'I'm not going anywhere until you answer my question!'

He put down the double brandy and turned and faced her. He looked tired; there were mauve circles beneath his eyes and his skin was flushed.

'All right. I can see that I won't have any peace until you've dragged it out of me! Not that there's very much to tell. The truth is that I'm not very good with flowery words and clever phrases; I never have been. But Tom is and he helped me out. When I wrote to you, before we were married, he made a few suggestions about what I should write.'

She was dumbstruck. '*He* told you what to write to me?'

'Does it matter now? Do you have to make such a drama out of it?'

'Does it *matter*?' She was close to tears. He'd just coolly told her that another man had composed all the love letters she'd always thought were his – Thomas Dreikhorn of all people! – and he didn't even understand why she was stunned and hurt. 'My God, Robin! No wonder he's always been laughing up his sleeve! All this time, and I never knew!' Suddenly, she was furiously angry. 'Robin, how could you?'

'Where are you going?'

She turned and ran out of the room and up the stairs. She burst into her bedroom to an astonished Grace.

'My lady! Is everything all right?'

Frances went over to the little writing desk in the corner of the room and pulled out the drawer. The two bundles of letters and cards were inside, tied neatly and lovingly with satin ribbon. Without hesitating she took them out and began tearing them into pieces, then threw the paper in handfuls on to the fire.

Robin had followed her upstairs and come into the bedroom behind her. 'Frances! You're being absolutely ridiculous about this!' She continued to ignore him. 'For God's sake, do you have to be so bloody childish?'

'Grace, would you please put more coal on the fire? It'll help to burn this rubbish more quickly.' She gave him one parting look of contempt before going to lock herself in the bathroom until he'd gone. 'Why do you look so shocked, Robin? It doesn't matter, does it? That's what you said to me downstairs.'

On the other side of the bathroom door she leaned against it, listening. He muttered a few unintelligible words to Grace, then went out. He'd spend the night in his dressing-room, but she was too hurt to care.

Grace had laid out her satin nightdress when she unlocked the door and went back into the room. When she was in bed, long after Grace had left, she lay on her side staring into the dying fire. A single piece of paper with Robin's writing had fallen out from the grate, its edges blackened and charred. All that was left of the letters she'd loved and treasured so much; the letters Dreikhorn had written. She turned her face into the depths of the pillow and silently began to cry.

<h1 style="text-align:center">44</h1>

Her mother looked up without pleasure; she was writing out invitations to a dinner party and Frances had interrupted her. The deep, impatient sigh she gave clearly showed her annoyance. 'You haven't picked your time very well.' Her long, elegant hand with its beautifully manicured nails hovered in mid-air, holding the platinum pen. 'Well, what is it? You look as if you've been crying.'

'I had a row with Robin last night.'

'An occupational hazard for married women, I would have thought. What am I expected to do about it?'

She'd get no sympathy from her mother about the letters; but that wasn't why she decided to come. She opened her lizardskin clutch bag and took out the photograph of Thomas Holland. She lay it down in front of her mother.

'Thomas Dreikhorn made certain insinuations about the likeness between us. Last night at the Hollands' dinner party he made some pointed remark about Marguerite and I looking like sisters.' She hesitated. 'As much as I detest him, every time I see this picture, I have to admit to myself that it's true. We are alike.'

'Dreikhorn!'

'Was Thomas Holland my real father? Please, Mummy. Tell me the truth.'

Katherine Cultrane's face was white with anger. She stood up, knocking aside the pile of half-written invitations. 'How dare you ask me such a question!'

'I have a right to know! *I loved him!*'

'You have no right to question me about anything that happened in my life!' At that moment before either of them could say anything else, the door opened and her brother Freddie burst in. 'Father's just telephoned! It's William Banbury; he's had a massive heart attack!' He stared from his sister to his mother. 'It happened just a little while ago, when he called in at Portland Place to collect some documents for this afternoon's debate. One of the footmen heard a terrific crash and they found him, collapsed, unconscious, on the study floor. Seddon called Theodore Mayerne and he says he's too ill to be moved!'

'I must go to Elizabeth,' Frances grabbed her bag and gloves. 'She must be in a terrible state!'

'Surely they'll have to get him to hospital?'

'Mayerne says he's far too ill. Any movement might kill him! Look, I've got my Lagonda outside. I'll drive you there straight away!'

'You take Frances. I'll come on afterwards.'

In a trance of double shock Frances followed her brother outside to the sports car parked in the square. He held the door open for her impatiently, then climbed in himself.

'Freddie, please, don't drive too fast!'

'Rotten bad luck for the old codger, what? Poor old Liz!' He turned the ignition and the engine roared. 'Not at all her style playing Florence Nightingale and nursing an invalid back to health. He could be laid up for months.'

'He worked too hard, he was always pushing himself. After the last heart attack, he should have taken things much more easily . . .'

Freddie stamped savagely on the brakes and she shot forward. She kept both hands on the dashboard to steady herself.

'His own fault, really; he wouldn't let up. And it wasn't just overwork that brought it on. Two sons in two years. That's going it a bit for a man of his age, what?'

'Freddie . . .'

'Can't have been easy, trying to keep up with Liz; she's always loved the high-life. Dancing, nightclubs. Not his cup of tea at all.'

'Do you think he'll be all right? Did Daddy say any more?'

They slowed down, swung left, then right towards Portland Place. He cursed as a cyclist crossed his path. 'Theodore Mayerne's a top man, Harley Street's best; he should be able to tell. If there'll be any permanent damage, I mean.'

He banged his horn loudly as they drew up outside the house. 'Who's parked right there? Damn nerve!' He leapt out and held the door open for Frances and she got out, grateful they'd arrived in one piece.

Inside the house every room seemed full of people. Colleagues, friends, members of the family who'd dropped everything as soon as they'd heard the news, to come over and be with Elizabeth. Theodore Mayerne was upstairs, with a specially trained nurse he'd brought with him. Her father was the first person she caught sight of.

My father. She stared at him as he came towards them from the drawing room, searching his face for any resemblance to herself, as if she was seeing him for the first time in her life. But all she could see was the face of Thomas Holland in the photograph.

'Freddie, Frances. Your sister's in a terrible state. Mayerne's given her something to calm her down and make her sleep. This has come as an awful shock . . .'

'Is he going to pull through?'

'He can't move, he's lost the power to speak. Mayerne's engaged a nurse to stay here night and day, and he'll be calling personally three times in every twenty-four hours, unless there's some change.'

'Surely he ought to be in hospital?'

'He's too ill to be moved. Mayerne won't risk it.'

'Damn shame and all that, so upsetting for Liz . . .'

Frances suddenly wanted to get away from them. 'I'll stay with her, for as long as she wants me to. Can you telephone Robin and tell him what's happened?'

'I'll tell him to get your maid to come over in a taxi with your things.'

Upstairs, she went to the nursery; Eddie Vaux was there with the nanny and Elizabeth's two boys.

'I didn't expect to find you here.' She came inside and closed the door. 'I was with Mummy when Freddie burst in and told us what had happened. We came right away.'

'Liz will be grateful.' It seemed strange to hear him calling her that; they'd never seemed close before. 'She hasn't had an easy time of it, you know.'

Frances wasn't sure what he meant. 'This is the third heart attack he's had in two years.'

'I didn't mean that.' He glanced behind him at the nanny; diplomatically, she went out. 'He's been keeping her on a tight rein for a long time. Checking her spending, checking up where she's been, that kind of thing.'

'She told you that?'

'Yes.' He was standing close to her sister's two boys and the likeness between the three of them suddenly struck her. Like her own striking resemblance to Thomas Holland she'd never noticed it before. 'She never wanted to marry him, you know.' His voice sounded extraordinarily bitter. 'Your parents and Henry Osborne pushed her into it.'

'I never realized, at the time; well, I was only fifteen then. All the society magazines and the press were saying it was the love match of the decade, and I never thought to wonder if it was true or not. But last summer, when Robin and I went down to see her at Greyfriars, she said as much.'

Vaux stroked the youngest boy's head. 'They're damn fine children. Liz is so proud of them.'

'Yes, I know. William is too. At least if the worst happens, he knows he has a son to succeed him.'

'Are you going along to see her now?'

'I thought Mayerne had given her a sedative, and she was asleep?'

'I think you'll find she's awake now.'

She was sitting in a chair, staring down into the street from the window. She glanced up as Frances came in.

'You ought to be lying down! You've had a shock.' Frances closed the door gently behind her. 'Didn't Mayerne give you something to make you sleep?'

'Yes, he did, the old fool, and I flushed it down the toilet.' She lit a cigarette. 'God knows why he thinks he has to drug me into insensibility! Does he think I'm going to turn hysterical because William's had a heart attack?' She got up and poured herself a large pink gin. 'It's getting to be a bit of a habit with him, isn't it? Having heart attacks.' She raised the glass and took a large gulp. 'Cheers, little sister. Let's hope this one finally kills him.'

'You don't mean that!'

'Don't I just! Well, what are you looking at me like that for? You're not shocked, surely? Not after what I told you last year. Disgusting old man. I expect the moment he dies the press boys will start digging up all the old bloody sentimental tosh and six-year-old wedding photos to feed the public with. The wedding of the year! That's a joke, isn't it? The wedding of the year with the bridegroom older than the father of the bride!' She nodded towards one of the pictures taken outside Westminster Cathedral in 1927. 'Look at him! My God, have I really managed to keep up this bloody masquerade for six whole years? That's damn good going, don't you think?'

'You're not yourself, Elizabeth. You're still in shock.'

'Oh, come on! We don't have to pretend to each other any more, do we? Daddy sold me into this marriage to further his own ends; I told you before, last summer. He wanted William to smooth the path to Baldwin for him . . . using my body. Just like a whore, really, wouldn't you say?' She was crying and laughing both at once. Her eyes were red-rimmed, bloodshot, unnaturally bright. 'I'd make a damn good actress, don't you think? They ought to have put me on the stage . . .'

He stared up at her, his eyes bloodshot and rounded. His mouth hung open and from the corner there was a trickle of foam. His sparse, greying hair, still heavily brilliantined, lay across his balding head, making a dark, greasy stain against the whiteness of the pillow.

Everyone who had been there that morning had gone now; only the nurse that Mayerne had brought with him, and Frances, had stayed.

Elizabeth came into the room, holding each of her sons by the hand. She paused at the side of the bed and looked down at him. He couldn't speak. He was unable to move. Only his eyes seemed alive in his useless, dying body. He swivelled them towards the small bottle of pills that Mayerne had left on the table beside the bed.

Elizabeth picked them up. 'There's really no point in you taking any more of these now, is there? After all, whatever medicine he gives you, you're still going to die.' Slowly, she unscrewed the top and began to drop them into the wastepaper basket, one by one. 'I just wanted you to see the next Earl of Banbury . . .' She touched her eldest son lightly on the head, then signalled for Frances to take them both away. 'I also wanted to tell you that neither of the boys is yours.' The bloodshot eyes in the sunken grey face seemed to bulge from the sockets. 'Yes, that's right. They're Eddie's. Eddie Vaux.' She smiled as he struggled to move his lips. 'I'm in love with him; I always have been. And he loves me.'

Behind her, in the doorway, Frances had gone rigid with shock.

Six years of forced living as Banbury's wife when she'd longed to be free had made Elizabeth cruel with the cruelty of the oppressed. She wanted to hurt him and she wanted revenge. 'I slept with him before I married you; I've been sleeping with him ever since. And his sons will inherit everything you've ever had.'

She could see the whites of her husband's eyes as they rolled wildly in the sunken sockets; the gurgling noise in his throat became louder. His face had turned puce.

'*Elizabeth!* Stop it, for God's sake; can't you see he's dying? I'm going to call the nurse!'

Slowly, without taking her eyes from him, Elizabeth moved away from the big curtained bed. 'I wouldn't bother, if I was you. It's too late.'

In the big bedroom the nurse had pulled all the curtains. She was on the telephone to Sir Theodore Mayerne.

'You don't have to stop with me, Frances. I've got the boys, and I can ran ring Eddie now. I'll do it as soon as she's gone.'

'I promised I wouldn't leave you.'

Elizabeth laid a hand on her arm. 'Go home. Robin's waiting, and you can tell him what's happened. Wait till Eddie gets here and he'll drive you back to North Audley Street. It's very late.'

'All right.'

'You think I'm perfectly heartless, don't you? Because I told the truth.'

'Look, I'm not judging you. I don't have the right . . .' Ever since last summer when they'd talked at Greyfriars, Frances had known that Elizabeth wasn't happy; she didn't *blame* her sister for falling in love with someone else. What young woman in her right mind would have chosen the squat, balding, ageing Banbury, nearly three times her age, over the tall, dark, suave Eddie Vaux with the matinée idol looks? She managed to smile. 'What are you and Eddie going to do? After the funeral? Surely you won't want to come back and live here?'

Elizabeth shook her head. 'I've always hated this house. For six years it's seemed almost like a prison. There are lots of other houses in London. It can be rented out, sold. I haven't decided yet. There's so much to suddenly decide. One thing for certain I can tell you. Eddie and I will get married as soon as possible.' A triumphant smile that altered her entire face. 'This time nobody's going to tell me what to do. And if Mummy and Daddy don't like it, they can lump it.'

They went downstairs together. Seddon was coming out of the drawing room into the hall, and he looked up and caught sight of them.

'Seddon.'

'I trust his lordship is a little better, my lady?'

'Seddon, Lord Banbury died a few minutes ago.'

His long face turned pale. His mouth was hanging slightly open from shock.

'And I shall no longer be requiring your services. She smiled at him; he'd always despised and disliked her, and she'd waited so long to say this. 'That's right, Seddon. You're dismissed.'

Eddie Vaux parked his blue Bugatti in front of the house and helped her out. She glanced up at the windows as they went up the short flight of steps to the front door; everywhere was in darkness, except for the single dim light in the main hall. A solitary footman was still on duty; another few moments and he would have bolted all the doors.

'My lady! Lord Rosslare wasn't expecting you back tonight. He thought you were staying with Lady Banbury at Portland Place.'

'Lord Banbury died earlier this evening,' Eddie Vaux said.

'My deepest condolences, my lady. Do you wish me to go and wake Lord Rosslare?'

Frances smiled wearily. 'No, that won't be necessary. I'll tell him myself.' She turned to Eddie Vaux. 'Thanks so much for bringing me home, Eddie. Do you want a brandy before you go?'

'No, thanks. I'd better tootle off, seeing what time it is. Don't want to leave Elizabeth on her own for too long.'

'Take care of her, won't you? And please tell her that I'll speak to her tomorrow.'

The footman let him out and began bolting the front door. 'Oh, my lady. I should perhaps mention that Lord Rosslare has a guest. Mr Dreikhorn. They worked very late on some urgent state papers, and Lord Rosslare instructed that one of the guest bedrooms be prepared for tonight.' He helped her off with her coat. 'His lordship was going to telephone you before he retired for the night, to see how Lord Banbury was, but he thought that you and Lady Banbury might already have gone to bed.'

'All right, Philipps. Thank you for telling me. You can go to bed yourself, now.'

She hesitated. There was a faint, but unmistakable noise of a car engine being crank-started in the street. 'Oh no!' She went over to the window and peered out. 'It looks as if Lord Vaux's having trouble with his car. I'm sorry, Philipps. Can you unbolt the front door and see if there's anything we can do? I won't be a moment.'

'Yes, of course, my lady.'

She went upstairs and quietly along the landing to the bedroom. As she'd expected, no light showed from beneath the door. Robin would be asleep, no doubt. Further along the landing the guest bedroom where he'd put Dreikhorn was also in darkness. She turned the handle on the door, slowly. If Robin woke up, she'd tell him about Banbury now. If not, it could wait until the morning.

Light from the hall and landing crept across the bedroom carpet and the half-tester satin bed as she pushed open the door. Then she stopped abruptly on the threshold of the room, stunned into immobility by what she saw. A cry escaped from her lips and the two

343

startled men drew apart from beneath the mound of rumpled bed-clothes. She heard Dreikhorn curse, then Robin call her name as she backed woodenly from the room, shaking her head from side to side in disbelief.

'*Frances, please* . . . !' He stumbled from the bed and grabbed his dressing-gown, but she'd already turned and fled back along the landing and down the stairs. An astonished Philipps was standing in the hall.

'My lady . . . !'

She grabbed her coat and handbag and ran out into the street. Eddie Vaux was still there, just about to close the bonnet of the Bugatti, wiping his hands on a handkerchief. She could hear the purr of the engine as she rushed towards him. He looked up suddenly when she appeared, as astonished as the footman.

'Eddie, please, help me! Please drive me home!'

'I say, what's up?'

'Please take me to Belgrave Square!' A single tear had welled up in the corner of one eye and it ran down her cheek. There was a terrible, tight feeling in her throat, and a dull, thudding pain had begun to spread across the front of her head; but for the moment she was still too shocked to cry. 'Please, just get me away from here.'

He stopped the car a few streets away from the entrance to Belgrave Square, and turned off the engine. The light from a street lamp cast deep shadows across her starkly white face. He put his hands on hers and turned to look at her. 'Do you want to tell me about it?'

For a moment she couldn't speak; she couldn't even look at him. While the words came out, hesitant at first, then tumbling one over the other, she kept staring at the foot-brake on the car floor. After what had happened she didn't know if she could ever look anyone in the face again. Everything was disjointed, unreal, like sequences in a nightmare; except that she was fully awake.

He listened to her without interrupting. 'Christ, Frances. I don't know what to say.'

At last, she turned her face towards him. There seemed to be no sense of time or place; Elizabeth was waiting for him back at Portland Place, no doubt wondering why he was taking so long; the whole city was asleep; but she was here, sitting in a parked car with her sister's lover, telling him that she'd just found her husband in bed with another man.

'I can't go back there. That's the only thing I *am* certain of at this very moment. I'm so grateful that you were still outside to help me.'

'Look, you're terribly upset right now. You've had a bad shock. You can't possibly decide anything while you're so emotional and tired.' He leaned forward and turned on the engine. 'We're nearly there.'

A stunned Madders in slippers and paisley dressing-gown unbolted, then opened, the huge front door. He was even more astonished when he saw who it was standing there at two o'clock in the morning. 'Lady Frances! Lord Vaux!'

'Madders, I'm dreadfully sorry about this, but I'm afraid I'm going to have to ask you to wake Lord and Lady Cultrane,' Eddie Vaux said, as they came inside.

'Right away, my lord.' Madders disappeared at the turn of the staircase, and Vaux took Frances into the empty drawing-room and turned on a light.

'Sit down, don't take your coat off just yet. I'll pour you a stiff drink.' He'd just handed her a double brandy when the door opened and Thomas and Katherine Cultrane came into the room in their dressing gowns.

'In God's name, what the dickens is going on, Vaux?'

'Daddy . . .' Frances said, half getting out of her seat. But Eddie Vaux gently eased her down again.

'Can I speak to you in private?' Eddie Vaux said. They went out, leaving Frances along with her mother.

'Are you going to tell me what this is all about? Elizabeth has already telephoned to say that Banbury's dead.'

'It has nothing to do with William dying.'

Frances swallowed. She rarely, if ever, touched spirits; she never smoked. *Little puritan*, Dreikhorn had mocked. She pushed away the picture of him, naked and in bed with Robin, and put a hand to her head. The brandy had burned her throat and made her feel dizzy.

'Elizabeth didn't need me to stop with her, after William died. She rang Eddie and he came back. He offered to drive me back home.'

She was still too distraught to notice her mother's disapproval; so Elizabeth and Eddie Vaux were going to spend the night together under the same roof, with all the servants knowing and her husband barely dead.

Frances continued, 'When we arrived at North Audley Street Philipps was still up. Eddie had trouble starting his car and I told him to help if he could . . . I felt so awful it wouldn't start after he'd left Elizabeth to run me back home. Philipps said Robin and Tom Dreikhorn had been working late and that Dreikhorn was stopping

345

the night as it was so late when they'd finished. So I went upstairs to bed. I was going to tell Robin about William if he was still awake.' She gripped the glass in her hands until her knuckles turned white. 'When I opened the bedroom door the light from the landing fell across the bed . . .' A loud sob broke from her throat. 'They were in bed together, Robin and Dreikhorn . . . !'

Outside in the hall she heard Vaux's voice, then the front door closing. Her father came back into the room.

'I couldn't believe what I was seeing, and I just stood there, staring at them. Then Robin jumped out of bed and grabbed his dressing-gown, and came towards me, and I turned and ran.' Her parents exchanged glances. 'Eddie had just got the car going again and I begged him to drive me away. We stopped somewhere, near here . . . and I told him what had happened.'

Neither of them said anything for a moment. She looked up at them, willing them to speak, to show some sign of understanding, shock, disgust, sympathy.

'Mummy, it was *horrible*! I don't know what I would have done if Eddie hadn't been there.'

'Have you told Madders to see that a room is made ready just for tonight?'

'Yes, just now.'

Frances went on staring at them. They both seemed so unruffled, so calm.

'Frances, control yourself. You're a married woman, not a child. I've telephoned Robin and told him I shall want to speak with him first thing in the morning when I reach Westminster. He understands, of course, that you're far too shaken and upset to go back to the house tonight.'

'*Go back?* Daddy, as long as I live I'll never go back to that house while he's in it!' She felt stronger now and she stood up. Her anger gave her sudden strength. 'Didn't Eddie tell you what happened? I walked into our bedroom and found my husband in bed with another man!'

'Keep your voice down! Have you any idea of the scandal you'd unleash if this ever got outside this room?'

'The scandal *I'd* unleash?'

'For God's sake, grow up! Do you really suppose that every married woman is happy with her husband? We all make our beds and we have to lie on them . . . irrespective of whether we like them or not. You and Robin are no different. All right; you're shocked and upset

346

but you'll have to get over it; it isn't the end of the world. And if you hadn't gone home unexpectedly tonight you would never have found out. He's a good husband in every other way, isn't he? You're happy. What you have to do now – tomorrow, when you've had a good night's sleep and you can think clearly again – is to carry on as if none of this ever happened. Your father will speak to him first thing in the morning and make sure that Dreikhorn keeps his distance.'

She turned to her husband. 'How long have I been suggesting that you and Henry get him moved to some post abroad, at one of the foreign embassies? If you'd listened to me in the first place none of this would have happened!'

'I'll go and see Baldwin. We'll pull a few strings . . .'

Frances couldn't believe what she was hearing. 'You expect me to go back to him? As if nothing had ever happened; as if nothing had changed? Well, I'm sorry to disappoint you, Mummy. But I won't.' She looked from one to the other. 'If you won't let me stay here, then I'll find somewhere else. I don't care where. But as far as I'm concerned my marriage to Robin is over!'

'Don't be so utterly ridiculous!'

'Have you any idea what people will say?'

'Other couples live apart, they have entirely separate lives. So shall we. Oh, don't worry. I won't cause any scandal that might damage the family reputation! I won't bring down any shame on the Osborne name. But when I left that house tonight I left behind anything that Robin and I might have shared. And nothing you can say will ever get me to change my mind.'

She picked up her handbag. She had enough money for a taxi, if she could find one at this time of the morning. She went to the door. 'You don't care, do you? It doesn't matter to you that the whole bottom has just fallen out of my entire life! Only that nobody finds out.'

'Frances, stop behaving like a fool! Isn't it bad enough that Elizabeth has invited her lover to spend the night with her, and Banbury's body not even cold yet?'

'At least Eddie Vaux's a proper man!' She pushed by them and ran out into the hall, then she opened the front door and went out into the deserted street. Her parents called after her to come back but she kept on running, only pausing to get her breath at the entrance to the square. Where could she go to, where did she belong? She'd walked almost a mile before she caught sight of a cruising taxicab, and she raised her arm almost unthinkingly to hail him, wiping the rain and the tears simultaneously out of her eyes.

'Where to, Miss?'

For a moment she thought of her sister and Eddie Vaux, then Marguerite and Jack Holland at Carlton House Terrace, then a hotel; she had to be alone to think, to try and marshal her wild tumult of thoughts without anyone influencing her. She closed her eyes and sank back against the cold leather seat. She didn't have enough money to pay for a hotel room, even for a single night. She gave the address of Laura's house in Holland Park.

It was dark and the rain was coming down much harder when the taxi finally drew up outside the front door. She wasn't dressed for bad weather, and her hair, legs, and feet were all soaked. It took several minutes after she'd rang the bell before a light went on in one of the rooms upstairs, and, finally, she heard the sound of somebody on the other side of the door drawing back the bolts.

When Laura's astonished face appeared in the open doorway, the tears that she hadn't been able to cry before poured down her face. She flung herself, sobbing, into Laura's arms.

'She won't come back! She's got Eddie Vaux to drive her over to Belgrave Square. Cultrane says that she's there now, that she's staying the night.' Robert Carr ran a hand through his thick, disordered fair hair. 'He wants to see me first thing in the morning. Christ, Tom! What the hell am I going to do? What am I going to say to him?'

'Do you really think the Osbornes care about anything except their bloody family name? She'll do what they tell her to, don't worry. And their motto, like all the upper classes, is that you can do anything you like as long as you keep it under the carpet. Just stay calm.'

'But she must have told Vaux something!'

'He won't talk, he knows the rules. Besides, when she's had a chance to cool down she'll soon come back. Outraged wives always do if they have nowhere else to go. And she hasn't.'

Carr's face was white. It was all very well for Dreikhorn to sit there so calmly, smoking a cigarette. But he was more than apprehensive now that Frances had found out the truth. She had always detested Tom and she'd been shocked, almost hysterical when she'd left; there was no telling what she might do. He thought of how close she was to the Hollands and his heart sank.

'Look, have a stiff drink. Go back to bed and get some sleep. The

Cultranes know how to keep their house in order. You should know them by now.'

Yes, of course, Tom was right. They would know how to manage their daughter.

Dreikhorn got up. He stubbed out his cigarette. 'It would really be best if I left, Robbie.'

'You can't leave now! It would look too odd.'

'You can think of something to say in the morning when the servants bring up the tea and find me gone.' But that was the trouble, Robbie's imagination was so limited. He sighed. 'Nobody knew it was her father who rang earlier. Say she was overwrought about Banbury and she just rushed out. Pretend it was her sister who telephoned. Or you could say a friend of mine was taken ill, and they called me up here. Sleep on it.'

Carr went with him to the door. The vast hall stretched behind them, dark and silent. They touched hands.

'Tom . . .'

'I'll see you tomorrow. At the Foreign Office as usual.' He let himself out without saying goodbye.

For once he was too preoccupied with his own thoughts to have noticed the slight, fair-haired young man lurking in the shadows opposite. It had started to spit lightly with rain, and there was no taxi in sight; too early in the morning for them to be plentiful. He turned up the collar of his coat, tipped his hat further over his eyes and went on walking in the direction of Henrietta Street and his second-floor apartment. Only when he heard the sound of footsteps some way behind him did Dreikhorn realize that he was being followed. He stopped immediately and turned round.

'*You!*'

Lawrence Rankin wasn't smiling. His hat and overcoat were both wet, his face was pale and drawn, and there were shadows beneath his eyes. Dreikhorn was taller and walked much faster and he'd had trouble keeping up with him.

'What have you been doing in there?' Rankin's voice was almost shrill. He looked for a moment as if he might burst into tears. 'You've been avoiding me, haven't you? After everything you promised, after what you said. That it was over between you and Rosslare! But it was all lies, wasn't it? I've been outside that bloody house for hours, since you got there; watching, waiting. You've been there all night!'

Dreikhorn's immediate reaction was anger; he didn't like being spied on. But his first concern was that they got off of the street; two men standing arguing at three o'clock in the morning would look highly suspicious to anyone, especially some zealous constable walking his beat.

'You'd better come back to my flat,' he said, taking Rankin by the elbow. 'We can't talk here.'

When they reached the flat Dreikhorn took off his wet outdoor clothes and poured two glasses of malt whiskey. He'd also realized that, in his hurry to get away after Robbie's scene with Frances, he'd forgotten to pick up his briefcase. But he couldn't go back for it now. He turned on the electric fire and sat down.

'Now listen. I told you before it wasn't a good idea for us to be seen too much together; you already know why. The only reason I went to North Audley Street tonight was to go through some papers with Robbie.'

Rankin stared morosely into his glass; he wished Dreikhorn wouldn't call Rosslare by his first name; it sounded too intimate and it hurt. He found it more and more difficult to control his jealousy. And his too-vivid imagination conjured up too many unbearable scenes of intimacy between them in the past that he hadn't shared. He hung his head while he listened.

'It got very late, and we were both tired. Robbie's wife had gone over to be with her sister at Portland Place; you must have heard that William Banbury had had another heart attack?'

'Yes.'

'Robbie suggested that I stay the night, and that we go over the rest of the papers at breakfast the next morning.' Dreikhorn took a gulp of whisky; he'd have to twist the truth a little now, or Rankin would make another jealous scene, and he was too tired for that. All he wanted to do was to get rid of him and go to bed. 'If you were watching the house, you must have seen Robbie's wife come back; we weren't expecting her and she was furious to find me there. They had a huge row and she stormed out.'

'Are you telling me the truth?'

'Of course. You saw her, didn't you?'

'Does she know about you and . . . and Lord Rosslare?'

'She knows how close we've been in the past and she resents it; she's always hated me.' He put down the glass and lit a cigarette. By the time he'd reached the end of it he hoped that Rankin would be gone. He had to be up early in the morning and it was already half-past three. 'The feeling's mutual. Anyhow, that's it. I told Robbie I thought it best if I simply left. So I did.'

Rankin desperately wanted to believe him, and he felt ashamed of his earlier doubts. So Tom was trying to break off things with Rosslare after all. 'I wish you didn't have to work with him.'

'I told you, it's necessary. I raised him up from nothing to begin with, and every time he rose higher, so did I. I have to hold the candle to the devil. You know that, Lawrence.'

'I can't understand why Lord Leith didn't want you as his private secretary. You're so clever. Much cleverer than Rosslare. It isn't fair. You should be where he is now. You're the one who really has the brains!'

'Ah, yes. But it wasn't Robbie's brains that Leith was interested in.'

Rankin was silent for several minutes. He kept twisting the glass round and round in his small, girlish hands. It irritated Dreikhorn unbearably.

'You really have finished with him, haven't you? There's nothing between you now? It's all over?'

He wanted reassurance and Dreikhorn gave it to him. What were a few lies more or less? 'How many times do I have to tell you? I'm only staying with Robbie for as long as it suits me.' He was reaching the end of his cigarette. 'Look . . . I hate to have to push you, Lawrence, but I have to be at Westminster half-an-hour earlier in the morning, and as it is I'll only get a couple of hours sleep.' He smiled at him and touched his knee. 'Why don't we meet at the club over the weekend? Robbie will be down in Kent with the rest of the bloody Osbornes burying Banbury. We can have a couple of days to ourselves.'

Rankin's face lit up. It was almost pathetic, Dreikhorn thought, how he hung on every half promise, every casual word.

'Yes, I'd like that.' They both stood up at the same time. 'I just wish I could stay here tonight.'

'I'm sorry. But that wouldn't be very wise, would it?'

'No.' He walked behind Dreikhorn to the door. 'I'm sorry about tonight . . . following you . . . waiting for you outside the house . . . but I simply couldn't help it, you see . . .'

When Rankin had gone Dreikhorn went over to the telephone; Robbie would probably be in bed but that didn't matter. He'd better remind him about the briefcase. And he wanted to hear his voice. He dialled the exchange and waited to be put through. It wouldn't ring for long and disturb the servants; Robbie had an extension, for

351

emergencies, beside his bed. A slow, drowsy voice eventually answered. 'Robbie? It's Tom . . .'

She opened her eyes; they were painful, sore, swollen from crying. Last night, when she'd poured out her misery and humiliation to Laura, she'd cried as if she would never stop. Now she felt drained and hollow, as if she'd woken from a bad dream. But it had all happened.

The little spare bedroom with its pretty, dainty chintz curtains and matching wallpaper comforted her, soothed her with its simplicity and ordinariness. The floorboards had been scrubbed, then stained and polished; a handmade rag rug lay in the middle of the room, a sea of bright, cheerful colours.

Laura had turned on the single bar of the electric fire and she stared into it, thinking of that other electric fire in that other room in Halkin Street that seemed another lifetime ago. Strange that someone turning on an electric fire could suddenly bring back that crowded rush of memories, thrilling, painful, happy and sad. She thought of Kit until it became an almost physical pain.

Laura came into the bedroom with a cup of tea. There were two aspirins in the saucer when she put it down on the little table beside the bed. 'Are you sure you don't want me to call a doctor?' She sat down and took Frances's hand. It felt very cold. 'We don't have a telephone yet, but they have one two doors along. I know they wouldn't mind.'

'I'm not ill, Laura.'

'But you're still in a state of shock.'

Frances sat up. The cup of piping hot tea felt warm and comforting in her hands. 'I'd feel guilty calling the doctor out when there are so many people who need him far more than I do.' Was she any better than they were at this moment? Where was 'home' now? She felt the overwhelming temptation to cry again, but that would merely be to give way to self-pity.

'It isn't the same and you know it.'

'Perhaps not. I don't know any more. All I do know is that I can't stop here, imposing on you and Maurice. It was bad enough having to wake you up last night.' She tried to smile, weakly. 'I'll find somewhere else today. I'll go back to the house while . . . while he's at Westminster.'

'You can stay here as long as you want to, Frances! You must know that. You're my friend, for God's sake!'

'But I'm not Maurice's. And it is his house.'

'You'd do the same for me, wouldn't you?'

A tear welled up in the corner of Frances' eye and ran down her cheek. Whenever she was in trouble, an Asmussen was there to help her; last time it had been Kit.

'Don't . . . Don't . . . It'll be all right. I'll help you. Maurice will help you. We'll do everything we can.' Laura hugged her while she sobbed. 'I'll call into Cavendish Street and tell them I won't be in today. They can cope on their own. Then we'll take a taxi and go back to collect some of your things. I'll help you to pack.'

'I don't want to go back to that house, Laura. I can't face the thought of walking into that room – but I know I have to. All my money is in a drawer in my dressing table, and I want my jewellery.' Suddenly, she remembered Grace. But could she afford to keep a maid now? 'I'll have to get a job.'

'*A job?*'

'How else can I support myself. Nobody can pay their way without money.'

All her life everything had been there for her; an army of servants to wait on her hand and foot. First her father had taken care of her, then Robin. Now there was only herself. But it wasn't impossible. 'Pity I can't sew. Maybe Anne Turner could offer me a job.'

Laura smiled with relief; she could still make a dry joke. But she knew it was only to cover Frances's real feelings of desperation and fear of walking into the unknown. She suddenly felt fiercely protective of her friend, as Kit had once done. 'Drink up, and get dressed. I'll go and get ready.'

'What the devil's going on? What's happening?' Maurice was waiting for her at the bottom of the stairs. She glanced back over her shoulder and put a finger on her lips.

'What do you think, Maurice? She's terribly upset. She was in a dreadful state last night! Well, you saw for yourself . . .'

'I don't mean that!' His voice was sharp, irritable. 'Look. She can't stay here, can she? I mean, it wouldn't be the thing at all. She belongs with her husband.'

'Maurice, for goodness sake, I told you what happened!'

'Well, her family then. Laura, I know she's your friend and you want to help and that's all very fine and commendable. But . . . well, it's dashed awkward for me. There's going to be a damned fine scandal over all this . . . I can smell it a mile off! And I have no intention of you or I being caught up in the middle of it!'

Laura brushed past him angrily and went into the dining room. She closed the door. 'Well, that's a good Christian attitude for a start! Which church did your mother say you went to?'

'There's no need for sarcasm, Laura. You understand exactly what I'm talking about. It's one thing to let her stay here for the night when she was disorientated and upset, but quite another to offer her a semi-permanent home. What on earth will the neighbours think? And your parents and mine? We'd have to tell them, at least, part of the truth. And it's simply too sordid to go into details! I don't want to be any part of it and I certainly won't allow you to be.'

'Oh, I see. It was one thing to boast to all the chaps in the office that your wife's friend was the Countess of Rosslare; to regale your mother and your sisters with stories about my friendship with her so that they can boast to the vicar's wife and the ladies' guild members that we're on tea-sipping terms with the aristocracy . . . but quite another thing when Frances is in real trouble and needs our help. How could you be so callous, Maurice?'

His eyes had become very hard and his chin was set in that stubborn look that he had sometimes. Upstairs, she heard Desmond crying.

'I'm not prepared to enter an argument with you over this, Laura; if I don't leave immediately I shall be late and I shall miss my train. And Mr Gorston is a stickler for punctuality. I've told you that I won't permit you to get mixed up in this business, and I mean what I say.' He went out into the hall and put on his hat and coat, then picked up his briefcase. The crying from upstairs grew louder. 'I suggest that you go and see to your son; Lily appears to be deaf this morning.' He didn't kiss her on the cheek as he usually did when he left the house in the mornings, and he slammed the front door without even saying goodbye.

Lily appeared at the top of the kitchen steps. 'Sorry, Mrs Flavel! Just givin' a hand with the washing in the scullery.' She nodded towards the ceiling. 'Looks like Lady Rosslare has beaten me to it; she's a wonder with Desmond, she really is. He always stops cryin' when she picks him up.'

'Lily, we'll be out for most of today, so there's no need to lay the table for lunch. But go on with dinner as usual.'

'Will Lady Rosslare be staying for dinner, then?'

Laura hesitated for a moment. 'You'd better lay the table for three. If there's any changes I'll let you know later.'

Frances was holding Desmond in her arms when she went back

354

upstairs. 'Are we going to take him with us? I don't mind carrying him if he gets tired.'

Laura managed to smile. 'He'll make your arms ache.'

'I don't mind.'

<h1 style="text-align:center">45</h1>

The façade of the house looked white, cold and forbidding as they walked from the taxi to the front door. Laura had told the driver to wait for them. Taking Desmond's small hand in hers, she followed Frances into the vast marble-floored hall.

Rosslare's butler was back on duty and he looked at them with surprise. 'My Lady! Lord Rosslare informed us that you would be staying with Lady Banbury for several days. May I express the staff's deepest condolences on the death of Lord Banbury yesterday.'

Yesterday; so much seemed to have happened since then. Was it only yesterday that Banbury had died? The funeral would be at Greyfriars, and she would have to go, she knew that, even though it would mean being forced to see Robin. 'Thank you. I've come back only to collect some luggage.'

'Grace has been waiting for instructions, my lady.'

'I'll speak to her.'

She went upstairs with Laura close behind her. Only when she came to the door of their room did she hesitate. For a moment she stood there with her hand gripping the doorknob; then she turned it and opened it and they went inside.

The large, half-tester satin bed was immaculately tidy; nothing in the whole room was out of place. She couldn't look at it. She went straight to one of the enormous double wardrobes and flung the doors open wide. An entire row of Laura's painstakingly designed creations stared back at her.

'I can't leave any of these behind, can I?' With swift, rapid movements she began to pull them from their scented hangers. 'Laura, will you call Grace and ask her to bring the suitcases from my dressing-room?'

'Are you taking her with you?'

Frances was down on her knees pulling open the wardrobe drawers. Immaculate layers of silk, satin, and crêpe de Chine underwear stared back at her. So many things to take, and there was so little time. 'It's best if she stays here for the time being. Until I know what I'm going to do.'

Frances heard Laura go out; the door closed behind her. Desmond was gazing in rapt fascination from the window, watching two gardeners spear fallen leaves from the billiard-table-smooth lawn; strange how the presence of unsullied childish innocence ameliorated some of the ugliness that had happened in this room. She went to her dressing-table and began picking up her cosmetics, face creams, hairbrush and silver-backed combs. She unlocked the drawer where her jewellery and money were kept. Then the door behind her opened again.

'This should last me for a little while; I think I should book myself a room in a hotel and leave everything there. I can't dump it all in your spare room; Maurice would have a fit. I'll be able to think more clearly when I've got settled.'

'Frances?'

She spun round at the sound of Robin's voice. For a moment she was so shocked to see him standing there that she couldn't speak.

'We have to talk.' Across the room, Desmond suddenly looked up at the sound of the strange voice.

'There's nothing for us to talk about, Robin. I'm leaving you.'

'You can't do that, there's far too much to be considered, far too much at stake . . .'

'Like your career, for instance?'

'Whatever you think of me, I do care for you. I've always cared for you.'

How much she wished she could believe him!

'I never meant you to find out about Tom; I didn't mean to do anything to hurt you.'

'You disgust me!'

'I know it's too much for me to ask for you to understand, so I won't try. But please listen to me. You must listen to me, Frances.'

'Whatever you say won't make me change my mind.'

'Your father telephoned me this morning. He said that you didn't spend the night at Belgrave Square. That you just ran out without saying where you were going! I was so worried . . . !'

Her face held open scorn. 'Really? And did he also tell you *why* I ran out without telling him or Mummy where I was going? Not that I even knew at that point myself! Because they both said that I should go back to you!'

He rubbed his eyes. He looked pale, drawn, awful, as if he too hadn't slept. 'Banbury's funeral is on Friday; we must be seen together. Frances, please. Don't make any decisions until after we've come back. I know it's useless asking you to forgive me; I suppose that's too much. But for the sake of appearances and everything else . . . if there was a scandal, even a breath of it . . . you know as well as I do exactly what that would mean for all of us.' He came towards her and she moved back against the dressing-table.

'Don't touch me.'

'I went to see your father this morning, but Baldwin was with him. I have to leave now; he insists on seeing me. Can I tell him I've talked to you and you've agreed to come back?'

'Our marriage is over, Robin.'

They stood looking at each other for several moments. He'd always been so clumsy with words, and there was no brilliant Dreikhorn to help him with them now.

'I know that. But you know that there can never be any question of divorce. We can live entirely separate lives, you can do whatever you want to do, go your own way. To everyone else it will look as if nothing has changed between us. Other couples do it, you know that. And we have to stay together for appearance's sake.'

She suddenly felt an overwhelming contempt for him. 'I can see that you and my parents have it all neatly worked out. You seem to have thought of everything; except for me. When I walk out of this house today, Robin, I walk out of your life as well. And I don't intend to ever come back.'

'You hate me, don't you?'

She could almost feel a grudging pity for him; between the vital, eager, self-confident rising young political star of three years ago who had sent her poetry and flowers and the tired, hollow-eyed man standing in front of her now begging her not to leave him, there was an unrecognizable, unbridgeable gap; and yet had he ever really been what he seemed? Had it been Robert Carr or Dreikhorn's puppet who had courted and married her? Perhaps he didn't even know himself.

'I wish I could hate you, Robin; it would make everything so much easier, somehow. But I can't.' She could hear voices coming towards the room, Laura's and then Grace's. 'I'll come to the funeral, of course; I'd do that anyway because of Elizabeth.'

As she finished speaking the door opened and Laura and Grace came in. Laura looked stunned to see Robin. 'Good morning, Lord

Rosslare.' Her tone was perfectly respectful but her eyes were as cold as ice. She went over and stood next to Frances.

'Good morning, Mrs Flavel. I was just leaving.' Grace had disappeared into the background. 'How your son's grown.' He smiled nervously at Desmond. 'He's a fine little boy; you and your husband must be very proud of him.'

'Thank you.'

'Frances, will you give me an address where I can reach you? A telephone number, even? I have to know because of the funeral . . .'

She pulled herself together, conscious that they weren't alone any more. 'I'll be at the Grosvenor Hotel. For a few days anyway. Probably until we get back from Greyfriars.'

He nodded, slowly, aware that they were all watching him, wondering how much Laura Flavel already knew and if the servants were already gossiping downstairs. He guessed correctly that he could rely on Laura's discretion, and the staff knew that to spread talk about what they saw or heard would be more than their jobs were worth. But he wasn't looking forward to the interview with his father-in-law and Lord Henry Osborne, so recently discharged from Charing Cross Hospital. 'If there's anything you need, anything at all . . . you know where to reach me.'

He went out and Frances sank down on the dressing-table stool. 'Grace, will you please go downstairs and ask Philipps to come up for the suitcases in a few minutes? There's a taxi waiting for us outside.'

'Am I to come with you, my lady?'

'You'll stay here until I send for you.'

'Did you mean it?' Laura asked as soon as she'd gone. 'The Grosvenor Hotel? You know you're welcome to stay as long as you like with me.'

'Yes, I do know that. But you have Maurice and Desmond to consider. No arguments, Laura. You helped me last night when I really needed it, and you know how grateful I am for that. But it wouldn't be fair for me to impose on you any longer.'

'But . . .'

'I'll stay at the Grosvenor just until after the funeral, and then I'll have to look around for somewhere else. I shall sell my jewellery.'

She thought with complete detachment of all the pieces Robin had given her that she'd treasured, the pieces that no longer meant anything now. They were suddenly all worthless, except in terms of what someone else would pay her for them. 'That should keep me going for a while. I told you before. I'll look for a small flat, and then a job of some sort.'

'But you've never worked before, you've never had to fend for yourself!'

'Then maybe it's time I stood on my own two feet. You've done it. Perhaps I can, too.' Laura could see that there was no dissuading her. Something in her dogged determination reminded her of Kit. 'I'll be there when you need me.'

'You always are.'

When Philipps had carried the bulging cases down to the car and put them inside, they both got in. Laura sat Desmond on her lap, and looked at the tall, elegant Regency façade of the house as the taxi drew away from the kerb. Only Frances never looked back.

46

Frances stood beside Robin with her head bowed beneath the wide brim of her black velvet hat, and stared down at the coffin as it was slowly lowered into the ground. Across the yawning gap she saw her parents, her brothers, Lord Henry Osborne; and Elizabeth, supported by Eddie Vaux, sniffing into a white lace handkerchief beneath a thick dark veil. It was impossible to see her face clearly; every now and then during the funeral service she would make a strange, gasping sound as if someone was strangling her, and reach for Vaux's hand. But Frances was convinced that under the heavy dark veil, the concealing hat, her sister's eyes were dry.

She looked at each of their faces in turn; her father's solemn, her mother's inscrutable; her brother's and Vaux's respectfully neutral; her great uncle's as if he had suddenly been brought face to face, after his own sudden illness, of the mortality of man; what were each of them really thinking? Not of William Banbury, of that she was almost sure.

The breeze was cold, penetrating; she shivered. She could sense Robin's eyes on her, anxiously; she went on staring straight ahead of her. She couldn't look at him. She couldn't speak. In front of them, the first shovelful of earth had been sprinkled on Banbury's coffin.

The priest's robes were blowing gently in the breeze. The wreaths of flowers looked like a sea of bright, gaudy colour against the sable and black of the mourners' garb. Elizabeth was dabbing at her eyes under the heavy veil with the white lace handkerchief. Was she feeling guilty, ashamed, was she sorry that she hadn't waited for Banbury's death before sleeping with his nephew? Frances wondered.

She thought, watching the bent head of her sister from across the grave, that today of all days was ironically appropriate for Banbury to be buried. April Fool's Day. Perhaps Elizabeth had also realized that last, bitter joke.

She shut the door and lay against it exultantly. She tossed back her veil; she'd always hated black. Then she smiled and he smiled back at the sudden happiness in her face. She ran to him and threw her arms around his neck and they embraced and kissed.

'Darling, I'm free! *Free*. Can you believe it? After six bloody years.' She wanted to dance around the room. 'Don't think badly of me, Eddie. Dancing at his funeral. It seems too callous and cruel. But I've been so wretchedly unhappy!'

'I know.'

'I've waited so long for us to be together, openly. No more meeting in corners, telling lies.' She ran her hands lingeringly through his thick, dark, wavy hair. 'I love you so much!'

'I know what you've been through. It couldn't have been easy, being married to my uncle. You, thrown away on an old man!' He stroked her hair, her face. He kissed her again. 'Are you sure you want to stay down here when they've all gone? Wouldn't you be happier back in London?'

She sat down and eased off her shoes. The wonderful sense of a weight being lifted, of freedom, lightness, hope, of being able to choose; for the moment she couldn't get used to it. But she would; she would. 'If I stay her until you and the Hollands get back from Le Touquet I won't have to endure any more of Mummy's moral lectures. I don't think I could bear that!'

He came and sat down beside her on the bed. He held her hand. 'We won't have to wait to get married. All that tosh about decent mourning! You know I've rented a little cottage near the airfield at Le Touquet, for when I fly the plane there? Well, while I'm gone why don't you pack what you and the boys need and then be ready to leave with me when we get back? I'll make all the arrangements. I'll get a special licence from the local notary and the Hollands can be witnesses? Well, what do you say?'

'*Eddie!*'

'He smiled. Does that mean no or yes?'

'What do you think, you idiot?' She leaned against him happily. 'No woman in her right mind could say no to you!'

The both laughed together.

'Well, I think your mother might be the exception; she'll be absolutely furious when we tell her. The whole Osborne clan will doubtless expect you to show the proper widow's respect by trailing around in black for at least a year or two!'

Slowly, reluctantly, Elizabeth stood up. 'I suppose we ought to go down; they'll be serving tea. And cakes and little three-cornered sandwiches. I've always thought there's something terribly indecent about sitting down and consuming food after you've just buried someone. Everyone should be too upset to eat anything.' She threaded her arm through his. 'But I do need the tea. Hot and very strong. And so will Frances. Darling, Mummy and Daddy and Uncle Henry are going to try to bully her into going back to Robin, and I think we ought to support her. After all, it isn't fair. And it's been such a dreadful shock for her. I mean, she was so in love with him.'

'Curious, isn't it?' He held the door open for her. 'I would never have thought that he was queer. Or Dreikhorn, for that matter. Squiring all those rich, single, society women around London a different one every time. Got himself quite a reputation, I can tell you, as a ladies' man. Obviously did it as a smoke-screen. Just goes to show, doesn't it?'

'I can hear their voices downstairs.'

Frances knew that she and Elizabeth were going to be cornered the moment the other guests had gone and her mother had sent away the servants. There was only the seven of them left in the room; her parents, Lord Henry Osborne, Robin and Vaux. Elizabeth and herself. But her sister seemed utterly unconcerned. In the sudden yawning, ominous silence, she took out her platinum lighter and lit herself a Turkish cigarette.

'Hadn't you and Daddy best be getting back to town? It's quite a long drive, isn't it?'

Katherine Cultrane stood up. 'We'll leave at the same time as Frances and Robin. And Edward.'

Eddie Vaux knew what was coming and he went and stood protectively beside Elizabeth. Frances felt a sudden, but not a grudging, stab of envy for her sister. She would be safe with Eddie Vaux.

'I'm not leaving,' he said firmly, looking from each of them to the

361

other. 'Not yet. I'm meeting the Hollands in Le Touquet in two days' time. You know I keep a plane there. And I'm in no hurry to drive down to the coast tonight. Liz and I have talked it over and I'm not leaving until tomorrow morning.'

'That would be most ill-advised,' said Lord Henry Osborne with a tight smile that didn't quite reach his eyes. 'After all, my niece has just been widowed; if you spent the night under this roof a few hours after her husband has been buried, what would people think?'

'With respect, neither of us much care what anybody thinks. And what we choose to do now that Elizabeth is free at last is our business; no one else's.'

The smile that hung about Henry Osborne's lips disappeared. Vaux was obviously not to be browbeaten.

'Let's dispense with the hypocrisy, shall we? You forced her to marry my uncle for your own selfish reasons – and she bent the knee and did what you expected her to do. Now he's dead she deserves a little happiness. With me. You might as well know – if you didn't know already – that we've been lovers since before she married. And that both Edward and Thomas are mine.'

Nobody moved. Nobody spoke. Smiling, Elizabeth flicked the surplus ash from her cigarette on to the carpet. It had been Banbury's favourite.

'You might also care to know that while I'm in Le Touquet I intend to get a special licence from the local notary. When I come back for Elizabeth and the boys to take them back with me, we intend to get married.'

Katherine Cultrane was shocked. 'Don't be absurd, Eddie! You can't possibly get married yet. Banbury's hardly cold in his grave and you're planning a wedding to your uncle's widow! In God's name, whatever will people think? Imagine the scandal!'

'It's out of the question,' Thomas Cultrane and Lord Henry Osborne said almost together. But her father was more shocked than her uncle. 'You can't possibly even think of remarriage for a year at least, perhaps longer . . .'

'Oh? And why not, Daddy? Have you and Mummy got some other prospective husband lined up in the wings, someone to enhance your political career? Like William Banbury, old enough to be my father?' Her voice was heavy with sarcasm. 'Well, I'm sorry to disappoint you; but this time I intend to choose for myself. I'm in love with Eddie, he's the father of my sons, and I'm going to marry him whether you like it or not.'

'If you go ahead with this with your husband barely dead and buried, everyone will know exactly what's been going on, you do realize that? Or are you too selfish to care about the honour of the family name?'

Elizabeth hooted with derisive laughter. 'That's all you really care about, isn't it? The family name. The Osborne family honour. No gossip, no whispering behind hands, no scandal. Well, I daresay all families have at least one skeleton in their cupboard.' she had the satisfaction of seeing her mother flush. 'As for being selfish . . . let they without sin cast the first stone. What else was it but selfishness and pure self-interest that made you marry me off against my will to a geriatric with one foot in the grave and my sister to a poof?'

There was a horrified silence; Rosslare turned scarlet in the face. 'The pity of it is that she loved you, Robin. Frances really did love you. But you had to let her come home and find you in bed with your male secretary. Now, there's a man who knows what ambition means!' Finally, she turned to Frances. 'You really should have married Iden, you know. He might have seemed tongue-tied and dull, but at least he doesn't prefer boys.' The clock boomed in the hall. 'That late already?' She got up and turned towards her parents with a mocking smile. 'You really ought to go now, oughtn't you? It's such a long drive back to town!'

They walked out without another word, without even saying good-bye. But Elizabeth didn't care any more.

She walked away, a solitary figure in black, towards the waiting cars. Their chauffeur was standing ready to hold open the door. Someone was running after her. She turned, a few feet away from the Bentley, and saw that it was Robin.

'Frances, please wait.' He was slightly out of breath. 'We have to talk.'

She got into the car. 'I thought we said all there was to say back in London.'

'Your parents want to talk to you. To us. After that little scene with your sister they could hardly do it here.' He climbed in beside her and the chauffeur closed the door. 'We have to drive back to London together. At least let's be civilized about it.'

She looked at him sharply from beneath the wide brim of her hat, and pushed back the veil. 'Are you so anxious to get back because of your job at the Foreign Office, or because you can't bear to be parted from Thomas Dreikhorn?'

Her voice was bitter, but he'd expected that. 'If Mummy and Daddy still think they can twist my arm to go running back to you, then they're as mistaken as they were about manipulating Elizabeth. What she said about them said it all.'

He gave a deep, almost painful sigh. 'Look. I didn't ask them to try and help me get you back, if that's what you think. I wouldn't because you've already made it plain that you won't come. I've accepted that, I don't want us to argue. And I know that everything that's happened is my fault.' The Bentley glided forward gently, and turned from the courtyard into the sweep of the drive. 'All I'm asking is that you be reasonable . . .'

'*Reasonable?*'

'I realize that you and Tom never really got on. I suppose Tom's the kind of person you either love or you hate. Not everyone appreciates his particular brand of humour. But then I've said that before . . .'

'Robin, what are you trying to say to me?'

'We have to co-exist, somehow. And I'm not saying it'll be very easy for either of us. There'll be a little talk, at first, when it becomes known that we both live in different places.'

'So do a lot of respectable married people. Look how many married women the Prince of Wales escorts to nightclubs, and invites down to Fort Belvedere for long weekends. Invariably without their husbands.'

'This can never come out . . . about Tom and me. You do know that? It simply can't . . . we both know the consequences . . .'

There was a tight constricting feeling in her throat, as if someone was strangling her. 'Do you really imagine that I want other people to find out the real truth why I've left you? What do you think would happen to my father's political career?'

He was silent for several minutes. They both stared out at scenery without seeing it.

'Your father and your uncle are going to hint in certain quarters that . . . that there's another woman . . .'

Frances almost gave way to the desire to laugh, the irony was so great. 'I should have guessed . . .'

'It wasn't my idea, Frances.'

When they reached London it was dark and the car dropped Frances off at the entrance to her hotel. She had barely had time to take off her coat and hat when she received an unexpected visitor.

The clerk at the reception desk telephoned her suite to tell her that the Countess of Cultrane was on her way up.

She was expecting the encounter with her mother to be unpleasant, and it was.

'Couldn't you have said what you wanted to say to me today, Mummy, after the funeral?'

'It was neither the right time nor place. And after Elizabeth's bombshell, you and Robin disappeared before we had a proper opportunity to talk.'

'I'm sorry that you and Daddy don't approve of Elizabeth's relationship with Eddie Vaux. But she was right. After six years of being married to a man you chose for her, she has the right to be happy.'

'Not at the expense of the family's good name.'

Frances was tired; the long drive back to London and the strain of having to spend it with Robin after everything that had happened had made her nerves frayed and raw. 'Mummy, did you come here to talk about Elizabeth or to say something specific to me? Perhaps you and Daddy were hoping that if we shared a car for the journey to Greyfriars and back, we'd patch up our differences on the way. Well, if you were then I'm sorry to disappoint you; but nothing's changed.'

'Maybe it will when you've heard what I have to say.' They faced each other across the floor. 'We're all in complete agreement that a scandal of any sort has to be avoided at all costs. True, many other couples choose to live separate lives and also to live apart, without comment if they are sensible enough to be discreet. But this is different. With Elizabeth determined to go ahead with this ill-advised marriage and Freddie behaving like a frivolous fool with some showgirl, for you and Robin to suddenly separate so publicly would invite far too much unwanted comment. That is the last thing we want. I've come to tell you that if you refuse to go back to him immediately, your allowance will be cut off. And I intend to take back all the jewellery that he gave you since your wedding.'

'You can't do that!'

'I doubt if he'd have much trouble proving that the jewellery belonged to the Rosslares and not to you personally. For you to keep it and no doubt sell it would not only be a serious breach of trust but also theft.'

She was a stranger, almost an enemy. She no longer even seemed to be flesh and blood. Where was the young, laughing, carefree

Katherine that Thomas Holland had loved? Without another word, Frances went over to the jewel-case on her dressing-table and picked it up. She placed it in her mother's hands.

'And this is your final answer?'

'Yes.'

'I see. May I enquire what you think you're going to do for money? Or have you found some lover to pay for this no doubt very expensive suite?'

'Coming here was only a stop-gap. I intend to look for a small flat and also find myself a job.'

Her mother laughed. 'Really?'

'It might surprise you, but I'm not entirely without friends.'

Katherine Cultrane went to the door and opened it. For a moment she paused in the doorway and they looked at each other. Then it closed and she was gone.

Frances went to the bed and sat down with her head in her hands. Losing the jewellery was a blow that she hadn't reckoned with and for a moment she felt afraid; she had only enough money to last until the end of the week. There were several people that she could ask for a loan to tide her over, but that would have been too humiliating, and in any case she was far too proud to let anyone know the depth of her desperation. There was nothing else for it; tomorrow she had to go out and find herself some kind of job. In that who she was would no doubt be more of a hindrance than a help, but it had to be done.

She lay down on the bed and stared up at the ceiling. During the whole journey to Kent and back, Robin had made no mention of taking back her jewellery; that, she was certain, was her parents' idea. Whatever else he was Robin wasn't petty and he wasn't cruel.

For a moment she thought of him as she remembered him when they'd first met, before the dark shadow of his intimacy with Thomas Dreikhorn had crept across her life. Silently, she wept.

A sudden shower of rain beat upon the windows and Laura shivered. While Ethel was clearing away the cakes and tea cups, she picked up Desmond and sat him on her lap, then drew closer to the fire.

'It's turned quite chilly,' she heard her mother say to Maurice on the other side of the room. I expect you'll soon have to be getting back; it's nearly Desmond's bedtime.'

'I don't feel well, Mummy,' he lisped, putting his arms up and around her neck.

'Too much cake,' Laura smiled, stroking his dark wavy hair lovingly. More and more he reminded her of Kit. 'I told you too much would give you tummy-ache.'

'But it hurts me *here*,' he wriggled out of her arms and touched his head.

'Sit down quietly like a good boy until it's time for us to go home,' Maurice said severely.

Her father had come back into the room and for a moment she could sense that they were all looking at her, expecting her to speak. The moment Ethel had taken away the tea things and they were alone, her mother came and sat down beside her.

'Maurice is right about . . . well, about Lady Frances. Laura, it really isn't any of your business, you must realize that. Whatever's happened between them, nobody should ever interfere between husband and wife.'

'Mummy, I'm not interfering, for heaven's sake. Frances is my friend. She needed help and I gave it to her. She had nowhere else to stay.'

Richard Asmussen came and stood beside the fire. Slowly, he began putting tobacco into his pipe. 'Your mother's perfectly right. Other people's quarrels are not your business. Or Maurice's. And once you get involved with this kind of thing, you never know where it might end.'

'She must have dozens of people she could have gone to stay with,' her mother said. 'I mean, someone in her position . . .'

Laura was trying to hold on to her thinning patience. 'Mummy, that's just the point. There *was* nobody she could turn to for help. If you knew what this was really about . . .'

'Laura!' Maurice's voice was sharp. 'I think we've said quite enough on the subject. And it's high time we were going. Desmond is almost falling asleep.'

'Poor little chap, he looks quite worn out,' her father lit his pipe and threw the match into the fire. 'Just like puppies, children. Dashing about one minute and then sound asleep the next.'

'I'm not surprised that all of us aren't half asleep.' Maurice looked at her accusingly. 'To be woken up at three o'clock in the morning with someone banging on the door . . . !'

'Well, you've certainly changed your tune, haven't you?' Laura said furiously. 'Before any of this happened, you were the first one to rush over to your mother at Cricklewood and regale her with the latest news about Lady Frances Osborne, Countess of Rosslare! And

367

what about Mr Forster the senior partner, and all the chaps in the office? Don't tell me that you haven't enjoyed boasting to them that your wife's best friend is a prominent member of the aristocracy, and that her photograph appeared in *Vanity Fair* wearing one of my exclusively designed gowns in the Royal Enclosure at Ascot last year, because I know differently!'

'*Laura!*'

'But it's different now, isn't it Maurice? When my friend comes to us for help it's quite another story! She's left her husband and you're terrified that you'll be involved in some sort of sordid scandal!' They were all staring at her, in horrified silence. 'It's a true saying, isn't it? A friend in need is a friend indeed. Well, she *is* my friend and whatever you say I intend to stick by her. She'd do exactly the same for me.' She knew by Maurice's face how furious he was with her and that there would be an argument the moment they were alone.

'My head hurts, Mummy!'

Turning away from his wrath and her parents appalled expressions, she picked Desmond up in her arms. 'Do you think Ethel could bring down the coats, please? His head does feel a little hot.' She could feel their disapproval of her going against Maurice's wishes like another presence.

'You really must do whatever Maurice says,' her mother whispered to her in the hall. 'He is your husband, Laura.'

'Goodnight, Mummy.' She kissed her, then her father. 'We'll come and see you again soon. I'm so busy at Cavendish Street all during the week.'

Maurice kept up an ominous, stony silence all during the journey home. He was visibly annoyed that she insisted on helping Lily undress, wash and tuck Desmond into bed.

'We do employ her to take care of him, Laura. She is capable of doing her job, believe it or not. You were simply staying upstairs as an excuse because you don't want to have this damn matter out.'

'As far as I'm concerned, there's nothing else to discuss, is there?'

'On the contrary. I suppose you haven't given this much thought – obviously – but if Frances Rosslare has left her husband, she'll hardly be in a position to patronise you any more.'

'I hadn't thought about that possibility, no. But does it really matter? I have plenty of other clients and if Frances needs new clothes I'd be only too happy to make them for her.'

'For nothing?'

'The whole idea of friendship, Maurice, is that you don't expect to be paid for it. You're forever telling me that you come from a staunch, church-going family, aren't you? What's the prayer that says, "To give and not to count the cost"?'

At this point he lost his temper. 'How dare you quote things at me! I simply won't have it, Laura. It's just too much. Ever since that damned friend of yours turned up here the other night there's been nothing but trouble. It isn't enough that she comes here and disrupts the entire household, but that you must take her part without knowing the rights and wrongs of the matter.'

'She came home and found her husband in bed with another man, Maurice!'

He turned white. Her voice was loud and angry enough to be heard in the kitchen and upstairs.

'Will you keep your voice down, for God's sake!'

'Oh, don't worry! If there is a scandal it won't involve you!'

'I should have known this friendship of yours would lead directly to trouble. I felt it coming from the very beginning. The upper classes and the middle classes simply do not mix. The scandalous way some of them go on is beyond thinking about!'

'Don't be such a hypocrite! How can you stand there and self-righteously say that? When you were the one who repeated everything I told you about the Osbornes to your family, to people in the office. You boasted about my friendship with Frances to everyone you knew.'

'Laura, all this started when she persuaded you to take on this business of yours – it was her idea, wasn't it? Ever since it got off the ground, you've been different. You've neglected your duties in the home, you haven't been here to give adequate supervision to the staff, you've neglected Desmond and you've neglected me. A wife's place is in the home and with her husband. Perhaps both of you would do well to remember that.'

For a moment Laura was speechless. Then her pent-up anger, the rage she'd been holding back all day, burst out in a torrent of furious words. 'Don't ever accuse me of neglecting my son! That isn't true and you know it. When I've been in Cavendish Street Lily has full charge of him; and I take over the moment I come home. I take him with me whenever I can, you know that. His welfare comes before anything else!'

'And what about *my* welfare? At the end of the day when I might reasonably expect to enjoy the company of my wife, where is she?

Upstairs sitting behind a sewing machine or drawing women's dresses!'

'You were all in favour of me doing this, Maurice! If you'd been against it at the start I would never have taken it on.'

'Then perhaps you'd better think about doing just that. It's high time that you realized where your priorities lie, Laura.' He stormed out and slammed the sitting-room door.

She waited for several minutes and then went upstairs and into Desmond's room. Lily glanced up. 'He's dropped off, bless him, while I was washing his hands and face . . . sleeping like a little lamb, he is.'

Laura smiled and bent over to kiss him. She frowned. 'His forehead feels very hot, Lily. He hasn't really seemed himself all day. If he isn't back to normal in the morning, I think I'll have to have the doctor.'

'Could be he's sickenin' for somethin', Mrs Flavel. There's a lot of measles and croup about. My sister's boy's got it.'

'Oh, goodness, Lily, I hope not!' She stood up, still looking down anxiously at him. 'That's all I need!'

'You'll be goin' to Cavendish Street in the morning, ma'am?'

'Yes, I must, Lily. So many things to do. And three appointments for fittings in the morning alone. I can't possibly cancel them; but if Desmond has to have the doctor, you hold the fort and I'll get back home as quickly as I can. If only we had a telephone here!'

Maurice was surly when she mentioned it.

'It would be so much easier if you arranged to have one installed; if you were ever working late at the office you could let me know straight away. Or if one of the senior partners wanted to contact you outside office hours.'

'That isn't the real reason you want a telephone so much, Laura, and we both know it. If I capitulated and had one of the damned things put in, there'd never be a moment's peace! We'd have your confounded clients ringing up at all hours! No. Definitely *no*. You have one at Cavendish Street and that is quite sufficient. They can telephone you there.' His voice was getting louder by the minute and she knew it had been a fatal mistake to mention the subject when he obviously had no intention of giving way. 'A man's entitled to some peace in his own home. Consider the matter closed.'

They went to bed without kissing or saying goodnight. Laura lay for a long while, her ears straining for any sound coming from Desmond's room, but thankfully there was nothing. Finally, exhausted, a dozen things whirling round and round in her mind all at once, she fell asleep.

47

She wandered through the little churchyard near Belgrave Square, drawing the huge collar of her coat up around her face to shield it from the wind. The grass was wet, muddy; she could feel it sticking to the heels and soles of her high-heeled shoes. But it didn't matter.

Most of the gravestones were long-neglected; overgrown, crooked, their inscriptions half-erased by time and weather; green, smothered with ivy and lichen. She walked slowly past, glancing down at each one. They were all at peace, whoever they had been.

She was alone with her misery and pain. She walked on, picking her way through the puddles and clumps of grass, thinking of her father, her real father. If Thomas Holland had been alive she would have gone unhesitatingly to him now. He would have supported her. He would have understood.

She pushed open the little rickety gate and walked on towards the street ahead. Behind her, the tall white house that seemed to tower above all the others in the elegant Georgian square became hidden by the trees. She would never think of it as her home any more.

Thomas Dreikhorn signed his name at the foot of the page with a flourish, and handed it to the waiting clerk. 'Before you take that, I want you to see that these others are sent on to the appropriate departments for Lord Rosslare.' He opened a brown folder in the wire tray on his desk and flicked through the documents. 'These are for the Attorney-General's office, these are for the personal attention of Lord Reading. See to it, will you?'

'Yes, sir. And the confidential memo on the Import Duties Act for Mr Chamberlain? Shall I take that now?'

Dreikhorn didn't look up. 'Lord Rosslare hasn't finished with it. He's only just got back from the Banbury funeral in Kent. I doubt whether he'll be able to deal with it today.'

'Very good, sir. I'm surprised that his lordship came in at all.'

'Life must go on, Benson. The country doesn't run itself.'

'Yes, sir. Of course. Oh, by the way, Mr Dreikhorn, there's a Mr Lawrence Rankin waiting downstairs to see you. He's very insistent.'

'Wasn't he here yesterday?'

'Yes, sir. He said it was a personal matter of some importance.'

Dreikhorn hid his annoyance and went on writing. 'Get rid of him. I'm far too busy to see anyone without an appointment today.'

'And Sir Rodney Bilson? His private secretary telephoned this morning to ask when he can expect to see Lord Rosslare. He's been waiting for several days now.'

'Bilson's too concerned with his own importance!' He waved his hand in a gesture of dismissal. 'Get back to his office and say Lord Rosslare won't be able to see him until the beginning of next week. I'll take a look in his diary later and check on the time and day. Leave it with me.'

'Yes, Mr Dreikhorn.' The clerk picked up the papers and went out.

He drummed his fingers on the desk, doing some quick thinking; Rankin was rapidly becoming a nuisance and a liability; now that Robbie was completely his again, somehow he must think of a way to get rid of him. He was far too astute to think that would be easy. Rankin was besotted, jealous, demanding more and more of his time. When Dreikhorn had first subtly cold-shouldered him he'd telephoned his office several times a day to try and speak with him; then he'd started to send messages. If he began turning up as he'd done just now, uninvited, unexpectedly, he could make things very awkward, and people might start talking; that was something to be avoided at all costs.

Dreikhorn looked at the clock on the wall and picked up the telephone receiver. He'd leave early this evening; Bilson and the stack of papers marked 'Urgent' would have to wait until tomorrow, or the day after. He needed to see Robbie.

He got out of the car and paid the driver, then looked into his pocket for his keys. He had no valet to worry about, the maid would have done her work and finished for the day. He took his personal mail from the uniformed porter and went upstairs, where he threw down his briefcase and poured himself a drink. Then he sat down and opened the letters. A noise outside his flat door, like someone waiting for entry, made him look up. But when he went to investigate, there was no one there. It mut have been his imagination; he wasn't expecting Robbie for another hour.

When dusk fell he went to the windows to draw the curtains himself. One hand raised on the pulley, he stopped suddenly and looked down into the street. Had it also been his imagination, or had someone been standing opposite the apartment block, staring up at his window? He looked again, but there was no one there. He closed the curtains and went back to the pile of half-opened mail. A few moments later, the telephone rang. He smiled as he went to answer it; Robbie had said he would ring first to make sure no one else was there. But when he lifted the receiver it went dead.

He'd been expecting Robbie to be as delighted as he was that he and Frances were now living apart. But his doleful look of depression angered him. 'It couldn't have worked out any better, surely? You're rid of her, you can come and go as you want. It'll be child's play for us now. We can meet as often as we want.'

'I didn't want to hurt her, Tom.'

'What are you worried about? Women like the Osborne females don't have hearts – haven't you learned that much yet? The only thing that's hurt her is her pride.'

'You don't know Frances like I do.'

Dreikhorn was angry now. 'Oh? And what's that supposed to mean? Don't try and tell me that you *miss* her? That she ever meant anything to you? Christ, who was it said that they were dreading the bloody honeymoon? Now you've got rid of her at last you turn round and try to pretend that you're sorry!'

'No, it isn't like that.' Robbie looked miserable. 'I could never want her . . . in that way. But I did . . . do care for her. In spite of everything you think about the rest of the family, she isn't like them. She deserves better than I've given her.'

'I don't believe this!'

'Please, don't get angry. I'm trying to explain how I feel. I'm not like you; I don't like hurting other people's feelings.' He went on staring into the half-drunk glass of brandy in his hands. 'I accept that the marriage, such as it was, is over; I even prefer living apart. But her parents have given her an ultimatum: either she comes back to me or they make things very difficult.'

'What do you mean?'

'Elizabeth and Eddie Vaux are planning to get married, straight away more or less, in Le Touquet; Freddie Osborne's been seen around town with a showgirl from the Majestic on his arm. Now we've separated and some people are bound to talk. Cultrane's put-

373

ting it carefully about that I've been seeing another woman . . .' He hesitated as Dreikhorn laughed. 'Frances has taken a suite at the Grosvenor, just for a while. But her mother's furious. Frances won't do what she wants, and after the funeral she told her that her allowance from me would be cut off completely, and she took back all her jewellery so that she can't sell it to live on.'

Dreikhorn shrugged. It was pleasing to think of Frances Osborne cast off by her family and virtually without a penny. But he could see the complications. 'I always told you Katherine Cultrane was a bitch! But why not dissemble a little? Think, Robbie! Think what's best for you and me . . . not the Osbornes. Let Frances find a flat somewhere and you pay the rent, with nobody the wiser. That way she stays away and her parents will never know.'

'Don't be silly; it would be obvious. And then I'd lose my position at the Ministry.'

Dreikhorn smiled; so Robbie cared more for his own well-being after all. 'There's nothing you can do, then, is there?' He got up. 'Let me pour you another drink. By the way, did you try to telephone earlier?'

'No.'

'Strange. I thought it might be you to see if the coast was clear, or to say you couldn't come. Probably a wrong number.' He lay a hand on Robbie's shoulder. 'I missed you. I missed you so much . . .'

48

Laura left her assistant to close up the shop for lunch, and made her way to the little restaurant near Hyde Park where they'd arranged to meet. Frances was already there, and she was smiling.

'I'm sorry!' They kissed on the cheek and Laura sat down. 'I was late getting away. Gosh, my feet are killing me! Is everything all right?'

'I've got a job.'

'Marvellous! Whatever is it?'

'You'll never guess. It's crazy, really. I wasn't even expecting to get it. I needed to think and I went for a walk . . . the park near Belgrave Square, the old churchyard . . . then I just wandered almost by accident into the sweetest antique shop. I was just aimlessly picking things up and looking at them when I overheard the manager saying that they were going to advertise for an assistant, so I asked them if I could apply. They were so astonished when they realized who I was, for a moment they thought it was a joke!'

'When do you start? What do you have to do?'

'On Monday. I just keep everything dusted and spick-and-span, and be charming to prospective customers, hopefully persuading them to buy. They get a lot of Americans and I suppose they think having a countess as a sales assistant will be an enormous asset. Whatever their reasons, I can't tell you how relieved I am. I went straight to the nearest letting agents and enquired about flats. I've got one to look over in Lupus Street this afternoon at four o'clock. Can you come with me?'

'Golly, you haven't wasted any time! Frances, I'm so glad you've managed to get back on your feet!'

'Let's order, while I tell you about the little surprise mother sprang on me when I got back from the funeral.'

Laura listened in growing astonishment as she talked.

'So, she said that if I didn't go back to Robin, that was that. No money. She and Daddy wouldn't have me back home. I know it was all her idea, because Robin didn't say a word about taking back my jewellery on the way back to town in the car. He may not love me, but he isn't cruel. Mummy never was averse to a little emotional blackmail. I suppose that was what made me so determined to get a job.'

'How could she treat you this way? For heaven's sake, you're her daughter!'

'And that fact comes a very poor second or third to Daddy's career and the Osborne family name. Elizabeth announcing that she was going to marry Eddie Vaux was simply the last straw. I thought Mummy and Daddy, and Uncle Henry, were going to have a blue fit!' She managed to smile. 'I wish you could have been there. Elizabeth was obviously enjoying every minute of it. I never realized how unhappy she was.' She caught the sudden look that came into Laura's eyes. 'Is anything wrong? Between you and Maurice, I mean?'

'We've been quarrelling a lot more than usual lately, that's all. And it all boils down to the fact that I'm away at Cavendish Street for most of the day. Maurice didn't seem to mind at first, but the designing seems to take up more and more of my time. Of course, when he has to bring mountains of papers home from the office, or work late because one of the senior partners wants something important finished off, I'm supposed to understand. But if I'm late home, even a few minutes, that's a different matter. And Maurice was so reasonable in the beginning. He thought it was such a good idea for me to have an outside interest. Not to mention, between you and I, the satisfaction he got from name-dropping to his mother or in the office. Men. And they say women are the impossible ones!'

'Tell me something I don't know.'

'What makes me absolutely furious is that my parents *and* Maurice's – with a sudden agile shift of their opinions – are entirely on his side. When I first started they were all wildly enthusiastic. But now that Maurice has decided I ought to be put on a chain like an obedient wife, *I'm* the one who is in the wrong.'

Frances leaned across the table towards her. 'But he wouldn't seriously expect you to give it all up?'

'I have thought about it. Anything to make him happy. I love him so much, but I can't seem to get through to him. Then he accuses me of neglecting Desmond, and that's when I go quite mad!'

'Surely he can't mean that? You couldn't be a better mother if you tried. And you take Desmond to Cavendish Street almost every day.'

'Maurice says it isn't good for him to be surrounded by women's clothes all the time. He wants him to go to a nursery school after Easter. We can afford it, and I'm all for it, of course, but I know why he's really doing it. To make me feel guilty because I shan't see him all day. Lily would have to take him and pick him up in the afternoons. I simply wouldn't have the time to make the journey.'

'You'll sort something out.'

'Yes . . .'

'The waiter brought their food and they both ate with relish.

'This flat . . . have you told Robin about it?'

'I shall give him the telephone number and the address. In case he needs to contact me.' Frances sighed and lay down her knife and fork. 'I still feel so confused . . . still hurt. I don't want to make things difficult for him, but I could never go back. I know there are some things that I simply won't be able to get out of, like those ghastly family occasions when one just has to attend . . . pretending, going on as if nothing has changed. I loathe the hypocrisy of it all!'

They had paid their bill, and the cloakroom attendant had gone to fetch their coats when a smart, fair-haired woman dressed in black brushed by their table; they both glanced up and they were both equally surprised. Anne Turner's blue eyes were cold as they rested on Laura's face.

376

'Mrs Turner . . . !' Laura half got up from her chair but something in the other woman's expression halted her where she stood.

'Well, what an unexpected surprise.' The chilly blue eyes went to Frances and then back again. 'Laura Asmussen . . . or is it Flavel now? Of course; you only design under your maiden name.' She made no attempt to disguise her hostility. 'But then you've become quite adept at surprising people, haven't you? And I thought your husband wanted you to leave New Bond Street because he objected to you working for me after your wedding. His objections don't extend, apparently, to you setting up in opposition.' She smiled icily. 'Do tell me, how are Lady Airlie and Lady Iden these days? I haven't seen them since they transferred their patronage to you.'

Frances was the first one to recover from her surprise. 'Any of your former patrons, Mrs Turner, who order their gowns from Laura instead of from New Bond Street came to her entirely of their own volition. As no doubt patrons of other *haute couture* establishments in the past transferred their custom from their previous dressmakers to you.'

Anne Turner's scarlet lips curved in a chilly ghost of a smile. 'All's fair in love, war, and business, Lady Rosslare. I was so sorry to hear of your brother-in-law's death. Dear Elizabeth must be prostrate with grief. Do give her my regards when you next see her.' She walked on through the restaurant into the street.

Laura sank back into her chair and heaved a sigh. 'Well, she's certainly got her knife into me! Thanks for coming to my rescue. It was one of those awful moments when you just can't think of anything to say, even though I wanted to say so much. Does she really think Maurice made me leave her so that I could set up on my own? Surely not! But if he'd been here I know exactly what he would have said; and without a shread of sympathy: *I told you so.*'

'She just resents anyone else's success, that's all. And she knows full well what an asset she lost when you got married and left New Bond Street. I shouldn't let it bother you. Sour grapes.'

Laura smiled gratefully.

'I'm so glad that things have started to come right for you after everything that's happened. If anyone really deserves to be happy, then it's you.'

She took a taxi from Hyde Park Corner and spent barely an hour in her office at New Bond Street; the advance orders that Blanche Stephens had left in a file on her desk made depressing reading; the sudden, unexpected meeting with Laura Asmussen had made her bad mood blacker still. She lit a cigarette and snapped at her secretary for being late back from lunch. Then sat down and flicked through the file. It was monthly becoming ever more thinner.

Lady Airlie and Lady Iden had got their husbands' secretaries to telephone, cancelling orders that had been in the design stage; both of their excuses were barely plausible. Then half-a-dozen more had rapidly followed suit. In the very beginning she'd thought that she could snap her fingers at them, that it was merely a passing phase; after all, she already knew from experience that such things happened in the world of high fashion. It was only when Princess Hélène von Sondburg, the Countess of Westmorland, and the Duchess of Devonshire called to tell her that they'd had second thoughts about her designs for new ball gowns for the Season, and that not even an implied reduction in price had changed their minds, did she realize how serious things had become. She'd taken a taxi and instructed the driver to go slowly past the Asmussen shop in Cavendish Street, and she'd seen several well-known faces – all recently her own clients – on their way inside. In cold anger she'd gone back and closeted herself in her office, plotting how best she could make them return. But nothing she'd done to entice them back had worked.

She sat looking around her; at the rich furnishings, the antique desk, the fashionable Art Noveau lights; all the little expensive touches that were an outward statement of her rapid rise to wealth, fame and success. She was not born to be a loser; second place in the high-fashion hierarchy was not enough. Anne Turner was only at her best when she was first.

Her egotism and her vanity refused to believe that it was in any way her fault; that someone younger, cleverer, more talented, someone with fresh ideas – the girl she herself had discovered and recognized as something special – had finally usurped her place in the *haute couture* world. That Laura Asmussen's designs were better, unique and far more inspired than Anne Turner's had ever been was not the point; the pill was too bitter for her to swallow.

She mixed herself a pink gin and drank it in a single gulp. She lit another cigarette. She needed a scapegoat, someone else to blame, and who else could it be but Frances Osborne? No doubt it had been her encouragement that had made the Asmussen girl start designing on her own, and now to even bigger and greater things. She'd started it all three years ago when she'd married Robert Rosslare and given

378

Laura Asmussen private commissions. Now everyone who mattered was following suit.

Anne Turner ground out her cigarette in the onyx ashtray and picked up her snakeskin bag. She went out and instructed the door-man to hail her a taxi without even leaving word to her secretary where she could be found.

She got out at Oxford Street and wandered through the busy stores, looking at things without really seeing them. At closing time she went to a restaurant and sat there drinking pink gins, without touching her meal.

She finally got another taxi to take her to Simon Forman's house in Bayswater.

He looked surprised to see her. 'Anne, darling! This is delightful, of course ... but I wasn't expecting you for another hour. Jane's only just left the house.'

She sat down and poured out her tale of woe, while he mixed cocktails. 'That underhanded little bitch. And to think that if I hadn't given her a job, she'd still be nothing. It was Elizabeth's sweet little sister who put her up to it, I've no doubt.'

'But you still have a tremendous reputation, and a very long list of impressive clients. Say "Turner" to anyone, and they know exactly what you mean.'

'The list is dwindling, Simon. And my orders for this Season are less than half what they were same time last year.'

'I see.'

'I'm getting tired of London. I've had ten years of bowing and scraping to the spoiled bitches of the aristocracy, and I'm sick to the teeth of them all. Flattering their vanity, telling them the exact opposite of the truth that any fool could see if she looked in the mirror. That the short and dumpy, the skinny and tall have figures like Venus de Milo or some Hollywood film star. And they believe it! My God, how I despise them!' She drank down the cocktail and held out the empty glass for more. 'They wouldn't know style, smartness or chic if it hit them in the face!'

'You *are* angry, my darling!'

She looked at him intently for several minutes without speaking. 'I want to leave and go to Paris, Simon. You promised.'

He was too suave and too practised a liar to show any glimmer of surprise. 'Anne, darling, surely this is just a storm in a teacup. Everything will change, you'll see.'

'That's what I told myself six months ago. But all that's changed is that things have got worse. I think it's time to move on.'

'At this precise moment in time that would be very difficult. I have assets to realize, plans to be laid. One simply can't pack up and leave at a moment's notice . . .'

'It's her, isn't it? Your wife.' She stood up. 'You said that she didn't mean a thing to you, but she does. You don't want to leave her after all.'

'Of course not! I told you. Would I ever lie to you? Really, I'm not the marrying kind. Too fond of women . . . one woman was never enough . . .' He came over and lay his hands on her shoulders, and she wanted him. 'I wanted to sleep with her and she wouldn't go to bed with me unless I married her first. So I did.'

'And you're tired of her now?'

'I was tired of her the moment I first set eyes on you. As if you ever needed to ask . . .' Slowly, deliberately, he began to unbutton the silk dress, and it fell softly to the floor around her feet. 'We'll go to Paris, I promise . . . just the two of us . . . when I judge the moment to be exactly right . . .'

Jane Forman had been about to close the back gate and turn in the direction of the station when she'd noticed the taxi draw up a few yards from the house. Moving back against the hedge, she'd watched Anne Turner climb out, a little unsteadily, pay the driver and then go up to the front door. It was the housemaid's evening off and her husband had answered; she'd continued watching as they'd kissed, and Anne Turner had slipped inside.

She had been on her way to visit her lover; she'd long ago ceased to care that her husband had affairs with almost every female patient that he had; but the liaison with Mrs Turner had been going on since their marriage, and, she guessed shrewdly, was cemented by far deeper ties than simple lust. For the last few months, when she'd watched and waited, she was beginning to realize what those ties might be.

It took her only several minutes to retrace her steps and go back into the house the way she came. Removing her high-heeled shoes she went quietly along the tiled passage and then hesitated, holding her breath, outside the consulting room door.

It was well known that Mrs Turner was a celebrated court dress-maker with a rich, sophisticated and aristocratic clientele; and she knew from her own observations that the vast majority of her husband's patients came from that particular category. Simon Forman was discreetly described as a 'woman's doctor', but Jane Forman had some time ago formulated her own opinion as to what exactly that all-embracing term really meant. One day when he was out she'd taken the keys to his desk and private files, and seen enough evidence to convince herself that Mrs Turner had been recommending certain of her own clients with 'problems' to her husband for treatment, and that he had been performing illegal abortions at extortionate rates. Traces of a white powder that she'd noticed in his surgery had convinced her that he was also running an equally profitable sideline in supplying cocaine and other drugs to the sophisticated and fashionable clientele who could afford his prices.

Jane Forman smiled to herself as she pressed her ear closer to the door; from the sound coming from the other side she had no doubt in her mind what her husband and Anne Turner were doing. But she no longer cared.

Not long now, her lover had said; just a few more months before his *decree nisi* was made absolute, and the divorce was final. Then she could proceed to the final stages of her so-carefully laid plans.

Elizabeth had been in the middle of packing when the telephone rang. The two boys were with her, sitting playing with wooden soldiers in the middle of the floor. Trunks and suitcases were littered around the room, and her maid was busily folding her underwear and laying it away ready for the journey to France, together with the little scented sachets that Elizabeth loved.

She knew that the caller wouldn't be Eddie or Marguerite; they'd both telephoned earlier to tell her that everything was ready, and that they would be flying back from Le Touquet late this afternoon. By her reckoning, they would already have left. If it was her mother, after all these weeks of silence, trying to persuade her to change her mind about the wedding, then she was wasting her time. Elizabeth picked up one of her favourite evening gowns and held it up in front of the mirror.

Evans the butler knocked and opened the bedroom door. The bright, expectant smile on her lips vanished as she saw the expression on his face. When he spoke the whole room whirled. 'My lady . . . a message has just come from the airfield . . . shortly after it took off, the plane's engine caught fire, and it crashed . . . both Mr and Mrs Holland and Lord Vaux were killed.'

PART FOUR

49

Pulling her cardigan closer around her shoulders, Laura wandered back through the long, narrow, immaculate garden and into the house. Her mother was playing with Desmond and they both looked up as she came in.

'Daddy and his garden. He's so proud of it. But I must admit it does look very pretty. Maurice has hired a gardener to come in for three days a week, but in the summer even that isn't enough. I wish I had time for it.' A wistful sigh. 'Gardening is so peaceful and soothing, somehow.'

It was small, aimless talk, masking what they really wanted to say. Laura wanted to talk to her mother about Kit, and she wanted to say what she'd come to say before her father came back.

'You have told him? About Kit coming to London?'

'It seems so strange, after all this time . . . six years. I have a son and I haven't seen him or spoken to him for six years . . . he's never sent us any photographs, no real news . . . all his letters, such as they've been, are about his work.'

'That's what matters to him most, Mummy. Haven't you realized that yet?'

'He was never like other boys, always different. Always wanting different things. You must understand that it's hard for your father and I to just carry on as if he'd never gone away to America . . . it hurt us both so much when he left home, then went away . . .'

'But, Mummy, he's done so well. If it hadn't been for Kit do you think I could have started up designing on my own?'

Her mother's face set in lines of immediate disapproval. 'Trust Kit to be behind another hare-brained idea. You told us it was largely Frances Osborne. Well, it doesn't matter now. Except that we both agree with Maurice that you should give it up. Laura, I'm serious. Maurice has been promoted again, and you'll have to entertain more. He tells me that you've been invited to dinner with one of the senior partners and his wife and you told Maurice you were too busy to go. How much longer do you think he can put up with that kind of thing?'

'Mummy, he gave me forty-eight hours notice! I had commitments to my clients!'

'Your husband comes first, Laura. And I always thought you were the sensible one. But all this proves that you can be just as irresponsible about your obligations to your family as Kit!'

'Mummy, that simply isn't fair! Or true. Maurice was so keen to begin with . . .'

'Well, he isn't now. And you should do as he wishes and put a stop to it.'

There was a long, awkward silence. She'd wanted to talk to her mother about Kit playing at the Savoy, but it had merely degenerated into a quarrel about the shop.

'Look, Daddy will be back in a moment. Can we discuss what I really came here for? I want to know why you say you can't come and hear Kit. For goodness sake, Mummy, he's so well known in America, and now here, with this special appearance with the Savoy Orpheans . . . I would have thought you and Daddy would have been thrilled to come.'

'Laura, you misunderstand. Of course your father and I are terribly proud of Kit, pleased that he's done so well. But the sort of music that he plays . . . well, you know as well as I do that it just isn't your father's cup of tea. And we'd feel a little out of place at the Savoy . . .'

'But he'll expect you to be there!'

'We can see him here just as easily.'

'Then you won't come?' There was a harsh note to her voice. 'Maurice doesn't want to come, either. His excuse is that that kind of music gives him a headache. But I think he's just sulking because we've had another argument about me carrying on with the designing business.'

'Maurice is a good man, Laura.' Her mother took a deep breath as if she was finding great difficulty in what she wanted to say. 'And if you want a happy marriage then you really will have to decide where your priorities lie.' They were exactly Maurice's words, and Laura wanted to scream with frustration.

'Look at Lady Frances Osborne and the Earl of Rosslare; they seemed the perfect young couple when they were first married. Now you tell me that they're living apart. That simply can't be right! Husband and wife belong together.'

'Mummy, you don't know the real reasons why they separated . . .'

'The reasons are unimportant. What matters is the marriage itself. I feel I must warn you, Laura, that unless you agree to abide by

Maurice's wishes, you're going to find your own marriage in a great deal of trouble.'

It had been a shock when Robin had telephoned. Ever since their separation, the brief meeting at Banbury's funeral and then again after the terrible accident to the Hollands and Eddie Vaux, they hadn't communicated. This was the first time that they'd spoken to each other in more than five months.

He'd sounded awkward, embarrassed. Then he'd asked her if it was convenient for him to come to see her. He needed to talk. She'd hesitated, strongly suspecting some plot motivated by her mother, but he'd told her that it was something personal, and he needed her help. After she'd put down the telephone receiver she'd had second thoughts, wishing that she hadn't agreed for him to come; but it was too late by then to change her mind because he'd already left. Thankfully he'd picked Grace's evening off.

Frances opened the door of the flat when he rang the bell slowly, reluctantly, and they'd stared at each other like strangers. Robin looked curiously different somehow, as people one hasn't seen for some time often do: older, a little heavier in build, lines around his eyes she hadn't seen before; the jovial, boyish Robin gone. She asked him if he would like a glass of wine and he accepted, but when she'd handed it to him he just stood there, cradling it nervously in his hands.

'You're looking well. How are you?'

'What do you want, Robin?'

There was a long silence, and then he spoke. 'I need to ask you a favour.' Another awkward pause. 'You remember my cousin Irene Treowen and her husband Ian? They came to our wedding. Ian was posted to Singapore, then Hong Kong and Melbourne a few weeks afterwards . . . they've been abroad ever since.' She could guess what was coming.

'They're back in London?'

'Yes. Ian's been attached to the Colonial Office and they've taken a rented house in Manchester Square. My aunt's health has been a great cause for worry for the last few months or so, and Irene's gone up to Scotland to visit her.'

'What are you saying, Robin?'

'They don't know about . . . us. About the separation.'

'I realize that you can hardly tell them the truth.'

'No.' He went on swivelling the wine glass in his hands. 'The thing

387

is . . . when Irene comes back next Friday, they want us to join them for dinner at the Savoy.' He couldn't quite look at her. 'I told them that we'd come.'

For a moment she didn't say anything. How easy he made it sound just to pretend. A single evening, nothing more. But he was still asking too much.

'Robin, I'm sorry. But I can't. I couldn't go through with it. You'll have to make my excuses.'

'Frances, *please*. What can I say to them? I've already accepted. If I say that you're ill then Irene will want to come and see you, and then they'll know that you no longer live at the house.'

'They're bound to find out that we're not together, Robin. That we live separate lives . . .'

'If it was anyone else, I could simply say that we'd separated, and that would be enough. But not to Ian and Irene. She's my cousin and she'd ask questions, don't you realize that? Families don't observe the polite conventions. Besides which, Ian will be working at the Scottish Office from next January, so that Irene can be near her mother. We won't have to see them again . . .'

'You can't go on lying to them forever. At some stage they're bound to find out the truth. Supposing someone tells them that we've been living apart while the're in London?'

'Frances, I'm not asking you to come back to me.' He put down the glass of wine, untouched. 'I know that you wouldn't; nor would I expect you to, after what happened . . . but if other couples can lead civilized separate lives, just meeting occasionally when it's necessary, I don't see why we can't do that, too . . .'

'How long are they stopping in London?'

'Until next month, when they go up to Ian's estate in Argyll for the shooting. They'll probably spend November in London, while he's temporarily attached to the Colonial Office. As I said, he's due to take up his new appointment in Scotland early in the new year.'

There was another long silence while all the doubts she felt about agreeing jostled for supremacy in her mind. She sat down wearily. 'All right, Robin. I'll come. But only for Irene's sake. I didn't have a chance to get to know her very well before they went overseas, but she was very kind to me, and Ian was very sweet.' A pause. 'Not that I don't have serious misgivings . . .'

'I'm grateful,' he said awkwardly, woodenly; Robin never did have a way with words; only when he'd been Dreikhorn's puppet with

388

ready-written lines had he seemed articulate at all. 'I'll contact you in a day or two and let you know what time I'll be here.'

'Why don't we just meet in the foyer at the Savoy?'

'They want us to go to Manchester Square first for drinks.'

'I see. You seem to have counted on my saying yes to all this.'

'No, I didn't. Frances, I swear it. I just hoped when I'd explained that you'd agree.'

She saw him to the door.

'I meant to ask . . . how Elizabeth is. Your parents refuse to talk about her; nobody's seen her for months, not since the accident . . .'

'She's still in a shocking state, as if she can't really believe that Eddie Vaux's dead. You know I spent three months with her after it happened, but I couldn't stay any longer because they wouldn't have held over my job. I was lucky as it was that they agreed to get someone temporarily to take over. I thought she might start to make a new life, once she was back in London. But she seems to have given up, nothing seems to matter to her any more. Not even the boys.'

'I'm sorry.'

When he'd gone Frances went and wound up her gramophone. She mixed herself a cocktail and sat down with a copy of *Vanity Fair* on her lap while she listened to Cole Porter. Already she was afraid that she'd made a terrible mistake. But for Irene and Ian Treowen's sake she couldn't go back on her word.

Elizabeth was lying sprawled across the rumpled bed when the maid come to her door. When she tapped, softly, then more loudly and there was still no flicker of response, she pushed it open and went inside.

'My lady . . . I'm sorry to disturb you . . . but there's a gentleman waiting downstairs . . .'

Elizabeth rolled over, pushing back her untidy hair from her staring, red-rimmed eyes. Her face was dirty, tear-streaked. She couldn't remember the last time that she'd washed. But it didn't matter now. Nothing mattered. There was no longer anyone to wash for; no longer anyone to love.

'I can't see anyone. *Nobody!* Do you understand? Whoever it is, tell them to go away!'

'He's most insistent, my lady . . .'

'Are you deaf?' She grasped an ornament on the bedside table and hurled it at the girl, wildly. But she ducked. It missed its target and crashed, shattering into pieces against the wall. 'Tell him to get out of my house!' Elizabeth buried her head in the satin eiderdown and burst into tears.

The maid who had replaced Sabine was terrified of her mistress's unpredictable rages, but she managed to stand her ground.

'He said to tell you it was Dr Forman, my lady.'

Abruptly, Elizabeth stopped crying. 'Dr Forman? Simon Forman? Why didn't you *say*? For God's sake, bring him up here . . . !'

The door closed very quietly behind her. Elizabeth could hear the maid's footsteps dying away along the landing.

When he came into the room it was so softly that she didn't realize for a moment he was standing there. 'Hello, Elizabeth.'

Shaking, her blue eyes bloodshot, she raised her head and looked at him. '*Simon . . . !*' A sob broke from her throat, a terrible, heart-rending sound. '*Help me . . .*'

He came across to her and sat down on the bed. Then he reached out and took her hand; it was cold, limp, lifeless. It lay in his hand like a stone. He was rarely shocked, but the awful change her grief and self-neglect had wrought shocked him now; but how Anne would have laughed.

She wore no make-up; her face was dirty, streaked with the stains of dried tears. Her eyes were dull, dead, devoid of any expression except utter hopelessness. Her hair – the wonderful bright, silver-blonde hair that he'd secretly longed to touch – fell lifelessly across her face, a pathetic shadow of the self-confident, striking beauty who'd come to his house in Bayswater with Anne Turner six years before, dressed immaculately in the height of fashion. Except for the fact that she was still breathing, she might have been dead.

Any other man would have pitied her; but Simon Forman could not quite bring himself to do that. His practice had been built on the exploitation of the weaknesses of others; casualties were inevitable and guilt was not his concern. He had only come here for a reason. Anne Turner would have come to gloat.

'My dear . . .' the smooth, professional, practised smile exuded reassurance and trust, 'I've been away, in Paris. With Anne, as a matter of fact. I guessed that you'd need a new supply when I got back.' He took something out of his pocket, glancing over his shoulder towards the door. 'She sends her love, of course. And she's so sorry that you refuse to see her . . . but she does understand. Grief can do terrible things . . .'

390

There was an anguished choking sound from the prostrate figure slumped across the bed.

'Bitch . . . *bitch* . . . she told me Eddie was seeing other women . . . Eva Scott-Montagu . . . and it was all lies!'

'A genuine mistake, my dear . . . Anne simply made a mistake. It was someone else, of course . . .'

'I don't want to see her. I never want to see her.' She suddenly reached out and gripped his hand with surprising strength. 'Have you brought the stuff? I must have it . . . I need more stuff . . . the pain . . . must blot out . . . *the pain . . . Eddie* . . .' Sobs racked her body. 'I *loved* him, Simon! I loved him so much . . .'

'Something different this time . . . stronger. Something to help you blot out the pain.' He was holding a syringe in his hands. 'Shall I show you how to use it?' She lay there on her side, staring blankly. 'The cocaine . . . you mix it . . . you use the syringe . . . and then you inject the needle into a vein in your arm . . . you'll feel so much better when it takes effect, I promise.'

She reached out; her hand was shaking. Forman held it slightly out of her reach.

'The money first, Elizabeth . . . my suppliers, you understand? I must have the money first. Then it's yours.' A smile. 'Unfortunately, supplies are so very expensive now, and extremely difficult to obtain. I have to take risks . . . and risks don't come cheap.'

'My jewellery . . . the box . . . drawer . . . bottom drawer . . . over there . . .'

He was a tall, blurred shadow. As he stood in front of the window he momentarily seemed to blot out the light. She didn't see him open the box and take out the entire contents. Impossible to sell here, in London; but in Paris it would be easy. For a moment he held them in his cupped hands, looking down at them as they winked and sparkled in the light; then he slipped them into his pocket and turned back to the prone body slumped across the bed.

'Shall I help you into the bathroom? It'll be easier to do it there.' He helped her up; she was light, skeletal. He could see the sharp bones showing through the fine skin of her face. 'I'll do it for you this time; then you can do it on your own. It's easy when I've shown you how . . .'

Robin collected her from the Lupus Street flat at seven o'clock and they drove to the Treowen's rented house in Manchester Square. On the short journey they barely spoke, but she could see the way he kept turning to glance at her anxiously, every few moments. As the car drove through the large open wrought-iron gates, they saw Ian and Irene appear together at the top of the steps.

'I *am* grateful, Frances,' he said, simply. 'I know this isn't easy for you.'

'I'm glad you realize it.' The chauffeur opened the door and he helped her out, to an ecstatic reception from Irene.

'Frances, darling! How simply stunning you look!' They kissed on the cheek. 'Do come inside for cocktails, it's getting quite chilly now.' They linked arms and the two men walked behind them, chatting. 'Goodness, I'm so thrilled to see you and Robert again . . . it's been absolutely *ages*.'

'I'm so sorry your mother hasn't been well. Robin told me that Ian's temporarily at the Colonial Office, then at the Scottish Office in the new year.'

'Poor Mummy; she's frightfully brave, even though her doctor says she's in such ghastly pain. Of course, since we left England three years ago, it's been difficult to get back to Argyll to see her . . . but now she's worse, and something just had to be done. I simply couldn't bear anything to happen to her and us not be there.'

'No, of course not. But it is good to see you both again.' Frances wanted to steer the conversation towards Irene's life, not hers; if it came to it would she be able to lie to Robin's cousin to her face if any awkward questions were asked? 'It was so kind of you to invite us this evening.' She looked all around her as they went into the enormous drawing-room. 'This is a *lovely* house!'

'Oh, it's quite bearable, I suppose; but renting is never quite like having one's own. Well, it's simply a short-term measure, and we did it before, when Ian was first posted to Singapore. Being surrounded by other people's possessions, other people's taste in furniture, isn't quite our cup of tea. But it'll do. Irene smiled brightly as she mixed cocktails and Ian Treowen handed them around. He raised his glass.

'Here's to your good health, happiness, and to your continuing career in the corridors of power, Robert! My word, it *is* good to be back in London! It's more than three years now; unbelievable how time flies.

'Does anyone else want another cocktail before we leave? Darling, is it that time already? Heavens, I must rush upstairs and powder my nose before we go! Robert, do let Ian mix you another screwdriver . . .'

Frances followed Irene upstairs into a large, pastel-pink bedroom with a huge pink satin canopied bed.

'I'm *so* looking forward to the Savoy tonight, and Christina Stanley says they have this absolutely marvellous American band. Apparently their bandleader is English . . .'

Frances kept her face expressionless because of her reflection in the mirror.

Irene went on dabbing her face with her powder-puff. 'They come from . . . now, where was it Christina said? Ah, yes. Chicago. I think. Or was it New Orleans? Oh, I'm such a duffer at remembering things.' She got up and smoothed down her silk evening gown in the mirror. 'At any rate, they're terribly famous in America and have made dozens of records. Tonight at the Savoy they're making just a one-off special appearance.'

'I didn't know that.' It was merely a coincidence, a chance in a thousand; it couldn't possibly be *him* or Laura would surely have said.

'Ah, that's it. It'll have to do.' She threaded her arm through Frances's, gaily. 'When you reach my age, my dear, you seem to spend every fifteen minutes rushing to the ladies' room to check that your face is still the same. Not you, of course – you're absolutely ravishingly beautiful. Lucky old Robert!'

They caught sight of each other at exactly the same moment; Frances and the Treowens were walking towards the ballroom from the hotel entrance; Kit with the others behind him had come down in the lift from his suite on the second floor.

In the middle of the noisy, crowded foyer she stood out; in the flesh she was so much more beautiful than the picture that he'd carried in his mind. For a moment he couldn't speak or move. He'd forgotten everyone else; Rudy, Maurice, even Laura.

He saw her hesitate with sudden shock as she saw him; then she recovered her composure and began to walk slowly towards the group that he was with. Quickly, his sharp eyes took in the other couple, the tall, good-looking, fair-haired man; clearly that was her husband because Laura had already described him.

'Hello, Frankie.' Her face was very pale, luminous; paler than he remembered. He wanted to reach out and touch her, kiss her, draw her into his arms; but he was six years too late. All around them he could sense everyone except Laura wondering how they knew each other and where they'd met. The jazz musician and the Cabinet Minister's daughter.

'Hello, Kit.' She recovered from her surprise before he did, turning to introduce him to her husband and their friends. She introduced Laura.

'Frances, darling! What an absolutely unbelievable coincidence! Ian, isn't it just? Mrs Flavel used to work for Anne Turner at New Bond Street, and now from all accounts she's taking London fashion by storm single-handed! *And* she's the famous Kit Asmussen's sister – it's quite incredible!'

Kit smiled, his eyes still on Frances. 'I wouldn't say that I'm as famous as all that.'

'Good heavens, one can tell instantly that you're British, even if you have lived in America for the last six years! So modest . . .' she unleashed one of her all-embracing smiles. 'You must all come back to Manchester Square after the show's finished. We've invited simply *everyone* . . . they'll be absolutely thrilled if you'd play for us . . .'

Beside him, from the corner of his eye, Kit saw Laura almost imperceptibly shake her head, but he took no notice. 'Thank you, we'd all like that.' He couldn't pass up any opportunity to be near her.

Under the evening suit, he could feel the sweat beginning to break out around his middle, along his back. His dark, wavy hair was already damp with perspiration; beads of it stood out along his forehead. Usually the clapping and the cheers of appreciation, being on the centre of the stage elated him, uplifted him, spurred him on beyond his own limits of endurance, pushing him to go on and on playing when he was exhausted, empty, tired. But not tonight. It was the sight of her, not the deafening cheering, that motivated him; sitting barely a hundred feet from where he stood but still out of reach, he couldn't tear his eyes away from her face. All his anger, unhappiness, emptiness and hopelessness took expression from the instrument that he held in his hands.

When he'd played the last solo, he put it down abruptly on the piano and told the others to carry on. Then ignoring all the women who clustered avidly around him wherever he went, he started walking towards her across the floor.

'Isn't he absolutely brilliant? What a wonderfully talented young man! And so dreadfully good-looking. Gracious me, the women simply won't leave him alone. Robert! Look, over there . . . isn't it that chum of yours? Heavens, he's with Elvira Bouverie!'

Frances turned cold as she followed Irene's eyes and saw the tall, dark figure of Thomas Dreikhorn, his companion clinging to his arm, making their way towards the Treowens' table through the crowds of dancing couples. Dreikhorn, the shadow across her life. He cast his arrogant, charming smile across everyone at the table, but his eyes were bright with malice as they met hers.

'You didn't say you were coming here tonight,' Robin said.

Dreikhorn pulled out a chair for his companion. 'It was all Elvira's idea. She's mad about this Kit Asmussen.'

'I think he's perfectly *divine!*'

'Isn't he just? And what a surprise we had when we first got here and bumped into him in the foyer! His sister is a friend of Frances'. Laura Flavel. She designs all these wonderful clothes! Ian and I have invited them back to the house . . . you and Thomas simply must come, I insist! I've even persuaded him to play for us . . .'

'Oh, I'd adore meeting him!' She plucked at Dreikhorn's sleeve. 'Tom, darling, Irene and Ian are having a party after the show and we're invited. Do let's go!'

'Of course.'

She twisted suddenly in her seat, astonishment all over her face. 'It's him! He's coming over to our table!'

He saw her surprise, her sudden panic. The others were all staring at him, wondering why he was there. But he didn't care about them; they might just as well have been invisible. The only face he could see was hers.

He stopped in front of her table. 'Will you dance with me, Frankie?'

She heard the little muffled whispers behind her; the girl Dreikhorn had brought with him gasped. She felt herself stand up, her lips framing a wordless refusal. But he'd reached down and taken her hands. 'Please, Frankie. I'm going back to Chicago the day after tomorrow.' He was already drawing her onto the floor. People were staring at them. 'I can't go without saying goodbye.'

'You did last time.' He deserved that and he knew it.

'Last time was a long time ago.'

She was light, graceful, floating in his arms. He loved the feel of her, the warmth of her skin through the exquisite gold lamé dress. He longed to make passionate love to her. He never wanted to let her go. But she was another man's wife. There was so much he

395

wanted to say to her. That he'd never stopped thinking about her, that he'd been a fool to let her go. But he couldn't say any of those things because he no longer had any right to.

'I'm glad you're happy now.' Had she hidden her misery so well, then? 'You look beautiful. More beautiful than any other woman in this room. More than anyone I've known.'

'That must be quite a few.' She was hurt by the sight of women crowding round him, though she knew she had no right to be. 'Laura didn't tell me you were coming back.' Already she'd guessed the reason why.

'It was a spur of the moment thing; it just happened. We got the invitation and it seemed like a good time to come. I haven't seen my parents for six years.'

She didn't want the music to stop, she didn't want the dance to end. She just wanted him to go on holding her.

Suddenly, he smiled. 'You've cut your hair.'

'Yours is exactly the same.' It was still thick, dark, luxuriant; it still fell slightly over the left-hand side of his forehead. She longed to reach up and touch it, to feel it clinging to her fingers. She wished that they were back in the second-floor room in Halkin Street, sitting on his piano stool, face to face. Now they were here, surrounded by hundreds of other people.

The music stopped and they drew apart. Slowly, he let her go and they stood there for a moment looking at each other. In a moment he would walk back to his table near the bandstand and she would walk back to hers; later, at Irene Treowen's party, they'd meet again but there was nothing left to say, only things that could not be said. *I love you. I need you. Stay with me.*

She reached the table and sat down on her chair. Then she glanced up into Thomas Dreikhorn's questioning, mocking eyes.

'Oh, Kit . . . *please* play for us!'

'I think you're absolutely wonderful . . . Daddy bought me all your RCA records when he was at the Washington Embassy . . .'

'You must have incredibly powerful lungs to play for so long without even stopping to draw breath . . . golly, it makes me go all shivery when you do those top notes . . .'

'Can I sit next to you on the piano stool? I can do accompaniment with two fingers . . .'

'Shall I turn the pages of your music over? Oh, *do* let me!'

They crowded around him at the piano, giggling, pressing against him, plying him with questions, while he played a medley of songs from memory from all the latest Broadway shows. But when he looked up from the keys he looked straight at Frances, leaning against the wall on the opposite side of the room.

'We're in London, now,' he said, still looking at her. 'So I'll play something English. Noël Coward recorded this the year after I left the Pavilion.' Ignoring the chorus of shrieking débutantes, he played *Mary Make Believe* from *This Year of Grace*, and this time sang the words himself.

She walked slowly forward towards the piano, and then stopped when she reached it, and their eyes locked together. She could sense the girls swarming around him staring at her, resentful that only she had his attention, but she no longer cared. When one of them tried to join in the song in a flat, wobbly, high-pitched voice, she felt so angry that she immediately intervened in her beautiful, rich soprano that very few people had ever heard. Kit's mouth curved into a wide smile. The girl with the flat, wobbly voice faded away, frowning, and they finished the song together. Everyone cheered and clapped.

'Frances, darling, I'd forgotten that you sang so divinely.'

'Keep an eye on her, Robert, if Charles B. Cochran hears her he'll snap her up for one of those shows of his!'

'Kit . . . is it true that he seduces all the new chorus girls?' There was an outburst of laughter among the débutantes.

'Why . . . are any of you girls thinking of going to work for him?' More laughter. He was still looking at her and she knew she had to get away before she betrayed herself. When she looked round, Laura was at her side.

'I'm sorry, Frances. I should have told you that he was coming home . . . but I never dreamed that you'd be at the Savoy tonight. I swear it.' They moved back together, away from the crowd. A footman carrying a tray of champagne cocktails paused as he came past, but they both shook their heads. 'He's only here for a few days. HMV wanted him to come. He's going to their studios tomorrow to record some numbers with the band.'

'It's none of my business, is it?'

'I didn't know your friends were going to invite us back.' She glanced across the press of admiring young women milling around the Treowen's grand piano to where her brother sat, playing beautifully and ignoring them all. Whenever he played he was always in a world of his own, isolated from other people. Except just now when he had sung for her.

'You weren't to know. It wasn't your fault.'

'We should be going. Maurice is giving me dark looks.' Frances glanced across the room to where Maurice Flavel was standing, talking with Ian Treowen. 'He isn't used to late nights like this. And I had such a terrible job even persuading him to come.' There was a groan of disappointment from around the room as Kit got up from the piano stool. 'Look, I'll telephone you tomorrow at the flat.' He was coming towards them; he paused halfway as Irene Treowen came up to thank him.

'Laura, please don't tell him about Robin and me . . . that we've split up . . .' Why had she said that, when it made no sense? Was it pride, shame, embarrassment? Was it simply that she couldn't bear Kit, more than anyone, to find out the truth? Was it a misplaced sense of loyalty to her family, who were determined that nobody except themselves would ever know the real reasons for her split with Robert Carr? Her grip tightened on Laura's arm. 'Laura, you won't tell him?'

'I promise, I won't.'

Suddenly he was standing beside her and the proximity between them made her feel weak, dizzy. 'Frankie, I *must* see you. Meet me tomorrow.'

'Kit, I *can't.*'

'*Please.* I told you. We're only here for a few days.'

The young American with the straw-coloured hair who she remembered from Halkin Street came up behind him. 'Hi! Say, haven't we met some place before?' A nudge in the ribs from Kit's elbow silenced him.

'Rudy, tell the others we're leaving. It's late.' She watched him go, walking side by side with Laura down the steps to the waiting cars. He turned and looked back at her.

'Goodnight, Frankie. Meet Laura tomorrow for lunch at the Savoy. I'll be there.'

The evening began to break up. More people left. Irene and Ian Treowen had gone into the hall to say goodbye. The footmen began collecting the empty glasses on the piano.

She wandered into the empty morning-room and leaned against the windows, staring out into the night. There was a full moon and stars. The perfect night sky. When the door softly opened and then closed behind her, she thought it was Robin coming to tell her that

398

it was time to leave. She turned round and came face to face with Dreikhorn.

He held a cocktail glass in one hand; there was a cigarette in the other. He smiled. 'Well, the party's over now. Did you enjoy yourself, Frankie?'

She was furiously angry, outraged. 'Don't ever call me by that name, do you understand? *Never!*'

Maddeningly, he laughed. 'Dear me, have I touched on someone's raw nerve? Or simply on an unmentionable subject? So. Only the good-looking young musician has the unique privilege of using this particular sobriquet. I wonder why? Am I mistaken or would I be right in assuming that you have met somewhere before?'

'What exactly do you mean by that?'

'My dear Frances, Robbie may be your estranged husband and not particularly observant when it comes to such things, but I assure you, I am. I saw the way he was looking at you, and the way you were looking at him, particularly when you danced. Have you ever been to bed with him?'

She hit him across the face with all the force she could muster, and his cocktail went flying. 'How *dare* you! Kit Asmussen is my best friend's brother!'

'And hasn't been in England for the last six years?' There was a livid red mark on his cheek where Frances had struck him, but the arrogant, taunting smile was still in place. 'How old would you have been when you saw each other last?'

She pushed past him towards the door.

'A particularly precocious fifteen-year-old, perhaps? Carnality would appear to run in the Osborne blood, wouldn't you say? After all, your sister was Eddie Vaux's mistress before she married that old fool Banbury, and for the last twenty years your mother's slept with every prominent man in London. Oh dear! Didn't you know that?'

She swung round and faced him. 'You're disgusting!'

'Such an ungovernable temper! And I always thought it was red-heads who ranted and raved. Still, all women are alike, aren't they? They never think, they can only feel. No brains.' He dotted the ash from his cigarette with insolent slowness. 'They lurch pathetically from moment to moment, existing only on their emotions. Like you. And now you're angry with me because I know all about your little secret.'

Her hand was on the handle of the door. She could hear voices coming from the next room.

'Checkmate. I also know a little secret about you.' She strode into the now almost deserted drawing-room; from the expressions on the Treowen's faces she knew that they'd heard the raised voices.

'Frances, is anything the matter?'

'It was a lovely evening, Irene, Ian. Thank you so much. Robin, will you please take me home?'

Behind her Thomas Dreikhorn appeared in the open doorway. She saw him exchange glances with Robin. 'I'm afraid there's been a little accident, Irene, one of your glasses has got broken. I'm so sorry. Too clumsy of me.'

She sank back on to the seat of the car, waiting for the inevitable rush of questions.

'Frances, for God's sake, what was going on? I heard you shouting at Tom!'

'I'm tired, Robin. Just get your driver to drop me at the flat, please. I don't want to talk about it.'

'But Irene and Ian heard . . . and Elvira. What were you arguing about for heaven's sake?'

'Do you really care?'

'Look, I know you and Tom have never got on . . .' a derisive laugh interrupted him. 'I know he can be difficult, that he rubs people up the wrong way, but did you really have to make a scene in someone else's house? Irene will want to know what happened!'

'I'm sure he'll think of a suitable lie to satisfy her curiosity.'

He let out a long sigh and stared from the window into the darkness. Buildings, trees, flashed past as they drove by. 'I didn't know he was going to be at the Savoy tonight. I was as surprised to see him as you were.'

'Can we please drop the subject?' The car turned into Lupus Street and she moved forward in her seat to climb out.

'Frances . . .' He reached out and touched her bare arm; she felt nothing. How different it had been with Kit when they'd danced together; just the lightest touch of his hand on her skin had sent all her pulses leaping. 'I want to thank you for coming with me tonight . . .'

The chauffeur was already standing on the pavement, holding open the door.

'I'm glad I came. But not for the reasons you wanted me to.'

'Laura, it's late. I think we should go straight home. I brought a briefcase full of papers home from the office with me that I have to read over the weekend. Gorston wants them on his desk first thing Monday morning.'

'You take a taxi, Maurice. I want to talk to Kit. He'll see me home, won't you?'

'Right to the front door.'

'He smiled at Maurice but he'd taken an almost instantaneous dislike to him; he was all wrong for Laura. Stiff, starchy. He reminded Kit of his father. 'Thanks for coming, Maurice . . . I appreciate it, especially since you have so many calls on your time.' Was he being sarcastic? Maurice frowned. Kit was too glib, too free and easy and far too attractive to women to be trusted. Their dislike was mutual. 'Don't worry. I'll take care of Laura.'

Maurice hesitated. He would have liked to insist that Laura accompany him back to Holland Park there and then, but he could scarcely cause a scene in the foyer of the Savoy Hotel. He'd tell her exactly what he thought of her brother tomorrow.

'Come on,' Kit said, taking hold of her arm. 'Rudy?' They went up to the second floor in the hotel lift and Kit unlocked the door of his suite, then tossed his clarinet case on the bed.

'Get me a drink, Rudy. I'm dead beat.' Across his head, Rudy Loew and Laura exchanged glances.

'Don't you think you've had enough for tonight, Kit? Don't want to wake up in the morning with a busted head.'

'Rudy, will you get me the bloody drink or shall I get it myself?' Rudy disappeared into the adjoining room.

'Kit . . .'

'Oh, no! No lectures, Laura. I didn't ask you to stay behind for that. I want to talk.' He sat down heavily on the bed. 'You didn't tell me Frankie was going to be here tonight. Was that your idea?'

'Of course not! I was just as stunned as you were when I saw her in the foyer . . . after I got your letter saying you were coming over and when, I didn't tell her. You must know why.'

'I know you still think that I treated her badly. And I did. Even though I did it for all the right reasons, like I told her, we both belong in different worlds.' He ran a hand through his thick dark hair. 'Christ, she's beautiful! And I turned my back on that.'

Laura was silent for a moment. She sat down beside him and put her arm around his shoulders. 'Kit, I won't stay long. I know you're tired and it's been a long day and you have another long day tomor-

401

row. I'm . . . sorry that Mummy and Daddy didn't come . . . I explained why . But I know they were thrilled to see you.'

'Yes, weren't they?' The sarcasm had come back into his voice. 'And that husband of yours, too. I could see just how he was sizing me up. We're not on the same planet.' He smiled, wearily. 'But I can see where Desmond gets all his good looks and charm.'

'Frances thinks he looks like you.'

The smile faded. Rudy came back with the drinks and then diplomatically disappeared again.

'Laura . . . are you happy with him? Really happy, I mean. Don't try and fake it, please; not with me. Tell me the truth, OK?'

'I love Maurice, Kit.'

'Sometimes that isn't enough.'

'I don't know what you mean.'

'He doesn't approve of you having your own designing business, does he? The whole set-up in Cavendish Street . . . he's dead against it. I suppose that's partly the reason that he doesn't like me. I was the one who gave you the money.'

'He just doesn't approve of married women going out to work, unless they have to.'

'Is he making life difficult for you?'

'Kit, I know you mean this for the best, but please don't interfere. I want you and Maurice to like each other.'

He drank down the glass of brandy. 'I think you're asking too much, little sister.' He put his arm round her. 'Listen, this is really what I wanted to say, and why I didn't want that husband of yours around when I said it. On the way here we drove up through Surrey . . . strange, I'd forgotten how beautiful the English countryside can be at this time of year. I caught sight of a big house, with a "For Sale" sign, laying back off the road. So we stopped the car and I went to take a closer look at it. We had time so I drove into the town and looked up the agents who were selling it . . . I bought it, Laura.'

Her eyes grew bright. 'You're coming home!'

'No. I bought it for later. For me, maybe. But for you, too.'

'I don't understand.'

'It's in my name, but I want you to think of it as yours, too. A bolt hole, if you ever need it. I bought it with all the furniture, and the agents are sending someone in to see to the garden.' He smiled. 'It was a little . . . overgrown.'

'What are you saying?'

402

'If you ever decided that things between you and Maurice won't work out, you have somewhere to go. Don't kid yourself, Laura. Not all marriages last forever; people change, things that you thought you could bear once become unbearable; that's when you need somewhere to run to. And you know as well as I do that you could never go back to Kilburn. Mum and Dad would never let you. They're the old school . . . remember? However miserable you are you stay married. And together. Till death do us part, and all that tosh.'

She was suddenly horrified at what he was saying. 'But I'd never leave Maurice! It's unthinkable! And he'd never let me take Desmond . . . Kit . . .'

'I know it's easy for me to say. But I know about people much more than you do. You're a novice, Laura. But you're all I've got in the world and I won't stand by and see you hurt.'

She kissed him.

'I'll give you the name of the agents. And see that you have a key. But remember. This is just between the two of us. OK?'

'I love you.'

He stared down morosely into his empty glass. 'It's a long time since anyone's said that. Anyone that I care about, that is.'

Rudy Loew had come back into the room and he was standing watching them in the frame of the doorway. Laura glanced up and they exchanged a smile. 'I've had a wonderful evening . . . I can't remember when I've enjoyed myself so much. If only you were staying longer.'

'Hey, I like the sound of that offer! And you still look the dead spit of Louise Brooks!'

Kit got to his feet. 'Do something for me, Laura? Besides thinking about what I've already said? Call Frankie and invite her to lunch. Tell her . . . one o'clock.'

'Kit . . . do you really think this is a good idea?'

'I want to see her, Laura. I just want to see her again, and talk. You'll be there as chaperone.' A pause. 'Except I don't want you to arrive until two-thirty.'

'Kit . . .'

'Please, Laura. Just do as I ask.' He helped her on with her coat, then he turned back to Rudy as they reached the door.

'Wait up for me, will you? I'm just going to take my sister home.'

He came back from Holland Park three-quarters of an hour later and threw himself down full-length on the bed. It was two o'clock in the morning and he was mentally and physically exhausted, but he knew that if he went to bed he wouldn't sleep. Ever since he'd seen her again tonight, he hadn't been able to get her out of his mind.

He sat up cross-legged in the middle of the bed and reached for the brandy and a glass.

'Don't you think you've had enough of that stuff, Kit. Come morning and you won't be able to see straight. And we have to be at HMV by eight.'

'Go to bed, Rudy.'

'Hey, look. Will you take some good advice for once? You've been laid off that witch's brew for more than a month before we sailed, and now you're floating in it again; don't think I don't know why. This is me, Rudy Loew, Kit. Who the hell do you think you're tryin' to kid? We've been pals a long time, remember? It's *her*, isn't it? The blue-eyed dame with the cut-glass accent that you ran into in the foyer tonight? Don't think I don't remember her from when she used to visit you in Halkin Street; she's got a face a guy just doesn't forget. You were in love with her, weren't you? And you still are.' There was no answer. 'Just one big difference now; she's married. Or have you conveniently forgotten about that? And married dames spell trouble, Kit.'

Kit poured the brandy into his glass until it was almost full to the brim, then drank it down. 'You think I'm drinking this to try and forget her, is that it?' A short, bitter laugh. 'Forget it. I've tried. And it doesn't work. Nor going to bed with other women, either; I've tried that too. I made a choice, six years ago, I did what I did because I thought it was for the best. For her. For me.' He glanced up, with dull, hopeless eyes. 'I'm drinking this because I can't face the truth I know now. That the choice I made was the wrong one for both of us.'

'Have you any idea of what time it is?' He was standing there, at the bottom of the stairs, a dressing gown over his pyjamas. She was only aware of the loud, echoing tick of the sitting-room clock.

'Maurice, please keep your voice down! You'll wake everyone in the house.'

'I'll raise the roof if I want to! And I think I have a perfect right to object.' He came into the room and shut the door, none too gently, behind him. 'My God, I can see now exactly what your parents meant when they said that brother of yours was completely irresponsible! Not content with dragging you off to their riotous party after the show, he then takes you back for more carousing into the early hours at his hotel. I dread to imagine what the neighbours think of you coming home at this ungodly hour!'

She was suddenly very angry. 'Have you any idea of how pompous you sound, Maurice? And what a kill-joy you are! I haven't seen Kit for more than three years, when Aunt Jessie and I went out to stay with him in Chicago – you even objected to that, if I remember! He's my *brother*, damn it!' She tugged off her coat and gloves and tossed them on a chair. 'You really don't want me to enjoy myself at all, do you? That's what this is all about. You don't want me to do anything or go anywhere without *you*.'

'Laura, don't be absurd!'

'Perhaps you think I ought to be a prisoner, housebound for twenty-four hours a day. Would that suit you better? No Cavendish Street, no lunch with friends, no evenings out at the theatre. Just Sunday tea at Kilburn or Cricklewood with your parents or mine, or a summons to dinner with one of the senior partners!'

'How dare you speak to me in that sarcastic tone of voice!'

'I can't believe you're behaving like this, Maurice; you've changed so much, I don't know you any more. You're certainly not the Maurice Flavel I first met and fell in love with.' She'd shocked him but she was too upset to care. 'You were another person then. We had fun, we did things together. You made me laugh. But ever since you started rising in the firm, everything is different. You want me to give up everything that I enjoy, all the things that I care about. Why, Maurice?'

He drew himself up to his full height; his face was taut, hard, unyielding; in that moment he bore a striking resemblance to his father. 'After your brother has gone back to Chicago, I believe you have a great deal of serious thinking to do.' She stared at him without understanding. 'I admit, in the beginning, I agreed for you to go ahead with this dressmaking business; but I see clearly now that that was a mistake and I should never have allowed it. What started as a mere time-filler has taken over your life, and it's become quite intolerable. I won't have it, Laura.'

'What are you saying?'

'I'm saying that you'll have to make a choice. Cavendish Street, or your marriage.' She couldn't believe he was saying this. 'I don't think I need to remind you that as your husband you owe me obedience. And under the circumstances I believe that I've been more than forbearing to put up with the frivolous way you've been carrying on.' He paused, to give effect to his final shot. 'If I chose to, I could obtain a judicial separation on the grounds of your neglect, both to your marital duties and to your son. And I think we both know that any court would deny you custody of Desmond under the circumstances.'

She was suddenly very frightened. 'No! Maurice, you wouldn't do that! You couldn't even consider doing anything so cruel . . . !'

'The choice is yours, Laura. Your place *here*; or in Cavendish Street.' He turned away and went back towards the stairs. He looked back at her over his shoulder. 'I shall sleep in the spare-room tonight. And Mr and Mrs Gorston will be coming here for dinner next Monday.'

He left her standing there in her evening dress, too devastated even to cry.

50

Robert Carr sat down very slowly in the chair opposite his father-in-law's desk; he felt like a schoolboy summoned for some unknown fault in front of his headmaster. Lord Henry Osborne, still looking pale and gaunt after his weeks in hospital, was sitting beside him. They both fixed him with unwavering, solemn stares.

He shifted uncomfortably on his seat. 'I'm sorry, Robin; but this has been coming for a long time now. Dreikhorn will have to be got rid of. And the sooner we can arrange a new appointment for him, the better.'

Carr had never had a way with words. He knew exactly what he felt, what he wanted to say, why he had to protest. But somehow the words he needed wouldn't come.

'We all know that he's been more than useful to you,' Lord Henry Osborne said, taking over. 'Yielding place to you at the Scottish Office, introducing you to Lord Leith, helping you along every stage of your career; we all appreciate that he's . . . been a valuable aid, and also . . . a personal friend. But nothing stands still in politics, Robin; you of all people – and Dreikhorn – know that.'

'I can't . . . he won't understand . . . he'll think that now I have no further use for him I'm simply throwing him aside . . . he'll be furious . . .' A confrontation with Tom, more than anything else, was something he dreaded and feared. All his life he'd hated scenes and done everything to avoid them. They were placing him in an impossible position, couldn't they see that? That far from appreciating his removal as a political necessity he would see it only as a personal betrayal. Knowing Dreikhorn as well as he did he knew that that was something he would never forgive.

'Surely it isn't necessary for him to go, just because he's offended a few people? Let me talk to him . . .'

Thomas Cultrane held up a hand. 'I'm sorry, Robin, but the time for talking is long past. If he stays where he is then he'll rapidly undermine *your* position. You're trying to duck the whole issue, and you can't. Admit it . . . Dreikhorn's always been self-opinionated and arrogant; since you were appointed to the new Ministry he's been well nigh intolerable.' Cultrane paused and looked at his son-in-law severely. 'You seem also to have forgotten that it was Dreikhorn who caused the rift in your marriage. It may well be, once he's been sent to Berlin, that you and Frances can sort out your differences.'

'I doubt it.' Surely they knew her better than that? 'She won't come back to me.'

'We'll see about that.'

There seemed little left to say; he hung his head, overcome with a sense of hopelessness and despair at his own inability to save his friend. Tom would be so angry!

At last he looked up into their waiting faces. 'I . . . I don't think I can face breaking the news to him myself . . . do you think that possibly you . . . ?'

Lord Henry Osborne and Cultrane exchanged glances. How spineless Rosslare was! They looked at him in mutual contempt. 'Don't worry. Leave it to us. We'll tell him that the Foreign Secretary has given him a new appointment at the British Embassy in Berlin.'

The dining-room in the Savoy was less crowded than she had expected it to be. As the waiter showed her to the table only Kit rose to greet her; there was no sign of Laura. For a moment they looked at each other.

'I'm glad you came, Frankie. I was half afraid that you somehow wouldn't.'

'You said Laura would be here, Kit.'

'She's been unavoidably detained.' He smiled and they both sat down. 'Actually, I wanted to see you alone first. Not for the reason you might think. I know that you're married now.'

'Kit . . .'

'I know you and Laura have always been close; that's why I have to ask you this because maybe you're the only one who really knows the answer. Do you think Laura is happy with Maurice Flavel?'

She hadn't expected him to ask her such a question and for a moment she hesitated, caught between her loyalty to Laura and wanting to tell Kit the truth.

'Don't you think that's a question you should be asking her, not me?'

'Do you really think she'd give me a straight answer?'

Frances was silent for a long while before she finally spoke. 'He doesn't want her to go on with the designing business. I think he resents the amount of time it takes up in her life, and he feels . . . threatened by it. He thinks that she ought to spend all her time in the home, doing ordinary, mundane things, like most housewives do. Most men are like that, aren't they?'

'I'm not.' They both smiled. 'Frankie, you've been close to her for the last six years; I haven't. What do you think is most important to Laura . . . I mean, besides her son.'

'Being happy. I think that's what is most important to her. But it isn't always that simple, is it?'

'No.' How well he knew that. He looked up into her face; she was beautiful, and he longed to tell her that he loved her. But he knew that he couldn't because she belonged to someone else. He wasn't going to make a fool of himself. 'Do you think Maurice resents me because I was the one who put up the money for Cavendish Street . . . or is it something else?'

It was her turn to smile. 'I think Maurice would have resented you anyway; he finds it very difficult to cope with other people's success. And, you must admit, neither of you are exactly compatible types.'

He laughed out loud. 'Why the hell did she marry him?'

'She thought he was different, then.'

Her own smile faded; how different she'd been with Robin, in the very beginning. And how different he'd seemed. Ironical, that she and Laura had both been caught in the same trap. How hopeless it was to even think how to break free. For both of them, divorce was unthinkable; the disgrace, the social stigma, the everlasting shame; and Laura had Desmond to think about. It was like being imprisoned in a tiny, doorless cell, with no way out. She had to stop thinking about it, she had to change the subject.

408

She waited while he ordered for them both, watching his face as he concentrated on the wine list; he still had the strong, chiselled features of a matinée idol, that same lock of hair fell across the left-hand side of his forehead that she remembered; his smile, gestures, the way he laughed were still spontaneous and boyish; no wonder women swarmed around him. She remembered her jealousy of last night, the way she'd hated to see them pressing against him and touching him as he'd played Irene Treowen's piano. She wondered how, when he went back to Chicago the day after tomorrow, she could ever bear to let him go without telling him how much she loved him. She already knew she never would.

'How did your recording session go at HMV this morning?'

'If it hadn't been for Rudy, it wouldn't have gone at all. I overslept.'

'I'm not surprised. What time did you go to bed last night?'

'I don't remember; I just passed out.'

There was so much she wanted to say to him still, things that could only be said while they were alone. Even Laura, as much as she loved her, would have been an intrusion at this moment. It was magical, precious, something she wanted to savour and never let go.

'Just before Robin and I . . . before we became engaged . . . I went to Paris with a friend. We went to a party one evening, the last evening we were there.' It seemed like yesterday; now Marguerite was dead. 'They were playing a record on the wind up gramophone. I knew the moment I heard it that it was you.' She smiled. 'And I was right.'

'Which one was it?'

'I don't remember; but I know how proud I felt. Of you. That you'd done so well. I always knew that you would, Kit.'

They looked into each other's eyes for a long moment.

'That reminds me, Frankie; there's something special that I wanted to give you. A new song, that we recorded just before we left Chicago; it hasn't been released here yet.' It was underhanded, reckless, but he didn't care. 'The record's upstairs in the suite; when we've finished this we'll go and get it. A little gift to you from me.'

'*Berlin!*'

'Tom, it has nothing at all to do with me! I swear it. The appointment was made by the Foreign Secretary!'

'And the Osbornes are behind it! And you just stood by and let them do it!'

'Tom, I tried to get it quashed, but they'd already signed the papers . . .'

'Don't lie to me, Robbie! You don't have the imagination.'

It was worse, much worse than he'd ever imagined; for a moment he closed his eyes. Dreikhorn's rage was so intense that it was overpowering. He felt helpless, inarticulate, floundering. He was trying to make him understand. He hadn't wanted it. He'd done everything he could to persuade them to let him stay. But they'd all been adamant. And Tom was still blaming him.

'I should have expected this, shouldn't I? That after everything I've done for you, after everything I've sacrificed for your career, you'd turn round and stab me in the back?' His dark eyes blazed furiously. 'Just how far do you think you would have got, Robbie, if it hadn't been for me?'

'Tom, you know how grateful I am for everything you've ever done.'

'Oh yes . . . you've got the looks, the golden hair and the blue eyes that Leith loved. He was so besotted with you that it didn't matter to him that the space between your ears was full of nothing except empty air! He couldn't wait to get his hands on you. And I wasn't supposed to mind, was I? That you belonged to me, that you'd got the place that ought to have been mine. I loved you and I wanted to do everything in my power to help.'

'For Christ's sake, do you think I want this? But it's out of my hands now. You've offended too many people, Tom.'

'I've offended the bloody high-and-mighty Osbornes! Don't try and tell me that they're not behind all this, because I know differently; and you're their puppet now! The old man or Cultrane pulls the strings, and you jump.'

'No.'

'After you'd won that Osborne bitch *through my letters*, everything gradually started to change; now you think that because you have them behind you, you don't need me any more. In return for everything I've done for you, when they want to exile me in Berlin you don't even raise a finger to stop them.' His voice had grown dangerously soft. 'You've just made a big mistake, Robbie. The biggest mistake of your life. Because if you don't get this posting in Berlin pushed aside, I'll tell you exactly what I intend to do.' He smiled, but his eyes were as hard as flint. 'I intend to put down in a letter everything that's been between you and me, from the very first day. And I promise you that nothing, no detail, no names, will be left out. I think the Prime Minister would find it very interesting reading, don't you?' Arrogantly, he lit a cigarette. 'Now why don't you run along back to your precious Osbornes, little lap-dog, and tell them that?'

They went up in the hotel lift to his suite on the second floor. He unlocked the door and then stood back to let her walk inside. She hesitated on the threshold of the enormous room, looking around her. There was a piano in one corner; a wind-up gramophone and a pile of records beside it on the floor. There was a general air of untidiness; various items of his clothing and sheets of music were scattered around the room.

She turned to him and smiled. 'It isn't like your room in Halkin Street.'

'Funny, I liked that better.' He closed the door and asked her to sit down, then he went over to a chest of drawers and began opening them one by one. 'That's the trouble with having to put things away in other people's furniture; you forget where it all goes.' He found the record and came over to sit beside her. 'Here. I want you to have it.'

It was as Frances reached out to take it from him that their hands touched, and he leaned over and kissed her lips. For both of them the entire room reeled; she felt her arms slide up around his neck and her fingers entwine themselves in his thick, dark, wavy hair; her mouth opened under his. Then he was kissing her face, her eyes, her hair, her throat; his arms held her to him like a vice.

As they drew, very slowly and breathlessly away from each other, the telephone across the room rang. A moment later Rudy Loew and Laura burst into the room simultaneously. Laura was holding a newspaper and waving it wildly.

'You'll never guess what's happened! I just can't *believe* it!' She paused and tried to get her breath, then she thrust the paper into Frances's hands. Rudy rushed across to pick up the telephone. 'Anne Turner! She's been arrested ... with a doctor called Simon Forman ...' She pointed to the three-inch high headlines on the front page. 'He's been accused of supplying illegal drugs to his patients and performing abortions ... and *she's* been cited as an accomplice!' They all stared at the large photograph of Anne Turner together.

'Kit, I can't *believe* it. I simply can't take it in!'

'How did they find out?' He was trying swiftly to compose himself.

'His wife. It says here that he was reported by his wife ... she had suspicions and she told the police. They raided his consulting room and found all the evidence.'

Frances was leaning against the wall. She and Kit were staring at each other. Across the room, Rudy Loew had put down the telephone receiver.

'Sounds to me like she wanted to get rid of the guy . . . turning him in. Maybe she got green-eyed over all those lady patients!' He coughed. 'That was the reception clerk, Kit. Lord Rosslare's downstairs in the foyer to collect his wife.'

'Irene, I'm *so* sorry! What can I say? You told me your mother was ill, but I never realized how seriously.'

'If only we'd come back to London a month sooner . . . we were going to spend Christmas together . . . Frances, it was so long since we'd seen her . . .'

Irene Treowen wiped her eyes with her lace-edged handkerchief; Frances suddenly thought of Banbury's funeral, then the sudden, stunning news of the Hollands' and Eddie Vaux's deaths. She went over and put her arm around her shoulders.

'You have to try to be strong . . . I know it's easy for me to say that . . . her housekeeper spoke to Ian on the telephone and said that she'd died peacefully in her sleep . . . that there was no pain . . . you have to think of that.'

'I feel only guilt at this moment.' She looked up, her grey eyes swimming. 'Last night. Here. At the Savoy. Laughing, gay, enjoying myself. And all the time she was dead.'

'You can't blame yourself for that. And she would have wanted you to be happy.'

Irene sniffed and gripped her hand. 'I'm not very good at times like these . . . mother always used to say that I was a happy times person, like my father. When there's some tragedy or other I simply can't cope.'

Frances stared beyond her to where Robin and Ian Treowen were talking in low voices in the adjoining room. Kit would still be at the Savoy now; she wondered what he was doing, thinking. She thought of the way he'd kissed her; what would have happened between them if Laura and Rudy Loew hadn't suddenly burst into the room. Would she have committed the unthinkable sin of adultery without even caring what she was doing? Fate had intervened and she would never know.

'You'll come up with us, of course, for the funeral? Ironic, we were leaving next month for the shooting on the estate . . .' She smiled, sadly. 'Mother would have so loved to have seen you and Robert . . .'

They walked side by side through the trees, for a long time without speaking. It was so peaceful here now, at the end of the summer and the beginning of autumn, with the first leaves already gradually falling from the trees, casting a carpet of green, gold, red, and amber across the ground.

They walked on, past the war monument, nannies wheeling prams, a businessman with a rolled-up umbrella and briefcase taking a short-cut across the park.

'I'm so sorry about Irene Treowen's mother. I know you weren't close to her, but when anyone dies it always casts such a shadow . . . your sister Elizabeth's husband, then the Hollands and Edward Vaux . . . now this. I felt as if someone had died when we saw Kit off at Southampton. I felt so miserable and depressed that I wanted to cry. I did try hard not to; Maurice would only have accused me of being silly.'

Frances was silent. 'I don't want to go to Scotland for the funeral; but everyone expects me to. There's no way I can really get out of it. Not the funeral; I wouldn't mind that. Having to go there with Robin, as if nothing ever happened; having to pretend. I can't bear it.'

'It's only for a little while.'

'Yes, I know.' They sat down on a vacant seat. 'What about you and Maurice? Surely he didn't mean what he said? He couldn't have.'

'Oh, but he did.' Laura gave a short, bitter little laugh. 'Either I give up Cavendish Street, or . . . I give up everything.' She swallowed; there was a lump in her throat. 'If it was just me, and no one else mattered, I'd defy him. But I can't do that because of Desmond. Frances, if Maurice applied for a legal separation I could lose my son!'

Frances put a hand on her arm. 'Have you told your parents what he said?'

'How could I? They're both on his side. They think that I should give up my designing straight away and stay at home like a good obedient little wife, being bored to death.' 'She leaned forward and covered her face with her hands. 'Ever since the scandal about Simon Forman and Mrs Turner, Mummy and Daddy have been going on at me as if it was somehow *my* fault! I worked for her, I was associated with her – as if that makes me partly guilty, too. They were even

413

terrified that we'd have a visit from the police – god knows why! – asking me questions about the days when I was at New Bond Street ... if I saw anything happening that I thought might be suspicious ... it's so absurd. And Maurice is being even more unreasonable than ever! People in the office have been asking him if we ever socialized with Mrs Turner, and you can imagine how he reacted to that! He even had the nerve to suggest that my working at New Bond Street had jeopardized his reputation!'

Frances sighed sadly. 'Your troubles sound even worse than mine!'

'When you come back from Scotland, let's meet for lunch. Go to a matinée ... anything! There'll be no Cavendish Street by then.'

'I'm sorry, Laura.'

They parted at the park gates; Frances kissed her friend on the cheek and they both walked away in opposite directions. A little way along Laura turned round and waved, and Frances waved back.

It was the last time they would meet in freedom for more than two years.

It was almost dark now but Dreikhorn was so intent on the large sheets of paper covered with his tall, bold, scrawling hand in front of him, that he'd barely noticed. Every now and then he stopped, wiped his eyes and then went on writing furiously. There were dried tear-stains on his cheeks; tears of rage and despair. Ever since their last angry, bitter confrontation, he'd shut himself away from everyone, except Lawrence Rankin. The young man stood over him now, watching what he was writing. Then he leaned forward and turned on the light.

'Have you almost finished?'

'No! No, I haven't written half of what I intend to write ... but I will. I will write it. Every bloody single word!' He dipped his pen in the inkwell impatiently, and a shower of tiny black inkspots stained the pages. He cursed angrily. '*I* introduced him to everyone that mattered; *I* was the one who was always there when he needed me, day or night. He'd ring me up, at two or three in the morning if he had a problem he couldn't deal with, and *I'd* tell him what to do. Whatever questions he asked *I* always came up with an answer.' A tear ran down his face and he dashed it away angrily with the back of his hand. 'I should have known, shouldn't I? I should have realized the truth. It's true, that old saying ... put a beggar on horseback! And that bloody ungrateful, turncoat beggar is bloody Robbie Carr!'

Rankin put a hand on his shoulder, gently. 'I knew you'd turn to me; that you'd come back again when you found out what he was really like . . . Tom, I knew you would.'

'Stand back, for Christ's sake, you're blotting out the light!' He dipped the pen into the ink again and scribbled furiously.

Rankin had poured them both drinks. He sat down while Dreikhorn read the endless sheets of scrawl.

'He used you, I told you he was using you. He used your brains to get himself the positions that should have been yours.'

'Yes, I know that now. But I don't intend to let him get away with it.'

'Are you really going to send that to the Prime Minister?' Rankin paused. 'He's got you tied, hand and foot, hasn't he? If you expose him, you expose yourself as well; is he really worth all that?'

Dreikhorn gulped back the double whisky. He felt sick with rage, anguish, disbelief. Robbie had done this to him. Robbie had betrayed him to his enemies after everything he had done. Had there ever been such betrayal?

'I'll pay him back. He'll be sorry. He can't do this to me and then walk calmly away. Nobody just uses me and then casts me aside like that; not even Robbie.'

Rankin felt a sudden, sharp stirring of jealousy; was Dreikhorn so devastated and upset because he was being sent to Berlin or because that would mean enforced separation from Robert Carr? Which did he find most unbearable?

He pushed a newspaper towards him, carefully. 'His aunt has died . . . a few days ago, at Renfrew . . . his cousin Lady Irene Treowen is travelling up there for the funeral . . .' He pointed to the particular line of newsprint. 'It says here that he's going, too . . . with her . . .'

51

Frances tramped across the lumpy, boggy ground behind the others, keeping her eyes on the circling swarm of birds above the distant line of trees that bordered the woods. Behind her, the servants were busy setting up the portable tables and chairs for the midday picnic; Irene Treowen and most of the other ladies were some way ahead. She had always hated any form of blood-sports and she had come only reluctantly to the shoot this afternoon.

'The beaters have gone down into the other part of the wood, now,' Irene turned and called to her. 'By the time we've had lunch they should be driving them towards the guns . . . oh, look, here come the men!'

'Of course, darling,' someone said, laughingly, 'They can positively smell the food! And there's Angus right at the front of the bunch, always on cue!'

'Golly, it's turned devilishly chilly! Anyone for a dram?'

Frances stood at the top of the sloping ground shading her eyes from the harsh early afternoon sunlight, trying to spot Robin. But when the group of men came nearer to the picnic tables, she saw that he wasn't there. 'Has Robin gone back to the house?'

'He was with us a moment ago,' Ian Treowen turned in the direction of the woods and shaded his eyes, like her, against the glare of the sun. 'He may have stopped to reload his gun.'

'I'll go and find him.' She gave him a ghost of a smile and broke into a run. She wanted to get away from the heaps of lifeless grouse, the noise and laughter of the others gathered around the picnic tables.

It was cool and darker when she reached the edge of the woods; sunlight filtering through the thick branches of the overhanging trees dappled the grass and bracken. Carefully, stepping over little potholes of muddy ground and twisted roots, she made her way forward through the trees. Some way ahead of her, she heard a loud crackling sound, as if somebody had stepped on a broken twig. 'Robin?' She called into the sudden eerie stillness. But there was no one there.

It seemed so long since he'd been here in Scotland; another lifetime away. He was tired from the long, tedious journey, but the fresh, crisp pine-scented greenness of the woods somehow refreshed him, spurring him forward with new strength. He had written the letter as he'd said he would; it had helped somehow to set it all down. But the letter didn't matter now. Rankin had been right; if he brought down Robbie and the Osbornes, he brought himself down, too. And Robbie wasn't worth going to prison for.

What else had young Rankin said? That men are more ready to repay an injury than a benefit, because gratitude is a burden and revenge a pleasure. He smiled as he skirted the deserted road and came upon the edge of the wood. Yes, faithless Robbie Carr, thirteenth Earl of Rosslare. Revenge.

It was suddenly much colder now; the air was stark, biting, making her shiver. She walked on through the trees, hands in pockets, wondering how Robin could have fallen so far behind the other men. In the distance she thought she could hear the sound of the beaters, driving the birds from their cover on the other side of the wood. Then she heard the sound of a single gunshot.

Instinctively, she began to run; overhead the screaming crows and rooks swirled in black clouds, disturbed by the sudden, unexpected noise. Then she caught sight of Robin, lying full-length in the thick carpet of fallen leaves.

His shotgun lay at his side; blood oozed from the gaping hole in his forehead, soaking his matted fair hair. Sobbing, trembling, fighting down the wave of panic and hysteria, Frances knelt down beside him, her hand on the gun.

It was then that the others suddenly appeared in the clearing beyond the trees.

'She didn't do it! She wouldn't have shot her own husband! Frances isn't capable of killing anyone in cold blood. For God's sake, Maurice, don't you think I know? We've been friends for more than six years!'

'During which time she's exerted a more than pernicious influence on you! Admit it. Everything she's done has merely given you similar ideas.'

'How can you say that? The problems we've had date from the first time you realized that you couldn't put a ball and chain on me. I wanted to so something that mattered to me, that made me feel useful; but you just couldn't accept that, could you?' She wanted to cry but she was determined not to in front of him. 'Well, I hope you're satisfied; I've given up designing. But not because you wanted me to, Maurice. I did it because I have no intention of letting you take Desmond.'

He turned away and picked up his evening newspaper. He sat down in front of the fire.

'Maurice,' she said into the yawning silence. 'I'm going to see her.'

He swung round immediately. 'That you most certainly are not. This murder is splashed across every paper in the country, and we're having absolutely no part of it. Do you understand me?'

'She has nobody else; her family have deserted her. And no wonder! They run like rats from a sinking ship at the first whiff of scandal! There was Lady Cultrane's friendship with Anne Turner, then Frances's sister Elizabeth being rushed to hospital after an overdose of drugs . . . they hushed that up pretty quickly; I suppose because Lord Cultrane and Lord Henry Osborne are on champagne clinking terms with every major newspaper editor in London!'

'Well, they won't hush this up. This time it's too much of a sordid mess even for people like the Osbornes to paper over. Nobody can hush up murder.'

52

She looked up as he was shown into her cell with her solicitor. She got up from the narrow prison bed and shook his hand. Strange, perhaps inappropriate and even comic, how even with bars on the single window and her dressed in prison garb, they still observed the polite social conventions.

She tried to smile at him. She wanted him to know that she was grateful. He was so celebrated, so sought after; she had been afraid that he would have to turn down the brief. But he was here, and that somehow made her feel better.

She sat down at the wooden table and looked into his eyes; they were kind eyes, honest eyes, sensitive and sympathetic. His was a face that she could trust. She felt that no matter how hopeless everything was, his stature and reputation alone would salvage something from the wreck of her life.

He had thick, smooth, well-kept hands. The brief lay on the table between them, and she could read the words upsidedown: *THE CROWN VERSUS FRANCES, COUNTESS OF ROSSLARE.*

She was seeing another paper now; old, yellowed cuttings from newspapers pasted into the pages of a book.

'You defended Edith Thompson, didn't you?'

A look passed over his face, and then it was gone. 'Lady Rosslare, my one concern now is that I have been briefed to defend *you*.' He gave her a smile of reassurance. 'I'm here today with Mr Lucas to go through your evidence once again, and the witness statements to the police.'

'I didn't do it, Sir Henry. I didn't kill my husband.' She swallowed. 'I know what they all thought, when they ran into the woods after the gun went off and saw me bending over his body . . .' he let her go on without interrupting her. 'But I came into the woods to look

418

for him, because he didn't come out with the other men. If I meant to kill him, would I have done something as blatantly stupid as that? And why, for heaven's sake? Nobody's told me *why!*'

'Lady Rosslare . . .'

'. . . Robin and I were estranged, it's true; for several months we'd lived apart . . . but I didn't hate him. He didn't hate me. It was just that the marriage was over, except in name; that we simply couldn't go on living together . . .'

'Lord Rosslare was a prominent politician; we all know that politicians, successful men, inevitably make enemies. Can you think of anyone who might have a motive strong enough for them to kill your husband?'

'No.'

'The real killer, then, must have been in the immediate vicinity, must have known the area extremely well; and also the district of Renfrew. Nobody was seen running from the scene of the crime afterwards; every member of the shooting party, including the beaters, gillies and household servants who served the picnic and waited on Sir Ian and Lady Irene Treowen's guests, was outside the immediate vicinity of the murder when it happened; and everyone was in sight of at least one other person for the entire time.' He paused. 'That means that we can safely eliminate every other person at that shoot.'

'But couldn't it have been an accident? Couldn't Robin have just fallen on his gun?' Her voice was beginning to sound desperate and she knew it.

'I'm afraid that the available evidence shows that it was not. The police report on the weapon confirms that your husband was shot at almost point-blank range.'

She looked up hopelessly into Curtis-Bennett's face. 'What are they going to do to me?'

'Lady Rosslare, it is not the duty of the defence to provide the prosecution with either a suspect or a motive; on the contrary, it is incumbent upon the prosecuting counsel to prove beyond any reasonable doubt that you had both the motive and the opportunity to kill your husband, and that you did so. Both sides will call witnesses to support their respective case. But with this difference, which I believe Mr Lucas has already outlined to you . . . as a peeress you will be tried in the House of Lords and not at the Central Criminal Court.'

'Do I have a choice?'

'No, I'm afraid that you do not. But let me assure you, you have

419

nothing to fear . . .' He smiled, and she somehow felt better. 'Justice will prevail in the Royal Gallery just as it would at the Old Bailey. Indeed, it may have certain advantages. You must be aware of the enormous publicity this case has generated . . . a peer of the realm is shot in the woods of a well-known estate in Scotland, and he happens to be a prominent Foreign Office Minister to boot. The accused is his wife, daughter of another peer of the realm, a leading figure in society and a leader of fashion. Such stuff, I fear, that the great English public loves. If the trial were to be held at the Central Criminal Courts no doubt the crowds would be so vast that it would take a battering ram for us to get through them. It will be a little easier having the trial held at Westminster, because security is a matter of course there, with the proximity to Parliament.'

'I see.'

'The trial has been set for the last week in October, which gives us three weeks to prepare our case.' He shuffled the papers in his hands. 'What I need to do now is ask you about your relationship with your husband both preceding your separation and also after it. I'm sorry if that will be painful for you . . . but I assure you that it is necessary.'

'Do you mean that the reason I left my husband will come out in open court?'

'It may be impossible to prevent that. I'm sorry.'

Slowly, she got up and walked around the little cell. 'This will ruin my family . . . and they'll never forgive me.' She was almost talking to herself. 'They tried so hard to make certain that nobody would ever find out. Mr Lucas has told me that the letter I wrote to my mother was returned unanswered. I think by that you can see I can expect no help from them. I have to face this alone.' She didn't want pity. 'Can you tell me why the Prosecution allege that I shot Robin in cold blood?'

He pressed his hands together as if he was praying. 'They allege that your original estrangement with Lord Rosslare arose because you discovered he was having an affair with another woman.' She gave a sharp intake of breath. 'They allege that although you were still very much in love with your husband, you left him in order to try to coerce him into giving her up . . . hoping that pressure from other sources would induce him to terminate the affair. They're alleging, in fact, that this is a crime of passion . . . and that your motive was purely sexual jealousy. You were unable to bear the thought of your husband's affair and finally, when the opportunity presented itself, you went into the woods and shot him with his own gun.'

She lay back against the dingy grey walls and shook with silent laughter. Tears ran down her face; she was laughing and crying both at once. Curtis-Bennett and Lucas both stood up, instantly. Lucas banged on the door and called for the lady wardress.

Frances held up a shaking hand. 'Please . . . no . . . it's all right . . . I'm not hysterical . . .' She kept her body flat against the wall to support herself. 'I've not suddenly gone insane . . . it's just the irony . . . you see . . .'

'Lady Rosslare, won't you sit down..?'

'. . . I did leave my husband because he was having an affair . . .' she hesitated, and took a deep breath. 'but not with another woman.' The two men stiffened to attention in their seats, both acutely aware that this trial was going to cause a public sensation. 'I left Robin because I discovered him in bed with another man.'

She was on the telephone when Cultrane came in. The top of his desk was tidy and bare. White dust-sheets covered all the furniture in the room. Slowly, he set down his Minister's briefcase on the floor while he watched her. That was the moment when she knew he'd gone against her advice and resigned.

She put down the telephone. 'So you did it?'

'I was with Ramsay MacDonald and Baldwin for more than an hour.'

'No doubt they didn't try to persuade you to stay?'

Her voice held ridicule, censure. But then he had always been so weak in a crisis; she had always been the strong one.

'They understood.'

'Resignation; after everything you've worked for, after all these years. They've only been waiting for a chance like this and you hand it to them on a golden platter!'

'What else could I do, for God's sake? What with Elizabeth being rushed to hospital after an overdose of drugs, Freddie wining and dining showgirls and behaving like a frivolous fool . . . and now this. We managed to avert a major scandal when Frances caught Carr and Dreikhorn in bed, but this murder is the biggest blow of all! We simply can't survive it. God alone knows what filth and scandal will come out at the trial. How can I go on in office, while Frances is in prison, waiting to be tried for her life?'

'You simply dissociate yourself.' He stared at her. 'Yes, that's

421

right. When you have a rotten branch on a healthy tree, what do you do? You cut it off, just as I cut off Anne Turner before it was too late. I've already written to Lucas telling him that we want nothing more to do with the matter, and I returned her letter without a reply. Yes, it may seem cruel. But what happened she brought on entirely by herself. If she'd compromised with Robin, if she'd relented just a little, she wouldn't be where she is now.'

He was aghast, incredulous, shocked. 'Katherine, she's our daughter for Christ's sake!'

'She's *my* daughter, yes.'

For a long moment they looked at each other. He couldn't move. He couldn't speak.

'You never guessed, did you? That she wasn't yours.'

'Who is it?' His voice was very soft, a whisper that she barely heard.

'Was. He's dead now. Surely you know the answer.' She wanted to hurt him. She wanted to punish him for throwing away everything that she'd worked for. 'I first saw him when my father took me to India, when I was seventeen. He looked like a god in his uniform . . . that weak, tubercular narrow-faced American nobody he was married to . . . how I hated and despised her. I could been the next Vicerine . . .'

'Thomas Holland.'

'Dear God, I loved him so! I wanted to be with him so much. But he was married already and it was too late.' She looked away, as if he was no longer in the room. 'Then when she died, I was married to you.' She sat down suddenly, as if the burden of telling him the truth at last was too much to bear. 'All those years later, when he was going to marry Grace Duggan, I asked him why . . .' She smiled, but to herself, not Cultrane. 'He said, 'Because I can't have you.'

His face was pallid, almost grey. Suddenly, he looked ravaged, tired and old.

'I was going to have an abortion when I first found out . . . but I changed my mind. Perhaps I shouldn't have.'

'Did he know?' His best friend. Katherine had loved his best friend and had his child. 'Did you ever tell him?'

She smiled again. 'I didn't have to. She was always his favourite godchild, and she was so like him to look at . . . you never noticed that, did you?'

He had never really understood her. The streak of cruelty, ruthlessness, side by side with something else that, perhaps if her life had taken another, different turn, would have cancelled out the fatal faults and redeemed her. Something he would never find out.

'I should have known, shouldn't I? I should have guessed the truth. At his memorial service in Westminster Abbey . . . it was the only time I ever saw you cry.'

She waited until Maurice had left for work before she opened the letter. It was not written in Kit's hand. Her fingers trembled as she tore open the air mail envelope, then spread the single page in front her her and read the short, brief note from Rudy Loew. She had written to Kit as soon as Frances had been arrested.

. . . For the last seven weeks, Kit has been in the clinic . . . it was the drinking that caused the collapse . . . and he would never listen to good advice . . . Nobody had written, nobody had told her. But then, Kit would never let them. She read on. *. . . I told him that you needed the money for yourself, but, because of the mental state that he's in, I didn't think it wise to show him the newspaper cuttings you cabled, and I'm sure you understand . . . he could be here for a very long time. Strange, he started drinking again heavily as soon as we left England . . . but, don't worry, the money will be sent on straight away . . .* Rudy.

She folded the letter and replaced it in the envelope. Then she tore it, slowly, into pieces. There was nowhere to put it, now that she no longer had the business in Cavendish Street where it could be kept free from the risk of Maurice reading it. And she was determined that he'd never know. She went over to the little red brick grate, and threw the pieces into the flames of the fire.

They sat looking at each other across the wide, scrubbed table; at either end of the room a wardress stood. When Laura had first seen her and burst into tears, then gone to throw her arms around her neck, one of them had told her sharply that she and the prisoner were not allowed to touch. 'It's inhuman!' she'd burst out, suddenly angry at the stupidity of the rules. 'Do you think I've smuggled a file and a bunch of keys in my suspender belt so she can break out?'

'Regulations, madam.'

'It's all right. It doesn't matter.' Frances smiled wanly, and she sat down.

She was shocked by her pale appearance; the dour, ugly prison clothes. All the things that she'd come to say, the bracing, cheering things she'd rehearsed on the way here, wouldn't come. She couldn't

423

remember any of them. She sat there, her hands lying on the table in front of her, tongue-tied for the first time in life.

'You mustn't worry. I'm sure everything will be all right. Sir Henry Curtis-Bennett is one of the best barristers in London.'

'I expect Edith Thompson thought so, too.'

'Frances, you mustn't say that. This case is entirely different! No one in their right mind could believe you were capable of killing Robin. Why should you, for goodness sake? You left him months ago. You only went with him to Renfrew because of the funeral . . .'

'Yes, they know all that. But they're saying it was a crime of passion. Don't laugh. The prosecution are saying that I left Robin when I found out he was having an affair . . . with another woman. I left him to try and force him to give her up. When he wouldn't, I pretended to forgive him, or simply not to mind; then when the chance presented itself I shot him. It sounds so neat and tidy, doesn't it?' A tear welled up in the corner of her eye and she wiped it away. 'I'm sorry. I meant to be strong when you came. I mustn't cry, otherwise I might not be able to stop. And then they really will believe that it was a crime of passion because I'm just a weak, unpredictable, hysterical woman.'

Laura leaned across the table toward her and the wardress gave her a warning glance.

'But they have no evidence!'

'I was in the wood, the only person known to be in the vicinity where Robin died. He was killed by a single shotgun bullet that penetrated the skull, and then the brain. Whoever did it shot him at point-blank range.' Her blue eyes wandered. 'God, how they must have hated him to do something like that!'

Suddenly, a flash of intuition brought Laura almost jerking to her feet. Her heart was beating very fast. 'Or hated you,' Frances stared at her, blankly. 'Perhaps whoever pulled the trigger of that shotgun did it not so much because they hated Robin . . . but so that *you* would get the blame.'

53

Her footsteps and the heavier tread of her escorts' beside her rang out, echoing, as they walked along the fan-vaulted corridors towards the Robing Room, and beyond it to the Prince's Chamber that adjoined the Royal Gallery; here the trial would be heard. She held her head high and went on staring straight ahead. But her hands in the black suede gloves were trembling.

Her face was pale, virtually devoid of any trace of make-up; that would have seemed both inappropriate and incongruous. Lipstick, the faintest touch of mascara. That was enough. Her severely cut black moiré silk costume emphasized her pallor and the weight she had lost; she wore no jewellery except her wedding ring and the little pearl brooch that Laura had given her for her birthday so long ago. Wearing it comforted her, somehow. Her dark gold hair was swept back into a simple chignon, held in place with a single tortoiseshell comb. She had chosen a sober, wide-brimmed black velvet hat.

Sir Henry Curtis-Bennett had explained gently to her what would happen, but she was still afraid. Until now, everything that had happened to her had seemed curiously unreal; now she was walking towards the Peers' Court reality had come back to her. A prison wardress walked on one side of her; a Court Usher on the other.

'When a Lord High Steward has been appointed and made known to the House of Lords,' Curtis-Bennett had said, the day before yesterday, 'an order is made summoning the accused peer or peeress to the bar of the House on the day appointed for the trial in order to answer the indictment. The Clerk of the Parliaments is authorized to summon such witnesses as may be desired by the Crown and the accused peer.

'On the day of the trial, the lords wearing their robes assemble in the House of Lords, and the Clerk of the Parliaments calls them to adjourn to the place where the trial is to be held . . . in this case, in the Royal Gallery. The Commission under the Great Seal appointing a Lord High Steward to preside over the trial is then read by the Clerk of the Crown in Chancery, after which the Lord High Steward is presented with his staff of office by Garter King of Arms and the Gentleman Usher of the Black Rod.'

Frances had smiled nervously. 'Perhaps it would have been better at the Old Bailey, after all.'

'. . . only the formalities will seem a little different . . . and instead of a jury of layman you have a jury of Peers. As soon as all the evidence has been heard, the Lords will adjourn to consider their judgement. But in view of the amount of evidence and the number of prosecution witnesses, I should prepare you for the fact that it may go on for several days. That is always a strain.'

'You said that Thomas Dreikhorn is one of the chief prosecution witnesses.'

'Yes.'

'After what I told you . . . his relationship with my husband . . . even though he'll be under oath, I know that he'll deny it.'

'And I shall do all in my power to disprove his testimony. Lady Rosslare, the penalties for perjury in a court of law are rightly very severe; the penalty for sodomy is even higher . . . for this particular man. Not only can he be sent to prison; his political career would be in ruins. No doubt he knows exactly what is at stake. Unfortunately, it is only your word against his. Lord Vaux, who could have corroborated your testimony, is unfortunately unable to be here. The plane crash in which he was killed earlier this year was a terrible tragedy in more ways than one.'

'He would have told my sister Elizabeth.' She'd sighed heavily and then looked away. 'Of course . . . she can't give evidence. Not where she is.'

As she walked on with the wardress and the usher on either side of her, Dreikhorn's image came to her, dark and mocking, transfixed against the awesome splendour of the hall. The life-sized paintings depicting allegorical scenes of justice, the gilded roof and walls, the gold statues on their plinths, the royal portraits, the double row of massive chandeliers. His face was taunting, his laughter cruel. Here was the daughter of the Osbornes who he so bitterly resented, envied and despised; the hated rival, the wife who had supplanted him in his lover's bed. Her family had deserted her, her name was strewn across every newspaper in the land. Now, today, here, she was on trial for her life. How much he was going to enjoy her public ordeal and humiliation.

His laughter echoed around the hall in her imagination, it filled her head, his mocking face danced vividly before her eyes. *Noblesse oblige.* He would be so certain that she would hide the truth because of duty, loyalty, family honour.

426

How little he had really known her at all.

'Frances, Countess of Rosslare, how will you be tried?'

'By God and my Peers.'

'Frances, Countess of Rosslare, how say you? Do you plead guilty or not guilty to the felony of which you are charged?'

She swallowed. But her voice was firm and clear.

'Not guilty.' A ripple of voices along the vast hall.

'And you ask their Lordships to believe that?'

'Yes.'

'You are charged that on the afternoon of October 2nd, 1933, in the woods of Treowen House, in the grounds of the aforesaid Treowen House, Renfrew, that you did wilfully murder Robert Patrick Kieran Carr, thirteenth Earl of Rosslare. Do you plead guilty or not guilty?'

'Not guilty.'

'And you ask their Lordships to believe that?'

'Yes.'

'God send your ladyship a good deliverance.'

Sir Thomas Inskip, the Attorney-General, rose in his place. She gripped the side of her chair tightly and tried not to think of him as an enemy, but as a man doing a job. Her husband had been murdered; she had been found kneeling next to his body in the wood, her hand on his gun; it was the same shotgun that was later proved to have been the gun that killed him. It was logical, from his point of view, that she had committed the crime. Moreover, she was the only suspect. The deceased had had political opponents; what powerful politician had not? Those who had reason to hate him most – and political differences could surely not be akin to real hate – and hate that would motivate one man to kill another – had cast-iron alibies. Every member of the Treowen shooting party – including the servants, the ghillies, and the beaters in the woods – not only had no discernible motive to murder Robert Rosslare, but each one had been in the sight of at least one other for the whole of the afternoon. Only Frances had no one who could vouch for her.

He would prove to their Lordships, beyond any reasonable doubt, that Lady Rosslare had killed her husband deliberately and with malice aforethought, because he had withdrawn his affections for her in favour of another woman. He would shortly produce witness and relevant testimony in support of this.

He first called as witness Sir Ian Treowen. Sir Ian and Lady Irene

427

Treowen had recently returned to London from abroad; Lady Irene was the deceased's first cousin.

'Sir Ian, when you returned to London from a diplomatic post in Melbourne and the Far East in September of his year, did you and your wife invite the late Earl of Rosslare and Lady Rosslare to your house?'

'Yes, we did.'

'Did either Lord or Lady Rosslare inform you or your wife, or indeed indicate in any way, that there was any element of discord between them?'

'No. Not at that time. It was only later that we learned, with some degree of shock, that Robert . . . that my wife's cousin and Lady Rosslare had been living apart for some time.'

'May we go specifically to that evening when Lord and Lady Rosslare came to your house? Did you notice any tension or unusual behaviour on that evening?'

'I thought . . . they seemed very cool towards each other.'

'And did this fact strike you as unusual?'

'Their behaviour towards each other was very different when we last saw them shortly after their marriage in 1930. They were very much in love.'

'This was not in evidence at your last meeting with them?'

'No. They seemed barely to speak to each other.'

'During the time that they stayed with you and Lady Irene Treowen for the funeral of Lady Treowen's mother, Lady Janet Carr, did you see or hear Lord and Lady Rosslare quarrelling.'

'Yes, I did.'

'On how many occasions would that be?'

'On several occasions.'

'And were these arguments heated ones, as far as you were able to ascertain?'

'Yes.'

Sir Henry Curtis-Bennett rose to register an obvious objection. Almost all married couples were prone to arguments. The objection was allowed.

'Sir Ian, will you please tell their Lordships in your own words what happened on the afternoon of the shoot when Lord Rosslare died.'

'We spent the morning shooting grouse, then the servants brought the picnic tables and rugs from the house, and we walked up through the woods to join the ladies. Lady Rosslare was standing near to my wife, and I believe my wife made some remark to her, but I could not hear what that was. As we approached the group of ladies, I heard Lady Rosslare remark to my wife that Robert – Lord Rosslare – was not with our party. She began running towards the woods; I supposed in order to find him. I thought no more about this until we all heard the unmistakable sound of a gun.'

He paused. All through his evidence he had avoided looking at her. He glanced at her briefly now. 'The beaters were on the opposite side of the woods, driving the birds forward. Robert was the only man we knew for certain was still in the woods, and who had a gun. Everybody rushed into the woods in the direction from which the gunshot came . . . as we reached the clearing we all saw Robert lying on the ground, and Lady Rosslare bending over him. Her hand was on the gun.' There was a murmur among the Peers. 'She looked up, very startled and white, and said something like, 'There's been a terrible accident, Robin has been shot!'

'Was your first reaction to believe that this was in fact the case?'

'At that time we had no reason not to.'

'It was only later, when you knew that Lord Rosslare had been shot deliberately, that you assumed Lady Rosslare had been the person who pulled the trigger?'

'Yes.'

'To your knowledge, apart from the beaters . . . was there any other person . . . did you see any other person in the woods in the vicinity of where the body was found?'

'No one.'

The Attorney-General had no further questions. Sir Henry Curtis-Bennett rose in his place. 'Sir Ian. You have stated to their Lordships and to my learned friend that during their stay with you and Lady Irene at Treowen House, Lord and Lady Rosslare's attitude to each other seemed . . . cool?'

'Yes.'

'Did it not occur to you, since you had at that time no knowledge of their estrangement, that they had perhaps argued about something quite trivial on their journey to Scotland and that the aftermath of this – not any more sinister reason – was the resultant coolness towards each other?'

'No.'

'Would it not be reasonable to assume, given that after an argument, most married couples might appear not to be talking to each other, that Lady Rosslare's attitude towards her husband was simply the result of the strain and natural awkwardness she might be expected to feel at being thrust into the company of a man with whom she no longer lived?'

'I hadn't thought about it. My wife and I simply assumed they had had some sort of quarrel; it was only afterwards that we thought of it in a different light. One would, naturally.'

Curtis-Bennett shuffled the papers in his hands. 'How well, Sir Ian, were you acquainted with the deceased, Lord Rosslare?'

'He was my wife's cousin. Her first cousin.'

'That is not quite what I meant. Could you elaborate a little further? For instance, in the years preceeding your posting abroad, did you and your wife often find yourselves in the company of this young man? Were you on terms of intimacy?'

'My wife was fond of Robert, of course. As I myself was. He was infrequently a guest in our house.'

'Infrequently? So would it be correct to assume that you did not know his character . . . shall we say "extremely well"?'

Sir Ian began to look uncomfortable. 'I'm not sure what you mean by that.'

'What I mean, Sir Ian, is that you and your wife, though fond of Lord Rosslare – plain Mr Robert Carr as he was in those days – could not say that either of you had a deep knowledge of either his character or his morals?'

The Attorney-General rose to object, but Curtis-Bennett was ready for him. 'If I may crave the indulgence of Their Lordships and that of my learned friend, I will come later to the reason behind this line of questioning.' The objection was overruled.

Treowen coughed. 'Robert was a most pleasant and courteous young man; everyone liked him. He was held in extremely high regard by Lord Leith, whose private secretary at the Scottish Office he was for some considerable length of time.'

'But neither you nor your wife had any knowledge of his private life?'

'No.'

'After your appointment abroad . . . did you keep up any kind of correspondence with Mr Carr – if I may call him by the name by which he was then known?'

'My wife did write to him occasionally.'

'Can we turn to the evening of your first reunion with Lord and Lady Rosslare . . . you spent the evening firstly at the Savoy, then you returned to your house in Manchester Square.'

'Yes. We held a party there. My wife invited a great number of friends back to the house, and also some of the musicians who had played at the Savoy that evening.'

'I see. And this party went on until quite late . . . until the early hours of the following morning?'

'I can't quite remember the exact time . . . but it was very late.'

'And Lord and Lady Rosslare were among the last or the first guests to leave?'

'They were the last. Apart from Mr Dreikhorn, and the lady whom he had brought to the Savoy Hotel earlier that evening.'

'Mr Dreikhorn.' Curtis-Bennett paused. 'Did you know Mr Dreikhorn very well? Or was he invited at Lord Rosslare's instigation?'

'We knew Thomas Dreikhorn very well indeed; he worked with Robert in Edinburgh – they were both at the Scottish Office together. He was a guest in our house before my appointment abroad. He happened to be at the Savoy that evening and naturally we invited him and his lady companion to join our table.'

At this point the Attorney-General rose to enquire as to where this line of questioning was leading; was it at all relevant to the murder of Robert Rosslare? Curtis-Bennett gave assurance that all would be revealed in due course.

'I understand that shortly before Lord and Lady Rosslare left your house that evening, there was a violent argument – overheard by you, your wife, and the Honourable Elvira Bouverie, Mr Dreikhorn's companion? Not between Lord Rosslare and his wife. But between his wife and Thomas Dreikhorn?'

'Yes. They were in the adjoining room and we suddenly heard raised voices; very angry voices. A moment later Frances . . . Lady Rosslare stormed out of the room and asked Lord Rosslare to take her home immediately.'

'Did she seem upset?'

'Very upset, yes. And very angry.'

'The Rosslares left at once?'

'Yes.'

'And after their sudden departure, did Mr Dreikhorn enlighten you as to what their argument had been about?'

'No. He laughed it off.'

'So you have no knowledge of what that violent argument was about?'

'No.'

More papers were shuffled. 'A final question, Sir Ian . . . may we

431

return now to the day of the shoot, the fatal afternoon when Lord Rosslare was killed. You have already stated that after the single gunshot was heard everyone in your party ran from the area of the picnic into the woods, and you saw Lady Rosslare kneeling beside her husband's body?'

'Yes.'

'Can you please describe her appearance to their Lordships? Did she seem hysterical, close to tears, horrified at what had happened? Or did she appear collected and calm?'

'She was in a frightful state, of course.'

Curtis-Bennett smiled.

'Shocked, in fact, at being confronted with her husband's body?'

'Yes, she looked very shocked.'

'She looked to you, indeed, like a young woman would be expected to look confronted with such a terrible catastrophe . . . not like a woman who has just murdered her husband at point blank range?'

'Yes . . .'

'I have no further questions of this witness.'

Almost everyone at the shoot was called, a seemingly endless procession; all of them questioned by both Counsel and all gave identical accounts; although Frances had been alone in the wood with the body, her state on the arrival of the rest of the shooting party was one of near-hysteria, anguish, shock, disbelief. Curtis-Bennett had won the first round.

Dreikhorn walked slowly to the witness-box when he was called and then turned and looked at her directly in the face. He was wearing a dark, Savile Row suit and sober tie, and every detail of his appearance was immaculate; Frances immediately sensed the impression he made on the assembled peers.

After he was sworn in, the Attorney-General went through his early career; the Scottish Office with Robert Carr, the promotion to London, their friendship and political ties. They had first met Lady Rosslare at a garden party to which they had both been invited by her mother, the Countess of Cultrane.

'Mr Dreikhorn, will you please tell their Lordships what was the impression you first formed of the then Lady Frances Osborne?'

'I thought her a very pretty, charming and intelligent young lady.' He smiled at her, and she knew how much he was enjoying her ordeal.

'And your opinion was, presumably, shared by Mr Carr at that time?'

'I could see he was very taken by her, yes.'

'And after this initial meeting Mr Carr, as it were, paid court to Lady Frances?'

'Yes.'

'Followed by their engagement, and then their marriage in the autumn of 1930?'

'Yes.'

'And you were Mr Carr's – he was then Earl of Rosslare – best man at the wedding to Lady Frances Osborne?'

'I was, yes.'

Inskip shuffled notes. 'After returning from their honeymoon, as Lord Rosslare's oldest friend and close colleague, you would of course have naturally been in Lady Rosslare's company many times?'

'Yes.'

'And can you tell their Lordships what opinion you then formed of her after coming to know her much better?'

Dreikhorn's lips curved upwards in a ghost of a smile. 'I formed the opinion that she had a vindictive and jealous nature . . . and an ungovernable temper.' Loud murmurs rippled along the hall. Frances jerked forward in her chair, her knuckles white as they gripped the sides.

'And can you give their Lordships any particular instances of this?'

'There were far too many to mention in entirety . . . but Robbie . . . Lord Rosslare told me that he dare not make any reference to any previous lady acquaintances, because Frances would fly into a rage.'

'I see. Did you yourself have occasion to witness any of these . . . jealous outbursts?'

'I recall one evening at dinner when Robbie inadvertently mentioned a time when he'd escorted Lord Leith's daughter to a concert in Edinburgh; Lady Frances began calling the young lady all manner of quite dreadful names, implying that she was of low moral character . . . and she shouted that if Robbie ever mentioned her name again in her presence she would strike him.'

'That isn't true!' She rose from her chair, her eyes wild.

'Lady Rosslare, you will sit down and not interrupt the proceedings.' The Lord High Steward's voice was harsh. 'Sir Henry, would you kindly instruct your client that such outbursts are not permitted and not tolerated in this chamber?' A glance from Curtis-Bennett sent her sinking back into her seat. But her heart was hammering against her chest.

'Mr Dreikhorn, will you please tell their Lordships of the evening that you were present, which immediately preceeded the separation of Lord and Lady Rosslare? It was February 18th, 1933 . . . eight months ago . . . the evening on which Lady Rosslare's brother-in-law, the Earl of Banbury, died.'

'Yes. Lady Rosslare had gone to spend the night with her sister; Lord Banbury had had a severe heart attack a few days previously, and she didn't want to be left alone in the house.

'I arrived at Lord Rosslare's home in North Audley Street after she'd left. There were a great deal of urgent papers which Lord Rosslare wanted to go through with me, and he'd suggested earlier that day that I come for dinner and we read through them together afterwards. I could tell that he was upset because his attention wandered considerably; and in the end I asked him if anything was the matter.' Dreikhorn paused. 'He admitted that he'd been . . . having an affair with a certain lady, but that Lady Rosslare had become very suspicious and had now found out . . . he said that shortly before I'd arrived, they'd quarrelled bitterly and there had been a most unpleasant scene.'

Frances leaned forward on her chair, her face pale and taut, silently shaking her head, but Curtis-Bennett made a sign to her and she sank back again. It took all her iron self-control to stop herself from crying out; but hadn't she expected Dreikhorn to lie?

'It got very late, and we were nearing the end of the papers; Lord Rosslare suggested that instead of returning to my flat in Henrietta Street I stay the night and we complete our work over breakfast the following morning.' He glanced across the chamber towards where Frances sat. For a moment they looked at each other. 'I was dropping off to sleep much later in my room, when I was awakened by a loud shouting. I got up, put on my dressing-gown and opened my bedroom door, then I looked along the landing towards Lord Rosslare's room. I could clearly hear Lady Rosslare's voice; very loud, very angry. I went to the door of Lord Rosslare's room, which was wide open, and looked inside. She was hitting him with her fists, screaming the most obscene abuse, calling him terrible names. I quickly closed the door to prevent any of the servants hearing what was going on. A moment later she ran out of the room, crying, hysterical; Lord Rosslare ran after her to try to reason with her, but she struck him very hard across the face. Then she ran downstairs and out of the house.'

'Lord Rosslare was very shaken by this violent outburst?'

'Yes, he was extremely upset. I went downstairs and fetched him a large whisky.'

'And did he then tell you, or did you ask him, what was the reason for Lady Rosslare's behaviour?'

'He told me that she'd accused him of entertaining a certain lady in her absence . . . that she knew this lady had been in the house, in her bedroom, while she was at Portland Place with her sister. He'd denied this and she'd attacked him physically.'

'Did he say anything else?'

'He said that he could not longer bear living with Lady Rosslare because of her ungovernable jealousy and rages. He said that it was perfectly possible that she could cause a most unpleasant and highly embarrassing scene in public . . . this was his greatest fear. Because of his reputation, the reputation of the Osborne family. He was extremely concerned about that. He then said that when Lady Rosslare had calmed down, he would suggest to her that they quietly separate, and live apart.'

'I see. And this separation was effected almost immediately?'

'Yes, it was. Lady Rosslare took a flat in Lupus Street; Lord Rosslare continued to live at North Audley Street alone.'

Inskip shuffled more notes; then he turned to his junior. Whispers were exchanged.

'Mr Dreikhorn, I will turn now, if I may, to the evening of September 1st last, when you were at the Savoy Hotel with a lady companion. You arrived in the ballroom and were not long there, I believe, when you caught sight of Lord and Lady Rosslare together.'

'Yes. Earlier at Westminster, Robbie . . . Lord Rosslare, had told me of the return to London of Sir Ian and Lady Irene Treowen, and that they were attending a performance by an American band at the Savoy that evening.'

'And Lord Rosslare told you that he would be accompanied by his wife?'

'Yes. I was somewhat surprised at this – in view of their estrangement. But he was anxious that his cousin not find out that they were living apart. Her invitation had of course been for them to attend as a couple.'

'Did he not think it would have been better to have told Lady Irene the truth – that he and Lady Frances no longer lived together as man and wife?'

'He knew that if he did that she would have asked him certain questions as to the cause of the estrangement . . . and he had no wish to implicate the lady to whom he had transferred his affections. It seemed simpler all round.' Dreikhorn paused. 'He was a little embarrassed at having to confess at the failure of his marriage . . . and he knew that Lady Irene was very fond of Lady Rosslare.'

'I see. You then joined the Treowen's party at the Savoy. Relations between Lord and Lady Rosslare appeared to be amicable during that evening?'

'They were polite to each other.'

'And afterwards, when your party returned to Manchester Square, they kept up this pretence for the sake of their hosts?'

'Yes. Up to that point nobody would have guessed that they'd lived apart for several months.' Another pause. He glanced at Frances. 'Lady Rosslare was extremely accomplished at façades.'

"Shortly before the party ended . . . when there was only yourself, your lady companion, Sir Ian and Lady Irene and the Rosslares left, I believe there was a violent altercation between yourself and Lady Rosslare? Will you please tell Their Lordships why this was?'

'I went into an adjoining room to smoke a cigarette; when I glanced round, Lady Rosslare had come into the room. She accused me of encouraging her husband in his affair with the other lady, which I naturally denied since it was completely untrue. She then became very angry, said I had never liked her and wanted to wreck her marriage. She said that if I didn't use my influence with Robbie to take her back again and end his relationship with the other woman, she would do something that both of us would regret . . .'

'She in effect threatened you?'

'Yes. But she had worked herself up into a state of rage, and I thought nothing more of it. After all, she'd said similar things to Robbie many times.

'I told her that although I was deeply sorry that her marriage to Robbie had gone wrong, it was his business and not mine if he chose to see another woman. When I refused to use my influence with him to end the affair and go back to her, she became very violent and abusive; and then she struck me very hard across the face. After that she stormed out of the room and demanded that Robbie take her home.'

'Thank you, Mr Dreikhorn. I have only one more question. Shortly before Lord Rosslare's death, you were due to be sent to the British Embassy in Berlin . . . naturally, as you were needed as a witness, this posting has been delayed . . . at the time of the killing I believe you were in London, busy packing for the journey?'

'Yes. I was stunned, shocked . . . when the news came. At first I simply couldn't believe it. I knew Lady Rosslare had made wild threats before . . . but I *never* believed that she would carry any of them out.'

Inskip nodded towards Curtis-Bennett. 'Your witness, Sir Henry.'

'Mr Dreikhorn. You have told their Lordships and my learned friend, that you and the late Lord Rosslare had for many years been close friends, as well as colleagues. You have also told us how you and Lord Rosslare were first acquainted with Lady Frances, and that after their subsequent marriage she displayed ungovernable bouts of jealousy and violent rage. You have also given us your accounts of the evening of Lord Banbury's death, when, you allege, Lady Rosslare stormed into her husband's bedroom in the middle of the night and accused him of adultery before physically attacking him. You have also given us your account of the evening at the Savoy Hotel and the subsequent quarrel at the Treowen's house in Manchester Square, during which, you further allege, Lady Rosslare made certain serious threats.' Dreikhorn nodded. 'May I suggest, Mr Dreikhorn, that your accounts of the evening on which Lord Banbury died and Lady Rosslare burst in upon her husband, and of the evening when you and she violently quarrelled, are an utter fabrication; a complete tissue of lies?'

'Everything I've said is true.'

'May I put it to you, Mr Dreikhorn, that the jealous rages and bouts of violence which you would have us believe Lady Rosslare gave rein to at frequent intervals, are also utter fabrication and a complete tissue of lies, a pure malicious invention of your own brilliant but very vindictive mind?'

'No.'

'You would have their Lordships believe, would you not, that in the middle of the night when her husband was asleep, Lady Rosslare stormed into the house to threaten and attack him because of his affair with another woman, a woman of whom you tell us she was insanely jealous; but did not Lady Rosslare return to the house for quite another reason, and did not the subsequent violent scene with her husband take place for an entirely different reason to the one you give us?'

'I saw everything and heard everything that happened.'

'I suggest, Mr Dreikhorn, that Lady Rosslare – far from being unreasonable – had every right to exhibit profound shock and anger when she returned unexpectedly to North Audley Street that night. For when she walked into her husband's bedroom she discovered him not in the act of adultery with the mythical woman you have invented, but in the act of sodomy with you.'

The chamber erupted into a volcano of noise. It was several moments before order was restored.

'That is a monstrous and wicked slander!'

'The monstrous and wicked slander, Mr Dreikhorn, is the testimony you have given to us, the testimony that would have us believe Lady Frances left her husband because of a love affair with another woman, when she left him because she found it intolerable to continue living with him after she discovered the true nature of his relationship with you. The relationship, Mr Dreikhorn, that I suggest existed between you and the late Lord Rosslare since your first association several years before.'

'No!'

'Has not everything you have said about Lady Rosslare today merely shown that you were jealous of her from the beginning of her relationship with Lord Rosslare and that your extreme jealousy and dislike of her because she was your lover's lawful wife induced you to invent a malicious tissue of lies in order to blacken her name?'

'That isn't true!'

'May we return, Mr Dreikhorn, to the evening of the violent quarrel between you and Lady Frances . . . the quarrel which took place at Manchester Square? May I suggest that the reason for this argument was not the one you gave us, but because you baited her about certain other matters, and made insulting insinuations about her family and friends?'

'No.'

'It was then, when she could no longer bear your insolence, that she slapped you across the face and knocked the glass you were holding out of your hand.'

'I've already told you why she hit me. I have nothing further to add.'

Curtis-Bennett gave him a long, penetrating look. For the first time, Dreikhorn shifted uncomfortably. 'Reminding you that you are under oath, Mr Dreikhorn, do you deny that you had, at any time, an unlawful homosexual relationship with the late Earl of Rosslare, and that the discovery of that relationship by his wife was the real cause of their separation, and of her antipathy to you?'

'Certainly I deny it.'

Rumbling voices echoed around the hall.

'At the time of Lord Rosslare's death, you were preparing for your journey to Berlin.' Curtis-Bennett glanced down at the sheaf of papers in his hand. 'I understand that your presence in London at the approximate time of the killing has been corroborated by the police?'

'Yes.'

'Mr Dreikhorn, you knew Lord Rosslare extremely well . . . intimately, one might say, as close friends and political colleagues. Obviously, a man in his position would make enemies. Can you think of anyone at all who would wish to see Lord Rosslare dead, or benefit greatly by his death?'

'No.'

'Thank you, Mr Dreikhorn.'

She watched him step out of the witness box and make his way to the back of the court. As he sat down, he gave her one look, full of malice. Then he turned away.

She sank down on the hard, narrow little bed in her cell, lay back against the wall and closed her eyes. It seemed strange and claustrophobic after the light and colour and ceremony in the vast, gilded hall; almost peaceful. Far away in the distance beyond the cell she could hear the familiar sounds and hollow echoes that she'd almost grown used to, the heavy tread of footsteps, clanking doors and keys. She fell into an exhausted sleep in minutes.

He turned from the window and looked round as he sensed Rankin at the door of the room. He was holding a small tray with a bottle of malt whisky and two glasses on it, and without speaking he set it down. For several minutes Dreikhorn went on staring from the window, his hands gripping the sill until the strong knucklesgrew white.

'Bitch. Osborne bitch! She told him; everything. Somehow I thought she never would. I thought she'd be too bloody ashamed to want anyone else to know!' He felt Rankin's hand on his shoulder.

'Come on, sit down. Have a drink . . . Highland malt always makes you feel better. Look, whatever they said, it doesn't matter. You told them she was making it all up. Nobody will believe anything she says!'

'I was there. You weren't. I saw their faces. They were shocked, at first. When Curtis-Bennett came right out and said it. Then I

439

could feel their eyes watching me, wondering. Now whenever they look at me, they'll start wondering. Is it true? Whispers, Lawrence. Whispers can ruin any man if they get loud enough.'

'They've got no proof.'

'No.'

'You've always been so careful, Tom. So discreet. And so was Rosslare. And me. I'd never say anything, you know that. I love you.'

Dreikhorn picked up the whisky and swigged it back in a single gulp. 'We shouldn't be seen together, Lawrence. Not now. Not for a while. It's too risky. Too dangerous.'

The boy's face crumpled like a piece of paper thrown on a fire. 'We can meet at the club! You said it was always safe there!'

'Not even there. Not till all this has blown over.'

The sight of Rankin's pale, unhappy face irritated him unbearably. Robbie. Robbie. Why, why? He felt a terrible anger, a terrible loneliness. He'd loved him so much, with his heart, soul, body, mind; surpassing the love of women. And he'd trusted Robbie, but Robbie in his irresolution and weakness had left him naked to his enemies, the Osbornes. He put a hand up to his face and realized that he was crying, but he couldn't help that now. He'd done what he'd done out of blind rage, the thirst for revenge, but when he'd come face to face with Robbie in the Treowen woods, he'd almost faltered, and failed. The look of stunned disbelief on Robbie's face was a look that he'd remember until he died.

'Tom, don't. Please, don't. I won't let anything happen to you, I swear. On my life I swear. Let me come to Berlin with you. We can live together there . . . it isn't like London . . . you know that . . .'

'No. Not yet. It would look too obvious. And then they'd know.' His voice was stronger now. 'No, Lawrence.'

'Tom . . .'

'Do you want to go to prison, for Christ's sake?' He got up, abruptly. 'I'm sorry; I can't stay here. I must go back to my flat and pack. I have to be ready to leave at the end of the trial. You do understand, don't you? I'll . . . write to you, I'll tell you when it's safe for you to come over.'

'That letter . . . the letter you wrote to Carr . . . and the other one . . . the one you put all those things in, that you said you were going to send to the Prime Minister . . .'

Dreikhorn went to the briefcase propped up against the chair and opened it. He took out the thick envelope inside and slowly began

440

tearing it into pieces. 'We'll throw it on your fire. No point, now. Robbie's dead.'

'You say his name as if you still care. As if you still love him. You said you hated him, Tom. You said you loved me.'

'Yes.'

'You're not sorry, are you? He betrayed you. I would never have done what he did!'

'I know that.' He made himself smile. The boy was obsessed with him, he was stifling him. In a few weeks' time, safely in Berlin, he'd have at last broken free. Rankin had been amusing and very useful, but Robbie was the only one he could ever love. He closed the briefcase.

'Tom. Will they find her guilty, do you think? Will she hang? They still hang women, don't they? For murder. Like they hanged Edith Thompson. Just because they're women, they don't show leniency . . .'

'I don't know. I don't care.' He gripped the handle of the briefcase tightly. If Robbie had never met Frances Osborne, he would be alive now. Nothing would have come between them. *Robbie. Robbie.*

He took his overcoat from Rankin. He made smiling promises that he knew he would never keep. He walked up the stone steps of the basement flat and out into the street.

54

Four long, gruelling days had been taken up with the minor but crucial testimonies of the remaining witnesses; maids, footmen, the butler at North Audley Street, the chauffeur who had driven them home that night from Manchester Square. Today, November 5th, was the day when Sir Henry Curtis-Bennett was to put Frances herself in the witness box; she thought what an irony it was that she was to testify on the anniversary of the Gunpowder Plot. Like Guy Fawkes three hundred years ago, were her revelations about to erupt into the major scandal of the century?

Curtis-Bennett called her, and she walked steadily, head held high, to the witness box before the assembled peers.

'Lady Rosslare, at the beginning of your marriage to the late Robert Carr, were your relations entirely happy?'

'Yes.'

'After some time had elapsed, however, I believe this did not continue to be the case?'

'No.'

'Will you tell their Lordships why not?'

She cleared her throat. Her voice came out firm and steady. 'I was very much aware of the hostility of my husband's friend, Thomas Dreikhorn. He disliked me intensely and the feeling between us was mutual.'

'Can you elaborate a little further on that answer?'

'He seemed to despise all women . . . he made jokes about their intellect, their emotions, their dependence on men. I was in a very difficult position because my husband was very fond of him, and their friendship went back a long way. I was forced to tolerate his presence in our house, at my dinner parties and other social occasions.'

'Yet, I believe, Mr Dreikhorn escorted many ladies on these occasions and at other social functions?'

'Yes. He had quite a reputation as a ladies' man.' She hesitated. 'Which was why when I found out the truth about his relationship with my husband it came as an even more terrible shock.'

There were murmurs among the peers.

'Lady Rosslare. Is it or is it not true that your husband was having an illicit love affair with another lady?'

'No, it isn't true.'

'The bitter arguments which Mr Dreikhorn alleges that you had with your husband were not in fact about this "affair", were they?'

'No. They were about Thomas Dreikhorn.'

'You complained to your husband of his blatantly hostile attitude towards you?'

'Yes.'

'And your husband told you that because Mr Dreikhorn was his friend and colleague you would have to grin and bear it?'

'Words to that effect.'

'Lady Rosslare . . . can we go back to the night of Lord Banbury's death eight months ago? You were staying with your sister at Portland Place?'

'I thought it was best that she wasn't left alone . . . but later in the evening she told me that another friend was coming to see her, and I decided to go home. Lord Vaux, Lord Banbury's nephew, drove me back to North Audley Street and I thanked him and we then said goodnight. Our first footman was still on duty and he bolted the front door after Lord Vaux left; but Lord Vaux had trouble starting his car, and while I was on my way upstairs he rang the bell and Phillips, our footman, gave him some assistance. I went upstairs and opened the door of our bedroom. She took a deep breath before she spoke those next awful words. 'I found my husband in bed with Thomas Dreikhorn.'

'Silence in the chamber!'

'Please go on, Lady Rosslare. I know this is very painful for you, but we must hear your version of what happened that night.'

'Robin . . . my husband . . . scrambled up out of the bed, and grabbed his dressing-gown . . . I can't remember very clearly what he said to me or I what shouted back at him, but I turned and ran. Lord Vaux had just managed to re-start his car and I begged him to drive me to my parents' house in Belgrave Square.' She leaned heavily against the witness box. 'He stopped the car some way from the house and I told him everything.'

'Silence in the chamber!'

'Unfortunately . . . tragically . . . Lord Vaux was killed in an aeroplane accident near Le Touquet shortly afterwards, is that not the case? Otherwise he, no doubt, would be in this chamber today to corroborate your story?'

'Yes . . .'

'Lady Rosslare . . . after these shocking events you refused, did you not, to continue living with your husband, and you separated immediately?'

'Yes. I told him that I could never live with him as his wife again under any circumstances.'

'You took a flat in Lupus Street, and Lord Rosslare lived alone in the North Audley Street house?'

'Yes.'

'But on the return to England of his cousin, Lady Irene Treowen . . . for the sake of appearances . . . he asked you to accompany him to her home in Manchester Square and then to the Savoy Hotel?'

'I agreed reluctantly, yes.'

'Was there any degree of animosity between you and your husband at that time? Had you . . . forgiven him?'

'I'd forgiven, yes; but not forgotten. I was hurt far too deeply . . .'

'I am certain that their Lordships can understand that. But for your husband's sake, so that he could keep at least temporary face in the company of his cousin and her husband, you acceded to his wishes?'

'Yes.'

'When you returned from the Savoy Hotel, after the other guests had left the party at Manchester Square, you and Thomas Dreikhorn quarrelled?'

'He made certain provocative and very insulting remarks, yes. And I did strike him.'

'Would you say that you lost control of your temper?'

'He provoked me beyond endurance.'

'You then insisted that your husband take you back to your flat in Lupus Street?'

'Yes.'

'When your husband's aunt, Lady Janet Carr, died some months later, did he then come to you and ask you to accompany him to her funeral at Renfrew?'

'Yes.'

'Did you do so willingly?'

'I didn't want to go, no. But it was a duty.'

'During your stay at Renfrew, did you share a bedroom with your husband?'

'Lady Irene Treowen put us in a room with twin beds.'

'If your husband had indicated that he wished to resume your marital relationship, would you have acquiesced?'

'No. But he would never have asked nor expected me to do that after what had happened.'

'During your stay at Treowen House, did you and Lord Rosslare have any quarrels?'

'No.'

'You are certain of that?'

'Yes.'

Curtis-Bennett glanced down at the remaining notes in his hands. 'Lady Rosslare . . . will you now please tell their Lordships your own account of what happened on that fateful afternoon . . . when you found the body of your husband in Treowen woods?'

She paused, and looked at the assembled rows of peers; what were they thinking, she wondered? Some faces held curiosity, some censure, disapproval; some were kind, some expressionless, noncommittal. But at the very end of the trial would they believe Thomas Dreikhorn's version of what had happened, or hers?

'The men and the ghillies spent most of the morning in the

444

wood . . . at about midday Lady Irene sent the servants to fetch the picnic tables, chairs and rugs from the house . . . the beaters had gone into the furthest end of the woods to drive the birds towards the guns . . . while the men joined us for lunch.'

She hesitated, remembering the piles of dead birds that lay in heaps along the ground. 'When the men came out of the wood, I saw that Robin wasn't with them . . . I think I made some remark to Lady Irene Treowen that he wasn't there, and I think she said something like, "Perhaps he's stopped to check his gun". I can't remember now. I ran into the woods, and I stopped several times and called his name.'

'Then I heard the sound of a gun going off. I ran on, and came to the edge of a small clearing . . . that was when I saw him. I ran over to him and knelt down, and touched him. He was warm, but I could see blood all over the back of his head. I reached down and touched the gun . . . I don't know why, it was just instinct . . . then I looked up as the others came running towards me.' She covered her face with her hands. 'Someone . . . I don't remember who it was . . . came over and held his wrist. That was when I knew he was dead. Everyone was in a state of shock . . . nobody knew what had happened . . . how the gun could have gone off. When we got back to the house, Sir Ian called the police and Irene gave me a large brandy. A few hours later . . . I was arrested and charged . . .'

'Lady Rosslare . . .' Curtis-Bennett's voice was gentle, coaxing. 'Did you, at any time while you were in the woods, see or hear the presence of another person?'

'No. I . . . thought I could hear the sound of the beaters . . . a long way in the distance, in the other end of the wood . . .'

'When you heard the single gunshot, and then saw your husband's body lying on the ground, can you describe what your first thoughts were?'

'I thought the gun had gone off by accident. That it was an accident.'

Curtis-Bennett let his eyes move slowly over the rows of robed peers. 'Lady Rosslare, although you and your husband were estranged at the time of his death, would it be true to say that you bore him no ill-will in spite of everything that had happened between you?'

'No, I bore him no ill-will at all . . .'

'Can you think of any other person who might do so . . . to such an extent that they would be prepared to take his life?'

445

'No, no one.'

There was a momentary silence before Curtis-Bennett came to his final question. She gripped the edge of the box.

'Lady Rosslare, remembering that you are under oath . . . I have only this to ask of you now: did you kill your husband Lord Rosslare?'

'No, I did not.'

The Attorney-General rose to cross-examine. This, she knew, was where her real ordeal began. He fixed her with his severest stare. Several seconds passed before he asked his first question, seconds that seemed unending. 'Lady Rosslare,' his voice was brisk, chilly. 'You have given their Lordships an account of events which differs, as you must agree, substantially from the account given by Mr Dreikhorn. Would you care to comment on that fact?'

'Mr Dreikhorn's account of events is nothing but a tissue of lies!'

'On the contrary, Lady Rosslare, Mr Dreikhorn's version of these happenings seems to me to be perfectly plausible!'

Curtis-Bennett objected that this was a matter to be decided by the Peers. The objection was allowed.

'Is it not correct to say that you have always disliked Mr Dreikhorn – your late husband's colleague and valued friend – because you resented the high regard in which Lord Rosslare held him?'

'I disliked him because he made it perfectly plain from the very beginning that he disliked me. He despised women!'

'That accusation does not appear to be borne out by facts, however. Mr Dreikhorn had a large number of women friends, whom he regularly escorted. Is that true or untrue?'

'It's true, but he only did it so that nobody . . .'

'True or untrue, Lady Rosslare?'

She paused, and momentarily looked down at her clenched hands. 'True.'

'And many of these ladies, I understand, were brought by Mr Dreikhorn to your house during the period of your marriage to Lord Rosslare, as guests to dinner parties and other social functions?'

'Yes.'

'Did any of them seem to be, in your opinion, unhappy in his company? Did he treat them with anything but the courtesy and deference any gentleman would be expected to exhibit towards a lady?'

'Of course he treated them with courtesy and deference; he wasn't a fool!'

His questions were deliberately designed to goad her and she knew that he was succeeding. She glanced at Curtis-Bennett and took a deep, slow breath. Keep calm. Cool. Controlled. Every pair of eyes in the enormous chamber was watching her.

'Lady Rosslare. You have stated that when you decided to return home to North Audley Street on the night of your brother-in-law's death, that you surprised your husband and Mr Dreikhorn in bed together?'

'Yes.'

'Yet Mr Dreikhorn emphatically denies this scandalous and slanderous accusation . . .'

'I would hardly expect him to admit it when it would mean the ruin of his career, his social standing, and a long term of imprisonment.'

'If what you allege in fact took place, why did you not immediately denounce both your husband and Mr Dreikhorn? You could have summoned witnesses. Lord Vaux was in the street outside. The footman Phillips within call. The house was full of servants whom you could have roused from their various beds as witness to this heinous scene! Yet you did nothing.'

'If I'd denounced Thomas Dreikhorn it would have ruined my husband's career. My family name would have been splashed across every newspaper in the country; the scandal would have made every-body connected with it social outcasts, and worse. Do you really think I would have taken any action which resulted in that?'

'It seems to me, Lady Rosslare, that you took no action at all . . . except to leave your husband's house for good. And the reason for that, as we have learned from Mr Dreikhorn's testimony, is your violent argument with your husband over his extra-marital love affair with another lady.'

'I told Lord Vaux exactly what I'd seen only minutes after I'd run out of the house. I told him everything!'

Was that a smirk on Inskip's face? 'But Lord Vaux is unable to substantiate your story, Lady Rosslare.'

'Because he's dead!' She hadn't meant to lose control, to cry out. She harnessed her frustration and anger and clenched her fists tightly. *'He's dead . . .'*

'John Phillips, the footman on duty that night, has already given testimony to their Lordships that nothing unusual happened on that evening, with the exception of when you came back to the house and he heard raised, angry voices from upstairs . . . coming from your bedroom. The voices he heard were those of yourself and Lord

Rosslare. The other servants whose accounts we have also heard, tell us that on Lord Rosslare's orders, a bedroom was prepared for Mr Dreikhorn's use for that night only. Mr Dreikhorn tells us that he only left his room when awakened by loud shouting. Nobody saw Mr Dreikhorn enter, or leave Lord Rosslare's bedroom at any time. It is only you, Lady Rosslare, who allege that he did so.'

'Simply because nobody else saw him doesn't mean that he wasn't there.'

'There is no proof that Mr Dreikhorn was in that particular room; but the state of the bed in the room in which he was given on your husband's orders *does* prove that he was *there*, Lady Rosslare.'

Inskip took fresh papers from his junior counsel. 'May we now turn to the fact of your estrangement and separation from your husband?' He flicked pages over one by one. 'You have told their Lordships that after this particular episode, you refused to live with your husband again as man and wife?'

'Yes.'

And what was Lord Rosslare's reaction to that?'

'He pleaded with me to reconsider because of the possible gossip which would inevitably result from such a separation.'

'But you still refused to return to him?'

'I felt fully justified in not doing so.'

'I see. You spent several days . . . a week . . . at the Grosvenor Hotel, after which you rented a flat in Lupus Street?'

'Yes.'

'And presumably Lord Rosslare paid the rent for this establishment, and your general household bills?'

'No.'

Murmurs again rippled along the benches.

'May I ask who did, Lady Rosslare?'

'I paid the rent myself. I got a job.'

Inskip's dark eyebrows rose. 'Indeed? And did you and your husband continue to meet on fairly amicable terms after this separation? Or did you not meet at all?'

'We didn't meet.'

'You refused utterly to forgive him?'

'Yes.'

'Did you harbour bitter resentment?'

'I was hurt. Angry. All the emotions you would expect me to feel in the circumstances.'

'Did you at any time issue an ultimatum to Lord Rosslare after your separation? That you would return to him if he consented to give up his association with the other woman?'

'My husband wasn't having an affair with another woman.'

'Lady Rosslare, Mr Dreikhorn has testified that he was and that he had taken Mr Dreikhorn into his confidence. He complained of your jealousy, your rages, because Lord Rosslare refused to give her up. We have testimony from many of your household servants that violent arguments were frequently overheard . . .'

'But they didn't hear what they were *about*!'

'Two of Mr Dreikhorn's lady companions have also told their Lordships that on certain occasions during dinner parties your speech to Mr Dreikhorn was extremely objectionable.'

Curtis-Bennett rose; he reminded Inskip that the two ladies had also admitted that Lady Rosslare had spoken to Mr Dreikhorn harshly after he had spoken to her in such a way as to provoke a harsh answer. The Attorney-General withdrew the remark.

Inskip paused for several moments to confer with junior counsel, then he turned back and faced Frances for his final assault. 'I suggest to you, Lady Rosslare, that you have a jealous, suspicious and most vindictive nature; that you not only resented your husband's long-standing friendship with Mr Dreikhorn, whose testimony has in a large measure been borne out by other witnesses, but you deeply and bitterly resented his blank refusal to assist you in regaining the lost affections of your husband.'

'No!'

'This, I further suggest, is the whole basis of your intense dislike of, and prejudice towards Mr Dreikhorn; why, in fact, you have sought – and sought so maliciously – to purposefully decry his account of events; ruthlessly uncaring as to the gravely damaging effects of your baseless accusations upon his moral character and political career . . . accusations for which you have not one single shred of evidence.'

'Everything I have told this court about my husband's relationship with Thomas Dreikhorn is true!'

'You would certainly have their Lordships believe it so, Lady Rosslare!'

She clenched and unclenched her fists to stop herself from screaming.

'We have your testimony about the evening of the Savoy, the quarrel at Manchester Square, and your husband's request that you accompany him to the funeral of Lady Janet Carr. I wish now to

449

come to the afternoon on which Lord Rosslare met his death.' A deliberate pause. More shuffling of papers in his hands. 'All witnesses agree that you were seen entering Treowen woods, and that your husband was somewhere inside those woods. You have stated that you heard the single gunshot, that you ran towards the spot where you believed it to have come from, and that you then saw the body of your husband lying lifeless on the ground. When the other members of the shooting party arrived on the scene they are unanimous in stating that you were kneeling beside the body and that your left hand was on the gun.

'Police reports on both the body of Lord Rosslare and on the weapon state that your husband was killed at almost point-blank range and that it was not an accident, as you at first alleged. No member of the party either saw or heard any other person – except for yourself – in the vicinity of the body. By your own admission, you neither saw nor heard another person other than your husband when you entered those woods.

'Lady Rosslare, I believe the facts of this sorry case speak very eloquently for themselves. Your rage and jealousy against your husband for his transgression with another woman continued to simmer throughout the months of your separation. During that time your bitter resentment towards his friend, Thomas Dreikhorn, also continued to grow.

'Mr Dreikhorn did not wish to become involved in your marital quarrels, and you deeply resented that; for you knew that your husband held him in high regard and that he might, if he wished, exert himself on your behalf. That he held himself aloof from this tangled web is entirely to his credit; as is his conspicuous loyalty to your husband. I am sure that their Lordships will commend him for that.

'I suggest, Lady Rosslare, that you agreed to accompany your husband to Renfrew for a purpose other than family obligation. That you knew a shooting-party had been planned and were only too well aware that a means of visiting long-awaited revenge on your husband for his infidelity might well present itself. This proved to be the case.' He looked at her sternly.

'When your husband did not emerge from the wood that day with the other gentlemen in the party, you seized that opportunity – why else should you run into the woods and not walk? Why enter them at all when, one would suppose, Lord Rosslare would emerge from them at any minute? Fate intervened and presented you with the opportunity which you seized. You found your husband. But not in the manner that you would have their Lordships believe. I suggest that Lord Rosslare was very much alive when you came across him. I suggest, Lady Frances, that you shot your husband in cold blood, from point blank range, with his own gun.'

'No! I didn't kill him!'

'I have no further questions, my Lord.' Inskip sat down, satisfied that he had done his best.

'They're going to find me guilty, aren't they?'

Curtis-Bennett's hand was gentle on her shoulder. She looked so fragile, so pale, so vulnerable; his instinct was to shield and protect. But he couldn't lie to her. She deserved more than that. 'The Lord High Steward was scrupulously fair in his summing up, after our closing speeches. Inskip has, it's true, made the case for the Prosecution a very formidable one; a true crime of passion. It would be very wrong of me, and grossly misleading, to say that I think the peers will or will not convict. But after hearing your testimony, I can't believe that any court would demand the extreme penalty.'

She looked at him sadly, her eyes full of tears. 'Perhaps dying isn't so terrible. But to be locked up, for ever . . . that would be nothing less than a living death . . .'

'*Frances, Countess of Rosslare, rise . . .*'

She stared straight ahead of her, at the Lord High Steward.

'Do you find the prisoner at the bar guilty or not guilty?'

'*Guilty, upon my honour.*'

'Guilty, upon my honour.'

'Guilty, upon my honour . . .'

The inexorable voices went on and on, until every Peer had delivered his verdict.

'. . . *we recommend that mercy be shown . . .*'

The blood was beating in her ears. The stern voice addressed her.

'Frances, Countess of Rosslare, you have been found guilty of the wilful murder of Robert Patrick Kieran Carr, thirteenth Earl of Rosslare. Have you anything to say before sentence of law be passed upon you?'

The tears ran down her face into her mouth. The gilded walls, the paintings, the vivid scarlet of the peers' robes all merged together in one long, piercing haze of light. She put out her hands in front of her like a blindwoman, and gripped the rail.

451

'*I . . . didn't . . . kill him!*'

'Frances, Countess of Rosslare, it is the sentence of this court of Peers that you be imprisoned for the remainder of your natural life.'

55

It had been freezing cold in the exercise yard; sleet had started to fall and she was grateful to come inside to the comparative warmth of the workshop. The tasks that the women prisoners had to do each day were invariably monotonous and boring; in the beginning, with the insults and the cruel, thoughtless taunts some of the other prisoners had hurled at her, Frances had thought that she would go out of her mind. But she didn't blame them; to them everything was either black or white; how could she expect simple, rough, ill-educated and underprivileged women to understand?

'Cor, look out girls, it's Lady Muck 'erself!'

'Fuck me, it's bleedin' oxtail stew again today . . . not like what *you're* used to at the fuckin' Ritz, your ladyship . . !'

'Couldn' 'ave bin much good in bed, could she, if 'er 'usband preferred men!'

She'd gone back each day, exhausted and miserable to her solitary cell, thrown herself down on the hard, narrow little iron bedstead and cried herself to sleep. But slowly, gradually, she'd learned to be strong. Now, most of the women had grown to like her.

''Ere, love . . . you got a bloke waitin' for you when . . . well, is there somebody, like? You know . . . on the outside?'

She'd smiled at that. All that most of the women seemed to think about and talk about was men.

'It wouldn't do much good if I did have someone, would it?'

Two of the girls were sitting at one of the communal tables, sifting through the magazines and old newspapers.

'Bloody hell, look at that! Why is there always politics on the front pages?'

'Anythin' interestin' in yours?'

'Mrs Anne Turner . . . *everyone's* 'eard of Mrs Anne Turner . . .

'She was 'avin' if off with the doctor . . .'

'. . . 'is wife blew the whistle on 'im . . . reckon she caught 'im with 'is trousers down with one of them la-di-da lady patients of 'is one day . . .' They all laughed except Frances.

In the dinner-hall for the last meal of the day she took her place in the queue, holding out her enamel plate for the wardress behind the table to ladle in a large dob of unappetizing stew.

They sat down at the long tressle table side by side. Frances looked down into the plate dispassionately. It bore no resemblance to anything she had ever seen, much less eaten before. But it was hot and it was filling and there was nothing else. She dipped in her spoon.

'Tasted worse,' Nancy said beside her, shovelling in hers and talking with her mouth full. 'Blimey, what I wouldn't give for a plate of jellied eels! You ever 'ad jellied eels?'

Frances smiled and shook her head.

'No, I didn't think so. Every Friday, me an' me old man'd go down the pub in the Mile End Road and 'e'd buy me some. Good ol' stick, me dad; when 'e's sober. Once 'e gets too much drink in, 'e's a right ol' bastard, I can tell you!'

Frances had long ago got accustomed to the other women's rough language; she couldn't help smiling now.

'Pity the old bastard don't snuff it.' Nancy wiped her lips on her sleeve. 'Then maybe I'd get a special pass from then Gov'nor to go to 'is funeral.' Frances didn't answer. '''ere, that reminds me. You could 'ave got out twice, couldn't you, love? On one o' them special passes. Your uncle died last year an' your sister in January.'

'There wouldn't have been any point.'

Nancy tore off a piece of bread and crammed it into her mouth.

'Oh, yeah. That posh family o' yours. Didn't want to know, did they? Fuckin' bastards. Anyway, you got that friend from Holland Park what comes to visit you, 'aven't you? She don't care what you s'pposed to 'ave done.'

Frances pushed away her half-empty plate. She thought of Laura. 'I don't know what I would have done without her.'

56

The pain was bad this morning. It had taken him a long time to get up, wash, then dress. Nowadays, he never ate breakfast. He sat down slowly when he was ready and drank a small glass of water, then he looked at his watch. There was still more than an hour before his appointment, but it took him so long to do things on his bad days.

Outside, in the bustling, crowded street, he hailed a taxicab. Gone were the days when he would have walked to his doctor's in Maybury Street; even the slightest exertion, climbing a short flight of stairs, made him dizzy and out of breath. But it was the pain that made him suffer most. He glanced down with a bitter smile at the last letter Dreikhorn wrote, dated more than ten months before. He had known for far longer than that that he had never really had the slightest intention of seeing him again; of sending for him to join him in Berlin at all. It was the betrayal, the casting-off, that had hurt him far more deeply than the pain that racked his body day and night.

In the old days he'd rarely had need to visit his doctor's surgery but those days were long gone, like the distances he walked. At first he'd ignored the pain, and it had only come every so often, in spasms; in the last few weeks it had become so bad that he knew something must be wrong. So they'd taken the X-rays.

The walk from the street up the single flight of half-dozen steps to the front door made him feel physically sick; for several minutes he leaned against the pillar, closing his eyes tightly against the new wave of pain.

The nurse bustled about briskly and efficiently, giving him a short, impersonal smile when she caught his eye. Then it was his turn.

He knew that the news was bad by the doctor's face, but somehow he'd expected that and also he'd reached the point where he didn't care. Nothing mattered now. His parents were gone. His career, through ill-health, had long since finished. All that had been left was his obsessive love for Dreikhorn; and Dreikhorn, he realized now, had never cared at all.

He wasn't afraid, he wasn't dreading the inevitable. It was the agony in his mind for the last two years, not the agony in his body, that never ceased to torment him. And every time he'd taken out those torn, yellowing pieces of paper that Dreikhorn thought had long ago perished in the fire, he knew what he was going to do.

The doctor broke the news that he'd half expected very gently, very professionally, as he'd known that he would. He explained that the X-rays showed beyond any doubt that the growth was already too deep-rooted to be cured, or to respond to any remedial treatment. He had six months, a year at most; in a few weeks he would be on morphine. They would have to admit him to hospital. At least, he thought with a bitter irony, it was no less than he deserved; and if he was there then at least, unlike some others, he would not be left to die alone.

The tears ran down his cheeks. He had the insane desire to laugh. Of course, the doctor thought that it was the shock, disbelief at what he'd told him. He rang for the nurse and they gave him a glass of water, but he waved it away.

They didn't understand; they couldn't. Rankin wasn't crying for himself, except perhaps for the blind, pathetic, duped fool he'd been. He was crying for the girl who had been condemned to a life sentence because he'd been too obsessed with the man responsible for imprisoning her, while he'd gone free. Until now, Rankin had been too cowardly, too bound by absurd sentiment, too afraid, to save her. He was strong enough to do it now.

Her first thought when the Governor sent for her was that somebody had died. There could be no other reason that she could think of.

She doubted it was any member of the family; after her conviction in the Lords two years ago, they'd cut her off completely. None of them had ever written; it was as if she'd died, or had never existed. She guessed that the scandal of Robin's murder and then the publicity of the trial had turned them against her forever. And her mother had never been able to forgive.

As she was ushered into the Governor's office in between two wardresses, she felt nothing but a mild curiosity. No apprehension, no fear. She had no strong emotions now; everything that had happened had somehow drained her dry. She wondered if she would ever be capable of feeling anything again. But that, too, no longer mattered.

Towards her family her first feelings had been ambivalent; guilt, remorse, shame for the terrible public humiliation she'd brought down on them; her conviction, the commuted sentence of life imprisonment; an unforgiveable blot on the Osborne name. But they'd turned away from her and cast her off when she needed them, and the injustice of that had made her angry and very bitter. Now even those emotions had disappeared.

She stood up straight in front of the Governor's desk; the Principal of the Kensington School of Manners and Deportment to which her parents had once sent her all those years ago, would have been proud of her now.

'You sent for me, sir.'

'Lady Frances, I think it would be as well if you sat down.' Lady Frances. Yesterday she'd been only Osborne, with a prison number.

He didn't say anything at first. Then he simply picked up what looked like the proof page of the next day's *Times*, and pushed it towards her. It bore the date of the following day and three inch high banner headlines. She stared at it, as if the words she saw had been written about someone else.

'I don't understand.'

'Lady Frances, the Home Secretary has been on the telephone to me; papers are being prepared at this moment to authorize your immediate release.'

She went on staring down at the page proof. There was a photograph of a pale, fair-haired young man, beside pictures of Thomas Dreikhorn, Robin, and then herself. There was a vague stirring of memory as she tried to place the distantly remembered features; then she saw the name, *Lawrence Rankin*; that was when she knew.

'Please read it all.'

Woodenly, she drew the page further towards her and stared down at each sensational line with increasing incredulity.

'Your name has been completely vindicated; tomorrow morning, what you see there now will be banner headlines on the front page of every national newspaper. Thomas Dreikhorn murdered your husband, Lady Frances.' Slowly, she glanced up into his face. 'Rankin made a false statement to the police at that time which gave Dreikhorn the perfect alibi; but these two letters, in Dreikhorn's own hand, added to what Rankin now says really happened, prove beyond any doubt that he was guilty. The police sprang into action as soon as they received Rankin's new statement . . . Dreikhorn has been arrested in Berlin and at least two witnesses have been found who say they recognize Dreikhorn from his photograph as being strikingly similar to a man seen buying a ticket and boarding the Glasgow-bound train a week before the killing.' He sat down in front of her and smiled. 'I think in a very short while there will be a cast-iron case against him, proving that it was him, not you, who should have stood trial.'

'Berlin,' she said, faintly and still disbelievingly. 'He never forgave Robin for letting my family send him to Berlin. How he must have hated us.'

'Until further orders arrive, please consider my own accommodation at your disposal. I've already issued instructions for your comfort, and asked one of my staff to bring you your own clothes.'

She smiled back faintly. He was trying so hard to be normal, kind. It was probably the first and the last time in his entire career as a prison governor that he'd been thrust into such an incredible situation as this. She almost felt sorry for him because he was so obviously embarrassed and ill at ease, as if he alone had been responsible for her imprisonment.

'Thank you.'

'If you wish to use my telephone, please do. And do also ask for anything else you need. Of course, I understand that you'll want to contact your family and make arrangements for them to meet you when you leave. There will be . . . inevitably, I'm afraid, enormous public and press interest. Every stage of the case and the trial was followed avidly; now this sensational revelation . . . it'll give the newspapers headline stories for months to come. It will mean that when the date for your release leaks out . . . there will be masses of crowds and press photographers waiting outside the prison.'

'I understand that; but I won't be contacting my family.' She ignored his look of stunned surprise. Of course, she could never make him understand; how could he? 'As far as I know after my father's resignation, my family are in the south of France. I doubt if they have any plans to return to England.'

'But . . . surely this news changes everything? They'll know now that you never committed this crime!'

How impossible it was to explain to someone who didn't know the Osbornes; but how could anyone know except herself?

'It was the shame, the scandal, the weeks of terrible publicity, that alienated my family. Not the crime itself. If I'd killed my husband and got away with it, they could have lived with that. They could have lived with anything I might have done as long as nobody ever knew.' He looked horrified. 'As strange as that may seem to you in your eyes, it was the trial, not the murder, that turned them against me. Nothing can change that now.'

457

For a few moments he seemed lost for words. 'But . . . if you don't go to your family, where will you go?'

She thought about her answer for a little while. She had a little money put by; not much, but enough. Laura would help her to find a room somewhere. She'd once got herself a job; she could do it again. It would be hard, but not impossible to make a new life, bereft of all the privileges she had once enjoyed. Prison at least had taught her how to survive. And she was grateful for that.

'There isn't anyone I want to telephone, except Mr Lucas, my solicitor. But I would be grateful if I could send a telegram to a friend. Mrs Flavel.'

He smiled at her. There was something about her that prison hadn't touched, something that shone through the pale, tired face and hopeless eyes, something he supposed, for want of a better word, he'd call spirit.

She was still beautiful. And he'd never quite been able to believe that she'd been guilty, anyway.

'Laura, I absolutely forbid it.'

'But she's *innocent*! Dreikhorn murdered Robert Rosslare . . . for God's sake, Maurice, you've read all the newspapers!'

'That's exactly the point that I'm trying to make. The newspapers. These banner headlines, the furore of publicity when they release her from prison. The entire press will be out in force outside Holloway jail when they let her out. Do you really suppose that I would permit *my* wife to be seen in public outside such a place, after all the disgusting scandal that was generated at the trial? In heaven's name, Laura, have you absolutely no thought for me? Have you any idea of what my position would be if your picture appeared in the newspapers, and one of the senior partners happened to see it? God forbid!'

She looked at him as if he was a stranger. She knew that there was no point in arguing; Maurice never changed his mind, not even when he was wrong. She should have known even before she told him what she wanted to do what his reaction would he. She wondered how she could ever have thought she loved him.

'She has her own family; let them be outside the prison gates to meet her.' His eyes were hard, like pebbles on a stony beach. 'Laura, I mean what I say. And I insist that you obey me. I absolutely forbid you to be at that gate when Frances Osborne comes out.'

He turned away from her abruptly and went out into the hall. She heard him pick up the telephone and ask the exchange to place a call; ironical, that when she'd had the business at Cavendish Street he'd refused to instal a telephone in the house, complaining that they'd never have a moment's peace from her customers; but as soon as he'd coerced her into giving her designing up, he'd had one almost instantly installed. She could hear him talking to Mr Gorston, the senior partner in his firm. His voice was light, cheerful, obsequious, displaying the charm he never bothered to display at home. Then he replaced the receiver, picked up his briefcase, and went out of the front door without saying goodbye.

She had waited a long time to do this. She had bottled so much anger, resentment, and regret up inside herself; for the sake of Desmond, of peace, harmony; his parents and hers. Wouldn't they all be the first to tell her that a wife's duty was to love, honour and obey? The trouble was, there was no longer love, or honour. No woman could honour a man she had grown to despise. He could have asked anything of her and still she would have done it, out of duty. But this one thing he asked, for her to abandon her friend, she could not do.

When he'd left for his office the following morning, she went upstairs and packed a single suitcase. She'd already washed and dressed Desmond, and sent him on in the taxi with Lily to her new address.

She came down and propped the envelope up against a vase on the table, so that he would see it the moment he came in the front hall. She lay her door key beside it.

Going out into the bright autumn sunshine, she closed the front door for the last time.

57

Getting out from the taxi, Laura told the driver to wait, then she began to push her way through the massive, jostling crowds. Up ahead of her, she could see the journalists and photographers from the press, skirmishing with each other outside the prison gates for the best positions, ready to descend on Frances when she came out. As Laura reached the edge of the crowd, a policeman stepped forward and pushed her back.

'Please, let me through.' Behind her, they were pushing and shoving to get a better view of what was going on. 'I'm here to meet Lady Frances Osborne.'

For a moment she thought that he didn't believe her; then he released her and let her through. At that same moment, the door in the main prison gate came open and Frances stepped out into the sunlight. A huge roar of cheering went up from the enormous crowd. Then the reporters and photographers descended on her.

Somehow they managed to reach each other. Laura grasped her hand and with all her strength pulled her through the wall of bodies to the back of the crowd, then bundled her into the waiting taxi. As it sped away, Frances turned and looked back.

'Don't.'

'I can't help it. I spent two years of my life in there. And all those people . . . look at them running after us . . . ! Perhaps they thought that I let them down. The Governor told me that the crowds had started to arrive outside the gate at six o'clock this morning. The press wanted to have interviews and take lots of pictures; the people wanted me to make a speech. All I want to do is go away and try to forget it.'

Laura held her hand. 'We're both in the same boat, aren't we?'

'What do you mean?' They both looked down on the taxi floor at the little suitcase. Frances frowned. 'Laura, what is it?'

'I've left Maurice.'

'He found out that you were coming to meet me?'

'That isn't the real reason. We've been drifting apart for such a long time . . . the only thing that's held us together has been Desmond. And I know that when he finds I'm gone and that I've taken him, he'll fight me for custody; but I thought about that very hard, and I think I'm strong enough now to fight too.' She laid her hand on Frances's. 'I should have told him sooner; but I suppose I didn't have the courage . . . or was it that I still thought there might be some hope that he'd change? For a long time, he's seemed like some other person, a person I don't understand any more; or love. Sometimes I thought that perhaps it was me. But I don't think I've changed from what I was when we got married, do you?'

Frances smiled. She looked so pale, so fragile. She'd lost weight. 'You're the one person in my life who never has. And I'm grateful for that.' The taxi slowed down and turned into an unfamiliar main road. She glimpsed a signpost to Surrey. 'Laura, where are we going? You told me in your letter that you'd explain it all on the way. The way to where?'

460

She told her about The Laurels, Kit's house. She opened her handbag and took out the key. 'That night, in the Savoy, when we talked. I knew he'd guessed about Maurice and me . . . Kit would. I could never hide anything from him. What was it he said? I can read you like a book. It seemed pointless not to tell him the truth.'

'Kit gave you the house?'

'It's his, but it's there for as long as Desmond and I need it. And you. I didn't write anything in the letter before you were released because I thought the press might find out. I didn't want the newspapers to get hold of the address.'

'I don't know what to say.'

'There's only one thing . . . we have to stop halfway there. I have to see someone who's been ill, and they're having treatment in a private clinic. But it won't take long.'

'You don't have to apologize to me.' She remembered the long, winding, leafy lanes, much like this one, on the way to Greyfriars and Audley House. 'I've always loved driving in the country. I still do.'

Laura went a little way ahead of her when the taxi left them at the top of the drive. Frances could see her on the steps of the terrace, smiling and gesturing and talking to a nurse. She saw the nurse nodding her head and pointing to something in the distance. When she looked, she could see patients in bath chairs, rugs over their knees, being wheeled onto the sloping lawns where the nurses were serving afternoon tea.

Laura waved and came towards her, stepping carefully in her high-heeled shoes over the shingle on the drive.

'It's this way. He's dressed and allowed to sit out on his own today.' They walked along the path, then across the lawn, side by side.

'It's so peaceful here. It's so beautiful. I want to keep on looking at everything as if I'm never going to see it again. The flowers, the grass, the bushes, the sky, the trees. It's like I never saw them before and everything seems new.' She couldn't cry. Not now, not yet. Perhaps if she could let loose all that terrible, pent-up emotion, she would feel better. But not here.

'Yes, it's a lovely place. The person I'm bringing you to see came back from America six months ago, and he's been here ever since. It takes a long time to cure a hardened alcoholic, the doctors tell me, because the will to stop drinking has to come from within.' Frances

461

was staring at her. They slowed down as they crossed the deeply sloping lawn towards the trees. 'They have to have a real reason to make them want to stop drinking. And this particular patient has, because of you.' She stopped walking and nodded towards a figure in the distance, sitting with a book on his lap under one of the trees. 'That's why I couldn't come here today without you, Frances. You're the only cure my brother needs.'

She knew she was going to cry, but she wanted to. He'd seen them walking towards him and he stood up. He laid the book down beside him on the seat. He could see Laura walking away, back across the sloping lawns and up the steps to the terrace.

She stood there, hatless, pale, her gold hair blowing behind her in the breeze. Then she called his name at the top of her voice, and began to run to him.